Men Of Honor Series

K.C. LYNN

Published by: K.C. LYNN

Second Edition

Contents

Dedication

This series is dedicated to the heroes who risk their lives every day to make the world a better place. Thank you for your service.

Fighting Temptation

Men of Honor Series

K.C. LYNN

Fighting Temptation

Published by K.C. Lynn

Second Edition

Cover Art by: Vanilla Lily Designs
Formatting: BB eBooks

Dedication

Dedicated to my grandmother who had a love for romance novels. I hope you have been wrapped in eternal love and sunshine since you left this world. Jaxson and Julia are for you.

CHAPTER 1

A Glimpse Of Our Beginning

Julia

I knew something was wrong the moment he said to meet him at our special place. My heart hasn't stopped twisting since I received his text a half hour ago. It's not uncommon for us to meet like this but his message was abrupt, said we needed to talk.

Please, God, whatever he's going to tell me, please don't let it be bad.

Reaching the beach, I slip off my sandals and start across the cool sand to where I can see a fire being started in the distance. I lift my long, white maxi dress as I walk along the shore, wetting my feet. Each step brings me closer to the man I'm secretly in love with, my best friend Jaxson.

We met when I moved here to Sunset Bay, South Carolina, just a little over two years ago. My mother had just passed away from cancer and I came to live with my grams. It still amazes me how fast I fell in love with this town, and how quickly I made some of the best friends I'll ever have.

A smile touches my lips as I recall the first time I laid eyes on Jaxson. My best friend, Kayla and I, had been sitting outside the ice cream shop, on a sweltering hot summer afternoon, when he came riding in on his motorcycle…

"Well, it looks like today is your lucky day, you're finally going to get to see the famous Jaxson Reid." Kayla's voice fades away as I watch him park across the lot, becoming captivated by the mysterious bad boy I've heard so much about.

He's dressed in loose, dark, faded jeans that have a few holes in them, and a snug black T-shirt that molds to his lean, muscular frame in all the right places. My eyes draw to the erotic display of tribal tattoos that are woven up his arms, getting cut off by the sleeves of his T-shirt. He takes his helmet off, and all the air sucks out of my lungs, my entire world tilting on its axis. Thick, dark lashes frame magnificent ice-blue eyes, his olive-colored complexion complemented by shaggy, dark brown hair. It's the kind of hair that makes my fingers itch to run through it, just to see if it feels as soft as it looks. His strong jaw is graced with a sexy five o'clock shadow.

I'd heard a lot about Jaxson since moving here, all the girls spoke about him as if he was some sort of god, and now I know why.

He unleashes a sexy smirk on me, and I soon realize that I've been busted openly ogling him. Heat invades my cheeks as I look away, only to receive the same knowing smile from Kayla.

"I know, right? If sex could walk, he would be it. Don't feel bad; you're not the only

one who drools around him. Most do, well, except for me. As sexy as he is, I have the major hots for his friend Cooper. I have big plans for that boy, just you wait."

She goes on to tell me that Jaxson is two years older than my sixteen and that he just graduated before the summer. I'm disappointed to learn that I won't see him around school.

"He did live with Cooper's family for a while, but now they have an apartment of their own," she explains.

"What about his parents?"

"His mom left when he was a kid, his dad a few years ago. I don't know where; he was a real asshole—the town drunk."

That information explained a lot later on. Little had I realized at the time, but Kayla really did have a plan laid out for her and Cooper. A year later, and they're still dating.

Unfortunately, I didn't get to meet Jaxson that day, he was there meeting Melissa Carmichael. My blood heats just thinking her name. She's always been such a bitch to me, especially after I became close with Jaxson. I hate to even think about what they did together after they left the ice cream shop that day. Although, that's been the story of my life for the last two years – watching Jaxson with random girls. He's not the relationship type, or so he says. I have a sneaking suspicion his mom leaving has something to do with that.

The night I finally did get to meet him, well… it was the scariest night of my life.

It was two weeks after seeing him at the ice cream shop. I had snuck out of my bedroom window after Grams went to sleep and walked to the cemetery to visit my mom. I had sat at her grave and talked to her. It was something I always found comforting and still do. I told her how scared I was to be starting a new school, worried people weren't going to like me, and more than anything, I told her how much I missed her. My mother was my best friend. The pain I felt when she passed hadn't faded, and I'd wondered if it ever would. I don't remember how long I'd been crying for before I heard some rustling and laughter…

I turn around to find two guys stumbling up behind me. They're big, their builds reminding me of linebackers. By looking at them, I guess they're a couple of years older than me. They smile as they approach; smiles that have terror skittering down my spine. I stand up quickly, my shaky legs barely able to hold me up.

"Well aren't you pretty. Isn't she, Jace?"

Suddenly feeling exposed in my yoga tank and shorts, I fold my cardigan over my breasts that they are openly staring at; the action only seems to amuse them.

"Yeah, she's really pretty, I'm glad we happened upon her."

Ignoring them, I start forward, but the one referred to as Jace steps out in front of me, blocking my escape. I attempt to calm my wild heartbeat while figuring out how to get out of this mess I've found myself in. I know I won't be able to outrun them, but my hope is to at least make it to the street and pray someone hears me scream for help.

Unfortunately, it's exactly what they anticipate. I don't make it far before one grabs a fistful of my hair and yanks me back against him. His hand clamps over my mouth with brutal force, muffling my screams.

"You stupid bitch. Shut the fuck up!"

With every bit of strength I possess, I fight against him, kicking and shifting, trying to break the hold he has on me, but none of it makes a difference; he's too strong.

He drags me back to my mom's grave while his friend Jace watches, his hand stroking over the front of his jeans.

My eyes close in disgust as bile inches up my throat.

"Come on, fucking help me, man! This bitch is squirmy."

Jace snaps to attention and grabs my kicking legs to help carry me. They drop me on my mother's grave, the hard impact knocking the breath from my lungs. The one behind me pins my struggling arms above my head while Jace sits on my legs, restraining them. His hand wraps around my throat as he leans in close, a malicious smile curling his lips. "I'm going to fuck you right here on your mother's grave, you little bitch."

It's now, I realize they must have been watching me for some time to know this is my mother's grave. For the first time since they showed up I feel something other than fear. Anger swells inside of me, bubbling over, and I spit in his face.

It's my first mistake.

Fury washes over his expression, his fingers tightening on my throat. "You're a brave little whore." He rears back and slaps me, the impact is so hard that blood pools in my mouth and black spots dance before my eyes. "After I'm done fucking you, my buddy is going to get a turn, then we're going to beat some manners into you."

He tears at my tank top, ripping the strap from my shoulder.

"No! Please don't do this," I beg, but quiet quickly when I realize my pleas only excite him further.

As his hand moves to his belt, I close my eyes and begin to pray. It's the first time I've prayed since my mom died. I am praying so hard that I don't realize my legs are suddenly free. Soon though, I clue in to the sound of shouting and painful grunts.

My eyes spring open and I see Jace on the ground with another guy on top of him, beating the ever-livin' crap out of him.

The guy holding my arms eventually releases me to help his friend.

"Watch out!" I scream, warning the mystery guy.

He turns around just in time to land a solid right hook, causing my attacker to hit the ground unconscious.

This guy packs a serious punch.

As he rises to his full height and turns toward me, I realize the dark avenging angel is none other than the town's bad boy, Jaxson Reid.

Rage twists his expression as he starts toward me.

I cower against my mother's headstone, fear gripping me for a second time. He's so fierce, it frightens me.

When he senses my alarm, he slows his steps and approaches me with more caution, lifting his hands in the air. "I'm not going to hurt you. Everything is going to be okay. I'm calling the police now."

After calling it in, he sits a short distance away and waits with me. Awkward silence fills the air around us. I want to thank him, but I can't form words, my teeth are chattering like crazy, my body shaking.

He catches me off guard when he leans over and gently brushes his fingers across my bruised cheek. "Sorry I didn't make it before this happened," he says quietly.

His tenderness surprises me. I've been told Jaxson was dangerous, and someone you don't want to screw with. After witnessing what he did to my two attackers, I can see why.

"Don't be sorry. Thank you for coming when you did, because if you hadn't, well... you know what was about to happen."

The horrific event comes rushing back with a vengeance. I wrap my arms around my legs, hugging my knees to my chest and begin sobbing.

He moves a little closer to me and awkwardly pats my shoulder. "Everything is fine now."

I can tell he's uncomfortable trying to console me and doesn't know what to say.

"Listen, I know now is not the time to be a dick, but what the hell were you thinking coming to a graveyard this late at night by yourself?"

His disapproving tone has my back going up. "I was visiting my mother. I didn't think coming here would almost get me raped," I snap, then feel bad, especially after everything he's done for me. "I'm sorry, you're right, it was stupid. I won't be doing it again, at least not in the middle of the night."

"I don't recognize those assholes. I'm assuming they were driving through, maybe back to Charleston." He shrugs. "Either way, probably a good idea if you come during daylight."

"I will," I say quietly.

He extends his battered hand to me. "I'm Jaxson Reid."

I put my shaking one in his. "Julia. Julia Sinclair."

Pulling myself back to the present, I try to shake the memory. What had started out to be one of the most awful nights of my life turned into one of the best. Because the sexy, dark, and mysterious bad boy I was warned to steer clear of became my best friend. Since that night, Jaxson has taken care of me – protected me. He brought me back from the brink of pain and heartbreak after losing my mother. He reminded me what it was like to be happy again.

People have a misperception about him, mainly due to the reputation of his father. Grams once told me his father was a terrible man and Jaxson was better off without him. That's all she had said but I didn't need her to elaborate, because I can tell just how deeply his father had hurt him. At times when his guard slips for a brief moment, I can see flashes of it, and he doesn't realize anyone is looking. I know any physical scars he bears are nothing compared to the ones left on his heart.

Don't get me wrong, Jaxson has earned some of his reputation. He can be arrogant, aggressive, and angry. He's guarded and damaged yet he's also beautiful, strong, and honorable. Our friendship surprises a lot of people because, other than Cooper, he has never befriended anyone else, and he definitely doesn't have any friends that are girls. But Jaxson and I formed a bond, one so strong, it is unbreakable. I unconditionally and irrevocably love every damaged part of him. And for the boy who doesn't believe in love, he will always and forever have mine.

My steps slow as I come up to him sitting by the fire; he stares into the bright flames, lost in thought. I watch him for a moment, his troubled expression glowing from the firelight.

When he hears my approach, his eyes lift to mine and his expression softens; he looks almost relieved to see me. Sometimes when he looks at me the way he is now, I think maybe he does love me the way I love him. But whenever I let the silly thought in, I shove it away and remember whom I'm talking about.

Flashing me a sexy smirk, he stands and walks over, pulling me into his arms. "Hey, Jules." He greets me with a familiar kiss to my forehead.

For whatever reason, he has kissed my forehead from the moment we became friends. It's something that he's reserved just for me, and I savor the intimate contact with him.

"Hey, Jax." I hug him back tightly, breathing in his comforting scent.

He breaks the connection much too soon, his hand grasping mine as he leads me to sit next to the fire. We rest back against the log behind us; both of my arms wrapping around one of his as I lean into him, seeking his warmth.

The tense silence filling the air has lead settling in my stomach and my earlier fear comes rushing back swiftly. "You're going to tell me something bad, aren't you?"

His somber expression says it all. "It'll be all right. It's not that bad." He pauses, expelling a heavy breath. "I'm leaving town. I've decided to enlist in the Navy. I want to be a SEAL."

My heart plummets, a million questions plaguing me at once. "Okay, and what does that mean exactly? Where would you go? Don't you have to qualify first, before you can even be accepted?"

"I already have been," he admits quietly. "I had to do some written exams and evaluations, but I passed. I'm going to their training facility in Coronado, California."

"What? Just how long have you thought about this?"

He clears his throat. "I started the process about six months ago."

"Six months?" I shriek, rearing back. "How could you keep this from me?" Betrayal thickens my throat, a sharp pain infiltrating my chest.

He blows out a breath, his eyes turning to me, pleading with me to understand. "I'm sorry, Jules. I didn't want to upset you if I wasn't going to make it," he apologizes, his words heavy with regret. "Please understand. I need to do this. I need to get out of this fucking town; I don't belong here. The only thing that kept me here as long as it has is you."

"How can you say that? This is your home, Jaxson. You grew up here."

"That's exactly my point. Everyone knows my shit. They know what I come from. Don't tell me you don't see how many people look down on me, especially when we're together. Everyone wonders why sweet little Margaret Sinclair's granddaughter is friends with a fuck-up like me."

I shake my head. "No you're wrong and even if you aren't, who cares what they think? Don't leave because you think you need to prove yourself."

"This has nothing to do with them. I don't give a shit what they think of me; I'm doing this for myself. I think I've found something that I'm going to be really good at. I did so well on the evaluation that the superior officers are excited to meet me."

"You're good at a lot of things. Can't you choose something else? Something that isn't so dangerous? How about being a mechanic? Or owning your own motorcycle shop? You would be really good at that, and that would be fun," I say, trying to sound upbeat.

Unfortunately, he doesn't take the bait. His eyes are lit with amusement as he stares down at me.

"It was worth a try," I grumble.

Chuckling, he slings his arm around my shoulders but sobers quickly, his blue irises holding mine. "I have a chance to do something good with my life. Tell me you understand."

"I'm trying, it's just hard. I don't want to lose you." My voice cracks as I struggle to hold onto my composure.

He rests his forehead against mine, his jaw flexing as he holds in his own emotions. "You won't lose me, Jules, we'll still see each other. Obviously not as much as we do now, but we'll figure something out."

"When do you leave?" I ask.

He straightens nervously, sending another dose of panic through me.

"Jaxson?"

"Saturday morning. I take the ferry to Bradsford then fly out from there."

"This Saturday? As in three days from now?" I screech.

"I'm sorry. I just found out yesterday. They don't give you much time."

I shake my head, having a hard time grasping that any of this is happening right now. How am I supposed to go every day without seeing him?

His hand caresses my cheek, the touch pulling me from my torment. "Are we okay?" he asks.

We are okay, *I* am not. But I don't tell him that. Instead, I cover his hand with mine, and nod because my throat is too tight to speak.

"Listen, I have a lot to get done before I leave, but how about we go out on Friday? We'll grab supper then come hang out here for the night."

"Sure, that sounds good," I agree, wanting any time I can get. "Anyway, I better head home. I'm later than what I told Grams I would be, and I don't want her to worry."

And I really don't want to completely lose it in front of you.

"All right, come on, I'll walk you to your car."

I falter, knowing he's not going to like what he's about to hear. "Um, I didn't drive here, I walked."

His eyes narrow in disapproval. "Damn it, Julia. You know better."

"Relax. It's a beautiful night and I want the fresh air."

"You know the rules. No walking at night by yourself." Letting out a frustrated breath, he drives a hand through his hair. "Come on, I'll take you home."

"I don't have my helmet and I'm wearing a dress," I argue, but know it's pointless.

"I don't care. Either I drive you back or I follow you home, it's up to you."

My eyes roll at his bossy attitude but I relent and follow him to his bike.

He puts his black helmet on over my head, making sure the strap is tight then straddles the seat. When I don't follow suit, he tosses me an impatient look.

Geez, he can be grumpy.

I hike my dress up just enough to climb on behind him, my arms wrapping around his waist. My irritation quickly vanishes, peace invading my soul. One of my favorite things to do is ride with Jaxson. I love getting to be so close to him.

The bike roars to life, a second before it kicks forward, starting our short journey home.

I turn my face to the side, resting my cheek against his hard back and try really hard not to think about the fact that he's leaving me in just three days.

Three days.

Does Kayla know? I'm sure Coop does, but I would like to think that if Kayla knew she would have told me.

I don't get much time to think about it before we arrive at my house. Once Jaxson comes to a stop, I climb off the back, missing his warmth. I hand him back his helmet without making eye contact and flick him a quick wave, needing to get out of here. My fragile composure is close to shattering.

However, I don't get the opportunity, because as soon as I take that first step he grabs my wrist and yanks me against him, enveloping me in his arms. "It's going to be okay, Jules," he whispers into my hair. "I promise."

The tears I've managed to hold at bay finally unleash. "I'm going to miss you so much," I cry, burying my face into his neck.

"I'm going to miss you too, Jules." He holds me close, his large hand rubbing comforting circles on my back. Once my tears subside, he curls a finger under my chin, lifting my face to his. "I'll pick you up at six on Friday, okay?"

I offer him a small smile and nod. When he releases me, I walk into the house and decide that I can't let him leave without telling him how much I love him. Even if the consequences could potentially be damaging.

CHAPTER 2

Once Julia's safely inside, I start my bike back up and take off. I knew that would be hard, but that fucking sucked. I hate that she's hurting because of me but I know I'm doing the right thing, not only for myself but her, too.

She thinks I don't know about the shit she gets from people for being friends with me, but I do. If it's not the rich assholes who think they're too good for someone like me, then it's the jealous bitches who hate the fact I'm close with Julia and not them. They don't understand that she's different; she always has been.

I'll never forget the first time I laid eyes on her. I had heard about the new girl, all the guys spoke about how hot she was, and even placed bets on who was going to fuck her first. When I found out she was at the ice cream shop with Kayla one night, I changed my plans and had Melissa meet me there instead. I had to get a look at the girl everyone was talking about. When I rode in, I immediately spotted her and Kayla sitting outside at one of the tables. I parked across the lot then took my helmet off to get a good look at her. It was like a jolt of electricity shot through my body and straight to my dick.

Julia was not *hot*, she was fucking beautiful.

Her gaze held me captive; her eyes, an exotic blue-green color that hid behind long, dark lashes, shone of beauty and innocence. Right then I knew she was not for me, but I couldn't stop myself from taking in the rest of her. She had long, brown hair that fell past her bare shoulders and laid against the best looking tits I'd ever seen. Her short yellow sundress enhanced her smooth, olive skin, and although there was nothing revealing about it, I still got a glimpse of her small, lithe body, one that I desperately wanted to feel wrapped around me.

She had stared back at me with appreciation, something that I was used to. Yet, she caused a strange sensation in my chest – one I'd never felt before, and I fucking hated it. I learned at a young age that feelings and emotions were dangerous; they only made you weak. So I gave myself a mental slap and acknowledged her appreciation with a cocky smirk. When Melissa climbed on the back of my bike I took off and fucked her all night, trying to get the new girl out of my head… It didn't work.

Two weeks later, I walked out of Big Mike's gym and heard a terrified scream echo from the graveyard across the street. A white-hot rage constricts my chest, just like it always does when I think about those fucking perverts on top of her, holding her down.

Little did I know, that night would change my life forever. The girl I had tried so hard to forget, the one I tried to stay away from, became my best friend. I knew she would be better off without me, but I couldn't stop myself from getting to know her. She was different from anyone I'd ever met. I never thought someone so good and genuine existed until her. The more I saw of her, the more addicted I became. Every time I was around her, she would destroy some of the darkness that lurked inside of me. She made the bad shit in my life seem not so terrible. Then before I knew it, I had fallen for a girl from another world.

As badly as I wanted her, I tamped down my feelings and kept my dick in my pants, because I knew I'd never be good enough for her. Unfortunately, my father's blood runs in me, and I refuse to taint her. She deserves everything good, everything I'm not.

Even though I didn't ever plan to take her, I made sure no one else had her either. I know it was an asshole move, but the thought of her with someone else rips my fucking guts out. So without her knowledge, I laid claim. I warned every guy to stay away from her, and they all did because no one was brave enough to fuck with me.

As much as I'm going to miss her, it's a good thing I'm leaving. My precious control is slipping and every day I'm finding it harder to be around her and not touch her the way I want to. The way I've dreamed about.

Relief surges through me when I pull up to the apartment I share with Cooper and don't see Kayla's car. Tonight, out of all nights, I don't feel like hearing the bed pound against the wall from the two of them fucking each other senseless.

Letting myself into the apartment, I find Cooper sitting on the couch, drinking a beer and watching TV. He looks up at me with a stupid grin. "Hey, SEAL boy."

My arms cross over my chest as I lean against the counter. "Not yet, but when I do pass, I'll put your rookie ass to shame," I fire back with a smirk.

He's gotten so cocky since he finished the police academy over a year ago. Graduated top of the class, as he always reminds everyone. He wants to be sheriff one day and knows the opportunity will arise when the current one retires in the next few years. He's the perfect guy for the job. He's more than my best friend, he's the best guy I know. If it weren't for him and his parents, I'm not sure where I'd be.

"No Kayla?" I ask.

"Not tonight. I told her I would meet up with her tomorrow. Figured you might need a beer, or four. Something you better appreciate, because not only will I not be getting laid tonight, I will probably lose my balls when she finds out I knew about you leaving and never told her."

I grunt. "Yeah, well, no need to keep it a secret anymore." Grabbing a beer from the fridge, I drop in the chair on the other side of the room.

"So how did Jules take it?"

"Pretty much as I expected. She was hurt, and pissed when she found out how long I have been planning it. She's still talking to me though." I feel uncomfortable confessing this to him, but I continue. "I didn't want to lose her over this."

"Did you really think you would? This is Julia we're talking about. That girl is as forgiving as they come."

He's right, she is, but I also know what it's like to have the people who you'd least expect abandon you. But she isn't one of them, and I should have known that.

"I need you to keep your promise to watch out for her and take care of her. I mean it, Coop, if something happens to her because I wasn't here, I'll never forgive myself."

He leans forward, his expression hard. "Have I ever broken a promise to you? I told you I'll watch out for her, and I will. Although, I can't promise I'll be able to control her dating life," he adds with a smirk.

I tense, my eyes narrowing. "Who in the hell said anything about dating? She'll be too busy with school to worry about that. Besides, why would I care? As long as he's good to her, I don't give a shit who she sees." The lie flows easily from my lips.

He grunts, knowing I'm full of shit. "Yeah, right. You know Wyatt Jennings is going to move in on her as soon as your ass hits that ferry."

My stomach sinks like a heavy anchor, dread snaking around my chest at the thought. Wyatt has wanted Julia since she first moved here. I warned him long ago not to go anywhere near her. It's no secret the shit he's done to half the chicks in this town, I've seen the bruises. The thought of him laying one finger on her makes me fucking violent.

"He's already been warned to stay away from her. If he doesn't, you better remind him."

"I'm a local cop now, Jaxson. I hate the thought too, but I can't just beat the shit out of the guy. I'll do what I can to stop her though, and if he hurts her in any way, well, everything I just said to you goes out the window. I'll take him out. You know I will. I'll just need to do it more inconspicuously is all," he says matter of factly.

I nod. "Thanks for doing this. It makes it a little easier for me to leave, knowing you got her back."

"Jaxson, again this is Julia we're talking about. You don't need to thank me. She's my girl's best friend; I care about her, too. Don't worry about this. I'll take care of her. You're doing the right thing, man. Go for it, and show those fuckers at BUD/S what you're made of."

CHAPTER 3

Julia

"I can't believe I am going through with this," I say to Kayla as I add the finishing touches to my hair while trying to calm the butterflies in my tummy.

"You can do this, Julia, don't chicken out now."

I've decided I'm going to tell Jaxson how I feel tonight and right now I am so thankful for Kayla's support. She's always known my feelings for him, and thinks I should have said something long ago, but I couldn't. Even now, I am so scared this is going to ruin our friendship.

No, I won't let that happen.

I know he probably doesn't feel the same way, and it will hurt to hear, but I can't let him go without telling him that I love him. I've thought long and hard about this. If something were to ever happen to him, I would always regret not telling him how I truly feel.

"If he tells you he doesn't feel the same way, he's lying," Kayla says, coming up behind me in the mirror. Leave it to her to say exactly what she thinks. It's something I've always admired about her.

"I'm not so sure about that, you know how Jaxson is, he doesn't believe in love."

"That's his daddy issues talking, Jules. Believe me, I have seen the way he looks at you. If he denies it, he's lying."

Letting out a nervous breath, I shrug. "I guess I'm not expecting him to say it back. I'm doing this so I have no regrets."

"Well, if he says he doesn't feel the same way, you could always say 'just kidding.'"

The suggestion has us both bursting into a fit of laughter.

Kayla sobers quickly, her laugh softening into a smile. "He's lucky to have you, Jules, and believe me, when he sees you tonight he's going to flip his shit. You look amazing."

"Thanks, Kayla," I reply softly, my throat feeling tight at her compliment. I decided on a short, faded denim skirt that shows off a little more leg than I'm used to. Soft pink lace edges the hemline which matches the tank top I borrowed from Kayla. I went against straightening my hair, letting my long, chestnut brown locks fall in loose waves past my shoulders. Kayla helped me with my makeup, making my aquamarine eyes really stand out with a smoky eye shadow. It made me think of my Mama. She always loved my eyes; said they reminded her of the Caribbean Sea.

Grams tells me all the time that I look like Mama, and although we do have some similarities, I don't hold a candle to her. I have yet to see anyone as beautiful as my mother.

Thinking about this, reminds me of the night I fell irrevocably in love with Jaxson. It was almost a year after we had met. We were at our usual spot on the beach, where I would sneak out at night to meet him. We'd hang out and talk, oftentimes until sunrise...

We're lying side by side, staring up at the stars, when out of the blue he asks if I'm happy living in Sunset Bay.

"Yeah, I am. I think it's a great town. I just wish the circumstances of what brought me here were different," I tell him, unable to hide the sadness in my voice.

"You've never mentioned your dad before. You can tell me to mind my own damn business, but I'm curious why you aren't living with him."

"Because I don't know who my father is." Before he is able to get the wrong idea about my mother, I rush to explain. "To make a long story short, my mother fell in love with my father in college and got pregnant. He didn't feel the same way, and didn't want a baby." I shrug, but can't deny the sting of abandonment I feel when thinking about him. "She said if I ever wanted to know anything about him I could ask, but, to be honest, I never thought too much about him. My mother was everything I needed. My pappi died before I was born and my mother never dated, so I never had any male figures growing up."

I shift, feeling nervous for what I'm about to share. He lays quietly, allowing me the time I need.

"But there were a few times I wondered if I was missing out. Like when I was young, living in our old house. There was a girl close to my age who lived next door. She had this big tree in her front yard, and her dad hung a wooden swing from it for her. He would push her on it every night after supper; they would laugh, and she would beg him to go higher. Oftentimes I'd watch them out my window, and wonder what that felt like. But I wouldn't let myself dwell on it because no one had a mom out there like I did."

With a soft smile, I pull my gaze away from the stars to look at him and am surprised to find him staring at me, his intense blue eyes penetrating my soul.

Before I can ask what he's thinking, he looks away, breaking the connection. "Well trust me when I say, sometimes it's better not knowing who your father is." There's so much pain in those few words, and it's now I realize that he harbors something much greater than anyone knows.

As badly as I want to know more, I don't push. Family is territory that Cooper warned me to never step in and I'm happy that he has even divulged this much to me. Instead, I tentatively reach out to touch his hand, hoping to offer some comfort.

His fingers curl around mine, interlocking our hands. My heart dances in excitement, and butterflies flock in my tummy. It feels like the greatest victory I have ever achieved.

A few precious seconds pass before he changes the subject back to me. "What was your mom like?"

It's the first time he has ever asked about her. Even though we have become close, I haven't spoken much about her because it hurts too much. He knows she passed away from cancer, but that's about it. I decide it's time to share her with him.

"She was beautiful, Jax, and not just on the outside, but the inside, too," I start, feeling the sting of tears in my eyes. "She was graceful and sweet, she never judged anyone. She was the kindest and most forgiving woman you would ever meet. Sometimes I think God took her because he needed her as one of his angels." I realize how silly that probably sounds to

him and shake my head. "I'm not making sense. I'm trying to describe how amazing she was, but no matter what I say, you will never fully understand how beautiful she was."

When a tear slips free, he leans over and wipes it away with his thumb. "Actually, I know exactly what you're saying, and I can picture it… because she sounds just like you."

Once again my eyes find his, the startling blue irises captivating me. In that moment, something shifted in me, something monumental, and I soon realize it's me giving Jaxson my entire heart.

I'm thrusted back to the present by Kayla ranting about Cooper. "I still can't believe that fucker kept this from me. He said he knew I would have told you. Can you believe that?"

"Well, would you have?"

"Of course!" she says, without missing a beat.

Her loyalty brings a smile to my face. "Then why are you mad at him?"

"Because he is supposed to tell me everything anyway, that's why," she replies, as if the answer is obvious. "I told him he isn't getting a piece of ass for at least a week. Although I may have to take that back, it's only been two days and I might die if I don't get him naked soon," she admits, making me chuckle.

Kayla and Cooper are the all-American couple. Kayla with her long, blonde hair, big blue eyes and witty personality. Before Cooper joined the sheriff's department he was the town's football hero, and let's just say that next to Jaxson, he is definitely the hottest guy I've ever laid eyes on. With his warm green eyes, brown hair and killer smile that girls fall all over themselves for, much to Kayla's dismay. I smile when I think of all the seductive tricks she used to snatch him.

"Don't be too hard on him, he was just being loyal to Jaxson. You would have done the same for me," I say, taking pity on Cooper.

"Yeah, you're right; I'm going to make him sweat it for a bit longer though," she snickers.

Smiling, I shake my head at her.

"Are you ready for this?" she asks.

I take a deep breath, nerves dancing in my belly. "As ready as I'm ever going to be."

CHAPTER 4

Jaxson

I arrive at Julia's house just a few minutes before six and try to pull myself together. These past few days I've been in a shitty mood; leaving her is bothering me more than I thought it would. Even Coop has had enough of me.

Just as I lift my hand to knock, Julia's grandma, Margaret Sinclair, opens the door. "Jaxson, I thought that was your bike I heard. Come here and give me a hug."

I do so, awkwardly. I'm not used to affection, but she's a really affectionate lady and likes to hug a lot.

"How are you doing, Miss Margaret?" I've never cared much about my manners, but Margaret has been good to me. She's never treated me like I wasn't good enough to be friends with Julia.

"How many times do I have to tell you to stop with the 'Miss Margaret' and call me Grams?" She scolds lightheartedly.

"Sorry," I mumble.

"You're forgiven, handsome. Now come on into the kitchen, Julia will be down in a minute, Kayla's up there with her. They should be done soon." I follow her into the kitchen and sit at the table where she places a plate of cookies in front of me. "Julia and I baked them this morning."

I don't hesitate taking one, the lady makes the best cookies.

Sitting down next to me, she cuts right to the chase. "So I heard you're leaving us."

I nod. "I'm heading off for training and hoping to make it into the Navy."

She watches me silently, making me feel uncomfortable then silently gets up and walks into the living room. She grabs a big photo album, shifting through the pages, then pulls out a picture and brings it back to me. "Julia's Pappi, my Ben, was in the Navy. He was a sailor, a darn good one, too."

Sure enough, the black and white photograph is of a young man in a sailor suit who looks even younger than me. I turn the picture over and read: *Benjamin Sinclair, 1952, 18 years old.*

"He served ten years before he was honorably discharged. He could have stayed, but after I had Julia's mother, Annabelle, I wanted him home safe with us. Who knew it would end up being a drunk driver that took him from us."

I stare down at the picture, unsure of what to say. My eyes snap back up to her in surprise when she puts her hand on mine.

"You remind me a little of my Ben, Jaxson. You're fierce, loyal, and strong. I think the Navy would be lucky to have you help serve this country."

It was probably the nicest thing anyone has ever said to me. "Thank you."

"Now tell me, are you going to come back to my Julia?"

Jesus, speaking of Julia… Where the hell is she? What am I supposed to say to that when I don't know the answer?

"I'm not sure what will happen, but I do expect to see Julia again. I care about her; she's a good friend. I'll miss her, but it will be good for her, too. I know it's been tough at times for her to be friends with me."

Next thing I know, she comes to stand in front of me. I stare up at her warily, wondering what in the hell she's going to say now. This conversation is way too much for me.

She takes my face between both of her hands and gives me a kind smile. "You're a good boy, Jaxson, never think any differently. Julia is lucky to have you; she's much stronger than you give her credit for. She needs you in her life, though, you make sure you come home to her, you hear?"

I nod, but feel bad doing it because I'm not sure I will be able to keep that promise. Finally, I hear Kayla and Julia bound down the stairs.

"We're in the kitchen, girls!" Margaret yells, patting my shoulder.

I push to my feet and stand, thankful the conversation is over, and suck in a sharp breath when Julia walks in.

Ho-ly shit!

All the blood from my head rushes south to my cock, and I immediately regret that I'm standing. Every time I see Julia I'm always struck with the reminder of how beautiful she is, but right now it's more than that. I have never seen her look this way. She's showing way more skin than I have ever seen, and now I don't want anyone else to, either. The way her hair and makeup is fixed, she doesn't look like beautiful, wholesome Julia. No, she looks like a sexy vixen.

"Oh, Julia, dear, you look beautiful."

"Thanks, Grams." Julia kisses her on the cheek then looks at me. "Hey, Jax." She fidgets with the bottom of her skirt, and my eyes are drawn to her long, smooth legs. Legs that I want to feel wrapped around my waist while I drive myself into her.

Fuck me!

"Hi," I croak out then clear my throat when I hear how gruff I sound. "Hey, Jules, you look nice."

That's a fucking understatement.

My attention pulls to Kayla next and I find her watching me with a sassy smirk.

"Hey," she greets me with a small wave. "Well I'm outta here, folks. Have fun and call me later, Jules." She gives Julia a hug and whispers something in her ear before looking back at me. "Good luck with the Navy thing, Jaxson. I'm sure you'll do great."

"Thanks, Kayla. Make sure to keep Coop in check. Don't let him get too big of a head while I'm gone."

Laughing, she bids us all one more wave then heads out the door.

"Are you ready?" I ask Julia.

She nods. "Is it all right if we take my car instead? I'm not really dressed for the bike."

No shit.

"Yeah, that's fine."

"Where are you two headed tonight?" Margaret asks.

Julia looks over at me, unsure.

"I thought we'd go get a pizza at Antonio's. Then head to the beach later?"

"Sounds good to me." She gives me a smile, one that always hits me like a blow to the chest.

When we start to the front door, Margaret grabs me again and wraps her thin, wrinkly arms around my waist. "You take care of yourself now, Jaxson, I have no doubt you're going to do great. You remember what I said, okay?"

"Thanks, I will. You take care too... *Grams.*"

She smiles when I add that last part.

"I'm not sure what time I'll be home. Don't wait up for me, just in case I'm late," Julia says, her cheeks turning pink as she avoids eye contact with me.

What's up with her?

"Actually, dear, don't wait up for me. My knitting club and I are partying it up tonight at Joyce Becker's. She's making monster margaritas."

Julia snickers at her excitement. "Be careful, and call if you need a ride."

"Oh you know me, I'll be fine, and I have a ride home. You kids have a good night."

Once we step outside, Julia turns to me with a smile and hands me the keys. "I imagine you want to drive," she says, rolling her eyes playfully.

I never sit shotgun. I need the control in every aspect of my life.

My jeans tighten further at her sassiness. Before I can think better of it, I reach out and slip my finger in the waist band of her skirt and yank her against me.

She gasps at the feel of my hard cock against her stomach.

"You look really good tonight, Jules."

"Thanks." The response is breathless, her cheeks flushing with desire.

Leaning down, I press a hard kiss to her forehead then drag her to the car before I do something really dumb, like hike up that skirt of hers and fuck her right here on the front porch.

CHAPTER 5

By the time we pull up to Antonio's Pizza Parlor, my senses are still reeling from what happened on my front porch, my skin burning from Jaxson's possessive touch.

Maybe tonight will go better than I anticipate.

"Did you want to order it to go and eat at the beach?" Jaxson asks as we get out of the car.

"Yeah, that sounds good." Smiling, I link my arm easily with his as we walk into the restaurant.

"Well, well, well, if it isn't my favorite customers," Antonio boasts loudly. He's a very loud, happy Italian man who makes the best pizza in the state.

"Hi, Antonio," I greet him with a smile, walking up to the counter.

"Come on over here, beautiful, and lay one on me." He pats the side of his face.

Pushing myself up on the counter, I give him a loud smooch on the cheek.

He turns to Jax next and shakes his hand. "How you doin', Jaxson? I hear you're leaving us to become a SEAL. Aren't you dangerous enough?"

"We all know you're the dangerous one in this town," Jax replies with a smirk.

Antonio proudly puffs out his chest. "You know it, kid. What can I get you two?"

Jaxson glances down at me. "A large cheese pizza, thin crust, to go."

I flash him an appreciative smile for ordering my favorite.

"Grab some drinks and take a seat. It'll be a few minutes."

We both grab a Coke then slide into an empty booth.

"Are you packed and ready for tomorrow?" I ask him, taking a sip of my soda.

"Yeah, mostly. Cooper is going to put the rest of my stuff in storage next week."

A moment of silence ensues, my heart heavy at the thought of him leaving. I'm not ready to lose him. I never will be.

The bell jingles above the door, announcing someone's arrival. Jaxson's gaze moves over my shoulder, and all easiness vanishes, his jaw tightening in anger.

"What is it?" I ask, glancing behind me. My body tenses when I see it's Wyatt Jennings. He looks directly at us, a cocky smirk curling his lips as he starts forward.

Oh shit!

Turning back around, I find Jaxson's eyes cold, fury pouring from him.

"Jaxson," I warn cautiously.

"Well hello, Miss Julia," Wyatt greets me, trying to get under Jaxson's skin.

"Hi, Wyatt," I respond for the sake of pleasantries, but my eyes remain on Jaxson.

Wyatt has always been polite to me, so I would never be rude back.

"You look really nice tonight. Where are you headed?"

"None of your fucking business," Jaxson growls.

"I wasn't talking to you. I was asking her." Wyatt places his hand on my shoulder, his fingers caressing my bare skin.

Before I'm able to move away from his touch Jaxson is on his feet, knocking Wyatt's hand off of me. "Don't fucking touch her."

Oh god!

I stand up too, but neither of them notice. They're too busy glaring at each other, looking ready to strike at any given moment.

"I hear you're leaving soon, Reid. It'll be nice to finally get to know Julia. This town will be better off without you, and so will she."

I glare at Wyatt, angry on Jaxson's behalf. Right when I'm about to say something, Jaxson moves me to the side then grabs Wyatt by the shirt, slamming him into the wall.

Oh shit.

"Jaxson, don't!"

"I fucking warned you, Jennings, and I mean it. If you go anywhere near her, I promise you will live to regret it. Are you fucking listening to me?"

Everyone in the restaurant is quiet, watching the scene unfold. When I see someone grab their cellphone, I worry they're about to call the police.

"Jaxson, please. I don't want our night to end because of this. Let's grab our pizza and get out of here." I try to reason with him, not wanting him to spend his last night in jail instead of with me. Wyatt's father is on the city council and is very influential in this town.

Thankfully, Antonio walks out from the back and breaks them up. "Okay, you two, that's enough. Jennings, you got a death wish? Go get a table. Jaxson, let him go, son. Your pizza's ready, take Miss Julia and go wherever y'all are headed for the night."

Jaxson's fists remain curled in Wyatt's shirt, his furious face only a mere inch from his. "I mean it, you stay the fuck away from her." He releases Wyatt with a hard shove before stepping back.

Antonio hands me the pizza and puts his hand on Jaxson's shoulder, trying to calm him further.

"Let's go, Jax," I whisper, tugging on his arm.

His feet stay planted and he looks at Antonio. "How much do I owe you?"

"Nothing, it's on me. Good luck out there, kid, make sure you come back."

"Thanks, Antonio. Sorry about this."

Antonio accepts the apology with a nod then turns his attention to me. "Take care, Miss Julia, I'll see you soon."

Everyone's eyes are on us as we walk out the door. Once we get into my car, Jaxson loses control, his fists pounding on my steering wheel. "Fuck!"

I flinch, not expecting the outburst.

His hard eyes train on me, pinning me in place. "Jules, you have to promise me that you won't go anywhere near that asshole. Not ever."

"What is it with you two? Why do y'all hate each other so much?"

"Just promise me you'll stay away from him. If he gives you any problems you go to Cooper right away, okay?"

I'm a little surprised at how intense he is about this. "I'll be fine. I'm pretty sure he only talks to me now just to get under your skin. He's always been nothing but polite to me."

"That's because he wants in your fucking pants! Christ, Julia, will you just trust me on this? I know shit about him that you don't."

He looks so panicked that I lean over and hug him. "All right, I promise. Don't worry. I'll go to Cooper if I need to, but I'm sure it'll be fine."

He reaches over the console of the car and wraps his arms around me, pulling me to him and hugging me tightly. "I don't know what I'd do if something happened to you," he murmurs.

My heart warms, and throat tightens. I'm curious what he knows about Wyatt that has him so concerned for my safety. "Nothing is going to happen to me. You're the one who's going to be a SEAL, you're in more danger than I am." Sadness washes over me as I'm reminded about him leaving. It's easy to forget when I'm in his arms. "Come on, let's go, and in the future please don't beat my car again."

"Sorry." He smirks, not looking very apologetic.

I'm really going to miss that sexy smirk – I'm going to miss everything about him.

The evening is warm, the cool ocean breeze a welcome relief to my heated skin. We eat mostly in comfortable silence, the crash of the waves washing over me and soothing my nerves as I debate when to pour my heart out. Should I wait until the end of the night or do it soon? But what happens if it doesn't go well? I don't want our night to end too quickly.

I don't want it to end at all.

"When do classes start for you?" Jaxson asks, breaking into my tormented thoughts as he cleans up our garbage from supper.

"In three weeks. I just purchased my textbooks yesterday." I'm attending college in Charleston to get my teaching degree and am really excited about it. "I'm not really looking forward to four more years of school, but I'm hoping the elementary school will have a position for me when I'm done," I tell him.

"You're going to be a good teacher, Jules."

"Thanks," I say softly, giving him a smile. "So tell me what all this training is going to entail for you?"

He cocks a brow, looking at me doubtfully. "You really want to hear about it?"

"Of course I do." Scooting closer to him, I get into our usual position of me wrapping both my arms around his one, and lean back on the log behind us.

"Well BUD/S, which stands for Basic Underwater Demolition/SEAL, is a six month process with different stages. The first eight weeks are the roughest on recruits, both mentally and physically, or so I've heard. The third week being the toughest of all, which is why they call it 'hell week.' They put us through a lot of shit to see how much our mind and body can endure. I've heard a lot of people drop out before the first eight weeks are finished because they can't handle it. But—" His words stop abruptly when he looks down and sees my horrified expression. "Okay, that's enough info for you," he chuckles.

"Why would you put yourself through that? What if something happens to you?"

"Jules, they're not going to kill us. They're just going to make us wish we were dead." He jokes.

"It's not funny," I whisper, my heart heavy with worry.

He drops his arm around my shoulders, pulling me in close. "I'll be fine; I can handle it, Jules. Nothing is going to happen to me, I promise."

I turn my face up to his, our mouths so close that I can feel his breath on my lips. As if sensing my thoughts his eyes drop to my mouth. I think about making my move now, but he looks away, breaking the moment.

Things become kind of awkward, so I decide now is a good time to give him his present.

"I have something for you," I tell him, sitting up to reach for my purse.

"What? Why? I don't need anything," he grumbles.

He doesn't like receiving presents, but I don't care.

"Stop your grumbling, it's nothing big, and it's important to me for you to have this." Pulling out the small velvet black box, I hand it to him.

He eyes it for a long moment, looking uncomfortable.

"Don't worry, it's not an engagement ring," I tease.

Chuckling, he accepts the gift and opens it, revealing the stainless steel chain with the metal pendant.

"It's a medallion of Archangel Michael," I explain. "It's for protection. I had Father Gabriel bless it for you. Promise me you will always wear it, no matter what you're doing or where you are, you'll always have it with you."

He watches me with an emotion I can't decipher, and I start feeling unsure, thinking he might not like it.

"How much was this?" he asks oddly.

"Not much. I already had the pendant, I just bought the chain."

"The pendant was yours?"

I nod, knowing he's not going to like what I say next. "Yeah, my mom gave it to me."

He drops the necklace back in my hand so fast I barely have time to register it. "Fuck that, Julia. I'm not taking something your mom gave to you."

"Stop! It's my pendant, and I will do what I want with it. I know my mom would be okay that I'm giving this to you." I shift now so I'm sitting right in front of him. His ice-blue eyes are burning with frustration, and I'm worried he's not going to accept it. "Please take it, Jax, you need it more than I do. It gives me comfort knowing you'll have it."

"Damn it, Julia," he breathes, resting his forehead on mine.

I place the necklace back in his hand and close his fingers around it. With our faces so close, I know now's my chance. Before I can chicken out, I tentatively brush my lips across his, giving him a gentle kiss. His eyes flare in shock, but he doesn't pull away. Taking this as a good sign, I press my lips against his again, more firmly this time.

"Julia," he growls out the warning. "Ah, fuck it!" Grabbing the back of my head, he crushes his mouth to mine, kissing me with an intensity that steals my breath.

Oh god!

His tongue thrusts past my lips, taking what I so eagerly want to give him. My senses reel, head spinning as I become intoxicated with the taste of him. Gripping my hips, he lifts me to straddle him. My arms wind around his neck, fingers threading through his soft, messy hair as I match him stroke for stroke.

His warm hands glide up my bare thighs, slipping under my skirt to cup my bottom. A low growl rumbles from his chest, vibrating against my lips.

I move against him, feeling like I can't get close enough. That's when he reverses our positions, flipping me to my back, his hard body covering mine. I moan against his lips, feeling how hard he is between my legs. His rough jeans rub against my satin panties, causing the best sensations to ripple through my body. I raise my hips, craving more of him.

"You taste fucking incredible," he mumbles, his lips traveling down the column of my throat, nipping and tasting. I take the opportunity to suck in lungfuls of much needed air as he cherishes the skin he passes.

He slides the straps of my tank top down my shoulders until the lace material is bunched at my waist. His eyes ignite as he stares down at my hot pink, satin bra; his fierce expression robbing me of air.

"Touch me," I plead impatiently. I feel like I've been waiting my whole life for this moment.

"Oh, baby, don't worry, I fucking plan on it."

My stomach tightens at the erotic promise. Sliding his hand up my stomach, he grazes over one breast before flicking the front clasp of my bra. The cups fall open, baring me to his stare, the warm ocean breeze triggering yet another incredible sensation to my already aroused body.

"I knew you'd be beautiful." he murmurs. Leaning down, he closes his hot, wet mouth over my stiff nipple.

I gasp, feeling the delicious pull between my legs. "Jaxson." My back arches, offering him more. His hand cups my other breast, pinching and rolling the tight tip between his fingers. He gives just enough pressure that the pulse between my legs becomes agonizing.

Reaching between us, I start tugging up his shirt. "Please, I want to touch you, too."

He sits up, swiftly pulling the material over his head before taking his place once again. My gasp and his groan mingle in the air between us as his hot skin falls upon mine.

"Jesus, Julia, you have the softest skin I've ever felt."

His back ripples and flexes under my touch as I hold him desperately close; scared if I don't, this won't be real. Moving his hand down between our bodies, he gently runs one finger down the center of my panties.

"So fucking wet." Pulling my panties to the side, he runs his finger through my wet heat and stills. "You're bare?" he says, sounding surprised. "I might actually die from this."

A harsh cry parts my lips as his fingers begin stroking, skillfully massaging the bundle of nerves that ache for attention.

"I can't wait to feel you come," he growls.

"Jaxson." His name falls on a harsh whimper, my impending orgasm inching closer by the second. I wait for the mind numbing pleasure to take me but he moves his finger away, stealing my chance. "No, please don't stop!"

He reassures me by sticking one finger inside then quickly follows with another. I cry out at the beautiful invasion, my legs clamping around his arm, trapping his hand inside of me.

"Easy, baby, let me in. Trust me, I'm going to take care of you." He pushes my legs apart, pumping his fingers in and out of my wet heat. "Fuck. You're so hot, so tight."

His rough voice in my ear adds to the sensations overtaking my body. I grab his wrist, holding his arm in place and ride his skilled fingers, each thrust taking me higher and higher. He changes the position of his hand, his palm exerting the perfect amount of pressure.

"Open your eyes, Julia, I want to see you when you come."

My eyes snap open, his possessive gaze consuming me, stealing my heart a little more.

"Let go, baby, I've got you." Leaning down, he takes my nipple between his teeth, the sharp graze sending me hurtling over the edge of destruction.

Pleasure slams into me, an army of sensations exploding through my body as I soar to a place I've never been before. One so powerful and life changing, I know my heart will never recover from it. Jaxson holds me through it all, his fingers relentless until I'm limp and sated.

I become aware of my surroundings once again, hearing the crash of the waves against the shore as Jaxson's hard warm body keeps me anchored.

Lifting my face from his shoulder, I stare up into his ice blue eyes, my heart pinching at the vulnerability I see there. Before I lose the chance, I reach up, tracing the perfect outline of his lips and reveal the one secret I've been keeping from him. "I love you, Jaxson."

His body tenses above me, horror washing over his expression.

Uh-oh.

Dread twists my stomach into a painful knot, my heart sinking at the quick rejection.

Jaxson remains stock still; it's as if he's frozen in place.

"Say something," I choke out softly.

He pushes off the ground, jumping to his feet, my voice snapping him out of his shock. "Shit, shit, shit. What the fuck am I doing?" he mutters, pacing back and forth like a caged animal.

Feeling cold and exposed, I put my bra and shirt back into place then sit up, hugging my knees to my chest. Once he's done talking to himself, he finally turns to me, his expression full of regret.

Ouch.

"Jules, I'm so fucking sorry, I don't know what the hell I was thinking. I got carried away."

I stare back at him, wondering if he's serious. "That's what you have to say right now? What exactly are you sorry for?"

"What we just did... it shouldn't have happened," he says, shattering my soul into a thousand pieces. "Fuck, I can't believe I did this."

Anger begins to override my hurt, my teeth grinding. "Well, you know what? I think what just happened was pretty amazing, and I'm not sorry. Do you not recall it was me who kissed you first?"

"Listen, our emotions are all over the place right now. I should have stopped—"

"Do you really think I just told you I loved you because my emotions are all over the place? Seriously?"

He drives his hand through his hair in frustration. "I know you care about me but—"

"No, Jaxson, I told you 'I love you', there's a big difference!"

"You don't love me. My leaving is screwing with both our heads."

"Don't you dare tell me what I feel. If you think I said 'I love you' just because you had your fingers inside of me, then you don't know me as well as I thought you did."

"Damn it, Julia. Listen, you may *think* that you love me—"

"Don't fucking patronize me," I scream back, finally reaching my breaking point. Shaking my head, I begin packing up the blanket, realizing this was a huge mistake. "I've been in love with you since I was seventeen years old, but I kept it to myself because I didn't want to mess up our friendship." I turn on him, trying to mask my pain with anger. "Are you really that disgusted with me?"

Fury hardens his expression. "Watch it, Julia, you don't know what the fuck you're talking about."

"Oh really? I don't? Then tell me why you have screwed almost every girl in this town and act like it's no big deal, but then you touch me and you have so much regret and disgust on your face it looks like you're going to be sick."

"I do not feel disgust. You're different than everyone else!"

"Yeah, I finally figured that out." Turning my back, I start to walk away, not wanting him to see the tears building behind my eyes.

"Oh, for fuck's sake! I didn't mean it like that." He charges after me, his fingers gripping my arm as he spins me around to face him. "This is about me, Julia, not you. I'm too fucked-up to love you," he says, his voice completely broken. "Why tell me now, huh? Why would you tell me the night before I have to leave?"

"Because I didn't know if I would ever see you again, and I knew I'd always regret it if something happened to you and you never knew how much I loved you," the last of my words fall on a sob, my heart too broken to hide my pain any longer.

The agony that reflects back at me, has me crying harder. "I'm so sorry, Jul—"

"Whatever, I just want to go home," I cut him off, not wanting to hear his apology anymore. With the blanket tucked under my arm, I head back to my car, hearing his muttered curse as he grabs his shirt and follows me.

The ride home is filled with angry silence. I stare out my window, fear overshadowing all else. I'm worried the damage is irreparable and we won't be able to fix this – that I will lose him forever.

Once we arrive at my house and climb out of the car, he turns to me, handing me my keys. I wait for him to say something, anything to fix this between us.

"Remember, if you need anything, go to Cooper."

I stare back at him, his eyes cold and distant; he's completely closed himself off to me. I can't believe that after everything we've been through together, that's all he's going to say.

It drives the final nail into my heart.

"I don't need a damn babysitter, I can take care of myself. Good-bye, Jaxson." I manage to hold in my sob until I'm safely in my house. As soon as I close the door behind me, I shatter, knowing I just lost the one person who will forever hold my heart.

I watch the one person who means the most to me in the entire fucking world run out of my life, and I don't stop her because I know in the end it's for the best.

Jesus, I can't believe I did this.

I love you, Jaxson.

It's the first time anyone has said those words to me, and it makes my chest hurt so fucking bad that I want to rip my heart out.

I fight the urge to go in after her and tell her how much she means to me because I know in the end it still won't change why we can't be together. I wish things were different, I wish I had different blood running through my veins.

I wish I were good enough.

After looking at the house one last time, I climb on my bike, my throat feeling so tight I can't swallow.

What the fuck is happening to me?

I haven't cried since I was seven years old, and I swore I never would again. But that's what Julia does to me – what she has always done to me – makes me feel shit I thought I was incapable of feeling. And I just fucked it up.

I lost the best thing that's ever happened to me.

CHAPTER 6

Julia

The sound of my phone ringing pulls me from my deep slumber. Moaning, I crack an eye open and squint at the screen to see it's Kayla.

Oh god, what time is it?

I glance at my bedside clock and see it's 7:40 a.m.

Shit! The ferry leaves in twenty minutes.

Dashing from my bed, I take a quick peek in the mirror and wince at the sight of my red, puffy eyes. Since I don't have time to make myself presentable, I toss my hair up in a messy bun, and throw a cardigan over my black tank and matching yoga shorts. On my way out of my room, I swipe my big sunglasses off my dresser to shield my bloodshot eyes and bound down the stairs.

As I'm putting my flip-flops on, Grams pokes her head out from the kitchen. "Julia, where are you going so early?"

"I don't have time to explain right now, Grams, but I need to see Jaxson before he leaves. I have to make things right." I feel bad running out the door when she calls my name, but time is of the essence right now.

My foot is heavy on the gas pedal as I speed through town, driving as fast as I dare without getting pulled over. I arrive five minutes later at the harbor and almost forget to shut the car door in my haste. There's a small crowd gathered on the dock, waiting to board the ferry. I spot Jaxson quickly, and see he's about to walk on.

"Jaxson!" Yelling his name, I start running faster than I ever thought possible. After the third time of calling out to him, he finally hears me; stopping, he turns around to see me charging at him. He's stunned for only a moment then drops his bag and strides toward me, meeting me halfway.

I throw myself at him, my arms wrapping around his neck and legs around his waist. "I'm so sorry, please forgive me," I cry. "It's okay that you don't love me back. I just need you in my life. Please don't leave hating me." Every word falls on a desperate plea as I try to make things right again.

He puts me down on my feet, cradling my wet cheeks between his hands. My tattered heart squeezes painfully when I see his eyes are brimmed red with unshed tears.

He rests his forehead on mine, giving me the intimacy I always crave to have with him. "I could never hate you, Jules. You mean more to me than anyone else in my life. If I had it in me to love someone, it would be you."

The crack in his voice sends my already emotional heart into a frenzy. I grab him, sobbing hysterically into his chest. "I love you, Jaxson, you will always be my best friend. Promise me you're not going to leave forever."

"I promise." He holds me close until the final boarding call is made. "I better get moving," he says against my hair.

"Okay," I whisper back but contradict my words by hugging him tighter.

Laughter rumbles in his chest, vibrating against my cheek. "Julia, you have to let go of me."

Sighing, I breathe him in one last time before stepping back. I frame his face between my hands and say one more thing before letting him leave. "I'm going to miss you. But I want you to know that when you come back, you will always have someone here waiting for you."

His jaw locks as he keeps his emotions reined in. "I'll miss you too, Jules. I'll text you when I get in, okay?"

I nod, my throat too tight to speak. He presses his kiss to my forehead, lingering longer than usual then picks up his bag, slinging it over his shoulder, and boards the ferry.

My feet remain planted, heart heavy as I watch the boat begin its journey. He turns back to me on the deck, giving me one last wave before walking inside where I can no longer see him.

Feeling lost and alone, I turn to walk back to my car, and find Kayla and Cooper waiting for me at the end of the dock. The sight of them brings me a small measure of peace, it's the familiarity I need right at this moment.

Kayla and I start toward one another, our feet bounding down the wooden dock as we run into each other's arms.

"How did you know I was here?" I ask, swiping at my wet cheeks as I step back.

"When Coop got home this morning there was a hole in the wall. I figured things didn't go well with Jaxson. Since you didn't answer your cell, I called the house and Grams told me. I'm so sorry, Julia, I shouldn't have pushed you into telling him."

I shake my head. "It isn't your fault. It was my decision, and I don't regret it; I'm glad he knows." My gaze moves to the ferry where it sails farther away, taking the one man I love most with it. "I miss him so much already."

She pulls me into her arms again, holding together my broken pieces.

Cooper eventually joins in, wrapping his arms around the both of us. "He'll come back, Julia. Trust me."

I wish I felt as confident as him.

"Come on, I'll take you girls out for breakfast," he says, throwing an arm around each of our shoulders.

I begin walking to what feels like a new life for me, one that doesn't seem whole – one without Jaxson.

CHAPTER 7

Giving In To Temptation

Julia

Five Years Later

"Can I get you something to drink, miss?"

I glance up at the flight attendant as she puts her hand on my shoulder. She's been very attentive, and I'm sure it's because she can tell I'm a total wreck, even though I've been trying to hide it.

"Vodka on the rocks please," I respond quietly. Right now, any alcohol would be welcome. I need something to calm my rattled nerves.

Her smile is warm as she sets the small bottle and glass with ice on my tray. "Let me know if I can get you anything else."

"Thank you."

With a shaky hand, I pour the bottle into the glass and take a hefty sip, relishing in the burn that coats my throat. My head drops back on the headrest behind me, my eyes closing as I think back to my phone conversation with Kayla that happened less than ten hours ago…

My cell rings as I carry groceries in from my car. Placing the bags down on the table, I pull my phone out of my purse and smile at the picture of Kayla and me on the screen. I answer as I head back outside for the next load. "Hey, can I call you back in a few minutes? I'm just bringing groceries in."

A long moment of silence fills the line before she finally responds. "Julia."

I falter at the sound of tears in her voice. "Kayla? What is it, what's wrong?"

"It's Jaxson, something has happened."

My heart plummets straight to my stomach, my legs giving out beneath me as I drop to my knees. "No!" I whisper brokenly.

"Listen, he's alive, but he's been hurt really bad."

"What's happened? Where is he?"

"I don't know much, and Coop is going to kill me when he finds out I called you. The only reason I know is because I was with him when he got the phone call last night. He must be Jaxson's emergency contact. All Coop knew was that he was on a rescue mission that went bad. He's at a hospital in Germany. It sounds like he is in rough shape."

My world shatters with every devastating word she breathes.

"Cooper left early this morning to go see him. I'm sorry I didn't tell you sooner, but

Jaxson wanted this kept from you and I had to make sure Coop was gone before I said anything. I think you have a right to know."

At the moment I can't even be hurt that he tried to keep this from me, all I can comprehend is that I need to go. I need to be with him. "I'm going. I don't care if he wants me there or not."

"I figured you were going to say that," she sighs. "I've already looked at flight options for you, and there's one that leaves in six hours. Do you think you can make that? The next one after that isn't for a few days."

"Yes, book it." I rush back into the house and begin packing.

"I'm doing it as we speak. I'll be there soon to help you pack, then I'll drive you to the airport."

"Thanks, Kayla," I whisper, valuing her loyalty and friendship more than ever. "I'll try to smooth things over with Cooper for you when I get there."

"Don't worry about Coop, I'll deal with him. He's going to be spittin' mad, but he'll forgive me, eventually. You deserve to know."

Damn right I do and if I wasn't so terrified for him I would be angry that he wanted it kept from me. Instead, I plead with God for him to be okay.

I'm pulled back to the present when the elderly gentleman next to me asks a question. "Are you going to Germany for business or pleasure, sugar?" He winks, giving me a flirtatious grin.

I try to return a smile but don't have much luck. "Neither, actually. I'm going to visit a friend who's in the hospital there."

His easy demeanor changes, expression sobering. "A soldier?" he asks, surprising me.

"Close, a Navy SEAL. How did you know?"

"I'm an ex-Marine. I've had to visit a few of my men in Germany a time or two," he tells me, his expression dark. "How bad is he?" He shakes his head before I'm able to respond. "Never mind, that was rude of me to ask."

"No. It's all right. Honestly, I'm really not sure. I haven't spoken to him, he doesn't even know I'm coming."

A low whistles hurdles past his lips as he tries lightening the moment. "If he's a SEAL he must have a pretty big ego." He chuckles, and this time I do smile back.

"Sometimes, but he's a really good guy, the best I've ever known," I answer, swallowing past the ache in my throat.

"It seems that this fellow may be more than a friend?"

"It's complicated."

"Love can be complicated, I agree with that."

Unsure of how to respond, I nod then lay my head back again, remembering Jaxson's graduation. I had found out about it only a few days before from Cooper. He wanted to go, but couldn't leave work. I was hurt that Jaxson never told me about it but there was no way I wasn't going to be there for him. So I had booked a flight to leave that Saturday morning and decided to stay the night in hopes Jaxson would be able to do something after.

It was a night that changed my life forever…

My nerves are a jumbled mess by the time I arrive at the training center. I'm hoping the soft purple maxi dress I'm wearing is appropriate. I have no idea how formal the ceremony is going to be. My fears are laid to rest when I walk in and see everyone else dressed in relatively the same manner.

They are all seated with their cameras, waiting proudly. It makes me sad to think if I hadn't found out about it then no one would have been here for Jaxson.

I choose a spot in the middle. I want him to see me, but not too easily. Cooper promised not to tell him I was coming.

When the graduates finally walk in, my breath locks in my chest at the sight of Jaxson. It has been six long months since I laid eyes on him and he looks incredibly sexy in his formal Navy uniform.

As he takes his seat, I see him laugh at something the guy next to him is saying. It's something that is rare for him to do and I can't stop from smiling with him. He looks so at ease, so… himself. Emotion wells inside of me when I realize this is what he was talking about when he said he didn't fit in back home. The only time I've ever saw him like this was when he's with Cooper or me. But in this moment, among all the other graduates, he looks like he is exactly where he's meant to be.

A senior officer makes his way to the podium and begins his speech. He congratulates the men on their hard work, and the importance of where their lives are headed. The speech is incredibly moving, and it's impossible not to respect all the men who are seated there, waiting to be awarded for their accomplishment.

When he finishes, each of the men are called up one at a time and given a certificate and medal. There are so many cheers and pictures being taken from loved ones that I make sure my camera and lungs are ready for Jaxson. He hasn't looked into the crowd once, thinking no one will be here for him. My heart pinches at the thought.

"Before I call out the next name, I want to give special recognition to this new SEAL," the senior officer says. "He's graduating top of this class, and may be one of the strongest men I've ever had come into this program. His dedication and hard work impressed not only myself, but many other senior officers and fellow SEALs. Every man sitting here has proven himself, but this officer made history by setting record times in his physical training. So with that being said, I'd like you all to congratulate Officer Jaxson Reid."

My jaw hits the floor as the crowd erupts in applause. The other graduates give a standing ovation while I stand there with my mouth hanging open. He told me he was doing well in training but I had no idea he set records. I am so proud of him and make sure I cheer loudly so I am heard over the others… It works.

Jaxson stops mid stride, his gaze whipping to the crowd. He spots me instantly, his ice blue eyes striking my very foundation. Complete and utter shock steals his expression. Time stands still, everyone else falling away in this moment but us.

Tears burn the back of my eyes but I push through them and grace him with a small smile before blowing him a kiss.

It knocks him from his shock. He shakes his head but rewards me with one of his sexy smirks, the same one that always makes my tummy flutter.

I snap a few pictures of him receiving his award, and can see he's uncomfortable with the recognition. It's typical Jaxson.

After the speeches and awards are done, the graduates join their families, hugging and smiling. I wander around looking for Jaxson, having lost sight of him in the crowd. When someone grabs me from behind, I yelp, startled, but relax quickly, recognizing whose hard body I'm up against.

"I guess I'm going to have to kill Cooper," Jaxson murmurs in my ear, his deep voice

sending a delicious shiver down my spine. "What are you doing here, Jules?"

I pull myself together and spin around to face him. My heart tumbles as I look up into his ice-blue eyes. "If anyone has a right to be mad, Jaxson, it's me. How could you not tell me about this?"

"Because it's not a big deal and you have a lot going on with school. You just told me you had exams coming up this week. You should focus on that, not this."

It's exactly the answer I expected, but it still doesn't make me happy. "I disagree, I think it's a very big deal. I would have been heartbroken if I missed this. But…" I sigh dramatically. "If you don't want to see me I guess I'll be on my way then."

As I turn away he grabs my arm with a growl. "I never said I wasn't happy to see you, I'm just saying you didn't need to go to the trouble to be here."

I peer up at him, wishing he knew how important he is to me. "It's no trouble, I want to be here. I've really missed you."

"I've missed you too, Jules. So fucking much." He pulls me into his arms and holds me close, giving me the safe haven I've had to live without for over six months.

"I'm really proud of you, Jax," I whisper, my faced buried in his strong chest.

"Thanks." He shifts, uncomfortable with the praise.

Lightening the mood, I step back and grab the lapels of his uniform. "I must say, Officer Reid, you look very handsome in your uniform."

He doesn't smile like I expect him to, instead he stares down at me with his intense steel blue eyes that always take my breath away. "And you are still so fucking beautiful."

My heart skips a beat, his words melting my insides to goo.

Unfortunately, our moment gets interrupted. "Well, well, well, let me guess – Julia, in the flesh. I started to think maybe you weren't real, but looking at you now I can see you're very real."

My attention is drawn to the left where the deep booming voice came from. Two attractive men are walking toward us. The one who spoke has a cocky grin and looks me over with blatant appreciation. The other one is the opposite. He has a hard expression and doesn't look friendly at all.

"Come on, buddy, aren't you going to introduce us?" The cocky one asks as he slings an arm around Jaxson.

Jaxson glares at him but introduces us. "Jules, this nosey, annoying dickhead is Sawyer Evans."

I giggle at the introduction.

"And the less annoying one is Cade Walker, both are my roommates. We were also grouped together as a team during training."

Sawyer reminds me a little of a surfer with his shaggy, dirty blond hair, green eyes, and olive skin. He was the one Jaxson was laughing with when they first walked in. Where Jaxson and Sawyer are long and lean, Cade is a little bigger, more muscular, but they all stand close in height. His hair is a tad shorter than Sawyer's and darker like Jaxson's. He looks partially Hispanic with his warm skin tone and hazel eyes. I can tell he has a past; his eyes have the same haunted look in them as Jaxson's.

"Hi, it's nice to meet you guys." I wave shyly.

Cade nods his greeting, whereas Sawyer grabs my hand and raises it to his mouth "Believe me the pleasure is all mine."

Before he makes contact, Jaxson slaps him upside the head, and rips my hand from his.

"What? I'm just trying to be nice to your Jules."

I quirk a brow at Jaxson. "Your *Jules?"*

He shakes his head. "Never mind him, he's just being an idiot, as usual."

Sawyer chuckles, not the least bit offended. It's obvious they banter a lot. "All right, I'll knock it off… for now. Are we still hitting O'Rileys tonight to celebrate?"

Jaxson meets my gaze. "How long are you here for?"

"I leave in the morning," I tell him regretfully.

He turns back to Sawyer. "Count me out."

"No, Jax, it's okay. Go ahead and celebrate, you deserve it." Of course I'm only being half truthful. I really want to spend time with him, but I don't want to interrupt his celebration either.

"No, I'm staying with you." His tone brooks no further argument.

"Why don't you bring her along?" Sawyer asks.

"No."

I'm not sure if he doesn't want me there or if he wants to spend time alone. I'm hoping it's the latter.

Sawyer flashes him a cocky smirk. "What's wrong? Worried one of us sexier SEALs are going to steal her away?"

I can't help the small giggle that escapes. I don't know why Sawyer thinks Jaxson feels more for me than a friend. If he only knew the truth… "We can go for a bit if you want. I don't mind," I tell him.

He searches my gaze before finally relenting. "Fine, we'll go for a bit."

Sawyer claps him on the back. "That's what I'm talking about. See you in an hour?"

Jaxson agrees then they walk away, leaving us alone again. "You sure about this, Jules? Because just say the word and we won't go."

"It's fine, really." As long as I am with him, I don't care what we do.

"All right, we'll go for a bit, then we'll catch up, just the two us."

I can't stop the smile that takes over my face and as much as I don't mind hanging out with his friends, I can't wait until we are alone.

We walk into O'Rileys an hour later, an Irish pub that seems to be at capacity. Sawyer waves us over where he sits in the back with a group of other graduates, some who have girls seated on their laps that I assume are their girlfriends.

Jaxson guides me toward the table with his hand on my lower back, the small touch searing the patch of skin beneath my dress.

"Well hi again, Julia!" Sawyer greets me as I take the seat next to him. He moves to sling his arm around my shoulders but Jaxson catches him quick enough and throws it away.

"Knock it off, Evans. I mean it, you're pissing me off."

Most people would be intimidated by Jaxson, but not Sawyer, he only seems amused by it all. If he only knew that Jaxson wasn't jealous, just protective, I'm sure he would stop.

Once I'm settled at the table and introduced to everyone, Jaxson gets up to get us drinks. Most of the girls give me the cold shoulder but I just ignore them and chat with people who aren't rude.

Cade is quiet and stares into his drink, looking like he'd rather be anywhere but here.

"Hi again, Cade," I greet him quietly.

His head jerks up in surprise and it makes me wonder if everyone usually ignores him. The thought hurts my heart.

"Hey, Julia," he responds, his hard expression a little softer.

I smile, appreciating I got words back and not just a nod like last time.

His eyes tighten in confusion, as if assessing me, trying to figure me out.

Jaxson interrupts the exchange when he comes back with our drinks.

Conversation flows steadily as the night wears on. I get to hear a lot about their time in training, which was grueling by the sound of it. But it's also clear that Jaxson has made some very good friends, especially Sawyer and Cade. I am happy for him, really happy, but also a little jealous. Other than Cooper, I'm his best friend and I'm not quite sure where I fit into his life anymore.

When Jaxson gets up to use the bathroom, Sawyer leans over to me. "So, what is it with you two?"

"What do you mean?" I ask.

"I'm trying to figure you guys out. Are you friends or more? I've tried asking Jaxson, but he's tight-lipped when it comes to you."

"There's nothing to figure out, we're just friends. Actually, he's my best friend," I add softly.

"Really? I didn't know best friends carry pictures of each other in their wallets," he says with a smirk.

I rear back. "Jaxson has a picture of me?"

"You didn't know? I thought you gave it to him."

I shake my head.

Now it's Sawyer's turn to be surprised. "Unbelievable." He chuckles.

"Leave her the hell alone!" Cade fires, inserting himself into the conversation.

"What? I'm just asking about the picture. You're my best friend and I don't carry a picture of you."

Before any of us can say more, Jaxson returns, ending the conversation. However, it doesn't stop me from wondering what picture Sawyer is talking about. I'm completely floored to know he has one. It warms me and also eases a little bit of my earlier worry about where I stand with him.

About an hour later Jaxson asks if I am ready to leave. I don't want to sound too eager but I don't hold back either, because the truth is, I need to be with him. Just the two of us.

"Yeah," I respond with a smile.

"What hotel are you staying at?"

"The Delta. It's not far from where the ceremony was."

He nods. "I know which one."

We stand up and are saying our good-byes when a girl comes stumbling toward us, her blood shot eyes on Jaxson only.

I feel him stiffen as she approaches.

"Hi, Jaxson, I didn't know you were going to be here tonight. Lucky me," she croons, her finger running down his arm.

I feel like someone has punched me in the stomach.

"Kat. We were just leaving," he replies stiffly.

She moves her attention to me, her eyes narrowing. "Who's the whore?"

Before I'm able to tell the bitch where to go, Jaxson steps in front of me, getting in her face. "Back off! You don't know anything about her. You got a problem with me, fine, but you fucking leave her out of it."

It takes her down a notch. She shifts on her feet and takes a nervous swallow. "I'm sorry, Jax, I've just missed you."

Jax?

No one calls him that but me and it sends my already heated blood rising to a dangerous temperature. I hate that I'm caught up in this embarrassing scene and everyone is staring. But most of all, I'm mad that Jaxson is nothing more than a manwhore.

I decide it's time to leave before the situation gets more out of hand. But first, I turn to the table of guys and offer a quick wave, not wanting to be rude. "Well it's been fun, nice meeting y'all, and good luck with your new career."

I don't wait for their goodbyes before I get the hell out of there.

The moment I step outside into the fresh air, I inhale a deep breath and try to shove aside the angry hurt that is lodged in my throat.

Jaxson races out the door after me but I take off, walking in the opposite direction.

"Julia, wait!"

I ignore him and keep my pace, the fast clicking of my heels matching the angry rhythm of my heartbeat.

"Damn it, Julia. Get your sweet little ass back here."

If he thinks by calling my ass sweet that I'm going to come strolling back, he has another thing comin'.

He catches up to me, spinning me around to face him. "Where the hell are you going?"

"To my hotel!" I yank my arm back and continue on my way.

"You're not even going the right way."

Damn!

Stopping, I turn back around and start in the other direction.

"Why the hell are you mad at me?"

He is so oblivious it makes me want to slap the stupid out of him. Instead, I round on him, my angry eyes colliding with his. "Did you screw her?" The question flies out of my mouth before I'm able to stop it. I put my hand up at his stunned expression. "Never mind, don't answer that. I already know the answer, because you're a stupid manwhore! I'm glad to see how easy it's been for you to start a new life." I know that isn't fair to say, but I can't seem to stop. I'm so angry and hurt.

"What the fuck does that mean?"

"It means that all of you have moved on but me. For the longest time it was always the four of us – Kayla and Cooper, you and me. Kayla still has Cooper. You moved here and made new friends and started a new life so easily. I just had it thrown in my face that what happened between us six months ago means nothing to you. While back home I can't move on because I can't stop thinking about you and missing you. I know it's not your fault that you don't care for me the same way I care for you, but it still hurts damn it!" The last of my words fall on a sob.

"Jesus, Julia." His voice is gruff as he pulls me into his arms. "You're wrong. Yes, I've moved on in some ways, but don't think for one second that I've moved on from you. I think about you every damn day. That night with you on the beach fucking haunts me, and that bitch means nothing to me, just like the rest of them. I know you don't understand that but it's the truth."

"She called you Jax," I whisper.

"What?"

"She called you Jax. Only I call you that." I don't care how dumb it sounds. That is something between the two of us.

"I didn't even notice; she's someone I went home with months ago when I was drunker than shit, and she hasn't left me alone since. You know I don't repeat women. She means

absolutely nothing to me, and she now knows to stay the fuck away from me."

"I'm so humiliated," I admit, hating that this is the first impression his friends have of me.

"The only one who should be embarrassed is her, not you, Julia," he says, pulling me into his arms.

It feels so good to be held by him that it is impossible to stay mad. "I'm sorry I called you stupid, Jaxson. You're not stupid; you're the smartest person I know," I apologize. "And I'm sorry I called you a manwhore, even if you are, I shouldn't have said it. I was just jealous."

Chuckling, he rubs his hands up and down my arms in a soothing gesture. "It's okay, Jules. Believe me, you have nothing to be jealous about, no one will ever mean more to me than you."

I wish he meant it the way I want him to, but I know he doesn't.

"I knew you liked me more than Cooper," I tease, hoping to lighten the mood.

He grunts. "Believe me, what I feel for you is completely different than what I feel for Coop." Before I have a chance to think about that, he puts his arm around me and kisses my forehead, just like old times. "Come on, let's get the hell out of here."

We make it back to my hotel fifteen minutes later. I head into the bathroom to freshen up and wash my tear-streaked face. I'm still a little upset about what happened at the bar, but I know I don't have a right to be angry with him. I decide to push it all aside and enjoy the rest of our time together. I'm hoping he will stay the night. I want to spend every second that I can with him.

My heart races at the thought of sleeping in his arms, but I tamp it down.

"Just friends, Julia, just friends," I remind myself. Hopefully one day my heart will believe it, too.

I change into my usual shorts and tank that I sleep in then step out of the bathroom. I switch the main light off but keep the lamp on, leaving the room in a soft glow. My steps falter when I see Jaxson pacing back and forth, looking edgy. "What's the matter?"

His head snaps up and he sucks in a sharp breath at the sight of me. "Why aren't you wearing any clothes?"

I stare back at him like he has two heads. "What are you talking about? These are my pajamas."

His eyes dart around the room warily, looking everywhere but at me. "Maybe we should go downstairs to the lounge to catch up."

"Why?" I ask, wondering what has changed.

He doesn't answer and remains rooted to his spot.

"Jaxson, I'm tired, let's just stay here and relax," I say, crawling on the bed.

His pained groan fills the room.

My head twists in his direction and I find his eyes glued to my ass. His expression is filled with sheer dominance and… restraint.

It's now that I finally realize what has him so uncomfortable. Rather than ignoring it like I've done every other time, I decide to call him out on it, asking the one question that has been burning inside of me since that night on the beach with him six months ago.

"You say that I mean more to you than any other girl, but then why do they get a part of you that I don't?" His eyes finally lift to mine, but before he can say anything, I continue, "It's no secret I'd give myself to you. I've wanted you for so long that some days I worry I'm going to die a virgin because you're the only one I want to be with. It's you who doesn't want me."

"Are you fucking crazy? I want you more than I want my next breath, but I can't do that to you. You ask about those other girls and it's because I don't give a shit about them, but with you, I care. I care too fucking much."

My heart squeezes painfully at his tortured admission. "I'm not better than you, I'm better with *you."*

I know if anything is ever going to change between us, now is the time to push. By the tormented look in his eyes I can see he wants me as badly as I do him. Who knows when the next time will be that I'll see him?

Gathering up all the courage I can muster, I stand from the bed and start toward him. He glances at the door nervously, as if considering running out. I don't give him the chance. My arms wrap around his waist as I reveal something to him that we both already know. "I want my first time to be with you, and I want it to happen tonight."

His eyes briefly close, jaw locking in restraint. "Julia, don't do this. You don't know what you're asking, and I only have so much control."

"I know exactly what I'm asking. I don't want to be a virgin anymore."

"What's wrong with being a virgin?" he asks gruffly.

I glare at him, irritated that he is denying us what we both want. "Fine." I unwind my arms from his waist, breaking the moment. "I'm not going to beg you. I guess when I get back, I'll just have to find the first willing guy to take me home," I say sweetly, knowing it will get under his skin.

When I head for the bed again he walks up behind me, his hands gripping my hips to yank me back against him.

I suck in a startled breath when I feel how hard he is against my bottom.

One of his arms locks around my chest and the other around my waist, keeping me close. "Be careful, Julia, you're playing with fire. I've tried hard for a long time to do the right thing, but you're about to make me throw it all away." His rough warning has a shiver dancing down my spine.

My breathing speeds up in anticipation for what is about to happen.

I turn back to face him, letting him see my truth. "I want it to be you, not someone else. I know you can't give me forever, but you can give me who I want it to be with."

A battle rages in his eyes, exposing all of his demons he always fights so hard against. I pray I know what I am getting us both into. My hands shake as I grab the hem of my tank top and pull it over my head, dropping it to the floor. His eyes melt into liquid fire as I stand before him in my lilac, lace bra. I fight through the urge to cover myself, ready to finally give myself freely to him, body and soul.

A curse pushes past his lips as he jerks me against him and claims my mouth in a ruthless kiss. The taste of him, mingled with beer, floods my senses and sends my head reeling. I decide the next time someone asks me what I want to drink it will be a beer, the one I'm getting the luxury to taste now.

Our kiss is desperate and consumes us from the beginning. I pry my fingers from his belt buckle and slide my hands under the hem of his shirt, gliding them over the smooth, hard plains of his stomach.

A whimper escapes me with the need to feel more of him, to feel his skin upon mine again. He severs our connection only long enough to get rid of his shirt, and the moment the material is shed from his body, I gasp, my heart stopping at the sight before me.

My hand moves to his chest, lifting the St. Michael pendant that is hanging around his neck. "You're wearing it," I whisper.

"I promised you I would."

He did, and I should have known he would never break that promise. Emotion clogs my throat, stopping me from speaking. Leaning in, I press a kiss to the pendant, then another right over his heart, feeling its fast beat against my lips. His breath quickens as my tongue slides along his chest, loving the salty taste of his skin. It's like an aphrodisiac, sparking the fire already burning inside me. When my teeth graze his nipple, he groans, the vibration powerful.

He cups my bottom in his large hands and effortlessly lifts me up. My legs hug his waist and my arms hook around his neck.

"Be sure about this, Julia," he says, his eyes holding mine. "Because once we start I don't think I'll be able to stop. I've been restraining myself for far too long, but I can't anymore. I know I don't deserve you, but the thought of someone else taking this from you makes me fucking insane."

I rest my forehead against his, forcing him to the see the truth. "I've never been more sure about anything in my life. I need it to be you, Jaxson. This is right… we *are right."*

Without further argument, he carries me over to the bed and lays me down before him. He stands above me, his eyes vulnerable. "I know you deserve all that romantic shit. Like flowers and candles, everything that I don't have right now, but I swear I'll be good to you, Julia. I'll take care of you."

"I don't need any of that stuff. I just need you." I offer him my hand to take, needing his trust in this moment.

He gives it to me and I pull him down, his hard body covering mine as his lips descend upon my skin, kissing the swell of my breasts. My body reacts to his touch like always, and goose bumps break out across my fevered skin.

Sighing, I thread my fingers through his hair, loving the feel of his soft, firm lips. He trails his mouth over my taut nipple and grazes it with his teeth through the lace of my bra.

A heated moan parts my lips and I arch up, begging for more.

His hand comes around my back and unhooks the clasp of my bra. The cups fall away and the way he looks down at my exposed body steals my breath, washing away any insecurity I felt earlier. "You make me feel beautiful when you look at me like this."

"Jesus, Julia, you have no idea," he breathes. "If you only knew how beautiful I think you are, you would never question it again."

A smile steals my lips, but it vanishes the moment he cups my breasts, kneading my soft flesh.

"Your tits are fucking perfect," he growls. "The memory of them torture me when I lie in bed at night, remembering how they filled my hands." He rolls my nipples between his fingers, feeding the hunger that burns within my blood. "And how good they felt against my tongue." He bends down, lashing the fiery tip before his lips close around it.

A harsh whimper spills past me, my body igniting like an inferno.

He slides down my body; trailing wet kisses across my stomach before grabbing the waistband of my shorts. I lift my hips as he pulls them down slowly, leaving me in only my matching lavender, hipster panties.

"I think purple is my new favorite color," he groans, tossing my discarded shorts behind him as he kneels on the floor between my opened legs. His lips place a hot, openmouthed kiss to my quivering stomach, leaving fire in its wake. "You know what my biggest regret is from that night, Julia?"

I tense, hating to hear the word regret from his mouth when it comes to the two of us. But my fear is laid to rest with what he says next.

"I regret not tasting you," he admits, his voice as rough as sandpaper. "I smelled your

sweet scent on my fingers that entire night when I got home and hated myself for not taking the chance I had to taste this." His knuckles skim down the center of my wet lace, passing over the spot that has slight tremors traveling through my body. "Are you still bare, baby?"

My cheeks flame with his question, but it also turns me on. I nod; worrying my voice will betray my nervousness.

"I was hoping you were going to say that." He brings his nose against me and inhales a deep breath. "You smell even better than I remember," he growls. His lips brush the inside of my thigh before he slides my panties down, baring every inch of my body for his view.

My legs begin to close on their own accord, but Jaxson grabs my knees, keeping them apart. "Don't hide yourself from me, Julia. You are way too fucking pretty and I want to commit this to memory."

I do what he asks because I, too, never want him to forget a second of this moment.

I never want him to forget me.

Once he gets his fill, he leans in and begins trailing his tongue up the inside of my thigh. Heat licks up my skin as anticipation builds low in my belly, but I'm also nervous. Really nervous. I rise to my elbows and look down at him between my parted legs. "Jax, I'm not so sure about this."

He glances up at me, his lips poised over my most intimate part. "Trust me, you're going to like this, and so am I."

All of my thoughts and hesitations vanish when his tongue glides through my hot flesh.

"Oh!" I fall to my back, my hips involuntarily lifting to his mouth, greedily seeking a pleasure I have never known.

He drops an arm across my lower tummy, holding my hips in place, while his mouth devours me. "Jesus, you taste fucking incredible," he says, his voice husky.

I tangle my hands in his hair, begging for something I don't quite understand. My breath races as one sensation collides with the next. "Jaxson, I think I'm going to come," I whimper.

His groan vibrates against my clit, and sends me careening over the beautiful edge of destruction. Lights explode behind my eyes as sweet ecstasy soars through every nerve ending of my body. My cry of pleasure tears through the room, ricocheting off the walls but I'm too lost to care.

When I finally join reality again, I open my eyes and find Jaxson undoing his belt, muttering something to himself I can't quite catch. Embarrassment starts setting in when I realize how loud I was, my throat raw from the pleasure that ripped from me. "I hope the people next door didn't hear that," I mumble.

His heated gaze snaps to mine. "Christ, Julia, I'm pretty sure the whole fucking hotel heard you."

Covering my face with my hands, I groan from humiliation.

He grabs my wrists, pulling my hands away. "Don't. Don't be embarrassed, not with me. It was so damn hot I almost came in my fucking pants."

I give him an appreciative smile and reach up, tracing his lips with my fingertips. He circles my wrist with his fingers and turns my hand over, his lips brushing a kiss to the palm of my hand. Deep affection is laced amongst the stark hunger in his gaze and it makes me feel cherished.

I spot the condom in his hand and the reality of what we are about to do sets in. I begin to feel unsure. Not from giving myself to him, but of losing him.

Concern darkens his expression as he senses my hesitation. "What's wrong, baby? Did you change your mind?"

I shake my head and swallow past the knot in my throat. "Promise me, that after this, no matter what happens, you'll still be my friend." My voice cracks and I close my eyes, dread curling around my heart at the thought.

"Look at me, Julia."

My eyes snap open at his harsh demand, his fierce gaze pinning me with the truth of the moment.

"I may not be able to give you the forever you deserve, but I fucking promise you, I will never stop being your friend." He seals the promise with a kiss, obliterating my biggest fear. His lips trail across my cheek, stopping at my ear. "Are you ready, baby?"

"Yes," I reply softly but with certainty.

When he stands up I scoot back to the middle of the bed and suck in a startled breath at the sight of him sheathing himself with the condom.

Is that size normal?

I have never really seen one before, but that seems awfully big. I take a hard swallow, an entirely new brand of fear taking over me.

"Seeing your horrified expression while staring at my dick is not good for my ego," he says with a smirk.

My expression does nothing to his ego, he knows exactly what I'm thinking.

"I don't think this is going to work. I don't think you'll fit," I admit, heat invading my cheeks as I speak the words.

He leans over me, bracing himself on his elbows, and I feel his erection on the inside of my thigh. "It'll fit," he says with certainty. "I'll go slow, but you have to know, Julia, it's going to hurt."

I can tell it bothers him to know I will feel pain, and I don't want him to change his mind. With a shaky breath, I nod and give him what I hope is a reassuring smile. Then I hook a hand around his neck, and bring his mouth down on mine.

It's all I need. The last of my worry disappears at the first touch of his perfect lips against mine.

He reaches between us and wraps his hand around his erection, gently pushing the tip of himself inside of me.

I gasp and he groans at the first beautiful moment. Although it is tight and uncomfortable, it's not so bad; I can handle it. But then he pushes in further and the pain steals my breath. I hug him tightly, my face burying in his neck at the snug invasion.

"Breathe, baby, relax a bit, Julia," he gently urges, pushing my knees apart that have a tight grip on his hips.

I shake my head, not knowing what to do. It hurts much more than I thought it would.

"Do you trust me?" he asks, his body tense as he stares down at me.

"Yes." That one word falls from my lips without any hesitation. I trust no one more in the world than him.

"Hold onto me, baby, I'm going to get this over with before it kills us both."

I tighten my arms around his shoulders, and before I can ask what he is going to do, he pushes himself inside me with one fast thrust.

A cry of agony tears through me, a blinding white-hot pain exploding behind my eyes.

Jaxson groans in pleasure but all I feel is pain.

"God, Jaxson," I whisper.

"I'm sorry, baby, so fucking sorry," he chokes out, kissing my shoulder.

The guilt in his voice snaps me out of my pained state. "It's okay." I brush a kiss across his lips and wiggle my hips to reassure him. That's when I feel more discomfort than pain.

"You sure?" he asks through hard breaths.

"Yes, just go slow."

Straightening his arms, he rises above me and begins to rock slowly back and forth. The first few strokes are tender but the more he moves inside me, the better it feels, and I begin feeling a different sensation. I even begin lifting my hips to meet his thrusts.

"That's it, baby. Does it feel better?"

I nod, staring up into his ice-blue eyes that are filled with an emotion I can't quite name. One that makes me feel desired and cherished. "I love feeling you inside of me," I tell him.

His forehead drops on mine. "You feel fucking incredible, Julia, I've never felt anything more perfect than you."

We've always had a strong connection, one I've never shared with anyone else. But now it's so much more – deeper, because right in this moment, we are one. Our bodies were the only way we hadn't connected yet, and now that we have I know he will not only own my heart but also my soul.

"I want more of you," I whisper, wrapping one of my legs around him, bringing him deeper than I thought possible.

"Shit." His jaw flexes as he pushes back up on his arms and begins thrusting a little harder and faster.

My hands roam his hard flesh, anywhere I can reach, loving the way his strong body ripples as he moves inside me. His hand reaches between our sweat-slicked bodies, his finger finding my throbbing clit.

I whimper, my gaze snapping to his in surprise at the pleasure I'm feeling again, especially after the powerful orgasm I'd just had.

"I want you to come again, Julia, I need to feel you come around my cock, baby."

My breath races as his finger strokes faster, his hips pushing deeper, and it isn't long before he sends me once again hurtling over the edge, leading me into divine oblivion.

"Fuck yes, me too," he groans, then stills, spilling himself inside me. I love getting to see this side of him, what he looks like when he lets himself go. His walls are gone, all that is between us is a connection and pleasure that only we can create.

I hold him close as our breaths begin to even out, our hearts beating together as one.

"Thank you," I whisper, my lips brushing his ear, feeling the need to express to him what this just meant to me.

His head lifts, face hovering above mine. My heart pinches at the vulnerable expression on his handsome face. He stares down at me like he is about to say something monumental that will change our lives forever. I foolishly hold my breath waiting for words I long to hear.

"I'm really glad you came today, Jules."

My hope deflates quickly and I give him a simple smile back. It may not have been exactly what I wanted to hear but I know better and I'm not going back on my word to him. He gave me something tonight that I will cherish forever.

After pressing *his lips to my forehead, he pulls out of me and I instantly miss the connection. As he makes his way to the bathroom, I pull my panties back on then grab his shirt from the floor, throwing it over my head.*

Once the door closes, I bend down and grab his wallet out of his jeans, on a mission to find what Sawyer was talking about earlier tonight. The moment I flip it open, my breath catches. There, staring up at me, is a picture of myself that I'd never seen before, but I remember the day. I had been waiting for Jaxson at our spot on the beach. My long, cream beach dress rested high on my thighs, my arms wrapped around my knees as the cool water rushed over my feet. My face was turned up to the sky, basking in the warmth of the sun, the long locks of my hair cascading down my back. The way the sun shone down on me gave me an ethereal glow.

I swallow thickly, amazed that the beautiful girl in this picture is me.

"If you needed money, Julia, you should have just asked."

I gasp, Jaxson's voice startling me out of the moment. I was so caught up in the picture that I never heard him come out. He doesn't seem all that mad, just… embarrassed maybe?

"How did you take this?" I ask, lifting the wallet.

He clears his throat. "With my phone."

"I look beautiful," I remark quietly, my eyes moving back to the photo.

"That's how you always look to me."

My gaze drifts back to him, his admission shocking me yet warming me at the same time. "I think you're beautiful," I whisper, my eyes roaming down his half naked body. He really is nothing short of perfection; the man looks like he's been carved from stone. The black ink that is woven up his cut arms only makes him sexier. He looks like heaven and sin wrapped in one package.

He grunts. "I am not beautiful, Julia. Attractive, sexy, good looking. You could even say hot, but not beautiful."

His grumbling has me smiling. Setting his wallet back down, I stand and ever so slowly start toward him. His eyes darken as I close the distance between us, devouring my body that is only covered by his shirt. Lifting to my tiptoes, I hook my arms around his neck. His hands mold to my bottom, pulling me flush against him.

"Mmm, you are sexy," I murmur, burying my nose in his neck to breathe in his delicious scent, "and beautiful." My lips slide up his throat and across his jaw, peppering soft kisses.

Growling, he hoists me up, his fingers digging into my soft flesh. "Keep that shit up, Julia, and I'll forget how sore you are and we'll go for round two," he threatens, walking us back to the bed.

"Promise?"

He swats my butt playfully. "Behave."

A laugh tumbles past my lips as he tosses me on the bed. He follows me down a moment later, stretching out and lying next to me, propped up on his elbow. His eyes hold mine, depicting something I can't quite decipher.

"What is it?" I ask.

"Nothing, I just… I love your laugh and I've really missed hearing it."

His words send my heart into a tailspin. Reaching up, I cup his jaw. "I've really missed you."

He drops a kiss on my forehead but not before I see the longing in his eyes, the same one I harbor deep inside of me.

I hug him close, wishing this night would never end. "Are you going to stay?"

My heart sinks when I feel him stiffen. He pulls back to look down at me. "Do you want me to?"

I contemplate lying to him, saying that I don't care either way. I don't want to sound needy, but I have never been a good liar and for just tonight, I want all of him. No holding back. "Yes. I want to sleep in your arms, all night."

I wait with bated breath as he stares down at me, his blue irises saying everything he would never voice. "Then, I'll stay," he says.

I relax, my imprisoned breath escaping me.

His brows pull into a frown. "What, did you think I would say no?"

"I wasn't sure. I hoped you'd say yes."

"Don't you know by now, Julia, I'd give you anything you wanted if I could?"

I wish I had the courage to confess that all I want is him, completely and in every way, but I'm too afraid after his rejection last time. Instead of saying that, I rise up and brush my lips against his. He reciprocates with another toe curling kiss that takes my breath away.

Eventually, we move beneath the covers and get situated for the night, his arms wrapping tight around me as I lie across his chest.

"I really enjoyed meeting your friends today. Sawyer and Cade both seem nice," I tell him.

"Yeah they're cool but Sawyer needs a good ass-kicking, which he's going to get when I'm back tomorrow."

I smile as I remember how much Sawyer ribbed him earlier, but it fades when I begin thinking about Cade. "What's Cade's story?"

"What do you mean?"

I shrug. "I don't know. He comes off intimidating, but he seems… vulnerable somehow."

He grunts, thinking I'm ridiculous.

"There's a pain in his eyes, Jaxson, the same one I see in yours sometimes. I can tell he has a past and I just wondered what it is."

He's quiet for a moment and I begin to feel bad for asking. Before I can offer an apology he speaks. "I don't know much. He and Sawyer are best friends; they enlisted together. He had a sister who died when he was younger. I don't know the story. It's something he doesn't talk about. Sawyer says it was really bad and fucked him up good. I don't ask Cade about it because I know what it's like to not want to talk about shit."

"That's horrible," I whisper, my heart breaking to hear that. "I feel bad for him. It seems like he's in the background a lot, and I'm sure it gets lonely."

"He's not lonely, Jules, trust me. He likes being on his own, and the three of us hang out on our free time."

I don't respond, because I disagree. Who would like being alone all of the time?

"I can tell he likes you too," he says, "and that's saying something because he doesn't like anybody."

I smile, glad to hear I make the exception. Contentment settles over me as I listen to Jaxson's steady heartbeat beneath my cheek while his fingers drag across my lower back. Being with him like this feels so… right. It's the most peace I've felt since my mother passed away, and I wish we could stay like this forever.

His hand stills a few minutes later, his breathing slow and even. I lift my cheek to look at him and see he's sound asleep. He looks so peaceful, something that is rare to see. I press a gentle kiss on his mouth, then whisper the words I didn't dare say when he was awake. "I love you."

My head rests back down on his chest, and as I drift off, a dream hits me fast, one where I swear he whispers the same words back to me.

I startle awake when the pilot announces our descent and realize I must have dozed off while thinking back to Jaxson's graduation. It had been the best night of my life. It was also the last time I saw Jaxson. We kept in touch with emails and phone calls but neither of us could get away to see each other. He was sent out on missions shortly after, and it seemed he's stayed gone since. Sometimes I think he's avoided me because, obviously, our relationship changed that night, no matter how much we hoped it wouldn't.

He calls me at least once or twice a month, and I send him packages of baked goods, which he says Sawyer and Cade also enjoy.

I smile, thinking how crazy it is, the three of them getting to be a part of the same SEAL team. Then my heart pinches, wondering if they're the other two who were with him. I feel like it's a safe bet to assume they were.

Please, God, let them all be okay.

As I'm walking off the plane, the elderly gentleman who was sitting next to me stops me with a hand on my shoulder. "Good luck with your friend, miss."

I offer him a smile. "Thank you."

After retrieving my luggage, I hail a taxi and direct the driver to take me straight to the hospital. I'm too anxious to wait any longer to see Jaxson; I need to know he's all right.

My stomach is one giant knot as I walk into the hospital and ask for Jaxson. I'm grateful to discover the nurses speak English.

"I'll have to check if he can have visitors. There are restrictions on his room. Please have a seat in the waiting area, miss…?"

"Julia. Julia Sinclair."

Nodding, she walks off.

I head into the waiting room and take a seat, my knee bouncing as I wait anxiously for her to come back. She doesn't. Instead, I'm met by an enraged Cooper, his long legs striding toward me. "I'm going to fucking kill my girlfriend!"

Anger begins overriding my fear. Standing, I advance on him, meeting him halfway. "I don't think so, Cooper," I seethe, poking my finger in his chest. "How dare you keep this from me, how dare both of you keep this from me!"

Toe to toe, we glare at each other but amongst the anger reflecting back at me, is fear and it has me taking a step back. With a shaky breath, I ask the question that's been haunting me since Kayla's phone call.

"Is he okay?" A terrified sob tumbles past my lips before I can stop it.

Cooper releases a heavy breath of his own, pinching the bridge of his nose, something he often does when he's stressed. "He's going to be okay, over time. He's really fucked up, Julia, you shouldn't have come."

"He's my best friend. How can you say that to me?"

He shakes his head. "Please don't make this harder than it has to be."

"How am I making it harder by wanting to be here for him?"

"Because he doesn't want you here."

I flinch, feeling like I've been slapped.

"Christ! He doesn't want you to see him like this. He needs time."

My temper flares, and I stand toe to toe with him again. I try to look intimidating, but that's pretty hard to do with someone the size of Coop. "You listen here, Cooper McKay, I'm seeing him one way or another, even if I have to physically go through you. So you tell him I'm here and that I'm not leaving until I see him."

He shakes his head again.

"Fine, have it your way." I storm past him but don't make it far before he grabs me from behind, his arms banding around my body so I can't get free. "Hey, what the hell do you think you're doing?"

The nurse behind the desk watches us anxiously as he carries me away, heading toward a side exit.

"Let go of me, Cooper, or I swear I'll scream," I warn, struggling to get free.

He grunts, unconcerned, and it only pisses me off further.

Panic grips me when he blows through the large double doors that lead outside, taking me farther away from Jaxson. Since reasoning hasn't worked with him, I turn my head and bite his shoulder.

"Ow, fuck!" He places me on my feet and grabs my shoulders, giving me a shake. "Goddamn it, Julia, listen to me! He knows you're here, and he's refusing to see you. No matter how hard you fight you're not going to see him. I'm sorry." The fierce determination in his eyes has fear slamming into my chest like a sledge hammer.

"Please, I've come all this way, Cooper, I need to see him," I plead, trying to hold onto my fragile composure as tears stream down my cheeks. "You of all people, know how much he means to me. Please don't do this."

A curse flees from him and he pulls me into his arms, holding me tight. "I'm sorry, but I respect his decision."

Stepping back, I look up to see his eyes dark with regret. "You tell him if he doesn't allow me to see him then he can forget about ever speaking to me again," I say, meaning it.

"Don't be foolish."

"Me be foolish! Are you kidding me?" I shriek. "I'm sick of this macho bullshit. I've gone through a lot to be here, and I haven't seen him in five fucking years, Cooper! I'm serious; if he sends me away after everything we've been through, then… I'm done."

"This isn't about macho bullshit!"

"The hell it isn't, you're allowed to see him."

"It's for the best, Julia, I know you don't understand that right now, but it is."

I stare back at him, unable to believe that Jaxson would do this to me. My heart has been split in two, and I know I can't do this anymore, I just can't. The realization that our friendship is over has a sob shattering my chest.

"Goddamn Kayla," he snaps furiously.

"No! Goddamn you! And goddamn Jaxson! Kayla's my only true friend."

I don't bother sticking around any longer, knowing it's useless. I storm off, ignoring Cooper when he tries calling me back and leave behind every beautiful memory I ever had with Jaxson.

At the sound of my door opening, I look over and brace myself, praying it isn't Julia. My body relaxes when I see it's only Coop.

"Well, that sucked."

"How bad was it?" I croak, pain slicing through me with just those few words.

The remorse in his eyes, says it all. "Pretty bad. Are you sure about this?"

My eyes narrow at the question. "Would you let Kayla see you like this?"

He shakes his head, his hard expression easing. "No, you're right. I just feel like shit, you didn't see her when she left."

"I'll make it up to her."

"I hope you do, man, because as mad as I am at my girlfriend right now, I know she's going to be way more pissed at me when Julia tells her I sent her away."

I'm pissed at myself but I can't let her see me like this. It will ruin what's left of me.

"I will, I just don't know when. After here, they're sending us to a rehabilitation clinic to make sure our heads get back on straight."

I'm dreading that the most. The last thing I want is some doctor trying to get into my fucking mind and push feelings out of me.

"I'm warning you now, Jaxson, it's not going to be easy. Not this time."

"I know." Julia is the most forgiving person I know, but I realize I'm going to have to work hard to make her understand.

Another wave of nausea suddenly hits me. Leaning over, I throw up into the small pan next to me, agony ripping through my broken body as I shake violently.

"I wish you wouldn't refuse the drugs," Cooper says, taking the bowl from me.

"Nothing else is getting pumped into my fucking body. Not ever again,"

He looks like he's about to argue, but thankfully he's smart enough to back off. "All right, I'll forget it. Do you want me to get you anything before I make my phone call to Kayla? It's going to be ugly, so it may take a while."

"No, but thanks, man… for everything."

He nods, heading toward the door. "By the way, I saw Sawyer not long ago. He told me to tell you that you're a pussy." It's obvious he enjoys delivering the message by the stupid grin on his face.

"I guess that means he's doing all right?"

He shrugs. "He looks like you. Both he and Cade are refusing the drugs, too."

"I figured they would." I take a deep breath before asking about the other person, "How about Anna?"

He clears his throat, his expression sobering at the thought of the battered fourteen year old girl. "They just reached her parents, and they're trying to get here as soon as they can. The nurse says she's been asking for you though; said she's scared and wants to stay close to you."

I have no idea why she would want to. It's not like I made it in time.

Guilt threatens to choke me at the thought. "Tell them she can see me if she needs to."

He nods then heads out the door.

Lying back, I close my eyes and think about Julia. For the last week, it was the memories I have of her that kept me alive. Every time one of those assholes came in to torture us, I would retreat into my mind and think about her. I'd think about our nights together on the beach. I'd remember the way her eyes lit up when she smiled, and the peace I always felt from just being around her. And most of all, I'd remember the sound of her laugh. I'd let the beautiful melody wash over me as I felt every lash that tore down on my skin.

There were times I thought I'd never see her again, and that was when I decided if

I ever got out of there alive, I wouldn't stay away. Not anymore. I stayed away as long as I did because after knowing what it felt like to be inside of her, I couldn't trust myself not to do it again. It's going to be hell on my control, but I need her in my life. I've seen so much bad shit over the last few years; I need her to remind me of the good again.

CHAPTER 8

Some Things Are Worth Fighting For

Jaxson

1 Year Later

I pull up to the small, southern-style house and look down at the address Cooper gave me, making sure that I'm at the right place. It's something I should know, but in all fairness, she moved here not that long ago and I've been away from civilization for a good long while. Something that I'm happy to be a part of again.

As I climb out of the truck, I take in my surroundings. It's a nice place, even with needing some fixing up, but I hate how secluded she is. Even though it's only a few minutes from town, her closest neighbor is a mile down the road. With so many trees you can't even see the house. If she were ever in trouble, no one would hear her call for help.

Don't go there, man, you have enough shit to worry about when it comes to her.

Shaking my head, I walk up the front porch and knock, my fist heavy on the door.

"Come in!"

My muscles tense and eyes narrow. *She has no idea who's here and she just yells at them to come in?*

Feeling pissed now, I let myself in and hear Julia moving around upstairs.

"I'm sorry, I must have gotten the time wrong. I thought you said seven. Go on into the kitchen and grab yourself something to drink. I just need a few minutes, I'll be right down."

Hearing the sound of her voice, after being gone so long, stirs up emotions I haven't felt in a really long time. It's obvious she's expecting someone. I check the time and see it's just after six. I have less than an hour to plead my case.

Walking straight ahead, I find the kitchen and see cookies on the counter. They're still on the baking sheet, warm from the oven. Snatching one, I pop the whole thing in my mouth and groan at how good it is.

Damn, Margaret taught her well.

Taking one more, I sit down at the kitchen table and wonder if it's Kayla she's expecting. I'm about to shoot Coop a text when I hear Julia's soft steps coming down the stairs. I take a deep breath and stand, bracing myself for the shit-storm that's about to hit.

Julia

I can't believe I got the time wrong, I could have sworn he said seven. Thankfully I started getting ready early. My steps are slow and cautious as I descend the stairs, holding the massive vase of flowers he sent me earlier. I'm hoping the outfit I have on is dressy enough. I figured the soft yellow, strapless sundress would be perfect for the hot, humid night, but I guess it's depending where he takes me.

Smiling, I round the bottom of the stairs and head into the kitchen. "Thanks so much for the flowers, you—" I come to an abrupt halt, my breath locking in my throat as I stare at the person leaning against my counter.

"Hey, Jules." Jaxson greets me with his arms crossed, looking arrogantly determined. His eyes sweep down the length of me, lingering over certain parts as I stare back dumbstruck.

"Jaxson?" I whisper, wondering if I'm hallucinating. The vase slips from my shaking hands and shatters all over the floor by my feet, but I remain frozen, shock rooting me to my spot.

"Don't move," he orders and maneuvers around my kitchen, searching my cabinets for something.

"What are you doing here?" I ask numbly, stepping toward him.

He moves quickly, picking me up around my waist. "Damn it! I said don't move."

My arms hook around his neck as I look down to see glass crunching under his boots.

"Where's your broom?" he asks, setting me on the counter. When I don't answer, he grabs my bare calf and lifts my foot to examine it. "Are you okay? Did you step in any?"

My attention anchors on his hand, the warmth of his warm touch beginning to invade my shock.

Why is he here? Why now?

"Julia! Will you fucking answer me? Are you hurt?"

I shake my head and open my mouth to say something but then close it, not knowing where to start. So many emotions suffocate me right now. Relief, sadness, but most of all, anger as the painful memory from a year ago comes rushing back with a vengeance.

Clearing my throat, I try again, this time getting words out. "What are you doing here?"

"I came to see you."

I stare back into his ice-blue eyes, the same ones I haven't seen for six long years, and try to gauge any emotion from him. There's something in his gaze that wasn't there before, something harder. But I don't see anything else – no remorse, no apology, nothing.

Feeling irritated, I push him out of my space and hop off the counter, grabbing the broom from the pantry.

As I start sweeping up the glass, he crowds my back, his hand gripping the handle. "I'll do it."

Not letting go, I yank it back in my direction. "No! I'll do it!"

His eyes narrow but he backs off.

I redirect my attention to sweeping again. "Did Cooper not give you my message a year ago?" I ask, bending down to brush the glass into the dustpan.

"Yeah, he did," the reply flows easily past his lips, obviously not caring.

I brush past him to dump the glass in the trash and notice cookies missing off the baking sheet. It takes my annoyance up another level. Turning, I glare at him. "If you think I wasn't serious, Jaxson, then you're very mistaken."

"Come on, Julia," he says, as if I'm being irrational.

"No, you *come on*! How dare you think after what happened a year ago that you can waltz right into my house like nothing is wrong and eat *my cookies*." I point at the baking sheet, noting the two that are missing. "These are for someone else, not you!"

"I didn't just waltz into your house, you fucking invited me in, not even knowing who was at your door. What the hell is wrong with you? I could have been anyone."

"Obviously I thought you were someone else. Believe me, Jaxson, if I had known it was you, I wouldn't have invited you in." I toss him an extra hard glare, hoping to hide the lie.

"I don't give a shit if you were expecting someone or not, don't ever do that again," he commands, pointing his finger at me.

Oh the nerve! I slap his hand away but really want to slap the arrogance right off his sexy face. "Just who the hell do you think you are? You have no say in how I answer my door. You have no say in anything I do in my life. Not anymore. So you can take your self-righteous ass and get out of my house."

I brush past him to show him to the door but he grabs my arm and pulls me back, his hard face only inches from mine. "I don't think so, baby. We have unfinished business, and you're not going anywhere until you hear me out." His words are filled with determination, and I hate it when I catch myself drawn to his full lips.

I take a step back, not trusting myself to be this close to him. "Fine, you want to talk, let's talk. Let's talk about the fact that before Germany I hadn't seen you in five years. Five fucking years, Jaxson! I received short phone calls, but that's it. Then I spend almost all of my savings to come see you, and you refuse me. I went through a lot to be there for you, it's not like you were just in the next state!"

His angry expression softens. "I'll pay you back for—"

"This isn't about money," I scream, finding it harder by the second to hold on to my control. Taking a deep breath, I say the one thing that hurts most. "When I got that phone call from Kayla, telling me you were hurt, my whole world stopped because nothing mattered to me more than you. Even after you stayed away from me for so long, you still mattered to me. Do you have any idea what it felt like when you had Cooper get rid of me? It was a shitty way to find out I didn't mean anything to you anymore." My voice catches, but I will myself not to cry. I swore a year ago I would never shed another tear over him again.

"Julia." His voice is gruff as he starts toward me.

I hold up my hand, warding him off. If I let him touch me I'll give in, and I can't. Not this time. Not anymore. "Are you even sorry at all? Do you regret it?" I ask, fearing for his answer.

He drives a frustrated hand through his hair, my heart pinching at his tortured expression.

Stay strong, Julia.

"I'm sorry I hurt you, Jules, more than you will ever know. But I don't regret my decision to send you away."

I guess I'm not surprised, but it still hurts. My eyes fall to the floor, needing to focus anywhere else but him. "Then we have nothing more to say to each other."

"Goddamn it! Would you try to understand? I didn't want anyone to see me like that."

"Even me?" I yell back.

"Especially you! How can you not fucking understand that?"

Silence fills the air as we glare back at each other, hurt and anger swirling between us. Before either of us can say more, my front door swings opens.

"Julia, where are you?" Kayla yells, her voice panicked.

"In the kitchen," I call out, my eyes remaining on Jaxson.

"You are never going to believe who's ba—" She stops short, her gaze moving between Jaxson and me. "Uh, never mind, I guess you know."

I nod, appreciating she had my back once again.

"Everything okay in here, Jules?" she asks, her eyes narrowing on Jaxson.

He flicks her an annoyed glance. "Everything's fine, *Kayla*."

"I wasn't asking you, I was asking Julia," she bites out.

Kayla can be pretty intimidating when she wants to be. Of course not to Jaxson, but I don't think anyone intimidates him.

"I'm okay," I reply softly, appreciating her concern.

"Are you sure? Because I'll fuck him up if you need me to," she offers, completely serious.

Jaxson grunts at this like it's ridiculous.

"What, you don't think I can? I'll have you know, Coop's been showing me some stuff. So I'd watch yourself, buddy."

My teeth sink into my lower lip as I suppress a smile. "Really, Kayla, everything is okay, but you'll be the first to know if I change my mind."

She finally swings her attention back to me, her eyes taking me in from head to toe. "Looking good, my friend. You ready for your hot date?"

My heart lodges in my throat, knowing exactly what she's trying to pull. I flick a nervous glance at Jaxson, his blue irises locked on me.

If he finds out who I'm going out with tonight, things are going to get way uglier than they are now.

"I will be once I'm left alone," I say quietly, hating to be rude but I need Jaxson out of here… now.

Thankfully, Kayla gets the hint and isn't the least bit offended. "Of course, I'm out of here." She pulls me in for a quick hug. "Don't come home early, if you know what I mean."

I bury my groan, not appreciating her not so subtle comments.

I'm rewarded with a wink before she drags her gaze over to Jaxson, flashing him a smug smile. "See you around, Jaxson."

He doesn't acknowledge her, his hard eyes remaining on me.

Her proud chuckle drifts through the air as she leaves the kitchen. The moment my front door closes, the silence becomes deafening.

Great, this is awkward.

"So that's who you thought I was, your date?" Jaxson asks easily, his tone a contradiction to his hard expression.

I nod. "He's going to be here soon, so you should go." Guilt settles over me, my heart squeezing painfully as soon as the words leave my mouth.

Stay strong, Julia, you have nothing to feel guilty about.

"We aren't done talking yet."

"There's nothing left to say, Jaxson."

"Bullshit! There's still a lot to say."

Great. It's obvious he's not going to leave easily. My eyes shift to the clock, seeing I only have five minutes. I have to get him out of here before Wyatt shows up.

"Who's your date? Is it someone I know?" he asks, suspicion coating his tone.

"What do you care?"

He shrugs. "I'm just curious."

"Are you shocked, Jaxson, that someone may actually want to date me?" As horrible as it is, I'm hoping the comment will piss him off enough to make him leave.

Of course I should have known better.

"Watch it, Julia, you don't want to play this game with me."

Glaring back at him, I give in. "Not that it's any of your business, but yes, you know who he is."

"Who is it?"

"I just said it's none of your damn business," I snap.

"Fine. Then I'll stay and see for myself."

"Oh no you won't, you're leaving right now." I grab his arm with the intention of dragging his butt to the door but he doesn't budge, no matter how hard I pull.

Ugh!

I stomp my foot childishly, then feel embarrassed.

A smirk plays at the corner of his ridiculously sexy mouth, knowing he has the upper hand. "Just tell me who it is and I'll leave," he says.

"You promise?"

His nod is halfhearted but I don't feel like I have much choice, it's my only hope.

Sighing, I take a step back, putting some distance between us. Really quietly, I mumble the name.

"What?"

I repeat the name again but still not loud enough, the power of my voice stuck in my throat.

"Speak up, I can't hear you."

"Wyatt." This time it's loud and clear.

He stares back at me with a calmness that scares the hell out of me. "That's not funny, Julia."

I swallow nervously. "I'm not kidding."

Before I can anticipate his move, he yanks me against him, his grip on my arm tight but not painful. My heart thumps wildly, echoing in my ears. His expression is filled with a rage I've never seen before, and I've seen him pretty damn mad.

"You fucking promised me. You promised me you would stay the hell away from him! What are you thinking?"

I rip my arm back, my own anger sparking again. "And I kept that promise. For five years he asked me out, and I always declined because of you… for you. But that promise went out the window a year ago when you threw me away."

I don't share with him that this is only the third and final date. The more time I spend with Wyatt, the more I realize I just don't have those kind of feelings for him. But I wanted to try one more time, just to see if there's something, anything, I can build on. He's asked me out for so long I feel bad.

"Jesus, Julia, I didn't throw you away. I'm sorry I hurt you, but don't do this, don't do this because you're mad at me."

"This has nothing to do with you, this has to do with me. I don't want to be alone for the rest of my life." I snap my mouth shut, regretting the words as soon as they're out.

"I'm not telling you to be alone for the rest of your life. I'm telling you to stay the hell away from him. He's dangerous. I thought you understood that."

"Listen, Jaxson, I don't know what went down with you guys all those years ago, but whatever you think of him, you're wrong."

"Have you fucked him?"

I flinch, his question a slap in the face. "None of your business," I seethe. "Actually, none of this is your business. I don't owe you any explanations."

He takes a menacing step forward, stealing my personal space. My back kisses the fridge as I retreat with nowhere else to go. His arms plant on either side of my head, caging me in. My traitorous heart skips a beat at his close proximity, the heat of his body warming me from the inside out. "You are my business and you always will be. Whether you like it or not."

I shake my head sadly. "Not anymore, Jaxson."

The sound of a car pulling up cuts through the silence.

Shit!

"Julia, you here?" Wyatt bellows, walking into my house without knocking.

Jaxson tenses over me, his hard body coiled tight. There's so much rage in his eyes that I consider calling Cooper before he can kill Wyatt.

"Please don't," I plead with a whisper.

"Julia!" Wyatt calls again, impatiently.

"I'm coming." I duck under Jaxson's arm and walk out to greet him.

"There you are, what's going on? Whose truck is that out front?" His eyes move over my shoulder, shock resonating on his face before fury quickly follows, and I know Jaxson has come out behind me. "What the fuck are you doing here?" His angry gaze swings back to me. "What the hell is going on, Julia?"

Before I can explain, Jaxson starts for him, each step calculating. "I should be asking you that question, Jennings. You don't listen very well. You must not value your life."

Oh god!

I step in front of Jaxson, my shaking hands pressing on his chest to keep him back.

"She's no longer your concern, Reid, she's mine now."

Wyatt's arrogant reply ticks me off. "Both of you stop, right now! Or I'll call Cooper and have him throw you both in jail. And, for the record, I am no one's concern but my own."

Wyatt grabs my arm, tugging me to stand beside him.

"Let go of her." Jaxson's voice is dangerously low.

I pull out of Wyatt's grasp to reassure him that I'm fine and insert myself between them. "Wyatt, please wait for me in the car, before this gets out of control. I'll be right out."

"I'm not leaving you alone with him."

"We both know I'm not the one she needs to fear," Jaxson says, his jaw tight.

"Wyatt, please, I'm asking you to do the right thing. Jaxson would never hurt me. I swear I'll be right out."

Thankfully he leaves but he's not happy about it. The door slams behind him, the crack echoing in my house.

My eyes fall closed and I place a shaky hand to my stomach, feeling sick with anxiety.

"Don't do this, Julia. Stay, let me explain." There's so much anguish and panic in those few words, it cracks my heart another fraction.

"I'm sorry, I'm not doing this to hurt you," I whisper, trying to hold back my sob. "Please, if you leave now I promise we will talk, all right? This is all so much for me right now. I need some time, Jaxson. I'm begging you, please don't cause a scene."

He invades my personal space once again, and surprises me by framing my face between his hands; his gentle touch a contradiction to the fury in his eyes. Leaning down, he presses a familiar kiss on my forehead. One that I feel through my whole body.

My breath catches and I close my eyes again, before he can see the tears.

"This isn't over. I'm not giving up." Without another word, he releases me and walks out.

My feet remain planted as I hear the door open behind me, my skin still warm from his lips.

I'm yanked from the beautiful feeling at the sound of Jaxson's angry voice. "I'm nowhere near done with you, Jennings. If you hurt her in any way tonight I will fucking kill you."

I hurry outside to find Jaxson climbing into his truck. He guns the gas, speeding out of my driveway, purposely spitting rocks at Wyatt's BMW.

"That son of a bitch!" Wyatt bellows, checking his car.

I get the familiar urge to stick up for Jaxson but I tamp it down. I've had enough arguing for one day.

Sighing tiredly, I lock up my house then meet Wyatt at his car. The last thing I want to do right now is go out but I continue to put one foot in front of the other, feeling Wyatt's angry eyes on me as I climb in. I flinch at the slam of his door.

"What was he doing here, Julia? I thought you guys weren't friends anymore," he questions, his tone accusing.

"I was just as surprised to see him as you were. I didn't know he was in town. I haven't spoken to him in a year."

"What did he want?"

"He said he wanted to talk about what happened between us, said he wanted to explain himself." I shrug tiredly. "We didn't talk much before you showed up."

Wyatt knows Jaxson turned me away when I went to see him in Germany but nothing else. It's not my place to say what happened. *I* don't even know the extent of what happened.

"I'm telling you now, Julia, I won't put up with it. If you're with me, then you won't be seeing him."

My eyes snap to his, anger beginning to override my exhaustion. "Don't, Wyatt. Don't make me choose, because if you do, it won't be you. I don't know what's going to happen with Jaxson, but no one tells me who I can be friends with."

There's a wild anger in his eyes that has a shiver of apprehension creeping up my spine. I've never seen him like this before. It's then that Jaxson's words invade me.

He's dangerous. I thought you understood that.

"Look, maybe this is a mistake," I say nervously, my hand reaching for the handle of the car. "Maybe we should do this another time."

He grabs my wrist, stopping me before I can open the door. "No, wait. Listen, I'm sorry. He just really gets under my skin. You know we have a past, but you're right, I shouldn't tell you who you can be friends with. I'll leave that up to you to decide. I just hope for your sake that you're smart about it. It's only a matter of time before he leaves again."

I'm well aware of that. I didn't need the sting of his words to remind me.

He takes my hand, his touch gentle. "Let's not let this ruin our night, okay? Let me take you for a drink. It will get your mind off your troubles."

I want to say no. All I feel like doing is going to bed and crying myself to sleep. However, in the end, I agree because I know deep down it will be the last one and I need to tell him that… later. "Yeah, okay," I respond, offering him a small smile.

I really do feel bad that I don't have feelings for him. He's attractive, charming and has a good career as a lawyer. It has always surprised me that he's wasted so much time asking me out when he could have his pick of women.

"Great." Lifting my hand to his mouth, he presses a soft kiss to my skin.

I wait for that spark. The one that I feel through my whole body, the one I get when…

Don't go there, Julia.

Damn, who am I kidding? I'm so screwed.

CHAPTER 9

My truck roars through town, my muscles wound tight with a dangerous rage. I expected a lot of shit, but not this. What the hell is she thinking?

I don't want to be alone for the rest of my life.

Her painful admission causes my chest to tighten. I need to stop this before something happens to her; she doesn't know what she's getting herself into. The thought of that bastard putting his hands on her makes me sick to my stomach.

I come to a hard stop on Cooper's driveway and barely have my truck shut off before I'm running up his front steps. My fist pounds on the door, and I decide if it doesn't open in the next few seconds I'm going to kick it in.

"What the hell!" he bellows, flinging his door open.

I grab him by the shirt, catching him off guard, and throw him into the wall. "Why didn't you tell me?"

He shoves me back. "Get the fuck off me, man. What the hell is wrong with you?"

With anger hot in my veins, I spring for him. He meets me halfway, our bodies colliding hard as we land of the floor.

Chaos erupts around us, the sound of glass shattering filling the air.

"What are you two idiots doing? Stop!" Kayla yells, panic thick in her voice but it does nothing to break through our rage. We continue to roll around, trying to pin one another, our fists powering out.

"How could you let her date that piece of shit?" I grind out.

"What the hell are you talking about?"

I still, and it's a mistake because I get a powerful fist in the jaw.

Shit!

When I don't strike back he stops too. Eventually, we both sit up, our chests heaving as we catch our breaths.

Cooper's furious eyes narrow on me. "What the fuck is wrong with you, man?"

"She just left with Jennings," I reply, feeling sick.

"Who?"

"Julia!" It's obvious he has no clue what I'm talking about but I find myself asking anyway. "You didn't know?"

"No, damn it! I would have fucking told you if I did."

Guilt grips my chest for what an asshole I was. "I'm sorry, I thought you knew."

Both of our eyes shift to Kayla where she stands looking nervous as hell.

"Why didn't you tell me?" Cooper asks.

Her shoulders straighten and chin lifts, as if she's ready to take us both on. "Because it's none of your business. It's especially not his," she snaps, pointing her finger at me.

Pushing to my feet, I try to make her understand. "She isn't safe, Kayla, she's in danger with him."

"Just because you don't like him doesn't make him dangerous."

Cooper stands too and advances on her. "That's not what this is about. Jaxson and I know shit about him that you girls don't."

"Tell me where they went," I demand, not wanting to waste another precious second.

Her fiery eyes snap back to me. "As if I'm going to tell you. You think you can just roll back into town and dictate who she can date after what you did to her. Just who the hell do you think you are, Jaxson? If you're so worried about her then where the hell have you been for the last six years?"

I know I deserve the wrath but the first person to get an explanation from me will be Julia, not her.

"Easy, Kayla, you don't know the whole story," Cooper cuts in, defending me. It makes me feel like shit even more for what I just did to him. I should have known he had no idea. He's always had my back, no questions asked.

"I know enough. I was the one there for her when she cried her eyes out, because he fucked her then never saw her again."

I tense, the truth of her words slicing my chest deep.

"What? You think I didn't know?" she asks.

I guess I shouldn't be surprised. Girls talk about shit like that.

"I've made mistakes, Kayla, and I'm going to make it up to her, I swear. But you have to listen to me; Jennings is not right in the head. I'm serious when I say she's in danger."

She begins looking unsure but she's still too pissed to let it go. "What kind of danger are we talking about here? Danger as in having her heart broken? Because that's no different than what you've done to her."

"No, damn it!" I fire back, sick of the back and forth with her. "I'm talking about physical danger. Coop and I have seen the bruises he's left on girls. If you want to protect her, like you say you do, then you will stop picking a fight with me and tell me right now where the fuck they went!"

Her eyes flare, both in disbelief and fear. "He's never laid a hand on her, I'm sure of it. Julia would never allow someone to do that to her."

"How long has she been seeing him?" Cooper asks.

Fear clenches my gut as I wait for her answer.

"This is only their third date."

"Then it's probably because he hasn't gotten the chance yet."

Because they haven't slept together yet—thank christ for that.

"It's still three dates too many," I say, cutting back in. "We're wasting time, tell me where they went."

"Hold on, don't answer that yet," Cooper says, his eyes tracking back to me. "What are you going to do, Jaxson? I don't like this any more than you do, but you causing a scene isn't going to help. It's going to piss Julia off more and force me to arrest you. As pissed as I am for what you just pulled, I really don't want to have to do that."

"I'm just going to keep an eye on her. You can't expect me to sit here and do nothing, Cooper, we both know what he's capable of."

Silence consumes the room but his eyes say it all. He knows I'm right.

"Where did they go, baby?" he asks, his attention back on Kayla.

She sighs, finally relenting. "The Oceanfront Tavern."

Her words have barely registered by the time my feet are moving for the door.

"Hold up." Cooper grabs my arms. "I'll come with you."

"Me, too," Kayla pipes in.

Coop turns on her. "No, you stay here."

"No way. Julia's going to know I told you where she is. If shit goes down I need to be there for her," she says, grabbing her purse.

"Damn it, Kayla."

"Save it, Cooper, I'm going. So either I drive with you or I drive myself." Swiping her purse off the chair, she pushes out the screen door and turns back to us impatiently. "Are you two coming or not?"

I offer Cooper a sympathetic shrug then get my ass in gear, meeting her on the steps.

"The woman doesn't listen to shit." His grumble reaches my ears as he follows out after me.

CHAPTER 10

Julia

I put my empty glass of beer down on the table and find myself feeling a little more relaxed. The Oceanfront Tavern is one of my favorite places to come in the summer. There are candle-lit ceramic tables scattered across the beach, tiki torches lit at dusk, and soft background music. It all comes together for a relaxing ambience. Tonight is quieter than usual, which I'm thankful for. I'm not in the mood for a big crowd.

"Another one?" Wyatt asks hopefully.

I really want to say no. I'm trying to be good company, but my thoughts are consumed with Jaxson. Over the last year I've worked hard at trying not to think about him. I went from thinking about him every second of the day to only once or twice in a twenty-four hour span.

Wyatt and I have only been here for thirty minutes, and I don't want to be rude so I relent with a nod. "Sure, maybe one more."

I'm hoping he catches on to the *one more* part.

He lifts my empty glass at the waitress, letting her know to bring another. "I have to say, Julia, I was surprised to find out you're a beer girl." There's nothing rude about his comment, but something about the way he says it seems like he disapproves.

If he only knew why I like it. It's a taste I acquired after that night six years ago. One I can't will myself to forget.

"Have you heard back about your interview yet?" he asks, stopping my traitorous thoughts before they can go any further.

"Not yet, but I'm hoping soon. Otherwise, I'll have to look into a different school. Which wouldn't be so bad, I just have my hopes set on Foothills. I really enjoyed doing my practicum there, and I want to teach elementary level."

"I'll get my dad to talk to the principal for you," he says, tipping his glass of whisky to his lips.

"Oh no. That's not necessary, but thank you."

"Why not? He's in a position of power, Julia, let him use it."

I completely disagree with that statement, but I tread carefully, not wanting to offend him. "No, really, Wyatt, it's important to me that I get it on my own. I want them to hire me because they want me there, not because of your father."

"Fine, suit yourself." He shrugs easily, but his tone says something different.

I shift in my seat, feeling uncomfortable now and decide to change the subject to something I know he enjoys talking about. "So how has work been going for you?"

"Great! I just landed a big client from Charleston. There were three of us fighting for this company, and I received the call yesterday that I got it. I'm getting quite the reputation already," he says proudly.

He only recently started up his own private practice specializing in corporate law.

"That's great. Congratulations." I'm about to ask another question but the words get stuck in my throat when my gaze lands on the three people walking in: Jaxson, Cooper, and Kayla.

What the hell?

Noticing where my attention is drawn, Wyatt turns around. "You've got to be fucking kidding me."

Kayla shoots me an apologetic look as they take a seat at the bar. Jaxson sits with his back to it, his gaze burning into the side of my face. When our eyes meet, my heart skips a beat. I hate that after all this time he can still make me feel this way.

"You told him we were coming here?" Wyatt asks accusingly, breaking our exchange.

"No, I didn't."

Jaxson's and Wyatt's eyes meet next, glare to glare. You can feel the hatred roll off them in waves.

Dread grips my chest at the thought of what could happen if we don't leave. "Maybe we should go."

"Fuck that, we aren't going anywhere," Wyatt snaps. "If that asshole wants to watch, then let him. He's going to have to get used to it anyway."

His last remark has my stomach sinking further. I have to be upfront with him tonight. I feel awful, but I don't want to lead him on. He already thinks this is more serious than it is.

Kayla gets up from her chair and motions for me to follow her. "I'll be right back. I need to use the ladies' room."

He nods distractedly, his fingers typing furiously as he texts someone on his phone.

Standing, I trail behind Kayla, following her into the bathroom. Once the door closes behind us she turns to me, regret heavy in her eyes. "I'm so sorry, Julia."

"What's going on?" I ask, knowing something had to have happened. Not much can make her squeal, she's a tough one to crack.

"Listen, Jules, Jaxson went ape shit, like I mean crazy. He and Coop got into a fist fight over this."

Guilt plagues me, hating that I'm the cause of it.

"He demanded to know where you guys went. Of course I gave him a piece of my mind and told him to go to hell. But… both he and Coop say you're in danger. I know they've said it before, but this time was different." She pauses, preparing me for what she says next. "They told me that Wyatt physically abuses the girls he's with."

"What?" I shriek, thinking I misheard her.

"I know, I told them that he's never laid a hand on you, but they're both swearing it's only a matter of time. Please don't be mad at me, I didn't know what to do. I was worried about you."

My expression softens. "I'm not mad. I just don't know what to think. Wyatt has never attempted such a thing. It has to be a misunderstanding," I say, desperately wanting to believe that. He's always been fairly calm around me, besides tonight that is. But still, I can't see him physically hurting a woman.

"I don't know, Jules, if this was just Jaxson then maybe. But we both know Cooper is pretty reasonable most of the time. I don't know why they never told us before. Even now it seems like they're holding something back."

"Well, you guys don't need to worry about me because this is going to be the last date for us. I really tried to have feelings for him, Kayla, but they just aren't there," I admit, guilt building inside of me once again.

"Don't feel bad, you can't change what you feel for someone."

Isn't that the truth.

"Anyway, Cooper and I are here to make sure Jaxson doesn't cause trouble. He promised he wouldn't."

"Yeah right, him just being here causes trouble." I sigh tiredly. "I'm going to get Wyatt to take me home after our drink. The sooner the better."

"I'm really sorry again, Jules," she whispers.

I pull her in for a long hug. "Don't be, I understand. I would have done the same thing for you." I offer her an easy smile, showing her I mean it.

"Good. Now let's get back out there before all hell breaks loose." She opens the door, gesturing for me to go first.

As we head to our separate tables, I feel Jaxson's eyes on me the entire time, beckoning me to look but I choose to ignore it. If I don't, I will find myself in even more trouble tonight.

"Everything all right?" Wyatt asks as I take my seat. I don't miss the annoyed glance he tosses Kayla's way.

I nod. "Yes, everything is fine. Unfortunately, Kayla just got bullied into telling them where we went." Which isn't a lie… it's just not the whole truth.

"It's none of their fucking business." His angry words make me tense. Reaching across the table, he grabs my hand, lacing our fingers together. "I'm sorry, I shouldn't have said that. Can we just ignore him? I don't want this to ruin our night."

Flashing him an easy smile, I remove my hand and grab my beer. "Yes, of course."

I suck back big gulps, wanting desperately to finish it and get the hell out of here. Disappointment crushes me when I notice Wyatt's glass is still half full.

"Another?" he asks as I place down my empty glass.

"No, I better not. I'm getting up early to go visit Grams at the senior home tomorrow morning. They're having a pancake breakfast to celebrate her birthday."

It's actually more of a brunch so it's not that early, but he doesn't need to know that.

"How old is Margaret turning?"

"Seventy," I reply with a proud smile. One would never guess her age; she looks at least ten years younger.

Wyatt doesn't offer anything more. His eyes shift around the restaurant, as if he's searching for someone.

"Everything okay, Wyatt?"

My question startles him out of his distraction. "Yes, sorry… so I have some big news to share. My dad has decided to run for mayor," he tells me.

Mr. Jennings running for mayor scares me, especially after Wyatt's earlier comment about his position of power. But I keep that to myself and fake a smile. I'm getting good at those tonight. "That's great. Are you going to help with his campaign?"

"Of course."

As he shares with me what their plans are, something pulls my attention over to the others. My stomach tightens when I see none other than Melissa Carmichael rubbing herself against Jaxson like a dog in heat.

This night just keeps getting better and better.

The black cocktail dress she wears is a few sizes too small and her heels are so high she can barely stand in them. Melissa used to be very pretty in high school, but the last few years have not been kind to her. She's Jaxson's age, so two years older than me, but she looks ten years older. I've heard rumors that she has a drug problem, and the way she's gone downhill, it wouldn't surprise me.

I watch on with jealousy as she whispers suggestively in Jaxson's ear, something I have no business feeling. His disinterest should make me feel better, but it doesn't.

"Go figure, those two are made for each other," Wyatt grunts, annoying me with his comment.

I tear my eyes away, not wanting to witness him go home with her if that's what he chooses to do. Just the thought of them together makes me sick. However, my attention is reverted back to them when Melissa's whiny voice rises above the restaurant's noise. "Come on, Jaxson. Don't you remember how good we used to be?"

He shrugs her off his shoulder. "Give it a rest. I mean it. Go home and sleep it off."

"Come with me and I'll show you what you've been missing."

I roll my eyes at her arrogance; someone needs to put her in her place. The two beers I just had are making me think I should be that person.

Leave it alone, Julia, this isn't your problem.

"I'm serious, Melissa, leave. You're only embarrassing yourself."

His rejection infuriates her. She steps back, her arms crossing over her chest as she cocks a hip. "Heard you couldn't cut it in the Navy, Jaxson. I guess you're not as tough as you thought."

A gasp shoves past my lips, her hurtful comment striking my heart as if it was directed toward me.

That's it! This bitch is going down.

I push to my feet, determination burning in my veins.

"What the hell are you doing, Julia? Stay out of it!" Wyatt hisses furiously.

Ignoring him, I march over to them, inserting myself in front of Jaxson protectively. "Back off! He said he's not interested, so stop trying to whore yourself out and take a hint." My voice is low, not wanting to draw more attention to the situation.

Her dazed eyes narrow into angry slits and I notice there's a wet, white substance on the bottom of her nose, confirming the rumors I've heard. "Mind your own business, bitch." She shoves me hard, knocking me back into Jaxson.

So much for not drawing attention.

Jaxson rights me quickly, his hands holding my shoulders as he pushes to stand behind me. "Watch it, Melissa. Don't put your fucking hands on her again," his warning is calm but no less intimidating.

"Of course. We wouldn't want anything to happen to your *precious Jules*, would we now?" she spits, her glare shifting from Jaxson back to me. "Do you really think you're any different to him than the rest of us?" She leans in close, her smile taunting. "After we were done fucking, we used to laugh at how pathetic you were. Why do you think he left in the first place? He couldn't wait to get rid of you."

Before I can even register her hurtful words, Jaxson reaches over my shoulder and grabs her wrist. "You're a fucking liar and she knows it. We had one night together, one that I regret. Don't make it out to be more than what it was. Now get the fuck out of here before you're thrown out."

She yanks her arm back. "I think you forget where you come from, Jaxson. You think just because you joined the Navy you're a better person? You're still nothing but trash, you always have been and always will be."

My fists clench at my sides as I take a forceful step toward her. "The only trash here is you, so do everyone a favor and go back to whatever street corner you came from tonight. And while you're at it, wipe your nose." I pick up the napkin next to me and throw it at her.

Kayla coughs, trying to muffle her laugh.

Melissa touches the skin beneath her nose and realizes what's there. Instead of being embarrassed, like most people would, she turns into more of a bitch. There's so much hatred in her expression that it causes a shiver to run down my spine.

I know things are about to get much worse.

"You think you're better than everyone else. You've fooled many with your innocent little act, but I've always known better. You're nothing more than a whore, just like your dead mother was."

I hear Kayla's gasp behind me, penetrating the blood rushing in my ears.

The comment is almost enough to bring me to my knees, a white hot pain striking my chest before a deep seated anger overrides it.

My fist pulls back then shoots forward like a sling shot, all of my fury in its power as I hit her square in the face. A sickening crack fills the air as her head snaps back. Gasps of alarm fill the air as blood sprays from her nose, pooling between her fingers where she cups it.

It's not enough.

I launch for her, fists swinging, but before I am able to make contact, Jaxson catches me midair. I fight against his hold, her comment still ripping apart my heart. "How dare you bring my mother into this, you bitch!" I cry, hating the tears streaming down my face.

She doesn't deserve them.

"I hate you!" she screams back. "Why does it always have to be you?" Her words make no sense but before she can spew more hateful garbage Wyatt grabs her arm and hauls her out of the restaurant.

Jaxson carries me to the opposite side of the parking lot from where she is. My kicking body ready to take another round out of her. "Easy, Julia, she's not worth it. Let it go, baby," he soothes in my ear.

"I can't believe she said that about my mother," I sob, pain replacing my anger once again.

"She knew it would hurt you. Don't let her win."

I close my eyes and breathe through the hurt trying to suffocate me. She does not deserve my pain and I know this, but it's hard. I've never hit anyone before but there are some boundaries you never cross and family is one of them.

Jaxson turns me to face him. His fingers curl under my chin as he tilts my head up, forcing my watery eyes to his. "When the hell did you turn into Mike Tyson?"

Laughter spills past my lips, lightening my heavy heart. "She deserved it," I tell him, my amusement vanishing when I think about her comment.

He nods, his own smile fading. "Yeah, she did."

Our eyes hold their connection, the last six years dancing between us for a fraction of a second before he pulls me into his arms. I return his embrace, breathing in his familiar scent that used to bring me so much comfort.

It still does.

My arms hug him tight while I forget about our problems—just for a little while.

"You didn't have to come to my defense, Jules," he whispers against my hair.

"Yes, I did, she was way out of line. And it's not like you can hit her. Besides, I had two drinks, so I felt like it was my place," I admit, mumbling the words into his chest.

He chuckles as his hands continue to rub soothing circles on my back. It's exactly what I need for the moment.

"What the hell are you doing? Get your fucking hands off of her!" Wyatt's rage breaks up our moment.

I twist to the side, panic thrumming through my veins. "Wyatt, calm down."

Jaxson pushes me behind him and starts forward, heading straight for Wyatt. Thankfully, Cooper and Kayla come running over at that moment.

"Easy, Jaxson," Coop warns, standing between them with his hand on Jaxson's chest.

Kayla throws her arms around me. "Are you all right, Jules?"

"I'm fine." I hug her back, wondering where they've been this whole time. I imagine Cooper was trying to calm down some furious managers.

"I can't believe what that bitch said," Kayla seethes. "If you hadn't broken her nose, I sure the hell was going to."

I have no doubt that she would have, and she would've done much more damage than me.

"Let's go, Julia, we're leaving right now," Wyatt bellows the order at me.

Jaxson reaches over Cooper and shoves him. "Watch your tone, asshole!"

"It's okay, Jaxson," I say, wrapping my arms around myself to ward off the sudden chill. One that took over me when he stepped away. "I want to go home now anyway."

I move to walk around him but his large frame intercepts me. "You don't have to leave with him. Come home with us instead."

A part of me wants to do just that, especially with Wyatt being so angry. But I've already made myself too vulnerable with Jaxson, and I need to end whatever it is Wyatt thinks we have.

"I need to go with Wyatt, I'm sorry. We'll talk later though, I promise."

Kayla's hand grasps my shoulder, her eyes darting to Wyatt nervously. "Julia, are you sure?"

"I'll be fine," I reassure her, offering a weak smile.

I don't miss Wyatt's smug smirk at Jaxson as we start for his car. Once I'm seated in the passenger seat, I can't help but glance at Jaxson as we pull away, guilt crawling up my throat at the helpless expression on his face.

"What the hell were you thinking getting involved with that shit?" Wyatt snaps, yanking me from my torment. "You completely embarrassed me. I have an image to uphold, especially for my father."

I gape at him, complete and utter shock rolling through me. "I can't believe you're mad at me for standing up for myself. Did you not hear what she said about my mother?"

"She wouldn't have said anything if you would have minded your own damn business."

"I was standing up for my friend. She needed to be put in her place."

"Right. The same friend who threw you away a year ago."

My teeth grind in regret, hating that I shared anything with him when it came to Jaxson and me.

"You know, Melissa didn't say anything to him that was untrue. Jaxson is a fucking loser. I don't know why you can't see that."

"He is not a loser! Don't talk about him like that," I yell, tears beginning to burn the back of my eyes.

His hands grip the steering wheel, knuckles turning white as he shoots me a furious look, one that has fear leaping into my throat.

I sit back in my seat and remain silent the rest of the way, my fingers gripping the handle of the door. It isn't long before we arrive at my house. The moment the car rolls to a stop, I jump out, thankful to be away from him. Unfortunately, he gets out, too.

"What are you doing?" I ask, stepping further away as he rounds the vehicle.

"I'm coming in, we aren't done talking."

"I have nothing more to say to you. I don't want to see you again, Wyatt, so stay the hell away from me!" I turn my back on him to flee into my house but he grabs my arm in a painful grip and spins me back around to face him. Terror seizes my chest at the thunderous expression on his face.

I lick my lips, trying to remain calm. "Wyatt, let go of my arm."

My body shoots forward as he jerks me against him. "You aren't going to fucking do this to me. I've been patient for years while you have been nothing more than a cocktease. I'm not letting you go just because that asshole is back in town."

"This has nothing to do with Jaxson."

"Don't fucking lie to me," he bellows. "It has everything to do with him."

I shake my head, panic robbing me of breath. "No, it doesn't, I swear I was going to tell you tonight after our date. I don't have the same feelings for you that you do for me."

"You're wrong and I'm going to show you how good we can be together." His eyes drop to my mouth, filling my body with revulsion.

"No! Stop. I mean it. Let go of me!"

The squeal of tires suddenly fill the night, bright headlights blinding my eyes. As I pull harder to free myself, Wyatt releases me at the same time and it sends me flying backward. I land hard, the impact knocking the breath from my lungs as I slide across the gravel. My head smacks into a large rock and I fist my hair as agony pounds in my ears.

CHAPTER 11

Jaxson

A white-hot fury pumps through my body when I see Julia hit the ground. I jump out of the truck before Cooper even comes to a stop. "I'm going to rip you apart, asshole. You're fucking dead!" My body slams into his at full speed, my fists striking out hard and fast.

"Enough, Jaxson!" Cooper reaches for me but I don't slow my blows. "Damn it! I said enough." He finally gets a good grip and rips me back.

"Julia, you're bleeding." Kayla's terrified voice penetrates my rage.

Looking over, I find her down on her knees next to Julia, trying to help her sit up. My boots slip as I kick off the gravel and rush over, dropping down next to her. "Let me see, baby." I tilt her face up to mine, fear burning in my gut at the sight of blood trickling from the corner of her forehead.

Kayla hands me the scarf from around her neck and I use it to compress the large gash.

"I'm okay," her assurance is weak and eyes disorientated.

"I want him arrested, McKay. I'm pressing charges," Wyatt yells as he stands, spitting blood from his mouth.

"No, don't," Julia cries, the sound making her flinch in pain.

"Shh, it's going to be okay." I scoop her up into my arms and head for the truck. "Let's move, Coop, she needs to see a doctor now." My swift feet falter and I spare a furious glance at Wyatt. "You *will* pay for this!"

"It was an accident. Julia, you know I would never hurt you, right? I love you."

What the fuck did he just say?

He starts forward, his eyes locked on her.

The guy has more balls than I thought.

Cooper stops him before he can come any closer. "Go home, Jennings. I'll pay you a visit later," he orders and ushers a crying Kayla into the truck ahead of him.

Climbing in the backseat, I hold Julia between my legs and cradle her head to my chest, making sure to keep pressure on the scarf.

"I'm so sorry, I should have listened to you," she whispers, her dazed eyes filled with regret.

Unable to find words at the moment, I lean down and carefully press a kiss to her forehead. Panic infiltrates my chest when her eyes begin to flutter close. "Hey, Jules, don't fall asleep. I need you to stay awake, okay? Come on, look at me."

"I'm so tired," she mumbles, her voice heavy.

"I know, baby, but not yet, you can sleep after the doctor sees you." I can tell she's trying but I'm not sure she's going to be able to hold off much longer. "Hurry up, Coop, what the fuck is taking so long?"

"We've only been driving for two minutes. We're almost there."

It takes less than that before we pull up to the entrance of the emergency room. Kayla swings open the door for me and I waste no time. The moment I breach the sliding glass doors a nurse spots me and hurries over with a bed. "What happened?"

"She fell and hit her head," Kayla explains as I reluctantly lay Julia down. My boots hit the hard floor as I follow the wheeling bed down the hall.

"Is she allergic to anything? Any medications?"

Is she? She never used to be… I don't think. Damn it! I should know this.

"No," Kayla answers again.

"Can you hear me, miss? What's your name?"

The loud questions have Julia moaning in pain.

"Jesus, lady, do you need to fucking yell like that, she has a headache."

"Easy, Jaxson, she's just trying to do her job," Cooper cuts in.

"Well she can do it quieter."

Once we reach the room, the nurse tries to prevent me from entering. "Sir, you can't come in, you have to wait out here."

"I don't think so, lady. I go where she goes."

"Sir, I'm sorry—"

"Please let him stay with me," Julia softly pleads, grabbing my hand.

My eyes narrow on the nurse, daring her to say no.

"All right, fine. But you better watch yourself or you're out," she warns, pointing her finger at me. "Sheriff, I want you in here in case I need him removed."

"I'll wait for you guys out here," Kayla whispers, tears staining her cheeks. "Just come tell me right away when I can see her."

Coop pulls her in for a kiss. "She's going to be okay, baby. Why don't you grab us some coffee from the cafeteria? Hopefully by the time you're back we'll have some answers."

I miss the rest of the conversation since I follow close behind the nurse, Julia still gripping my hand. She opens her eyes a little more when the lights are dimmed, the room falling to a soft glow.

"That better?" she asks softly.

Well at least she's stopped fucking yelling for the time being.

"Yes, a little. Thank you."

"On a scale from one to ten, what's your pain?"

"About an eight."

"Are you hurt anywhere else?"

"My ribs," she replies, pointing to her left side.

Shit, I didn't even think to check her for other injuries.

The nurse grabs a sheet to cover Julia's lower half, then lifts her dress, exposing her beautiful, toned stomach. A sharp inhale moves swiftly into my lungs at the sight of her ribs. They're already turning blue, road rash evident from her hip all the way up to where her bra is.

"Wow, what did you fall on, dear?"

"My driveway, well I more slid, I guess," she explains, her eyes drifting to mine anxiously.

I sit in the chair by her bed and bring her hand to my mouth, trying to control the violence threatening to consume me.

"The doctor will be here any minute. In the meantime, I'll go get you something for the pain."

Once the nurse leaves, Julia brings her attention back to me. "How did you know to come?"

"Kayla told me you were ending it with him. I knew it wouldn't go over well."

"I've made a mess of everything. I'm so sorry," she apologizes, touching my mouth that's cut from when Cooper and I got into it earlier.

I shake my head. "It's not your fault."

A knock on the door interrupts our conversation and in comes the doctor, one who looks really young.

"Hi, Julia." He greets her with a familiar smile.

"Hi, Dr. Carson."

"Call me Blake, remember?" he says, flashing her a wink.

Who the fuck is this asshole?

He glances down at Julia's hips where the sheet isn't covering. I rip it up, shielding half of her stomach and cast him a warning glare.

He loses some of his confidence. "And you are?"

"A friend," I tell him, my voice tight.

His eyes dart away nervously and back to Julia. "Nurse Debbie says you had quite the fall." He removes the scarf from her head. "This is going to need a few stitches."

He begins asking her simple questions, like her age and name. I decide if the prick asks for her phone number I'm going to lay him out.

Thankfully, he doesn't.

Next, he shines a light in her eyes, checking for a concussion, then starts probing around the cut with his fingers, making her gasp in pain.

"Watch it, asshole," I snap.

"Jesus, Jaxson, lay off. He's trying to help her," Cooper steps in.

Knowing he's right, I back off… slightly.

The nurse brings Julia the pain medication then the doctor starts on her stitches. She remains still and doesn't seem to be in much pain. Thankfully he finishes quickly.

"Well, Julia, you're all finished," he announces, stepping back. "Now you do have a minor concussion, so we have two options. Either you can stay here for the night, as you will need to be woken up every two hours, or if you have someone at home who can do this, then I can let you leave with them. I will also give you something for the pain to take with you. You'll probably need it for a day or two."

"I'll be taking care of her," I tell him before she has a chance to answer. No way is she staying here with the good doctor. Besides, she will rest better in her own bed.

"No. It's fine, Jaxson, I'll stay here. No need to keep you or anyone else up all night."

"Don't argue. I said I'd do it."

"Fine," she relents on a tired sigh.

The doctor turns to address me. "As I said, it's important to wake her every two hours. Ask her simple questions, like her name or her age. The drugs could make her drowsy and a little disoriented, so expect that. But she should be able to answer the easy questions. If she seems worse, bring her in, otherwise I expect a full recovery."

"Thank you, Blake," Julia whispers, making me tense at the use of his first name.

"No problem-o." He winks again at her.

What a jackass.

Noticing my look of disapproval, he clears his throat. "Nurse Debbie will bandage your ribs and show you how to care for the dressing. Take care, Miss Julia."

Once he's gone I look down at Julia, brushing aside a piece of her chestnut hair. "How are you feeling?"

"The pain has lessened. I'm just really tired," she admits. "Where's Kayla?"

"I'll get her now," Cooper answers, heading for the door.

The nurse enters as he leaves. "All right, dear. I'm going to put some ointment on your ribs and bandage you up. Keep this up for a couple of days; it will prevent infection. Cover it with saran wrap when you shower, okay? You will probably need some help with it."

"I'll help her," I assure her.

I watch and listen carefully to her instructions right up until she finishes.

"Okay, all set, you can leave when you're ready. Take your time."

"Thank you," Julia's voice is soft, her eyes heavy with exhaustion.

Kayla pushes through the door with Coop following close behind her, her eyes bloodshot from crying. "I'm so glad you're okay," she says, gently hugging Julia.

Cooper interrupts their exchange. "I need to know what happened tonight, Julia."

"Not now," I tell him firmly. "She's too tired. We can talk about it tomorrow."

He drives a frustrated hand through his hair. "Fine, but we can't leave it past then. I have a feeling I'll be having that dickhead's father on my ass, so I need to know details."

I can only imagine the shit he puts up with as the sheriff when dealing with arrogant pricks like the Jennings.

"Come on, Jules, let's get out of here," Kayla says, helping her out of bed.

"Whoa." Julia grabs on to her unsteadily as she loses her balance.

Bypassing Kayla, I scoop her up into my arms.

"I can walk, Jaxson, I just need a minute."

I ignore her protest and continue out of the room. By the time we reach the truck she's sound asleep. In the ten minutes it takes us to arrive at her house, I hold her close, my eyes drawn to her peaceful expression. My chest tightens when I realize just how much I've missed her.

Kayla and Cooper help me get into her house. "Her room is at the top of the stairs to the right," Kayla instructs quietly.

Nodding my thanks, I look to Cooper next. "I'll call you tomorrow when she wakes up."

"I'll be waiting."

I begin my climb up the long staircase when Kayla starts in on me again. "No funny business, Jaxson, or I will kick your ass."

My response is a grunt. Whatever Cooper has been showing her, he needs to tone it down. That's the second time she has threatened to cause me physical harm.

I enter into Julia's dark room, leaving the lights off for her benefit then lay her down on the bed. It isn't long before I'm left wondering what to do about her dress.

Shit!

I charge out of the room and down the stairs, hoping Kayla and Coop haven't left. The moment I burst through the front door, I catch the taillights on Coop's truck as they drive away.

Damn it!

I head back into Julia's room and stare down at her with indecision.

Just don't think about it and do it.

Turning her so she's lying on her uninjured side, I unzip her dress then roll her onto her back again. As I slide the soft material down her body, she moans. "Mmmm, Jaxson."

Every muscle in my body hardens. Looking closer, I see she's still sound asleep. With a heavy breath, I try to control the need pounding through my veins and continue my task, as fast as possible. Once her dress is all the way off I can't help but torture myself more, my eyes sweeping down the length of her beautiful body. One I remember so well.

I could never forget.

Her bra and panties match the dress she was wearing, the pale yellow complimenting her smooth olive skin.

Rage ignites inside of me once again at the sight of her bandaged ribs but I shove it aside for the time being and pull the blanket over her. I pick a spot on the floor by her bed and rest my head against the wall, watching her sleep. Minutes eventually turn into hours. When it's time, I move to sit next to her. "Jules."

She stirs, her face pinching in a frown.

My knuckles graze her soft cheek. "Come on, baby, I need you to wake up."

"No!" she mumbles and slaps my hand away.

"What's your name?" I ask, amused by her grumpiness. When I get no response, I give her a gentle nudge. "Come on, I need you to answer me."

A frustrated growl shoves past her delicate throat and she cracks an eye open. "My name is Julia, I'm twenty-four years old, and you are Jaxson… my *ex*-best friend. Now shut up and leave me alone." She rolls away from me and is out cold again.

Damn! She's pissy when she's tired.

I take my spot back on the floor once again. Clearly, by her *ex*-best friend comment, she's far from forgiving me. I will find a way to make this right. I would have made it up to her before now if I hadn't been holed up in that fucking rehabilitation clinic for all those months.

Stretching out my legs, I come into contact with something under her bed. I reach under to see what it is and am surprised when I pull out a framed picture of Julia and me from my graduation. All the memories from that day come flooding back. She looked incredible. I remember the shock I felt when I was called up and her beautiful unmistakable voice rose above the crowd of applause.

It was the best surprise I could have ever gotten and one of the reasons why I reciprocated, wanting to be there for hers. It had been three years since I'd last seen her. When I arrived back home I found out she had a boyfriend, someone more in her league, a med student. She had no idea I was there; I didn't want to fuck up her relationship. And if I was being honest, I didn't want her to realize just how different I was from that guy. How unworthy I was—even of her friendship.

From what Coop had gathered from Kayla, the guy was good to her. It drove me crazy thinking of anyone touching her, but all I cared about was her happiness.

Obviously it never lasted, something I'm grateful for, otherwise it would be him here right now and not me.

I'm yanked out of my thoughts at the sound of Julia's soft moan. I look over to see her holding her head. Putting the picture back under her bed, I move back up to sit next to her. "Hey, what's wrong?" I ask.

Her eyes narrow in confusion. "Jaxson?"

"It's me, do you remember tonight?"

She looks around disoriented. "Some… I think. What time is it?"

"Two in the morning."

"My head really hurts," she confesses on a painful whisper.

"Here, take some more of these." I grab her pills and shake out two, handing them to her, with the glass of water I got earlier.

"Thanks," she mumbles as I help her sit up. I'm about to move back down on the floor when she grabs my arm, her eyes wild with panic. "Don't leave me."

"I'm not. I've been sitting right over there." I point over to my spot on the floor.

"Lay here with me."

Jesus! This is a different Julia than the one I woke up an hour ago. Can I control myself? I peer down at her pleading eyes and find I can't say no. I don't *want* to either.

When I make my move she opens the blankets to invite me in, clearing not realizing she's in nothing but her underwear. "Don't do that, baby." I tuck the quilt back around her again. "I'll lie on top of the blankets."

Once my shoulder meets the mattress, she rolls on her side to face me. Her eyes are dazed and glassy as she reaches over and lays her hand gently on the side of my face. "I've really missed you."

My chest tightens at her admission. Grabbing her warm hand, I bring it to my mouth, giving it a soft kiss. "Me too, baby," is all I manage to say.

She scoots in closer, her face burying in my chest. She's the only woman I've ever held. It's a foreign concept to me, but feels natural and so goddamn good with her. Her sweet scent envelops me, and I try really hard not to think about what she's wearing, or rather, not wearing, beneath the covers.

The tips of my fingers trail along the smooth skin of her back as she finds sleep once again. This time I decide to set my watch and follow along with her, feeling at peace for the first time since the night I was buried deep inside her.

CHAPTER 12

Julia

As morning descends upon me, I wake up enveloped in the most amazing warmth. "Mmm," I moan, cocooning myself deeper in the comforting heat.

A loud growl penetrates the silence, a large hand gripping my hips to keep me in place. "Stay the fuck still!"

I stiffen, my heart in my throat as memories from last night plague me.

Oh god… Jaxson.

The mattress dips as he flies off the bed. "Shit." His palm meets the wall with a hard slap before he enters the bathroom and slams the door.

What the heck just happened? And why was he in my bed?

I try to remember anything after the hospital but can't, my memory is clouded. Lifting the blankets I see I'm only in my bra and underwear.

Oh sweet jesus!

Please don't tell me I tried to seduce him. Humiliation burns inside of me as I think of the way I just rubbed myself all over him. I'm no better than that two-bit whore Melissa.

Way to stay mad at him, Julia, he's really going to be sorry now.

The bathroom door opens a moment later. I sit up quickly, wincing from my bruised ribs, and pull the blankets up under my arms to cover myself as much as possible. Jaxson comes to stand in front of me, leaning against the wall, his fierce gaze penetrating, but I'm too embarrassed to look at him.

"Look, Jaxson, I'm really sorry," I start, deciding to get this over with. "I was out of it last night, I know it's no excuse, but I don't remember it."

"What the hell are you talking about?" he asks, confused.

Of course he's going to make me say it. "I'm sorry for trying to… have sex with you, all right!" My cheeks burn furiously as I wait for him to respond. When silence continues to fill the air I chance a look at him and find him watching me with an amused smirk.

"Let me get this straight. You wake up half naked with me in your bed. You don't remember shit, and you think it was you who seduced me?"

"Well, why else am I half naked?"

"Because I took your dress off while you were sleeping," he explains, as if I'm an idiot.

"Why did you do that?"

"Would you have rather slept in it?"

I think about what he just said, my foggy mind trying to catch up. "Wait, so I didn't try to have sex with you?"

Oh please let that be true.

"If you had tried to have sex with me, Julia, you would still be feeling me inside of you."

A current of heat sparks inside of me, his husky voice making my heart skip a beat. I glare at him, hoping to hide the effect and wait for a better answer.

"You passed out before we even got in the truck," he tells me. "I brought you up here, and Kayla left before I realized I would need help getting you out of your clothes. I stayed on the floor but then halfway through the night you asked me to lay down with you, so I did." The last of his words end on a happy note, clearly amused by my confusion.

"I'm glad you're finding this so funny."

"I don't understand why you wouldn't think I was the one who tried something."

"It never crossed my mind. I know you would never take advantage of me."

His amusement evaporates and he shakes his head.

"What?"

"Nothing," he says then changes the subject. "How's your head?"

"Not too bad, it's my ribs that hurt terribly this morning."

"We should probably change the dressing and put more of that ointment on. Do you want to shower first?"

I become uncomfortable as I think about him doing it. Then I remember Grams's brunch today. "Shit! What time is it?"

"Nine."

"Crap! I have to hurry, I need to be at the senior home in an hour."

"I don't think that's a good idea, Jules. You should stay home and rest."

"It's Grams's birthday. I'm not missing it, I'll be fine." I throw the blankets off then shriek, remembering I'm only in my underwear and yank the sheet back in place. "Do you mind?"

"Not at all," he replies, making no effort to leave.

I point at the door. "Out!"

"It's nothing I haven't seen before, Julia."

Our eyes lock, tension filling the room as we both remember that night. I look away, breaking the connection. "Yeah, well, that was a long time ago, things change."

We both know I'm not talking about my body anymore.

"Not everything changes," he replies softly.

I'm not ready to have this conversation yet so I ignore the comment. "I need to get in the shower so..." I gesture to the door again.

"You need to cover your bandage before you shower, remember?"

No, I don't.

"Where do you keep your plastic wrap?" he asks.

"In the pantry."

Once he leaves, I carefully climb out of bed and head into my closet, sliding on my silk robe. I'm in the midst of tying it when he walks back in, his large frame overpowering the confines of my room.

"Thanks," I say, reaching for the wrap.

He keeps it clutched firmly in his hand. "I'll do it."

His overbearingness really begins to grate on my nerves. “I can manage, Jaxson, now give it to me.” I rip the box out of his hand and head into the bathroom. The task proves harder than I thought it would and I want to kick myself for letting my pride get the best of me. In the end, I manage to get it done and step into the shower, a blissful sigh escaping me as the hot water pours down my aching body. As much as I’d love to stay in here forever, I wash quickly, needing to get to Grams.

After drying off, I throw on a pair of panties and bra, then adorn my robe once again. When I exit the bathroom I come to a hard stop at the sight of Jaxson sitting on my freshly made bed. He has gauze, bandages, and ointment next to him.

“Can’t a girl get some privacy?” I ask, annoyed.

“Quit your grumbling and get over here.”

The last thing I want is for him to touch me, especially my bare skin. Dangerous things can happen from that. “I’ll try and do it myself.”

“No. I know what to do, you don’t.”

“You can’t expect me to stand in front of you half naked.”

“It’s not a big deal, just come over here and we’ll get it over with.”

I remain where I am, not moving any closer to him.

“Now, Julia!” he demands.

With a frustrated huff, I start across the room, but glare at him, making sure he knows I’m not happy about it. I’m a pretty private person; only two people have ever seen me naked and Jaxson is one of them. Both were a long time ago.

Coming to stand in front of him, I turn to my injured side and try to figure out a way to let him see my ribs without having to fully open my robe. It doesn’t work so well.

“I can’t get to it like this. Take off the robe,” he says, his voice gruffer than it was a moment ago.

“No!”

“Jesus, Julia, I won’t look anywhere else but your ribs, okay? You’re wasting time. Don’t you need to get to Grams’s soon?”

Damn it, he’s right.

“Fine. But I mean it, Jaxson, don’t look anywhere else.”

I probably shouldn’t be so paranoid. The guy has stayed away from me for the last six years, it’s not like he’s going to jump at the first opportunity to see me naked. Loosening the knot on my robe, the silk material has barely slipped aside before he opens his mouth. “Jesus, that’s nice.”

“That’s it!” I clutch my robe closed and am about to storm off but he grabs my arm before I can escape, his laughter filling the air.

“I’m kidding, Jules.”

“It’s not funny.”

“I’m sorry, I couldn’t resist. I won’t do it again,” he promises but still has that stupid smirk on his face.

Fine, two can play at this game.

“You promise you won’t do it again?” I ask.

He nods. “I promise.”

I step between his opened legs, closing the gap between us. This time when I untie the robe, I allow it to slip down my arms and pool at my feet. His sharp breath fills the tense air, as I stand before him in my black satin bra and panties.

My earlier irritation vanishes when the smirk he had moments ago is wiped off his smug face. He keeps his promise to me, his eyes remaining only on my stomach, jaw flexing in restraint.

Not so funny now, is it, buddy?

"Hello? Are you going to start anytime soon? I'm a little cold here," I snap impatiently, enjoying his torment.

Shaking his head, he begins the task of re-bandaging my ribs.

A painful gasp parts my lips when he begins to peel the bandage off. I grab onto his broad shoulders as the sticky tape holding the gauze pulls excruciatingly at my raw skin.

"I'm sorry, I'm trying to be careful," he apologizes.

My pain fades at the feel of his hot breath whispering across my bare skin. I suddenly become aware of how close my body is to his, and how strong his shoulders feel under my fingers. It takes every ounce of my willpower not to squeeze my legs together to stop the ache that's building between them.

"Do you want to take some more pain medication?"

His question snaps me back into myself. I clear my throat and try not to let my voice betray what I'm feeling. "Maybe after Grams's. I don't want to be drowsy during brunch."

Once he gets the bandage removed, he gently applies the ointment. The coolness is a welcome relief to my overheated body.

Jaxson's shoulders tense beneath my fingertips as he applies it. "I'm seriously going to kill that fucker."

"It was mostly an accident," I admit on a whisper. It's unfortunate but I yanked away at the same time Wyatt let go.

"It shouldn't have happened in the first place."

I don't respond because I don't want to talk about Wyatt right now, especially with him.

"Cooper is coming by today to talk to you about last night," he informs me.

"Okay, but it will have to wait until after Grams's brunch."

He nods in agreement.

After he finishes the last of the bandaging, he grabs my good hip and drags me in closer to him. It catches me off balance, and my fingers tighten on his shoulders to steady myself.

His heated eyes slowly move up my body, passing over every inch, until the blue irises lock with mine, stealing my breath. "Next time you pull something like that, Julia, sore ribs or not, I won't let you off the hook so easily."

Oh the man is infuriating! Sexy, but infuriating.

"Then next time, Jaxson, don't start something you won't finish," I say with more confidence than I feel.

His grip tightens on my hip, fingers digging into my flesh. "Oh, Julia, you know me better than that. I always finish what I start."

My breath is stolen when he leans in and presses a gentle kiss to my quivering stomach. His confident hands glide up the back of my legs, cupping my bottom. A traitorous moan breaches my lips, my fingers tightening on his shoulders to ensure I don't buckle from the need coursing through me.

Right when I think there's going to be no coming back, his phone rings, dragging me back to reality.

A frustrated growl rumbles from his chest, his forehead drops to my stomach. I shove against his shoulders, stepping out of the dangerous territory and try to regain control of my body.

"What?" He snaps the greeting into his phone. His eyes meet mine as he listens to whoever is on the other end, seeing much more than I want him to.

Breaking the connection, I head over to my walk-in closet, feeling his eyes burning into my back as I disappear. I close the door behind me and drop back against it, all the air pushing from my lungs.

What on earth am I thinking? Why did I have to challenge him like that? It's like dangling a piece of meat in front of a bear. I'm disgusted with myself for how easily I caved to him; the man still has so much control over me.

I overhear him talking to who I'm assuming is Cooper. "She's visiting Margaret this morning, we'll call you when we get back then you guys can come."

Since when are *we* going to Grams's, I think, annoyed.

"I don't give a fuck what he wants, I'll kill him if he comes near her again."

Not wanting to hear the rest of the conversation, I move away from the door and get dressed. I was going to wear shorts, but change my mind, not wanting anything snug against my sore hip. Instead I throw on a short, black, cotton baby-doll sundress. When I don't hear Jaxson on the phone anymore, I pull myself together, open the door, and march straight into the bathroom without looking in his direction.

I'm applying my makeup when he comes to stand at the bathroom door, his eyes penetrating me through the reflecting glass.

"Running scared, Julia?"

Ignoring him, I flick on my blow-dryer and drown out anything else he might say. He doesn't walk away like most people would do. Instead he stays exactly where he is, waiting patiently, or not so patiently, with a narrowed gaze.

Once my hair is dry, I part it over my stitches, thankfully able to cover most of them.

"Are you going to ignore me all day?" he asks.

"Nope. Because you're not going to be here all day," I inform him then make an effort to leave but his large frame remains blocking the door. "Do you mind?"

"We're going to have to talk about this sometime, Julia."

I sigh tiredly, and it's only 9:30 in the morning. "I know, but not right now."

"Fine," he relents but isn't happy about it. "We need to call Cooper when we get back from brunch."

"Why are you saying *we*?"

"Because I'm coming with you."

"No, you're not."

"I'm not leaving you, Julia, so forget about it!"

"You already did!"

Damn! Why the hell did I have to say that?

I look away from him, angry with myself for letting him know just how hurt I still am.

He collects two steps closer and takes my face in both of his hands, forcing my gaze to his. For the first time since seeing seen him again, I see remorse reflecting back at me. "I promise, I'll make this right."

"Maybe it's too late?"

"It's never too late, because I will never give up on you."

My throat urns with emotion, all the words I want to say to him lodged inside.

"Let me come with you to Grams, I'd really like to see her."

I know Grams would be over the moon to see him, too. It's that thought that has me caving. "Fine. But let's get one thing straight, Jaxson," I say, my finger poking into his hard chest. "I'm saying yes because I know she will be happy to see you. I'm doing this for her, not for you. This does not mean that I forgive you."

His lips curl in amusement, kicking my annoyance up another level.

"Lose the smirk and let's go." I storm past him, my shoulder knocking into his in the process.

His chuckle trails behind me, making me want to turn back and slap his sexy face.

On the way over to Grams's, we stop by Jaxson's hotel first, so he can quickly shower and change. After what happened back in my room I figured it was safer for me to wait in the car.

He emerges from the hotel a few minutes later, his strides as confident as the man himself. A white T-shirt stretches across his defined chest, and he's added an unbuttoned, long-sleeved, navy henley over it, the sleeves rolled up enough to see some of the tattoos on his arms. His dark-washed jeans hang just low enough on his hips to visually tease me.

I swear the man is a walking orgasm. It's completely unfair.

"Like what you see, Julia?" he asks, a cocky grin gracing his face as he climbs into my car.

Heat invades my cheeks when I realize I've been busted gawking at him like an idiot.

God, I'm pathetic.

"I'm surprised you aren't staying with Cooper," I comment, evading his question.

"He offered, but I didn't want to intrude, or hear him and Kayla fucking each other's brains out. I remember what it was like living with that shit before. Besides, with the way Kayla has been acting toward me it's probably safer. She might just kill me in my sleep if she gets the chance."

I giggle, knowing that's probably true.

The short drive to Sunny Acres is silent as the tension hangs heavy between us. There's so much that needs to be said, but they're words I'm scared to say and questions I'm terrified to know the answers to. Once we arrive, I quickly exit the car, anxious to breathe in the fresh ocean air and blossoming flowers of the gardens nearby where residents sit and sip their afternoon tea.

"When did Margaret move here?" Jaxson asks, climbing out after me.

"About two years ago. It was difficult for her to leave her home, but she knew she couldn't keep up with all the yard work. She seems to really love it here. There's always an event going on—bingo, dances, and even margarita nights."

He flashes me a knowing grin. "I'll bet she likes that."

I return his smile, the first genuine one I've had today. "That she does, the woman loves her margaritas."

We walk inside, heading directly to the dining area that's filled with seniors. I spot Grams at the back of the room, laughing with a few of her friends. One of them points me out, and she turns around with a beaming smile that dies quickly when she sees Jaxson. She brings a shaky hand to her throat, staring at him in shock.

My heart swells when I look over to see Jaxson with his hands in his pockets, looking unsure of himself.

Grams starts toward us, her stunned gaze frozen on the man next to me. "Jaxson?" she asks quietly.

He clears his throat and nods. "It's me, how are you doing, Miss Margaret?"

"Oh, Jaxson!" she sobs, wrapping her arms around his waist. "I'm so glad you're okay, honey."

Her emotion sparks my own, tears burn the back of my eyes as I watch her cry against his chest. She knows about Jaxson getting hurt and everything that happened when I went to Germany.

His body is stiff from the affection but he pats her back. "It's good to see you, too."

She looks up at him, her hands grabbing either side of his face to pull him down for a kiss. "You're even more handsome than I remember. How is that possible?"

I roll my eyes; the man doesn't need his ego boosted any more.

"This is the best birthday present I could have gotten," she gushes.

Really? I knew she would be happy to see him, but I didn't think she would let him off the hook so easily.

Once she finishes fawning all over him, she finally acknowledges me. "I told you he would come back, sweetheart."

"Grams," I scold under my breath.

She snickers at my embarrassment. "Come here, honey." She hugs me tight, thankfully on my good side, but gasps when she leans in to kiss my cheek, spotting my stitches. "Julia, what on earth happened to you?"

"I had a little fall last night, but I'm fine, it's nothing to worry about."

Jaxson grunts, making me look like a liar.

"Julia Sinclair. What aren't you telling me?"

I guess she's going to hear about it sooner or later. Nothing stays quiet in this town. "I had a minor altercation with Wyatt is all."

"Wyatt did this to you?" she asks in outrage. "I knew that boy was trouble, he has always rubbed me the wrong way, same with his father." She swings her angry eyes over at Jaxson. "Did you kick his ass?"

"Grams!" I scold her again; knowing Jaxson doesn't need any further encouragement.

"Damn straight, and I'm not done with him either."

"Good boy," she praises, patting his shoulder.

"I'll be right back. I need to use the ladies' room," I mumble and start away, needing a moment to collect myself.

This is going to be a long couple of hours.

I watch Julia walk away, knowing she's pissed that I made Margaret aware of what happened.

"Come on, honey, have a seat." Margaret leads me over to an empty table. The moment I take a seat she slaps me upside the head. "That's for hurting Julia, mister," she says, shaking her finger in my face.

I knew it wasn't going to be that easy with her but I try my best to explain my actions. "I'm sorry I hurt her, but trust me when I say it was for the best. She wouldn't have been able to handle seeing me like I was."

Her expression softens as she lays her hand over mine. "I've told you before, Jaxson, she's stronger than you think. You hurt her really badly when you sent her away like that. I worried she was never going to come out of it."

My chest constricts with guilt and I swallow thickly. "I'll make it up to her."

"I know you will, but I'm warning you, it's not going to be easy."

"I know, but I won't stop until she forgives me."

"Good." She pats the side of my face, a lot more gentle than the pat that was just delivered to my head. "And while you're asking for forgiveness, you may as well tell her you love her."

My eyes snap to hers, panic seizing my chest.

"Oh don't look at me like that. I've always known you love her, Jaxson. I've waited a long time for you to come to terms with it, but you're a little slow on the uptake," she snickers.

I shake my head. "She needs someone who can love her the way she deserves. I don't know how to, it's something I was never around."

"Jaxson, love isn't always something you learn, it's something that you feel. And I know you feel it, I can see it in your eyes every time you look at her."

"I'm really messed up, Margaret, even more so after what happened in Iraq." I'm uncomfortable admitting this to her, but I'm trying to make her understand.

"Oh, honey," she sighs, laying her worn hand on the side of my face. "If you'd let her, she could help you heal. I don't know anyone else who will love Julia or protect her more than you. Just look at what happened with that no-good scoundrel, Wyatt."

Anger swells in my veins at the reminder of last night. I'm pissed at myself, knowing if I had been here in the first place none of it would have happened. I always thought I was doing the right thing by staying away, but look at the mess it created.

"All I'm saying is, for once think with your heart instead of your head. See where that leads you."

We're interrupted when one of the staff walks over to us. A girl that looks to be around Julia's age. "Hi, Margaret, is this your grandson?" she asks, flashing me a flirtatious smile.

"No! He's Julia's man, now get outta here!" Margaret snaps, surprising the hell out of me. She glares at the girl's retreating back. "That girl is a hussy. You should see some of the stockings she wears with her uniform."

The lady amuses the shit out of me. My attention anchors to the left as Julia makes her way back over to us, that usual shift in my chest happening at the sight of her. She's so fucking beautiful it hurts just to look at her, mainly because I have to force my dick to stay down whenever I'm around her.

I can tell by the way she's walking that she's in pain but trying to hide it. When she takes the seat next to me, I lean over to whisper in her ear. "I brought your pain medication in case you needed to take some."

She shakes her head. "I'm okay, but thanks." Before I have a chance to argue with her, she hands Margaret the present she brought. "Happy birthday, Grams."

"Julia, I tell you every year not to get me anything."

"And every year I do, so stop your fussin' and open it."

Margaret does and pulls out a big black book from the gift bag. Opening it, she gasps, tears forming in her eyes. "Oh, Julia, this is so beautiful, thank you."

"You're welcome."

Once Margaret finishes leafing through the pages, she hands it to me to look at. The book is filled with pictures of her and her husband, along with Julia and her mom. I've seen photos of Julia's mom before and am always taken aback by her beauty. Julia is a spitting image of her.

"That's my pappi, right after he got out of the Navy," Julia explains, pointing to a picture of him.

"Wasn't he handsome?" Margaret asks me.

I nod awkwardly, feeling weird to agree but don't know what else to say.

Julia chuckles, amused by my discomfort.

"The man took my breath away whenever he walked into a room," she continues, sadness creeping into her voice. "No matter how long we were together, I never got tired of looking at him. I miss him dearly."

Julia reaches over and grabs her hand.

"He would have liked you, Jaxson. I told you this before and I meant it, you're a lot like him. I knew the moment I met you, you were right for my Julia."

Jesus, the woman doesn't hold back, does she?

Julia scoffs and releases her hand. "Give it a rest, Grams."

Before any of us can say more, two elderly ladies come and sit with us, both of them smiling and eyeing me with curiosity.

"Margaret, who is this boy and where have you been hiding him?"

"This is Julia's Jaxson," she replies happily.

"He is not my anything."

I chuckle at Julia's growl.

"Why not? He's handsome, Julia. You have to hold on tight to men like him," one says, winking at me.

Okay, that's a little uncomfortable.

Julia smiles, noticing my discomfort, and slings an arm around my shoulders. "Well, Gladys, looks like it's your lucky day, because it just so happens that Jaxson here is single."

I glare at her, wondering what the hell she's up to.

"Oh really?" Gladys replies, eyeing me like I'm a fucking treat or something.

"Yep, and I promise to bring him here more often for you. I should bring him on your dance nights; he loves to dance, Gladys."

Oh she's going to fucking pay for this. She damn well knows I hate to dance. I glance over at Margaret, hoping she will help me, but she just looks amused as hell.

"You like to dance?" Gladys asks excitedly.

"Uh, actually, no."

Her face falls, making me feel like a dick.

I never thought the day would come that I'd have to worry about hurting an old lady's feelings by shutting her down. "It's just that I'm not a very good dancer is all."

Her eyes light back up. "Oh, honey, don't you worry. I can dance well enough for the both of us."

Is this lady for real?

Julia grabs the side of my face. "Oh don't listen to him," she coos, "Jaxson's just being modest. Believe me, this guy has some killer moves."

That's it! Grabbing the back of her head, I kiss the fucking smirk right off her face.

"Attaboy, Jaxson," Margaret cheers.

Julia gasps the moment my mouth collides with hers. I swallow the breathy sound, feeling it rush through my veins like the sweetest drug. She remains frozen at first, making no move to reciprocate. That's until I lick the seam of her lips. Her mouth parts on a sexy moan and I plunge my tongue, becoming intoxicated with her taste.

Fuck me! She tastes even better than I remember.

"Oh my!" someone says at the table, reminding me we aren't alone.

I reluctantly pull back and stare into her heavy-lidded gaze. Shit! I only meant to press a hard kiss to her mouth, not maul her in front of everyone. Not that I regret it.

Her eyes flash with anger, but it doesn't hide the need I see in them. "What the hell are you doing?" she hisses, pushing me back.

"What? I was just demonstrating some of my *killer moves* you were telling them about."

Margaret's snicker fills the moment. "All right. Come on, you two, food's ready."

The three of them get up and start making their way to the buffet table. "I gotta tell you, I'd like to see what that guy is packing," Gladys says.

I tense, wondering if I just heard her right.

"Don't you ever do that again," Julia snaps, shaking her finger in my face.

Grabbing her wrist, I yank her in close. "Then next time, think twice before you play games with me. When you challenge me like that, Julia, all it does is make my dick hard. I thought you learned that in your room this morning."

"You are so infuriating."

"Admit it, you liked it, and you want more."

I know I shouldn't push her, but I can't resist.

Her eyes drop to my lap, staring at my now hard dick through my jeans. She looks back up at me, her brow quirked in amusement. "You seem to be the one affected, Jaxson."

"Don't tell me that if I shoved my hand up that dress of yours right now, I wouldn't find your panties soaked."

Heat sparks in her eyes but she tries to hide it behind her smirk. "I guess that's something you will never find out." She stands and adds, "Take your time to settle down before you come and get your food."

She strolls away, leaving me with the urge to haul her to the bathroom and show her just who's in control.

Damn it!

The woman is testing my limits, and I haven't even been around her for twenty-four hours. Clearly, it's going to be harder to restrain myself than I thought. I need to keep a clear head; I'm trying to fix the mess I made, not screw it up more.

I track her over to the table where she stands in line, helping Margaret with her plate. My gaze zeroes in on her sweet ass when she reaches for the punch.

I'm so fucked!

CHAPTER 13

Julia

We leave shortly after eating because I needed to get away from Grams's knowing smile. I haven't been the same since that kiss from Jaxson. I shift in my seat, feeling restless, and cross my legs to stop the throbbing that's happening between them.

I'm pathetic.

It doesn't help that it's been a long time since I've been with anyone. Justin is the only person I have slept with other than Jaxson. That was almost two years ago, and for the man being a med student, he had absolutely no idea where a woman's clitoris was located. Or maybe he just didn't care. I dated him for nine months in hopes of getting over Jaxson. It didn't work, of course, but at least I wasn't alone and the company was nice.

Cooper's truck is already parked out front by the time we arrive at my house. He and Kayla climb out the same time we do, and I'm happy to see she came with him.

"Hey, how are you feeling?" she asks, greeting me with a gentle hug.

"Not too bad, my ribs are sore today but my head feels better."

"Good." She offers me a smile that doesn't quite reach her eyes.

I'm about to ask her if everything is okay but Cooper speaks first. "Mind if we talk about last night?"

"Sure, come in." Leading them into the house, I get everyone a drink before we all sit down together at my kitchen table.

"Okay, tell me what went down last night," Cooper starts. "Jennings is saying it was an accident, and he's demanding that I arrest Jaxson for assault."

Panic seizes my chest at the thought. "It was kind of an accident…or not." I shake my head. "I don't know, Cooper, I've never seen him like that before. I'm still trying to wrap my head around it. He was so angry when we left you guys."

I relay the rest of the events from that evening, up to when I told Wyatt I no longer wanted to see him. Jaxson tenses next to me when I tell them about Wyatt grabbing me and calling me a cocktease. "He said he was going to show me how good we could be together. I knew he was going to kiss me. I tried pulling away and that's when you guys showed up. He finally let me go, and I fell."

I glance over at Jaxson nervously and see him staring straight ahead, his expression hard as stone.

My attention reverts back to Cooper. "The thing is, I have no idea what he's talking about when he says I've been playing head games with him. I've barely had any contact with him. That was only the third date we've ever had. I've run into him here and there while I was going to school. He would ask me out and I'd always politely decline. It wasn't until recently that I ran into him again, and when he asked me again I said okay." I shrug, hating how wrong I was. I should have kept declining.

Kayla senses my thoughts and leans over to grab my hand. "Don't you dare blame yourself for any of this. This is his fault, not yours."

I can't help but feel partly responsible.

"Julia, you have grounds to press charges," Cooper says. "You wouldn't have fallen and gotten hurt if he hadn't forced you there to begin with."

I look over at Jaxson, my heart aching at the thought of him receiving any kind of punishment for this. His eyes narrow back at me, knowing exactly where my head is at.

"I'm not pressing charges," I whisper.

"Fuck that!" He slams his fist on the table, making me jump. "Yes, you are!"

"Don't yell at her like that!" Kayla snaps.

"Kayla, stay out of it." Cooper's tone is as angry as hers.

"Then you tell him too, this is Julia's decision, and hers alone. I will not let her be bullied into anything."

They glare at one another, the tension so thick you could cut it with a knife.

I drop my head in my hands, hating that everyone is fighting over this.

"Julia, I think you should reconsider," Cooper starts again.

"She doesn't want to press charges because of me. She thinks if she doesn't then he won't, but you're wrong." Jaxson's tone softens and he cups my cheek, turning my face toward his. "If he wants to press charges he will, no matter what you do. Don't let him get away with this, Julia."

"I don't want anything to happen to you because of this," I tell him thickly then look over at Cooper. "Couldn't you talk to him, Cooper? Tell Wyatt that I'll drop the charges against him if he drops his against Jaxson."

"No!"

I ignore Jaxson's protest and continue. "Trust me, he won't want me pressing charges, especially right now. He told me his dad is running for mayor. With the campaign starting up soon, he won't want bad publicity."

Surprise passes over Cooper's expression. "He said his old man is running for mayor?"

I nod.

"Fuck, that's the last thing we need. You're right though, it's leverage."

"Damn it, I said no! I don't give a shit what happens to me. She's pressing charges."

"Well I do care, and it's my decision," I argue back.

Jaxson stands, his chair slamming into the wall as he starts pacing angrily.

"Look, just calm down. Julia's right, it's something we can try." Cooper puts up his hand, silencing Jaxson's protest but his determined eyes remain on me. "But I think you need to consider putting a restraining order on him at the very least."

My eyes flare in surprise. "A restraining order?"

"The guy thinks he's in love with you, Julia. If you have had as little contact as you say you have, then that shit's not normal."

"I don't think that's necessary. I think putting a restraining order on him will just make the situation worse in the end."

"Listen, Julia. When I questioned him, the shit he said made me nervous. He's not right in the head, I'm telling you, you need this. I have no doubt he will not leave you alone unless you do."

"I'll fucking kill him if he goes anywhere near her." There's a terrifying calmness in Jaxson's voice, his words holding promise.

"Jesus, I did not just hear you say that," Cooper says, distressed.

I decide to relent, wanting this to be over. "I'll put a restraining order on him. But first I want you to try to get the charges dropped against Jaxson."

"For fuck's sake!" Jaxson's heated curse slices through the air but I ignore it.

Cooper nods his agreement then looks over at Jaxson. "You need to come to the station with me and do an official statement. We have a strong case to get the charges dropped either way, but we can use Julia's for leverage."

I feel much better after hearing that, but I can tell Jaxson is not happy about it.

"Julia shouldn't be alone right now. She's still healing," he says.

"I'll be fine on my own."

"I'll stay with her for a while," Kayla offers.

"You don't have to."

"I know, but I want to. We can catch up, maybe watch a movie while you rest."

I smile. "Sure, that sounds good."

"All right, let's go and get this over with," Cooper says, pushing to his feet.

The rest of us stand and Jaxson comes over to hand me my pain pills. "Take these, I know you're hurting."

I roll my eyes at his bossiness. "I'll be fine. I can take care of myself. Now go with Cooper and cooperate, or I'll be forced to call Gladys for your punishment," I tease, biting back a smile.

He grunts unamused. "You're such a smart-ass." His arm hooks around my waist, yanking me in close so he can plant a hard kiss right on my lips.

"I told you to stop doing that." I try to sound angry but it comes out breathless.

The arrogant ass just smirks, knowing his effect on me, and walks away.

"Who the fuck is Gladys?" Cooper asks as they walk out the door.

"Yeah, good-bye to you, too."

I look over at Kayla and see she's upset. "Is everything all right?"

"Yeah, Cooper and I have just been butting heads lately. That's all." She flashes me a reassuring smile that doesn't quite reach her eyes again.

"I hope it isn't because of Jaxson and me?"

"No." She waves away my concern. "Really, it's fine. Let's go pick a movie. Want to watch it in your room so you can rest in bed?"

"Sure." She heads for the living room but I grab her arm before she can leave. "You know I'm always here for you, right? You can call me day or night."

"Yeah, I know. Thanks, Jules." She hugs me tight, unfortunately it's on my injured side.

I suck in a sharp breath and wince.

"Shit, sorry. Are you going to take the medication?"

"No. I don't feel like I need them yet."

"All right. I won't push like Mr. Bossy," she teases.

"Thanks. I appreciate that."

After making some popcorn, we pick our favorite movie, *Dirty Dancing,* and go snuggle down in bed, becoming enraptured with Patrick Swayze like always.

Halfway through the movie, Kayla turns to me. "We should go out dancing one night, it's been a while. We can make it a girls' night and invite Grace, too."

"Sure, that would be fun. Let's do it soon. Grace could use a night off; she's been working herself into the ground. I saw her the other day and she looked ready to fall over."

"I know. I'm pretty sure it's because she needs the money."

I nod, agreeing.

Grace moved to Sunset Bay a little over a year ago. Kayla and I hit it off with her right away, and we all quickly became friends. There's still a lot we don't know about her, but we can tell something has happened to her. When she found out about my mom passing away, she opened up, telling us that she lost her mom too, but she never shared how. I didn't want to be rude and ask. As far as we know, Grace is alone with no other family. I'm hoping she will open up once she gets more comfortable with us.

"Depending on how you're feeling, what about next weekend?" Kayla asks.

"That works for me. I'm sure I'll be fine. I'm surprised how well I'm doing today, considering."

"I still can't believe we never knew about Wyatt. Why wouldn't Coop and Jaxson just tell us the reason from the start?"

I shrug, not having any idea and I don't try to figure it out either. It doesn't matter, not anymore.

"So fill me in on what's been happening with Jaxson. Your conversation looked pretty intense when I walked in yesterday."

"Yeah, and you didn't help by the way, talking about my 'hot date.'"

She chuckles. "Sorry, I couldn't resist. I wanted to make sure he knew you weren't just kickin' around waiting for his sorry ass. Believe me, I regretted it when he came storming over later like the Incredible Hulk."

We share a laugh, the nickname very fitting for Jaxson, but I sober quickly. "I don't know, Kayla. We haven't had much of a chance to talk about it. He says he's going to make things right, but he also said he doesn't regret sending me away. A part of me wants to forgive him, it feels so good to be around him again, but that's what scares me the most. He still affects me so strongly. I've worked really hard trying to get over him, and all of it just crumbled the moment I laid eyes on him again. What if I forgive him and he eventually leaves?"

"Well I guess that's what you need to find out. I don't know what the right thing is to tell you, Jules. I do believe that in his fucked-up head he thinks he did the right thing and believes he was protecting you. Listen to what he has to say about his future plans. If it's something that includes you, then maybe make him work at your friendship, don't let him off too easily."

We're interrupted when she gets a phone call. I hold my breath, praying it's news about Jaxson.

"Hello… What? I'm supposed to have today off, can't someone else take them?" It's obviously the massage clinic where Kayla works.

What's taking them so long?

"Fine, I'm on my way." Hanging up, she looks over at me regretfully. "I'm sorry, I gotta go. Someone called in sick and I need to take her appointments. It'll only be for a few hours."

"It's okay, thanks for staying as long as you did. Come on, I'll drive you over," I say, climbing out of bed.

"Are you sure? I can ask Coop to come get me?"

"No, it's fine. I need the fresh air."

After dropping her off, I decide to go visit my mom for a while. I sit and talk to her about Jaxson being back and ask her for guidance. Once my heart feels a little lighter, I leave and find myself pulling up to the beach.

I start across the warm sand, heading toward the one place I haven't been to in over a year—our spot. I used to come often, especially when I was missing Jaxson. But after Germany I tried to rid myself of any reminders of him, it was too painful.

Sitting down, I lean back against the log and take a deep breath of the ocean-filled air, letting the crash of the waves soothe me. I close my eyes, trying to clear my head, and the next thing I know I'm being startled awake.

"Where the fuck have you been?"

My eyes spring open and I sit up in a panic. Jaxson stands over me, looking like he's ready to commit murder. I lay a hand over my thundering heart. "You scared me to death." The sun has started to set and I notice it's visibly cooler out.

How long have I been here?

"I scared *you*?" he shouts in outrage. "Do you have any idea how long I've been looking for you?"

I shake my head, a little scared to ask.

"Almost two fucking hours, Julia! I checked here before and never saw you."

"I visited my mom for a bit then I came here. Geez, calm down."

"Are you kidding me? I find you sleeping on the beach and you tell me to calm down. What the hell is the matter with you?"

That's it! Grabbing my shoes, I push to my feet. "Screw you! I don't need to listen to this shit," I start across the beach without looking back.

His frustrated breath sounds behind me. "Shit! Julia, wait."

I ignore him and keep walking, my bare feet stomping through the sand.

He catches up to me, grabbing my arm before I can make it too far. "I'm sorry, okay? You scared the hell out of me when I couldn't find you. All of this shit with Wyatt has me going crazy. I thought something happened to you."

I soften when I realize how scared he is. "Why didn't you just call me? My number is still the same, although, I imagine you forgot it after all this time." I can't resist adding in that last part.

He looks at me like I've lost my mind. "Julia, I called it about a hundred fucking times."

"What?" Reaching into my purse, I grab my phone and see twenty-seven missed calls and eighteen voice mails, all from Jaxson. There's also a text from Kayla.

Kayla: *Hulk Alert! Jaxson's going crazy looking for you.*

Turning my phone to the side, I see it's on silent. *Oops!* "Sorry, it seems my ringer was off."

"Jesus!"

I clear my throat sheepishly. "So… how did it go at the station with Cooper?"

His expression is filled with disbelief, clearly not feeling the change of topic. He shakes his head, an exasperated chuckle leaving him. "Damn it, woman." He pulls me against his chest, wrapping me in his arms. His heart thumps against my cheek, proving just how scared he was. "You shouldn't have fallen asleep on the beach, Julia, it's dangerous. Promise me you won't do that again."

"I didn't mean to. I'm sorry I scared you." Stepping back, I look up at him and repeat the question that's been plaguing me since he left this morning. "Did everything work out with Cooper?"

He gestures over to our spot.

I trudge back through the sand and we sit next to each other, just like old times. It has me feeling a little panicked so I inch away, leaving a small gap between us.

"Well, you were right," he starts, his eyes focused on the ocean in front of us. "He dropped the charges when Cooper told him you were going to press them if he didn't."

"Good," I sigh in relief.

Annoyance flashes in his eyes. "I still don't agree with it, Julia, that bastard should have some consequence for what he did to you."

"I think you smashing his face in was consequence enough."

"No, it's not. You need to go in and get that restraining order."

I clear my throat, knowing he's not going to like what I say next. "You know, I was thinking about that and I really don't think it's necessary. I mean what if—"

"Julia," my name falls on a warning growl.

"All right, calm down, I'll go tomorrow."

"I'll pick you up in the morning and take you to get it done."

"That's okay. I can manage on my own," I mumble.

"I'm sure you can, but I told you, I'll take you."

I shake my head, too tired to argue with him.

Things fall quiet between us, the sound of the crashing waves filling the tense silence.

"Well, I should go," I say awkwardly.

He grabs my wrist before I can stand, his touch burning my skin. "Not so fast. No more stalling, it's time you hear me out."

Damn. I knew it.

"What's the point, Jaxson? You sending me away in Germany is not something we are ever going to agree on, no matter what you say to me."

"Why can't you just try to understand that I didn't want anyone to see me like that?"

"Cooper did!" I point out angrily.

"That's because he was my emergency contact; I didn't really have a choice. Believe me, if I could have prevented him from seeing me like that too, I would have. But I also knew he could handle it. You don't get just how fucked-up I was."

"Of course I don't, because you never gave me the chance to."

"I'm sorry, but it was for the best, trust me."

"Well that's a really shitty explanation. Did you come back thinking it was going to be that easy, Jaxson?"

"No. I know it's going to take time for you to forgive me, but I'm asking you to at least give me the chance to make it right."

"It's not just about Germany. Why did you stay away from me for so long?"

Guilt flashes in his eyes before he looks away. I wait for him to say something, to explain himself, but he doesn't. His casted armor firmly in place, preventing me from seeing anything.

"Was Melissa telling the truth last night?" I whisper.

That gets a reaction out of him. He whips his head in my direction. "What are you asking me?"

"Did you leave in the first place because of me?"

His expression hardens, jaw locking in anger. "You know better than that. Nothing that bitch said last night was true."

"Then answer my question! Why did you stay away from me for six years?"

"Because I didn't think I could keep my dick in my pants, all right?"

I rear back in surprise, not expecting that admission.

"Christ!" Shoving to his feet, he begins pacing angrily. "Let's face it, Julia, that night changed everything between us."

"Are you saying you regret it?" Just the thought makes me want to throw up.

"No, damn it! I probably should, but I don't. That was the best fucking night of my life." I can tell he immediately regrets letting that out.

"Mine, too," I admit quietly.

His hard expression softens, eyes holding mine and reflecting everything that I'm feeling.

"You promised me that night that you would stay my friend, and you broke that promise." I look away as tears form in my eyes.

Kneeling down, he cups my face in both of his hands, forcing my gaze to his. "I'm sorry I fucked up. I thought I was doing the right thing. Believe me, if I could go back and change the way I handled things I would."

Emotion clogs my throat as I try to keep my tears at bay. "Why do you feel differently now? What's changed?"

Something dark and heartbreaking steals his expression. "Because there was a point when I didn't think I'd ever see you again, and the thought fucking ripped me apart."

A sharp pain seizes my chest and captures my breath.

"I swore to myself that if I got out of there alive I'd fix the mess I made with you. I can't live without you, Julia. I'll fix this, even if it kills me trying."

His tortured admission breaks me. Sliding off the log onto my knees in front of him, I wrap my arms around his neck, sobs racking my body.

He lifts me to straddle him and holds me close as all the years of hurt pour out of me. I cry over our loss of years together. I cry for him, that someone hurt him. I cry until the energy to cry any more has been completely drained out of me. Eventually, my tears subside, leaving only the sound of my labored breathing.

"I'll get us back to what we had, Julia, I promise," he whispers, making me believe him.

"Okay."

He pulls back, framing my face again between his hands. "Okay?" he asks, unsure if he heard me right.

I nod, my throat too tight to speak.

A breath of relief leaves him. "Okay."

Pressing a soft kiss to my temple, he rests his forehead on mine. I close my eyes, savoring the intimate contact with him.

"Are you going to be okay?"

My eyes spring back open at the gruff sound of his voice and I become intimately aware of our position. My dress is hiked up to my hips with his warm hands resting high on my bare thighs. I shift a little, only to feel how hard he is beneath me. His jaw flexes and grip tightens. My labored breathing is for a whole other reason now. His eyes draw to my mouth when I lick my dry lips.

Groaning, he drops his head on my shoulder. "Jules, this is one of those times where my control is being tested, so I need you to get up before I rip your panties off."

My breath stalls in my chest. "What if I want you to rip them off?"

"Oh fuck, don't say that to me right now. I'm trying to do the right thing and fix my mistakes. Help me out, Jules."

He's right, as much as I want him, now is not the time. If we are ever intimate again, it will be his move and his alone.

I begin to stand but his grip tightens, holding me in place. "Answer my question first. Are you okay?"

"I will be, I'm just tired. It's been an eventful few days."

He nods. "I know. Come on, I'll drive you home."

"I drove here, remember?" I remind him as I stand to my feet.

"Don't worry about it. Coop and I will drive your car back later."

I'm grateful he offers, because I'm too tired to drive right now anyway.

"Thanks." My arms wrap around his one as we start back to his truck. "Whatever happened to your bike?" I ask curiously.

"I still have it, it's in storage." He cracks a sexy grin. "Why? Want to go for a ride?"

"Yeah, I do. I miss it. I haven't been on a bike since you left."

"Good," he grunts. "I'll take you out once you're better."

"I'd like that." As much as I love his bike I have to say his truck is very nice too. It's black with chrome trim and tinted windows, but it's way too tall.

My head cranes back as we approach it, wondering how the hell I'm going to get in. "Geez, Jaxson, your truck doesn't quite reach the streetlight. I think you need to jack it up some more. How the heck am I supposed to get in this thing?"

"Get over here, smart-ass, and I'll help you," he replies, opening the passenger door for me.

Giggling, I move in front of him. His hands span my hips, but before giving me the lift I need, he leans in close, his mouth brushing my ear. "When you're lippy like that, Julia, it makes me want to do things to that smart-ass mouth of yours."

Heat surges through my blood when I think of all the things he would do to my mouth. His knowing chuckle tickles my ear before he boosts me up into the truck, making sure to be mindful of my sore hip. Walking over to his side, he hops up gracefully, the height not being an issue for him.

Sexy jerk.

Smiling, I lean my head against the window, feeling lighter and happier than I have in a long time. My tired eyes flutter close, and the next thing I know I feel myself being lifted. I come awake with a gasp, my arms flailing around in a panic as I grab on to something solid.

"Shh, it's okay, it's just me. I've got you."

Releasing a breath, I wrap my arms around Jaxson's neck and rest my head on his shoulder, falling in and out of consciousness.

"Where are your keys?" he asks softly.

"The door's unlocked."

His body tenses, a growl escaping him. "Damn it, Julia."

I ignore his outburst, too tired to argue.

Once in the house, he makes the climb up my stairs, keeping me in his protective arms… ones I've missed so much. My body eventually meets the cool hard mattress and I snuggle in with a moan as he drapes the blankets over me.

"Jesus." I hear him breathe out.

What is his problem now?

He digs in my purse on the nightstand, fishing out my car keys. "Is your house key on here so I can lock the door behind me?"

"Mmm hmm," I mumble sleepily.

He chuckles. "I'll be back in the morning to take you to the station."

Before he can leave, I reach out and grab his wrist. He looks back at me, his blue eyes meeting mine in the shadows of my room. "Don't ever leave me again, because if you do I might not survive it." I hate admitting that to him, but I need him to understand. I can't have him do that to me again.

His expression softens. "I'm not going anywhere." He promises, his voice sure. Leaning down, he gives me one more kiss on the forehead. "Good night, Julia."

This time I let him go and fall into a blissful sleep.

CHAPTER 14

Jaxson

I lock the door on my way out then hop in my truck and head to the station. The lust burning inside of me is hard to ignore but I remind myself to keep focus on what's important and fix the mess I've made with Julia. Not get into her panties, no matter how bad I want back in them.

When I arrive at the station, I park next to Coop's truck and head inside. The receptionist from this afternoon jumps to her feet, eye fucking me like she did earlier. "Hey, Jaxson, back so soon?" she purrs, leaning over to give me a view of her cleavage that comes from a great looking pair of fake tits.

"Uh yeah, is Coop around?"

"He's in his office, go right in."

"Thanks." I start forward but turn back around when she calls out to me.

"I'm off in an hour, wanna hook up?"

I consider it for all of three seconds. I haven't been with anyone since Iraq; it's been a really long year. But I know from experience that fucking any other girl won't do anything to satisfy my need for Julia.

"Maybe another time," I say noncommittally.

"Let me know."

Heading into Coop's office I see him bent over a file, looking pissed. There's a coffee and a half-eaten doughnut next to him.

Typical.

"Hard at work with your coffee and doughnuts, I see."

His head snaps up. "Jesus, I didn't even hear you come in."

That's one way of knowing he's upset about something. "What has you looking like you're ready to kill someone?"

He pinches the bridge of his nose, something he always does when he's stressed. "Nothing, just some shit I found on someone's past I wish I didn't know."

"Anyone I know?"

"No, but you will probably meet her. She's a friend of the girls. Now shut up and don't ask me any more questions, because I can't answer them."

"Is it something Julia can get hurt from?"

"No, lover boy, so calm down."

I glare at his 'lover boy' comment as I take a seat in the chair across from him.

"So what brings you back here? Don't tell me you're turning yourself in for murdering Jennings."

I grunt. "I wouldn't turn myself in, I know exactly what to do with that prick's body so he was never found."

"Jesus, Jaxson, don't say shit like that to me."

I chuckle, loving that I get a rise out of him. "I need you to help me get Julia's car home for her. I gave her a ride earlier."

He relaxes back into his chair, crossing his arms with a knowing smirk. "So you finally found her. I was right, wasn't I? She was hiding from you."

"No, asshole, she wasn't. I found her sleeping on the beach."

He sobers, all earlier amusement wiped from his face. "Seriously? What the hell is wrong with her?"

"Believe me, I asked the same thing…a little more pissed off, mind you. It didn't go over very well."

He grunts. "I bet not."

"Speaking of which, what have you been teaching your girlfriend?"

"What are you talking about?"

"She's been constantly threatening to kick my ass and seems to think she can do some serious damage to me. She says you have been *showing her stuff.* Whatever the hell you're doing, tone it down."

He shakes his head. "I showed her how to get out of a few holds if someone ever tried to attack her. She seems to think she's Rocky now or some shit."

"Yeah, well, I swear she's more pissed at me than Julia is."

"Ignore it. She's been pissed at me lately for something too, and I don't have a fucking clue why. I don't know what's going on in that head of hers."

I can tell he's bothered by it. "Everything okay?"

He shrugs. "It will be. Come on, I'll help you take Julia's car home."

"Thanks."

As we walk out of his office, the receptionist stands up again, shoving her tits out.

"I'm gone for the night, Jenny, you can transfer all calls to my cell."

"You betcha, darlin'. See you around, Jaxson." She tosses me a wink as we head out the door.

"Jesus, that's quite the receptionist you have there. Has Kayla met her yet? Maybe that's why she's pissed at you."

He grunts. "Yeah, she's met her all right. Kayla put the gears to her when she started and the girl barely made eye contact with me for the first month." He looks over at me. "Be careful with her, she's a persistent one. And she's been banged more times than a snooze button on a Monday morning."

A beat of silence stretches between us until we both crack into laughter.

Damn. It's good to be back.

CHAPTER 15

Julia

I wake up the next morning feeling almost like myself again. My ribs look worse today but thankfully they feel better, which is most important.

After my shower, I throw on a pair of black capri leggings and an off-the-shoulder white shirt that's loose and comfortable, then throw my natural wavy hair into a high, messy bun. I have no idea what time Jaxson's coming, all he said was morning, so I don't want to take too long getting ready. My stomach does a little flip at the thought of getting to see him again so soon, but I shove the dangerous feeling aside and concentrate on making my morning smoothie. Just as the blender finishes its racket my doorbell rings. I expect it to be Jaxson, so I'm surprised when I open it to find Grace.

"Grace, this is a pleasant surprise."

"Hi, Julia." She steps in, giving me a gentle hug. "I heard what happened, are you okay?"

"You heard already?"

"Yeah, Kayla told me."

"Oh good, at least I know you got the right story then," I say with a chuckle. "Come in, I'm just making myself a smoothie, want one?"

"Sure." She follows me into the kitchen and sets a pie down on my counter. "I made this for you, it's fresh from this morning."

Grace is an amazing baker, her specialty is pies, but she can bake anything. She creates and names them all herself too.

"It's only nine in the morning and you already baked this for me?"

She shrugs like it's no big deal. "I had an itch to create something, and when Kayla told me what happened I created something with all of your favorites."

My heart warms. "That's really sweet, thank you. What did you call it?"

Her shoulders straighten and expression hardens. "I named it, Wyatt Is An Ass-hole Pie."

We burst into a fit of laughter, my heart lightening further.

"That's a great name," I tell her.

Her smile fades. "You know, Julia, I'm happy you ended things with him. After your guys' first date, he came into the diner, and the way he acted with me… Well, it scared me a bit," she admits nervously.

"Oh, Grace, why didn't you say something?"

"Well I didn't want to jump to conclusions, I thought maybe I took it wrong. You and Kayla grew up with him; I figured you knew him better. I'm sorry, I wish I would have said somethin' now."

"Don't be sorry, just know you can always tell me anything."

Our conversation is interrupted when my front door opens and slams. Jaxson storms into the kitchen, looking angry as hell.

Grace grabs my arm with a gasp, scared spit-less.

"What the hell did I tell you about locking that damn door!"

I cock my hip and glare at him. "Well good morning to you too, ya jerk. And why on earth would I lock it? I'm home for heaven's sake."

"That's why you should lock it."

I roll my eyes. "Give it a rest and watch your mouth. I have my friend here, and you're making a terrible first impression."

For the first time he looks at Grace. Her grip on me has loosened, realizing I know him. But I notice she's quite shaken up.

"Jaxson, this is my friend, Grace."

"Nice to meet you. Sorry about that, but the woman doesn't listen about locking her doors," he says as an explanation, glaring at me.

Grace's eyes roam down Jaxson, and I can't help but smile. I have a feeling I know exactly what she's thinking.

She gives him a nervous wave and clears her throat. "Um, hello. Ah, what was your name again?"

"Jaxson," we both reply at the same time.

Grace snaps her head in my direction. "Jaxson?" she asks in shock. Leaning in, she whispers, "*The* Jaxson?"

I guess Kayla left that part out this morning. Nodding, I give her a look, telling her I'll explain everything later. Thankfully, she gets the memo.

Jaxson interrupts the silent exchange. "Are you ready to go to the station or should I come back?"

Grace jumps in. "Oh no, I need to get to work, I just stopped in to check on Julia and give her this pie."

"Did you walk here or take a cab?" I ask, knowing it's one or the other because she doesn't own a car.

"I walked."

"You walked here?" Jaxson asks in exasperation.

"Um, yes?" she replies, looking unsure.

"Do you have any idea how dangerous that is?"

"Lay off, Jaxson. What are you, the safety police?"

"You live in the country and she's walking alone on a gravel road."

"It's not that far," Grace argues back defensively.

He shakes his head. "Whatever. I'll drive you back in and drop you off wherever it is you work."

Her back straightens and chin lifts. "No, that's all right. I enjoy walkin'."

I take pity on her, knowing it's a battle she won't win. "Trust me, Grace, the argument is pointless. Let us drive you back, we're headed that way anyway."

She nods but it's a bit stiff. "All right, thank you."

Grabbing two travel mugs, I fill them both with the smoothie then hand one to Grace.

"Thanks." She accepts it, smiling again.

As we head out of the kitchen she grabs my arm and leans in close to me. "Wow, Julia, you and Kayla weren't kiddin'. The man is sexy. A little scary and arrogant, but damn sexy."

A laugh tumbles past my lips. "I know."

Jaxson stands at the front door, impatiently waiting for us to follow. We quickly snap out of our giggling and get moving.

Once we arrive at the station, Jaxson comes over and helps me out of the truck. He seems to be in a better mood since I promised him on the way here that I would start locking my doors all the time.

I stare at the building in front of me, my stomach twisting anxiously for what I'm about to do. Jaxson laces his fingers with mine and gives them a reassuring squeeze. I look up to see his gaze warm and understanding. "It'll be all right, Jules, you're doing the right thing."

I nod even though I feel unsure of that.

When we enter through the front doors, Jenny stands and gives Jaxson a flirtatious smile. "Hi, Jaxson, miss me already?"

I tense, jealousy heating my blood.

She looks down at our joined hands, her nose lifting in distaste. "Julia, what are you doing here?"

I don't get the chance to respond because Jaxson does. "That's none of your business. We're here to see Cooper."

I stand a little taller by the way he puts her in her place. She glares at me a second longer before pointing in the direction of Cooper's office. Jaxson gives my hand a tug, leading me across the station.

"Wow, you've been busy. First Gladys, now Jenny," I tease, unable to help myself.

He quirks a brow. "Jealous, Julia?"

I scoff. "Yeah, right…"

Deputy Wilkinson comes walking out of Coop's office. "Well hello, Miss Julia, you're looking lovely today."

Now it's Jaxson's turn to tense, and I can't help but rub it in just a little. "Why thank you, Trevor, you're not looking too bad yourself today either."

With a growl, Jaxson propels me forward.

"Jealous, Jaxson?" I mock, a smug smile tugging at my lips.

"You're pushing it, Julia."

I giggle as we enter Cooper's office.

"Hey," he greets us, looking exhausted.

"You look like shit," Jaxson points out rudely.

"Thanks, asshole."

Seeing Cooper like this reminds me of how sad Kayla was yesterday. I hope everything is all right between them.

"Hi, Coop. Thanks for driving my car home last night with Jaxson."

"No problem." He rises out of his chair and points for me to sit in it. When I do he places a pile of papers in front of me. "I need you to fill all of this out."

Picking up the pen, I hesitate and again try my best to get out of doing this but they won't hear it.

"Trust me, Julia, when I say this is necessary," Cooper says.

"I do trust you. I'm just scared this is going to make things worse, but if you think it's that important I'll do it."

Reluctantly, I fill out the paperwork, then hand them over to Cooper when I'm finished.

"It takes anywhere from twenty-four to forty-eight hours for this to process. I will speed it up as quickly as I can. You need to tell us right away if he tries to contact you. I mean it."

"I will."

We walk out of his office and a moment of panic strikes me when he hands the papers off to Jenny. "I need you to fax this to the number attached right away."

She glances down at them, before her shocked eyes lock on mine. "You're putting a restraining order on Wyatt Jennings? Aren't you dating him?"

My heart plummets at her outburst, embarrassment heating my cheeks.

"Jenny, you have no right to ask questions," Cooper snaps. "Do I need to remind you what your job is?"

She shifts nervously. "No, of course not. I understand."

Swallowing thickly, I storm out of the station.

Jaxson rushes out after me and tugs me against him. "Forget about her, Jules."

"Everybody is going to think what she just said," I mumble into his chest.

"Who gives a fuck what anyone else thinks? You did the right thing."

"Can you just take me home?" I ask.

"Yeah, come on." He slings an arm around my shoulder and leads me to his truck.

We arrive at my house a few minutes later. Jaxson leaves his truck running, the motor idling loudly as he climbs out to help me down. I try to ignore the way my skin tingles where his hands grip my waist.

"What are you doing tonight?" he asks, slamming the door behind me.

"Nothing at the moment."

"Want to go out and do something? Maybe grab supper?"

A smile dances across my lips at the way his feet shift. If I didn't know better I'd think he is nervous. "Yeah, I'd like that," I tell him.

"I'll pick you up at six, okay?"

I nod then clear my throat, feeling nervous for what I'm about to say next. "You know, Jaxson, you don't have to stay at the hotel, you could stay here with me if you want to." I notice his body visibly stiffen but before he can get the wrong idea I rush on to say, "I have more than enough room, I have three spare rooms."

I see the answer before he even responds. "I don't think that's a good idea, Jules."

My eyes fall to the ground where I kick at the gravel. "Okay," I reply quietly, then shrug, acting like it's no big deal. "Just thought I'd offer. I'll see you at six."

When I turn to leave, he wraps his arms around me from behind and pulls me back against him. A gasp parts my lips when I feel how hard he is against my bottom.

"I appreciate the offer, Julia, but the problem is, your bedroom door will do nothing to stop me from coming into your room at night and sinking into that sweet, hot pussy of yours."

Oh lord!

A current of heat explodes through my body like an inferno. Unable to stop myself, I push back against his erection, a fiery whimper breaching my lips at the contact.

A groan rumbles from his chest, his grip tightening on my hips. "Be a good girl,

Julia, and go into the house before I lose control and fuck you right here on your driveway."

I try to move, I really do, but I'm completely rooted to my spot, need pounding through every nerve ending of my body.

Growling, Jaxson spins me around, his lips dropping a hard kiss on my forehead. "I'll be back at six." He walks off without another word.

Once he's in his truck again I manage to get my feet moving and hightail it into the house. Closing the door, I drop back against it.

Holy crap!

My breath races and senses reel. My back still burns hot from where he was pressed against me. I turn my head and look at the lock on my door, another smile curving my lips when I click it in place.

CHAPTER 16

Julia

As I'm folding laundry later that afternoon, there's a knock on the door. I glance at the clock wondering if it's Jaxson, but know it's too early. Bounding down the stairs, I open the door to see Kayla with tears streaming down her face. "Kayla, what's wrong?"

"You're never going to believe this," she chokes out on a sob, her arms wrapped around her stomach as if trying to keep warm.

I pull her in and usher her to my couch, forcing her to sit down. "What is it? You're scaring me to death."

She looks at me, her blue eyes filled with devastation. "I'm pretty sure Cooper is cheating on me."

"What?" I gasp. "No way, Kayla, he'd never do something like that to you, he loves you."

"I've suspected something for a couple of weeks now, but I shut the thought down because, just like you, I thought he would never do that to me." Her breath catches as she tries to compose herself enough to speak. "I caught him lying to me. The other night he called me at six and told me he was working late at the station. I decided to surprise him and bring him supper. When I got there he wasn't there, Jenny said he left at five. Julia, he didn't get home until ten that night."

I rub her back, trying to soothe her. "Did you ask him where he was?"

"Yeah, he said he got a call and had to meet with another officer at the department in Charleston. I could tell he was lying, but I dropped it because a small part of me hoped he was telling the truth." She shakes her head, a bitter laugh escaping her. "I've caught him a few times whispering into his phone, but as soon as I walk in he hangs up. Anytime I asked who it was he'd say it was the wrong number."

That does seem suspicious, but this is Cooper, he's one of the most honest men I know.

"Today the moment of truth came out," she continues. "His phone rang when he was in the shower. I didn't recognize the number but saw it was from Charleston. When I answered someone gasped then hung up. So I called it back a few minutes later from my cell, blocking my number, and a woman answered. When I didn't say anything, you know what she said?"

I shake my head, afraid to ask.

"She whispered, 'Cooper, is that you?' She whispered it, Julia! Like it was a secret."

"What did you say?"

"Nothing, I couldn't speak. I was frozen because my heart had just broken in two."

I wrap my arms around her as another sob shreds from her throat. "You have to talk to Cooper about this. There has to be some explanation."

"He's meeting her this Friday at a motel on I-90 between here and Charleston."

"No!"

She nods. "I scrolled through his text messages after and found the number. There wasn't much, except that she looked forward to seeing him and what room she would be in."

"Oh my god!" I can't believe this is happening, I never thought Cooper would do this in a million years. "Are you going to confront him?"

Her back straightens and eyes flash with anger. "Damn straight, this Friday at the motel when I bust him and his whore."

I suck in a sharp breath. "Oh, Kayla, I'm not sure that's a good idea."

"I have to. I need to see it with my own eyes. If I ask him, he'll just lie to me like he has been for weeks." Her hand rests on her stomach, looking like she might be sick. "I can't believe this is happening. I thought we were going to get married and have babies, Julia. We've been together for years. How could he do this to me?"

She breaks down again, and I can't stop my own tears from falling, her devastation shattering my heart. "I'm so sorry."

I think back to seeing Cooper this morning, remembering how awful he looked. Maybe the guilt is eating at him.

The bastard!

"I'll come with you on Friday."

She gives me a sad smile. "I was hoping you would say that."

"Of course, I'd never let you go through this alone."

"Thanks, Jules," she whispers, her voice sounding as sad as her eyes look. "Anyway, I better get going. I work evenings this week, and I need to make myself somewhat presentable."

"Maybe you should take a few days off?"

She shakes her head. "No, it's good for me, it will keep me busy and away from Cooper."

"Okay. Call me if you need anything. I mean it, Kayla."

"I will, I'll text you the details for Friday."

We give each other one last hug before she heads out the door. I drop down on my couch again, my mind reeling.

A few minutes later, another knock sounds on my door. I answer it, thinking it's Kayla again until I open it and see Wyatt. My heart sinks to the pit of my stomach. He looks terribly angry, his face black and blue from Jaxson's fists.

"You're putting a fucking restraining order on me?"

"Cooper thought it was necessary," I tell him anxiously, deciding it's best to leave Jaxson's name out of it.

"How could you fucking do this to me, after everything we've been through."

I gape at him, my mouth ajar. "This is why, Wyatt. We've had three dates and you act like what we had was serious."

It was the wrong thing to say.

His fists clench at his sides, as if he's going to hit something. I'm praying that something isn't me. "Don't give me that shit. We've been in love with each other for years. I waited patiently, because I know that son of a bitch brainwashed you to stay away from me."

Oh my god!

He's completely serious; he really believes this.

"You're going to drop the restraining order," he says firmly.

"No, I'm not. You need to leave, Wyatt, right now." I start to close my door but he shoves his foot inside. "Don't make me call Cooper," my threat is weak and shaky, shredding my brave facade.

His expression softens as he reaches up to touch my face and I flinch at the unwanted contact. "Don't be scared. I'd never hurt you."

"You already did," I choke out.

His jaw flexes in anger. "That was an accident."

I shake my head. "It doesn't matter."

"Don't throw away what we have for him, Julia. It will only be a matter of time before he leaves you again."

"This isn't about Jaxson."

"Bullshit!" he barks, making me jump. "It's always been about him."

A gasp flees me, panic thrashing through my veins as he grabs my arm in a painful grip.

"Have you spread your legs for him already? Have you let him have what's mine?" His expression is full of violence, but his eyes are glazed over, almost as if he's not there.

He's crazy. Absolutely certifiably crazy.

"Answer me now!" he bellows, giving my shoulders a shake.

I tread carefully, realizing that he's completely irrational. Tears stream down my face as I shake my head.

His expression eases again. "Good girl."

My body stiffens when he leans in closer, putting his mouth to my ear. "Wyatt, what are you doing?" I ask, stifling my sob.

"Shhh." He inhales deeply through his nose and groans, the sound has bile inching up my throat. His hand runs up my spine and grabs a fistful of my hair, yanking my head back. "Drop the restraining order or I will make your life hell."

I stumble back a step when he shoves away from me. The moment he turns his back and starts down my steps I slam the door and lock it. It isn't long before I hear his car peeling away.

An hour later my body is still trembling violently. I threw on sweats and a blanket, but can't seem to get warm. Icy terror has ruthlessly taken over me and won't let go. Fear leaps into my throat when there's another knock on the door. Standing, I approach slowly, my heart thundering, praying it's not him again. Peeking through the peephole, I see it's Jaxson. Unlocking the latch, I swing the door open.

"I'm glad to see the door is locked," he says with a smirk that vanishes the moment he sees me. "Jules?" He grabs my shoulders in concern. "What's wrong? What happened?"

I shove him off of me, anger bubbling up to the surface hot and fast and it overrides everything else. "I told you! I told you both that it was a mistake. But you didn't listen to me and now everything is worse." My fists strike out, hitting him in the chest as I release my anger and fear on him. "Why didn't you listen to me?"

"Goddamn it, stop!" He spins me around, my back to his front, and locks his arms around me so I can't get loose.

My knees give out beneath me as a sob shatters my chest.

He falls with me, holding me tight. "Talk to me, baby, what happened?"

"He came here," I choke out.

He turns me to face him, his hands gripping my arms firmly. "What did he do? Did he fucking hurt you?"

I can't answer him, because I'm crying too hard.

"Answer me, are you hurt?"

I shake my head, my emotion robbing me of breath.

"God, Julia, breathe, baby, it's okay." He pulls me into his chest, trying to talk me through whatever is happening to me. Eventually, the deep baritone of his voice, and the comforting circles he's rubbing on my back begin to calm me enough that I'm able to catch my breath.

Leaning back, he takes my face between his hands, his expression lethal. "I'm going to fucking kill him."

I grab his shirt, panic seizing my chest at the thought. "No, you can't! Jaxson, you have to listen to me! He's crazy. Like I mean, seriously crazy. He thinks I'm his. He thinks we have been in love with each other for years, he thinks… Oh god." I start losing control of my breath again.

"Stop, just calm down."

He tries to stand but I cling to him. "No! Don't leave me."

"Fuck me!" Picking me up, he carries me into the kitchen with him and sets me on the counter. He fills a glass of water and hands it to me. "Drink this, just a little at a time."

I do as he says, the cool water a welcome relief to my raw throat.

Once I'm finished he takes it back and comes to stand between my legs, his hands cradling my face. "I need you to tell me exactly what happened and what he said." My mouth opens to blast him with the information but he cuts me off, his hand covering my mouth. "Calmly, everything is going to be okay."

Closing my eyes, I take a deep breath then relay everything that was said. A dangerous rage fills his expression when I tell him about Wyatt asking me if I spread my legs for him. "I told you this would happen," I say through a fresh wave of tears. "I'm dropping the restraining order."

"No, you're not! Julia, listen to me, he's trying to scare you."

I laugh bitterly. "Yeah, well it worked, I'm fucking scared. I'm serious, Jaxson. I'm dropping it and there's not a damn thing you or Cooper can do to stop me."

"Damn it! Listen to everything you just told me. Now more than ever, you should understand just how much you need that restraining order."

"No. If I drop it everything can go back to the way it was, and I'll just stay clear of him."

"Do you really think it will be that easy?"

"I don't have any other choice!"

"Yes, you do! You stand up to him. He's a rich asshole who's used to getting his way, by either paying people off or threatening them. Don't let him push you around."

"I'm scared" I whisper. "You didn't see him, he's crazy."

He wraps me in his arms, holding me close. "I won't let him hurt you. He might be crazy, but he's a fucking coward. It's why he came to you and not me."

I shake my head as tears stream down my face.

"What do you think he's going to do once you lift that restraining order? Do you really think he will just leave you alone? He's infatuated with you. Lifting it is only going to cause you more harm."

He's right. I know he is but it doesn't make it any easier. "How did he find out about it already? I thought Cooper said it would take a couple of days."

His jaw hardens. "I don't know, but I'm going to find out." Fishing his cell out of his pocket, he dials Coop's number. "Yeah, hold on a sec." He covers the phone to speak to me. "Go ahead and get your shoes on. I'll meet you at the door."

"I don't want to go out anymore."

"We're not, we're going to my hotel so I can get my things and check out."

"Why?"

"Because I'm staying here with you."

His explanation brings me a small measure of peace. I really don't want to stay by myself, especially tonight.

Hopping off the counter, I head to the bathroom first and wash my face, the cool water stinging my hot eyes. Afterward, I slip my shoes on and walk back into the kitchen to see Jaxson still on the phone with Cooper.

His tone is quiet but harsh. "Oh come on, we both know she told him."

I'm assuming he's talking about Jenny. I figured it was probably her, too.

"I don't fucking care! I'm telling you now, Cooper, if he comes near her again I won't tell you first, I'll deal with him my way." Icy disdain drips from his promise. "Fine, get back to me after you do." He hangs up and slips the phone back in his pocket. "Fuck!" His angry curse pierces the air as he braces his hands on my counter, head hanging in defeat.

My steps are slow as I approach him. His muscles tense as I lay my hand on his back before wrapping my arms around him, wanting to ease his fury.

A few beats pass before he turns to face me, reciprocating my hug. His heart thunders against my cheek, chest heaving in anger.

"I'll keep the restraining order," I tell him quietly.

His stiff muscles relax. "Thanks, baby. You just saved us from having a really big fight." The corner of my mouth lifts in a smile as he kisses the top of my head. "Come on, let's go. We'll pick up something to eat on the way home."

CHAPTER 17

Jaxson

Later that evening, we're sitting on Julia's couch eating supper and watching a movie. All my stuff is piled in the guest room upstairs, right next to Julia's bedroom. From here on out, I will be getting no sleep, my hard dick will be keeping me up all night. I just hope I'm not plagued by any nightmares. I haven't had one for some time now, but every once in a while, one will sneak up on me.

Looking down at Julia, I notice she still hasn't touched her food. "Eat," I demand, pointing to her untouched burger.

"I'm not very hungry," she responds quietly. She's wrapped in a blanket, her face pale and eyes bright with fear. I want to kill that fucker. The only thing stopping me is I don't want to leave her, especially right now; she scared the hell out of me with her panic attack earlier. Cooper promised me he would deal with the asshole. It's his only shot. Then the bastard is mine.

"Eat, Julia!" I say again.

She rolls her eyes and takes a dramatic bite of her burger. "There, happy?"

I grunt. "I will be when it's gone."

She finishes most of it, so I let her be. Eventually she lies down, putting her feet across my lap while she watches the movie, some chick flick I haven't been paying attention to. My mind is too busy conjuring up images of beating Jennings to death. I knew the fucker wasn't all there, but even Cooper and I didn't realize it was this bad. The fact that Wyatt thinks Julia is his goes to show just how crazy he is. Everyone in this town has always known she's mine.

It makes me rethink my decision about this just friends bullshit. Clearly, we already have a hard time controlling our emotions. Staying here with her is only going to make it worse. But I know it's not fair to Julia; she deserves to have a life, a family. That's something she can never have with me, because no way in hell do I ever plan on having kids. My bloodline stops with me, the thought of fucking a kid up like my father did to me makes me sick.

Glancing back down at her, I see she's sound asleep. She looks so small and fragile like this that it makes me want to lock her in here forever so no one can hurt her.

I turn off the TV then pick her up effortlessly; she doesn't stir. Climbing the stairs, I carry her into her room and lay her down. Putting her to bed is seeming to become a ritual for the two of us, one I could definitely get used to, but one that's dangerous. I decide to leave her in her sweats, knowing I'll have a hard enough time sleeping tonight as it is.

After locking up, I head to bed and settle in for a long fucking night.

CHAPTER 18

Julia

I wake up in my bed the next morning, still in my sweats with a blanket draped over me and realize I must have fallen asleep watching the movie last night. Stretching out my tired muscles, I think about yesterday's events and still can't believe how delusional I was about Wyatt.

How has he gone so long in this town without people realizing how crazy he is?

The thought is interrupted when my phone chimes with a text. Reaching over, I grab it off my nightstand to see it's from Kayla.

> **Kayla:** *Be ready for 7 on Friday. Make sure you dress in dark clothes and wear a hat. We're going to bust this fucker.*

After everything that happened with Wyatt yesterday, I had forgotten all about her, which makes me feel terrible. I'm still reeling over the thought that Cooper could do this. I've thought about mentioning it to Jaxson but I know he won't keep it from Cooper.

The sound of the shower turning on down the hall in the guest bathroom alerts me Jaxson is awake. I get up and take one myself, but make it quick, wanting to cook him breakfast before he's done.

After changing into a pair of faded jean shorts and a soft pink tank, I head out into the hall and peek my head into his room when I see the door slightly ajar. "Hey, what do you want—" My words die in my throat and I suck in a sharp, painful breath at the sight before me.

Jaxson stands faced away from me without a shirt on, a massive tattoo covering his defined back. It's the most beautiful angel I've ever seen. Her detailing so distinctive you would swear she was real. There's a darkness that swirls around her, but it does nothing to take away from her beauty. The image is mostly black and shaded, except her eyes. They're a bright aquamarine—the same color as mine.

Although the tattoo is large, it does nothing to cover the horrendous scars that mark his skin. It looks like someone whipped him or cut him… I don't know which, and I'm not sure I want to.

My burning, watery eyes roam up his back and collide with his hard ones. Tears soak my cheeks as my heart swells painfully in my chest. I try to speak, to say something, but the words are lodged in my aching throat. They end up invading me a moment later. "I-I'm sorry, I didn't realize you were changing." Closing the door, I make my way downstairs and head into the kitchen, my blood rushing in my ears. I lean over the sink and put a shaking hand to my stomach, feeling like I'm going to be sick.

How could someone do that to him? To anyone? What does the tattoo mean?

I snap out of my thoughts when Jaxson walks in. Clearing my throat, I swipe my tears away and busy myself around the kitchen. "What do you want for breakfast? I can make eggs, pancakes—"

"Julia."

I continue to move about and talk over him. "I don't have any bacon but I can make French toast, or if you like we can go into town and eat at the diner."

"Julia, stop!" Reaching out, his fingers curl around my arm as he pulls me against him, his strong arms holding my shattered pieces together.

My sob breaks free, exploding past my lips. "What did they do to you?"

He lifts me off my feet and sets me on the counter, coming to stand between my legs. My arms hug his neck as I keep him close, wishing I had the power to heal what I just saw a moment ago.

"Don't cry for me, Jules," he says, his voice gruff as he rubs my back.

"I hate that someone hurt you."

"We made it out, that's all that matters."

When he says *we* it reminds me he wasn't the only one hurt. I lean back to look at him. "Were Sawyer and Cade the other ones with you?"

He confirms the question with a nod.

"Are they okay?" I ask on a painful breath.

He drops his forehead on mine. "Yeah, baby, they're okay. We all are. We're a little fucked-up maybe, but what else is new?" He grins, trying to make light of the moment, but there's nothing funny about it.

"Don't make jokes."

His expression sobers, a dark pain entering his eyes. "Do you understand now, Julia? Do you get why I sent you away. I see you hurt like this and it fucking kills me. Trust me when I say what you would have seen in that hospital was a hundred times worse than what you just saw."

I think about this for a moment then nod. "I understand, but it doesn't change that I wanted to be there for you. Yes, it would have hurt me to see you like that, but I wanted to help you. I wanted to make it better for you."

"After seeing the tattoo don't you understand that you did? The angel is you, Julia. You were always there with me in the darkness. Every time those fuckers came in to torture us, I went into my mind and thought about you."

My breath seizes in my lungs, his words stealing my breath.

"I would think about your smile and your eyes," he says, his thumb brushing my cheek. "Then I would think about the night I was buried inside your warm body, and I'd completely lose myself in you. It made everything I went through bearable, it made me fight to get the fuck out of there."

His beautiful words are my undoing. Grabbing his shirt, I seal his mouth over mine, but that's where my control ends. His fingers thread in my hair with a firm grip, tilting my head back, to deepen the kiss. All of our pent up desire unleashes, our mouths aligning in fevered hunger.

I suck in air as his lips move down my throat, scalding my sensitive skin. His hand presses on my chest, coaxing me to my back. He tugs down my tank top, freeing my breasts. The cool air whispers across my fevered flesh, my nipples pebbling beneath his heated gaze.

A low growl rumbles from his throat as he leans down and latches on to one aching point. Heat sweeps through my body like a desert storm, stealing my senses.

Moaning, I arch off the counter, my fingers threading in his still-damp hair. I thrust against his hard stomach, seeking friction for the throbbing between my legs.

Reaching between our bodies, Jaxson snaps open the button to my jean shorts, and shoves his hand in my panties. "Ah yeah, you're so fucking wet," he groans, gliding his fingers through my arousal before entering two of them deep inside of me.

A heated cry breaches my lips and I grab onto his biceps, my fingers getting lost in the grooves of his muscles.

"Jesus, I love seeing you burn for me, baby."

My fiery moans fill the air around us. I'm so lost in the pleasure that I don't hear the knock on the door until Jaxson tenses.

I still and listen again, praying it's not… yep, it's my door.

"Are you fucking serious?" he asks, exasperated.

Disappointment crushes me, tears leaking from my eyes at the need torturing my body. I gasp when Jaxson's fingers return to their delicious thrusting.

He peers down at me, a wicked grin curving his lips. "I won't leave you hangin', baby, but you only have a few seconds here, so try not to be too loud."

With a smile of my own, I pull his mouth down to mine and rock my hips to the rhythm of his fingers. My fast breaths tumble past my lips with the anticipation of my climax.

"That's it, baby. Let go and come all over my fingers."

My orgasm slams into me and I fall apart, a total shaking mess. He claims my lips, smothering my cries of pleasure.

Once I'm limp and sated, I notice the knocking has stopped. I yelp, startled at the vibration between my legs.

"It's just my phone," Jaxson chuckles.

He removes his hand from my shorts then shocks me by putting his fingers to his mouth, sucking my arousal off them, his eyes never leaving mine. A growl rumbles from him, his face savage. "Go to the bathroom and get decent; it's Cooper." Without another word, he leaves the kitchen.

Righting my shirt, I hurry into the bathroom, my legs feeling like jelly from the intense orgasm that just crashed through me. I splash water on my face, trying to rid my flushed skin tone.

Jaxson's and Cooper's voices carry from the kitchen. Exiting the bathroom, I head into the kitchen to find them in a heated discussion. I have a hard time looking Cooper in the eye. I'm sure he has a pretty good idea what was taking us so long to answer. It also doesn't help that I'm furious at him for what he's doing to Kayla, but I try to mask that, not wanting to give anything away.

"Hey, Julia."

"Cooper," I acknowledge with a tight nod, failing miserably at my attempt.

He frowns at my less-than-friendly greeting. "I came by to let you know that I served Jennings the restraining order today, and I also laid into him about coming over here last night. He shouldn't be bothering you again."

"Thank you," I reply, my words a little softer this time.

He nods. "I found out it was Jenny who told him about the restraining order. I fired her this morning."

"You didn't have to do that."

Jaxson grunts. "The bitch is lucky that's all she got."

"If Wyatt comes anywhere near you again I want you to call me right away. If you run into him somewhere by chance, he has to leave immediately, not the other way around."

"He must have been pretty mad, huh?" I ask, chewing my nail nervously.

He shrugs. "Doesn't matter. I think he was hoping he scared you enough yesterday that you would drop it. I'm glad you didn't. He knows now that you're serious, so I do believe he'll leave you alone. Either way, I think it's good Jaxson stays here for a while with you."

My attention anchors on Jaxson, his expression void of any emotion. His armor is back in place. I can tell we won't be picking up where we left off, much to my disappointment.

"Anyway, I better get back, but I wanted to come by and tell you in person that it has been taken care of."

My eyes narrow suspiciously. "Where are you going?"

"Back to work," he answers slowly.

"You sure about that?"

Ugh, shut up, Julia!

He looks at me like I've lost my mind. "Yeah, I'm sure. Why?"

"Just curious." I shrug easily, hoping to cover the lie. "Thanks for stopping by." Walking over to the sink I grab myself a glass of water. Out of the corner of my eye I see Cooper and Jaxson exchange a look.

Damn, I hope I didn't ruin anything and he's figured out that I know.

With a shake of his head, Cooper mumbles a good-bye then leaves.

I feel Jaxson's gaze burning me but I ignore it and pay close attention to the glass of water in my hand. "What was that all about?"

"What?" I feign ignorance.

"Your suspicious questions, that's what."

"I just wondered if he was going back to work."

"Where else would he be going?"

"I don't know, Jaxson, *do you*?"

Shit! Now I'm accusing him, too.

"What the fuck is with you?"

"Never mind, forget I said anything." I decide to change the subject to a topic that's no less easy to talk about. "So, are we going to talk about what just happened?"

He shrugs. "Nothing much to say. Heat of the moment, we got wrapped up in our emotions."

"Really, that's how we're going to play this?"

"What do you want me to say, Julia? Do I want to fuck you? Yeah, I do, but what do we do after that?"

"Why do we have to decide? Why can't we just see where it goes?"

"I don't know how to do that. I've never had a fucking girlfriend before."

"Well it's quite easy, Jaxson. You see, it would be exactly how we are now except we get to have sex, lots of sex. Sounds like a damn good deal to me."

He doesn't smile like I hope for him to. "And what do we do when our time is up? Because once we change our relationship there's no going back to just being friends."

"Why does there have to be a time limit?"

"Because one day you're going to want to get married and have kids, something I never plan to have."

Pain slices through my chest, my heart twisting at his words. "Yeah, well, as much as I really want kids one day it's never going to happen, because I can't have children." My words come out as raw and painful as the wound in my chest.

"What the hell are you talking about?"

"I have polycystic ovary syndrome," I tell him, my throat tight. "I found out after I came back from your graduation. I had a physical with my doctor after we… well you know, and it came up. I don't ovulate because I don't have regular menstrual cycles. It's why I am on the pill. The doctor told me my chances of ever having children are slim to none."

"Shit." His long legs eat up the distance between us, his arms banding around me. "I'm sorry, Jules, you would make a good mom."

I shrug and stay silent, not wanting to talk about the painful topic.

"Look, let's get back what we had before, then we'll go from there. I don't want to lose you again."

I peer up at him, his startling blue eyes striking me deeper. "You never lost me, Jaxson, you pushed me away. There's a difference." Slipping out from his grasp, I walk away.

He does nothing to stop me, but I didn't expect him to. I'm tired of being rejected, and I decide from here on out there will be no more attempts on my part. The rest is up to him.

CHAPTER 19

Julia

A few days later I'm standing at my kitchen sink, cursing up a storm, as I try to pry up the handle on the tap but can't. The darn thing is stuck.

"What's wrong?" Jaxson asks, walking up behind me.

"The stupid tap is jammed. I should just buy a whole new sink, the damn thing is like a hundred years old anyway."

He nudges me to the side. "Watch out, I got this."

My eyes roll at his arrogance, but I step aside. At first he tries to pull it up firmly, but not too hard. When he has no luck with that, he gives up and really yanks on it. A loud pop pierces the air.

I gasp and jump out of the way as water sprays out, all over Jaxson.

"Fuck!" He tries screwing the handle back on while water soaks his chest and face. Finally, he manages to get it back on. "Shit," he mutters with a heavy breath, looking a little stunned.

I stand with my hand cupped over my mouth, my body shaking as I try to hold in my laughter.

He turns to face me, eyes narrowing. "Are you laughing?"

I shake my head but a snort escapes me, outing the lie.

"You think this is funny, Julia?" he asks with a gleam in his eye.

Uh-oh, I know that look. Shoving from the counter, I haul ass out of the kitchen. His heavy steps gain on me but I push myself harder, barreling up the stairs for my bedroom. Of course I'm nowhere near fast enough. Jaxson's arms snag my waist, holding me tight as he carries my flailing body up the remainder of the stairs, hauling me into the main bathroom.

"What are you doing?" I shriek, trying to kick free as he leans down to start the shower. "You wouldn't dare!"

"Yeah, I would."

I manage to break free for all of a second before he has me back against him. "Jaxson, don't you do it! I mean it, I will kick your ass."

He grunts, unconcerned by the threat, then lifts me into the shower, forcing me under the warm water.

"I hate you, I hate you, I hate you!" I grind out and give him my best glare.

He chuckles, proud of himself. "What are you going to do about it, Julia?"

The challenge fuels me. My eyes track down his body, his wet shirt showing every line and curve of his muscles. The perfect idea forms and I grace him with a smirk of my own. His smugness disappears as I saunter closer to him. "I can think of a few things to do," I say breathlessly, dragging a finger slowly down his chest to the waistband of his jeans.

"What are you doing?" he asks, voice gruff.

Reaching down I grab his hard length through his wet jeans, giving it a gentle squeeze.

"Shit," he breathes, dropping his head against the wall.

"You know, Jaxson, I owe you for the other day, and I'm thinking now would be a good time to repay you." I drop to my knees before him and unsnap his jeans.

"Ah fuck!" the curse flees him on a hiss, his muscles tense.

Even though I'm only messing with him, I can't help it when my own breathing speeds up, desire igniting in my blood. Unzipping him, I push open the flaps of his jeans then lean in and press a soft kiss to his hard length over his black boxer briefs.

A loud groan rumbles from him, and I can't deny that my clothes aren't the only things wet right now. I look up to see his jaw locked and eyes shut, waiting for me to take him in my mouth.

"Oh wait, what am I doing?"

His eyes snap open as I stand.

"I totally forgot... *friends only*," I give myself a tap on the head and let out a dramatic sigh. "Well, I guess I better go and change now." Giving him a pat on the chest, I move to step out of the shower when I'm yanked back.

"I don't fucking think so."

His mouth descends hard.

Claiming.

Branding.

Moaning, I kiss him back with the same passion, letting the taste of him settle deep into my bones.

His hands cup my bottom, hoisting me up. My legs hug his waist as he shoves me up against the shower wall. He pulls back, his eyes holding mine beneath the hood of his dark lashes. "It's time you learned just who is in control here, Julia."

He drives his hip against the apex of my thighs, dragging a fiery whimper from my throat.

Lord, he can be really sexy when he's arrogant.

His head dips, teeth grazing my stiff nipple through my thin, wet tank top.

"Oh god, Jaxson, please," I beg shamelessly, my nails digging into his shoulders.

"You want it so bad, don't you, baby?"

"Yes," I manage through short breaths.

"Not as bad as me." His hips push forward again, giving me more but it's still not enough.

My fingers grip his wet shirt, dragging it up his back, needing his skin upon mine. I feel him tense and he stops his delicious assault.

"What?" I ask breathlessly.

Then I hear it... a knock on my door.

This is not happening.

"What the hell?" he asks in disbelief. "Are you expecting someone?"

I shake my head.

Someone bangs on the door again, and not all that gently.

"Ignore it," I say, taking his mouth again in a desperate attempt to make him forget he heard anything.

The insistent knocking finally stops but instead of leaving they ring the doorbell.

"Shit!" Jaxson pulls his mouth free, regret burning in his ice-blue eyes. "We should answer it, it might be Cooper."

If it is Cooper again, I'm gonna kill him. My body slides sinfully down Jaxson's as he releases me. I want to cling to it and beg him to never let go.

"Who's going to answer it?" I ask, looking down at our wet clothes.

His eyes lock on my plastered tank top. "Definitely not you. I'll answer it, you go change."

Giggling, I grab a towel and dash out of the bathroom and into my room. I dry my hair as best as I can then trade my wet tank top and capris for a light denim jean skirt and sage green, lace tank top that shows some cleavage. Hopefully, it will tempt Jaxson to finish what we started. I know I said he had to be the first to make the move from now on, but that doesn't mean I'm going to make it easy on him.

As I descend the stairs, I hear a couple of male voices that I don't recognize. Wondering whom it could be, I enter into the kitchen and come to an abrupt halt, gaping at the men before me. "Oh my gosh! Sawyer? Cade?" I ask, unsure if what I'm seeing is real.

"Holy shit, look who went and got even hotter," Sawyer boasts with that charming smile of his, one I've never forgotten. His arms open invitingly. "Get your pretty ass over here."

Smiling, I run into his outstretched arms, hugging him tight. Tears sting my eyes, relief filling my chest to know he's okay.

He places me back on my feet and grabs a lock of my damp hair. "Did you get nice and wet just for me, *Jules*?"

"Oh you!" I laugh, slapping him in the chest.

"Watch yourself, Evans!" Jaxson growls.

Sawyer chuckles, not the least bit intimidated. Turning, I face Cade. He hasn't changed a bit, his expression still cold and hard, maybe even harder but I know better.

"Hi, Julia." He nods the greeting.

"Oh, Cade." With a teary smile, I walk up to him and wrap my arms around his waist. His body stiffens but he pats my back awkwardly. "I'm so glad you're okay; I'm glad you're both okay," I blubber, my arm reaching to bring Sawyer in too.

"You want to get in on this group hug, Reid? I'll be nice and share Julia."

A giggle tumbles past my lips and I look over at Jaxson to find him glaring at Sawyer, clearly not finding it as funny as we do. Stepping back, I grab a tissue to wipe under my eyes. "What are y'all doing here?" I ask with a sniffle.

"We came to see you and figured while we're here we'd see what this jackass has been up to," Sawyer explains.

I shake my head, a knowing smile curving my lips.

"All right. We actually went to see Jaxson at the hotel we thought he was staying at, but they said he checked out. Then we ran into your sheriff, and he told us he's living with you now," he says, his green eyes filled with questions.

My attention shifts to Jaxson and I see him tight-lipped, still pouting.

Whatever!

"Jaxson is staying with me… in the guest bedroom, by his own choice," I add, feeling his disapproving gaze on me but I ignore it. "How long are y'all here for?"

Sawyer shrugs. "I don't know, we're playing it by ear, but so far I like it here. I may just stay a while," he admits, his lip kicking up in a dirty grin.

"Oh fuck off," Jaxson mumbles.

I toss him a silent warning before retracting my eyes back to Sawyer. "Well you both can stay here."

"No, they can't!" Jaxson barks.

"Yes, they can. I have more than enough spare rooms, and it's my house!"

"Yeah, it's her house," Sawyer steps in, backing me up. "And if there aren't enough rooms I'll just crawl in bed and sleep with her…since you aren't."

I burst into a fit of laughter, unable to stop myself.

"You're seriously pissing me off, Evans."

"Oh lighten up, Jaxson," I scold. "Are you boys hungry? I was going to see if Jaxson wanted to head to the diner in town for supper, want to come?"

"I could eat, I can always eat," Sawyer answers.

Cade shrugs, not caring either way.

I look over at Jaxson next. "Are you coming, grumpy, or are you going to stay here and pout?" I really shouldn't antagonize him, but it's annoying that he acts all territorial over me and then says we can only be friends.

"I'm coming, just let me change," he grumbles, walking out of the kitchen.

Sawyer flashes me another smirk. "This is going to be fun."

I shake my head, biting back a smile.

Jaxson comes down in record time, his scowl still in place. Sawyer slings an arm around my shoulders as we start for the door but Jaxson shoves it off of me. "You, asshole, can drive yourself. Julia and I will go in my truck."

Sawyer feigns offense. "Why don't I take Julia and you take Cade?"

"Why don't we all just drive together?" I suggest before Jaxson has the chance to throttle him.

"Sounds good to me," Sawyer agrees. "Julia can ride in the back with me. I'll be nice and give Cade shotgun."

Jaxson shakes his head, his jaw locked in annoyance.

I hold back a laugh, knowing it won't be appreciated. I have a feeling this is going to be a long night, but I couldn't be happier right now.

CHAPTER 20

Julia

We arrive at the diner and are lucky to get a booth since the place is packed. I watch poor Grace running her butt off, looking flustered and realize they must be short-staffed, again.

Looking around the crowded diner, my eyes land on one person, one that has my stomach bottoming out.

Ray Jennings, Wyatt's dad.

He sits at the counter, his disapproving eyes on our booth. Jaxson senses my unease and follows my gaze. I feel him stiffen next to me but I don't look over at him. I can't. My attention is rooted on Mr. Jennings, my belly twisting anxiously.

Jaxson's warm hand cups my cheek and forces my eyes to his. "Forget about him. It's fine."

Nodding, I open my menu, chewing on my thumbnail.

"What is it?" Sawyer asks, glancing back at Ray.

"Later," Jaxson's tone is clipped, shutting down the conversation before it can even start.

Grace comes over at that moment, her head down as she tries to find her pad of paper. "Hi, y'all, sorry about the wait. What can I—" She looks up, finally noticing me. "Julia, hi," she greets me with a kind smile.

"Hi, Grace." I stand and give her a hug.

Her smile disappears and eyes widen when she takes in Sawyer and Cade.

"Grace, this is Sawyer and Cade," I introduce her. "They're friends of Jaxson's from the Navy. Guys, this is my good friend, Grace."

"Hi." She waves shyly, her cheeks pink.

Cade greets her with his usual nod, while Sawyer, of course, lays on the charm. "Well heya there, Grace, nice outfit," he compliments with a dashing smile.

She looks down at her uniform dress with a frown, her cheeks heating. "Thanks, I guess," she mumbles then brings her attention back to me, blatantly dismissing him. "What can I get y'all to drink?"

"Sweet tea for me please," I say, ordering my usual.

Once everyone else gives her their drink order, she walks away. Sawyer's eyes track her, his brows furrowed deep in thought.

Jaxson relaxes back into our seat, a smug grin on his face. "What's wrong, Evans, losing your touch?"

"I don't know, that's never happened to me before," he says, completely serious.

Jaxson grunts. "Well there's a first time for everything."

When Grace brings us our drinks and takes our order she doesn't glance at Sawyer once. I can tell it really bothers him.

This could get interesting...

Once she leaves us again, Sawyer snaps out of his mood and changes the subject. "So the admiral called me," he tells Jaxson, something flickering in his green eyes. "He's wondering why you aren't answering his calls?"

"What calls?" I ask.

"Not now, Sawyer." Jaxson's voice is tight as he refuses to discuss the topic.

Annoyance sparks inside of me and I can't help but feel a little hurt. It's obvious he doesn't want to talk about it in front of me.

Before I can give it too much thought a bigger problem forms when I catch sight of Ray Jennings making his way over to us.

My anxious fingers curl around Jaxson's wrist and I become terrified for the confrontation that's about to ensue.

Ray stops next to Jaxson, but his eyes are only on me. "Well, Miss Julia, I can't say I'm surprised. Disappointed maybe, but not surprised."

"Well, no one asked you, asshole, so get the fuck out of here," Jaxson says, his icy tone sending a chill through the air.

Ray ignores him and keeps his attention on me, the silent fury in his eyes making me more uncomfortable by the second. "I tried to tell my son you are who you hang out with, but he assured me you had enough class to be seen with him. I'm sad he had to learn the hard way."

Jaxson begins to stand up but I tighten my grip on his arm. "He's trying to goad you, don't take the bait."

Ray smirks, looking rather amused. "I remember your mother, Julia, she too was very pretty. I can only imagine the disappointment she feels from beyond the grave."

His hurtful words barely have time to register before Jaxson is out of the booth and has him by the lapels of his expensive suit. Sawyer and Cade both stand and flank him.

Oh lord!

"I told you to get the fuck out of here—"

"Jaxson, stop!" I insert myself between Sawyer and him, placing my shaking hand on his chest.

"Listen to her, son, you don't want to mess with me."

Jaxson leans in closer to Ray, fury hardening his expression. "Wrong, dickhead, you don't want to fuck with me. I'm trained to kill with my bare hands. I also know what to do with your body so no one would find you, so don't fucking tempt me. You and your crazy son better stay away from Julia, or you'll find out exactly what *trash* like me is capable of."

There's no denying the fear in Ray's eyes; he knows Jaxson not only means it but is capable of it.

"Julia, should I call Cooper?" Grace asks, her timid eyes moving from Ray to Jaxson.

"That isn't necessary, sweetheart," Ray says before I can answer. "I was just leaving."

I apply pressure to Jaxson's chest. "Come on, Jax. Let him go."

"I mean it, you leave her the fuck alone," his warning slices through the air as he steps back.

Ray straightens his suit, his jaw tight as he walks out the door.

"Jesus, who the fuck was that asshole?" Sawyer asks.

"Ray Jennings," I tell him quietly, my voice shaky. "He's on the town council. I had to put a restraining order on his son."

"Town council? The way that arrogant prick spoke you'd think he was President of the United States."

A laugh tumbles past my lips, my anxious heart a little lighter. Leave it to Sawyer to lighten the mood.

When we take our seats again, Jaxson turns to me, concern bright in his eyes. "You okay?"

I nod but my heart still beats a million miles a minute.

"You know what he said about your mom is bullshit, right?"

I smile. "Yeah. I do." My mother would never be disappointed of my friendship with Jaxson. Actually, if she were still alive, I know she'd love him just as much as Grams does.

"Good." He presses a hard kiss to my forehead, calming the storm of emotions that took over my body moments ago.

I really love it when he does that.

"All right, here's your food," Grace announces, laying the plates out in front of everyone. "Can I get y'all another drink?"

I shake my head. "I'm okay, thank you."

"I'd love another one," Sawyer says, tossing her another panty dropping smile, one Grace misses because she doesn't look at him.

Her very apparent dismissal seems to really bother him. In fact, he looks kind of pissed off, something I've never seen on him before. He's always so funny and happy.

Conversation flows throughout the rest of dinner, all the earlier tension evaporating, besides Sawyer and Grace that is. Once we finish our meals, the guys leave Grace a generous tip, one she tries refusing but eventually accepts due to Jaxson's demand.

I give her another hug before we leave and tell her I'll see her on Saturday. I'm hoping Kayla will still be up for it after tomorrow night. If not we can have a girls' night watching movies and veg out on junk food. Either way, I won't be leaving Kayla to sulk alone.

When we arrive back at my house, Cade and Sawyer start for their truck.

"Aren't you guys going to stay here?"

Sawyer smirks over at Jaxson, a silent challenge happening between them. "That's all right, Julia, but thanks for the offer. Cade and I are going to stay at the motel where Jaxson was. But I hope it's all right we come by and visit a lot while we're here?"

I glare over at Jaxson, knowing it's because of him they aren't staying. "Of course. Come over as much as you like. You're always welcome, and you can always change your minds, too."

"Great! Then I'll see you tomorrow." he swoops in, planting a kiss on my cheek until Jaxson shoves him back.

"Lips to yourself, asshole."

Laughing, Sawyer hops into his truck while Cade gives us a quick wave. Then they're driving away, leaving me with a grumpy Jaxson.

CHAPTER 21

I climb out of the shower the next morning and hear familiar voices coming from downstairs.

Of course that fucker is already here this early. I'm sure he set his alarm just to piss me off.

Throwing on some clothes, I walk downstairs and into the kitchen to find Julia serving the asshole breakfast.

Sawyer turns to me with a grin. "Well good morning, sleepyhead."

"What the hell are you doing here already?"

"Boy, you're grumpy. What's wrong—didn't sleep well? I hope Julia and I didn't keep you up last night. I tried to keep her quiet—"

Julia gasps and slaps his shoulder. "Sawyer!" She scolds with a giggle.

The guy is going to get his ass kicked soon. "I'm not in the mood for your shit this morning, Evans, so lay off." I know he's only doing it to get a rise out of me, but the thought of him laying a hand on Julia drives me insane.

"Okay, you two, that's enough," Julia says. "Jaxson, what do you want? I have pancakes made, but I can make you something else if you'd like?" she offers, busying herself around the kitchen.

My eyes track her every move, my cock swelling in my jeans. Even this early in the morning she looks fucking good enough to eat. Her yoga pants and tank top fit her lithe body snugly, leaving nothing to the imagination. She has the best ass I've ever seen, and I want to punch the shit out of Sawyer when I see him staring at it as she bends down to grab something from the fridge. Instead I settle for a slap upside the head.

He chuckles, unashamed for being busted.

"Pancakes are good," I finally answer her and go grab a plate off the counter to dish my own food. "You didn't have to feed these assholes. Especially him." I jerk a thumb at Sawyer.

His cocky smirk spreads. "What can I say, she likes cooking me breakfast."

Shaking my head, I try to ignore the mouthy shit and load my plate with pancakes before I take a seat at the table.

"I don't mind, I like cooking breakfast… for *everyone*," she adds, smiling at Sawyer.

I don't want her to smile at him like that. It will give him ideas and fuel his obnoxiousness.

"Do you guys have a gym here?" Cade asks.

"Yeah, but I don't know what condition it's in though. They used to have a sparring ring and all," I tell him then glance back at Julia. "Does Big Mike still own it?"

"Yep, he does, but I know he's been thinking of selling. He told me he's getting too old. His son moved to Florida and has no interest in taking it over, much to Mike's disappointment."

"We can go by there later today if you want?" I tell Cade then look over at Sawyer. "I'd love to go a couple of rounds with you, asshole."

"I'm in for that. Wanna come, Julia? You can see me put your man to shame."

I can't wait to take his ass down.

"I think I'll pass," she declines with a smile, then swings her pretty eyes to me. "What do you have planned tonight?"

"Not sure, why?"

"I was just wondering because I'm going out with Kayla."

"I thought your girls' night is tomorrow night?"

"Girls' night?" Sawyer pipes back in. "Where? Is Grace going to be there?"

"It is, but Kayla and I have plans tonight, too," she tells me before looking over at Evans. "And yes, Sawyer, Grace is going to be with us."

"I'm in, I love girls' night. Where is it?"

"We're going out dancing. It's a *girls'* night which means you can't come if you have a penis."

He grunts. "If you're going to a club dancing, Julia, guys will be there."

Exactly! It's all I've thought about and it pisses me off.

"That I can't control." She shrugs.

No, but I can…

Sawyer, Cade, and I walk into Big Mike's gym later that afternoon. It looks the same as it did when I was here last, but more run-down. The place has a lot of potential, if he would put the money into it.

"Well I'll be damned, if it isn't Jaxson Reid!" Big Mike bellows, striding over to us. He, too, looks mostly the same but older—much older. By the tired lines around his eyes I can understand why he's looking at selling the place. He's got to be well into his sixties now.

Mike was a huge influence on me. When I was younger and got busted for fighting a lot, he brought me in here to train with him. He let me work my aggression out, something I had a lot of at that age.

"How are you doing, kid?" he asks, slapping me on the back.

"I'm good. It's great to see you again."

"You too. What are you doing here? You on leave?"

"I've been discharged." He has to know that after only being in the Navy for five years there's a reason why I've been discharged. Thankfully, he doesn't ask questions.

"You here to stay?"

I shrug. "Maybe."

"Well I'll bet Miss Julia is real happy about that."

Nodding, I end the topic there and gesture to the guys next to me. "These are some friends who are visiting. We were hoping to come work out and do some sparring."

"Of course. Come on in, the ring is free."

"Thanks."

"You bet, good to have you back." He claps me on the shoulder one more time before walking back to his office.

We head into the locker room to change and Sawyer wastes no time bringing up the admiral. "So why aren't you answering his calls?"

"Because I don't care what he has to say," I answer truthfully.

"Yeah, well, when you don't answer he comes for me next." He pauses, his eyes lifting to mine. "He wants us to do another mission, he put together a team and wants you to run it."

"Yeah, and how does he suppose that's going to work, since we're no longer in the Navy."

He shrugs. "He said he'd take care of it. Someone he knows specifically asked for the three of us."

"Why?"

There's a tense moment of silence and I can tell I'm not going to like this.

"Because it's a sex trafficking ring."

Disgust settles in my gut, heavy and hard. I drop down on the bench, feeling sick and glance over at Cade to see he looks much the same, his body tense and jaw locked. "What did you tell him?" I ask.

"I didn't tell him anything, I said I had to talk to you guys first." His eyes shift between Cade and me. "But we're done, right? I mean, I don't know about you guys, but I'm still fucked-up. And personally, after what the admiral tried to pull on us last time, he can go fuck himself for all I care."

I'm glad I'm not the only one still messed up.

"What are your thoughts?" I ask Cade.

"I don't care. I'll go if you guys want. I owe you at least that much."

His response is one I expected but it still pisses me off. "You don't owe us shit, man, how many times do we have to tell you that? It was our choice to follow you."

He remains quiet, his hard eyes on the floor.

"Have you spoken with Faith since the hospital?" I ask, treading carefully.

Pain darkens his expression and his jaw hardens. "No. It's for the best." He gets up, ending the conversation. "You guys discuss it and let me know. I'm going to hit the weights." He leaves without another word, leaving us with our demons brought to the surface. Although, his just might be worse than ours.

"Don't bother," Sawyer says, breaking the tense silence. "I've tried to talk to him about her, but he's an idiot, like you. Doesn't know what's right in front of him."

"You don't get it, Evans, it's not about us not knowing what's right in front of us. It's about trying to do the right thing. We don't come from the same family you do."

"Oh fuck that! I've had my issues too, man, life isn't perfect for anyone. You guys need to pull your heads out of your asses, because one day it might be too late. If I had someone that wanted me, like Julia does you, there would be no doubt I would take that shit, issues and all."

"Yeah, because you're an arrogant son of a bitch who thinks he's God's gift to women."

He grins, spreading his arms wide. "Hey, I can't help it that women find me irresistible."

I grunt. "Whatever. Let's go. I've been waiting since yesterday to pound the shit out of you." I stand, grabbing some gloves.

"Bring it," he counters, up for the challenge. "So what do I tell the admiral?"

I shake my head. "I don't know, let me think about it."

I want to help. The thought of another girl like Anna out there needing our help eats at me, the guilt almost unbearable. But the consequences this time could be even greater than the last.

CHAPTER 22

Julia

At seven o'clock sharp, Kayla comes walking through my door, looking like a fierce, sexy spy all decked out in black. She has on dark leggings, thigh-high leather boots, and a black tank top. Her long, blonde hair is pulled into a low ponytail through the back of a black, military-style hat. She's also sporting a pair of aviator sunglasses, even though the sun has started to set.

"Wow, you look amazing," I tell her, glancing down at my own attire. I chose a dark pair of blue jeans with a black tank top and a similar hat with my hair pulled back in a ponytail.

"Thanks." She drops the backpack she brought with her and starts pulling stuff out. "I figured I may as well look good when I kick his ass, since this will be the last time the asshole sees me."

This fiercely pissed off woman is much better than the devastatingly sad one I saw a few days ago.

She hands me a walkie-talkie. "Here, I stole this from the top of our closet, turn it to channel nine."

"Why do we need these?"

"Just in case we get separated. Especially if I need you to be on the look-out while I try to bust the fucker."

I nod in understanding.

"You look great, too. Do you have a pair of sunglasses? I don't want him noticing us."

"Sure, I'll go get them." I dash upstairs into my room, snagging them off my nightstand. I also grab my boots from my closet and put them on since Kayla is wearing hers.

"Where's Jaxson?" she asks as I make my way back down the stairs.

"I don't know. He made himself scarce when I told him we were hanging out tonight. He's probably out with Sawyer and Cade."

"Did he suspect anything?"

"No, but I almost messed up when Coop was over here the other day." I tell her about how hard it was to keep my anger in check and act like nothing was wrong.

"Tell me about it. I've been trying to work as much as I can, taking other people's appointments then pretending to be asleep when he gets home. The other night he tried getting some and it took major self-control not to cut his dick off. In the end, I feigned being sick." She shrugs, sadness pinching her expression. "It sucked because I still wanted him, even after knowing what I do. I'll probably always want him," she whispers.

I pull her in for a hug, my own throat feeling tight. "You never know, Kayla, maybe we will find out tonight that we're wrong. There's still that possibility."

"I don't think so, Jules. I can feel it. All the lies he's told and her hanging up on me, there's no other explanation." Shaking her head, her back straightens, fierce determination brightening her eyes again. "Forget it. No more tears. Let's do this!"

There's a black SUV sitting out front as we step outside. "Whose is this?" I ask.

"A co-worker's, we switched vehicles. We're going to be parked right in front of the motel when he shows up. I had to take a vehicle he wouldn't recognize, so that leaves out either of our cars."

I nod again in understanding, all of this feeling so surreal.

Twenty minutes later, we pull up to the motel, which is just off I-90. It's a seedy looking place, mainly where trucker's stop over for the night. The bar attached next door doesn't look much classier.

We end up parking at the gas station that's just across the street. Kayla shuts off the car and its lights, blanketing us in darkness except for the neon pink flashing sign. I'm feeling a little silly with my sunglasses on, but since Kayla is still wearing hers I keep mine in place.

"Right there," she says, pointing to a door across the way from us. "Room twenty-three is where the text said she would be."

We stare at it as if it's our lifeline.

"Shit! There's Cooper, get down," she hisses.

We hunker down in our seats as Cooper pulls into the lot across the way, his truck blocking half of our view of the door. I notice Kayla begin to shake so I grab her hand in silent comfort. Lifting our heads just enough to peek out the window, we both gasp when Cooper's passenger door opens first and Jaxson steps out.

"What the hell?" Kayla mumbles.

What on earth is he doing here?

Kayla and I exchange a confused look, before her eyes widen in shock. "Oh my god, do you think they're both fucking her?"

Pain strikes my chest and I instantly feel sick. After I give it some good thought, I come to my senses and shake my head.

"Yeah, you're right, that sounds a little too messed up. But what's he doing here then?"

I shrug, having no idea.

We watch Cooper as he exits the truck next. He waves at Jaxson as he makes his way over to the motel while Jaxson heads to the bar next door.

He's going to go drink while Cooper sleeps with her? How could he do something like this?

Kayla scoffs. "I really shouldn't be surprised."

Silence descends on us as Cooper knocks on the motel room door. We both wait with bated breath, waiting to see what happens. It swings open a moment later to reveal a beautiful brunette that looks close to our age. Dread sinks to the pit of my stomach when Cooper enters and closes the door behind him.

"Oh my god," Kayla whispers, sheer agony thick in her voice.

"I'm so sorry, Kayla."

"Did you get a good look at her? Do you recognize her?"

I shake my head.

"Me either," she spits, jaw tight. "Come on!" She climbs out of the SUV with purpose.

I follow suit and have to jog to catch up to her. "What are you going to do?"

"I want to get closer, hopefully I can see something in the window. Go stand by his truck and watch for Jaxson. Radio me if he comes out," she says, holding up her walkie-talkie.

"Okay, be careful." I take my spot by Coop's truck, making sure I have a good view of the bar door. "Anything?" I ask a moment later, whispering into the radio.

"Not really, but if I listen closely enough I can hear a little bit. The bitch is giggling a lot," she says, sounding pissed.

I'm so caught up in watching her that I miss Jaxson walking out of the bar. "Oh shit!" I duck behind Coop's truck, dropping to my hands and knees. I crawl around it, praying he didn't see me and bring the radio to my lips. "Kayla, get out now! Hurry, Jaxson is out."

"Julia?"

Shit!

I swing my head around and find Jaxson standing directly behind me.

"What the hell are you doing?" he asks, looking at me like I'm a complete loon.

Standing, I glance toward the motel room but don't see Kayla. Looking back at Jaxson my eyes narrow. "I can't believe you would do this, you should be ashamed of yourself!"

He rears back, *pretending* to be confused. "What the hell are you talking about?"

"Oh don't give me that. I know—" I gasp, my words dying in my throat when I hear glass shatter behind me. Running over to the other side of Cooper's truck, I find Kayla with a bat. She just smashed in the driver side window and now she's whacking the shit out of the door and side mirror.

Oh no!

"Holy shit, Kayla, what the fuck are you doing?" Jaxson's eyes are wide with shock, his hands on top of his head.

I remain frozen, not knowing what to do.

He reaches for the bat but jumps back when she raises it at him.

"Stay back, asshole, or you're next!" She walks around Coop's truck, smashing out his taillights and anything else she can hit.

"Damn it, Kayla! Stop!" Just when Jaxson starts for her again, Cooper hauls ass out of the motel room, the girl following close behind him.

Oh god, this is so bad.

"What the fuck?" Cooper bellows, his expression filled with disbelief. His quick feet stop at Kayla and he reaches for the bat but she turns around and swings at him, just missing his shoulder.

"You lying piece of shit!" she screams, taking another swing at him.

Cooper spins her around, his arms wrapping around her, trying to restrain her. The bat flails wildly behind her as she tries to strike him.

They get closer to me as they struggle but I'm unable to move. I'm completely frozen, watching their battle.

"Jesus christ!" Jaxson pulls me out of the way before I can get caught in the crossfire.

Cooper finally manages to pry the bat out of her hands and throws it across the parking lot. "What the hell do you think you're doing?"

"You lying, cheating bastard!" She continues to fight against him, tears streaming down her cheeks. Her anguish is completely devastating.

Spinning her around to face him, Cooper grips her upper arms firmly. "Stop!" He orders, giving her a hard shake.

I start toward them, scared for Kayla with seeing how mad he is, but Jaxson stops me. He also looks pretty pissed right now.

A bunch of people stand outside the bar, watching the scene unfold.

"How could you do this to me?" Kayla cries. "After everything we have been through!" Her foot strikes out, kicking him in the shin.

"That's enough. I'm not cheating on you!"

"You're seriously going to lie to me again, after I just busted your sorry ass?"

"You don't know anything, you have this all wrong!"

"Oh yeah, then who the fuck is this whore?" She points to the shocked looking brunette.

"This is Sarah Miller, my sister's friend. She's a jewelry designer. I'm here picking up your fucking engagement ring from her."

Shock slams into my chest like a sledgehammer.

Oh shit!

Kayla's entire body stills, her face paling. "My engagement ring?" she mumbles.

Cooper nods, his jaw locked so tight I'm surprised it doesn't snap.

"But the text, she hung up on me when I answered your phone, you told me you were working late when you weren't," Kayla rambles, trying to absorb what's happening.

"Yeah, I kind of wanted to keep it a fucking surprise and all," he bites out, shaking his head. "You really thought I was cheating on you?" His tone is furious, but you can see the hurt in his eyes. It makes me feel horrible, so I can only imagine what Kayla is feeling right now.

"I'm so sorry," she whispers.

He pushes away from her. "You're sorry? Look at my fucking truck!"

"I'll pay for it to get fixed—"

"Forget it! Go to the fucking car and wait for me."

"Cooper, please, will you just—"

"Now, Kayla!" He orders, pointing her away.

I tug on her arm. "Come on."

She stares at Cooper for a few more seconds then allows me to pull her away.

"Follow them," he tells Jaxson.

I link my arm with Kayla's, trying to comfort her as much as possible.

Jaxson steps in front of us, opening the back door of the SUV. "Get in. I'm going to help Cooper clean up the truck and let him know what vehicle you're in, since you aren't driving your own."

Kayla climbs in first. I glance at Jaxson to see him looking as mad as Cooper and decide it's best not to say anything and follow in behind Kayla.

Once the door slams, Kayla breaks down, gut wrenching sobs ripping from her chest. "Oh god, Julia, what have I done?"

My arm wraps around her shoulders. "Shh! It's going to be okay. You didn't know. The evidence was damning. I would have thought the same thing." I leave out that I probably wouldn't have beaten his truck in. I think she feels bad enough.

"He's so angry. He's never going to forgive me."

"Yes, he will. We'll explain it to him. We'll make him understand."

Minutes later, the driver's side door opens and Jaxson gets in. My eyes anchor on his furious ones in the rearview mirror while Cooper climbs in on the passenger side. He slams the door so hard both Kayla and I jump.

I grasp her hand as she continues to cry.

Angry silence fills the vehicle as Jaxson pulls away. I debate whether to say anything, but I'm scared. I've never seen Cooper this angry before, and I don't want to make it worse.

However, he ends up breaking the silence a moment later. "You know, girls, I just have to ask. What the fuck is with the outfits? Especially the sunglasses?"

Since Kayla is crying too hard I try my best to explain. "We didn't want you to notice us."

A bitter laugh barrels out of him. "Oh yeah, because I'm not going to notice two fucking chicks wearing goddamn sunglasses in the dark. Smart one, ladies."

My back straightens at his sarcasm. "You know, Cooper. I get that you're upset, but you don't need to be so rude. The evidence was pretty incriminating."

"So that makes it okay for you girls to dress up and play Charlie's fucking Angels for the night?"

I decide not to respond. He's too angry to understand where we were coming from.

When we arrive at their house, Cooper gets out and yanks open the back door that Kayla is leaning against. "Get in the fucking house."

"Don't talk to her like that!" I get out and meet Kayla around the other side. "Why don't you come sleep at my place tonight? Give him a chance to calm down," I suggest quietly, but not quiet enough because Cooper hears me.

"Stay out of this, Julia!"

"No, you're being irrational, Cooper. You're not even trying to understand where we're coming from—"

He advances on me, his expression hard as stone. "Just shut up, you have caused enough shit!"

Jaxson suddenly appears in front of me, his hand moving to Cooper's chest. "Watch it, Coop, I know you're mad and I don't blame you, but no one talks to her like that."

"Of course, this is where your loyalty lies."

"This isn't about loyalty, man—"

Cooper shoves him. "Whatever, you're so fucking pussy-whipped by her, and the worst part is she doesn't even give it up to you."

"Cooper!" Kayla gasps in horror.

Jaxson's fist slams into his face.

Oh god!

It's obvious that Cooper not only anticipated a fight but is also happy about it. He charges at Jaxson, primed and ready. They take each other down and roll around on the lawn, trying to pin each other.

"Both of you, stop, right now," I cry, my heart pounding in terror.

"Cooper, please, let's just go inside," Kayla pleads.

Finally, Jaxson gets the upper hand and manages to pin Cooper. "You need to stop picking a fight with me. Take your girlfriend into the house and figure out why the hell she thinks you're fucking cheating on her." He shoves himself off Cooper, getting to his feet.

Kayla runs into the house crying as Cooper stands. He glares back at Jaxson with so much anger I'm worried he's about to go after him again, but thankfully he has enough sense to walk away. He starts up the front steps, his fist smashing into the side of the house on the way in. The door slams behind him, the loud crack in the air leaving my blood cold.

"What do we do?" I cry, tears clogging my throat. "I can't leave her here with him while he's like this."

"Jesus, Julia, he's not going to hurt her. He's just majorly pissed off, with good fucking reason."

He's right. Cooper might be furious but he would never hurt her.

"Let's go," Jaxson says, climbing back into the SUV.

I follow hesitantly, guilt gripping my chest at the mistake we made.

The car ride home is silent, except for the sound of my tears. Jaxson doesn't spare me one glance until we finally walk into my house. "What the hell were you girls thinking? I mean christ, Julia, this is Cooper we're talking about here."

"I know, believe me, we feel terrible. This isn't something we just assumed over petty jealousy. The evidence was damning." I tell him about everything that happened and why we thought he was cheating.

"Okay, fine, but what about after you saw me there with him? I mean, didn't that clue you in?"

My eyes fall to the floor as I remember what our first thought was.

"Holy shit! You guys thought we were both fucking her, didn't you?"

I don't bother to confirm it, knowing my expression says it all.

A bitter laugh escapes him. "This is too fucked up, even for me. I'm going to bed." He starts up the stairs, leaving me without another word.

Locking up, I head up to bed and can't help worrying about Kayla. I send her a quick text telling her to call if she needs me, then I cry myself to sleep.

CHAPTER 23

I don't know if it was from the fucked-up night with Kayla and Cooper, or from Sawyer bringing up what the admiral wants from us, but that night, a nightmare plagues me.

I'm back in that hellhole, the cold, damp cell reeking of blood and death. My wrists are chained above my head, as my broken body burns and aches from the pain I had endured earlier. A part of me almost wishes they would keep pumping those drugs into us that they did at the beginning, at least then I would be too fucked-up to feel all of this.

No. It's good they stopped; I need to keep a clear head if I'm going to get out of this. I peer over at Sawyer and Cade. If I look as bad as they do, then I know why those assholes think they don't have to worry about incapacitating us anymore.

Sawyer groans, his swollen battered face lifting to mine. "You look like shit."

I grunt, then immediately regret it when pain slices through me. "Yeah, well, you don't look too fucking pretty either."

I'm hoping Cade comes around soon. They really did a number on him after what he did to that sick bastard who was rubbing Faith in his face.

My head drops forward, too weak to remain up. Panic floods my system when I see my chest bare, the necklace Julia gave me gone. "Fuck!"

"What?" Sawyer mumbles.

"My chain, it's gone."

"They ripped it off of you," a quiet female voice says.

My head snaps to the cell on my left and there I find a girl chained to the bed.

When the hell did she show up here?

"How long have you been here?" I ask.

"I'm not sure, a few hours, I think." Her voice trembles in fear and I realize she's American. She also sounds really young.

"How did you get here?"

"I don't know," she cries. "I'm traveling with my school. A friend and I snuck out at night to go to the beach. These boys were trying to take my friend home, she was drinking but something didn't seem right with her. I only had soda, but now I don't remember anything, and the next thing I know, I woke up in the back of a van, and I haven't seen my friend since."

"Your school traveled to Iraq?" Sawyer asks the question I was just thinking.

What school travels to a fucking war zone?

"Iraq? No, we're in Thailand."

Well shit. Knowing she was shipped here from Thailand confirms my original suspicion, that we're smack fucking dab in the middle of a human trafficking ring.

Her whimper cuts through the silence. "We, we aren't in Thailand?"

"No, you're in Iraq," I inform her regretfully.

"Oh my god, they're never going to find me. I'm never going to see my parents again." Her desperate sobs fill the bleak air.

My chest constricts at the sound of her agony, and something builds up in me that I haven't felt in a long time… protectiveness. "Listen, everything's going to be okay. What's your name?"

"A-Anna."

"I'm Jaxson and these are my buddies, Cade and Sawyer." I'm hoping she doesn't consider addressing Cade since he's still out of it. "We're Navy SEALs, do you know what that is?"

Her sobs begin to settle. "I think so, isn't that like soldiers?"

"Yeah, kind of."

"Except we're way more badass," Sawyer adds.

She giggles but soon quiets and I hear her crying again.

"How old are you?" I ask.

"Fourteen."

Jesus! "Well, Anna, we have every intention of getting out of here, and I promise we won't leave without you, okay?"

"O-okay."

"Where are you from?"

"South Carolina."

"No shit. So am I. What part?"

"Summerland."

"That's only a few hours from where I grew up."

She falls silent, and I think she's fallen asleep until she says, "It was the fat, smelly one."

"What's that?"

"The guy who ripped your necklace off. He's fat, smelly, and his teeth are disgusting. Do you know which one I'm talking about?"

"Yeah." The asshole whose nose I broke when he stole my picture of Julia and made the comment about fucking her.

"Was it special?" she asks quietly.

"Yeah."

"I'm sorry."

Me fucking, too.

"What are they going to do to me?" Her fearful question hits me like a blow to my chest.

"Nothing if I can help it."

A few minutes later, her exhaustion takes over and she falls asleep.

"You need to keep working on Irina," I whisper to Sawyer. "She's our only hope of getting the fuck out of here."

He nods. "I know."

We fall into a state of unconsciousness again and wake up some time later to a fearful scream. "No, don't touch me! Ow, stop!"

My head snaps up to see two guys grabbing Anna, one of them whose nose I broke. The bastard has her by the hair, dragging her from the bed. "Come on, bitch, we have a customer who can't wait to break you in."

Oh shit.

Anna's screams become louder. "No! Jaxson, help! Please, help me!"

I shoot awake, my body knifing up off the bed, drenched in sweat, my heart pounding so fucking loud it's all I can hear. I drop back down until I get my pulse under control.

Glancing at the clock, I see it's five a.m. and know I won't be going back to sleep. I get up and take a shower, hoping to wash away the fucking guilt that eats me alive every day.

CHAPTER 24

Julia

The next morning, I roll over and look at my phone, hoping Kayla texted me back. She didn't. I send her another one asking her if she's all right, then get out of bed and throw on my robe before heading downstairs.

Jaxson is already up, sitting at the kitchen table with a cup of coffee and the paper. He doesn't acknowledge me as I walk in, and it makes me want to cry all over again.

Walking over to him, I take his face between my hands and force him to look at me. "Please don't be mad at me anymore."

He lets out a heavy breath and pulls me down on his lap.

I wrap my arms around him and bury my face in his neck. "We didn't know, Jaxson, all the evidence pointed to what we thought."

"I know, Jules." His hand slides under my robe, rubbing comforting circles on my upper thigh.

Lifting my face, I rest my forehead against his and gently touch the wound on his lip from his fight with Cooper. "This is my fault," I whisper, pressing a soft kiss to the corner of his mouth.

His eyes darken, fingers tightening on my skin. "No, it's not."

The doorbell rings, interrupting our moment.

"I'll answer it, you get yourself something to eat," he says, pressing a kiss to my forehead before letting me stand. The magic touch eases so much of my heavy heart.

I'm fixing myself some toast when Kayla comes in on a rush, still in her pajamas. Her eyes look the same as mine—red and puffy—but she has a huge smile on her face.

"Oh thank god!" I throw my arms around her, hugging her tight. "I've been so worried about you. Are you okay? How's Cooper?"

Cooper comes walking in at that moment with Jaxson trailing behind him. The sight of his busted lip hurts my heart as much as Jaxson's does. "Hey, Julia," he greets me with a nod.

"Hi, Coop." My greeting sounds as nervous as I feel.

I look back at Kayla who still has a huge smile on her face. "Everything's okay." She lifts her hand, showing me her finger.

Gasping, I grab her wrist and study the massive rock. "You're getting married?!"

She nods, her smile infectious.

"Oh my gosh, I'm so happy for you guys." I pull her in for another hug then look at Cooper, his easy smile telling me we're okay.

A sob builds in my throat as I walk over and wrap my arms around him. "I'm so sorry I thought you were a cheating bastard, Cooper," I apologize, blubbering into his chest.

He chuckles and hugs me back. "It's all right, Jules. Sorry I told you to shut the fuck up."

Cooper lifts his other arm for Kayla and pulls her in, too. "Don't you have something else to say, Cooper?" she says, sparing a glance at Jaxson.

"No."

"Coop, apologize to Jaxson, too," she orders quietly.

Jaxson smirks, enjoying Cooper's torment.

With a frustrated breath, he walks over and puts his hand out to Jaxson. "Sorry, asshole," he grumbles.

"Cooper!" Kayla scolds.

Jaxson accepts his hand smugly but remains silent.

"Jaxson, don't you have something to say back?" I urge.

"Why the fuck should I say sorry?"

"For punching him."

When he remains silent, Cooper cuts back in. "It's okay, Julia, I'm used to being the bigger man."

Jaxson puts him in a headlock, which he gets out of easily, and they start roughhousing.

Kayla and I roll our eyes at their barbaric way of apologizing. Her smile returns as she takes my hand. "Will you be my maid of honor?"

My heart melts into a giant puddle. "Of course I will. I'd be honored."

Unable to contain our excitement any longer, we start jumping up and down. "This is going to be so much fun!" I squeal excitedly.

"I know. I'm so fucking excited!"

"We can reschedule our girls' night if you want," I offer. "I understand if you want to celebrate with Cooper."

"No, he has to work for a bit tonight anyway. You, Grace, and I can celebrate. Katelyn told me about this great club that just opened in Charleston."

"Sounds good to me."

"How are you guys getting there?" Jaxson asks.

I shrug. "We'll take a cab."

"Coop said he will come get us after," Kayla adds, sending him a heart stopping smile.

"Perfect."

We make our plans and decide to get ready together here at my place.

"All right, let's go," Cooper says to Kayla. "I have plans for you for the rest of the day." He tosses her over his shoulder, making her squeal with laughter, and hauls her out of the house.

"See you later," I call out just before the door closes.

I turn back to Jaxson, my excitement close to bursting. "Oh my god, Jaxson, they're getting married!" I squeal enthusiastically, launching myself into his arms.

He catches me with a chuckle.

"Isn't this so amazing? I'm gonna call Grams and give her the news." Pushing out of his arms, I dash out of the kitchen and up to my room, happy that my terrible morning has turned around to be one of the best.

CHAPTER 25

Julia

That evening, Kayla, Grace, and I are in my room getting ready. Kayla pulls a short, black cocktail dress out of her bag and slips it on. The strapless silk hugs her in all the right places. With her long, blonde hair flowing down her shoulders in big curls and smoky eye makeup, she looks like she just stepped out of a magazine.

"Wow," Grace and I say in unison.

"Why thank you," she says, her face glowing with happiness.

Grace looks over at me, her fingers fidgeting nervously. "Um, Julia, do you think I could borrow a dress from you? I don't really have anything nice enough for the club we're goin' to."

My heart pinches in guilt. Kayla and I should have thought about that and asked her earlier. Especially since we know she doesn't have the money to afford much.

"Of course, I have a couple you can pick from."

She ends up choosing my soft yellow, silk dress, which looks stunning against her golden skin. Grace is beautiful, but simple. Most of the time her long, blonde hair is tied back and her face free of makeup. One of her best features are her eyes. They're a unique, warm amber color, almost the same color as whiskey.

"Would you like Kayla and I to help with your hair and makeup?"

"Sure, but my makeup selection is kind of pathetic," she replies, embarrassed.

"Don't worry, we got you covered." Kayla pulls out her massive makeup bag. While she starts her foundation, I grab my curling wand and get to work on her hair.

"I still can't believe you're getting married, Kayla. I am so happy for you," Grace says, her excitement mirroring my own.

We told her earlier about our little escapade last night. We were all able to laugh about it, even though it wasn't very funny at the time.

"Thanks, Grace. I'd love for you to be a bridesmaid. It would mean a lot to me to have you and Julia by my side."

"Oh my gosh, really?"

Kayla nods at her with a smile.

"Oh I would love to. Thank you for askin' me." I pull the wand back as she hugs Kayla.

"I want to have a celebration supper for you and Cooper," I tell her. "Are you guys free two weeks from now?"

"That works for me. I'll make sure Coop takes it off."

"Me too," Grace says. "I'll make sure to book the entire day off so I can help you prepare."

"That'd be great. Thanks."

My doorbell chimes, interrupting our conversation. Both girls look at me in question.

"It's probably Sawyer and Cade. They're coming to hang out with Jaxson tonight."

"Ah, the famous SEAL boys I have yet to meet," Kayla muses. "Glad I'll finally get the chance. They're all I've heard about the entire week from clients who have spotted them around town."

"Oh they're somethin' all right," Grace mutters under her breath.

I smile, remembering the way Sawyer acted at the diner with her. "I think Sawyer has a crush on you, Grace."

She scoffs but her cheeks turn pink. "I think Sawyer is the type to have a crush on anythin' with boobs."

I laugh but don't deny her impression. He does seem that way, but there's something about the way he looked at Grace. It bothered him that she didn't melt into a puddle like every other girl does when he's near.

"Anyway, I'm not his type, at least not anymore," she says, her voice soft.

Kayla and I exchange a look. "Why would you say that?" I ask, treading carefully.

She shrugs. "I can just tell. He's a confident guy, which means he's into confident girls. Girls who know what they want and aren't afraid to go after it. Not girls who are… damaged." She pauses and clears her throat. "There's a lot I haven't told y'all."

"You can tell us anything, Grace," Kayla says. "You can trust us."

"Absolutely." Putting the curling wand down, I move to sit next to her. Kayla does the same, sitting on the other side and we take her hand, waiting patiently for her to continue.

"I told y'all that I lost my mother when I was seventeen, but I didn't tell you how. She was…raped and murdered."

Kayla and I suck in a sharp breath but remain silent, not wanting to interrupt her.

"We were really close, and she was all I had. I came home when it happened; they almost killed me, too."

My heart swells painfully at the devastation in her voice. "I'm so sorry, Grace. I know what it's like to lose someone you love so much."

She gives me a sad smile. "I know you do." Taking a breath, she continues. "The man who hurt her, hurt us, is in prison back in Florida; that's where I'm originally from. I came here to find my father; I've never met him. He lives in Charleston but I haven't had the courage to contact him yet. He's kind of a big deal… he's the lieutenant governor," she confesses quietly.

"Holy shit! Your father is John Weston, Jr.?" Kayla asks in shock.

She nods. "That's why I'm nervous. He knows about me, but has never contacted me. He has a family—a wife and two daughters. I'm scared of what his reaction will be if I reach out to him."

I give her hand a gentle squeeze. "He's lucky to have a daughter like you, Grace."

"Damn straight," Kayla adds.

She smiles but it's sad. "Thanks, I'm really glad I met y'all. You both have come to mean an awful lot to me."

"We feel the same way," I confess past the lump that has formed in my throat.

Kayla and I wrap our arms around her, offering comfort.

"Oh darn, we need to stop this," she says with a sniffle. "I didn't mean to put a damper on our girls' night. I'm sorry."

"You didn't. We're glad you opened up to us. I know there's more you probably haven't told us." Her expression confirms my suspicion. "Just know we're always here for you. You can trust us with anything."

"Thanks," she whispers.

"All right, let me fix your makeup before we take you to a mirror," Kayla says, standing once again.

I touch mine up too, since my cheeks are blotchy from the few tears that escaped.

After we finish, we take Grace into the bathroom with Kayla covering her eyes. When she removes her hands for the reveal Grace gasps. "Oh my gosh, I look... pretty," she says, sounding surprised.

"Of course you do, you always look beautiful, Grace."

"Thanks, Julia." She offers me a smile but I can tell she doesn't believe me and it breaks my heart further.

Heading out of the bathroom, I grab my dress hanging at the top of my door. It's almost identical to the one Grace borrowed, but hot pink. I haven't had a chance to wear it yet, so I'm excited to break it in. After slipping on my strappy, silver heels, I walk back into the bathroom.

The three of us stand in front of the mirror, taking in our appearances. "We look fucking hot, ladies!" Kayla comments, slinging her arms over our shoulders.

I have to agree. We clean up nice.

Kayla smirks, her eyes meeting mine in the reflecting glass. "How much do you want to bet we're going to see the Hulk come out when we go downstairs?"

"Probably, he's been pouting all day," I mumble. But I can't deny how eager I am for Jaxson to see me. I like it when he gets territorial, and tonight I'm ready to test his control again.

"Well then, let's get this show on the road. I love irritating that guy," Kayla says, rubbing her hands together in glee.

This shall be interesting.

CHAPTER 26

Jaxson

Sawyer, Cade, and I are at the table having a beer. I'm trying to be social, but I'm in a pissy mood about Julia going out tonight. Why can't their girls' night consist of staying in the house and watching a movie? Do they really need to go to the club? It pisses me off to think about all the guys who will be sniffing around her all night.

It doesn't help that it's been a long fucking week. Being around her constantly and not burying myself inside her like I want to has been hell. I haven't jerked off this much since I was fourteen years old. I'm not sure how much longer I can hold back.

"Ho-ly shit!" Sawyer's outburst and gaping expression has lead settling in my gut as his attention becomes riveted on something behind me.

Turning around, I see the girls walk into the kitchen. My gaze zeroes in on Julia, and I suck in a sharp breath at the sight of her. My dick rages along with my temper. "What the fuck are you wearing?"

She cocks a sassy hip. "It's called a dress, haven't you ever seen one before?"

"You're not leaving looking like that."

Shit, I didn't mean it to come out quite like that.

Her eyes narrow, but before she can say anything Kayla cuts in. "Easy there, Hulk, we don't want things going smash."

The girls giggle, like it's some private joke.

Sawyer joins in too, acting like her comment is the funniest thing in the world. "Well, I personally think you girls look incredible."

"Thank you." Julia smiles, soaking in his attention.

He's such an asshole.

She gestures to Kayla. "Sawyer and Cade, I'd like you to meet my friend Kayla, Cooper's fiancée," she adds.

"Ah, yes, the famous fiancée," Sawyer says. "I heard you girls had quite the evening last night."

Both Kayla and Julia groan, knowing they won't ever live that down. Julia points to Grace next. "And y'all remember Grace."

Cade nods and Sawyer tries laying on the charm. "Of course, I never forget a beautiful woman. How are you doing, Grace?"

"Fine, thank you," she responds without making eye contact, which only seems to piss him off again.

His torment slightly eases my shitty mood… until I look over at Julia again.

"Will you stop glaring at me?" she snaps, making me glare harder. "Whatever," she mumbles, moving her attention to Kayla. "Want to go wait outside? The cab should be here soon."

I tense. "I told you I'd drive you."

"And I said, no thank you."

"Why the hell not?"

Kayla answers before she can. "Because if you take us they won't let us in after the scene you'll cause." She follows up her comment with a shitty impersonation. "Hulk like Julia. Hulk smash anyone who look at Julia."

Everyone bursts into laughter, Sawyer being the loudest of them all. "I fucking love this girl," he says, trying to catch his breath.

Dickhead!

"See ya later, boys, have a good night!" Julia blows me a kiss over her shoulder as she walks out.

I consider hauling her sweet ass upstairs and fucking the sass right out of her. Throwing my chair into the wall, I start pacing, wondering what the hell I'm going to do.

"You bring this shit on yourself, you know that, right?" Sawyer says, opening his big mouth.

"It's not that simple, Evans. I care more about her than I do about fucking her."

"Actually, it is that simple, take both. It doesn't have to be one or the other, you idiot."

"Lay off him, I get it," Cade says, stepping in to defend me.

Sawyer grunts. "Of course you get it because you're an idiot, too. I tell you boys, if I had women like Faith and Julia after me I wouldn't be fucking it up like you dumb asses," he says, giving us a smirk. "I'd be fucking them all night long."

Both Cade and I nail him in the shoulder. It only makes him laugh harder.

Eventually he gets control of himself, his expression sobering. "I'm telling you, Jaxson, somebody is going to fill that position sooner than later. You can't expect her to be alone for the rest of her life. So if I were you, I'd pull your head out of your ass and lay your claim before it's too late."

He's right. I can't expect her to be alone forever, and the thought of anyone else having her makes me sick. I stare back at him, watching a knowing smirk morph on his face.

"We're going, aren't we?" he asks, already knowing the answer.

"Yeah, we're going, just let me change."

"All right, busting up girls' night!" he cheers.

I send Cooper a quick text, telling him to meet us at the club rather than come here first. The time I spend getting ready I pray I know what the hell I'm doing.

CHAPTER 27

Julia

"This place is awesome!" Kayla yells to be heard over the loud music.

It is pretty great. Thankfully, Katelyn's name got us in quickly. The line outside is long, and it's packed in here.

We head right up to the bar to order a shot, and the handsome bartender welcomes us with a charming smile. "What can I get you ladies?"

Kayla leans over the counter and orders for us all. "Three lemon drops please."

I'm just about to ask her what that is but Grace beats me to it. "What's in that?"

"Trust me, you're going to love it," she says, giving no further explanations.

The bartender comes back with three shots and lemon wedges with sugar on them. Or is that salt?

Kayla grabs hers first and raises it. "Bottoms up, ladies."

"Wait!" I stop her before she can down it and raise my drink to make a toast. "To the future Mrs. McKay."

"Oh, yours is much better," she agrees with a smile.

Clinking our glasses, we throw back the clear liquid.

Yuck!

Grace and I both cough in disgust then grab our lemon wedge and suck them clean like Kayla. The citrus actually brings a nice flavor to the after taste and I find myself licking my lips for more.

"See, it's good, right?" Kayla says, as if hearing my thoughts. "Come on, ladies, let's dance."

We follow her out to the dance floor and for the next hour we drink and dance our asses off. After four shots and two drinks I'm quite tipsy, and it feels fantastic, freeing even. It's rare I ever get out like this and let loose. We're all having a blast, especially Grace, and it makes me so happy to see a genuine smile on her face. I laugh when a group of guys come up to dance with us and Kayla flashes her hand in front of their faces, making them back off respectfully.

Guys have been lining up to dance with Grace, some she has accepted, others not. I don't mind anyone dancing with me, as long as they don't grab inappropriately. There's nothing more annoying than being treated like a piece of meat.

The next song that plays is Kesha's "Die Young" it sends our bodies moving and hearts soaring. The guy behind me grabs my hips, and it's then that a feeling of awareness skitters down my spine. Even before I turn around I know exactly who is the cause of it.

Oh, this is going to be fun.

Jaxson

"Jesus, this place is insane," Cooper yells next to me, as we make our way through the club.

"No shit!"

After waiting in line outside for almost forty minutes, a friend of Kayla and Julia's spotted Cooper outside and got us in. If she hadn't we would have waited at least another hour.

It's just the three of us, Sawyer, Cooper, and me. Cade decided to bail and go to the gym. Sawyer said he's been spending most of his time there lately, putting his energy into working out. I have a feeling I know *who* he's trying to work out of his system.

My gaze searches for Julia as we weave in and out of people, making our way across the crowded bar. Some chick purposefully rubs her tits into my chest as she passes by.

"Sorry." She giggles annoyingly.

I ignore her and keep walking. We line up along the bar and order a round of beers.

"Holy shit, there are some grabby skanks in here; my junk has been grabbed twice already," Sawyer says, acting as if it bothers him to be assaulted.

"Like you care." The guy has fucked more than I have, which is saying something.

"Hey, I do. I have standards you know."

I grunt, and I'm just about to say something when the breath gets knocked out of my lungs at the sight of Julia on the dance floor, looking like every guy's wet dream. A new song starts that her and the girls go crazy over.

I become enraptured, watching her dance. Her arms are thrown over her head as her hips move in rhythm to the beat. There's a group of guys not far from them and when one comes up behind her, grabbing her hips, anger spikes in my veins.

The fucker is dead.

I slam my beer down and am about to storm over there but Cooper stops me with a hand to my chest. "Hold up, don't go getting us all kicked out now."

My pulse hammers, blood pumping with fury from seeing someone touch what's mine. As if feeling my furious gaze on her, Julia stills and turns around. There's a second of surprise in her eyes before her pretty lips curve into a sassy smile. She knows exactly what it's doing to me to see this guy with his hands on her.

I shake my head, warning her what will happen if the asshole doesn't back away. Turning around, she says something to the guy that has him making eye contact with me. He raises his hands in surrender and moves to the next girl.

Julia starts for me, her hips keeping rhythm with the beat. Heat explodes through my body, coiling low in my stomach, and everyone falls away as I watch her dance her way over, my cock hardening at every dip of her hips.

Once she reaches me, she turns around, shoving her tight fuckable ass against me.

I grab her hips firmly, my fingers digging into her soft flesh. She tosses me a smile over her shoulder, feeling how hard my cock is for her. One of her arms lifts, curling around my neck and bringing my mouth down close to her ear. Her scent penetrates my senses; the smell of lemons mixed in with her usual, sweet scent, races through my blood like a fucking drug.

I nip her pierced earlobe, and she lets out the sexiest fucking moan. My mouth continues down her slender throat, feeling the rapid beat of her pulse against my lips. I suck and lick her delicate skin, wanting to brand her so every fucker in the place will know she's mine.

Her fiery whimper reaches my ears and she grinds against me, her sweet body eager for more. I'm so fucking turned on, it's taking every bit of control I have not to slip into her from behind and fuck her senseless right here.

When the song comes to an end, she turns to face me and wraps her arms around my neck. Her eyes flash with surprise when I pull her flush against my body.

"What are you doing at my girls' night? I thought I said no penises allowed."

A growl erupts from my throat before I can stop it. "What about the prick who just had his hands on you? He has a dick."

Smiling, she lifts a perfectly arched brow. "Why, yes, he does. What are you going to do about it, Jaxson?"

My blood pressure spikes along with my dick at her challenge. I lean in close to her ear so she can hear me over the thundering music. "I'm going to take you home and bury myself so deep inside that sweet pussy of yours. My scent will cling to every part of you. Then every fucking guy in the world will know you're mine."

I've barely registered her gasp before my mouth descends, finally taking what I've been denying myself for far too long. She whimpers against my lips, giving me the access I crave. My tongue slides in, seeking.

Tasting.

Her flavor explodes in my mouth and settles deep in my chest. It's time to get her out of here. This night has been coming for a long time, and I can't wait anymore. Pulling back, I stare into her glazed eyes that are burning with questions.

"Is that what I am, Jaxson, yours?" she asks, her voice hesitant.

"You've always been mine, in every way that matters." My chest tightens at the uncertainty in her eyes. She doesn't believe me, and I don't blame her. "I don't know what the future holds for us, Jules, but I think this week has proven we can't go back to what we had before."

Her slender fingers wrap around my wrist as she turns her face to the side, pressing her lips to my palm. "Then we'll make a new us."

I nod and tamp down the panic threatening to choke me.

Please don't let me fuck this up.

"Let's go home," I say, my arm hooking around her waist to bring her in closer. "I can't wait anymore."

Her eyes search mine for a solid two breaths before giving the answer I want to hear. "All right, let me go say good-bye first."

I press a hard kiss to her mouth then release her. Looking over at Sawyer, I see his hard eyes glued to the dance floor, glaring at the guy dancing with Grace. "I'm taking off. You okay to catch a ride with Coop?"

"Yeah." He waves me away, not once sparing me a glance.

After saying good-bye to Cooper, I start for Julia and see the asshole who had his hands on her earlier, eyeing her with eagerness, thinking she's come back for him. His hope deflates fast when he sees me charging at them. With quick strides I grab her from behind.

"What the hell are you doing?" she shrieks as I lift her up off her feet.

"Time's up, Julia, say good-bye to your friends."

She sputters in protest as I turn and head for the exit.

"It's about damn time," Kayla yells at my retreating back.

"Put me down right now, Jaxson! You're embarrassing me."

I ignore her and continue on. The cool night air hits us as I push open the doors and head over to my truck. Opening the passenger door, I toss her inside, her hair tangling around her pissed off face.

"Ugh! You are such a Neanderthal, what the hell—"

I claim her mouth, silencing her protest and her response is instant. Her hands fist in my shirt, yanking me closer and I swallow every sexy moan that falls past her lips. My hand slides under her dress, cupping the sweet spot between her legs.

A groan rips from my chest at the damp feel of her silk panties. "I'm done waiting, Julia, I need to get you home and sink into your hot pussy before I lose all control."

She arches against my touch, her eyes hooded with lust. "Oh, okay then."

I chuckle at her breathless response and drop one more kiss on her parted lips then remove my hand and slam the door.

Sweet, hot anticipation fills the truck most of the drive home, every second passing is torture on my control and dick.

Feeling her eyes on me, I glance over and find her staring at me with a knowing smile. "Wanna know something?"

"What, baby?"

"I'm just a wee bit drunk," she admits with a giggle, holding her thumb and finger up with a small gap between them.

I grunt. "Tell me something I don't know."

I feel her shift next to me. "Does it make you want to take advantage of me, Jaxson?"

My eyes retract their path back, the seductive tone of her voice beckoning me to look.

Oh jesus!

Her body is angled toward me, her back leaning against the door. One leg is propped on the seat, bent at the knee, giving me the perfect view of her sweet pussy hidden behind a pair of black silk panties. Air becomes trapped in my lungs when she trails a single finger up the inside of her thigh.

My jaw locks, not finding her cute anymore. "Stop that shit, Julia. I mean it. Turn around and sit properly until we get home."

She bursts into laughter, finding herself fucking hilarious.

Thankfully, it's not long before we pull up to her house. I come to a hard stop and barely have the truck shut off before I jump out. My feet eat up the gravel as I move for her, a dark primal need hammering through my veins.

It's time to finally claim what I have so foolishly kept from the both of us.

Julia's still trying to climb down out of the truck when I grab her around the waist. Slamming the door, I pin her against it and take her mouth, inhaling everything that belongs to me.

God, I fucking love the taste of her. I could kiss this girl for the rest of my life and it still wouldn't be long enough.

My hands slip under her dress and mold to the soft flesh of her ass. A fiery moan purges from her and I inhale the beautiful sound. When her teeth sink into my lip, it awakens the beast within me.

Growling, my hips drive forward, my aching cock begging to be released from its confines. "You want it, rough, baby?" I pull down the top of her strapless dress, revealing her black bra. My head dips, lips skimming across the swells of her tits as I descend to one tight nipple beneath the fabric and give a sharp nip.

"Jaxson!" My name falls on a heated cry, her nails digging into my shoulder.

I love the way she comes apart for me.

Unable to wait a second longer, I head to the door, keeping her in my arms as I dig in my pocket for the keys. Her lips kiss along my jaw while I try to unlock the door, but the goddamn thing is nothing but a hassle.

"See, Jaxson, this is why we shouldn't bother locking the stupid door."

My efforts cease and my eyes find hers, the sassy challenge reflecting back at me driving my need higher. Reaching up, I grab a fistful of her long silky hair, gently tugging her head back to stare into her seductive eyes. Eyes that are screaming for me to fuck her. "What did I tell you about that smart-ass mouth of yours, Julia?"

"Maybe you should shove something in it then to shut me up."

The breathless taunt sparks something dark and rich inside of me, calling it to the surface. I'm assuming my facial expression is comical by the way she laughs her ass off again. It fades the moment my fingers tighten in her hair. "Is that what you want, baby, my dick in your mouth?"

"God, yes."

Her needy response makes me whimper, fucking whimper like a pussy. I focus on the door again and finally get the damn thing unlocked. Once inside, I kick it shut and haul her sexy ass up the stairs to her room.

I slide her down my body until her feet touch the floor, then I collect a step back. "Take off your dress."

She raises an eyebrow at my command but does as I ask. Before she unzips the dress though, she bends down to take her shoes off.

"Leave them on."

Her head snaps up, a smile curving her pretty pink lips. "Mmm, bossy, bossy, you're lucky I like you like that."

She wants to see bossy, I'll fucking show her bossy.

Her eyes never leave mine as she unzips her dress, letting it pool at her feet. My cock jerks at the sight of her body, minimally covered by black satin and silver, fuck-me heels.

A low growl erupts from my throat. "Damn, woman, you're fucking sexy." I reach out to pull her to me, but she steps back before I can make contact.

"Uh-uh." She tsks, shaking her finger at me. "Not one step closer until you take some clothes off, too."

Reaching behind my shoulders, I pull my shirt off and stalk toward her but her sharp inhale halts me in my tracks.

"Oh my god, Jaxson," she breathes, her eyes locking on my chest.

I'm thinking her shock is from the scars. They're not as bad as my back, but it's still not a pretty sight. Until she grabs the beat-up, worn pendant that's hanging around my neck.

"I had to get a new chain for it, it got a little beat-up," I tell her, hating to think why it needed a new one to begin with.

She gives me a sad smile, her throat bobbing in emotion. "I guess it didn't do much good, huh?"

I shrug. "I don't know about that. I'm still here, aren't I?" I say that for her benefit because the truth is, I don't believe in that shit, but the thought of Julia losing her faith bothers me. She doesn't need to know how cruel the world really is.

"Yeah, you are, and thank God for that because I would die without you." Her choked words send a sharp pain through my chest, making it hard to breathe. No one has ever cared for me the way she does, and as good as it feels, it also scares the living shit out of me.

My abdominal muscles twitch as she lays her warm hand on my stomach. "Let me touch you, Jaxson. I want to know your body," she says, her eyes pleading.

Control is something I never give up, but for Julia, for a few moments, I will give it up for her.

At my nod, she glides her smooth palm across my chest as she walks around to my back. I feel her delicate fingers trace the angel before they are replaced with her lips, kissing all of my scars, as if trying to erase them from my body. She wraps her arms around me from behind, her breasts pressing against my back. A beat of a second passes before my skin becomes wet with her tears and it makes me feel as if someone just punched me in the fucking throat.

Even though it's hard for me to do, I let her hold me because I know she needs this, and well… maybe I do, too.

Eventually, she makes her way back in front of me, tracing the scars on my chest. Her warm lips press to every single one, her shoulders trembling with her sadness and it rips me apart.

My fingers thread through her hair and I bring her pained gaze to mine. "Please don't cry, Jules."

"I wish I could take them away."

"You do." It's the honest truth, no one calms the darkness inside of me but her. She's always been able to do that for me.

My mouth descends, closing the remaining distance between us as I pull her in my arms again. I consume every salty tear that falls, taking it as my own until there is nothing left but us and the dark desire claiming us.

Her hand trails down my stomach and she makes quick work of my belt and pants. My head drops back on my shoulders, a tortured groan vibrating in my throat when she reaches in and grabs my painfully stiff cock.

She strokes me firmly from base to tip, her soft thumb running over the smooth tip. "I want to taste you." She drops to her knees before me and it's the sweetest sight I've ever seen. Freeing my cock, she leans in and presses a soft kiss to my shaft. "I like knowing I affect you like this," she confesses with a smile, her warm breath hitting my flesh and making it jerk against her lips.

"Baby, my dick is in this state whenever you're in the same room as me."

"Well then, you should have let me take care of you long before now." With that smart-ass remark, she licks me from base to tip then closes her warm, wet mouth around my cock, knocking the breath from my lungs.

"Fuck me!"

She takes me as far down as she can before sucking her way back to the top, swirling her tongue around the tip, her fist pumping where her mouth can't reach.

Grinding my teeth, I try not to think about how she got to be good at this; the thought makes me see red.

Her eyes find mine beneath the hood of her thick dark lashes as she continues to drive me insane. I've pictured this countless times, but none of them came close to the pretty sight that's before me now.

Wrapping her long, thick locks around my fist, I begin controlling her rhythm, pumping my hips into her mouth with fast, steady strokes. "You have no idea what it does to me to see you on your knees, sucking my dick."

She moans, the vibration enough to make me come and I'm far from ready for that.

"Stop!" I tug her hair, pulling her mouth away, then haul her up against me.

"What is it, what's—"

Spinning her around, I lift her up and pin her against the wall, stealing her mouth in a ruthless kiss. I flick open the clasp of her strapless bra, letting it fall away from her body.

A groan rumbles from deep within my chest at the feel of her soft tits against my skin. I swoop down and take a soft, pink nipple into my mouth, grazing the tight tip with my teeth.

"Oh god, that feels so good," she whimpers, her wet panties sliding against my stomach as she tries to find release. A disappointed moan spills from her when I move away from her efforts. "Please, Jaxson."

"Easy, baby."

I carry her over to the bed, laying her out in front of me. Her brown hair fans out around her, high, firm breasts flushed and red from my mouth, begging for me.

"Jesus, you're a fucking sight." Dropping down in front of her, my face aligns directly in line with her pussy. I kiss her soft, toned stomach just above her panty line, a smirk pulling at my mouth when she tries pushing my head down. My eyes lift to hers. "What do you want, Jules?"

She moans in frustration. "You know what I want."

"Maybe, but I want to hear you say it."

She looks down at me, her teeth sinking into her bottom lip shyly. "I want you to kiss me."

"Where?"

She slides a shaking hand to the black satin. "Here."

I lean in and press a kiss to the wet material, her scent penetrating my senses.

She shakes her head. "I need more."

"Then tell me exactly what you want, Julia. I want to hear you say it… all of it."

Her cheeks flush a brighter shade of pink. "I want you to lick my… pussy."

Growling, I grab the side of her panties and rip the thin silk from her body. Her gasp of surprise turns into a pleasure-filled moan when I bury my tongue in her hot, wet flesh, the sweet taste of her exploding on my tongue.

"Oh god, yes!"

I fucking love how loud she is.

I groan in approval when she lets her knees fall open, giving me complete access. Her back arches, fingers roughly pulling my hair as I fuck her with my tongue. Her cries of pleasure and needy moans are enough to make me come. I can feel she's close, the small nub growing firmer with every fiery lick. My lips close around the bundle of nerves and it sends her flying.

She cries out my name, her body trembling as I drink every bit of pleasure that spills from her. She's still gasping for breath when I pull my mouth away and kiss my way up her body. I try to regain some measure of control before I humiliate myself and blow my load all over her stomach. However, she makes it extremely fucking difficult by moving restlessly under me.

"Easy, baby, we have all night," I murmur, tasting the delicate skin of her neck.

She grabs my face between her hands, angling me to look at her. "No! Listen, Jaxson. I don't want you to go slow. I want you to fuck me right now—hard and fast."

Well fuck me!

My control snaps. Rising up, I grab under her knees, positioning myself at her entrance. "Do I need to wear a condom, Julia?" I've always worn one, but knowing she can't get pregnant, I want to have nothing between us as I take her.

"No, I want nothing—" She loses her breath as I drive myself right into fucking heaven, a heated cry escaping her.

I still, worried I hurt her. "Are you okay, baby?"

"God, yes! Don't stop!"

She doesn't have to tell me twice.

I pound into her relentlessly, my dick surrounded in the hottest perfection I've ever felt. She wraps her legs around my waist, her heels digging into my back. I grind my teeth, the sting of pain sending heat to lick down my spine.

Our gazes remain locked as I completely lose myself to her. Reaching up, she touches my lips, something painful passing over her expression.

I still deep inside of her and rest my forehead against hers. "Talk to me, baby, what's wrong?"

"I just can't believe this is happening. I've waited so long to feel you inside of me again."

Her words strike me deep, my buried guilt rising to the surface. "I'll never stay away again, Julia, I can't. I need you as much as I need my next fucking breath, so get used to feeling me, because you're mine." I resume my pace, thrusting into her possessively with slow, hard strokes.

"Yes, yours. Always yours."

Damn fucking straight.

I take her lips, savoring her taste before descending down her delicate throat. Her nails rake along my back and her mouth finds my shoulder. When her teeth sink into my flesh, I come unglued and begin fucking her with a desperation I've never felt. The bed pounds against the wall with each hard, frantic thrust.

"Oh god, Jaxson, I'm coming," she screams, her pussy locking down on me.

"Fuck yeah, you are!" Feeling her spasm around my bare flesh is like nothing I've ever experienced. I fuck her through her orgasm, stealing every cry of pleasure from her until there's no more left. Then I let go, and take my own pleasure, losing the only part of myself I had left. She now owns all of me.

I drop down on top of her, trying to catch my breath as we lie in a sweaty, tangled mess.

"That was… wow," she says, her breath racing against my shoulder.

"That's the biggest fucking understatement ever."

I never want to move from this spot, I want to stay inside of her for the rest of my life.

I'm in serious shit.

"Jaxson?" she whispers.

"Yeah?"

"I can't breathe very well."

"Shit! Sorry." Rising up on my arms, I pull out of her, the disconnection making me want to cry like a pussy.

Like I said, I'm in serious shit.

After we clean up, we lie together in comfortable silence. Julia's sweet, soft body is draped over my chest while she traces the tattoo that runs from my arm to my shoulder. My hand does its own exploring along her lower back and soft curve of her ass.

"Jax?"

My hand stills in surprise. It's the first time she's called me that since I've been back, and I didn't realize how much I missed it until now. "Yeah, baby?"

"Can I ask you something?"

Trepidation sweeps over me, wondering where this conversation is about to go. "Yeah, Jules, you can ask me anything."

"What scares you the most about doing this with me?"

I frown in confusion. "What do you mean?"

She releases a nervous breath. "I mean, what scares you the most about us changing our relationship? Is it… is it not to have the freedom to be with anyone else?"

She barely finishes her sentence before I have her flat on her back under me, the quick action making her gasp. Frustration pumps through my blood but it fades quickly when I see the vulnerability in her eyes and realize she's serious.

"Is that what you really think?"

She shrugs. "I'm just asking. You can't really be that surprised I would think it. I've only been with one other person and—"

I cut her off with a hand over her mouth. "First off, Julia, don't ever mention you and your ex again. I know I wasn't around, but I don't want to fucking hear about it… ever. Got me? Secondly, I thought you understood you were different to me than everyone else. I mean christ, I have you fucking tattooed on my damn back."

She rips my hand away, her eyes narrowed in anger. "*First off, Jaxson*," she mimics back to me with sass. "I do know that I mean more to you than your fuck buddies. That's not what I was asking. I can tell you're scared to do this with me, and let's be real, it's no secret how much you like women, or your freedom to do what you want with them. Secondly, buddy."

Buddy? Did she just fucking call me buddy?

"You're right, you weren't here for *six years*. So don't you dare tell me that I can't mention my ex, Justin is his name to be exact, and—"

That's it.

I claim her mouth, silencing whatever else is about to come out of her sassy mouth. The kiss is angry, desperate, and fucking soul crushing. "I told you I don't want to hear about him," I grind out, and reach between us for my hardening cock. "I'm going to fuck him right out of your mind. By the time I'm done with you, you won't even remember his fucking name."

Aligning myself, I push forward with one hard thrust, her hungry pussy accepting me eagerly. I take her without abandon, fucking her harder than I have ever anyone in my entire life.

"Oh god!" Her cry of pleasure pierces the air, her hands clawing at my shoulders, desperately trying to keep their grip. I feel her muscles contract around me, loving every frantic thrust I deliver.

"Look at me, Julia." Her eyes snap open at the command. "You feel this? Do you feel how perfect this is? This is the only pussy I want to feel around my dick—the only one. I could be the last man on the fucking planet having my pick, and I would always, only, pick you." I stare down at her, willing her to see the truth.

A smile takes over her face, and it's the biggest one I've ever seen on her. "Well, you certainly know how to make a girl feel special."

A laugh barrels out of me but it trails into a groan. "Jesus, woman, you drive me crazy."

"Good," she says, her smile still in place. "Now finish the statement you were making."

"I fucking plan on it." Grabbing her legs, I place them over my shoulders, driving myself in deeper.

By the time I'm finished with her, there's no way she remembers Dr. Med student whatever the hell his name was.

CHAPTER 28

Julia

The next morning my phone chimes with a text message, pulling me from my blessed sleep. I moan at the painful throbbing behind my eyes.

Too much to drink.

When it blares a second time, sounding way louder than it usually does, I grab my pillow and throw it over my head. The sound of a muffled chuckle meets my ears.

Pulling the pillow away, I squint against the powerful sunlight and am met with the sexiest sight of my life. Jaxson stands at the end of my bed, freshly showered, wearing only a pair of kick-ass jeans that hang low on his hips. The top button has been left undone, probably for my torture.

I ogle his naked chest, remembering how every taut muscle felt beneath my hands and lips. Then I remember where I had my mouth and have to squeeze my legs together. There's a glorious tenderness, muscles aching that haven't been used in a long time, especially as well used as last night.

My eyes lift to his ridiculously handsome face, and I find a cocky grin lifting his lips. I glare at him and his sexiness. "What are you doing looking so sexy and chipper this early in the morning?"

His grin spreads to a full-fledged smile.

God, the man is beautiful.

"Jules, it's noon."

"What!" I sit up with a gasp then instantly regret it when the room spins. Groaning, I grab my head, praying I don't humiliate myself and throw up the entire contents of my stomach.

"Easy, Jules," Jaxson soothes, sitting next to me. "Here, take this." He hands me a glass of water and two aspirin that I never even noticed he had. Probably because I was too busy looking at other places.

"Thanks." I toss back the white pills and drink half the glass of water, the cool liquid refreshing my parched throat.

When he takes the glass from me, I drop back down on another groan and close my eyes. At the sound of his chuckle, I peek up at him and can't help but smile.

"Hi," I whisper, reaching up to touch his face.

His warm fingers circle my wrist and he turns his face, kissing the inside of my wrist. "Hey, baby." He yanks the sheet from my body and sees me covered in his button-down shirt that he wore last night. A low growl erupts from his chest. "You look fucking sexy in my clothes."

I'm pretty sure I don't look any kind of sexy at all this morning.

Leaning down, he buries his face in my neck, nipping and tasting my skin. "Mmm." I thread my fingers in his freshly damp hair and breathe him in, loving the clean scent of his shampoo. He aligns his mouth to mine, but I slap my hand over it before he can make contact and shake my head. "Morning breath," I mumble.

His eyes narrow and he rips my hand away. "I don't give a shit about morning breath."

He tries to descend again, but I turn my head away. "No! I care—"

Grasping my chin, he forces my face back to him and swoops in for the kill. I keep my lips tightly shut, but he presses down on my chin to give him the access he needs. Once his tongue slips in, I'm lost in his world and I succumb to it completely. It's a a crazy whirlwind of a world that I would gladly live in for the rest of my life.

"Morning breath, my ass. You taste amazing," he mumbles, making me giggle. His forehead rests on mine, thumb stroking my cheek as he smiles down at me with an easiness that I haven't seen since he's come back. "What are your plans today?"

I'm just about to respond when my phone beeps with another text. Reaching over, I grab it and see six messages from a group text with Kayla and Grace. They want to meet up at the diner for brunch. A laugh tumbles out of me when I read the last text from Kayla.

> ***Kayla:*** *Damn, Julia, tell that man to take his dick out of you already. You can make up for lost time after. I'm fucking hungry!*

I glance up at Jaxson to find him watching me in question. "It's just Kayla and Grace, they want to meet me for lunch at the diner."

"What's so funny about that?"

I clear my throat. "Nothing."

He rips the phone out of my hand and stands.

"Hey, give it back!" I jump from the bed and try to get it back but he holds it above his head to read.

The man is a freaking giant.

His arm curls around my waist, stopping my pathetic attempt of retrieval. "Jesus, that girl has a mouth on her," he says.

I scoff. "Coming from the guy who swears like a sailor." Realizing what I just said, I laugh at the irony of my comment.

That sexy grin of his steals his lips. "Maybe that's why I made such a damn good one."

"Mmm, maybe." I push up on my tiptoes to wrap my arms around his neck. "Or maybe it's because you're really smart, strong, and honorable." My lips pave a path across his shaven jaw, stopping at his ear. "Can I have my phone back now?" I ask, grazing the tender flesh with my teeth.

Growling, he hoists me up and pins me against the wall, his erection hitting me between the legs. The fire that burns in his eyes ignites in my own body. "You tell Kayla that I'll let you go for now, but don't plan on being gone too long. My dick and I have plans for you later." He follows up his dirty words with a pump of his hips.

"Okay, I'll pass the message on," I tell him, my voice breathless.

Chuckling, he sets me down on my feet, hands me back my phone, then presses a soft kiss to my forehead. By the time I open my eyes, he's gone, leaving me with a silly smile on my face.

An hour later, Kayla, Grace, and I are all seated in a booth waiting for our lunch. The diner is steady but not overly busy. It's nice to sit with Grace in here and have her eat with us rather than serve us.

"I still can't believe after all these years, Jaxson has finally pulled his head out of his ass," Kayla says, sipping on her sweet tea. "Okay, give us the details. How was it? I mean obviously it was good, given the I-was-just-amazingly-fucked look on your face, but was it sweet and romantic or hot and desperate? My guess is hot and desperate. Grace, what do you think?"

"Um, I'm gonna say sweet and romantic," she guesses. "Jaxson doesn't seem like the sweet kinda guy, but you can tell he and Julia have somethin' special."

My heart warms at her insightful comment. "Actually, you're both right. It was all of the above, it was… perfect," I sigh, probably looking as dreamy as I feel.

Kayla drops back against her seat with a smile. "Damn, girl, I'm so happy for you. Okay, next question, how many times did you come?"

Grace gasps at the personal question.

"Oh as if you weren't wondering, too."

"Okay, you're right, I was," she admits with a giggle.

They both look at me expectantly, waiting for an answer.

"Four," I confess, feeling my cheeks heat.

"No way," Grace says, her eyes wide with disbelief.

I laugh. "Yes way."

Kayla nods in approval. "Not bad."

"You're serious?" Grace asks again.

"Yes."

"Wow."

"Why?" Kayla asks her. "How many times have you in one night?"

Her face turns the shade of a tomato. "Um, well, uh… never actually."

"What?" Kayla and I both shriek at the same time, drawing customers' attention to our table.

Oops.

"What do you mean, never?" Kayla hisses, leaning in close. "Are you telling us that you have never had an orgasm, Grace? Are you a virgin?"

She shifts, clearly uncomfortable, and it makes me feel horrible.

"It's okay, Grace, you don't have to tell us."

"The hell she doesn't!" Kayla says. "You can't tell us you've never had an orgasm and that's just the end of the conversation."

"I don't mind telling you guys," she says, biting her lip nervously. "I'm not a virgin, but I'm not real experienced either. I've only been with one person and although it wasn't horrible I wondered what all the fuss was about. I love romance novels, and I've heard other women talk about it like you and Julia do, but my experiences certainly weren't anything like what y'all talk about."

"Well no shit. If you've never come, then yeah, it isn't all that great," Kayla says.

"Either he didn't know what the hell he was doing or he was too selfish to care."

"Or maybe it's me? Maybe there's something wrong with me?" she muses quietly.

"I doubt it. But have you tried to give yourself one?" Kayla is so blatant about the question that she may as well have just asked Grace what her favorite color was.

The girl has no shame.

Grace shifts uncomfortably. "Uh, no, I haven't."

"This is fucking insane!" Kayla mumbles, still not believing Grace's unfortunate circumstance.

"Well how many have you had in a night?" Grace asks.

"Six," she replies proudly. "And that was the night I smashed Coop's truck in. I'm considering doing it again sometime soon."

We bust into laughter, drawing everyone's attention over to us again.

Kayla leans in close. "We need to get this rectified, Grace, and fast. And I know just the person." A smile takes over her face as we wait with anticipation for who she's going to name. "Sawyer Evans."

"No way!" Grace rejects the idea quickly, shaking her head vehemently.

"Why not?" I ask, agreeing with Kayla.

"Because he is the most arrogant man I've ever met."

"Exactly," Kayla counters back. "He's arrogant for a reason, Grace. I mean, look at him. Don't get me wrong, I think Coop is sexy as hell but I'm not dead, and you can tell Sawyer is the kind of guy who can back up that mouth of his. I'll just bet that cocky mouth could do all sorts of things to you."

"Oh god, stop!" Grace groans, covering her ears.

"And look what happened last night? I'll bet he would be more than happy to help you out with your little problem."

I frown in confusion. "What happened last night?"

"After you left, Sawyer got all sorts of possessive and cranky when some guy got a little too touchy with Grace," Kayla explains with a smirk. "He wouldn't lay off when she told him to. Sawyer almost came to blows with the guy while defending Grace's honor."

Grace scoffs. "Yeah, but then he was all moody at me like it was my fault, which really ticked me off, by the way. It's not like I knew the guy was gonna try to have sex with me right on the dance floor, for cryin' out loud! I'm tellin' you, no way. Sawyer is out of the question, that man drives me crazy."

I smile as I recall Jaxson's words to me last night.

Jesus, woman, you drive me crazy.

I have a feeling Sawyer isn't all that out of the question.

CHAPTER 29

Julia

Anticipation hums through my body as I head back home to Jaxson. Even though I enjoyed my time with Grace and Kayla, I missed him like crazy. I love that when I get home I don't have to hold my feelings in anymore. That I can freely walk up to him, wrap my arms around him and plant a deep kiss on his sexy face.

I never thought this day would come, but as happy as I am, I'm also scared. Because I know if something happens to end this—to end *us*—there will be no going back to being just friends. And the thought of not having him in my life again is unbearable to even think about.

As I pull up to my house, my gaze becomes riveted on the sleek black motorcycle parked out front. Excitement takes hold of me as I exit the car and race up my porch steps. "Jax?" I call, bolting through my front door.

He appears in the kitchen entry with a lopsided grin, wearing jeans, a T-shirt, and his riding boots. I run for him, launching myself into his arms. He catches me with a grunted chuckle that dies when I attack his mouth, showing him just how much I missed him.

My hands frame his face as I pull back to look at him. "Are you taking me riding?" I ask, hopefully.

"I was going to until you just did that. Now I'm thinking I should just take you upstairs for a ride instead."

"How about bike first, then bed?"

"Deal," he agrees with a smirk. "Do you still have your helmet?"

I nod.

"Bring it to me, I bought a Bluetooth for it."

"We can talk to each other now?"

"Yep, so run grab it for me and I'll install it while you get dressed," he says, placing me on my feet.

I clap my hands in excitement then run and grab him the pink helmet with the black face shield he bought me for my seventeenth birthday. After passing it off to him, I bound up the stairs and into my room.

Hmmm, what am I going to wear?

I dig through my fall clothes and decide on a pair of dark skinny jeans, a white tank top, and my thigh-high black boots. Grabbing my black leather bomber jacket, I throw it on over my tank then secure my hair in a ponytail at the nape of my neck so it won't interfere with my helmet. A few minutes later, I'm bounding back into the kitchen where Jaxson sits at the table bent over my helmet.

"I'm ready. Let's go."

He looks up at me with a smirk that vanishes the moment his eyes land on me, the light blue irises darkening as they sweep down my body from head to toe.

Leaning against the wall, I quirk a brow at him. "Like what you see, Jaxson?" I ask, throwing back the words he always says to me when I'm busted ogling him.

Silence fills the air as he pushes to his feet and starts toward me, his determined strides reminding me of an animal stalking its prey.

My heart thumps wildly in my chest, a familiar ache building between my legs. His arms come around me, his hands cupping my bottom to bring me flush against him. I bite back a moan at the feel of his erection pressing into my stomach.

"I always like what I see, Jules, but fuck me. Right now you look like every biker's fantasy. I want nothing more than to fuck you right now with nothing on but these boots you're wearing." He seals his words with a toe curling kiss.

My fingers grip in his disheveled hair as I succumb to the sensations this man instills in me. All too soon, he's breaking contact. We gaze back at one another, our breaths mingling in the air between us.

"Let's get the hell out of here before I change my mind and fuck you right up against this wall." He places me back on my feet, grabs my helmet, then takes my hand and drags me out of the house behind him.

Once we reach his bike he props the helmet over my head and makes sure the strap is secure. Even though I can fully manage to do this myself, I let him, because sometimes I really like it when he takes care of me.

After putting his own helmet on, he straddles the bike, looking as badass as I know he is. Since both of our visors are still up I'm totally busted for my appreciation. "Stop looking at me like that and get your pretty ass on the bike."

Giggling, I flick my shield down and climb on behind him. My feet land on the pegs as I wrap my arms around him, crushing the front of my body against his back.

His hard abs flex beneath my hands. "Christ, this is going to be a long fucking ride."

I smile when I hear his mumble through the Bluetooth. The loud roar of the bike starting up sends a long forgotten rush of adrenaline through me. The dull ache I had moments ago from his kiss in the kitchen comes pulsing to life from the vibration between my legs.

Jaxson's right, this is going to be a long ride.

The bike creeps forward and we keep a slower pace as he turns out of my driveway and onto the gravel road. Once we hit the interstate, Jaxson drops the throttle and the bike kicks forward on a rush.

I squeal in laughter and tighten my arms around his waist as we speed down the long stretch. The feeling of freedom washes over me, the one I've always gotten when I'm on the back of this bike with him. The thing I love most about riding, besides being so close to Jaxson, is how the whole world feels different. The fresh air feels cleaner, the sun feels warmer, and everything just seems more… peaceful. You get a whole new appreciation for the everyday things around you.

We drive for so long that my cheeks begin to ache from smiling so much. Eventually we leave the interstate and head up a curved road, the ocean below us getting further away as we weave up the steep hill.

"Where are we going?"

"You'll see." Is the only response I get.

A few minutes later, a lighthouse comes into view, sparking another rush of excitement through me. "Are you for real right now? Are we going there?"

His chuckle meets my ears through the bluetooth and my question is answered when he pulls into an opening off the road that leads to the stunning lighthouse.

I jump off the bike before he even has it turned off and remove my helmet as I walk closer to the edge of the cliff. The view is absolutely breathtaking, I've never seen anything like it.

I turn back to Jaxson, who's still sitting on the bike, holding his helmet on his lap, his signature sexy smirk curving his lips. "How on earth did you find this place?" Ever since I moved here, I've wanted to visit a lighthouse. You would think with us being so close to the ocean there would be a lot around us, but there's not.

"Coop told me about it. He discovered it coming back from a party he had to break up just a few miles up the road from here."

"I can't believe this has been here the whole time and we never knew about it." I look up, my head craning all the way back as I take in the tall, white lighthouse with black trim. The sun has started to set, making the beam of light at the top more prominent.

Jaxson comes up beside me and takes my hand. "Come on." He pulls me toward the entrance and we start making our way up a long flight of stairs.

I slow every time we near a window and try to get a peek of the view, but Jaxson tugs on my hand, not giving me the chance. "Patience, we're almost there."

Sure enough, a few more steps and we reach the top. My legs and lungs burn from our lengthy climb, but I don't let it slow me down. I run through the small opening at the top and gasp at the view before me. The Atlantic Ocean stretches out before us, the crystal blue water seeming to go on forever. Orange and pink hues dance across the glowing sky as the sun descends beyond the horizon.

Wanting to soak up everything about this incredible moment, I take off my leather jacket and lean forward against the railing with my arms out at my sides. My eyes fall closed as I take in a deep breath. Even from this high up, I can hear the crash of the waves as the warm ocean breeze blows gently across my face. I have never felt anything so warm and peaceful in my entire life, and for one fleeting moment, I think about my mother, and hope this is what she sees and feels wherever she is, every single day.

Right when I think this moment can't get any better, I feel Jaxson's strong arms come around me, proving me wrong. His body heat seeps into my back and his scent mingles with the salty ocean air. He slips my ponytail loose, freeing my waves from their confines and sweeps my blowing strands to the side so his lips can claim their place on my throat.

Reaching up, I curl my arm around his neck as his warm hands slip underneath the bottom of my tank and glide up on either side of my stomach. Goose bumps break out across my skin even though his touch brings only warmth.

"You're so beautiful, Jules," he whispers, his soft breath hitting the shell of my ear.

Smiling, I turn to face him and wrap my arms around his neck while his lock around my waist. The way he looks down at me makes me feel like the most beautiful woman in the world.

At this moment I desperately want to tell him how much I love him. Tell him that I never stopped, and I never will, because it's the god's honest truth. I will love this man until the day I die, but I know he isn't ready to hear that, not yet. So, instead, I swallow past the lump in my throat and try to put into words what I'm feeling. "I love that I am living out another beautiful moment of my life with you. Thank you for bringing me here."

"You deserve a lifetime of these moments." His head dips as he places his lips on mine, giving me a soul touching kiss.

Soon, we're shredding each other's clothes off and making love under the warmth of the sunset. He makes love to me with a tenderness I have never known, and I know in this moment, with every fiber of my being, that Jaxson Reid loves me as much as I love him.

CHAPTER 30

Julia

Three weeks later, I'm in the kitchen starting the preparations for Kayla and Coop's engagement supper. I pushed the date back a week since Grace had a hard time getting off work. I didn't want her coming here drained after a long day at the diner.

As I'm peeling the potatoes, my phone rings, the screen flashing an unknown number. I answer it politely, even though I'm not expecting an answer.

This past week I've been getting a hang-up call at least once a day. Sure enough, the same thing happens again. Annoyed, I hang up and move back to my spot at the counter. At first I thought it was a wrong number or kids, but now I realize that's probably unlikely. I know it's something I should mention to Jaxson, but things have been amazing between us the last few weeks, and I really don't want anything to strain it.

Bending down, I grab a baking sheet from underneath the oven when something big and hard crowds me from behind, startling me. I reach up and grab onto the counter to balance myself.

"You can't stick this pretty ass in the air, Julia, and expect me not to do something about it." Jaxson's husky voice sends a delicious shiver through my body.

Unable to stop myself, I push back against his erection. He groans, his fingers digging into my hips.

Smiling, I force his hands away and turn around. "Behave. Kayla and Grace will be here soon."

Ignoring me, he spans my waist and lifts me on the counter, coming to stand between my legs. "Then I guess we better make it quick."

My giggle trails into a fiery moan when his tongue laves at the sensitive skin of my neck, leaving a path of heat in its wake. He gently squeezes my breast through my thin tank top, my nipple straining against his touch. I arch against his heated palm and slide my hands under his shirt, scoring my nails across his toned stomach.

Growling, he tugs the top of my tank down with my bra, freeing my breasts, and sucks an aching nipple into his mouth.

A harsh cry breaches my lips and warmth gathers between my thighs. I wrap my legs around his hips to reel him in closer. Just when I reach for his belt, the doorbell rings.

Of course.

"For fuck's sake." Jaxson's heated curse slices through the air, his frustration mirroring my own. He captures my mouth in one more fiery kiss, which is interrupted again when someone begins pounding on the door. Another growl rips from his throat as he pulls back. "We are fucking moving, Julia, and we aren't telling anyone where we live."

Chuckling, I right my top and trail behind him as he storms to the door. He swings it open aggressively, forcing Grace a step back, but not Kayla.

She cocks a hip and returns his glare. "You know, Jaxson, you and this door locking business is starting to piss me off. There was a time where I could just walk into my best friend's house when I showed up. I didn't have to knock."

"Well, Kayla, sorry to inconvenience you, but my door locking business is to keep your best friend's ass safe. Don't tell me Coop doesn't make you lock your damn door."

She tilts her head. "Wow, you're grouchy today. Is the Hulk going to be gracing us with his presence the whole time?" She walks past him, giving him a quick pat on the chest. "Coop's waiting for you in the truck to head to the liquor store whenever you decide to get over your tantrum."

Covering our mouths, Grace and I burst into muffled giggles.

Jaxson mutters to himself as he puts his shoes on, then walks over and gives me a quick, peck on the lips. "You need to find new friends."

"Ha!" Kayla fires back. "You would still have to put up with me because I'm marrying your best friend. Sorry, big guy, but you're stuck with me."

He shakes his head, but I don't miss the twitch of his lips before he heads out the door.

They secretly love each other.

I swing my attention over to Kayla to find her looking rather amused. "I love screwing with that guy."

Our laughter fills the air as we make our way into the kitchen. Grace places a tote bag on my counter and pulls out three freshly baked pies that look absolutely divine.

"Wow, these look great, Grace. Thanks for bringing them."

"No problem, they're nothin' fancy. I made an apple, a raspberry, and a blueberry."

"I'm sure they'll be delicious, as always."

"Have you heard from Katelyn?" Kayla asks. "Is she able to come tonight?"

"Yeah, she's coming. Between her, Sawyer, Cade, and Grams we will have a full house."

"I'm so glad Grams could make it. I haven't seen her in a while."

"You know Grams, she's always in the mood to celebrate, especially if there are margaritas."

Kayla snickers. "We'll make them nice and strong for her tonight."

We start to set up, pushing together tables and adding chairs. My back screams every time I lift anything. Since my fall from Wyatt it hasn't been the same, and it wasn't great to begin with.

"You all right, Jules?" Kayla asks, when I twist my body to relieve pressure.

"Yeah, it's just my back. It's a mess."

"I thought yoga was helping?"

"It was, but since my fall it hasn't been doing well. I've been meaning to come see you, but I've just been caught up in stuff."

"More like someone has been caught up in you," she mumbles. "Come on, I'll give you a quick fix to hold you over."

"Oh no, that's okay. I'll be fine. I'll make sure to come see you next week."

She gives me the *look,* the one that brooks no argument. "I'll be quick, come to the living room."

"All right, thanks." I follow her into the other room where she makes up a little spot on the floor with the throw blankets and pillows.

"Take off your tank and lie face down. Grace, I'm going to get you to hold certain points on her lower back while I work on her top. Between the both of us it won't take long."

Removing my shirt, I do as she instructs, making myself comfortable. As soon as she puts her hands on me, sweet oblivion claims me.

"Who's Katelyn?" I ask Cooper on our way back to the house.

"She's the girls' hairdresser. And… waxer," he adds, looking over at me with a smirk.

"Waxer? What kind of waxing are we talking about?" Sawyer asks from the backseat. He and Cade had pulled up just before we left to the liquor store.

"None of your damn business."

I'm not letting that shithead know anything about Julia's waxing.

"Oh, so it's that kind of waxing. Nice."

I turn back and glare at him, daring him to say more.

"She's the one who spotted us outside the club that night and got us in," Coop explains further. "She's nice, but dates some real douche bags. Especially this most recent one. He owns that club, which is how she got us all in. I met him at Big Mike's one day when I was there sparring with a deputy. I never wanted to kick someone's ass as much as I did his."

"Speaking of Big Mike," Sawyer cuts in. "He approached Cade and me the other day, and asked us if we wanted to buy his gym."

"What?" I ask, the information rocking me to my core.

"No bullshit. Actually, he said he wants the three of us to buy it. I'm considering it."

"You want to move here?" I couldn't be more surprised right now if the guy told me he had a pussy.

"Why not, I'm kind of digging this town. And with a little money we could do some pretty cool shit with that place."

I look over at Cade. "What about you?"

He shrugs. "I'm not sure I want to settle in one place, but I agree with Evans. We could do a lot with the place."

"It doesn't surprise me he asked you guys," Cooper says. "He's been wanting to sell it, but only to the right person." His eyes shift to me. "I think it's something you should consider."

I haven't thought much about what I'm going to do. I've only been thinking about Julia and fixing shit with her, but I have to admit, as shocked as I am about Big Mike's approach, the thought does appeal to me.

The conversation ends when we pull back up to the house. As we climb up the front steps, Sawyer looks down at the margarita mix I'm carrying and smirks. "In the mood for pussy drinks tonight?"

"It's for Julia's Grams, you asshole. She loves margaritas."

He chuckles. "Sure, sure, I'll just bet…" His words trail off when we walk into the house and hear a pleasure-filled moan.

It's a moan I'd know anywhere.

What the fuck?

"Oh yeah, right there, that's the spot," Julia says, her voice soft and seductive.

I'm about to storm through the place like a fucking tornado but Sawyer grabs my arm, stopping me. He puts a finger to his mouth, telling me to be quiet.

"Damn, Julia, you're tight. Grace, move over so I can get better access."

Sawyer's green eyes light up like it's fucking Christmas. "Ho-ly shit!" Shoving against my chest he heads for the living room.

I charge after him with Coop and Cade on my heels and yank him back. I don't know what the hell is going on, but I don't want anyone to see Julia moaning about anything.

All of us shove at each other to get through the entrance of the living room but freeze mid-struggle when we get a look at the sight before us. Julia lies face down on blankets, wearing no shirt. Kayla is on one side of her and Grace on the other with their hands on her back. The side swell of her perfect breast is visible and rage pumps through me, knowing everyone else can see it, too.

"Hey," Julia greets me with a smile, acting as if it's perfectly normal to be lying on the floor half naked for everyone to see.

"What the hell are you doing?"

Her eyes narrow at my harsh tone. "I'm getting a massage, what does it look like I'm doing?"

Sawyer's laughter pierces the air. Turning around, I shove him back a step. "Get the hell out of here. And you…" I point over at Julia. "Get your clothes back on."

She bristles at the order and awkward silence falls over the room.

Kayla fastens up her bra then stands and glares at me. "Come on, Grace, let's go finish setting up."

She storms past me with Grace and everyone else following behind her.

"You can be a real asshole, you know that?" Julia hisses, throwing her top back on. "What the hell is your problem?"

"You want to know what my problem is? I don't like coming home with a bunch of friends to see my girlfriend half fucking naked and moaning on the living room floor for everyone to see."

She crosses her arms, pushing her perfect tits up for my viewing. "Oh please, Jaxson, I was getting a massage. You act like what we were doing was inappropriate."

"It sure the hell sounded like that when we walked through the door."

"So that gives you the right to yell and embarrass me in front of everyone?" She turns away, but not before I see the hurt in her eyes.

Well shit!

Releasing a guilt-stricken breath, I walk over and pull her in my arms. "I'm sorry, you're right. I'm an asshole. I shouldn't have reacted like that. I was caught off guard when I walked in and heard shit that's only for me to hear."

She looks up at me, her cheeks pink. "Did it really sound that bad?"

"Baby, if I wasn't certain Kayla and Grace were in here with you, there would have been major destruction left in my path."

"Oh lord," she groans, hiding her face in my chest.

Grasping her chin, I bring her gaze back to mine. "I am really sorry. We good?"

She nods. "Yeah."

"Good." I drop a kiss on her forehead then release her.

"But just so we're clear, Jaxson, the next time you talk to me like that you'll be finding yourself a new place to sleep, and the moans I'll be making won't be coming from you. Got it?" She doesn't wait for a response before she sashays her sweet ass out of the room.

CHAPTER 31

Julia

Kayla, Grace, and I are in the kitchen mixing the salads and getting things ready when the doorbell rings. Leaving my task, I go open the door and let Grams in.

"Hello, my sweet girl," she greets me, reaching up to kiss my cheek.

"Hi, Grams, come on in. Everyone's out back. We're just waiting on Katelyn."

I link her arm with mine and escort her into the kitchen. Grace and Kayla drop what they are doing and greet her with a big hug. Grams kisses and fusses over them, as always, then she grabs Kayla's hand to admire her ring. "I'm so happy for you, sweetheart. And I want you to know, I heard about what happened at the motel."

Kayla groans. "I'm never going to live that down, am I?"

"Now don't you be getting all embarrassed," Grams gently scolds, shaking a finger at her. "Desperate times call for desperate measures. It's important to show your man you will fight for him."

We share a laugh before I lead her out back where the guys are barbecuing. I take her over to Sawyer and Cade first. "Grams, this is Sawyer and Cade. They're friends of Jaxson's from the Navy."

"Well my goodness, aren't y'all both so handsome," she coos, kissing their cheeks. Cade tenses at her affection but tries to hide it and nods politely, but Sawyer soaks it up, loving every bit of the attention.

She turns to Jaxson next who stands over at the barbecue. "There's my favorite boy, come here, honey, and give me some love," she says, opening her arms.

It melts my heart when he accepts her affection comfortably and hugs her back.

Grams takes his face between her worn hands, making him have to bend down. "Miss Gladys wants me to give you a kiss for her, but I told her only on the cheek because you're Julia's now."

A laugh spills past my lips and it earns me a glare from him.

Next, she makes her way over to Cooper. "Cooper, you handsome devil. I'm so proud of you for making an honest woman out of Kayla," she praises, kissing his cheek. "Now I have something I need to tell you, honey. Something happened to me on the way over here."

I frown and start over to her. "Grams, what's wrong? Are you okay?"

She cuts a hand through the air, waving away my concern. "Now don't worry, I'm all right, but a man was blaring his horn at me, and driving like a maniac in his fancy-schmancy car. When we pulled up to a red light he rolled down his window and started yelling at me, told me I was driving too slow and to get off the effin' road."

I gasp, not liking to hear someone spoke to her like that.

Cooper doesn't like it either. "Did you get a good look at the guy?" he asks.

"Actually, I did one better, I wrote down his license plate number for you. I told him that I knew the sheriff personally and that he was going to get into some major trouble. He laughed and started yelling more profanities at me. So then I pulled out the big guns, I told him my grandson was a Navy SEAL, and he was going to kick his ass."

A small smile cracks my lips as I picture Grams threatening someone with Jaxson. But Jaxson doesn't find it funny. In fact, he looks down right pissed.

"There was a girl in the passenger seat," she continues. "I couldn't see her well, but she was yelling at him to stop. Whoever the poor girl is, I feel bad for her, being with someone like that can't be all that fun."

Cooper takes the paper from Grams. "No, I bet not. You did a good job writing down the license plate number, Miss Margaret. I'll look into this first thing tomorrow."

Grams pats his shoulder. "I know you will, honey."

I help Grams into her seat and offer her a drink. "Can I get you a margarita?"

"That would be lovely, thank you, dear."

I head back inside and fill Kayla and Grace in on what Grams just told us while I mix her drink.

"Oh my gosh, that's terrible," Grace says, sounding as upset as I feel.

Kayla's reaction is the opposite. She's furious. "What an asshole! I can't wait for Cooper to find his sorry ass."

Before either of us can say more the doorbell rings. The three of us go answer it and open the door to find Katelyn, and some guy who I'm assuming is her new boyfriend.

"Hey, Katelyn, come on in," I greet her with a smile but it fades when I notice her eyes are red and glassy. It looks as if she's been crying.

She steps inside, hugging Grace and Kayla before coming to me. "Hey, Jules. Um, so it turns out that Vince didn't have to work tonight. I hope it's okay that I brought him along?"

Something in her voice gives me the impression she didn't necessarily want to bring him but I don't want to make things awkward, so I paste a smile on my face and nod. "Of course, no problem. Hi, Vince, it's nice to meet you. I'm Julia, and this is Grace and Kayla."

His eyes sweep down my body, slowly and deliberately, blatantly checking me out. When his gaze finally makes it to my face he gives me a sleazy smile. "Hi."

Kayla, Grace, and I exchange a look.

So much for things not being awkward.

Katelyn clears her throat. "Can I use your bathroom?"

"Sure, follow me. I'll show you where it is. Kayla and Grace, can you guys get Vince a drink and take him out back?"

"Sure, right this way, Vince." Kayla leads him into the kitchen as I walk Katelyn down the hall toward the bathroom.

"Oh god, Julia, I'm so sorry," her choked whisper stops me in my tracks.

I turn around to see tears streaming down her face. "Are you okay?"

She shakes her head. "He is such a jerk. We had this huge fight on the way here.

I'm seeing a side of him I didn't know he had. I tried to get rid of him, but he wouldn't listen. In the end I figured it was easier just to bring him and then deal with him later."

Just as I open my mouth to respond we hear a commotion out in the backyard. Katelyn and I rush outside to find Grams yelling and pointing at Vince. "That's him, Cooper! That's the guy who was yelling and cussing at me. I told you I knew the sheriff. You're in big trouble now, mister!"

"Oh no," Katelyn cries.

"You have got to be fucking kidding me," Vince mutters, annoyed.

"So you're the one who was harassing Miss Margaret." Cooper gets up from his chair, his eyes furious. I spot Jaxson across the yard with Sawyer and Cade and see them coming toward us.

"The bitch shouldn't be behind the wheel. She can't drive worth a shit."

I tense at Vince's cruel words and round on him. "Don't you talk about my Grams like that!"

He steps into my personal space and leans in close, his eyes wild and angry. "Listen, bitch. She—"

I'm yanked back and Vince vanishes before my eyes. Big hands grip my shoulders to steady me. Looking over my shoulder, I find Cade behind me. "Thanks," I say, my voice shaky.

Turning back around, I see Vince pinned against the house by a very pissed off Jaxson, his beer bottle shattered at their feet. "I don't know who the hell you are, but if you don't get off this property in ten seconds I will kick your fucking teeth through the back of your skull."

Vince's angry eyes take in the lot of us, considering his options. He's a big guy and I'm sure he can handle himself, but he's no match for Jaxson.

It's obvious he realizes this and raises his hands in surrender. "No problem, man, just let me get my girl and we're out of here."

Jaxson releases him but stays close.

"Let's go!" he barks at Katelyn, starting toward her.

I step next to her and reach for her hand. "No! She's staying here."

Katelyn gives my fingers a grateful squeeze.

"I don't think so, bitch. You better—"

Jaxson brings his knee up into Vince's gut, making him double over. "Time's up, asshole."

"I'm not leaving without my girl," Vince wheezes through painful breaths.

Cooper comes to stand in front of Katelyn. "Do you want to leave with him?"

She shakes her head. "No, I don't. Leave, Vince and don't ever contact me again."

"That's all I needed to hear." Cooper turns his back on us and helps Jaxson drag him out.

Tears slip down Katelyn's cheeks when she walks over to Grams. "I'm so sorry, Miss Margaret. I tried to tell him to stop. I feel even more terrible knowing it was you."

Grams pulls her in for a hug. "It's all right, dear, you have nothing to be sorry about. He's responsible for his own actions."

Katelyn turns to me next. "I'm sorry, Julia, I didn't mean to ruin anyone's night."

"You didn't. I'm glad you stayed."

"Me, too," Kayla says, giving her a hug.

"And me." Grace follows Kayla's lead and joins in on their hug.

"And me," Sawyer adds, enveloping all three girls in his arms, making all of us chuckle.

Leave it to Sawyer to lighten the heavy moment.

Feeling someone's eyes on me, my attention shifts to the back door and I find Jaxson leaning against it, watching me. I give him a small smile, appreciating what he just did for Katelyn. He returns it with one of his own and the beauty of it makes my heart skip a beat.

Our silent exchange needed no words. With just a look and a smile, the words we have yet said to each other were spoken.

Later that evening, when Sawyer and Cade are the only ones left, I decide to call it a night. I walk over to Jaxson where he sits at the kitchen table and wrap my arms around his neck. "I'm going to bed, y'all need anything before I head up?"

His hand strokes the inside of my bare leg, eliciting goose bumps across my skin. It's a touch of promise for what's to come later. "Nah, we're good. I'll be up after this," he says, lifting his beer.

"That's fine, take your time." After giving him a kiss, I move to Sawyer and Cade next and give them both a hug. "Good night, boys. Take that leftover pie."

Sawyer sneaks a kiss on my cheek. "Night, Jules, thanks for having us."

Jaxson kicks the bottom of his chair. "Lips to yourself, asshole."

Giggling, I shake my head and make my way upstairs. As I'm getting changed, I realize I left my cell down in the kitchen and I want to check in on Katelyn. Grabbing my thin sweater, I throw it over my tank top and make my way back down the stairs. Just as I reach the bottom I catch a glimpse of the guys' conversation.

"I can't hold the admiral off anymore, Jaxson. We need to make a decision and we need to make one now, are we going to help with this mission or not?"

I come to a hard stop, dread sinking into the pit of my stomach.

"I don't know. Instinct is telling me yes, we need to go help, but after what happened and the way things ended… I don't know if we are the right ones for this. Cade, what do you want to do?"

"Like I said, I'll do whatever you guys want."

Unable to listen to another word, I charge into the kitchen, shaking with hurt and anger. "How can any of you even consider this?"

All their eyes snap to me in surprise.

"Shit," Jaxson mumbles, shaking his head.

I stomp closer to him. "What are you thinking? Haven't you been through enough? Haven't you all been through enough?"

He reaches for me, but I step back. "Calm down, baby, come here. We haven't decided anything."

"Calm down? How could you keep this from me? What else are you hiding?"

"Damn it, Julia, nothing. You're overreacting."

"The hell I am! You promised. You promised you wouldn't leave again. You lied to me!"

Before I completely lose it in front of them all, I run back upstairs and into my room. Slamming the door, I crawl in bed and curl into a ball. The thought of Jaxson leaving again—and possibly getting hurt or worse—breaks something inside of me, something I may never get back.

CHAPTER 32

Jaxson

"Shit!" I jump to my feet, my chair slamming into the wall behind me.

"I told you to tell her, man."

I glare over at Sawyer, not appreciating his two fucking cents at the moment. "I didn't want to say anything until we made a decision."

"Yeah, and because of that she just got blindsided. Listen, Jaxson, you need to think hard about this. Is this something that's worth hurting her over? I feel the same way as you do—I want to help. But let's face it, if we don't go, someone else will. It isn't like the mission will fail if we say no. If we were still in the Navy then this wouldn't even be a question, we would haul our asses out there and do what we needed to do. But we aren't anymore; and for a damn good reason too, if you ask me."

I run my hand through my hair, angry at myself because he's right. I should have told her, but things have been so good lately I didn't want to fuck it up.

Sawyer stands and claps me on the shoulder. "Think about it. You know we'll go along with whatever you want to do. Just remember what I said—someone else will do it if we say no."

Cade nods his agreement, then they both bid me goodbye before walking out the door.

I lock up behind them and head upstairs, wondering what the hell I'm going to encounter once I walk into the room. Bracing myself at the door, I open it and am met with darkness. Through the shadows of the room, I see Julia curled up on her side of the bed with her back to me. If it weren't for the quiet sniffles, I would think she was asleep. I switch on the lamp, bringing the room to a soft glow.

"Jules?" I call softly, my steps slow. When she doesn't answer, I kneel on the floor next to her. A tissue is clutched in her hand as she buries her face in the pillow, her shoulders trembling with her pain.

It rips me apart to see her like this, especially knowing I'm the cause of it. "Please don't cry, Jules. Everything's going to be okay."

She shakes her head. "No, it's not. It's not going to be okay, Jaxson. You lied to me. You promised you wouldn't leave me again."

"I'm sorry, I should've told you. But you need to know, if we decide to do this, if I leave, it won't be forever. I'll come back to you."

Her head snaps up and she fists my shirt with a strength that shocks the hell out of me. "Don't make promises you can't keep! You can't promise you will come back to me. Something could happen to you. Look what happened last time." Her anger quickly turns to agony. She drops back down, her shattered sobs slicing me right down the middle. "I've never asked anything from you. I've supported you in everything you've chosen to do, even if I didn't like it. But I'm begging you now, please don't do this, please don't leave again. I won't survive if something happens to you."

Her agonized plea destroys me, but also brings clarity. Leaning over, I cover the top half of her body with my own and trail my lips across her wet cheek, bringing my mouth to her ear. "Okay."

She falls completely still under me. "What?"

"Okay, I won't go. I'll do anything to not have you hurt like this."

It's the damn truth, nothing or no one matters to me more than her.

She lifts her chin, her devastating eyes wide with surprise. "Really? You won't leave me?"

I shake my head. "Never."

Her breath catches, a small sob of relief escaping her. She reaches up, her fingers fanning my jaw as she gazes back at me with an emotion I'm too scared to name. But I don't need to, because she breathes the words a moment later and they rock me to my fucking core just like they did six years ago. "I love you, Jaxson."

My heart swells so fucking much it hurts, emotion gripping the hollow organ in a tight vise. They're words I've longed to hear yet feared at the same time.

Her hand covers my mouth before I can respond. "Don't say anything. I don't want you to say anything back. I just… I need you to know that I still love you. I never stopped and I never will."

She deserves to hear those same words, but they remain stuck in my throat. I'm too much of a pussy to say them because the last woman I said them to left and never came back.

"I don't deserve you." The truthful words sound gruff even to my own ears.

She sits up on the edge of the bed, her legs dangling on either side of me. "Yes, you do. You deserve all of me, including my heart." She grabs the bottom of her tank top and pulls it over her head, baring me to the most beautiful sight of my life.

Since I can't say the words I feel, I show her, my hands gliding up her smooth, toned stomach and cup the full weight of her breasts.

"Jaxson." My name breaches her lips on a fiery whimper as she leans back on straight arms, arching into my touch.

"You're so fucking pretty, Julia. Every perfect inch of you." I take a taut nipple into my mouth, licking and sucking the velvet tip.

With a harsh gasp, her hand curls in my hair, fingers gripping. The sting shoots straight to my cock and sends lust roaring through my veins. Her hips rise off the bed, her hot, covered center grinding against my stomach as she tugs at my shirt with urgent hands.

Leaning back, I get rid of the material quickly then lift her off the bed. Her arms cling to me, skin warming mine as I reverse our positions. I fall back onto the bed, my shoulders meeting the mattress as I bring her down on top of me.

A low growl shreds my throat when she takes the opportunity to grind her hot pussy down on my stiff cock. Spanning her hips, I inch her further up my stomach until she's sitting on my chest. Then, I fist the side of her tiny shorts and shred them from her body.

She sucks in a sharp breath, and grabs onto my shoulders to steady herself, her bare pussy only inches from my face.

My mouth waters at the sweet smell of her, the urge to taste her overwhelming. "Come here, baby, and grab onto the headboard."

"What are you going to do?" she asks, uncertainty shining in her eyes.

I smirk up at her. "You're going to ride my face while I fuck your pussy with my mouth."

Her cheeks flame, but there's no denying the need in her eyes, it's the same one raging in my blood. Tentatively, she grabs onto the headboard. I slide down a little more, bringing her soft, warm thighs on either side of my head, my mouth coming in direct line with what I crave most. Rising up, I burrow my mouth into her hot, wet flesh and groan when the taste of her explodes on my tongue.

"Oh shit!" Her cry of pleasure tears through the room. It fuels my efforts—challenging me. Her trepidation forgotten, she tangles one hand in my hair and fucks my mouth with greedy thrusts of her hips.

Groaning, I apply more pressure, my tongue working her clit, the nub getting harder and firmer. Her breath quickens and her movements become more frantic. Knowing she's close, I bring my hand up behind her and coat my fingers with her arousal before slipping two fingers inside her, and that's all it takes.

She sobs out her orgasm, trembling against my mouth and I drink every last fucking drop from her. Her legs begin to shake as she fights to hold herself up. My hands span her hips but before I can lift her, she grabs my wrists, stopping me. Our eyes meet between her legs and a seductive smile curves her lips. "Stay right where you are."

Slowly, she moves down my body, and I kiss every inch of golden skin that passes. When her perfect tits come in line with my mouth, I nip at one tight bud, dragging a heated moan from her throat.

Her lips meet the skin on my chest, tongue dipping and tasting the hard lines of my body. Need coils low in my stomach, my cock aching for release.

"Baby, as much as I love your mouth on my body, if you don't speed this up we're going to be in serious trouble."

She giggles, but thankfully moves with more urgency. Sitting on my thighs, she works the button on my jeans and lowers them enough to free my cock. Her fingers wrap around the thick base, stroking me with a firm grip.

"Fuck me!" My hips jerk off the bed as I pump myself into her hand, my dick charged and ready. "Julia, now!" I order.

She aligns herself over me and slowly begins to sink down on me. I grind my teeth, my fingers digging into the soft flesh of her hips. "So hot, so tight."

Her heat surrounds me, my whole body going warm, especially the spot in my chest. With her hands braced on my stomach, she begins riding me, her movement slow and unsure. But she's a fucking sight to behold.

Long brown hair tumbles past her slender shoulders, framing her perfect tits while a light sheen of sweat covers her skin, giving it a glowing affect. With her eyes closed and face tilted up, her expression soft and sweet, she looks like a goddamn angel.

My angel.

"God, I love how you fill me up," she moans.

My teeth grind so hard with restraint that my jaw begins to ache. Reaching up, I cup both of her tits and she arches into my touch, her rhythm picking up.

"That's it, baby, fucking ride me." I jerk my hips up into her, burying myself so deep I'm not sure I'll ever find my way out.

"Oh!" She gasps, lips parting.

"You like that?" I repeat the motion but even harder, giving her more.

She whimpers. "I love it. I love everything I do with you. I… I love you."

My chest tightens with a mix of pleasure and pain. I still can't believe that I was lucky enough to meet this girl, to have her become my best friend, and then to become… mine.

She deserves better; she deserves more.

Wanting to silence the stupid, but truthful, voice in my head, I sit up and wrap an arm around her slender body. My hand anchors in the back of her hair as I bring her lips to mine, selfishly taking everything she has to give me.

This is my favorite place to be in the world, surrounded by Julia—her taste, her scent, to be inside of her. I constantly ache for her, body and soul. I have no idea how I went so many years without this, but I know I never will again.

I'd die without her.

"You own me, Julia, every fucking part of me." I look up at her, letting her see what I so cowardly can't say.

She gives me one of her beautiful smiles. A smile that always tightens my chest and proves to me that the world can be a good place. "I know," she whispers, before pressing a soft kiss against my forehead, just like the one I always give her. Then she drops one at the corner of my eye, my cheek… she doesn't stop and continues to heal all the broken parts of me with just a brush of her lips.

I bury my face in her soft skin, my throat burning like a motherfucker. Our bodies stop moving, my cock seated deep inside of her as we hold each other. As if sensing my internal battle, she leans down, bringing her mouth to my ear. "This is right, Jaxson, this has always been right. Something that feels this good could never be wrong."

Her words of truth destroy me and it all becomes too much. Needing to move on, my lips meet her warm skin as I coast them across the swell of her breasts, brushing them across her stiff nipple before sucking it into my mouth.

"Yes," she moans, her hips finding rhythm again.

I lie back down and keep one hand on her breast and the other on her hip, helping guide her. My hips pump up inside of her, driving my cock deeper.

"Oh god!" She braces her hands on my chest, further leaning over me, her full tits swaying inches from my mouth. "More, I want more."

My fucking pleasure.

Giving her what she wants, I drive up inside of her again and again, her inner muscles gripping my cock. "Your pussy is so greedy, baby. I fucking love it."

She whimpers, her teeth sinking into her bottom lip. I reach up and tug at the tender flesh. Her tongue darts out, curling around my thumb before she sucks it into her mouth.

It shreds the last of my control.

I fuck her hard, like I've been dying to. Her screams fill the air, nails digging into my flesh as she takes every hard, frantic thrust. Within seconds, she's shattering above me.

Her head falls back on a cry as ecstasy washes over her face. It's the most beautiful sight I've ever seen. Fire spreads through my body as I follow along with her, losing a little more of myself as I do.

It takes us a good few minutes before we're able to move and clean up. Julia walks out of the bathroom, looking rumpled and sexy as hell in my shirt. A soft smile curls her lips as she approaches the bed.

Reaching out, I catch her off guard and haul her on top of me. She squeals in laughter and accidentally kicks something off her nightstand.

"Oh crap!" Scrambling off of me she reaches over to pick up a framed picture of her and her mom on a Ferris wheel at some fair. Her expression is soft as she lies down on top of me, holding the picture up so we can both look at it. "Wasn't she beautiful, Jax?"

"Yeah, baby," I agree, holding her a little tighter. "Just like you."

She makes a fist on my chest, resting her chin on it, and smiles up at me. "She would have loved you."

I grunt. "I'll just bet she would've loved the guy that fantasized about all the ways to screw her daughter from the moment he laid eyes on her."

Giggling, she presses a kiss to my chest then stares up at me somberly. "She would have loved my best friend. The guy who helped take my pain away and made me smile again. The one who watched out for me, protected me." She reaches up, her fingers grazing the side of my face. "I've always believed she sent you to me that night in the graveyard."

My muscles tense, rage igniting in my blood as the memory of that fateful night resurfaces.

"It was the first time I had prayed since my mother died. I was so scared, thinking of what they were going to do to me, not knowing if they were going to kill me after. I was sad for Grams, thinking she was going to lose the last family she had left. So I prayed to my mom for help. I prayed so hard for something, anything, to stop what was happening. Then you showed up and saved my life, in more ways than one."

Little does she know it was her who saved me that night, not the other way around.

"I'll always protect you, Julia." I may not be able to give her everything she deserves, but I'm more than capable of giving her that.

"I know." She reaches up and drags her fingers along my lips, her expression sobering. "Are you going to resent me later for asking you not to go?"

I shake my head. "No. It's not something I have to do, and I wasn't sure I was going to do it. That's why I never told you, but seeing you hurt like that..." I shrug. "It just made the decision that I was struggling with easier. I'm surprised the admiral even asked us; the three of us aren't his favorite people."

"Why?"

"Because we went against his order," I tell her.

Pain enters her eyes, knowing it was that order that lead me to a week of hell. "How did it happen? How were you guys held for so long? Didn't they know where you were?"

With a heavy breath, I focus on the ceiling and think about how much to share with her. "We had just finished a mission that we were sent to do in Iraq. We were there for two weeks, learning the territory that we needed to cover and coming up with our plan of action. During that time, Cade would leave in the evenings. Wherever he was going had him tied up in knots when he came back. Some nights he came back, I don't know… relaxed? Then other times he was moody and restless. Sawyer and I didn't have a clue what the fuck was going on with him."

"He met someone, didn't he?" she asks.

I look down at her in surprise. "Yeah. How did you know?"

"Because he's a lot like you," she says, smiling up at me.

Huh, well if that isn't a little true.

"Anyway, moving on, Miss Know-It-All."

She chuckles.

"The day before we were supposed to come home, Cade was moodier than usual. Something went down the night before in his room. That's when Sawyer and I realized he was seeing someone, which was a big deal because the guy never sees the same girl twice."

After I say that, it strikes me again how similar he and I really are.

"Sawyer and I took him to the local bar we had gone to a few times, and tried to talk to him. In the middle of our beers a kid came running in, crying. He was yelling at Cade, half in English, the other half in Arabic—*'He took her, he took her.'* Cade understood more than we did and seemed to know the kid from somewhere. He went crazy. I've never seen him like that. Don't get me wrong, the guy is lethal but always in control."

I pause, remembering that day so vividly and what followed after.

"It turned out the girl he was seeing was an American. She was there on a mission trip with her church. Cade got into it the week before with some local asshole who was harassing her. As it turns out, that asshole was part of some pretty serious shit. He took her to punish him."

"Oh no," she whispers, but can't begin to understand just how bad it was. No one could, not unless you were there to hear the screams and the pain that was inflicted.

"Cade took off half-cocked and ready to shed blood," I continue, my voice harder—darker. "I held him back and told him we would go to the admiral to get backup. He agreed. But the admiral said no, told us that it wasn't our problem and we were to have our asses ready to ship out. Sawyer and I knew Cade wasn't going to leave her there, and we sure as hell weren't going to bail on him. So we loaded up with what weapons we could, and the kid said he would take us to her. But it was a fucking setup, he led us right into an ambush."

"Why would he do that?" she asks, her question thick with tears.

"He didn't have a choice, he was forced to do it. He was the son of one of our captors." My stomach churns when I think about what ended up happening to that poor kid.

"So in the end the Navy finally found you guys?"

A bitter laugh escapes me. "No, we got out on our own. With help from someone on the inside. The only reason we were honorably discharged was because we made our team look good. They didn't want it revealed that we were ordered not to help another American, so disclosures were signed and the three of us walked away with a big settlement."

"Did you guys get the girl out?" she asks softly.

My chest tightens as I think about more than one American girl. "Yeah, but not before she was hurt."

"Why isn't Cade with her now?"

"I don't know. He doesn't like to talk about it."

A moment of silence settles between us before she speaks again. "Jax?"

"Yeah."

"The men… the ones who hurt you, are they dead?"

"Most of them."

"Good," she says firmly, hugging me tighter.

I hold her close as she drifts off into a deep slumber. Meanwhile, sleep evades me and instead I'm left with the sound of tortured screams and the smell of death.

CHAPTER 33

Julia

"Julia."

I moan from Jaxson's urgent whisper. "Again? Lord, man, don't you ever sleep?" I mumble, teasing.

"Julia, get up now."

My eyes spring open at the harsh tone of his voice, realizing something's wrong. Sitting up, I see he's out of bed, throwing on his jeans.

I glance at the clock and see it's only three a.m. "What is it, what's wrong?"

"Someone's in the house."

"What?" I screech.

He claps a hand over my mouth. "Listen, baby, everything's going to be all right, but you need to be quiet, okay?"

I nod.

Removing his hand, he reaches under the bed and pulls out a gun.

"Oh my god, you have a gun? In my house?" I whisper harshly.

He looks at me like I'm stupid. "Of course I have a gun."

I guess I shouldn't be surprised, but I deserve to know if I'm sleeping over top of one for goodness' sake. I climb out of bed quietly and follow Jaxson to my bedroom window that looks out over the front yard.

A loud clanging noise sounds from downstairs, startling me. I gasp and grab his arm, fear gripping my chest.

He hands me his cell phone. "Call Cooper, tell him what's going on and to bring backup."

"Where are you going?"

"I'm going down to find out who the fuck is in here."

"No! Jaxson, please just stay here with me. We have no idea who's down there or how many there are."

"I can handle myself, Julia, I promise. But I need you to be strong right now and do what I ask, okay?"

I resist the urge to argue and nod, tears lodging in my throat.

He hands me the gun but I step back and throw my hands up. "No way! I have no idea how to use that. I hate guns."

"Listen to me!" he snaps. "The safety is off, all you do is point and pull the trigger. You probably won't need it, but just in case."

The cold steel is placed in my hand as he forces me to take it.

"You stay right here. Don't fucking move from this spot. If anyone comes through that door you shoot first and ask questions later, got it?" he says, pulling another gun from behind him.

When the hell did he put that there?

"What if it's you?" I ask.

"I'll make sure you know it's me."

The sound of the front door slamming comes from downstairs. Jaxson's head snaps to the window. "Fuck! Call Cooper now!" he orders, charging out of the room.

Looking out the window, I watch someone dressed all in black running across my yard and disappearing into the woods. A second later Jaxson bolts out of the house, barefoot with no shirt on, gaining on the person quickly.

With my hands shaking and tears building behind my eyes, I struggle to dial Cooper.

He picks up after the second ring. "Do you have any idea what time it is, asshole?"

"Cooper?" His name trembles past my lips on a sob.

"Julia? What's wrong?"

"You need to come quick. Someone broke into my house and Jaxson took off running after him. He has a gun and—"

"Okay, calm down. I'm on my way, stay on the phone with me, all right?"

Tears stream down my face as I nod my head.

"Julia, you still there?"

"Yes, sorry, I'm here. Just please hurry. I'm scared for Jaxson."

"I'm heading to my truck now, I'll be there in a few minutes, can you…" His voice fades out when I hear another noise come from downstairs.

"Shhh!" I tell him to be quiet and listen more closely. Slowly, I walk to my bedroom door, the sound getting more profound. "There's a noise coming from downstairs, it sounds like whimpering."

"Julia, just stay where you are. I'm almost there."

"What if someone is hurt?"

"I'll deal with it when I get there. I mean it, don't move!"

I know I should heed the warning but my instincts have me pushing forward, my steps slow and quiet as I descend the stairs.

"Damn it, Julia, are you fucking listening to me?"

"I'll keep you on the phone," I promise.

I ignore his heated curse, and pay close attention to my surroundings, the gun still firmly in my hand. Once I reach the bottom of the stairs, I'm able to pinpoint where it's coming from. "It's in the kitchen," I whisper and now realize that it isn't a whimper but a squeaking sound.

My heart is pounding so loud I'm surprised I can hear anything else besides its thundering beat. On shaking legs, I enter the kitchen, and what I see has my blood running cold and bile rising in my throat.

The phone slips from my hand as a scream shatters my chest.

Jaxson

Gun in hand, I charge down the stairs and out of the house to see the guy running into the woods. My bare feet pound the earth, gravel biting into the bottoms as I push forward, keeping him in sight.

"Jennings, is that you, you motherfucker?"

At first, I thought maybe it was that asshole Vince from tonight. But this guy isn't big enough to be him. My heart pumps faster, lungs working harder, as I gain on him.

You're mine, you son of a bitch.

A piercing scream rips through the night, stopping me in my tracks. I look back toward the house, realizing it's Julia. Fear grips hold of me and I start back the way I came, running faster than I thought myself possible.

"Julia?" I call out, barreling through the door. I move for the stairs at break neck speed but stop when I hear her in the kitchen. Dread curls its icy fingers around my heart as I enter inside and find her on the ground, retching and crying. I drop down next to her, my hand pushing aside her hair. "Julia, what's wrong? What happened?"

Before she has a chance to answer, my attention draws to the left and I see a gutted coyote hanging from the ceiling, a chain wrapped around its neck as it sways above the table.

"Jesus!"

Half of the kitchen is a fucking bloodbath from its insides, including the large window where blood spells out: *You're next, whore.*

Rage pumps through my blood with unrelenting fury. The sound of Julia's cries yank my attention back to her. "It's okay, I got you." Scooping her up in my arms, I carry her into the living room and that's when Cooper bolts through the door, almost throwing it off its hinges.

"Is she all right? Damn it, Julia. You scared the shit out of me. What happened?"

I jerk my head toward the kitchen, indicating for him to see for himself and take a seat on the couch. Julia curls into me, my arms vibrating from her trembling body.

Cooper walks back out of the kitchen, his jaw locked and eyes tight. "I guess you didn't catch the son of a bitch."

I shake my head. "I almost had him, but then I heard her scream and left him in the woods to run back here."

A couple of deputies come running in shortly after. "Sheriff?"

Coop orders them outside. "Get out in the woods across the way and search for him. He's probably gone by now, but look for anything that can link us to him." His eyes shift back to me. "What was he wearing?"

"All black with a hood over his head, medium build, about six feet tall. He's armed with at least a knife," I tell him, thinking about the gutted animal in the kitchen.

Once the deputies leave, I force Julia to look at me, hating the pain and fear that are in her eyes. "Why did you come down here? I told you to stay put."

"I'm sorry. I thought someone was hurt. I didn't know it was… that." She covers her ears, trying to block the sound of the swinging chain. "God, please make that sound stop!"

"I'm sorry, Julia, but we can't touch anything in here until the forensics team comes in," Cooper says regretfully.

I pull her into my chest and kiss the top of her head. "Let's go pack a bag and stay somewhere in town for tonight."

"You guys come stay at my place," Cooper says. "I need to call Kayla anyway, she was out of her mind when I flew out of the house."

Before I can accept his offer, Cade and Sawyer burst through the open front door.

"What the hell are you guys doing here?" Cooper asks.

"Kayla just called me freaking out," Sawyer explains. "She asked if I was with you guys. She wanted to know if Julia was okay."

"Jesus, that woman is fucking impatient," Cooper growls. Pulling out his phone, he steps out to call her.

"What the hell happened?" Sawyer asks, taking in the sight of Julia in my arms.

I nod toward the kitchen.

He and Cade both go check it out for themselves. By the time they walk back out, they look as angry as me, their expressions hard.

"Who?" Sawyer asks.

Just one word but it was the most important one.

"Meet us at Cooper's," I tell them.

They give me a tight nod then head out the door.

Standing with Julia in my arms, I start for the stairs. Vengeance burns in my blood, promising retribution.

The son of a bitch will pay for this.

CHAPTER 34

Julia

I walk into Kayla and Cooper's house, feeling cold and detached from my body.

Kayla takes my bag from me and pulls me in for a hug, one I cannot feel. "Come on, let's take this into the spare room," she says, ushering me with an arm around my shoulders.

Jaxson trails behind us, his anger silent yet deafening at the same time.

As we bypass the kitchen, I see Sawyer and Cade sitting at the table, looking as furious as Jaxson. They both greet me with a tight nod. I smile in return, or at least I try to but it's weak at best.

Once we enter the spare room, Kayla drops my bag on the bed and turns to me, concern bright in her eyes. "Can I get you something? Some tea maybe?"

"Yeah, that would be great, thanks."

The guys' heated conversation drops as we enter back into the kitchen.

"Come here, baby." Jaxson opens his arms for me and I don't hesitate, walking into them, my body curling into his as I settle on his lap. His strong arms bring me the warmth and security I crave.

The front door slams and Cooper comes walking in a moment later, looking tired and stressed. "Forensics are going through things now," he says, his eyes moving from Jaxson to me. "Julia, who has a key to your house?"

"Just Kayla. Why?"

"Are you sure about that?"

"Yes, I'm positive. Not even Grams has one."

His attention moves to Kayla next. "Go check your keys to see if it's still there."

"What's this about, Coop?" Jaxson asks.

"No one broke into that house. They got into it with a key, there's no way they even picked the lock."

What?

Kayla comes back a moment later with her keys in her hand. "Yeah, it's still here."

Silence and tension consumes the kitchen while everyone ponders their thoughts.

"Do you think it was that prick from earlier tonight?" Sawyer asks.

"Vince?" Kayla and I ask at the same time.

He shrugs. "Why not? The guy was pissed about getting tossed out, plus it gave him an opportunity to swipe a key from somewhere."

"It wasn't him," Jaxson says, his tone filled with certainty. "The guy I ran after wasn't big enough. Besides, I already know who it was."

Wyatt!

A chill races up my spine at the thought. When Kayla hands me my tea, I wrap both of my hands around the steaming mug, trying to soak in its warmth.

"I don't know, Jaxson," Cooper says, doubtful. "Things have been quiet for weeks. Nothing out of the ordinary has happened. Why start trouble now?"

It's at this very moment that I remember the phone calls. "Well, something out of the ordinary has been going on," I tell them quietly.

Jaxson tenses, and everyone's eyes snap to me.

Regret plagues me as I focus only on Jaxson. "I'm sorry, I should have told you sooner."

"Tell me what?"

"I've been getting phone calls all week."

"Jesus, Julia! All fucking week and you're just now telling me?"

"Well, at first I just thought it was the wrong number, or kids playing a prank. No one said anything, they would just hang up. But the last two times I could hear someone breathing and—"

"For fuck's sake!"

"How many did you get?" Cooper asks.

"About one a day, all on my landline, not cell phone."

"I'll go question him tomorrow."

"Come on, Cooper," Jaxson snaps, his voice harsh. "It's not like the asshole is going to admit to it. He went too far this time, I'm dealing with him myself."

"No, you're not! I'm serious. Don't you do something stupid and make me have to arrest my best fucking friend."

Tense silence fills the air as they glare back at each other.

I rest my forehead on Jaxson's, my hand moving to his hard jaw. "He's right, Jax, please just let him handle it."

He remains silent, too angry right now to listen to reason.

A tired sigh escapes me and I press a soft kiss to his lips. "I'm going to go to bed." I climb off him and walk over to Cooper to hug him. "Thanks, Cooper, for everything."

"You're welcome but next time, you listen to me when I tell you to stay where you are."

"I will. I'm sorry." I turn and offer Sawyer and Cade a wave before heading out of the kitchen with Kayla following behind me.

"Do you want company?" she asks.

"Sure, I'd love some."

With a smile she follows me into bed. We both curl up on our sides and face each other.

"Are you going to be all right?" she asks quietly.

"Yeah, I just wish I could erase the image I have in my head. It was terrible, Kayla."

She reaches for my hand, her fingers folding around mine. "Don't worry, Jules. Coop will make the son of a bitch pay."

I hope she's right because if not, the next time it might not be an animal hanging from the ceiling. It could very well be me.

Jaxson

Cooper and I argue for a long while before I finally give in and let him handle things—for now. The fury that pumped through my body earlier has now settled in a low simmer, always there but controllable.

"Call us if you need help. You know we have your back," Sawyer says as he and Cade stand from the table.

I climb to my feet also and decide now is a good time to tell them about my decision about the Admiral. "I'm turning down the mission, especially now. I'm not leaving Julia."

Sawyer nods. "It's a good decision. I'll deal with the admiral."

"Thanks." I head out of the kitchen and stop short at the entrance to the spare room, a grin tugging at my mouth from the sight before me. "Hey, Coop, come get your woman out of my spot."

All three guys approach the doorway and peek in to see Kayla and Julia curled on their sides facing one another, their hands linked between their bodies as they soundly sleep.

"Aw, and look, they're both wearing your shirts. Someone take a picture," Sawyer chuckles.

Cooper walks over and lifts Kayla in his arms. "No, Coop, not with Jaxson and Julia here," she mumbles.

The three of us burst into muffled chuckles.

Grinning, he turns back to us and shrugs. "What can I say, I'm always on her mind."

Once he walks out, I close the door behind me and start removing my clothes.

"Jax?" Julia whispers, stirring awake.

"Yeah, baby."

"Did you and Cooper work everything out?"

"Yeah." I crawl into bed and pull her to me, needing to feel her warmth.

She buries her face in my neck, her lips planting heated kisses. Lust begins to stir in my blood, mixing with the deep seated rage. Groaning, I palm her ass in both of my hands, bringing her closer.

She sits up in a flash, straddling my hips and swiftly pulls my shirt off her body, bringing my dick to life with a jolt.

"I need you. I need to feel you right now." Her voice is frantic and hands urgent. "I can't get the image of that poor animal out of my head, and—"

I flip her over, cutting her off before she can fall into hysterics. "I've got you, baby." I pull her against me, her back to my front then lift her top leg and bring it back over mine. Grabbing her hip, my fingers curl in the silk fabric of her panties and I shred them from her body.

A harsh moan parts her lips. "As hot as that is, you really need to stop doing it or I'm not going to have any panties left."

"It's faster, and right now I don't have the patience to take them off of you any other way." I slide my hand between her legs, our groans mingling in the air when I feel her soaked and ready. "Always so wet and ready for me," I whisper, trailing my lips along her shoulder.

"Always for you."

I pull my underwear down just enough to free my cock, then enter her in one hard thrust.

She gasps, her head falling back on my shoulder. "God, yes. I need you."

"You have me." My lips brush the shell of her ear, teeth grazing as I pump into her warm body. Sweat builds between our skin, my hands palming her breasts as I fuck her hard and deep. "Feel me, baby. Only me."

"I do. It's all I feel," she whimpers, pushing back greedily with each thrust.

Reaching in front of her, I slide my finger through her wet slit, finding her swollen nub.

"Jaxson." My name is the only warning I get before her orgasm claims her. Her pussy locks down on me, gripping my cock like a tight vise and sucking it greedily into its hot depth.

"Good girl, come all over my cock." The dirty words drag another moan from her throat. Once I know I've claimed every bit of pleasure she has to give me, I allow myself my own release.

Afterward, I hold her close, my arms banded tight around her. "I'll take care of this, Julia, I promise."

I'll give Cooper his time, but after that, the motherfucker is mine.

Lifting my hand, she brings it to her mouth, her lips pressing a soft kiss to my palm. "I love you, Jaxson." The words are only a soft murmur in the dark but have the power to heal and destroy at the same time.

I drop a kiss on the back of her neck, a burning ache taking up residence in my chest. Once again I hate myself for not saying it back.

CHAPTER 35

Julia

A week later I'm in the very place I thought I'd never be able to step foot in again—my kitchen. Jaxson took care of making sure it was thoroughly cleaned; he even bought me a new table. I can even still smell the fresh paint on the walls and I shudder when I think about why it needed a paint job to begin with.

Things have been strained between us lately, to say the least. Ever since we found out from Cooper that Wyatt had an airtight alibi for that night, Jaxson has been on edge. There's a quiet rage about him now that wasn't there before. He's always on guard, not letting me go anywhere by myself, and gets angry if I even suggest it.

He's been having nightmares, too, but anytime I try to talk about it with him, he says he's fine and closes himself off from me. Before all of this, things were so amazing for us. I could feel him opening up to me, letting me in more than he ever has before, but since that night he's completely shut me out and it breaks my heart. To make matters worse, I've been feeling terrible lately. The stress is really starting to get to me.

My phone rings, pulling me out of my depressing thoughts. Before I can answer it Jaxson comes charging in, throwing his hand up at me, to stay put and let him answer it.

"Hello." He snaps the greeting into the phone, his icy tone annoying me.

What if it's my grams?

"Who's this? Yeah, hold on."

He hands me the phone. "Some Don Thomson from Foothills Elementary."

Gasping, I rip the phone from him and pray this is the call I've been waiting for. "Hello, Mr. Thomson?"

A huge smile takes over my face as Don tells me I got the job. I start dancing around silently, fist pumping the air. He tells me I'll be subbing until Christmas, but after that my position will become full-time, and I'll be teaching second grade. I thank him for the opportunity and hang up.

I look up at Jaxson to see him leaning against the counter, watching me with a smile. "I got the job! I got the job! I got the job!" I cheer, launching myself into his arms.

His chuckle rumbles against my ear as he holds me tight. "Congratulations, Jules, you're going to be a great teacher."

It's the first time in a week I've heard his tone soft and genuine. It warms my heart and makes my throat tight. I rest my forehead against his and bring my lips to his, showing him how much I've missed him. When I pull back, there's a fire in his eyes that I haven't seen since we came back. He leans in for another taste but I push away from him, my stomach suddenly rebelling.

"Oh no!" Covering my mouth, I run to the bathroom and slam the door behind me. I barely make it to the toilet before emptying the contents of my stomach. Moaning, I lean my head against the side of the toilet, the cold porcelain bringing me a small measure of relief.

I startle when a wet cloth touches my forehead. My eyes spring open and I see Jaxson staring back at me in concern.

"Oh god, did you really just watch me throw up?" I groan. "That's so not hot."

He chuckles, finding my distress amusing. "There's nothing you could do that would make you '*not hot*.'" His hand cups my clammy cheek, his expression sobering though. "How long has this been going on?"

I shrug. "Not long. I think it's just the stress running me down."

"Make an appointment for the doctor, Jules."

"I'm fine, it's just the flu or something."

"I still want you to book an appointment, just in case, all right?"

"Okay." I relent with a sigh.

"Can I get you anything?"

I smile, my heart warming at his kindness. "No, I'm okay but thank you. I'm going to call Grams and tell her my good news."

He helps me to my feet and stays close while I rinse my mouth and splash cold water on my face. Once I feel a little more refreshed, I head upstairs and call Grams. She shares in my excitement and makes plans for next week to take both Jaxson and I out for supper to celebrate.

After my phone call with her, I go online to check my bank account. I had a decent amount in savings but without a steady paycheck until after Christmas, I may need to look into a part-time job. When I click on my balance, my eyes widen in shock, bugging out of my head at the number before me. "What on earth? This can't be right." Going through my history, I see there's no mistake, someone deposited ten thousand dollars into my account.

Who would do that? Grams? No, she would have told me, wouldn't she?

Logging off, I head down into the kitchen and grab a Coke from the fridge. I lean against the counter and think about why Grams would deposit money and not say something.

"What's wrong?" Jaxson asks from the kitchen table.

"Someone deposited ten thousand dollars in my account. It could only be Grams, but why would she not—"

"It was me."

I tense, a frown pulling between my brows. "What? Why would you do that?"

"Because I told you I would pay you back for Germany."

My eyes narrow, anger igniting in my blood. "First off, Jaxson, it was nowhere near ten thousand dollars. And secondly, I told you I didn't want your damn money."

He shrugs easily. "Don't worry about."

His blatant attitude only angers me further. I slam my drink down on the counter. "Are you listening to me? I am not taking it, so you can forget about it."

"Yes, you are."

My teeth grind at the order. "No. I'm not. I'm going to the bank tomorrow, withdrawing that money, and giving it back."

"What's your problem? Just take the damn money."

"No! I am not your whore."

He shoots to his feet, knocking the chair over in his haste. "What the fuck are you talking about?"

"Just because you're screwing me, it doesn't give you the right to deposit money into my account. Who the hell do you think you are? How could you…" I trail off and grab onto the counter for support, suddenly feeling lightheaded.

"Will you calm down?" He starts over to me in concern but I throw my hand up, holding him back.

Once the dizziness passes, I straighten and push away from the counter. "I'm giving the money back and that's final." Without another word, I head upstairs to my room and slam the door.

An hour later when I'm still too angry to face him, I decide to run a bubble bath, hoping it will help calm me. Throwing my hair up in a messy bun, I turn on my iPod for music and climb into the hot, sudsy water. It isn't long before my tight muscles begin to ease and I feel slightly more relaxed. The big, claw foot tub is my favorite place in the house, and when I say big, I mean massive. I could stretch out at the bottom of it and my feet still wouldn't hit the end.

Resting against the pink bath pillow, I close my eyes and hum softly to the song playing, Pink's duet with Nate Russ, "Just Give Me A Reason".

A moment later, I hear the click of the door and the air around me becomes hotter, awareness seeping into my body when I feel someone's gaze on me. Already knowing who it is, I open my eyes and find Jaxson leaning against the closed bathroom door, watching me; his fierce expression making my heart skip a beat.

"Are you still mad at me?"

"Yeah," I answer truthfully but softly.

His lips twitch with a smile before he starts toward me, his strides slow and confident as he peels his shirt off, revealing absolute perfection. His body is hard and strong, capable of both pleasure and pain.

My pulse races as I wait for him to take off his pants and join me, but he doesn't. Instead, he kneels on the floor beside the tub then leans over and cups the side of my neck, his thumb stroking over my thrumming pulse. The simple touch is electrifying; goose bumps break out over my body, even though I'm surrounded by hot water.

"Please take the money, Jules." His soft tone contradicts the fire that's in his eyes.

My gaze narrows. "No! And don't think for one second that I don't know what you're up to."

"I don't know what you're talking about," he says, leaning in to kiss my neck.

I hold him back. "Yes, you do. Now get your sexy lips away from me."

Chuckling, he pulls my hand away, holding it captive as he presses his lips to the base of my throat. His skillful tongue tastes and teeth nip the sensitive skin.

Oh god!

Heat surges through my blood, desire flooding every part of my body.

He trails warm kisses up my neck, moving for my lips. I try to turn my head to the side but he grasps my chin firmly between his thumb and finger, holding me in place, while his lips descend upon mine. My mouth remains soft and slack, as I try not to give in to the temptation but oh god, it's difficult.

"Come on, baby, kiss me, I know you want to."

"Uh-uh."

He continues his teasing assault, swiping his tongue across my top lip then grabbing my bottom between his teeth. And it's the little sting that breaks me. Moaning, I wrap my arms around his neck and kiss the ever-loving heck out of him.

A feral growl erupts from him, my lips tingling from the vibration of it. One hand dips into the water, grabbing my hip, then slides up my stomach to my breast. He circles my nipple with his finger, teasing but never touching.

When I pull away to take in air, he moves to my throat. "Come in here with me," I plead breathlessly, gripping his bare shoulders.

"I'm not much of a bath guy, Jules, but fuck do you make me wish I was." He sinks both hands in the water and spans my hips. "Sit up a bit, baby." He helps me move into a higher position, bringing my breasts out of the water, bubbles lightly surrounding them. "Seeing you all hot and wet like this…" A rough sound erupts from the back of his throat as he bends down, and sucks a stiff nipple into his mouth with heated force.

A heated cry spills from me, my clit swelling from the almost too much pain. He blows on the aching tip, soothing the sting before moving on to the next one, giving it the same greedy attention it thrives for.

"Please, Jaxson," I whimper, needing more.

"What do you want, baby?"

"Touch me."

"I am touching you."

"No, here." I shamelessly bring his hand between my legs, my hips lifting.

"My fucking pleasure." His fingers delve, immediately finding the spot that craves his attention.

A heated whimper shoves from my throat, my knees falling open to give him more access. "Touch yourself, Jules."

I tense at the rough command, my eyes lifting to his. "What?"

He grabs one of my hands and places it on my breast. "Touch yourself. Show me how you like it." Heat invades my cheeks at the thought and he senses my hesitation. "Don't be embarrassed, baby, it's just me."

As apprehensive as I am, I can't deny the way my body burns with the need to give him this. Closing my eyes, I let the sensation of his fingers take over my body, focusing on the pleasure. My hand begins kneading my breast, my sensitive nipple feeling like silk against my palm. A fiery moan leaves my lips as Jaxson's finger strokes a little harder and faster. I slide my other hand up and cup the other breast, freely giving into the pleasure I can bring myself.

"That's it, baby. Fuck, that's sexy." The rough arousal in his voice empowers me, and I completely abandon myself to my touch. I feel his eyes upon me, his hot gaze heating the air around us. "Have you touched yourself before, Jules?" He follows up the question by inserting a single finger inside of me.

I gasp and arch into his touch. "Yes," I answer breathlessly, "and I always thought of you when I did. Always imagined it was your hands on me."

"Jesus."

I cry out as he pushes a second finger inside of me. Pleasure soars through my body, and I vaguely hear Jaxson undoing his belt. My eyes snap open to see him stroking himself, and it's the most erotic thing I've ever seen. When pre-cum spills over the flushed tip I lick my lips, wishing it was in my mouth.

"Do you like watching me, Julia?" he asks, his fingers stroking that hidden spot deep inside of me.

"Yes," I moan, thrusting against his hand.

"Since the day I've laid eyes on you, you're all I thought about every time I stroked my cock. I'd imagine what you'd look like over me, under me, on your hands and knees in front of me," he growls. "And you're even fucking better than I imagined."

"Jaxson," I whimper, feeling myself teeter on the edge of destruction. He brings the heel of his hand against my clit and it's exactly what I need. A harsh cry flees from me, the intense orgasm crashing through my body and stealing the breath from my lungs.

"That's it, baby, come all over my fingers." He keeps his rhythm, dragging out the pleasure until I'm soft and limp.

I look down at his fist, as he pumps himself faster. Sitting up, I lean over the tub and stop his efforts. "I want to finish you with my mouth."

He stands in a flash, dropping his jeans a little more to fully free his cock. Before he can even guide it to my mouth I'm on him, sucking him as deep as I can possibly go, making sure my hand strokes where I can't reach. I glance up to see him watching me, his jaw clenched and eyes wild with lust.

His throaty groans spur me on as I slowly suck back to the head and give him a show, swirling my tongue around the swollen tip.

"That's it, baby, suck my dick, just like that." He pulls my hair from its hold on the top of my head and tightly wraps my loose strands around his fist, creating a delicious sting on my scalp. He controls my rhythm, pumping his hips, filling my mouth. When he hits the back of my throat, I hold him there and swallow.

"Shit!" He tries to pull my head back but I fight against it. "Julia, I'm going to come any second, so if you don't want to swallow, you better move your mouth."

I moan, letting him know I want it, and quicken my pace, sucking him harder and faster.

"Fuck!" His head falls back on a roar as his cock pulses, spilling a hot stream of semen down my throat. I keep my efforts strong and drink every bit of pleasure that spills from him.

"Jesus." He falls to his knees and gives me a mind numbing kiss before resting his forehead against mine, his hand cupping the side of my neck.

No words are spoken but none need to be. The love and devotion in his eyes says it all.

CHAPTER 36

That night, another nightmare plagues me and it's the mother of all nightmares—the night I finally got out of hell, but not before others paid the price…

I pull against the chains with all the strength I have left, my wrists feeling close to snapping. Little bits of gravel from the wall crumble around me, and I'm shocked to discover I still have this much strength left. Cade and Sawyer struggle as hard as I do, all of us fighting for Faith and Anna's sake.

Please let one of us make progress. The memory of Anna's screams fuel me with adrenaline and strength I didn't know I still possessed.

The sound of our cell being unlocked has me stopping my attempts; Sawyer and Cade immediately follow and go slack. Irina walks in, the wife of one of our captors, and the mother of the boy who set us up. She holds a finger to her lips, her gaze darting around nervously, tears streaking down her face. "Okay, I'll help you," she says, whispering to Sawyer.

My aching muscles tense, suspicion rearing inside of me. "Why now?"

We've been asking for her help all week, and each time she coldly refused; she also helped inject that shit into us in the beginning.

"Because they just killed my boy," she sobs, throwing her hand over her mouth.

"Shit!" Cade hisses. Even though the kid helped with the ambush, you could see he had a soft spot for him.

"Listen, I don't have much time. Something's going down in about an hour. I don't know how much I can help once they're in here, but if you guys can overpower them, I'll help get you out. There's only going to be six of them on the whole compound tonight. The rest are picking up a shipment at a location hours from here, and they're not due back until tomorrow."

"Where's the American girl, Anna?" I ask. When her eyes dart away, panic surges through my veins. "Where the fuck is she?"

She swallows nervously. "She's in one of the rooms at the other end of the building. Same floor as you. She's set to have a customer in less than an hour."

Dread sinks into my gut, heavy and hard. "You need to get her out of there, I won't make it in time."

She shakes her head. "I can't help her. They will kill me and then I will be no good to you guys."

"She's right, Jaxson," Sawyer cuts in. "Listen, we need to come up with a plan, then once we overpower the fuckers, we'll go get her. We have no other choice."

I grit my teeth, not liking that option.

"I will try to stall the customer," she says, trying to make me feel better, but it doesn't. Not one damn bit.

"Can you tell us what's happening? What their plan is?" Sawyer asks.

"I honestly don't know, but they're bringing his woman down with them," she says, pointing to Cade.

Cade's head snaps up, his eyes hard.

"They said they're going to test your loyalty and honor."

Well that doesn't sound good at all.

Someone barks out Irina's name, making her jump in fear. "Listen, I have to go, I will do what I can."

"Irina," Sawyer calls out before she can leave. "We'll take you with us. We can get you out of here."

She shakes her head, a sob tearing from her. "I don't care if I live or die anymore, I only lived for my boy. He wanted you guys out of here, that's why I'm going to help you." She closes the door, leaving us in silence with our thoughts.

"They're going to try turning us against each other," I say quietly.

"Yeah, and they're going to use Faith to do it," Cade grits through clenched teeth. "I'm going to kill them, every last one of them. We don't leave here until they're all fucking dead." His rage ignites a fire and fuels my own.

"What's most important is getting Anna and Faith out of here. That comes even before killing them. And we need to take Irina, too," Sawyer says, being the sensible one as always.

Less than an hour later, heavy boot-falls make their way down the hall to us. In the last week, anytime we heard this sound, pain and torture always followed.

Not this time.

A calmness settles over me, one that leaves me cold and detached from my body. One where I don't feel human… but like a machine.

"Where are you taking me?" A female voice cuts through the air, thick with tears but filled with strength.

Only four out of the six guys enter our cell. Two of them on either side of a slender woman that's dressed in a long, black silk nightgown. Bruises mar every inch of bare skin that's exposed, including her face.

"Cade? Oh god, oh no!" She rips free of her captors and runs to Cade, sinking to her knees in front of him. She wraps her arms around his neck and sobs into his shoulder. "I'm so sorry. I'm so sorry, Cade!"

Why the hell is she sorry?

I watch Cade's head dip, murmuring something in her ear.

"Not so fast, bitch." One of the assholes who brought her in grabs her by the hair, dragging her away.

"Let go of me!" she screams, kicking and fighting. The guy flips around and backhands her across the face, knocking her to the ground.

An enraged roar rips from Cade, ricocheting off the walls. "I'm going to fucking kill you, every single one of you motherfuckers are dead!"

Shit!

"Is that so, soldier?" The one whose nose I broke walks closer to him, getting into his face. "Wait until you see what I have in store for you. I'm going to fucking break you."

Cade peers back at him, a lethal smile lifting his lips. "You can't break something that's already broken."

His response has another sob spilling from Faith.

"We're not soldiers, you fucking idiot, how many times do we have to tell you assholes that? We're N-a-v-y S-E-A-L-s," Sawyer taunts, trying to deflect the attention off Cade.

The guard walks over to him and sends a blow to the center of his chest with his baton, the spikes at the end of it ripping the flesh from his body. Other than the slight flinch and his lungs fighting to pull in a breath, he makes no sound.

"Navy SEALs…soldiers," he spits the words. "They're all the same, you all live and breathe your honor. Well, boys, we're going to see just what it will take for you to break your so-called honor." He turns to the men behind him. "Set her up."

Two of the men grab Faith again, setting her to her knees. The guy walks up to her, leaning down to get in her face. Faith glares back at him, defiance raging in her eyes.

Glad to see the fuckers haven't broken her completely.

"We're going to have some fun with this man you seem so smitten with. Maybe you can show him some of the new tricks we have taught you." He straightens, looking over at Cade. "Did you know, soldier, that many of us fucked her?"

Oh shit!

"Tied her to a bed and fucked her while she begged us not to. And after we finished, she got to choke on our dicks."

Faith sobs, her head hanging in shame as their laughter fills the cell.

Hate boils in my blood, merging with the deep seated anger. I can only imagine what Cade's feeling right now.

"Akram! Get the soldier ready."

The one referred to as Akram walks nervously over to Cade.

Please let him keep his cool.

He keeps Cade's wrists chained but unlocks them from the steel in the wall and drags him over to the other end of the cell. He sets him up the same way Faith is, forcing him on his knees. Then taking his makeshift weapon, he starts beating the shit out of him, his flesh and blood tearing from his body and spilling across the cell.

"No, stop! Please stop!" Faith's desperate pleas echo through the stale air that rains with rage, fear, and death. Finally, the fucker tires out, and other than Cade heaving for breaths, he remains calm and still.

The one barking orders walks over, relieving a guard from Faith's side, and takes up his position before pointing to me. "Grab that one first. The one who broke my nose." He smirks at me. "I told you, you would pay for that."

I'm unlocked the same way Cade was, my wrists chained in front of me. I make it difficult for him to drag me, letting him think I'm weaker than I am. My body may be weak, but my vengeance is stronger.

The guard positions me in front of Cade so I'm standing over him.

"Tell me, soldier, would you ever turn on a fellow brother?" The one whose nose I broke asks.

I remain silent, trying to figure out what his plan is when I'm delivered a painful blow to my spine, making my legs crumble beneath me. My teeth grind as I breathe through the pain.

"Get up!" The guard yanks me back to my feet. "Now answer Allah."

Allah? He calls himself God?

"No," I croak out my answer.

"No?" He laughs. "There's nothing that would make you kill this man in front of you? What if it was to save this woman here—his woman?"

I shake my head.

"Give him the knife," he orders Akram.

Faith whimpers in fear as Akram hands me the dagger.

Sawyer's right, they're fucking idiots.

"Don't get too excited and fill that head of yours with any ideas." The leader who calls himself Allah pulls a knife and holds it to Faith's throat. "Now, let's just see how loyal and honorable you are. I want you to end this so-called broken soldier's life. If you don't we will fuck this woman in front of you and make you all watch her beg until the moment I end her life."

"Oh God, please, no!" The desperate sob that escapes Faith has fire burning my chest.

"Shut up, bitch!" he yells, backhanding her.

Cade's jaw locks, fury like I've never seen raging in his eyes. "Do it! Just fucking do it!"

Not yet.

"No! Don't," Faith screams. "Please don't hurt him. I don't care what they do to me. Don't hurt him!"

The bastard laughs. "He's even telling you it's okay. You must choose soldier—this bitch's dignity or your honor to your brother?"

I raise the knife over my head, the blade pointing down at Cade.

He nods, his eyes hard.

Not yet, wait for it.

"No! Stop, please don't!" she pleads again.

"Bitch, if you don't shut the—"

Now.

It happens so fast, my dagger going right in the center of their leader's forehead. The knife he was holding to Faith's neck goes slack and falls from his hand. Before the others have time to react, Cade and I are on them.

I turn on the bastard behind me; my chains going around his throat, pulling tight until his neck snaps.

Grabbing the keys from his pocket, I run to Sawyer, knowing we will need him when the others come. I hear Faith scream and Cade's roar behind me.

Quickly freeing Sawyer and myself, I spin around, charged and ready for battle, except I find nothing but a bloodbath.

Ho-ly shit!

Every single guard is massacred. Most of their insides lie on the cold cement floor, including the leader who I had already killed with the dagger. Their blood soaks Cade's body where he holds a hysterical Faith in his arms.

Irina comes running in, unaffected by the gory scene. "This way," she orders, waving us along.

"The girl—Anna—where is she?" I ask.

She shakes her head. "You don't have time. There are two other guards who are going to come in here any—"

I grab her arm and yank her to me. "Listen, bitch, I'm not leaving here without her, so tell me where the fuck she is."

She lifts a stubborn chin. "Down that hall and to the left, then it's the third door on your right. But you will not make it out of here in time if you do this."

My eyes shift to Sawyer and Cade. "Go. You guys get Faith out of here. I'll get Anna and meet up with you."

"I'm not leaving you," Sawyer says.

"I'll be fine." I toss him one of the guns I grabbed from the guards. "You cover Cade. I'll be right behind you guys."

Without another word, I haul ass, running faster than I thought possible in my condition. My thoughts only on Anna.

Please let me make it in time.

Her desperate screams assault my ears as I near the end of the hallway. "Anna," I bellow, my hand turning the locked door knob. Backing up I kick the door in, and what I see will forever be ingrained into memory.

I was too late.

The bastard on top of her turns around, making eye contact with me. "Wait your turn, asshole."

A white-hot fury fuels a rage so deep inside of me it coils around every part of my body like a snake, and I completely lose control. Pushing forward, I pull the son of a bitch off her, and land blow after blow to his face. His bones shatter under my fist as I pummel him hard and fast, unleashing a violence inside of me I've never felt.

"J-Jaxson?" Anna's panicked voice snaps me out of my rage, and I look down to realize I'm beating a dead guy. I drop him to the floor and turn around to find her huddled in the corner, a bloody sheet pulled around her naked body. Her face is swollen and bruised, tears mixing with blood.

Her innocence stolen.

I swallow past the guilt in my throat and push aside my emotions. "Where are your clothes?"

"They took them from me," she cries.

"Can you walk?"

"I don't think so. The fat guy hit my ankle with his baton and I think it's broken." She covers her face as a sob of defeat explodes from her.

"It's going to be okay." I say but know it isn't true. The damage has been done. I look back to the asshole I just beat to death and find his gun not far from him. Picking it up, I make my way over to her. "Let's go, we're getting out of here, kid."

She launches herself at me, keeping the sheet against her. "Thank you," she cries. "Thank you for not leaving without me."

I hug her back, pain searing my chest. "Tie the sheet around you, I'm going to carry you out." Once she does I hand her the gun, and she takes it without question. "Have you shot one before?"

She shakes her head.

"The safety is off. You're going to have to wrap your legs around my waist for me to carry you out. It's the only way I can cover what's in front of me. I need you to keep this trained behind me. If you see anyone, you aim and pull the trigger. Do you understand?"

Tears continue to spill from her, but she nods and does what I ask.

"Wait!" she says when I begin to lift her. She reaches under her pillow and pulls out my pendant. "I got it back from that guy. I saw it hanging out of his pocket when he was dragging me, so I grabbed it. He thought I was trying to take his keys, that's why he hit me."

I stare down at the tarnished medal in her hand, pain restricting my chest at the sacrifice she made for me. "Thank you," I choke out.

"You're welcome." She closes it in her fist then wraps her arms around my neck again. "Okay, I'm ready."

Picking her up, I get us the fuck out of there. I head the way Irina told me to. My limbs are heavy, the strain of my broken body fighting against me but I clench my teeth and push through it.

I will not stop now.

A scream of terror erupts from Anna and I feel her tense in my arms. Instinct has me turning around and pulling the trigger. A guard drops, my bullet hitting him in the head. Twisting back around, I push myself harder, faster.

"I'm sorry," she sobs. "I panicked."

I don't respond, not wanting to waste any energy I have left. Finally, I hit the side door and push through it into the night. It takes my eyes a moment to adjust to the darkness.

"Jaxson, straight ahead," Sawyer yells from a distance.

My feet pummel the earth as I try to keep a steady pace. Out of nowhere Irina comes running up to me. "Over here, you have to—"

Thwack!

She falls right in front of me, a bullet hitting her in the chest.

"Fuck!" I drop to the ground on top of Anna, not knowing what direction it came from.

Sawyer charges out of the bushes, his gun shooting wildly over top of me. He leans down to pick up Irina.

"Leave me," she chokes out, blood sputtering from her mouth.

"No!" He scoops her up in his arms. "Come on, man, we have no choice, we have to make a run for it."

Somehow I find the strength to get Anna and myself both up. With heavy limbs, I follow Sawyer into the bush, only to hear another shot go off.

I bolt upright in bed, my body covered in a cold sweat and heart pounding wildly.

"Jax?" Julia sits up beside me, her hand going to my shoulder.

"I'm fine. I just need a minute." Getting up, I head to the bathroom, needing the privacy. The last thing I want is for her to see just how fucked-up I really am.

Julia

I jump at the slam of the bathroom door and hate that he's shutting me out again. A heavy sigh leaves me as I lie back down. This nightmare was by far the worst one yet. I glance at the bedside clock to see it's four in the morning.

Do I go to him?

At the sound of the shower turning on, I make my decision. Throwing the covers off with purpose, I climb out of bed. All I can do is try, if he shuts me out then I'll try again next time. I'll keep trying until he lets me in.

Entering the bathroom, I close the door behind me and watch Jaxson through the shower glass door. His hands are braced on the wall in front of him and head hanging low in defeat as water pours down his strong body.

My trepidation vanishes when I see how much he's hurting. I pull his shirt from my body and slide off my panties. Opening the shower door, I step in behind him, the thick steam enveloping me.

He's fully aware of my presence, yet he still tenses when I wrap my arms around him. My lips press to the wet mangled skin of his back as I try to ease his pain. Kissing the angel and his scars.

"Not a good idea, Julia. I don't have a lot of control right now." The pain that laces his words has me coming around to stand in front of him. He keeps his head down and under the spray, avoiding my gaze.

"Look at me, Jaxson," I order softly.

When he shakes his head, I step closer and frame his face between my hands, forcing his tortured eyes to mine. What I see staring back at me shatters my heart—despair, guilt, and most of all, self-loathing. His eyes are brimmed red with tears that desperately need to be shed, but he won't allow them to.

"Talk to me. Please, don't shut me out." Water drips from his dark hair and thick lashes, falling onto my face; his pain heavy in the humid air. "It's me, Jax. Let me in. Let me help you," I plead.

"I tried to get to her in time," he grinds out, his jaw flexing. "I tried so fucking hard, but I didn't make it. I was too late." Every word that spills from him is gruff with agony, completely breaking my heart.

"Who? Cade's girl?"

He shakes his head. "Anna," he chokes out, as if I should know who this person is. "She was only fourteen."

Oh god!

I swallow past the bile rising in my throat. "Did she die?"

He shakes his head. "No, but they took her innocence, they robbed her of something she will never get back. I almost made it in time; if I could have gotten there ten minutes sooner I would have made it... Fuck!" he breathes out the curse; his chest heaving rapidly from holding in the pain that desperately needs to be let out.

"Jaxson. Cry. It's okay to cry. You're hurting yourself by keeping it in."

Panic flashes in his gaze and he quickly shakes his head, his eyes squeezing shut.

I'm about to lose him.

"Did you get her out in the end?" I ask, hoping to keep him from shutting down.

When his eyes open, I know it's too late. I've lost him. The pain and emotion that were in them, now masked.

"Yeah, I got her out," he answers.

"Then that's what matters. I know I don't know the whole story, and I probably couldn't even begin to understand if I tried. But you need to understand, you're only human. You can't control other people's actions. You did the best you could, and in the end it turned out to be enough because you saved her life."

He shakes his head, not believing me.

"Yes. You have to work through this or it's going to kill you." I wrap my arms around his body, my breasts pressing against his hard chest as I hold him close, wishing I could take his pain away.

My lips press against his chest, right over his steady heart as hot water rains down on us, my tongue catching the rivulets that run down his body.

His cock swells against my stomach as his arms come around me, bringing me in closer. "I need you," he rasps in my ear. "I need you to remind me of the good."

He picks me up, my legs wrapping around his waist as he pins me against the wall. We gaze at each other, steam billowing around us. It's as if we are in our own world and no one else can enter but us.

My hand moves to the side of his face. "All you need to do is look in the mirror and you'll be reminded of the good this world has to offer." He closes his eyes, wanting to shut me out, but I don't let him. I kiss across his jaw, bringing my lips to his ear. "You're the best man I've ever known, Jaxson. You're strong, honorable, and loyal. The best thing that ever happened to that little girl was having you in the wrong place at the right time. Just like me."

"Stop," he croaks, not wanting to hear my words. With his hand gripping the back of my hair, he tilts my head back and seals his mouth over mine.

It's devastating and beautiful all at the same time.

He arranges my legs so they hang in the crook of his arms, then in one smooth motion he enters me—completing me.

I sob against his lips at the perfection our bodies make. "You're so good. Perfect—perfect for me." I cry into his mouth as he thrusts deep inside of me. My arms cling to him as I let him use my body as an outlet for his pain. Water and tears mix down my face as I feel my orgasm begin to build.

Jaxson groans. "That's it, baby. I can feel it. You're close. So close." He speeds up his pace, slamming into me faster and deeper, hitting the exact spot that I need him to.

My orgasm washes over me, pleasure exploding through every cell in my body.

I open my eyes and collide with Jaxson's tortured ones, his expression soft with sorrow and vulnerability. I drop my forehead on his. "I love you, every amazing part of you." His breathing kicks up, his fingers imprinting into my wet skin. "Let go, Jax. I want to feel you come inside of me." Taking his bottom lip between my teeth, I nip the soft flesh sharply, knowing it's all he needs.

He burrows his face into my neck, groaning through the intensity of his pleasure.

We stay in our position, soaking in a state of bliss.

I feel myself starting to slip so I begin to unwind my legs from his waist, but he grips me tighter. "Don't leave me," he rasps, the desperate plea tugging at my heart.

I hug him close. "I'll never leave you. I'll stay for as long as you'll have me."

"Forever," he mumbles in my neck.

"Forever," I repeat the word, my heart filling with peace.

CHAPTER 37

Julia

"Well, Julia, I am happy to tell you that you're completely healthy," Dr. Bayer says, looking through my paperwork.

"So it's just stress then?"

"Actually, no. You're pregnant."

Shock slams into me like a freight train, my senses reeling. "Excuse me?" I choke out, swearing I misheard her.

She smiles. "You're pregnant."

"But… but that's impossible. You told me I couldn't get pregnant."

"No. I said your chances of getting pregnant were slim, but I didn't say it was impossible."

"But I'm on the pill."

Her expression sobers. "Yes, which is most likely how you got pregnant, it regulated your cycles, helping you to ovulate. This is very unusual, but I have heard of it happening before. However, you have to stop taking them now."

I'm pregnant.

My hand moves to my stomach, warmth spreading through my body.

"The last time we spoke you were not sexually active. Obviously that's changed?"

"Yes. It's very new, but he's someone I've known for a long time. Someone I've been in love with for a long time," I add softly.

Her smile returns. "Good to hear. I know how much it hurt when I told you about your diagnosis. We'll schedule you for an ultrasound so we can determine the due date." She writes something on a piece of paper and hands it to me. "This is the name of some prenatal vitamins you can pick up." She puts a gentle hand on my shoulder. "I'm happy this happened for you, Julia."

Emotion clogs my throat. "Me, too."

For as long as I can remember I've wanted to be a mother, and when I thought it would never happen for me, my heart broke into a million pieces. Finding out I am going to have the baby I've always wanted, and for it to also be Jaxson's…

Oh god, Jaxson.

Jaxson

I walk into Big Mike's gym to meet up with Cade and Sawyer. We set up a meeting with Mike to talk business. The more I've thought about buying into this gym, the more I want to do it.

Sawyer, Cade, and I have come up with some pretty cool ideas that we want to do with the place. And if I'm being honest, I like the idea of them sticking around. Yeah, Sawyer can drive me fucking crazy, especially when it comes to Julia. But other than Cooper, these guys are like the brothers I never had. We have been to hell and back together…literally. There are no other people I'd rather work side by side with than them.

"Hey, where's Julia?" Sawyer asks, he and Cade standing by the sparring ring.

"She has a doctor's appointment, then she's meeting with Kayla to talk wedding shit. Cooper said he'd bring her home after."

"How's she doing?" Cade asks.

I shrug. "Better, I guess. She found out the other day she got the job at the elementary school, so that has helped keep her mind off things."

"Are we going to deal with this fucker or what?" Sawyer asks.

I nod. "Yeah, we are. I just need to decide how I want to handle him. I don't want to make things hard for Coop."

"Just let us know when you have it figured out," Cade says.

"I will."

Big Mike pokes his head out of his office, a big grin eating up his face. "Come on in, boys, let's talk business."

Two hours later, agreements are made and things are set in motion for us to take over the gym. Normally, the thought of a commitment like this would have me freaking the hell out, but it actually feels good. Real good. And I can't wait to tell Julia.

CHAPTER 38

Julia

Anxiety surges through my veins, my heart beating rapidly the entire drive home.

"Everything all right, Julia? You seem quiet," Cooper asks as he turns down the gravel road that leads to my house.

Kayla grabs my hand, giving it a sympathetic squeeze. I wanted to tell Jaxson before anyone else, but Kayla knew right away something was wrong. So I cracked and told her, and I'm thankful I did. She was extremely happy for me and shared in my excitement, but I know she's also nervous about Jaxson's reaction.

We both are.

I try to paste a reassuring smile on my face. "Yeah, I'm fine. Just tired is all."

He doesn't buy it, but thankfully, lets it go.

Maybe I'm worrying over nothing. I know Jaxson said having kids was something he never wanted, but a lot has changed since then. And there's been a new peace over us since the night of his nightmare; the night he finally opened up to me. He told me he wanted me forever, surely that has to mean something.

My thoughts come to a halt when Cooper pulls into my driveway. "Thanks for the ride, Coop."

"No problem."

I give Kayla a hug. "I'll see you tomorrow morning, I can't wait to go dress shopping."

"Me, too," she says, then lowers her voice. "Call me if you need me."

I nod.

As I climb out of the truck, Jaxson walks out of the house to greet me, waving at Cooper as he pulls away.

"Hey, baby." He pulls me against him, his hands cupping my behind as he gives me one of his toe curling kisses.

My arms wrap around his neck and his scent envelops me, easing my anxiety. "Well, hello to you, too," I whisper against his lips.

"How was your appointment? What did the doctor say?"

My nerves come rushing back.

He picks up on it immediately. "Jules, baby, everything okay?"

I take a deep breath. "Yeah, but can we go inside and talk?"

He nods, his expression concerned.

Our hands link as we walk into the house and I lead him over to the couch in the living room. I turn to face him, my knee bouncing incessantly as I nervously chew on my thumbnail.

He pulls my hand away from my mouth. "Jules, you're freaking me out. What's going on? Did the doctor give you bad news? Are you sick?"

I shake my head. "No, it's nothing like that. Um… well…um…" I blow out a breath and steel myself. "I'm pregnant."

He doesn't move, doesn't even blink. He just stares at me, his eyes going flat.

Uh-oh.

"What did you just say?" he chokes out.

My heart thunders so hard I swear it's trying to crawl its way out of my throat. "I'm pregnant," I whisper.

He jumps to his feet, immediately pacing a hole in the floor. "How the fuck did this happen?" I assume it's a rhetorical question, so I don't answer. "I thought you couldn't get pregnant."

"I did, too. It turns out that my case is very unusual, but it has happened, and I'm one of the lucky ones."

His swift feet falter and he stops in his tracks, staring at me in outrage. "Lucky? Julia, there's nothing lucky about this. Fuck!" he bellows, storming into the kitchen.

I get up and follow after him. His arms are braced on the counter with his head down, his body vibrating with… well, I'm not sure what. Anger? Fear? Probably both.

Tentatively, I lay a hand on his back. "I know this is a shock, Jax. It was for me too, but everything will be okay. You'll see."

He throws my hand off him and spins around to face me. My heart drops into my stomach at the anger in his eyes. If I didn't know better, I'd swear he hates me right now. I try to push aside my emotions, knowing he's scared.

"None of this is okay, Julia. Not for you, not for me, and especially not for the fucking kid. Do you not remember who my father is?"

It suddenly becomes achingly clear what he fears most. "I know all about your father, and I'm glad I never had to meet him. But he has nothing to do with this. You're nothing like him, Jax." I reach for his hand but he pulls away from me.

"What the fuck are you talking about? I'm exactly like him, because that's all I knew growing up. Why do you think I said I never fucking wanted kids? What part did you not understand?"

My blood heats in anger, mixing with the hurt. "You're acting as if I did this on purpose for god's sake."

"Did you?"

My eyes narrow and I grind my teeth against the pain staking my chest. "Be careful, Jaxson, some things you can't take back once they're said. I am not manipulative or a liar, and you know it."

His jaw flexes.

With a deep breath, I try a different tactic. "Listen, I know you're in shock and probably a little scared." He scoffs but I continue, not letting him interrupt me. "So am I, but I'm also really happy. I didn't think this would ever happen to me. I thought I'd never get a chance to be a mother, and the best part of all, to me, is that it's yours. We love each other. We—"

"Don't put words into my mouth, Julia."

I flinch, his words slashing my heart like a cruel blade. Unable to hold them back any longer, the first of many tears spill down my cheeks. "Are you saying you don't love me, Jaxson? Huh? Is that what you're saying?"

"I'm telling you I don't want the fucking baby! But you're not listening to me, goddamn it!" He loses control. His fist slams into the fridge repeatedly before moving to grab my crystal vase full of flowers and throwing it to smash against the wall.

I cover my ears at the sound of glass shattering, my knees weakening in fear. "Stop it! You're scaring me!"

He grabs my upper arms firmly, but I keep my hands over my ears, trying to quiet his rage. "Good, it's about fucking time!"

I close my eyes, sobbing through his violence.

"I've told you for a long time that you should have stayed the fuck away, but you didn't listen, you kept trying to make yourself believe that—" His words die abruptly.

I take the chance at opening my eyes and what I see staring back at me makes me cry harder—fear, panic, and regret.

"Jesus, I'm so sorry," he says, pushing away from me. "I have to get the fuck out of here."

"No, Jaxson, don't leave," I beg, but it's too late. Within seconds the front door slams with his departure. I remain frozen, trying to absorb what just happened. When the pain is too much I crumble to my knees, his words ringing repeatedly in my head.

I don't want the fucking baby.

Time comes to a standstill as I cry amidst the broken glass around me. When my front door swings open I look up, thinking it's Jaxson, but see it's Sawyer and Cade.

Sawyer takes in the mess and hurries over to me. "Jesus, Julia, what the hell happened? Are you okay?"

I shake my head. I'm not all right, not with all of us hurting so much. Especially Jaxson.

"Will you please tell me what the fuck is going on? Jaxson called us to come here. As soon as we showed up, he tore out of here, without any explanation."

"He doesn't want the baby." Saying the words out loud is torture. "I'm pregnant, Sawyer, but he doesn't want us," I tell him, agony ripping through my already tattered heart.

His eyes widen for a fraction of a second before he expels a loud breath and takes me into his arms. "That dumbass motherfuckin' asshole."

"I thought he loved me," I sob.

"Don't think for one second that he doesn't. He's just an idiot who's fucked in the head. But trust me, Julia, he does."

"It's true, he does," Cade adds, speaking up for the first time.

I shake my head, not knowing what to believe anymore. I was so certain that he did, but after what just happened, I'm not sure anymore. Or maybe the sad truth is, it doesn't matter if he does, because maybe love isn't enough.

"Take her upstairs. I'll clean this up," Cade says.

"Come on." Sawyer helps me to my feet, keeping his arm around me as he walks me upstairs to my room. "Do you want me to call someone? Kayla maybe?"

"No, thank you. I'm just going to try and get some sleep. I need to be up early."

He nods but hesitates to leave, his eyes concerned.

"I'm sorry you guys got roped into staying here with me," I say, feeling guilty.

"I don't mind being here, Julia. I'm just sorry he's being such an ass right now."

I shrug. "I know he's scared. I just..." I pause, feeling another sob build in my throat. “I love him so much, Sawyer, that it hurts. I don’t want to lose him.”

He wraps his arms around me again, offering me the comfort I so desperately need right now. “Just give him some time. Let him get his head back on straight. But if I were you, I’d make the prick grovel his ass off when he does come back. And I know he will, sooner rather than later.”

I can only pray he’s right, because the thought of living without Jaxson completely destroys me.

CHAPTER 39

After driving through part of the night, I stopped at a motel just outside of my destination to catch a few hours of sleep, or at least, I tried to. But sleep proved impossible, because any time I closed my eyes, all I could see was her beautiful, tear-streaked face, pale with fear and twisted with agony; her body shaking while her hands covered her ears to quiet my violence.

I swallow past the knot in my throat, my teeth grinding against the ache in my chest. The one thing that matters most to me in the whole damn world, and I go and fuck it up. Who knew I could hate myself any more than I already did.

Now it's the crack of dawn, and I'm parked outside the one place I've been debating to visit since leaving the clinic—Anna's. The last time I saw her was in the hospital. She had asked me to come visit her. I'm not sure why last night, of all nights, I decided to finally come, but after I left the house, I drove for hours in a daze and this is where it took me.

She lives in a high-end neighborhood with big houses and vehicles that cost more than I ever came close to making in a year. Not surprising, since her father is a surgeon. I met her parents at the hospital. They seemed like really good people—good parents—which wasn't surprising considering the daughter they raised.

Glancing at the clock, I decide to wait another hour before knocking, not wanting to wake anyone up. I turn off the truck and drop my head against the headrest, trying not to think about the previous night, but it's impossible.

I'm pregnant.

Panic infiltrates my chest as the words float through my head. How the hell am I supposed to be a dad when my role model was an alcoholic who hated kids, especially his own. I doubt I'd be half as fucked-up if my mom had stuck around, but nope, she left because she was better off without my worthless father. I assume she thought she was better off without me too, since she didn't take me with her. I fight off the additional wave of pain that thought brings on.

Julia is the one person who's always been there for me whenever I needed her. And what did I do when she needed me? I threw a fucking tantrum and bailed on her. I hate myself so much right now I want to punch my own self in the face.

I'm yanked from my turmoil when Anna's mother steps out of the house in her robe to grab the paper.

Here goes nothing.

I climb out of the truck and make my way over to her. Once she notices me, she straightens, clutching the top of her robe. Her gaze darts around nervously before recognition dawns on her. "Jaxson?" she says, surprise clear in her voice.

"Hi, Susan. Sorry to drop by unexpectedly like this. I was hoping to see Anna."

"Of course. She will be thrilled to see you." She smiles, taking my hand. "Come on. She's just getting ready for church."

As I follow her into the house, Bill comes walking out of the kitchen in a suit.

"Look who came by to see Anna," Susan says, putting her hand on my arm as I awkwardly stand at the front door.

It takes him a moment before he recognizes me. "Well I'll be, how are you doing, Jaxson?" he asks, giving me a firm handshake.

"I'm doing good, sir. Sorry to stop by unannounced."

Susan waves away my apology. "Nonsense, you're always welcome in our home."

Bill nods. "Absolutely."

"Mom, who are you talking to?"

My chest seizes at the sound of Anna's voice from upstairs.

"Why don't you come down and see for yourself?" Susan says with a smile in her voice.

I stand in the entryway, directly at the bottom of the staircase and hear Anna's soft footsteps above us seconds before I see her. My breath stalls in my lungs, the wind getting knocked out of me. She looks beautiful. Innocent, and youthful. Not at all the damaged girl I saw a year ago.

She comes to an abrupt stop at the top, her brown eyes widening in shock. Seconds later, a big smile breaks out across her face. "Oh my god, Jaxson?" She bolts down the stairs, her excitement triggering a smile of my own.

My arms open for her and I catch her as she launches herself from the bottom step. "How are you doing, kid?" I whisper in her hair.

Her body trembles against me, quiet sobs racking her body.

My throat and eyes burn like a motherfucker as I hold her close.

"I'm so glad you came," she cries.

"Me, too."

"Honey, why don't you and Jaxson go catch up in the kitchen while your father and I get ready for church."

Bill is obviously ready, but he follows his wife upstairs, giving us privacy.

Placing Anna back on her feet, she looks up at me with a watery smile, and I can't stop myself from wiping the tears from her cheeks.

"Come on." She grabs my hand and drags me into the kitchen. "You want something to drink? Looks like my mom has coffee made."

I shake my head and take a seat at the table. "Nah, thanks anyway."

"About time you came and visited me," she says, sitting in the chair next to me.

"I only just got out of rehabilitation a couple of months ago."

"You look different," she muses softly. "You're kind of cute without all the blood and bruises."

I cock a brow at her. "Kind of?"

She giggles. "Oh whatever, you're hot and you know it. If I didn't love you like a big brother I would have a crush on you myself."

My chest tightens at her words. "Big brother, huh?"

She shrugs. "Yeah, well, I always wanted a sibling, and if I could choose a big brother he would be exactly like you." Her smile fades, expression sobering. "I think about you often," she whispers. "I've missed you."

"Me too, kid," I admit. "You look good. How have things been for you since coming home?"

A genuine smile transforms her face. "Really good. I'm in counseling and have joined a support group where there are other girls who went through what I did. It's helped a lot. I'm almost feeling like my old self again."

I let out a relieved breath, her words lifting some of the guilt that's been weighing heavily on me.

"I even have a boyfriend," she adds, blushing.

"Boyfriend?" I repeat, my tone harsher than I intend for it to be.

She nods, a shy smile curving her mouth. "He's amazing. Treats me well, and he's really cute, too," she says with a giggle.

I grunt. "What does your dad think about him?"

She groans. "Don't ask. You know what he said to Logan, when he came to pick me up on our first date?"

I smirk, waiting for her to tell me. By the look on her face I'm assuming it was pretty bad.

Coming to stand in front of me, she puts her hand on my shoulder. "He said, 'Just so you know, son,'" she mimics in a deep voice, "'whatever you do to my daughter tonight, I do to you later.'"

A throaty laugh barrels out of me.

That's a good one.

She groans again, but smiles. "Do not laugh. It was one of the most humiliating experiences of my life, I was furious. Thankfully Logan is not easily intimidated. My dad isn't a big fan; especially since he drives a motorcycle."

Shit! The kid drives a motorcycle?

Her voice drops to a whisper. "It's been real hard on my dad, everything that's happened to me."

I'll bet. It kills me so I can only imagine what it does to Bill.

"But he's trying for me, because he knows I really like him."

"Well as long as the kid is good to you, then that's what matters."

"He is, real good to me. You'll get to meet him; he should be here soon. He's joining us for church," she tells me, a giggle escaping her. "I don't think he's ever stepped foot in a church, but he's coming because he knows it will help my dad lighten up."

"Good. I'm glad I'll get to meet him."

Her eyes drop to my chest and she reaches out, fingering the pendant that's hanging around my neck. "Got a new chain for it, I see."

I nod, remembering what she did to get it back for me.

"Did you ever make things right with Julia?"

I told her about Julia in the hospital, it was hard not to when she was around me so much. "Yeah, I did. Actually, I just found out last night that she's pregnant, with my baby." Saying the words out loud brings on a fresh wave of panic.

Anna beams another smile, as if she also thinks this is great fucking news. "Jaxson, that's fantastic, congratulations," she says, hugging me. "Wow, your kid is so lucky."

I grunt. "How do you figure that?"

"Are you kidding me? From what you told me about Julia, she's going to be a rockin' mom. But having you for a father? Well, no one will love and protect that kid like you. If someone ever tried to mess with your child, I'd feel real sorry for the poor bugger. If I didn't love my dad so much, I'd totally pick you. Hence, naming you the big brother instead," she adds with a wink.

Her words hit me like a ton of bricks, the realization striking me to my core. She's right, I'd love that kid so fucking much, and I'd kick anyone's ass who tried to hurt him… or her.

I stare back at her, dumbstruck by the epiphany. "You're kind of smart for being a kid, you know that?"

"You're just figuring that out now?"

Chuckling, I stand and pull her into my arms. "Nah, I knew that a year ago when I met you."

She hugs me back, squeezing me harder than she looks capable of. "I'm really glad I met you, Jaxson. Even though it was under such awful circumstances."

Pain settles over me as I think about that fateful week. I clear my throat but my words still come out gruff. "I'm sorry, Anna. I wish I would have made it to you in time. You have no idea how much I regret that I didn't."

Her watery eyes lift to mine and she shakes her head. "Please don't. The last thing you should ever feel when it comes to me is guilt. If it weren't for you, I wouldn't even be alive right now, or God knows where I would be. Even if it was the most awful experience of my life, I'm not letting it define me and you shouldn't either. I've taken my life back, and it's all thanks to you."

Her words pull the guilt right out of my chest. She's right. She is okay—more than okay. I kept picturing the damaged girl I found a year ago, but that's not who she is at all. Instead, she's a smart, vibrant teenager who's living her life the way she deserves.

"You're one strong girl, Anna," I tell her, slinging an arm around her shoulders as we walk out of the kitchen.

"Yeah well, I could be stronger if you showed me how to fight like you." She starts punching the air, her tiny fists the least threatening things I've ever seen.

A chuckle escapes me, but it dies quickly when I think about what she just said. "You know, that's not a bad idea. I actually just bought a gym in my hometown. You should come down one weekend and visit. I could teach you how to kick some aaa—butt."

"Oh my gosh, really?" She gasps, excitedly. "Yes! I'd love that."

"Cool, we'll work something out with your parents."

Susan and Bill come walking down the stairs the same time the doorbell rings.

"That's probably Logan," Anna says, blushing again.

I notice Bill tense and I bite back a smile, thinking about what Anna told me he said to the kid on their first date.

"Hi, come in," she greets shyly, stepping aside for him to enter.

My first thought when I get a look at him isn't a good one. He stands tall, looking a little older than Anna. Wearing a black leather riding jacket, jeans, and a black T-shirt, he reminds me exactly of myself at that age. And if his brain is thinking the same things I was, I want to beat the shit out of him.

He throws a possessive arm around Anna's shoulders, his eyes narrowing at me, sizing me up.

Yep, just like me.

Anna stands next to him with a nervous smile, looking at me for approval. "Logan, this is Jaxson. He's the Navy SEAL I told you about who saved my life."

His tight expression eases and he extends his hand. "Hey, nice to meet you. Anna's told me a lot about you."

I accept his gesture with a firm shake. "Nice to meet you, Logan, Anna has said good things about you too." I grip his hand tighter and yank him closer to me. "Make sure it stays that way."

"Jaxson!" Anna scolds under her breath, then looks up at Logan. "He's just kidding."

"No, I'm not."

I hear Bill chuckle behind me.

Logan rips his hand away, not seeming fazed in the least. "Yeah, well, that's not something you need to worry about."

Huh, the kid has some balls. Okay, maybe he'll be all right.

"Good. Make sure that it's not and we'll get along just fine."

Anna groans. "Come on, I'll walk you out."

I wave good-bye to Bill and Susan as she tugs on my arm.

"Glad you came, Jaxson. Come by anytime," Bill shouts, a big grin plastered across his face that I see just before the door closes.

"I can't believe you just did that," Anna hisses under her breath.

"What? I was just looking out for you. That's what big brothers do."

Her expression softens, her smile returning. "All right, really, what did you think?" She chews her nails nervously, my answer clearly meaning a lot to her.

"Honestly, the kid reminds me of myself. So if he wasn't dating you I'd think he's pretty cool, but since he is… I hate him."

She throws herself at me with a laugh. "Well, personally, I think I could do a whole lot worse. And if he turns out anything like you, I'd say I'm a pretty lucky girl."

I hug her tight. "Nah, he's the lucky one."

"Thanks, Jaxson," she whispers, hugging me for a long moment before stepping back. "I better get back inside, god knows what Dad is saying to him."

"All right, go on. We'll talk soon and set up a time for you to come and visit me."

"I can't wait. I'd love to meet Julia."

A flash of pain strikes me, thinking about the mess I've made. "I'd like that, too."

If she ever forgives me.

Logan steps out of the house and waits on the porch for Anna. With a smile, she starts toward him, tossing me a final wave over her shoulder. "See you soon, Jaxson."

"Yeah, see you soon, kid."

Logan grabs her around the waist and pulls her to him. The way he looks down at her… it makes me want to beat the shit out of him.

Shaking my head, I climb into my truck, knowing what I need to do. I just pray I didn't fuck things up beyond repair.

CHAPTER 40

Julia

I wake up the next morning, and know before I even walk downstairs that Jaxson didn't come home last night.

Where could he be?

Sawyer and Cade are sitting at the table, arguing under harsh tones, as I enter the kitchen, their conversation stops abruptly when they catch sight of me.

"Hey, Julia." Sawyer stands, greeting me.

"Morning. Have you heard from him?"

They both shake their heads, confirming what I already expected.

"Me either."

"I'm sure you will hear something today," Sawyer says.

I wish I felt as confident as him.

The sound of my front door being unlocked, sends hope to fill my chest but it deflates when Kayla walks into the kitchen. She comes to an abrupt stop. "Uh, hey. I used the key because I didn't want to wake Jaxson up." Her gaze takes us all in before she notices my teary eyes. "He's not here?"

I shake my head, my throat too tight to speak.

"Well that son of a bitch. What did he do? I'm going to kick his ass."

Sawyer grunts. "Get in line."

She pulls me in for a hug. "You should have called, Julia. I would have come over and stayed with you."

"It's all right. Sawyer and Cade stayed with me, and we have a big day ahead of us. I didn't want you to be tired for it."

She steps back, her eyes sympathetic. "We don't need to go today. We can reschedule and just hang here."

I shake my head, rejecting the idea fast. "No. I'm looking forward to this. We are not going to let this ruin today. Besides, it will be good for me, help me keep my mind off him."

Yeah, right.

"If you're sure…"

"I am. Just give me a second." I grab a banana and an oatmeal bar to eat on the way then walk over and hug Sawyer. "Thank you for everything last night."

"No problem. You have my cell number, right? If you need anything today, make sure you call. Otherwise, if that dickhead isn't back when you get home, we will be."

"I have it. Thank you," I reply quietly, hoping that won't be the case. I move to

Cade next and he surprises me by taking me in his arms, returning my embrace. Once we break apart, I look up at them both. "Will you guys try finding him today? Just check in and make sure he's all right?"

"We will," Cade promises.

"Thanks." With a heavy heart, I follow Kayla out of the house, and pray that when I get back, Jaxson will be here waiting for me.

The car is filled with silence as we turn onto I-90, heading toward Charleston; I find it eerily odd that the highway is completely deserted. "Is it me or does it feel like we're the only ones alive on this planet right now?" I joke, trying to lighten the mood.

"It's Sunday, everyone's at church. I have to say though, it's nice driving with no other traffic."

It is nice, the sun is shining and we have Kayla's sunroof open. The warmth beams down on us along with a mixture of fresh air, bringing a little peace to my aching heart.

"Well damn, looks like we spoke too soon," Kayla says.

I look back and see a silver truck coming up behind us. Turning around, I rest my head against the window, getting lost in my troubled thoughts.

"Are you sure you're going to be okay, Julia?

"Yeah, I..." My words trail off on a gasp when my head jerks forward.

"What the hell?" Kayla shrieks in panic, her hands tightening on the steering wheel as she tries to maintain control of the car. "What is he doing?"

I twist around again and realize the silver truck just rear-ended us, and he's not easing up, he keeps right on our ass. Kayla pulls into the other lane to let him pass but he follows us, tailing close behind.

"What is his problem?" I ask, my voice trembling.

Kayla glances in the rearview mirror. "Do you recognize him? I can't tell."

"No, he's wearing a hat and sunglasses. I don't recognize the truck either."

He pulls up along Kayla's side next and turns the wheel sharply, side-swiping us.

We both scream as the car swerves.

"Julia, grab my cell and call 9-1-1. Hurry!"

Reaching into the console, I grab her phone where it's plugged into the charger. My fingers shake uncontrollably, barely able to dial the three numbers I need.

The asshole rams us again as I'm dialing.

"Son of a bitch," Kayla grits out in fury, stepping on the gas.

"9-1-1, what's your emergency?"

"We need help. My friend and I are on I-90, heading west to Charleston, there's a silver truck trying to run us off the road."

"Okay, ma'am, just stay calm and..."

That was the last I heard before he hit us again, this time causing the car to spin out of control.

Everything falls into slow motion around me, our screams fill the air, sounding distant even to my own ears, as the car tumbles into the ditch. We roll several times, glass shattering around us, nicking the delicate skin on my face.

The baby.

The quick thought has me throwing my arms around my mid-section, hoping to offer some protection. My seat belt bites into my hips, painfully restraining me in the seat. Finally, the car comes to a stop and we land upright in the ditch.

I sit, stunned, and try to get my bearings. Looking over at Kayla, I see her slumped forward on the steering wheel, blood trickling down her forehead.

"Oh god, Kayla?" I sob. "Kayla, wake up!" I shake her shoulder then remember I shouldn't touch her. With trembling hands, I undo my seat belt and look for her phone. Realizing I still have my purse around my shoulder, I dig through it to find my cell when my door flies open, startling me. I turn with a yelp to see Wyatt.

"Wyatt?" I scan my surroundings and realize he was driving the truck. "What the hell are you doing?" I yell. "Are you fucking crazy?"

He doesn't answer. His rough hands grab me, pulling me out of the car.

"Let go of me!" I scream at the top of my lungs and kick out at him repeatedly, trying to escape his strong grip. My body hits the ground with a hard thud, the impact knocking the breath out of my lungs.

Before I'm able to recover from it, he grabs a fist full of my hair and starts dragging me toward his truck.

"Ow! Stop it! Get off me, you son of a bitch!" I continue to struggle, feeling my hair being ripped from my scalp. "Kayla, wake up!" I cry out, willing her to wake up; terrified she's never going to.

Wyatt twists our positions so he's standing over top of me, his grip still strong in my hair. He whips his sunglasses off, his eyes filled with a wild rage I've never seen before. "Shut the fuck up, you dirty whore!" His fist smashes into my face, turning my world black.

CHAPTER 41

Jaxson

Sawyer sent me a text not long after I left Anna's telling me to meet him at the gym. I had wanted to see Julia first, but he reminded me that she and Kayla were gone dress shopping today.

Cade, Sawyer, and Cooper are all standing by the ring looking pissed when I walk in. I can already tell this is going to be messy.

Sawyer starts toward me, meeting me halfway. His posture is relaxed, but his eyes are hard. Before I can fully register his anger, he catches me off guard by throwing a left hook to the side of my jaw.

My head snaps back and I fall on my ass, not expecting the blow.

"You son of a bitch!" He moves for me again but this time I'm ready for him. Pushing to my feet, I block his next blow and throw a shot of my own.

"Take it easy, both of you," Cooper bellows and yanks me back while Cade grabs Sawyer.

Rage threatens to consume me but I keep it locked up because I know I deserved it. "Is she all right?" I ask quietly.

"No! She's not. What the hell is wrong with you? I walk in and find your woman on the floor, surrounded by broken glass. Crying her fucking eyes out that you don't love her or want the damn baby you knocked her up with."

I shake my head, a sharp ache seizing my chest. "I messed up."

"You're damn right you did. And I hope she cans your sorry ass."

My eyes narrow, my control slipping. "I'll bet you fucking do. I'm sure you loved being there for her last night, trying to console her."

"Fuck you! I have more respect for both of you than that. But I'll tell you something—it would have served your ass right. Have someone else step in and take care of her since you sure as hell can't."

Everything he says is the truth but I'll make it right. I'll do whatever I have to.

Cooper's radio goes off at his hip, interrupting the heated moment. "Sheriff?"

Keeping a hand on my chest he reaches down, grabbing his radio. "Yeah, what is it?"

"I'm sorry, sir, but you need to get over to the hospital right away. Kayla's been in a bad accident."

We all share a look; dread consuming the air around us.

Our fight forgotten, we scramble out the door and hop into Cooper's cruiser, hauling ass to the hospital.

The moment we enter through the emergency doors we can hear Kayla's pleading cry. "Please, you're wasting time. You need to find her!"

We follow the sound, charging into her room. A bandage is wrapped around her head, her face cut and swollen where she sits on the bed. Grace is beside her, holding her hand and crying, but doesn't look hurt.

"Where's Julia?" I ask, my gaze searching for her.

Cooper shoves me aside and rushes over to her. "Jesus, baby, are you all right? What happened?"

"Oh god, Cooper, you need to help Julia."

"Where the fuck is she?" I ask again, louder this time.

"He took her," Kayla cries, sending icy terror through my veins. "He fucking took her."

"Who damn it?"

"Wyatt! He ran us off the road. I passed out but I woke up to her screaming my name. He was dragging her by her hair to his truck, then he hit her." She starts sobbing uncontrollably. "Oh god, Cooper, he hit her so hard that she stopped screaming, he knocked her out."

Panic crawls up my throat, my knees threatening to buckle beneath me, until an overpowering fury consumes me, exploding through every cell in my body. "He's dead! I'm going to fucking kill him."

"Jaxson, man, take it easy. We'll find her." Sawyer's voice is distant to my ears as my fists strike out, destroying everything in my path.

A force knocks into me from behind, taking me to the ground. "Get control of yourself," Cade grits out, his face inches from mine. "You're trained for shit like this, Jaxson. Keep your head together or you're not going to be able to help her."

My chest heaves with fury as I fight to find my control, knowing he's right.

"You good?" he asks, through an exerted breath.

I nod.

He climbs off me then extends his hand, helping me to my feet. I take in our surroundings, seeing the damage I caused. A chair is splintered in a million pieces, a table and tray flipped on its side, its medical tools scattered all over the place.

I drive a hand through my hair, panic thick in my veins. "Shit, I'm sorry."

Grace nods at my apology, looking ghost white.

"Cooper, please," Kayla cries. "You guys need to go find her."

I kneel before her. "Kayla, did you hear anything else? Did he say anything about where he was taking her?"

She shakes her head, a sob escaping her.

One of the deputies come walking in. "Sheriff, we have the 9-1-1 recording Miss Julia made during the accident. The operator stayed on the line while the crash happened, we have her being taken on tape."

Cooper nods, then turns to Kayla. "Jesus, I don't want to fucking leave you right now."

"You have to," she says, taking his face in her hands. "I'm going to be fine. Julia needs you now more than I do. You're the best. Please go find her."

"I'll stay with her," Grace offers quietly.

Cooper drops his forehead on hers, his jaw locked in turmoil. "I love you."

His three simple words strike a chord deep inside me. I never said them to Julia, all because I was too scared. Now she's god knows where, terrified and alone, thinking I don't love her or our baby…

The baby!

The thought sends another bolt of urgency through me.

"Let's go," I bark at Cade and Sawyer, leaving the room and sprinting down the hall.

"Jaxson, hold up," Cooper calls, but I don't stop.

Time's running out.

"Goddamn it, I said hold up."

When he grabs my arm, I throw him into the wall and get into his face. "I don't have time to hold up. I need to find her now."

"And you're going to do it without me?" he asks, betrayal thick in his voice.

"I have no choice, Coop. Right now the law means nothing to me, and it's not going to. That son of a bitch took my girl and my baby; he's fucking dead."

"Listen, I get where you're coming from, I do. I want to kill the bastard myself. But right now you need the law on your side. I have resources that you don't. Working together is only going to find her faster."

"He's right, Jaxson," Sawyer says, cutting in. "Think about Julia and the baby, they need you when this is over."

My eyes remain locked with Cooper's. "Do you understand what I'm telling you? The only thing that matters to me is getting Julia and my baby back alive, and I will stop at nothing to do it, even if it means breaking the law. Are you prepared for that?"

"Do you really think my first priority isn't the same as yours? She means a lot to me too, Jaxson."

I step back, knowing he's right. "All right, let's go, time's wasting."

"Sheriff?" a deputy calls out, running out of Kayla's room. "I just got word from Reynolds that Wyatt's home has been searched and cleared, no sign of either him or Miss Julia."

"I want all property records pulled under Jennings, that includes his old man. Also, bring Ray in for questioning, we'll meet you there."

"Yes, sir."

The four of us hop in Cooper's police cruiser and head to the station. The entire drive over I have only one thought in mind… vengeance.

CHAPTER 42

Julia

I awake shivering, my body cold and aching; it feels like someone took a sledgehammer to me. Moaning, I try bringing my hand to my head but can't.

What the heck?

It takes only a moment for my memories to come flooding back.

Wyatt.

My eyes shoot open, a small whimper escaping me when I take in my surroundings. I'm in a cold, dark room lying on a cot, my hands chained to a wrought iron headboard. My mouth is gagged, making it difficult for me to pull in the deep breaths my lungs are desperately trying to inhale.

Looking down, I see I've been stripped down to my underwear.

Oh god!

I try to remain calm and find a way out of this, for both my baby's sake and mine.

Please let my baby be okay.

A loud noise has my head snapping to the right and I instantly regret it when pain radiates behind my eyes, making my stomach rebel.

Wyatt paces back and forth, his cell phone to his ear. "Come on, you bitch. Pick up!"

What I see beyond him has my panic escalating—candles are lit, highlighting an entire wall filled with pictures of me. Images of me walking around town, in my car, in my house, and worst of all, some are of me sleeping in bed. He was in my house while I was sleeping and I never knew.

"Well, look who's awake."

My attention snaps to him, his silhouette blurry from the tears streaking down my face. He walks over and sits next to me on the bed, trailing a finger from my cheek, down between my breasts.

I whimper behind the gag, trying to wiggle away from his unwanted touch. It only infuriates him. He backhands me so hard that my cheek splits on the inside, blood pooling in my mouth. Darkness dances in my vision, threatening to take me under again.

"You'll let that fucking trash touch you, but not me?"

I choke on my sob, the gag making it difficult to breathe.

Wyatt fingers the tie at my mouth. "If I remove this you're going to be good, right? Not that anyone will hear you scream, but it will get on my nerves. And right now my patience is thin when it comes to you, do you understand?" His voice is soft again, contradicting the wild rage that's in his eyes. "Answer me!" he snaps, his hand squeezing one of my breasts painfully.

A painful cry shoves past my throat and I quickly nod.

"Good girl."

When he removes the gag, I take in lungfuls of sobbing breaths. "Wyatt, please don't do this."

He cups my face, his touch gentle. "I hate that it had to come to this. I really do. You have no idea how much this pains me, I've loved you for so long…" His crazy words trail off as he gets a faraway look in his eyes.

I decide to try my own crazy. "I know that now. I'm so sorry. You were right, we had something special, and I should have given us more of a chance."

He stares down at me, searching for the truth. Whatever he finds isn't what he was looking for. Fury twists his expression, his jaw locking. "It's too late. You let that son of a bitch take you from me. You ruined my reputation with that fucking restraining order. Now you're both going to pay."

His hand tightens on my cheeks, making blood trickle down my mouth. He sucks in a sharp breath, his eyes filling with lust. A growl erupts from him and he crushes his mouth to mine with brutal force, thrusting his tongue past my lips.

It takes everything in me not to choke from the bile rising in my throat.

He pulls back, licking the smeared blood from his mouth. "Fucking beautiful. We're going to have some long, overdue fun, Julia. I'm finally going to have you. First though, we are going to teach that bastard a lesson for taking you from me."

Oh no, Jaxson.

CHAPTER 43

Jaxson

Ow! Stop it! Get off me, you son of a bitch! Kayla, wake up!

Listening to Julia scream and struggle from the 9-1-1 recording is almost too much to bear.

Shut the fuck up, you dirty whore!

Then everything falls silent.

"Motherfucker!" Cade seethes.

I close my eyes and swallow past the burn in my throat, my body shaking with a violent rage, waiting to be unleashed.

Cade, Sawyer, and I turn back at the two-way mirror, looking into the interrogation room where Cooper questions Ray Jennings.

"I'm tellin' you, you're wrong. There's no way my son took Miss Julia." Ray lifts his hand, pointing a finger at Cooper. "If I were you, I would look at Jaxson Reid, Wyatt warned her—"

Cooper's fist slams down on the table, silencing whatever other bullshit he was about to spew. "I have a 9-1-1 recording that says Wyatt kidnapped her, not Jaxson. You arguing is wasting valuable time that could spare Julia her life. So I am going to ask you again, do you have any idea where he could have taken her? What other properties do you own?"

Ray's eyes narrow. "I don't believe you. I want my lawyer… now."

Cooper storms out of the room and joins us on the other side. "Wright!" he shouts out the open door. "What the fuck is taking so long on the list of properties?"

"I should be getting them anytime now, sir."

I rake a frustrated hand through my hair. "We don't have time for this shit."

"I'm with Jaxson, maybe we should split up, and some of us can at least start patrolling. We can backtrack from where the accident happened."

I'm about to agree with Sawyer when my cell starts ringing. Pulling it out of my pocket I look at the call display, and my heart stops when I see the screen. "It's Julia's number."

"Put it on speaker," Cooper orders, slamming the door.

I hit the intercom. "Julia, baby, you there?"

"Oh, she's here all right."

White-hot fury ignites through my blood at the sound of Wyatt's taunting voice. "Where are you hiding, motherfucker?"

"Tsk, tsk, it isn't very smart, Reid, to be calling someone names when that person has something that means a whole lot to you."

"I'm telling you now, Jennings, I will find you, and if you have hurt any part of her, I will fucking gut you alive and feed you your own insides."

The son of a bitch laughs. "Oh, Jaxson, I plan to hurt her all right. And you are finally going to know what it's like to have her taken away from you. I'm just deciding though, do I record me fucking her, or would you rather I just keep you on the phone so you can listen to her beg?"

My violence reaches a whole new level, pumping through my body like hot lava.

Before I lose control, Cooper speaks up. "Wyatt, it's Cooper. It's not too late to change things around. Think hard, is it worth losing everything over this?"

He grunts. "Of course you're already with the good sheriff. Sorry about your woman there, Sheriff, nothing personal, she just happened to be in the way. I'm assuming she's okay though, if you already knew Julia was with me."

"This is between you and me, Jennings," I say, cutting back in. "It always has been, so leave Julia out of it, and we can deal with it one-on-one."

His cool façade shatters. "This has everything to do with her, you son of a bitch! She was mine and you took her from me. For years you kept her from me."

"You're fucking crazy. Julia has always been mine, and everyone in this town knows it, including you."

"No! You're wrong. Tell him, you bitch, tell him right now that you were mine, that *you are mine.*"

Shuffling fills the line before Julia's voice comes on. "Jaxson?"

Agony rips through my chest at the sound of her sobs. "Julia, baby, I'm here. Hang in there, okay? I'm coming for you."

A loud crack has her screaming out in pain.

"Tell him right fucking now!"

"Jaxson," she whimpers. "I-I love you."

"You whore!" The second blow he sends to her is louder than the first, her cry of agony tearing through me, shredding my insides.

A growl rips from me, my fist connecting with the wall. "Jennings, I swear to God, I'm going to kill you!"

"You are going to do nothing because you will never find me. I'm finally going to have her, and when I'm done, I'm going to light the place on fire. By the time you find her, she will be nothing but fucking rubble. Have a nice life, you son of a bitch!"

I hear the click but still call out his name. "Jennings! Jennings!" I drop the phone on the table. "Fuck!" My fist crashes in the two-way mirror repeatedly, the glass cracking. When I look through it at Ray, I lose all control.

"Shit! Grab him!" Cooper orders.

I escape the arms that reach for me, and in a flash I'm in the room next door. Grabbing Ray, I throw him down on the table, my hands wrapping around his throat. "Tell us where she is!"

His hands slap at me, his face turning purple, but I don't let up.

"Jaxson, stop! Come on, man, you're going to kill him," Sawyer tries reasoning with me, but my rage fuels a strength that makes it impossible for all the arms to rip me off him.

"If anything happens to her because you didn't cooperate, I will make you watch while I gut your son like a fucking fish." Hoping this got through to him, I let go, allowing myself to be pulled back.

"Are you crazy?" Ray chokes and sputters, his hands soothing his throat.

Cooper bends down, getting in his face. "We just got a call from your son saying he's going to kill Julia. She's pregnant, and her life is depending on you. So tell us where they are or I will leave Jaxson in this room with you and lock the door on my way out."

Ray shakes his head. "I have no idea where they are. I swear, I never thought he would do something like this."

"Properties, give us properties that you own," Cooper presses.

Before he can answer, a deputy comes barreling in. "Sir, Melissa Carmichael is here saying she has information on Miss Julia's whereabouts."

I bolt out the door with everyone following close behind me. Melissa stands nervously by the front desk, sporting a black eye. Suspicion quickly rears its ugly head.

I should have known.

She backs into the counter, looking scared shitless when she sees me charging toward her. "I'm sorry. We were only supposed to scare her—"

I grab her arms, yanking her to me. "What the fuck have you done? Where is she?"

Sobs begin to pour from her but I feel no sympathy. "Wyatt's holding her at some fishing cabin that's twenty minutes from here. He's expecting me to pick him up in an hour to take him to the airport. His private plane is waiting for him. I swear I didn't know it would escalate to this."

"Why would you help him? She's never done a damn thing to you!"

Anger flashes in her gaze, masking some of the fear. "She took everything from me. From the moment she moved here everyone flocked to her, especially you."

All this over fucking jealousy?

"You make me sick." I shove her back. "If anything happens to her, or my baby, I will make you fucking pay."

She pales. "I didn't know she was pregnant. We were only supposed to scare her. I didn't think he would take it this far."

"Directions, now!" Cooper orders, slamming down a pen and paper on the desk.

With a shaking hand she gives us what we want.

"Take her into custody," Cooper orders, snatching the paper from her. "And keep Ray here too, don't allow him any phone calls."

Chaos explodes around us, a flurry of activity ensuing as the four of us rush out the door to save the only girl I've ever loved.

Primed and ready, I keep my fury locked up until the exact moment I will unleash it, making the son of a bitch pay for what he's done.

CHAPTER 44

Julia

"Goddamn it, Melissa, pick up your phone. Listen, the cops already know I have her. It's only going to be a matter of time before they find the cabin. Get here, now!"

Wyatt's agitated voice brings me out of unconsciousness and I start coming around again. I'm not sure how many times I've faded in and out since he beat me with my phone repeatedly, shattering it against my face.

A strong smell penetrates my senses, burning my nostrils. Opening my eyes, I fight against the wave of pain it brings and look over to see Wyatt dousing the walls with gasoline.

So he was telling Jaxson the truth, he's going to burn me alive. I have begged, pleaded, and fought with everything I have left in me, but it has only ended with cruel taunts, inappropriate fondling, and severe beatings. I've come to accept that I'm not getting out of here, at least not alive. My broken body is already close to death, I can feel it.

Grief suffocates me, knowing that I couldn't protect the beautiful, little life inside of me. Knowing I'll never get to meet, hold, or kiss my baby. I knew I had taken a serious risk telling Jaxson I loved him in front of Wyatt. But I needed him to hear those words from me, needed him to know that despite everything that has happened, I still love him.

My heart aches, knowing I will never again feel his touch, see his ice-blue eyes, or his sexy smirk. And most of all, I ache knowing that this is going to kill him, because even though he acted the way he did about the baby, I know, with every fiber of my being, that he loves me.

"Ah, you're awake again. About time. It's no fun for me if you're asleep."

Instead of fear, Wyatt's taunting voice only fuels the anger inside of me. I hate him for doing this to me, for taking away everything I've always wanted.

He drops the gasoline can down and stalks over to me, pulling his shirt off in the process. "Unfortunately, I'm not going to be able to take my time with you, Julia. Plans have changed so we are going to have to make this quick," he says, flashing me a taunting smile. "But I promise it will still be good." He rubs the erection that strains the front of his jeans.

I turn my head away, not wanting to watch what comes next, and pray for the darkness dancing along the edge of my vision to take me under again. It's close; one more hit would probably do it.

I feel him crawl on top of me, his hot breath hitting the side of my face. I close my eyes and try to keep the numbness in place, not wanting to feel his naked chest on mine, or the erection that settles between my thighs. "Look at me, bitch!"

I ignore his demand, keeping my eyes tightly shut.

"I said, look at me!" He slaps my battered face.

My teeth clench from the pain, black spots dancing behind my eyes, but unfortunately, it doesn't pull me under.

Feeling a cold, sharp object along the curve of my breasts has my eyes springing open. Wyatt stares down at me with a cruel smile, dragging a large knife across my chest. I keep my face void of expression, knowing any fear I show will only give him satisfaction.

He slips the cruel blade under one of my bra straps and stills. "Tell me you want me," he pants heavily, his eyes raging with hunger.

"No." My response is quiet but firm. I will not let my last words be anything that will satisfy him and I'm hoping he will get mad enough to just end my life quickly.

He chuckles, enjoying my defiance. "Wrong answer, sweetheart." His hand wraps around my throat firmly, allowing only a small bit of oxygen through, then the sharp blade slices through my bra strap. "Tell me you're mine!" he seethes through clenched teeth, grinding his erection against me.

His pressure eases so I can speak, and I know the next words I choke out will be my last. "I hope when Jaxson finds you, he makes you die a slow and painful death."

My words have the effect I expected; a wild rage twists his face savagely. "You bitch!" He lands two more solid blows to my face.

Darkness taunts me cruelly, almost pulling me under. My eyes close again, but not because I'm forcing them to.

"I'm going to fuck you until my cock goes limp, then I'm going to light you on fire and watch you burn until there's nothing left of you but ash." His hand squeezes around my throat, cutting off all oxygen as I feel him fumble with his pants.

Darkness finally begins to close in on me, and I blessedly welcome it. Right when I am about to fade into nothing, an enraged roar rips through the room. "Motherfucker!"

Wyatt suddenly vanishes, his weight no longer crushing me into the mattress. I gasp and sputter from the released pressure on my throat. A loud crash sends a wave of heat exploding around me. I try to open my eyes and see what's happening, but can't.

Shouts and enraged curses fill the air, mixing in with the sound of crackling flames. I quickly realize that the candles have been knocked over, starting the fire.

A sickening crack fills the air then everything falls silent.

Hands scour my body, but it's a touch I welcome, one I thought I would never feel again—Jaxson's.

He made it.

My relief soon morphs into sadness when, no matter how hard I try, I can't open my eyes. I fight against the darkness that only a few minutes ago I wanted so desperately to consume me.

"Julia, baby, can you hear me?"

"Jaxson," I sob out weakly, not even sure if he heard me through my tender throat.

"It's me. I'm here, I'm going to get you out, just hang on." I feel him pull on my chains. "Fuck! Where's the key?"

I whimper when the heat starts feeling too close for comfort. My lungs begin to burn from thick smoke, making it impossible to breathe.

I feel him struggle harder to free me, my heart breaking because I know he'll die here with me if he waits too long.

"Leave me," I whisper.

"No! Don't say that. We're both getting out of here."

His words become distant as I feel myself drifting, my body giving up. I fight against it, just long enough to mumble what I want my last words to be. "I love you."

It's then the darkness finally takes me, sucking me into a sweet oblivion of nothing.

Jaxson

"Julia!" I shake her, fear squeezing my chest when I get no response. "Fuck!"

My eyes search frantically for anything to use to break through the chains, but the heavy, black smoke makes it impossible to see much. Knowing I'm running short on time, I lean back on my elbows and kick the shit out of the metal bed frame, particularly close to the pole that the chains are wrapped around. I put all my weight behind it, my heavy boot rattling the entire frame. Finally, it snaps.

A loud crash sounds in the distance. "Jaxson?" Cade yells, his voice barely penetrating over the roaring flames.

"Over here!"

I rip the broken pole out from the smashed bed frame then take Julia's chained wrists and throw them over my neck. Picking her up, I try not to think about how still her broken body is. "Hold on, baby, we're almost out," I whisper in her hair.

Cade, Sawyer, and Cooper come charging around the corner, emerging through the thick smoke. Cade holds an axe that would have fucking come in handy a minute ago.

"Where the hell have you guys been?" I snap. I had shot out of the cruiser before we even came to a stop, not wanting to waste another precious second, and thank God I did. Because a second longer would have been too late.

"We had to find another way in, the entrance burst into flames right after you ran through it," Sawyer explains. "We made a small opening in one of the rooms."

I watch Cooper's eyes fall to Wyatt's lifeless body on the ground, his head twisted awkwardly from where I broke his neck.

Another crash happens behind me, the heat at my back feeling a hell of a lot closer.

"We need to move, now," Cooper bellows, pointing behind me. "We probably have a minute before these flames reach the gas tank."

I follow Cade through the billowing black smoke, cradling Julia close to my chest. He leads me to a bedroom with a hole in the wall that's barely big enough to fit through. All of them make way to let me out first.

Once the fresh air hits me, I haul ass to get as far away as I can from the house before the explosion comes. I make it a good distance across the grassy field before the fierce blast happens, but the force of it still knocks me off my feet. I keep her close to me, twisting with just enough time to land on my back, taking the brunt of our fall.

Quickly, I roll her beneath me, covering her from any falling debris. Once we're in the clear, I sit up and look at her; really look at her. And what I see has my heart shattering in a million fucking pieces.

"Julia, baby, wake up!" My hands run along her battered body, noticing every bruise that marks her skin. "Julia! Wake up!"

She remains lifeless.

Pure terror grips my chest when I don't find a pulse, sending icy dread surging through my veins. "No, no, no!" Picking her up, I cradle her body against my chest, gently rocking her back and forth.

My eyes burn as bad as my throat, big ugly tears falling from my face and soaking her hair. For the first time since I was seven years old, I cry, the most excruciating grief ripping from my chest. "Please don't leave me, I'm so sorry, so fucking sorry. I love you so much. Please, Julia, wake up!"

I thought I had already experienced the most heart-wrenching pain that I'd ever feel in my life, but I was wrong. What I'm feeling now exceeds it by a thousand times more than anything I've ever felt. My heart fucking aches so bad I'm surprised it's still beating.

Seconds later, Cooper leans down, putting his hand on my shoulder. "Jaxson, man, paramedics are here, let them help her."

I lay her down, but remain close.

The paramedics drop down beside me. "Back away, sir. We need room to assess her injuries," one of them says.

I shake my head, refusing to let her go.

"Come on, man, give them space so they can help her," Cooper says, grabbing my shoulder again.

"Be careful with her, she's pregnant," I croak out, stepping back.

Sawyer and Cade come to stand on either side of me, but I don't look at them, my eyes never leaving Julia. I watch helplessly, my dread growing stronger with every second. "She's so still."

I ignore the one female paramedic's sympathetic glance.

Sawyer grips my shoulder. "She'll be all right, man, I know it. Have faith."

Faith.

Something I've never had, but Julia always did.

Bracing my hands behind my head, I start pacing back and forth and for the first time in my life, I pray.

"We have a pulse." The paramedic's shouted observation snaps me out of my silent plea.

"Holy shit!" I breathe, hope filling my chest.

Sawyer grins, clapping me on the back. "See? What the fuck did I tell you?"

"Let's move!" A paramedic orders as they lift the stretcher.

"I'm coming with her," I say, following them toward the ambulance.

I get a nod of approval and briefly notice the chaos of fire trucks and police cars before crawling into the ambulance.

"We'll meet you over there," Cooper says, just before they close the door.

I grab Julia's cold hand and bring it to my mouth. "Everything's going to be okay, Jules, just hang on."

CHAPTER 45

Julia

"Why isn't she waking up?"

I cling to Jaxson's voice, wanting to hold onto it but am surrounded by darkness, one that's constantly sucking me in. I try to fight it off, wanting to see him but can't. I'm too tired.

"Her mind has shut down so her body can heal. I know it's difficult, but be patient, Mr. Reid, she and your baby need rest."

My baby.

Relief swamps me right before I slip into oblivion once again.

The next time I come around, I'm frustrated to be surrounded by the dark again. This time I not only hear Jaxson but can feel him too, the warmth of his hand wrapped around mine.

"I know what you're thinking, so why not just get it over with and ask me." I hear him say to someone.

"Because I'm not sure I want to know the answer, and to be honest, I don't really care either way."

Cooper.

I fight off my exhaustion, wanting to know what they're talking about.

"Yeah, well, for the record, I didn't run in and murder the son of a bitch. We were struggling, it was self-defense. But I'm also not sorry, I'd kill him again in a heartbeat."

"Can't say I blame you."

Wyatt's dead.

All I feel from hearing that is sweet relief. To know I will never have to face him again brings on a peace that I let sweep over me.

This time, I fully awake. I'm groggy and still tired, but feel attached to my body. I know if I want to open my eyes I can. But I keep them closed for the time being, because right now I'm feeling peaceful and I'm not sure what awaits me when I open them.

A warm gentle pressure weighs on my tummy. It doesn't take me long to realize it's Jaxson's hand. "I'm going to let you know now, kid, I'm probably going to fuck up, a lot." I hear him whisper. "I had a real shitty father growing up so I never learned how to be a good dad. Thankfully, you have an amazing mom, so hopefully she overshadows all of the mistakes I'll make."

I force my eyes open and am grateful the room is relatively dark, only a soft glow from the bathroom light illuminating Jaxson. He's bent over the side of my bed, his chin resting low on his forearm while he looks at his other hand that's rubbing gentle circles on my stomach. His gentleness warms my heart, but the exhaustion and sorrow on his face makes me ache for him.

"I promise though," he continues quietly, "I'll try really hard to make those mistakes few and far between. I promise I'll always love you, and I'll always protect you. I'll kick anyone's ass if they try to hurt you, even if it's just your feelings."

I stifle a chuckle, not wanting to interrupt his moment.

He drops his head in his arms with a groan. "See, I'm already fucking up. Listen to how much I'm swearing. Your first word is probably going to be shit."

My giggle breaks free. "Actually, it'll probably be fuck," I try to say teasingly, but my voice comes out raw and hoarse, not sounding like me at all.

Jaxson's entire body stiffens before his head snaps up in surprise. "Holy shit!" He jumps up, moving to sit beside me on the bed. "Jules, you're awake." He takes my face between his hands, making sure to be gentle, and rains kisses all over it. "Jesus, I've been waiting for what seems like forever for you to wake up."

Tears streak down my face when I didn't even realize I was crying. With my reflexes sluggish, I bring my hand up to Jaxson's jaw, needing to touch him. Shock washes over me when I realize the tears aren't my own, but his.

He buries his face in the crook of my neck, his shoulders trembling. He makes no sound, his silent tears soaking my skin. I hold him close, rubbing his shoulders, his back, any part of him I can reach, and let my own emotion free.

Eventually, he lifts his face, gently resting his forehead on mine.

"You're crying," I say sadly, still stunned by the simple act.

"I know," he chokes out. "I started when I didn't think you were going to wake up and now I can't seem to stop. I've turned into a real fucking pussy, Jules."

Another giggle escapes me, but it trails off into a sob. I wrap my arms around his neck, hugging him close. "I didn't think I was ever going to see you again," I cry, my lips softly brush his ear. "He was awful, Jaxson, and I was so sure he was going to finish what he started."

"It's going to be okay now, all of it. The baby is all right and…" He pauses. "He's dead, Jules, he can never hurt you again."

"I know. I heard you talking to Cooper… at least I think I did," I add, feeling a little unsure now.

Maybe I dreamed it?

"You were awake then?"

I nod. "I could hear you but I couldn't open my eyes. This was the first time where I came awake and felt in control of my body."

"I'm glad you finally did."

"How long have I been out for?" I ask, a little frightened to know the answer.

"Two days. And it has been the longest two fucking days of my life." He runs his hands through his hair and expels a heavy breath. "I have so much I need to say to you. So much to say I'm sorry for—for the things I said and did that night."

I shake my head, not wanting to think about it. It hurts too much.

Jaxson cups the side of my face, his thumb stroking my cheek. "Please, just hear me out."

I swallow thickly and nod.

"I was so scared, Julia. The only reason I've never wanted kids is because I'm fucking terrified I'll turn out to be just like him." He doesn't have to say his dad, because we both know who *he* is. "Let's be real, we both know I have one hot temper, and where do you think I get that from?" I'm about to argue but he places his fingers gently on my lip. "Just wait, let me finish."

I remain silent and let him get out what he needs to.

"After the way I snapped like that…" He pauses and shakes his head. "I didn't think I could hate myself any more than I already did, but I was wrong. After I left that night, I never hated myself more. Because the truth is, Jules, I do love you. I've probably loved you longer than you've loved me; you're just the one who said it first. I wanted to tell you so many times. But I was too scared because the last person I ever said those words to left me, and she never fucking came back."

Tears begin to stream down my face again, my heart breaking at every single agonizing word that falls from his lips. It's the first time he has ever talked about his mom with me.

"It really messed me up when she left, but it didn't destroy me. But the thought of you leaving me… it would completely fucking break me." His voice cracks, making my heart shatter into a million pieces.

I pull him to me, holding him close.

"Please forgive me, I swear I'll make it up to you."

My breath hitches as I try to hold in my emotion. "Where did you go that night? I was so scared you were never going to come back."

"I'm sorry I left you like that, but it's also good that I did, because I went and dealt with something I should have dealt with a long time ago."

My curiosity piques.

"I went and saw Anna."

I gasp. "The girl you saved?"

He nods. "She lives just a few hours away in Summerland. Before we left the hospital she had asked me to come visit her, but I couldn't bring myself to. I didn't want to be reminded of how I failed her."

It kills me to hear the guilt in his voice.

"But I'm glad I did. She looked real good, Jules. She was beautiful and happy, exactly how a fifteen-year-old girl should be."

Smiling, I lay my hand on the side of his face. "It's all because of you that she had this chance to heal and be happy again."

Encircling my wrist, he turns his face, kissing the marks on my wrist from where the chains rubbed raw. "I know that now. I walked away with a whole new perspective on things, most of all myself."

He pauses and I wait patiently, knowing it's hard for him to open up.

"The thing is, I never felt like I was even good enough to be your friend, let alone love you. And honestly, I still think that. I know I'm not, but I also know that no one will love you and protect you like I will. If you give me another chance, I'll work every day at trying to be the person you and our baby deserve." His hand moves to my tummy now. "I'm still fucking terrified about being a father, but I promise I will love and protect our baby with everything I am. I already do love him… her—whatever it is."

I chuckle, my heart close to bursting.

His fingers gently wipe away my flowing tears. "Please forgive me."

"I do. I've loved you since I was seventeen years old, and I will love you for the rest of my life. But for us to work, I need you to trust me with your heart and your feelings. When you're scared or angry, talk to me about it, don't run away."

"I promise, Jules, I'll never leave you, or lose control like that again. I'll try really hard to tell you what I'm always feeling, just be patient with me, it's not something I'm good at."

"I will. And I'll make sure to tell you how I'm feeling too, because the truth is, I'm a little scared myself about having this baby."

"Yeah?" he asks, surprised.

"Of course I am. I mean, I love our baby so much already, but I have no clue what to do. What diapers are best to use, what formula is better, when should they start food? All of it. It's something I have to learn, but we'll learn it together."

"Jesus. See I didn't even think about any of that shit. Knowing me, I'd probably forget to fucking feed it."

I burst into laughter, my throat raw and scratchy. "No, you won't, but these are all things we'll learn together. And if we fail, well, we always have Grams. She will definitely know what to do."

He grins. "Yeah, she will." His hand moves to my cheek in a gentle caress. "But I have no doubt, Jules, you will be the best mom in the world."

"And you will be the best father," I tell him, tears thick in my voice. "You are so much better than you know, Jaxson, you're perfect, and I hope our baby turns out to be just like you."

A nurse walks in, interrupting our moment. She smiles to see me awake and does a quick check, taking my vitals and topping up my pain medication. After she leaves I notice how exhausted Jaxson looks.

"Have you been home at all to sleep?"

He shakes his head. "I'm not going back until you do."

"Come here," I say softly, patting the bed next to me. "I want to feel you beside me."

"Jules, baby, I want to be next to you too, but I'm a little big for that bed, and you need room to rest and get better."

"All I need to get better is to have you beside me." I tell him, making room next to me.

It's obvious he still doesn't think it's a good idea but he gives in, taking the open spot beside me.

Carefully, I turn on my side to face him and he drapes an arm over me. We lie in the dark, silently watching one another.

"How bad do I look?" I ask, knowing it's probably pretty bad since my face feels about three times its usual size.

"You're still the most beautiful woman I've ever seen. Nothing else matters, Julia, the rest will fade over time," he says, pressing his lips to my forehead. "Sleep, baby."

I bury my face in his chest and run a hand up his shirt, feeling his warm bare flesh. "I love you."

"I love you, too," I hear him whisper just before I fall into a blissful sleep.

CHAPTER 46

Julia

"Good morning, Julia, it's nice to finally see you awake. I'm Dr. Gordon, and I've been the one overseeing you the last few days. How are you feeling this morning?"

Dr. Gordon stands just inside the room, his hand resting on a machine that he rolled in with him. He must be new to the hospital, because I have never seen him before, and in a small town, you know everyone. He's an older man with a kind smile, and I instantly feel comfortable with him.

"I'm feeling all right. My throat is tender and raw, especially when I speak, but as long as the nurse keeps giving me what she has been, then I feel quite lovely actually."

He chuckles. "Yes, good old morphine always tends to make people feel that way, although, unfortunately, we will be changing your pain medication to something different soon. I'm sure the nurse told you though, that everything we are giving you is in smaller amounts, and is okay for your baby."

"Yes, sir. It was the first thing I asked."

"Ah, yes, the same as your young man here. Although, his approach was a little, shall we say… protective?" He chuckles.

My attention shifts to Jaxson and I shoot him a questioning look.

He shrugs, looking unregretful.

The poor nurses, I can only imagine what he was like.

"Anyway, I brought a little something in with me today that I think will brighten your morning," Dr. Gordon continues. "This machine is a portable ultrasound. Although the baby seems to be doing well after your injuries, I'd like to take a look, and thought you would, too."

Excitement barrels through me at the thought. "I'd love to."

"Will it hurt her?" Jaxson asks in concern.

"No, Jax, it's just a camera they put on my stomach so we can see the baby on that screen," I explain, pointing to the monitor.

"That's right," Dr. Gordon says, backing me up. "However, since you're in the very early stages of pregnancy this will be done internally. Are you okay with that?"

"Oh sure, no problem."

"Whoa, wait, hold the fuck up." Jaxson straightens, flipping his hand up. "What do you mean *internally*?"

"Jax, it's all right. This is normal."

"Yes it is," Dr. Gordon begins to explain it to him. "During pregnancy she will be having many things happen internally. This is still not going to hurt her and once she's further along, then the camera will be placed on her stomach."

"It'll be okay. You'll see," I assure him, taking his hand.

It's clear he doesn't like it but he accepts it. "Just be careful with her."

"I promise, she's in great hands." Dr. Gordon hits the button on the bed to lay me down before getting into position. Then he reaches under the blanket and inserts the camera.

Jaxson glares at him, looking ready to rip his head off any moment. I grab the side of his face, bringing his gaze to mine. "It's all right, Jax, I'm fine."

The sound of static and a fast thumping beat have both of us snapping our attention to the monitor.

"Let's have a look." Dr. Gordon hits a bunch of buttons and points to the screen at a small looking bean that flickers in rhythm.

"Holy shit, Jules, that's our baby," Jaxson says in awe.

Dr. Gordon chuckles. "Yes, it is, the flickering you see is the baby's heartbeat. It's nice and strong."

Tears fill my eyes, my smile big. "Isn't this so cool, Jax?"

"Yeah, baby, real cool," he says, bringing my hand to his for a kiss.

We both watch the screen with fascination and excitement as Dr. Gordon explains everything to us, measuring the baby at around six weeks.

"When are we able to find out the sex?" I ask.

"Around the eighteen week mark, which is when your next ultrasound will probably be scheduled for. Dr. Bayer is your physician, correct?"

I nod.

"Then I'll make sure she gets these results. Everything looks great though, your baby is strong and healthy."

I look over at Jaxson, and smile. "See. Just like you."

A storm of emotions pass over his expression before he drops his head in my lap. I run my fingers through his hair and don't say anything else and neither does the doctor. As he packs up his stuff, I thank him for everything, and then he's gone, leaving the two of us alone.

Jaxson moves up beside me and pulls me into his arms. "Our baby is going to be really fucking cool, Jules."

I snuggle in closer to him, my heart content. "Yeah, it will be."

CHAPTER 47

Julia

A week later, I'm thankful to be getting out of the hospital and going home. My discharge papers have just been signed and Jaxson is packing up the rest of my stuff.

I look around at all the flowers and balloons that fill my room and feel so blessed to have the friends that I do. This whole week I've had constant visitors. Grace and Kayla even set up a little celebration party with everyone in my room to congratulate Jaxson and me on the baby.

Jaxson, Sawyer, and Cade also shared the news about them buying the gym. I thought it was a great thing for Jax, but most of all I'm happy that Cade and Sawyer are going to move here. They have become like brothers to me, the same way Cooper is. We're all like one big family; even Jaxson and Kayla called a truce. Well mostly, Kayla still loves messing with him, and to be honest, I can't ever see her stopping.

Jaxson stayed with me most of the time, only the last few days did he step out for a bit. He made sure someone was with me every time he did. Sawyer, Cooper, and Cade always went with him. I know he is up to something, but I have no idea what.

"Okay, I think that's it," Jaxson says, walking out of the bathroom, looking his usual sexy self. "Cade and Sawyer are going to come by later and grab all the flowers and balloons for us." He drops my bag by the door and looks over to see me watching him.

His eyes close, jaw locking. "Stop looking at me like that."

"Like what?" I ask innocently, sitting on the side of my hospital bed, with my feet dangling close to the ground. My white, baby-doll sundress rests against my upper thighs. I'm still covered in bruises, but thankfully they have begun to fade.

Jaxson moves for me, coming to stand between my legs and braces his hands on either side of my hips, his lips only a breath from mine. "Like you want me to do things to you that I can't do, especially right now."

"There is something you can do," I whisper breathlessly.

"What's that?"

"Kiss me." Fisting his shirt, I close the small gap between us, moaning at the beautiful contact of his mouth against mine.

A growl escapes him but he keeps his pressure gentle, like he has been with me all week. As much as I love this side of him, I want his other side back, the aggressive one. We haven't spoken much about what happened with Wyatt; it's just as difficult for me to talk about it as it is for him to hear.

I've had an overwhelming desire to be with him, for him to be inside of me and erase the ugly memories of Wyatt's unwanted hands.

"Uh, knock, knock." Cooper's voice breaks up our kiss.

Jaxson pulls back, his eyes dark with the same need claiming me. He turns to face Cooper. "What are you doing here?"

Cooper doesn't look at him, he only addresses me. "Um, Jules, there's someone here who's been wanting to talk to you. Is it okay?"

"Sure, who is it?" I ask, wondering why he seems so nervous.

"Well…"

"Me," Ray Jennings says, walking in behind Cooper.

Fear snakes down my spine, my heart beating wildly.

Jaxson moves for him in a flash. "What the fuck are you doing here?"

Cooper grabs him before he can reach Ray. "Easy, man, he just wants to talk to her. He's not here to start problems. I wouldn't have brought him otherwise."

"I don't give a shit, he's not welcome anywhere near her."

"It's all right, Jaxson." I don't know why on earth he wants to talk to me, but I know Cooper wouldn't have brought him here if it were to start trouble.

"No, it's not. You don't have to listen to anything he has to say. You owe him nothing."

Ray ignores Jaxson and keeps his gaze on me. "He's right, you don't owe me anything, but I feel like I owe you. And I'd really like it if you would hear me out, Miss Julia."

I take in Ray's appearance and for the first time, the wealthy, powerful man looks unkempt. He has dark circles under his eyes from exhaustion, and his clothes are wrinkled, looking as if he's slept in them. He looks… sad.

I nod. "All right, go ahead."

He clears his throat. "Well, first off, I just want to say I'm sorry. Real sorry for what my son did to you. I knew he was quite taken with you, but I did not think he was obsessive. Over the last few days, I've learned things about him that I never knew, and for that I am truly sorry." He swallows thickly, his eyes beginning to well with emotion. "If I had known I would have gotten him help."

I can only imagine how hard it was for Ray to hear half of the things he did about Wyatt. Including dealing cocaine, which is how Melissa was supplied for her drug habit.

I feel bad for him because even though I'm not sorry Wyatt is dead, I am sorry Ray lost him. As far as I know, Wyatt is all he had. Wyatt's mom died when he was a baby and Ray never remarried.

"I know my apology doesn't make up for what he did, nothing will. But I'd really like to take care of your medical bills, if you'd let me."

"No!" Jaxson says, his voice hard. "We don't need your money."

Ray shifts nervously, his eyes remaining on me. "Like I said, I know this won't make up for anything, but I'd really like to do something to show how sorry I am."

I think about it for a moment then nod. "Thank you for your apology. I accept your offer to pay for my medical bills."

"Unfuckingbelievable!"

I glare over at Jaxson, not appreciating his outburst.

"Thank you," Ray says relieved. "And thank you for hearing me out. Again, I'm sorry and I'm glad you and your baby are all right."

When he turns to leave, I call out his name, stopping him at the door.

He turns around, and my heart breaks when I see a tear trickling down his worn cheek.

"I just want to say that I'm sorry for your loss. I know this entire situation has hurt a lot of people, not just me."

He watches me for a long moment, his sad eyes looking at me differently than he usually does. "Thank you," he croaks then leaves out the door.

Silence fills the room as I stare at the closed door, my breathing heavy from the pain in my heart. Covering my face, I sob into my hands, hating the conflicting turmoil battling inside of me. Wyatt's death was unavoidable, even necessary, but I can't help feeling bad for Ray, knowing he's all alone. So many lives were affected from Wyatt's actions, not just mine.

A second later, I hear the door shut, then feel Jaxson come to stand in front of me. He hunkers down in front of me, resting his hands on my thighs while my face remains hidden behind my hands.

"I know you don't understand me taking his money, and I know you don't like it," I cry. "But he's hurting too, Jaxson. He didn't do this to me, Wyatt did. And if letting him pay for my bill brings him a small measure of peace, then I'm going to accept it."

He places a gentle kiss on the inside of my thigh, offering me comfort. "You're right, I don't understand it, and I don't like it, but that's because you're a better person than I am."

"I just want everyone to stop hurting, including myself."

"I know, Jules. You'll get through this. I'll help you."

He waits patiently as I release everything I need to, his warm hands rubbing my legs in a comforting gesture.

Once my tears subside, he takes my hand. "Come on, baby, let's go home."

It was past suppertime by the time I had been discharged, so we stopped at a drive-thru and grabbed a bite to eat. Halfway home Jaxson pulled over on the side of the road and blindfolded me, telling me he had a surprise for me. For the last few minutes, I've been dying of curiosity.

"I have to say, Jax, this is kinda kinky, we should try this sometime," I tease, wishing I could see his expression.

"Julia," he growls.

I chuckle and feel the truck come to a stop. "Are we home? Can I take it off now?"

"Just wait, I'll come around to get you."

I hear him exit the truck, slamming his door, and wait for him to come to my side. I'm close to bursting from excitement, dying to know what he's up to. I'm assuming this has to do with the sneaking around he did this week when leaving the hospital.

As my door opens, I turn to the side and feel his hands span my hips. I find his shoulders as he helps me down. Once my feet touch the ground, I wrap my arms around his neck and feel him stare down at me.

"Kiss me," I whisper.

His groan pierces the air before his mouth claims mine. I sigh against his lips, the small feather of a touch spreading through every part of my body.

"Come on," he mumbles, breaking the beautiful contact much too quickly. Taking my hand in his, he leads me across the gravel, the shale crunching under my flip-flops until we reach grass where he comes to a stop.

The little pieces of hair that have escaped my ponytail blow gently into my face from the warm night breeze as he comes to stand behind me. His hands move to my bare shoulders, and my pulse races as he leans down, pressing his lips to the base of my throat.

He flattens his hand on my stomach, pulling me against him where I can feel his erection.

"Are you trying to kill me?" I moan.

He chuckles, his breath tickling my ear. "I love you, Julia."

I smile, warmth invading my heart. I will never tire of hearing him say those words. "I love you, too."

I feel his hands move to the back of my head as he unties the blindfold. I blink several times, my eyes adjusting to the fall of night and I try to absorb what's in front of me. My heart understands it before my mind because tears immediately spring to my eyes, the sight before me taking my breath away.

A massive tree has been planted in my front lawn. Strings of white lights decorate it, making it look beautiful and majestic. But my favorite part of all, the one that has emotion flooding my heart, is the handmade wooden swing that's attached to it.

"I can't believe you remembered this," I breathe, tears spilling down my cheeks.

"I remember every word you've ever breathed, Julia."

My breath catches as I turn to him. "You did this for our baby?"

His response is a sexy smirk before he takes my hand and leads me over to the swing. I grab the rope that's on either side of me, lit with white lights, and sit down.

Jaxson kneels before me. "I did this for you, and when our baby gets old enough I will push them too, every night after supper."

A sob explodes past my lips, my face burying in my hands as I become overwhelmed with emotion.

He remembered every word.

"Look at me, baby." He pulls one of my hands away from my face and I gasp when I see he's holding a square cut diamond ring.

"Are you serious right now?" I ask through a fresh wave of tears.

"Julia—"

"Yes!" I answer before he can finish, then rein myself in quickly. "Sorry, continue."

He chuckles, amused by my excitement. "Marry me."

"You're supposed to ask, not demand it," I say with a broken laugh.

Another sexy grin tugs at his lips. "You know me better than that. I'm someone who demands, not asks. But if you say yes, I promise to love you forever, and push you on this swing every night for the rest of your life."

Warmth invades my chest, my heart soaring. "You're right, I do know you better, and I like you bossy. So shove that beautiful, shiny rock on my finger then come over here and kiss me."

"Now look who's bossy," he grunts, sliding the ring on my finger.

Taking his face between my hands I kiss him, long, slow, and deep, feeling it all the way to my soul.

"I'll take good care of you and the baby, Jules," he says, pulling back to look at me. "I promise to be what you guys deserve."

"You already are. You always have been." Grabbing his hand, I stand up. "Swing with me," I say, reversing our positions.

Our gazes remain locked as he sits on the swing, bringing me down to straddle him, his erection hitting me where I crave him most.

He groans, his eyes turning to fire as he grips my hips where my dress has ridden up. I grab the ropes on either side of his head, my eyes never leaving his as we begin to gently sway.

"How on earth did you get this tree here and planted?" I ask softly.

"The guys helped me. The lights were Kayla's idea, and I have to say it was a good one."

"Yes, it was," I agree, staring into his ice-blue eyes that are warm with need, yet fierce with restraint. "I miss you, Jaxson," I tell him sadly, knowing we need to have this conversation.

He frowns. "I'm right here, baby. I'm not going anywhere."

"You're holding back, you're not giving me all of who you are."

Realization dawns on him. "Jules…" He trails off, shaking his head.

"I need you," I plead quietly. "I need all of you, because you're the only one who can make me forget. He was the last one to touch me, and I hate him. I hate that I can still feel it. Make me forget. I want—"

He cuts me off with his mouth, his lips possessive, claiming me body and soul.

Moaning, I thread my fingers in his hair, holding him captive to me. I wiggle to get closer, grinding down on his erection.

With a growl, his hands cup my bottom, encouraging me further. He pulls his mouth from mine; trailing his firm lips down my throat. "You're mine, baby. Feel me. This is the only touch you're going to feel for the rest of your life."

"Yes, only yours," I whisper, pulling at his shirt, desperately needing more of him.

He leans back, swiftly discarding the material to reveal perfection. My hands explore his hot, naked skin, loving the way his muscles ripple and flex under my touch.

His fingers slip under my straps, dragging them down my arms until my dress is bunched at my waist. Thanks to the built-in bra, I'm completely bared to him. The warm evening breeze creating goose bumps to break across my fevered skin.

I feel Jaxson tense, fury raging in his eyes as he stares at my exposed skin. Looking down I realize he's seeing the faded marks on my breasts.

I force his eyes to mine. "Don't let him come between us. Erase them with your touch."

He buries his face in my chest, exhaling a deep breath. "I'll never let anyone hurt you again, Jules. I swear."

"I know," I whisper.

Gently, his lips brush every mark, healing some of my wounded heart. A harsh whimper leaves me when he takes a peaked nipple into his mouth. I clutch his shoulders, my back arching in pleasure as he does exactly what I need him to… *make me forget.*

"Jaxson, I need you inside of me, I need to feel all of you."

"Fuck, yes," he growls.

Grabbing onto the ropes on either side of me, I pull myself up while he fumbles to undo his pants. He pulls them open just enough to free his smooth, hard cock. His hands span my hips, shredding my soft yellow panties from my body before running his fingers through my wet flesh, sending pleasure to explode through me.

"Always so fucking wet and ready for me, Julia."

He grabs his cock and runs it where his fingers just were, coating it with my arousal, driving me wild with need.

"Please, Jaxson, now."

He lowers me onto him—too slow. Fighting against his cautious grip, I sink down on him, a cry of ecstasy leaving my lips as he fills me completely.

"Jesus!" His fingers dig into my hips with restraint.

"Stop holding back, please," I plead.

"Baby, you just got out of the hospital. I don't want to hurt you even more." Every word is delivered between clenched teeth.

"You won't. Just… please, Jaxson, fuck me."

With a growl, he pumps up into me harder and faster. It's still not all he's capable of but it's exactly what I need.

"Yes!" I cry out, pleasure whipping through my senses. "Don't stop!

"Never. I'm never going to stop. I'm going to fuck you for the rest of my life. Sometimes it's going to be slow and gentle, other times it will be fast and hard but it will always, only, ever be me, Julia. Because you're mine."

"Yes, yours." I match him thrust for thrust, our rhythm so in sync I don't know who's driving it.

"That's right, baby. Fuck, you feel so damn good." He leans in, catching a nipple between his teeth as his hand moves between us, fingers seeking and exploring.

I whimper, feeling my impending orgasm build inside of me.

"That's it, baby, I can feel how close you are. Give me what I want, Julia. Let me feel your tight little pussy grip my cock." His husky, erotic words send me over the steep edge.

My head falls back on a cry, my gaze going to the dark night sky that's filled with stars, the bright spots blurring from the strength of my orgasm.

When I feel every last bit of pleasure leave my body, I bring my head forward and collide with Jaxson's fierce gaze.

"You're fucking perfect, and the best thing that's ever happened to me," he says.

I wrap my arms around his neck, bringing us chest to chest, our hot skin melding together as our hearts beat as one. My lips brush the corner of his eye as I deliver a gentle kiss. "You're the very best thing that has ever happened to me, too. And I promise, you're safe with me. I'll never leave you."

His eyes burn with too many emotions to name. A groan vibrates from his chest as I pick up pace again.

"Let go, Jaxson," I whisper, just before I lean down and sink my teeth into his shoulder.

"Fuck!" His cock pulses inside of me as his orgasm takes him.

I relax against him, my body limp with pleasure. His arms hold me close as we catch our breaths, our heartbeats slowing to normal.

"I have to say, Jules, I did not intend this swing for what we just did, but I'm sure fucking glad we will both be able to enjoy it."

I giggle against his shoulder. "I love it." Lifting my head, I look at him, our lips only a breath away. "Thank you, for everything."

"Thank you for agreeing to marry me."

"Well I thought I should give in, that tattoo on your back kind of ruins you for anyone else," I tease.

He doesn't laugh like I hoped he would; instead his expression sobers, his hand moving to my cheek. "Every other woman was ruined for me the moment I laid eyes on you. You have always been mine, and you always will be."

I swallow thickly, his words settling like a warm blanket over my heart. "I love you… forever."

EPILOGUE

Julia

7 Months Later

"No fucking way, I will not wear pink at our wedding," Cooper says heatedly.

The four of us sit in my kitchen having dinner, discussing Kayla and Cooper's wedding plans. Clearly, they are still having issues over the colors.

Jaxson shakes his head vehemently, his expression panicked. "I'm with Coop, no pink."

"Oh stop being ridiculous," Kayla says. "You guys act like I'm asking you to wear a pink suit, it's a tie for crying out loud."

"I don't give a shit, Kayla, I'm not a pink kind of guy," Cooper exclaims, seeming more frustrated by the minute. "There's a thousand other colors out there, can't you pick something else?"

Kayla shrugs. "Okay fine, purple."

"For fuck's sake" he grumbles.

I giggle at Coop's signature move when he pinches the bridge of his nose.

As excited as I am for Kayla and Cooper's big day, because I know it's going to be amazing, this wedding planning business can be stressful. I am thankful Jaxson and I did ours the way we did.

It was very small. Jaxson is a private person and isn't one for being the center of attention, which was all right with me. Besides, neither of us wanted to wait that long to make wedding plans.

One month after he proposed, we had the small ceremony, at the very place I fell completely in love with him... our spot. It was only close friends and family; it was beautiful, intimate, and perfect. The beach was dotted with a thousand glowing tiki torches and further highlighted by the full moon and twinkling stars. We danced the night away with our bare feet in the warm sand and the cool ocean breeze on our faces.

We thought about going on a honeymoon, but decided not to. We were too nervous to be away from my doctor, just in case. So instead, the next night Jaxson planned a romantic night under the stars at the lighthouse.

It was perfect. It was...us.

"Fine! We'll wear pink ties, but that's it. I mean it, Kayla, don't push it on us anywhere else."

"Thank you, baby," she replies, kissing Cooper.

Jaxson drops his head in his hands, groaning in defeat.

"Well I think you guys are going to look incredibly sexy," I say, trying to ease their egos.

Cooper grunts. "More like fucking pretty."

Kayla and I burst into laughter and that's when I get a kick in the bladder. My hand drops to my stomach, rubbing comfortable circles. Jaxson and I found out we're having a girl, and both agreed to name her after my mother, Annabelle.

Jaxson is incredibly protective over her already, and Sawyer's comments never help either. The first thing he said to Jaxson when he found out it was a girl was, *Ha, ha, you're going to have a daughter, and she's going to grow up and be hot, just like Julia.*

Of course Jax didn't find it as funny as everyone else, and if there was ever a time I thought he would kill Sawyer, it was then.

I'm brought out of my thoughts with another kick that has me needing to use the bathroom. I push on the table to try and get out of my chair, but the struggle is real.

Jaxson jumps to his feet, pulling me to stand.

"I can't wait until I'm no longer too fat to stand," I grumble.

He pulls me against him, my round belly making it complicated for us to be too close. His head dips as he brings his mouth to my ear. "You're fucking sexy and once they leave, I'm going to show you how much."

I shiver in anticipation, loving how much he still always wants me. I head to the bathroom, turning my back on the group before Cooper and Kayla can see my flushed cheeks. Just as I situate myself, Annabelle kicks me so hard I gasp, and a ton of liquid gushes into the toilet.

What the… I look down in shock, realizing my water just broke.

Oh. My. God.

I'm thankful it happened now and not at the dinner table.

Okay, Julia, keep calm and think.

What did I read about? I guess the minor cramps I've been having today make sense.

After cleaning up, I walk back into the kitchen to the three of them laughing about something Sawyer did. It dies abruptly when they catch sight of me, obviously my expression saying everything I am not.

"What's wrong?" Jaxson asks, jumping out of his chair.

"Well, nothing's wrong, per say. It's just, well… my water broke."

"What?" He and Cooper bellow at the same time.

Then chaos erupts.

"Shit, the bag. I'll get the bag." Jaxson is quick, running around the table in a panic.

Cooper stands at the same time, colliding right into Jaxson's haste. "Shit!" he grunts, falling back into the chair. He waits until Jaxson passes before standing back up. "I'll drive, I can put the sirens on."

They both flee out of the kitchen, Cooper running out the door and Jaxson up the stairs.

Kayla and I walk to the kitchen entryway and watch the chaotic scene unfold. Jaxson comes flying down the stairs a moment later with his hands full of things, including my blanket and pillow that I don't need.

He trips over the blanket at the bottom of the stairs and stumbles. "Fuck!" he curses but recovers quickly, then he's out the door.

At the sound of Cooper's sirens, Kayla and I look at each other. "Did they just leave?" she asks, exasperated.

I shrug, unsure. Everything feels surreal at the moment.

She shakes her head. "Unfuckingbelievable! Don't worry, Jules, I got you. Let me grab my purse and we're out of here."

Suddenly, the sound of tires skid to a halt outside, and Jaxson comes running back inside. "Julia! Why aren't you in the fucking car?"

"Don't talk to her like that, you asshole. She's having your baby," Kayla snaps. "If you and Cooper would calm the hell down, you wouldn't have left without us."

Jaxson takes a deep breath, trying to calm himself, then strides over to me, his long legs eating up the distance between us. "I'm sorry, baby, can you please get in the fucking car?"

I nod, since I can't seem to speak, too many emotions swirl inside of me. Excitement, happiness, but most of all, fear. Lord, I'm so scared right now.

"Come on." Jaxson picks me up as if I'm not a giant pregnant woman.

"Jax, I can walk."

He shakes his head. "This way I won't lose you."

Kayla scoffs. "You won't if you guys would calm down."

"What the hell is taking you guys so long?" Cooper bellows out his open window as Jaxson walks us through the front door and down the steps. "Let's fucking go, I don't want to have to deliver this baby on the side of the road."

Jaxson picks up pace, as if concerned the same thing might happen. Climbing in the backseat, he situates me so I'm sitting on his lap.

Kayla hops in the front, her finger jabbing into Cooper's shoulder. You need to calm down. Julia is going to have a baby and you're only—"

"Oh, ow." I gasp and grip Jaxson's shoulder when a painful cramp tightens my belly.

"Oh fuck! Hurry, Coop," he says, as if the baby is going to fall out of me any second.

My breathing comes out short and fast as I try to remember the labor classes I took. "Jaxson…" I trail off when another contraction hits me, this one stronger.

"It's okay, baby, I'm here. Keep breathing, you're doing good."

Once the wave passes, I quickly try to get out words before another one hits me. "Jax, I really need you to stay calm, okay? Promise me you will stay calm. Because I'm really scared right now, and I don't want you yelling or scaring any of the nurses away."

He kisses my shoulder. "I'm calm, baby, and I'll stay calm. I promise I'll make sure you're taken care of."

"Thank you." I smile, excitement masking some of my pain. "She's coming, Jax. I can't wait to meet her."

He grins back. "Me too, baby. You're going to do great."

He claims my mouth in a mind numbing kiss, right when another one hits, my cry of pain exploding against his lips.

He freezes, scared to move. "Cooper… please hurry the fuck up."

Oh god, I have a feeling this is not going to go smoothly.

"Ahh! Oh god. Oh god," I wail, not caring in the least who hears me like I did when we first got here. This hurts so damn much.

"Deep breaths, Julia, you're doing great." The kind nurse reassures me, standing next to my bed as she watches the machine measuring my contractions.

Jaxson jumps up out of his chair that's next to me, glaring at the nurses. "Where the fuck is the guy with the drugs? He was supposed to be here two fucking hours ago."

"Jax, you promised," I plead, reaching for his hand.

"I'm calm, baby, I'm calm. Don't worry, I got this shit under control."

A laugh escapes me, even though I'm in excruciating pain.

He smirks. "All right, well maybe not totally under control."

"The anesthesiologist is on his way, sir. You have only been here thirty minutes, so no, he wasn't supposed to be here two hours ago."

He glares at her, not liking that response. "Well, it's thirty minutes too long. This guy should be prepared and waiting for this shit to happen."

I shake my head, laughing in disbelief when another bout of pain slices through me. Jaxson keeps hold of my hand, whispering words of encouragement in my ear that I'm really starting to find annoying, which makes me feel bad.

Thankfully, the anesthesiologist comes in shortly after and brings me peaceful relief. Though not before Jaxson ordered him to 'be careful' with the gigantic needle in his hand.

A few minutes later the nurse checks me again, watching the fetal monitor, and instantly I know something's wrong.

"Get the OR prepped, stat!" she shouts out the open door then looks back at me, her hand remaining inside of me. "Miss Reid, we need to do an emergency C-section. The umbilical cord is wrapped around the baby's neck."

"What?" I gasp, fear gripping my heart.

"What the fuck does that mean?" Jaxson bellows, looking ready to tear the place apart.

A flurry of activity explodes through my room as the nurse rushes to explain. "It's all right, this sort of thing happens more often than not. Try not to panic, I know it's hard, but trust that we will take care of you both. You're still going to have a healthy baby, just not the way you were anticipating."

"Jaxson?" I whisper, looking up at him for reassurance.

He leans down, pressing a kiss to my forehead, his expression looking much calmer than I feel. "It's going to be okay, Julia, you heard what she said. Annabelle is going to be fine, you're just going to have her a different way. Trust me, baby, I won't let anything happen to either of you."

Even though that's a silly promise to make, I trust him completely.

"Sir, follow the nurse as you will need to get scrubbed up before coming into the OR."

His hand drops to my cheek, his thumb soothing over my clammy skin. "I'll be right there, everything will be fine, I promise."

I'm rolled away before I can respond, feeling lost without him.

Thankfully, it's only minutes that we're apart. Relief swamps me as Jaxson comes rushing into the OR. He sits down by my head, grabbing my cold hand in his big, warm one.

Everything happens quickly.

"You're doing great, Julia, everything is good on this end. I almost have your daughter out," Dr. Bayer says.

Jaxson rests his forehead on mine, reassuring me through all of it. It isn't long before the sound of a baby crying fills the air, causing my own tears to fall.

"Here she is, your beautiful baby girl," Dr. Bayer announces, placing this teeny-tiny, naked thing on my chest.

Her skin is a warm pink, her eyes big and blue, and she has the perfect amount of brown hair. "Oh my god," I sob. "Isn't she beautiful, Jax?"

I look up to see his head casted down and his hands clutched in his hair. He lifts his head to look at me, his eyes wet. It's the second time I've ever seen him cry.

"Yeah, Jules, she's beautiful. Just like you."

I smile, knowing he's going to be the best father ever.

"Oh my god, you're so beautiful," Kayla coos, kissing Annabelle's tiny nose. "Seriously, she is. This is the best looking baby I've ever seen. Don't you think, Coop?"

"Yep, only because she takes after her mom," he teases with a smirk.

"Actually, I think she has Jaxson's eyes," Kayla says, but quickly points her finger at him. "Don't take that as a compliment, buddy."

Jaxson grunts.

"Auntie Kayla is going to buy you so many pretty dresses. Yes, I am. You're going to be the best-dressed kid around."

I giggle, watching her fawn all over Annabelle.

"All right, time's up. Give her back to me now," Jaxson says, reaching for her.

Kayla pulls her in closer to her chest. "No. I'm not done yet."

"Come on. Once Margaret gets here, I'm not going to be able to hold her until she leaves, and who knows when that will be."

Kayla rolls her eyes. "Fine. Sorry, kid, your dad can be a real pain in the ass. Be prepared for when he turns all green and spittin' mad. You will probably see it when you bring your first date over to the house."

Jaxson glares at her as he takes Annabelle. "There will be no dating," he grumbles. Leaning down, he presses a gentle kiss to her tiny forehead, the sight completely warming my heart. "The only man you need is me, baby girl. So don't go getting any ideas from your Auntie Kayla. I'm going to show you exactly what to do if any boy asks you out."

"Between you, me, Sawyer, and Cade we got that shit covered," Cooper replies seriously.

I shake my head with a smile. Even though I'm excited for the others to get here, I love that it's just the four of us right now. The way it has always been. Cooper and Kayla are the closest Jaxson and I have to siblings, and the four of us have been through a lot together.

I decide now is a good time to ask them what Jax and I discussed the other day. "Jaxson and I were talking, and we would really like for you both to be the godparents."

"Oh my god, really? Of course we will, we would be honored!" Kayla says, her eyes becoming emotional while Cooper wears a big smile. "All right, give her back now." She reaches out for Annabelle again.

"No way. I just got her."

"So what? You get to live with her and see her every day, I don't."

"What the hell are you talking about? You're pretty much over every day."

Kayla glares at him, looking ready to battle.

"Fine, whatever," he grumbles, reluctantly handing Annabelle off to her.

He moves to lie next to me on the queen bed. We got a private luxury room at the hospital since I will be here for a few days to recover. "How are you feeling? Do you need anything?"

"Just you," I tell him with a smile.

"That's something you'll always have." Leaning down, he rests his forehead against mine, blanketing us in our own intimate world. "You did real good today, Jules."

"Thanks, so did you. You only got mad at two people, I'm very proud of you," I tease, though I know it's something to be proud of.

"Anything for you, baby," he says with a smirk but his expression quickly sobers. "I love you, Jules. We're going to have a good life, I promise."

I smile, my heart skipping a beat like it always does when he says those words. But I didn't need the reassurance. We have come a long way to get to where we are now, and I know it wasn't for nothing. I know with every fiber of my being that our life together will be nothing short of extraordinary.

Sweet Temptation

Men of Honor Series

K.C. LYNN

Sweet Temptation

Published by K.C. Lynn

Second Edition

Cover Art by: Vanilla Lily Designs
Editing: Wild Rose Editing
Formatting: BB eBooks

Dedication

This is for my mom because Sawyer is her favorite. Thanks for always being my biggest supporter. Sawyer and Grace are for you.

PROLOGUE

Grace

The afternoon heat is stifling as I jog home, my backpack and cheer bag swinging wildly in my haste. Guilt plagues me for being late, knowing it's going to run Mama and me behind on our drive out of town.

My phone dings with a text, the muffled chime barely penetrating my heavy breathing. Slowing down, I reach into the side of my backpack and pull it out to see it's from Adam.

> ***Adam:*** *Just wanted to say good luck and have a good weekend. I'll miss you. Bring me back any leftover pie. Love you, babe. :)*

My stomach does a little flip at the sweet message. A reaction I'm used to when it comes to him. We've been dating for almost a year, and lately he's been pushing to take our relationship to the next level. I appreciate how patient he's been, considerin' he isn't a virgin. I've been thinking about it a lot and I have decided, when I get back from the fair with Mama, I'm going to tell him I'm ready.

I send him a quick reply, letting him know I'll miss him too and I'll call as soon as we get home on Sunday. Hopefully, I'll come back $20,000 richer. The prize money from the bakin' contest will help Mama and I to start our dream; a dream we have been talking about for as long as I can remember.

Once my house comes into view, I pick up speed and run up my front steps. By the time I open the door I'm out of breath and have an ache in my side.

"Hey, Mama, sorry I'm late. Coach made us stay late at practice, but I'll be quick. Just let me change and we can start loadin' the car."

I toss my backpack and cheer bag off to the side then head into the kitchen to see the pies are stacked and ready, but there's no sign of her.

"Mama?"

A loud thump sounds above me, pulling my attention up to the ceiling. The eerie silence sends a skitter of unease down my spine. Slowly, I start toward the stairs, my approach quiet and cautious.

"Mama?" I call again, starting up the carpeted steps. "Are you up here?"

The higher I climb, the more I'm plagued with the feeling that something is very wrong. When I finally make it to the top, I find her bedroom door slightly ajar. I continue forward even though every instinct I possess is screaming at me to run. With my heart in my throat, I push open the door and find her room in disarray.

What on earth?

The closet door swings open with a bang, my mother barreling out onto the floor, naked and bleeding. A man follows out after her, holding a knife.

Fear paralyzes me, imprisoning me where I stand.

"Grace, run!" Her frantic scream pierces the air, snapping me back into myself.

I hesitate for only a second, not wanting to leave her but know I need to get help. Turning, I start for my room, my feet pounding the carpet.

"Hurry up and grab that bitch."

Someone grabs a fistful of my hair and yanks me off my feet. I land on my back painfully, the hard impact knocking the air from my lungs.

A man appears above me, his greasy, jet-black hair hanging into his dark malicious eyes—eyes that lack any emotion. "You're just as pretty as your mama. I think I'll fuck you, too."

My heart plummets straight to my stomach, the words he spews too vile to fathom.

"Leave her alone! Please don't hurt her." My mom's sobbing plea breaks my heart further.

I have to get us out of here; I have to get to the phone.

A strangled noise works its way up my throat as I'm pulled to my feet by my hair. The throbbing sting is dull compared to the pain that has taken up residency in my chest. Before I have time to anticipate what he's about to do, his disgusting mouth lands on mine.

I cry out against the brutal force and try to push him away but he doesn't budge. He's too strong. Instinct kicks in and I bring my knee up, nailing him between the legs.

"Fuck!"

The moment his grip loosens, I shove myself away and dash into my room, slamming the door behind me. I click the lock in place then push everything off my dresser, tipping it over to barricade myself in.

Reaching for the bedside phone, I quickly dial 9-1-1, my fingers trembling violently.

"9-1-1. What's your emergency?" Just as the operator answers, a forceful pounding starts against my door, almost throwing it off its hinges.

I dash into my closet, keeping the phone against my ear. "This is Grace Morgan, I live at 917 Lakeland Point. Two men have broken into my home, and they are hurtin' my mother."

My mother's screams penetrate the chaos roaring in my ears, and I hear her begging for her life.

"Please, you have to hurry!" I sob. "They're hurtin' her real bad."

"It's all right, honey. The police are on their way. Stay on the phone with me, okay?"

"Okay."

"How old are you, Grace?"

"Seventeen."

The relentless pounding on my door suddenly comes to a stop and so does my mother's fearful pleas.

I listen carefully, afraid to even breathe. A moment later a loud bang vibrates my walls and I hear wood splinter.

"Oh god! He's in my room."

My closet door swings open, revealing the furious man I escaped only moments ago.

A scream of terror shoves from my throat as he yanks the phone from me and throws it. I crawl under his arm as it smashes against the wall and push to my feet, attempting to escape his wrath once more, but I'm not fast enough.

His large body tackles me from behind, sending me to face-plant into the hardwood floor next to my bed. My lip splits open, the metallic taste of blood filling my mouth.

"You're not goin' anywhere, bitch." He pummels my back, every painful blow he delivers weakening me further. I fight against him only to be flipped to my back and struck across the face.

Pain explodes through my head and black spots dance in my vision. Groaning, I fight to remain conscious.

His rough hands grab the V-neck of my shirt and tears it down the middle, exposing my bra. Next, he fumbles with my spandex cheer shorts, trying to pull them down.

"No!" I buck against him, fighting with all the strength I have left.

"Stay still, bitch; this will be over quickly."

I don't submit to his command and it earns me another blow to the face.

My head snaps to the left and through watery eyes I spot my pink baseball bat from Little League. Reaching out, I grab it, curling my fingers around the rubber grip. I don't waste another second and swing hard, making solid contact with his head.

Grunting, he falls to the side.

I climb to my feet and swing again, harder this time, bringing the steel against his back. I continue to hit him, unable to stop, fear and anger fueling every violent blow.

Footsteps thunder down the hall, barely breaking through the dark rage that's consumed me. "Emilio, man, we need to get the hell out of here. Sirens are coming our way."

The guy who was in the closet with my mother comes to a hard stop just inside of my room, a bloody knife gripped in his hand. He takes in his friend who struggles to stand from my assault, his furious eyes snapping to me.

"You fuckin' bitch." He charges at me, fists swinging.

I raise the bat but miss his head by an inch. Before I can attempt again, he strikes out, his fist connecting with my temple. A tattoo on the inside of his wrist snags my attention before the force of his blow sends me into the wall.

He hauls his friend to his feet, draping an arm around his neck. "Come on, man, pull it together. We have to go."

I watch as they stumble out of my room and wait until I'm certain they are gone before managing to climb to my feet. My beaten body screams in protest as I go in search of my mother. I call out for her, but my voice sounds as weak as I feel.

Once inside her room, I falter at the sight of her lying naked in a pool of her own blood. Devastation seizes my chest, shredding it into a million pieces.

"Mama!" Running to her side, I slip in all the crimson liquid surrounding her, landing on my knees. I don't let it deter me and reach for her, cradling her lifeless body to my chest. "It's okay, Mama, just hang on, help is on the way," I cry, my sobs as broken as my heart.

My tears fall into her beautiful golden hair as I plead for her to hang on. No matter how much I reassure her that everything will be okay, I know it isn't. I know she's dead but my shattered heart refuses to believe it.

"I'm so sorry I was late. So sorry." Leaning down, I kiss her bloodstained forehead and bury my face into her hair.

Seconds later, chaos erupts around me.

At seventeen years old I had managed to live through the worst day of my life. Instead of finding peace and safety during my heartbreak I was sent to live with *him*—a man who is more evil than the devil himself.

CHAPTER 1

Grace

Three Years Later

"Order up!"

My tired feet ache as I rush over to grab the two hot plates filled with burgers and fries. It's only lunch and already exhaustion is weighin' me down. The twelve-hour shift I worked yesterday doesn't help.

"How are you doing out there, darlin'?" My boss, Mac, asks as he flips burgers over the flaming grill.

I grace him with my best smile. "You know me. I'm always great."

"I do know you, and if you weren't okay you still wouldn't tell me. I'm scared one day I'm going to look out there"—he points his massive flipper to the diner behind me—"and find you passed out, sleeping on my damn floor."

"Now, Mac, I barely get any sleep in my own bed, there's no way your floor is gonna cut it for me."

The tease earns me a grunt and shake of his head.

I take that as my cue and walk away to deliver the waiting couple their meals. I appreciate his concern but he needs the help and I need the money. It's a win-win situation for us both.

This might not be my dream job, but I'm thankful for it and even more thankful for Mac. The surly tough guy with dark hair, brown eyes, and a bunch of tattoos might look scary but he's nothin' more than a giant teddy bear. I'm grateful for everything he has done for me. Without him, I'd have nothing.

After delivering the plates of food, I attend to a few other tables and hear the bell jingle on the door, announcing more customers. In my peripheral vision, I see two men walk in and take a seat in the back. My heart skips a beat and awareness rolls through every nerve ending of my body. I already know who it is without looking over my shoulder.

Sawyer Evans.

Why does the arrogant, sexy son of a gun have to come in here to eat all the time? Why can't he go somewhere else?

Frustrated at myself for caring, I pull it together, and try not to look directly at him as I head for their table; otherwise, I'll make a fool out of myself. Instead, I focus on Cade. He's attractive too but he's also pretty darn scary. And he doesn't make my heart pound like it wants to fly out of my chest the way Sawyer does.

Stupid Sawyer!

"Hi, y'all," I greet quietly, reaching for my pad of paper. Not that I need it, but it will help distract me from making goo-goo eyes at Mr. Sexy.

"Hey, Grace," Cade replies, with his usual nod.

"Well, hiya there, Grace. Fancy seeing you here again, I didn't know you worked today." The deep, smooth baritone of Sawyer's voice sends a delicious shiver to dance along my skin.

Get a hold of yourself, Grace.

I let out a dramatic sigh. "I work pretty much every day, which you know, since you're in here every day."

"I don't come *every day*."

Scoffing, I pull my gaze up from the floor to his face and immediately regret it when I connect with the sexiest pair of green eyes I have ever seen.

Crap!

Heat creeps up my neck, turning my face the color of a tomato. My eyes narrow as I attempt to hide the effect he has on me. "Yes, you do."

His smug grin turns into a beautiful smile; one that girls drop their panties for in a heartbeat. "Nope, just on the days you're working, Cupcake."

My hands clench at the nickname he gave me a few weeks ago at Jaxson and Julia's weddin'. After watching the new bride and groom feed each other one of the beautiful cupcakes I had made, Sawyer yelled out, *"That's not how you're supposed to do it! You're supposed to do it like this."* He then grabbed his cupcake, coated my nose and mouth with the pink frosting, and proceeded to try to lick it off.

I, of course, dodged his attempt before he could make contact and thank god for that. Lord only knows what would have happened if I let him get those beautiful lips anywhere near mine. I probably would have given into temptation and embarrassingly mauled the man in front of everyone.

As the traitorous thought emerges, my eyes latch onto those perfect lips.

Gah! Snap out of it, Grace.

Yanking my gaze away, I direct my attention over to Cade. "What can I get for ya, Cade?"

Sawyer chuckles at my very apparent brush off. Cade's lips twitch, something that's rare to see. Usually he looks about ready to kill someone. "I'll get the special with mashed potatoes and a Coke."

I nod then flick an annoyed glance at Sawyer, making sure not to look directly at him. "You?"

There's a smile in his voice as he answers. "I'll get the usual. And, of course, throw in a slice of whatever delicious pie you baked for me today."

I roll my eyes at his arrogant assumption and walk away. Though, the sad truth is, every morning I do think about him as I make whatever pie I decide on for the day, because I know he'll be eating it. I've often wondered what his favorite one is, but of course I would never ask.

Hanging the slip up for Mac, I grab two cups and start filling their drinks. With a side-glance, I notice Sawyer stand and head toward the bathroom. No matter how hard I try not to, I find myself completely drawn to his every move. That sexy swagger of his makes my toes curl and knees weak.

It should be illegal for someone to look as good as he does. Today his messy blond hair is covered with a black Hurley cap, the longer strands brushing the tops of his ears.

He's wearing a black T-shirt that stretches across his broad shoulders and lean muscles. Loose, faded jeans that sport a few holes in them hang low enough on his lean hips that you can spot the edge of his boxer briefs…well, I'm assuming boxer briefs, they look like boxer briefs. Oh boy would I like to find out. Wait…no, I don't.

I'm yanked from my internal battle when I realize all that hotness has changed directions from the bathroom and is headed my way.

Uh-oh!

My head cranes back, eyes connecting with Sawyer's, and I find the biggest, most arrogant smile plastered on his handsome face.

"See something you like, Cupcake?" he asks, his smoldering voice as smooth as Tennessee Whiskey.

Heat invades my cheeks once again. Well now, this is embarrassin'. This is why I try not to look directly at him. Otherwise, I lose all common sense.

Rather than answer his question, I shove the drinks into his hands. "Here ya go. You can take these back to your table. Thanks for comin' to grab them." Without another word, I spin on my heel and storm into the kitchen.

His chuckle follows me—taunting me.

Even his stupid laugh is sexy.

CHAPTER 2

Sawyer

"What is with her? Why do you think she avoids me like the plague?" I ask Cade on the drive over to Jaxson and Julia's.

I'm feeling frustrated after leaving the diner. That woman tangles me up in knots and I fucking hate it.

"Maybe she's just not into you. You know that's possible, right?"

"No, it's not that," I say, dismissing the suggestion. It can't be. Not with the way her pretty amber eyes eat me up like I'm one of those delicious pies she makes. Christ, it makes me want to bend her over, hike up that waitress dress, and fuck her until we're both dying for air.

"Maybe it's because you're always messing with her. It really pisses her off."

I chuckle. It does but I can't seem to help myself, she's so fun to rile up. I love it when she gets all flustered; it's a hell of a lot better than witnessing the pain in her eyes that she tries so hard to hide, something I want to know more about.

Our conversation comes to an end when we pull up to Jaxson and Julia's.

Now I get to ruffle someone else's feathers.

A smile curves my lips as I climb out of the truck. Cade knocks first but we get no answer. Knowing Jaxson, he probably has his new wife in bed. So I make sure to knock again, louder this time.

The door flies open to a shirtless, scowling Jaxson.

Yep, I was right. He was trying to get laid.

"Do you always have to come at the worst fucking time?"

"It's nice to see you, too." I clap him on the back, passing him with a cheerful smile.

Julia pokes her head in from the kitchen, her hair rumpled, looking like she was just about to be fucked good.

Her greeting is much more polite than her husband's. "Hi, guys, come in."

"Hey, Julia," Cade replies, taking a seat at the kitchen table.

My greeting is a little more, shall we say, hands-on. "Well hey there, beautiful." I wrap my arms around her from behind, my hands resting on her slightly rounded stomach as I give her a kiss on the cheek. "I have to tell you, Julia, you're starting to make me have a thing for pregnant women."

"Oh, Sawyer." She giggles, delivering a playful elbow to my ribs.

Rough hands jerk me back, the collar of my shirt strangling me. "Get the fuck off my wife, asshole, and keep your hands to yourself."

I'm unable to control my laughter as I take a seat next to Cade.

"Oh, Jax, lighten up, he's just teasing."

"Yeah, *Jax,* lighten up."

The look he shoots me is a good indication that it's time to back off. He's only fun to rile up to a certain point.

We are now at that point.

"Are you guys hungry?" Julia asks. "I can make you something."

"We just came from the diner so we're good. But thanks anyway."

"The diner? Was Grace working again?" she asks, taking a seat on Jaxson's lap.

Cade answers with a nod.

"Of course she was," she grumbles. "I don't know why I even bothered asking. That girl has been working herself into the ground lately."

I noticed that, too. It seems all she does is work.

"Can I ask you something," I speak, knowing I shouldn't.

"Sure. Go ahead."

"Why does she always avoid me?"

"Because she's smart," Jaxson answers with a smirk.

Now it's my turn to scowl. "I'm serious. She doesn't even look at me half the time."

At least not when I'm addressing her, but I leave that out.

"Sawyer…" Julia starts, shifting uncomfortably.

"What is it? Tell me. Have I offended her in some way? I know I mess with her a lot, but I'm only kidding."

"Can I ask why you want to know? What is it you want with her?"

"Honestly, I don't really know. But it would be nice to at least be friends with her, talk with her."

Her shoulders deflate on a sigh. "You just have to be patient with her. She's guarded, she's been hurt, and I have a feeling I only know the half of it. It's taken her a long time to open up to Kayla and me."

I tense at the information. "What do you mean, 'hurt?' What kind of hurt are we talking about here?"

She looks away, her eyes dropping to the table. "It's not my story to tell."

"Is this something we should know about?" Jaxson asks. "Is she in trouble?"

"No, well, at least I don't think so. Like I said, I only know some of it."

We all stare at her, refusing to back down and she finally gives in.

"She lost her mother tragically when she was seventeen," she whispers. "And don't ask me for the details because I'm not sharing them with you, but it was really horrible. I also have a feeling that where she was, before coming here, was not a good place."

"What about her dad? Where is he?" I ask.

"Again, that's not my story to tell." Her eyes narrow at the hard look I give her. "Forget it. You're not going to bully me. Grace trusted me and I will not betray her. But, Sawyer, if you want to get to know her then do it, just…"

"What?" I ask when she trails off.

"Just whatever it is you want with her, whether it's friendship or more, I ask you to be sure about it. I don't want either of you to get hurt. You both mean a lot to me."

I nod, giving her my word.

I'd be lying if I said I didn't want to spend a long night with Grace in my bed, because I do, but I also want to get to know her, especially now.

All these unanswered questions aren't going to cut it for me. I will take Julia's advice and tread carefully but I refuse to back away from this. One way or another, I will get my answers, even if I have to break through every damn barrier she has.

CHAPTER 3

Grace

"Honey, don't take this the wrong way, but I'm sending you home," Mac says, his voice stern.

"Why?"

"Because you have been here for ten hours, Grace, and you worked twelve yesterday. You look about ready to fall over. You need to go home and get some sleep. Ruby's coming in; she'll be fine on her own now that the supper rush is over."

"I'm all right, Mac. Really."

His hand moves to my shoulder. "This ain't up for debate, darlin'. Go home and get some sleep. I appreciate all your help lately but it's important you get rest."

"All right," I relent quietly. "But just know I don't mind all the hours. I need the money."

"Oh," he says, his eyes narrowing, "and what exactly are you needing it for?"

"I've been thinkin' about taking some online courses for school. I haven't decided exactly what yet, maybe business or somethin'." I shrug. "But even online it can be costly."

"Well," he starts cautiously. "How much are we talking about? Maybe I can help."

"No!" My hand lifts, stopping him from going further. "You have already done too much for me. I will not accept anythin' more."

He becomes irritated at the quick rejection, a scowl forming on his worn face.

I close the space between us, wrapping my arms around the big lug. The last thing I want to do is hurt his feelings. "I love and appreciate everything you've done for me. Please don't be offended, and understand that I can't accept any more from you."

His burly arms hug me tight, a little too tight that I find it hard to breathe. "Fine, you stubborn-ass girl, I'll drop it for now. But you are going home, Grace, and I want you to get some sleep. That's an order."

I step back, giving him a sassy salute. "Yes, sir."

His lips twitch. "Go on and get outta here. I'll see you tomorrow, darlin'."

"Bye." Lifting to my toes, I give him a quick kiss on the cheek then collect my purse and jacket. Before leaving, I grab the table scraps that I sat aside throughout the day and head for the back door, hoping the sweet, homeless, chocolate Labrador is there.

I spotted him when I took out the trash the other day and he bolted in the opposite direction, absolutely terrified of me. I've tried everything to coax him closer but nothing has worked. He doesn't trust me yet; which is something I can understand. So

I decided to start leaving leftover scraps for him and hope he's been the one eating them.

Sure enough, as soon as I push open the heavy door and set the container down, I hear a clickin' sound on the concrete. It isn't long until the cute, but homely lookin' dog, comes trotting around the corner. He stops a good distance from me but doesn't run off.

I take this as a good sign and remain where I am, kneeling by the door. "Come on, it's all right, I won't hurt ya." My tone is calm and gentle. "Are you hungry?" I ask, pushing the table scraps toward him.

His head tilts, a low whimper escaping him.

What are you so afraid of?

Hope fills my chest as he starts toward me, his steps cautious. I remain still, barely taking a breath. He comes only close enough to eat the food I brought.

I raise my hand ever so slowly, making sure he can see it and gently lay it on the side of his neck. "Good boy. See, I won't hurt you." My fingers are gentle, stroking his greasy fur. "Where did you come from? Don't ya have a family?"

He whines again, the sound completely breaking my heart.

"It's okay. Don't feel bad. Families are overrated anyway. And they're stupid if they don't love something as special as you."

A chuckle erupts behind me, scaring the bejeezus out of me. I jump with a scream and land on my butt, smackin' my head against the door in the process.

The dog yelps and takes off.

"Shit! Grace, are you all right?" A concerned pair of green eyes comes into my view as Sawyer kneels in front of me.

"Sawyer? What the heck are ya doin' sneakin' up on me like that?"

"Sorry, I didn't mean to scare you. Mac told me I could find you back here. I didn't want to intrude on your conversation with your new friend there." He jerks his thumb over his shoulder, the beginning of a smile curving his lips.

I glare at him, hoping to conceal my embarrassment. "Well, thanks a lot for scarin' him off. Do you know how long it's taken me to get that close to him?"

His amusement fades, guilt taking over his expression. "I really am sorry. I didn't mean to frighten you or the dog. Is your head all right?"

"Yeah, I'm all right," I tell him softly. "What are you doin' back here anyway? Don't you ever get tired of eatin' out?"

He smirks, turning my insides into goo. "I'm not here to eat, I'm here to see you."

"Me?"

"Yes, *you*. I thought I would see what time you were off work and offer you a ride. Looks like I came at the right time, Mac told me he's sending you home."

"You want to give me a ride home?" I ask, suspicion rearing inside of me.

"Yeah."

"Why?"

"What do you mean '*why*?' Why not?"

Why would he want to? What does he get out of it?

He stands, offering me his hand. I look at it for a long second before accepting it. His warm fingers curl around mine, sending a tingle up my arm, spreading right to the tips of my toes.

I'm pathetic.

"Well, thank you very much for the offer, but I like walkin'."

And if I'm around you for too long, I could end up jumping your bones.

He shrugs, not the least bit put off. "Okay, I'll walk with you then."

"You don't have to do that, Sawyer. I can manage on my own just fine; I do it all the time."

His eyes narrow in annoyance. "I know you can."

I peer up at him, trying to figure out what he's up to.

"Listen, Grace, I just want to talk. I thought we could get to know each other better since we have mutual friends. That's all."

Oh! Well that's awful nice of him. Now I feel bad for being so suspicious.

"All right. If you really want to walk with me, I'd like that."

He flashes me a smile, but it's not his usual arrogant one, it's a genuine one, and boy is it lethal.

"I want to," he assures me.

"Come on then, we'll head out through the front."

We walk back inside, my body humming from his close proximity.

The walk home is going to be a long one.

"See ya tomorrow, Mac." I wave as we pass by him.

"Bye, darlin', and remember what I said—sleep, young lady!"

"Yeah, yeah, yeah," I grumble.

Once we get outside, I bundle my jacket up from the slight chill in the air. Nearing the end of October you can feel winter on the horizon.

"What did Mac mean about you getting sleep?" Sawyer asks, falling in step next to me. He slows his stride since my legs are not nearly as long as his.

"He's just bein' a mother hen," I say, cutting my hand through the air. "He thinks I work too much and don't sleep enough."

He grunts. "You do work too much."

I shrug. "Mac needs the help and I need the money."

"And sleep?" he asks.

"Sleep hasn't come easy for me in a long time," I confess softly, regretting the words as soon as they leave my mouth.

His questioning eyes burn into the side of my face.

I quickly change the subject. "Aren't you cold? Where's your jacket?" I ask, pointing to the same T-shirt I saw him in earlier today.

"Cupcake, this is not cold. I grew up in Denver, you haven't seen cold until you experience a winter there."

I find myself intrigued with this tidbit of information. "You grew up in Colorado?"

"Yep, born and raised."

"I've always wanted to see snow."

"Believe me, it gets old fast. It's colder than shit and a pain in the ass to shovel."

Shoveling probably isn't all that fun, but I'd still love to experience it at least once.

I feel his eyes upon me again but I don't look over at him because, well, I don't want to embarrass myself like always.

"What about you, Grace? Where are you from?"

"Florida." My answer is nothing more than a whisper. It hurts to speak about the place where I lost everything that mattered to me.

"Did you like it there?"

I nod, since my throat suddenly feels a little too tight.

"Do you miss it?"

"I miss what I lost there."

Gah! What the heck is wrong with me? I have a loose tongue tonight.

"But I really like it here, too," I continue. "It's a nice town, and I'm glad I met Julia and Kayla." My pathetic attempt to change the subject sounds lame, even to my own ears. "Do you like it here?" I ask, hoping to steer the conversation back to him.

Thankfully, it works.

"I do. And what I love most about it is getting to piss off Jaxson on a regular basis."

A smile plays at the edge of my lips as I think about all the ways he's always pokin' at Jaxson. "How's the gym comin' along for y'all?"

"Good. We should be up and running in another couple months."

"Julia has told me a little about it. Sounds like it's gonna be a great place."

"Yeah." Is his only response before he turns the tables on me again. "Tell me about yourself, Cupcake."

"Well…my name is Grace and I hate bein' called Cupcake."

There's a smile in his voice when he speaks again. "Sorry, but I can't help it, you just remind me of a cupcake."

I scoff. "I'm sure I remind everyone of a cupcake now, since you shoved one into my face at the wedding."

He chuckles, amused with himself. "That's not why you remind me of a cupcake."

My eyes shift to his, my curiosity getting the better of me. "Oh yeah, then why?"

"Because you're as cute as a cupcake, you smell as sweet as a cupcake"—his tone drops and turns husky—"and I'll just bet you fucking taste as good as one, too."

Whoa.

All the oxygen gets sucked out of my lungs, my heart kicking into overdrive.

Damn, the man is good. He's the master at flirting. He could become a professional and write a book on it.

I wish I could think of a witty comeback but I'm not nearly as smooth as he is.

"All right, your turn," he says, saving me from having to make a fool out of myself.

I look at up him, my head tilting inquisitively.

"What reminds you of me?" He elaborates.

Sex!

Yikes, hold that tongue of yours, Grace!

"What makes you think anythin' reminds me of you?" I return, hoping he doesn't see the truth in my expression.

"Come on, there has to be something? Let me guess, sex? Orgasms?"

Well that hits a little too close to home.

It isn't long before the perfect thing comes to mind. Smiling, I glance up at him. "You really wanna know?"

"Yep."

"Have you ever heard the song "I'm Sexy and I Know It"?"

His steps falter and smile vanishes.

I start to worry that I overstepped, but then he throws his head back and lets out the huskiest laugh I've ever heard. It's so infectious that I cover my mouth and laugh, too.

"Okay, Cupcake, that was a good one. I'll give you that."

"Thanks. I thought it was quite clever myself," I admit, pride thick in my voice.

He tosses another question at me. "Favorite color?"

"I have two—pink and yellow."

He nods. "I can see that. Mine's blue, since I'm sure you've been dying to know."

I shake my head, biting back a smile. That would have been my guess, since that is the color of his truck. The deep blue is so dark it almost appears black until the sun hits it.

"Favorite movie?" he asks.

"*27 Dresses.*"

"Never heard of it."

"I'm not surprised. It's a chick flick," I tell him. "Okay, my turn."

He lifts a brow, almost seeming surprised, his arms spreading wide. "Ask away, Cupcake. I'm an open book."

"Favorite food?"

"Any one of your pies."

I roll my eyes so hard I practically see my brain. "I'm serious."

"I am too. They are the best I've ever had and I've had many samples. Although, I have a feeling your taste would beat out all of it."

Holy moly!

My cheeks turn to what I'm assuming is a deep shade of red. I'm thankful it's dark out, but apparently not dark enough.

"I like making you blush, Grace."

I turn my head to the side, trying to shield the evidence with my hair. "Yeah, well, it don't take much. So don't let it go to your already oversized head, Evans."

The response makes him chuckle and again I find myself laughing with him. It's been a long time since I laughed like this. I'm smilin' so much that my cheeks ache.

Since we're on the subject, I finally ask the one question I've been wanting to know. "Which one is your favorite?"

"What?"

"What pie is your favorite?" I avoid eye contact with him, feelin' embarrassed for some silly reason.

"That's a tough one because I really like them all. The one I had just the other day comes to mind first. It has berries and chocolate and shit in it."

I burst into laughter. "I never, ever put shit into my pies, Sawyer."

"You know what I mean… So, what's it called?"

My smile fades, a heaviness settling over my chest. "Missin' My Mama Pie," I admit on a whisper, paying close attention to the pavement beneath my feet.

"Why did you name it that?"

"Because I was missin' her when I made it. It's what pulled me out of bed at three in the morning." I shrug. "Whatever I'm feeling at that moment is usually how I name my pies."

I'm startled out of the heavy moment when Sawyer snags my elbow, his steps coming to an abrupt halt. My mouth opens to ask if everything's okay and that's when he pulls me in for a hug, his strong arms banding around me.

I tense, caught off guard by his sudden affection, but it doesn't take long for my mind to register the embrace. My body relaxes against him, arms wrapping around his waist as I soak in the comfort he so graciously offers. His heat envelops me, warming me from the inside out, and for the first time in a long time, I feel safe. Something I didn't think I was ever capable of feeling again.

All too soon he breaks the contact, but his body remains close. His hands frame either side of my face, tilting my head up until our gazes meet. "I'm sorry about your mom, Grace."

"Thanks," I whisper, my voice thick with emotion.

"If you ever need anything you can call me," he says. "It doesn't matter what time it is, I'll always come."

"Why?" I ask, unable to stop myself.

"Because you're my friend, and I take care of what's mine."

Warmth blooms across my chest, my heart swelling at his kindness. Without wanting it to, a single tear slips from the corner of my eye. Sawyer is there to catch it with his thumb, refusing to let it fall. Then, he surprises me once more by dropping a kiss on top of my head. The simple gesture is almost enough to make me break down into a blubberin' mess.

He slings an arm around my shoulders and starts moving again. "All right, Cupcake. Back to twenty questions. What's your favorite pie?"

"Hmm," I muse, thinking of my answer. "Grace's First Kiss Pie."

He tenses, his body tightening next to me. "I'm not sure I want to know why it's called that."

His teasin' brings a smile to my face. "My mama created it, after my first kiss. It's a graham cracker crust with raspberries, whip cream, and chocolate, because it was a sweet kiss. She even made little heart shapes with the dough on the top."

He grunts. "Sounds like a sissy kiss to me."

Laughter tumbles past my lips but it fades the moment we turn onto my street. Disappointment strikes me, hating to leave him already. I really enjoyed his company. One of the reasons I like being at the diner so much is because I'm always around people. Being alone gets old real fast.

I think about the letter I mailed out a week ago. One I should have sent when I first came to Sunset Bay and hope it will change my life for the better.

"So this is where you live," he says, assessing the old house as we head up my driveway.

"Yeah, it's Mac's. He rents it out to me. Or at least he's supposed to. Our agreement was he'd garnish rent off my wages, but my checks always have the full hours I worked. If I bring it up to him he gets all grumpy so I just keep quiet and appreciate it."

When he remains silent, I look up and find him watching me with an expression I can't decipher.

"Give me your phone," he says, putting out his hand.

"Have you ever heard the word *please*?"

There's a smile on his face as I reach into my purse and pull it out. He takes it from me and enters in what I'm assuming is his number. It has my heart dancing in my chest like a silly schoolgirl.

"There, now you have my number and I have yours."

I take my phone back and see he sent himself a text. The contact name he gave himself has me bursting into laughter—*Sexy Sawyer.*

"You, Sawyer Evans, have the biggest ego of anyone I've ever met."

"Not ego, baby, just confidence."

I shake my head but can't hide my smile. "Goodbye, Sexy Sawyer. Thank you for walkin' me home. I enjoyed talkin' with you."

He grabs my wrist in a gentle grip, his expression somber. "I mean it, Grace. Call me any time and I'll come, no matter what."

Emotion burns the back of my throat. "Thank you."

His eyes are on me as I climb up the front steps. "I'll pick you up again tomorrow."

I toss him a look over my shoulder, my brow lifting at his bold statement. "How do you know if I work?"

"Because I know everything, Cupcake." After flashing me one of his panty droppin' smiles, he walks away, taking all of his arrogance with him.

It leaves me with a flock of butterflies in my tummy and warmth in my heart.

CHAPTER 4

Sawyer

My mind reels as I walk back to my truck. I'm starting to realize there are many sides to Grace. She's not only sweet but also sassy. I loved hearing her laugh tonight, something I know she doesn't do often. Yet, no matter how much she smiled that pain still lurked in her pretty eyes. Whoever put it there, I want to find them and rip their fucking throats out.

It took every ounce of control I possessed not to kiss those sad, pouty lips of hers when she spoke about her mom. She makes me feel shit no other girl ever has. Raises every protective instinct inside of me.

Not only do I plan to see her tomorrow but also every day after that. She is full of secrets, and I am going to find out every single one of them no matter how long it takes.

My phone chimes with a text, pulling me from my thoughts. I fish it out of my pocket, a smirk curling my lips when I see whom it's from.

Cupcake: *Thank you again for walkin' me home, Sexy Sawyer. Let me know when you make it to your truck so I know you get there safely. :)*

I grunt. What does she think I am, a sissy?

Me: *Cupcake, I'm badass. Believe me, I will make it to my truck safe and sound. Now let's be honest, you just wanted an excuse to text me. Miss me already?*

My phone dings again a second later with her response.

Cupcake: *Ha, in your dreams, Evans! Seriously, how do you manage to carry that big head of yours around?*

Yeah, she can be fucking sassy.

Me: *I've got big shoulders, baby.*

Cupcake: **Eye roll**

Me: *Have a good sleep, Cupcake. I know you'll be dreaming of me.*

Minutes tick by before I finally get a reply.

Cupcake: *Maybe! ;)*

My cock hardens, every muscle in my body tightening with lust. Very soon I will be doing all the things I've been dying to do to her, but it will be done the right way. No just fucking around. I promised Julia I'd tread carefully and that's what I'm going to do. The last thing I want to do is hurt Grace. Although, I have a feeling she's the one who holds the power to destroy me.

My steps slow as I come up to my truck and find Jenny leaning against it, a girl I was warned about the moment I came to town. She used to work for Cooper and apparently enjoys *company* often.

I'd be lying if I said I haven't thought about fucking her. I like to fuck, a lot and often, but she doesn't smell like a cupcake and since meeting Grace that's all I want.

She pushes off my truck as I approach, shoving her tits out for me to notice. "Hey, Sawyer."

"Jenny," I greet, not bothering to hide my annoyance. I've been brushing her off for weeks and she's obviously not getting the damn hint.

"Where were you just now?"

"Not that it's any of your business, but I walked a friend home."

"Grace?" She sneers the name, taking my irritation up another notch.

I don't confirm or deny and step around her to open my truck door.

"I have to admit. Your friendship with her surprises me."

"And why is that?" I ask, unable to help myself.

She scoffs like the stuck-up bitch that she is. "Come on, Sawyer. She's not your type and we both know it. She's pathetic; the girl doesn't even own a car. From what I hear, Mac found her on the street and gave her a place to live. She's nothing without him."

I can have a pretty bad temper when I'm pushed, and this bitch just went too far.

Slamming my truck door, I stalk toward her, fear washing over her smug expression. "You don't know me and you sure as hell don't know Grace. Keep your fucking mouth shut about her, or you and I are going to have major problems. Do you understand?"

She takes a nervous swallow but lifts her chin. "Just stating what I've heard. If you want to get messed up in that, that's your choice."

"Yeah, it is, and it sure as hell is better than getting mixed up with the likes of you." Without another word, I get into my truck and drive away before I do something I can't take back.

Mac pretty much found her on the street.

I have no idea what Grace's story is or what happened to land her where she is, but I have every intention of finding out and making sure no one hurts her again.

CHAPTER 5

Grace

I can't believe that after all this time I'm finally going to meet my father, a man I've longed for but don't know.

Since moving to Sunset Bay, I've been trying to work up the courage to contact him. It's what brought me here in the first place. Last week, I finally bit the bullet and sent him a letter, since I was too scared to receive his rejection in person. But he didn't reject me; he wants to meet me.

Earlier today his assistant called, asking if I would have dinner with him this Friday night at one of Charleston's finest restaurants. Of course I accepted, then I wanted to vomit. I've dreamed of this moment for years but now that it's finally going to happen I have no idea what to say.

The sound of Mac's coughing fit brings me out of my anxious thoughts. Glancing at the clock, I see it's nine, only an hour left until closing. "Mac, go home. Seriously, I got this."

"I don't like leaving you alone here at night."

"I'll be fine. Sawyer is coming in soon and walkin' me home, so I won't be on my own for long."

The thought has my heart leaping in my chest. It will be the third night in a row that he's walked me home. Every night he leaves me with a smile on my face and an ache between my legs. I never thought a guy like him could be into me. The girls I picture him with are exceptionally beautiful, like he is. They stand out amongst a crowd, looking like they belong on the cover of a magazine. Not someone as plain-Jane as me.

It's no secret Sawyer's a flirt but somethin' about the way he looks at me, makes me think he does feel differently about me. Maybe he feels this connection just as much as I do.

When Mac has another coughin' spell, I point my finger at him. "Go home and sleep. That's an order," I say, mimicking the words that he used on me the other day.

"All right, if you're sure."

"I am."

"Thank you, darlin'. Call me if you need anything and I'll come right back."

"I'll be fine. You just take care of yourself."

He mumbles something intangible and leaves out the back door.

I walk back out front to check on the table of high school guys who came in a half hour ago. All of them sport the same football jackets and arrogance. They're rude, obnoxious little jerks and I'm pretty sure they've been drinkin'.

"Hey, baby, bring your sweet ass over here and bring us more coffee," the blond one yells out at me.

His two friends break into laughter, finding his crude behavior funny.

I hate confrontations and try to avoid them at all costs but these guys have left me no choice. Instead of bringing him more coffee, I grab the bill and place it on their table. "Sorry, boys, but we're closin' early. It's time for you to leave."

"Come on now, don't be like that. Give us some more coffee." The mouthy one brushes his fingers along the inside of my leg, inching them under my dress.

I swat his hand away and step back. "Don't touch me! This isn't a bar, it's a diner. You need to pay your bill and leave now!" My heart hammers in my chest, adrenaline surging through my veins.

He pulls out a bunch of bills and throws them at my feet. "Here, bitch, and there's a little extra in there for you to suck my dick."

Their laughter fills the room, until the confrontation takes a fast turn.

Sawyer appears out of nowhere, yanking the blond guy from the table and forcing him to his hands and knees before me. "Pick up the fucking money and hand it to her nicely."

"Screw you, man! Mind your own business."

He shoves the kid's face into the floor, making him howl in pain. "I'm not into beating the shit out of kids, but I will make an exception if you don't pick up the money and hand it to her nicely."

The two other guys begin to stand until Sawyer snaps his furious eyes on them, pinning them in place. "Whatever you're thinking, rethink it."

They are smart enough to listen.

I've never seen this side of him before, and holy moly is it frightenin'. "It's all right, Sawyer," I coax gently. The last thing I want is for him to get in trouble for helping me.

"No, it's not. He's going to pick it up and give it to you nicely, or I'm going to rip his dick off and shove it down his own throat since he wants it in someone's mouth so bad." He leans down closer, bringing his face an inch from the guy. "What's it going to be, kid?"

The guy picks up the money and hands it to me.

"Now apologize to her." When he remains silent, Sawyer knees him in the ribs, making him curl over. "That's the last time I'm going to be gentle."

"I'm sorry," he wheezes out.

Sawyer hauls him to his feet, gripping a fistful of his shirt. "If any of you ever come in here again, I will work you over so bad you won't be able to even hold a fucking football, let alone play it. Got it?"

All three of them nod.

"Good. Now get the hell out of here before I change my mind."

They leave the restaurant in a rush, never looking back.

Releasing a shaky breath, I begin collecting their dishes, my hands trembling violently.

"You all right, Cupcake?" Sawyer asks softly, swiping his thumb across my wet cheek. That's when I realize I'm cryin'.

I wipe my tears away furiously, hating that I let them get to me. "I'm fine. I just hate confrontations." A plate drops from my trembling hand and smashes on the floor. "Shit!"

Before I can kneel down to get it, Sawyer pulls me against him, wrapping his arms around me. His warm strength has me breakin' down.

"Thank you for standin' up for me," I cry into his chest.

"You don't need to thank me, Grace. I told you, I take care of what's mine." He holds me close, rubbing soothing circles along my back. "You okay?"

Nodding, I step back.

"Come on. I'll help you clean up."

I ward him off. "No, I got it. Go on and sit down. It won't take me long, then we'll leave."

"You sure?"

"Yeah."

Once he takes a seat at the counter, I grab him a piece of today's pie along with a cup of coffee then head over to clean up the glass.

"What's this one called?" he asks with his mouth full.

The question brings a smile to my face. "Baby Love Pie," I tell him, dumping the broken glass into the trash. "It's an old recipe. My mama made it when she found out she was pregnant with me."

Turning around, I find him staring at me with questions in his eyes.

My gaze drops to the counter, focusing on the dishcloth I hold. "My father left her when he found out she was pregnant. She told me it never mattered because she was madly in love with me. That night she created this pie and decided to call it Baby Love Pie."

I feel him watch me, but I keep my head down and tell him something that I haven't shared with anyone except Kayla and Julia.

"I've never met my father. The only reason why I came here is because he lives in Charleston. I've been nervous to contact him. He's kinda a big deal, and already has a family of his own. But I finally sucked it up and sent him a letter." My eyes lift to his and I flash him a smile. "He wants to meet me Friday night for dinner. I guess I've been worryin' all this time for nothin'."

He returns my smile, but it doesn't quite reach his eyes. "I'm happy for you, Cupcake."

"Thanks." Clearing my throat, I start gathering his dishes. "Just let me put these away and leave out some leftovers for Chuckie, then we can go."

"Who's Chuckie?" he asks, a frown tightening his face.

"The chocolate Lab. I haven't seen him since the night you scared him off, but I still leave food out for him just in case."

"How do you know that's his name?"

"I don't, but he looks like a Chuckie, so that's what I call him."

He belts out a husky laugh, the infectious sound bringing a smile to my face.

"Are you laughin' at me, Sawyer Evans?"

"Never."

I shake my head, knowing he's full of it. "Just wait there. I'll be right back." I head into the kitchen, his laughter drifting in behind me.

The sexy bugger.

CHAPTER 6

Sawyer

"Would it be okay if we drove tonight?" Grace asks softly as we walk out the front door of the diner. "That way you don't have to walk home by yourself so late."

What is with her always worrying about me walking alone at night?

"It's up to you, Cupcake. I can drive if you want, but don't choose it because you're worried about me. I told you, I'm badass. Walking in this town late at night is the least scariest thing I've ever done."

She graces me with one of her sweet smiles that always causes a shift in my chest. "If it's all right with you, I wouldn't mind drivin'. My feet are a little sore from pulling a double shift."

My eyes drop to her scuffed-up white shoes, hating to think about how many hours she's worked in them. "That's fine, we'll drive."

I lead her over to my truck, opening the passenger door for her.

"What is it with you boys and high trucks? Not all of us are giants, ya know," she says, her head craned all the way back.

Smirking, I stand behind her, my hands spanning her waist to hoist her up. Her sweet cupcake scent penetrates my senses, making my cock harden behind my zipper.

What I wouldn't give for just a little taste, to know if she's as sweet as she smells. I have no doubt she is.

"Um, Sawyer? You can let go now."

I realize I still have a firm grip on her hips. My eyes lift to hers to see a blush staining her cheeks. I get the urge to rip off her dress and find out just how far that pretty pink color spreads.

However, I manage to rein myself in and fight the temptation. "Sorry about that, Cupcake. My thoughts strayed for a moment." I grin, not the least bit apologetic, then close the door and walk around to my side.

My good mood sours as I think about the little prick who was harassing her when I walked in tonight. He's lucky I didn't cut his hand off. It pisses me off to think what could have happened if I hadn't shown up when I did.

I slam my door harder than necessary, my expression hard when I look at Grace. "Where was Mac tonight? Why were you alone?"

She licks her lips nervously, wreaking havoc on my restraint. "I sent him home because he was sick and needed rest. I'd appreciate it if you didn't tell him what happened. He felt guilty enough about leavin' me."

"You shouldn't be alone there, Grace, especially at night."

Her back straightens, chin lifting. "I wasn't worried because I knew you were comin' in soon. And I would have called Cooper if I needed to." She pauses, softening her voice. "Please don't tell him."

Well shit, when she asks all soft and sweet like that I'm willing to do pretty much anything she says, which is dangerous. I should just hand over my balls to her right now.

"Fine, on one condition. If you're ever going to be there alone at night you call me so I can be there, or have someone else with you. Got it?"

"Yes, Sexy Sawyer, sir," she mocks, giving me a sassy salute.

Grunting, I pull away from the diner but drive really slow, wanting to spend as much time with her as possible. It's one of the reasons I like walking with her so much.

"Tell me about your family," she says softly, surprising me with the choice of topic.

"I have two younger sisters, both are a real pain in the ass, but I love them. My mom does a lot of charity work. She's pretty amazing, but of course you already know that because she had me."

She rolls her eyes, her soft laugh filling the truck. "What about your dad?"

My smirk slips. "He owns a construction business. We were close when I was growing up, but we don't see eye to eye anymore. He wasn't all that happy when I joined the Navy," I tell her, the bitterness tasting sour on my tongue.

"Because he was worried about you?" she asks quietly.

I grunt. "No. It's because I was a really good hockey player. I had scouts coming out to my games by the time I was thirteen; my dad had big dreams of me making it in the NHL. When he found out I picked the Navy instead I crushed his dreams."

"I'm sorry."

I shrug, not really wanting to discuss it anymore.

"I didn't dwell over not having a father, but there were times I often found myself thinking about him," she starts quietly, her eyes trained ahead. "When I was about six years old, Mama and I were invited to a weddin'. There was another girl there who was my age. She and her dad were really close. He had propped her up on his feet and danced with her all night long. I watched them with envy and to this day I still think about that moment, wishing I knew what that felt like."

The wistful note to her voice has an ache building in my chest. It pushes me to ask the one question I've been wanting to know. "Can I ask you something, Cupcake?"

"Sure."

I glance over at her, hoping I don't overstep. "How did your mom die?"

She flinches, as if I just slapped her.

"Sorry, I shouldn't have asked."

"No, it's okay. I'll tell you."

My breath stalls, dread coiling in my gut as I wait for her to speak again.

"She was raped and murdered." The words are barely above a whisper but I hear them loud and clear, the information rocking me to my core.

Julia said it was bad, but jesus…

"We were supposed to drive to the state fair a few hours away for a pie bakin' contest," she tells me. "But when I got home from cheer practice, I found two men in our home and they were hurtin' her. I almost suffered the same fate, but managed to escape for a few brief minutes to call 9-1-1. It was minutes that cost my mother her life."

The sorrow in her voice is one that I can't even begin to understand.

"Turns out her death was part of an initiation into a gang for them. We were just the random house that got chosen, no rhyme or reason. If it wouldn't have been for the tattoo I saw, on the guy's wrist when he hit me, they probably would have never been caught."

Hearing someone struck her makes me fucking violent. "Where are they now?" I need to know, because if they're still alive I'm going to hunt them down and kill them.

"One is still in prison, the other was murdered while awaiting trial."

They both should be dead and burning in hell.

"I'm sorry, Grace."

She peers over at me, the devastation in her eyes restricting my chest. "She was my best friend. We had plans to conquer the world with our pies. When they took her life they took mine too, in more ways than one. But as hard as it is, I know that life goes on and I need to be grateful for what I do have. Which is amazing friends and Mac… I'm not sure where I would be if it weren't for him."

She deserves more, so much more than the hand she's been dealt.

Too soon I'm pulling into her driveway but the last thing I want to do is let her go.

"So there you have it. My very sad and pathetic life, you're welcome for the depressing story," she tries to lighten the moment, playing it off as a joke but there's nothing funny about any of this.

"You're not pathetic, Grace. Far from it. You have a right to feel hurt."

She swallows thickly, tears glistening in her eyes. "If I let myself feel the full strength of my pain, it will kill me."

The admission hits me like a powerful blow to the chest, sucking all the air out of my lungs.

She reaches for the door, tossing me a look over her shoulder. "Thank you for the ride. Text me when you get home so I know you made it safely."

"You just want me to text you so you can dream about me again," I joke, hoping to elicit even a small smile from her before she goes.

I get my wish, her pretty lips lifting at the corners. "Goodbye, Sexy Sawyer." She hops out of my truck, her handing resting on the door.

"Hey, Grace," I call before she can close it.

"Yeah?"

"Can I ask you one more question?"

She hesitates for only a second before nodding. "Go ahead."

"Who did you live with after your mother?"

I didn't think it was possible to see a greater pain enter her eyes but I was wrong and it makes me regret asking the question.

Her throat bobs, face paling. "With the devil himself."

I tense, remaining locked in a stare with her. I have no idea what the hell that means and the last thing I want to do is ask her, not tonight.

She closes my truck door, leaving me with a knife twisting in my chest and vengeance burning in my veins.

CHAPTER 7

Grace

Julia, Kayla, and I sit in Julia's kitchen as I relay last night's events, telling them all about the altercation with those jerks and the way Sawyer lost it on them. "I've never seen him like that before. I'm tellin' ya, Julia, he could have given Jaxson a run for his money in the temper department."

"He should have cut the little pervert's hand off," Kayla seethes.

I'm surprised he didn't. In that moment, I saw murder in his eyes. He was capable of anything.

"I'm glad Sawyer showed up when he did," Julia says, concern edging her voice. "I've never seen that side of him, it's hard to picture."

"It's hard to picture what?" Jaxson walks in, inserting himself into the conversation. He plants a kiss on Julia's forehead, resting his hand on her stomach.

My heart pinches with envy. What I wouldn't give for someone to look at me like that one day.

"We're talking about Sawyer," Julia says then proceeds to tell him about my eventful night.

Jaxson's eyes shift to me, a scowl forming on his face. "Why were you there by yourself so late?"

Of course he would react just like Sawyer.

"I sent Mac home early because he was sick. I knew Sawyer was going to be there soon, so I didn't worry."

"Grace says he got so angry he could have given you a run for your money," Julia tells him, a smile twitching her lips.

Jaxson grunts. "I believe it. The only difference between us is it takes more to push him to that point."

"See? I told you, it was crazy."

Kayla chuckles. "We believe you."

Jaxson dips his head, giving his wife another kiss but this time on the lips. "I'm heading to the gym. I'll be back in a couple of hours." He glances up at Kayla and me. "Will you guys stay with her?"

"I don't need a babysitter, Jax, they can leave whenever they want. I'll be fine."

He shoots her a hard look, clearly not agreeing.

"Grace and I plan to be here for a while," Kayla says, reassuring him.

"Good. Then I'll see you girls later." He heads out the door, leaving us in silence.

"Lord that man can be overbearing," Julia grumbles but it lacks heat.

Kayla shrugs. "What else is new? He's always been that way."

"Yeah, but he's gotten worse since Wyatt."

Silence stretches between us as we think about the awful event that happened a few months ago.

Kayla breaks up the heavy moment, changing the topic of conversation. "Okay, enough stalling, Grace. What is going on with you and Sawyer?"

"Nothin' is going on with us. He started walkin' me home at night. Said he wanted to get to know me better, since we are both close with Jaxson and Julia."

"He's lying. He likes you."

"I agree," Julia says, backing her up.

I shrug. "I'm not so sure about that, but I've enjoyed getting to know him. There's more to him than just his striking good looks."

"No shit?" Kayla blurts out, making us all chuckle but I sober quickly, my heart warming when I think about just how amazing he has been.

"Yeah, he can be really sweet. He's been good to me; has said some awfully nice things." I pause for a moment before confessing, "I told him what happened to my mother and confided in him about my dad."

"Really?" Both girls blurt at the same time, their surprise evident.

"Yeah. He's really easy to talk to."

"I guess I shouldn't be surprised. I've always known there's more to Sawyer than his charm and insane good looks," Julia says. "He was amazing to me when Jaxson exploded about the baby…" She trails off, sadness entering her eyes. "Did he tell you about the time the three of them were held captive?"

I stiffen. "No. They were?"

She nods. "I don't know much of the story, and to be honest, I don't want to. Jaxson bears some horrendous scars from it. I imagine both Sawyer and Cade have the same ones."

My heart plummets at the thought of someone hurting Sawyer…or any of them for that matter.

A gloomy silence settles over us once again until I decide to drop another bombshell on them. "I contacted my father."

Both of their eyes snap to mine, mouths parting in surprise.

"I sent him a letter last week because I was too scared of being rejected in person. But his assistant called me yesterday; he wants to meet me for dinner tomorrow night. His driver is picking me up at seven."

"That's great," Julia says, sharing in my excitement.

Kayla, on the other hand, seems nervous. "Grace, you know I'm happy for you. But…have you thought about if it doesn't turn out the way you want it to? I'm sure it will, but I think you should be prepared, just in case. I don't want you to get hurt. Otherwise I'll have to bust heads and no one wants to see that, especially my husband."

I understand where she's coming from. "I have thought about it but I always come up with the same conclusion. Why would he meet with me if he didn't want some kind of relationship? You'd think he just wouldn't respond."

"You're right," she says. "I'm sure it will be great. I'm really happy for you."

"Thanks." Smiling, I revert my attention back to Julia. "Would it be all right if I borrowed one of your dresses again? This restaurant seems pretty fancy and I really want to make a good impression." I'd ask Kayla but I'm closer to Julia's size.

"Of course you can, but know matter what, Grace, dress or no dress, you'll make a good impression."

"Damn straight," Kayla adds.

My heart warms at their kind words. They are seriously the bestest friends I've ever had.

"All right, enough of this sappy shit," Kayla says, "let's move on to a more fun topic, like getting Sawyer to give Grace her first big O."

I groan, embarrassed with her not-so-subtle topic change.

"Wait, hold that thought," she says, lifting her hand. "First, I want to know, how have you not masturbated after reading the shit that you do? Because that book you lent me was seriously hot."

Heat invades my cheeks as I think about the romance novel I let her borrow. It is definitely one of the steamier ones I own.

"You have got to give me more of it. Even Coop wants to thank you. I attacked the shit out of him every time I picked the damn thing up."

"This sounds juicy, Grace," Julia says, intrigued. "Maybe I need to borrow it."

"You are more than welcome to. It's a great story."

"It's more than great. It's damn hot. Believe me, Grace, we need to get Sawyer going on this. The real thing is so much better than reading about it."

A current of heat sparks through my body as I think about Sawyer doin' anything to me. I have a feeling that man would do more than just pleasure me. He would flip my world on its axis.

The thought is both terrifying and exhilarating.

CHAPTER 8

Sawyer

"What's wrong with you?" Jaxson asks, the sound of his drill muffling the question as he drives another screw into the drywall. "You've been acting weird all day."

Cade and Cooper shoot me a look, clearly thinking the same thing.

Ever since Grace's confession the other night, I've been in a mood. A violent one where I want to do some serious harm to the fuckers who hurt her and her mother.

Then there's her devil comment. I've been conjuring up all sorts of terrible images of what that meant. On top of all that she's meeting her useless father tonight, and I have a bad feeling it isn't going to go well, not at all like she's expecting. Which means she will be hurt once again and then I am going to have to hurt him.

The three of them stare at me, waiting for an answer.

Instead of telling them, I ask Jaxson a question of my own. "Did Julia ever tell you about how Grace's mother died?"

"No, but I did try getting it out of her. She wouldn't budge; says she won't betray her trust."

I understand where Julia is coming from, and if it were anyone else in this room with me I wouldn't share this either but I trust no one else more than these guys in front of me.

"She was raped and murdered."

"Holy shit," he spews the heated curse, his shock and outrage mirroring my own.

Cade remains silent, his fist gripping the hammer so tight his knuckles turn white.

Cooper however, doesn't seem the least bit surprised.

"You knew," I say, calling him on it.

"Yeah. I knew even before the girls did. I looked into it when she first came to town. The details weren't hard to find. It's all over the fucking Internet as one of the most brutal murders the state of Florida has ever seen. I know, because I saw the case file."

Dread flares in my gut at the thought of seeing pictures of the heinous murder. "Do you know who she lived with after?" I ask.

"Yeah, some uncle who lives in Virginia. Why?"

"Just wondering." I'm not ready to share that piece of information just yet.

"What exactly are your intentions with her, Evans?" Jaxson asks, cutting back in.

Now if that isn't the million-dollar question. "I don't know, but I'm working on figuring it out," I tell him, being honest.

"Whatever you decide, don't fuck her around."

Annoyance strikes inside of me, the warning unnecessary. "If my intention was to hurt her I'd have already fucked her and been done with it."

He shrugs. "Fair enough. Just making sure we're clear."

I grunt, refusing to repeat myself.

"Did she tell you who her father is?" Cooper asks.

"No."

I guess I should have asked. She did say he was a big deal.

"He's the lieutenant governor."

I stare back at him, not liking the sound of that. "So what are you saying, Coop? You telling me it's not going to go well?"

"I don't know him personally, but I spoke with Kayla about it last night. Grace thinks he doesn't know about her mom. The guy has powerful resources, I'll bet he not only knows but has probably always known where Grace is. He has a family of his own, kids that are close to her age. His reputation is a big deal to him, so if I had to guess… No, I don't think tonight will play out the way she's hoping it will."

That's pretty much what I've been thinking too, and it leaves me even more pissed off than before. The problem is, I don't know how to stop it from happening.

CHAPTER 9

Grace

My hands are cold and clammy, fingers linked tightly as I sit in the backseat of the expensive car, being chauffeured to the restaurant by a driver who is not all that friendly. From the moment the older, gray-haired man picked me up he hasn't so much as even cracked a smile my way let alone speak to me. It has not helped my already jumbled nerves.

Kayla even tried to lighten the heavy moment of his arrival by cracking a joke. "*You make sure you bring her back in one piece to us, Alfred, no secret visits to the bat cave, ya hear?*" she said.

It made us all laugh, except him. I guess he didn't find it as funny as the rest of us but I have a feeling he doesn't find much humor in anything.

My cellphone chimes with a text, distracting me from my nervous thoughts. Pulling it from my purse, my heart leaps when I see it's Sawyer.

> ***Sexy Sawyer:*** *Good luck tonight, Cupcake. I'll be thinking about you. If you find yourself getting nervous just think about me naked, then you'll be too turned on to feel anything else. ;)*

Smiling, I shake my head.

> ***Me:*** *How am I supposed to picture you naked if I've never seen you without clothes on?*

I'm starting to get a little better at this flirtin' thing with him, which brings me pride since he's the king of it.

> ***Sexy Sawyer:*** *Trust me, I'm hot. But you're right; you won't be able to picture it, because even your wildest imagination couldn't dream up my perfection.*

A quiet giggle escapes me, my anxious heart calming. He's probably telling the truth; I'll just bet he looks all sorts of delicious when he's naked.

> ***Me:*** *I'm picturing you right now, dancing to "I'm Sexy and I Know It," kissing each of your biceps. That calmed my nerves right down so I will continue to picture it. Have a good night, Sexy Sawyer, I will text you later.*
>
> ***Sexy Sawyer:*** *Touché, my little Cupcake…touché. Text me the moment you get back.*

I end it with a heart emoji then put my phone back in my purse. When I look back up, I realize we're pulling up to the restaurant. The warmth Sawyer just instilled is replaced with anxiety once again, my thundering heart close to beating right out of my chest.

The driver turns the corner, parking in the back of the restaurant.

"Why are you parkin' here?" I ask.

"Mr. Weston prefers his privacy." He climbs out and comes around to open my door for me, not even bothering to look at me.

Sheesh, I wonder if he's like this with everyone or just me.

I step out of the car and smooth my hands down the black satin dress Julia lent me, trying to calm my nerves as I think about how I should greet him.

Do I hug him or just shake his hand? Should I start off the conversation by telling him about Mama or wait until we're further into dinner?

The back door swings open, displaying a man in a suit with an earpiece. His eyes shift back and forth, taking in our surroundings before landing on me. "Miss Morgan?"

I nod, too nervous to speak.

"This way, Mr. Weston is waiting."

I follow him inside and he leads me toward a private room, making sure to keep me out of view. A bad feeling settles in my gut, mixing with my already jumbled nerves.

I enter the room, coming face-to-face with the man I've longed to meet my whole life—my father. Time stands still as we both take each other in. He's dressed in a crisp gray business suit; his dark salt and pepper hair slicked back from his face revealing hazel eyes. We share very few resemblances.

"You sure do look like your mama," he says in greeting.

I nod, a nervous smile stretching across my lips.

He gestures to the table. "Come, have a seat."

I take the chair across from him and try not to let it sting that he doesn't offer anything else, not even a handshake.

"I already took the liberty of ordering for us; our food should arrive shortly."

I find it odd he would order for me since he has no idea what I like to eat.

Awkward silence fills the room as Grumpy Alfred stands by the door, watching us.

My father folds his hands in front of him, looking at me expectantly. "So tell me, what can I do for you?"

"Do for me?" I ask, thinking I'm missin' something.

"You contacted me with a letter, so I'm curious what it is that you want from me. What is it you're looking to get from our meeting?"

I thought it was obvious.

My heart pinches in my chest, feelin' hurt that he would even ask such a question. "Well, for starters, I wanted to meet you; I thought maybe we could at least get to know each other."

He sits back in his chair, letting out a weary sigh. "Listen, Grace, I'm going to be upfront with you. I cared about your mother a lot but we came from two very different families, and I had expectations I had to follow due to my family's political position. I now have a family of my own, and still have that same reputation I need to protect. If this"—he gestures with his hand between the two of us—"ever got out it would hurt the family I have now. Do you understand?"

Agony rips apart my chest as I realize how foolish I've been. I clench my teeth, fighting back my emotion.

Reaching into his suit jacket, he withdraws a folded piece of paper and hands it to me. "I want you to have this. Your mama refused to accept anything from me and that made me feel bad. Hopefully, this will help make up for some of the things I've missed throughout the years."

I don't accept whatever he's offerin', knowing nothing can make up for the pain he's caused me.

Letting out a breath, he opens the check and lays it down in front of me.

My lips part on a subtle gasp when I see the amount of $50,000.

"I'm truly sorry about what happened to your mama. She was a good lady and didn't deserve for that to happen."

My eyes lift to his, shock striking me to my core. "Wait, you know what happened to her?"

He nods, regret darkening his expression.

It pushes me over the edge. "You knew this whole time and you never came for me?"

He shifts nervously and is about to open his ugly mouth, but I don't give him the chance.

"Do you have any idea who I was sent to live with? What I had to endure because I had nowhere else to go? How could you just leave me with him? How could you not have come for me?" Every word that falls from my mouth drips with the heartache he has caused, a pain I will never forgive him for.

I don't bother to wait for a response, there's nothing he can say to make this right.

Standing, I pick up the check, ripping it into pieces then throw it at him. "The best thing that ever happened to my mother was you walkin' out on her, because she was way too good for your pretentious ass."

I stalk to the door, my furious steps forcing Grumpy Alfred to jump out of my way.

Grabbing the door handle, I turn around, taking one last look at the pathetic excuse I always gave the liberty of calling my father. "Enjoy your family. I hope you teach your children more morals and values than what you have." Those are the last words I speak to him before storming out of the restaurant.

Pain rips through my wounded heart, finishing whatever I had left of it. The tears I've been holding at bay spill down my cheeks with a vengeance as the horrible memories flood my mind. Every crack of the belt, burn from the pot, and cruel touch that came from his hands. All because I had no one who loved me.

CHAPTER 10

Sawyer

My feet tear up the tile floor of Jaxson and Julia's kitchen as I pace relentlessly. "Anything yet?" I ask.

"Nothing," Kayla answers, sounding as concerned as I am.

All of us have been waiting for Grace's text, but we've heard nothing. It's been hours; she should be home by now.

"Screw it! I'm just going to go there. If she's not home yet then I'll wait for her."

"I don't think that's a good idea, Sawyer," Julia speaks quietly. "What if she wants to be alone right now?"

"The last thing she should be is by herself!" My words come out harsher than I intended for them to.

"Watch your tone, Evans," Jaxson warns.

Shaking my head, I decide to leave before I get into a fight with one of my best friends. "I'm going over there. I'll text you guys later." I storm out of the house before anyone else can tell me it's not a good idea.

The entire drive over to Grace's I worry about what I'm going to find. A part of me hopes she's having a good time and that's why she's not home yet. But my gut tells me otherwise. It has all day.

I pull into her driveway less than ten minutes later and find her outside lights on. Climbing out of my truck, I round the corner and come to a dead stop, the sad sight before me stealing the air from my lungs.

A beautiful, broken girl sits on her front steps. She's bent over at the waist, her head buried in her lap, shoulders shaking in grief. I briefly register the empty bottle of wine that sits next to her.

"Cupcake?" The words are choked past the restriction in my throat.

Her head snaps up, the black tears running down her cheeks from her makeup strikes me in the chest like a sledgehammer.

"What are ya doin' here?" she asks.

"You never texted and I was worried."

She gazes back at me, the sorrow pinching her face as painful as the beating of my heart.

I remain where I am, trying like hell to be patient and not push her.

She shrugs, her breath hitching as she tries to compose herself. "He doesn't want me." Her head drops back down, the most agonizing sobs ripping from her chest.

Unable to stay away a second longer, I walk over, pick her up, and bring her down on my lap. She wraps her arms around my neck, soaking my shoulder with her tears.

I didn't even know it was possible for someone to cry this hard.

I remain silent, knowing no words will make it better. Instead I hold her close, letting her cry out what she needs to.

"He knew, Sawyer."

I have to strain really hard to understand the words she's trying to speak.

"He knew about my mama and he never came. He left me with him; this whole time I thought he never knew, because there was no way he wouldn't come for me. No way he would leave me with that monster, but he knew...he knew the whole damn time."

Her monster comment has my fury reaching a whole other level. Leaning back, I take her face between my hands, peering into her emotional eyes. "It's his goddamn loss, Grace, not yours. You hear me? You don't need him, you've made it this far without him and you will continue to."

She rests her forehead against mine, her hot tears spilling onto my face. "All I want is to belong to someone. It's not right, everyone should belong to somebody." The last of her words fall into another sob, cracking my fucking heart right in half.

"You do belong to people, baby. You belong to me, Julia, and Kayla...you belong to all of us."

She shakes her head. "It's not the same thing. I love you guys but it's not the same. Everyone should have some sort of family."

"Sometimes, Grace, people are better off without their families. Look at Jaxson—"

"But he belongs to Julia, he still belongs to someone. The only person who ever loved me was cruelly taken from this earth." Her tears fall faster as she speaks about her mother. "I miss her so much, Sawyer; some days the pain is so bad I wish my heart would stop beating."

The impact of her words knocks the wind out of me, gripping my chest in a tight vise. "Don't fucking say that," I grind out. "Don't ever say that again. Your friends need you. *I* need you. You will get through this, I'll help you."

She gazes back at me, her tortured eyes dropping to my mouth. It's the only warning I get before her lips land on mine, the contact rocking me to my core and kicking my heart into overdrive.

The longing I've had for this girl for the past several months surfaces and explodes like fucking dynamite. I dominate her mouth the way I want her body, our tongues dueling in a fevered game of pitch and take.

Her fingers spear through my hair while mine coast up her smooth, bare legs, slipping under her dress. A growl shreds my throat, my hands kneading her lace-covered ass.

"Sawyer," my name purges past her lips, her hot pussy burning me through my jeans as she grinds down on my stiff cock.

Amongst the sweet taste of her tongue, I also taste her tears, her agony, and...the wine. A war battles inside of me, right and wrong fighting for their place until I'm forced to make a decision I don't want to make.

Groaning, I pull my mouth away from the best thing I've ever had the pleasure of kissing, and hate myself for it. I rest my head on her shoulder, not wanting to look at her. If I do I'll lose the precious control I'm barely hanging on to.

"Cupcake," I whisper, the regret in my voice mirroring the one in my chest.

“Oh god.” She scrambles off me in a blink of an eye, the loss of her warm body leaving me cold.

I grab hold of her hips, keeping her steady so she doesn’t fall on her face. “Whoa, baby, calm down.”

She slaps my hands away. “Please, don’t. I’m fine, really,” she chokes out, barreling up her front steps.

“Grace, what the hell?”

“Please just go; I need to be alone.”

“I don’t think you should be alone right now.”

“I’ll be fine, I promise. I’ve been through far worse than this. I just need time.”

Before I can argue further she hightails it into the house, leaving me to wonder what the hell just happened.

CHAPTER 11

Grace

A distant pounding pulls me from my restless sleep, my swollen, gritty eyes burning as they flutter open.

"Grace, girl, open up," Kayla bellows. "Don't make me show you my ninja moves and break down this door."

Groaning, I pull my self-pityin' butt out of bed and go answer the door. As soon as I swing it open, I come face-to-face with my two best friends. They get a look at my red, puffy eyes and charge in, wrapping me in a hug.

"I'm so sorry, Grace," Julia whispers, her soft voice reflecting the sadness I have in my heart.

"Thank you. Come in. Y'all want some tea or somethin'?"

"No, we're fine," Kayla declines. "Come sit down and talk to us."

We take a seat on my living room couch. Both girls flank me, wrapping their arms around my shoulders.

"I guess y'all know how bad it went, since I never texted last night," I start quietly. "I'm sorry about that. I just needed some time to myself."

"It's okay. We understand," Julia says. "I tried to stop Sawyer from coming over but he was insistent on seeing you. He was really worried. We all were."

Humiliation burns deep at the mention of Sawyer but I shove it aside for now and tell them the story about my father. "To sum it up quickly, he doesn't want anything to do with me. He hid us in the back of the restaurant where no one could see us and offered me money to keep quiet, which I didn't accept."

"Bastard!" Kayla seethes.

"What hurt the most was finding out he knew about what happened to my mother. He knew and he still never came for me, and because of it I lived with a horribly cruel man." Unable to hold them in any longer, my tears run fast, streaking down my cheeks.

Both girls hold me tighter, offering me comfort.

"I know you're hurting right now, Grace, but believe me when I tell you that this is his loss, not yours," Julia says, her voice thick with emotion.

"She's right. He's an asshole. You're better off without him."

I nod, knowing they're right, but it doesn't stop it from hurting. "I thought my night couldn't get any worse, but then I had to go and humiliate myself even more."

"Why, what happened?" Kayla asks.

"Sawyer found me on my front steps last night. Of course, bein' the nice guy that he is, he tried comfortin' me, and what did I do? I attacked his sexy butt, then got majorly rejected." I shake my head, my cheeks heating at the memory. "I'm so embarrassed. I really misread things with him."

"I don't think you did at all," Julia says. "Sawyer cares a lot about you."

"Yeah, as a friend. I should have known better. I was stupid to think that someone like him would want me that way."

"Hey, enough of that shit," Kayla snaps. "Don't you dare talk that way about yourself. Any man, Sawyer included, would be damn lucky to have you."

I remain silent, knowing she's just being nice.

"Julia's right. You should have seen how worried he was when you didn't text. He was like a caged animal. I thought he was going to attack any second."

Because that's Sawyer. Fierce and protective. I've come to learn he has a big heart, but I am no fool. What was the best kiss of my life, and made me feel more than anyone ever has, was not the same for him.

"Can we talk about something else please?" I whisper, my mangled heart too fragile at the moment to rehash anymore.

"Of course," Julia says, "but please know if you ever need to talk, we're here for you. Always."

"Thank you. That means a lot. I promise I'll be okay. Yes, it hurts right now, but I'll get through it. I have gotten through much worse than this."

Kayla shifts next to me, clearing her throat. "Can I just say something real quick? You never told us where you lived before here, and I respect your privacy, but by the sounds of it, maybe you should talk to Coop about it. It sounds like where you were before wasn't a good place."

"No!" I shoot down her suggestion immediately, dread fisting my chest. "I just want to forget that part of my life."

"All right. You don't have to," she says gently, sensing my building hysteria. "Just know, like Julia said, we're always here for you if you ever want to talk about it."

Never.

I will never revisit that part of my life, not for any reason. That monster haunts me enough in my dreams.

CHAPTER 12

Sawyer

Pain explodes through my thumb as the hammer misses the nail. "Fuck!" I throw the tool across the room, sending it through the drywall.

Everyone's eyes are pinned on me, silence adopting the gym.

"Want to talk about it?" Jaxson asks, making shit even more awkward.

"No. I don't want to talk about it. There's nothing to say."

Except that all week Grace has been ignoring me. Other than some vague replies to my text messages, I get nothing. I've even shown up at the diner and she's had other people serve me, pretending to be too busy to talk to me. All I've gotten is the cold shoulder, and quite frankly, I'm fucking sick of it.

"By the hole that hammer made, I'd say you have a lot to say," Jaxson comments.

I do but not here and not to them.

"I'm out of here. I'm dealing with this shit right now!"

Jaxson and Cade blink back at me, having no idea what the hell I'm talking about and I don't bother explaining it. Hell, I can't even make sense of this damn mess with Grace to myself let alone explain it to anyone else.

Grabbing my jacket, I storm out of the gym and hop into my truck. It's not long until I pull up to the diner. The place is relatively quiet when I walk in, the dinner rush long over. I search for Grace but only see the new girl Mac hired.

I charge into the back and find Mac washing dishes. "Is Grace here?"

His head snaps up, eyes holding mine. It's obvious he's unsure whether or not to divulge the information to me.

"I'm not leaving until I see her," I tell him.

He relents. "She's out back, looking for that damn dog."

I push out the side door and make my way down the long hallway. Rounding the corner, I find Grace leaning against the doorjamb, her arms wrapped around herself as she stares outside, lost in her thoughts.

I step forward, accidentally kicking a box, and it startles her. She spins around with a hand on her throat, her eyes wide. "You scared the hell out of me. What are ya doin' here?"

"I came to talk to you."

She pushes from the door. "Sorry, now's not a good time. I need to get back to work."

The brush off has my temper flaring. "You plan to just keep ignoring me until I go away? Is that it?"

Her eyes drop to the floor, feet shifting. "What do you want me to say, Sawyer?"

"For starters, you could tell me what I did wrong."

"You didn't do anything," she whispers.

"Really? Because you're sure fucking acting like I have."

"I'm sorry. I never meant to hurt your feelings."

"For fuck's sake! Would you look at me?"

Her head snaps up, pain and anger prominent in her amber eyes. "Do I really need me to spell it out for you? I'm humiliated enough as it is."

"Humiliated about what?"

"For throwing myself at you, all right?" she yells, tears welling in her eyes. "I promise it will never happen again. Now let's just move on and forget about it!"

She blows past me but I grab her arm before she can make it far. She flinches, raising her arms protectively in front of her.

I quickly release her and step back. "You think I would hit you, Grace? Huh? Is that what you think of me?"

Her slender throat bobs with emotion. "No, I don't. It was just reflex."

A heavy breath leaves me as I fight to rein in my temper. "Look. I'm not sorry about the other night so you shouldn't be either."

"Don't lie to me. I got the rejection loud and clear."

"Did you ever fucking consider that I stopped because I was trying to do the right thing? You drank a whole damn bottle of wine, Grace. I wasn't going to take advantage of you."

She scoffs. "Right, coming from the guy that will screw anything." As soon as the words leave her mouth, she drops her head, her shoulders deflating. "I'm sorry. I shouldn't have—"

"You know what? Save it. I'm done. I don't need this shit." Before I say something I'll regret, I walk away.

Mac watches me blow through the kitchen and the new girl clears a wide path for me as I storm out the front door.

Try to be noble and that's what I get. Well, forget it. I'm Sawyer fucking Evans. I can have any woman I want. Why should I care about what some blonde chick who bakes delicious pies thinks of me?

Climbing into my truck, I slam the door and keep a tight hold on my anger, because it feels a hell of a lot better than the burn spreading through my chest. A pain I'm not used to feeling.

Grace

Tears stream down my face as I run into the kitchen and grab my coat. "Mac, I need to go. I'm sorry but I can't be here right now."

He nods, worry etched on his face. "You go on. We'll be fine. Did you want me to give you a ride?"

"No, but thank you. I need the fresh air. I'll be back tomorrow." Lifting to the tips of my toes, I plant my usual kiss on his cheek. I'm about to make my exit but he wraps me in a bear hug, squeezin' the life out of me.

"Watching you this last week is breaking my heart, Grace."

Guilt strikes the deepest part of me. I'm hurting everyone around me just because I'm hurting. I've never been a self-pitying person and I let my pain get the best of me.

"I'm sorry, Mac. I never meant to hurt any of you. I promise to be better."

"Don't be sorry, darlin', if anyone has a right to be sad it's you. But let your friends help you, all right? Don't push them away."

I nod, feeling terrible for what just happened with Sawyer.

Mac releases me. "Get out of here. Call if you need anything."

"I will. Thank you." I rush out of the diner, my steps quick as I walk home. Reaching into my purse, I pull out my cell and type a text to Kayla and Julia.

Are y'all busy? Can you meet me at my house? I need some company.

I hate to bother them but I really need their advice. I need to make things right with Sawyer.

My phone chimes a moment later.

Julia: *On our way.*

Her quick response has my heart warming in my chest. I may have had a lot of hurt come my way in the last three years, but I also have a lot to be thankful for, especially my friends. My mother always used to say, *If the bad starts to overshadow the good, baby girl, then dig deeper, because you'll end up havin' more of it.*

It's something I wish I was mindful of this past week. I've been a self-pityin' fool. I should create a pie called Feelin' Sorry For Myself Pie, one with yucky ingredients like oatmeal and parsley mashed together.

I finally turn down my street and see Julia and Kayla are already at my house, waiting for me on my driveway. I pick up speed, heading toward them in a slow jog. They can tell I'm upset and meet me halfway, folding me into a hug.

"Thank you for comin'."

"Thank you for texting us when you needed someone," Julia says.

"Yeah, and I especially want to thank you for pulling me away from my husband. The man-cold has hit my house, and I was about to start poisoning his soup if I had to hear any more about how serious a sore throat can be."

We burst into a fit of laughter, something we haven't done in a while and that's my fault.

My smile fades, throat growing tight. "I'm sorry I've been such a downer this week, and I'm really sorry if I hurt y'all's feelings."

"You didn't," Julia assures me, her expression soft with understanding. "We know you're going through a hard time right now."

"I am but no more. I promise."

"Why don't we go inside and you can fill us in on what's going on," Kayla suggests. "I brought wine for the two of us, in case this was a crisis alcohol can fix, and I brought Jules some sparkling juice. She can pretend it's wine."

We head inside to my living room and I tell them what happened with Sawyer, guilt spreading through my chest once again when I relay what my last comment to him was.

"You should have seen his face, I've never felt so awful in my life. I'm a terrible, terrible person," I spit out, angry with myself.

"Whoa, easy there, Mother Theresa, I wouldn't go that far." Kayla pops the cork off the wine and hands me the bottle. "Here drink this. Trust me, it will make things a whole lot better."

Grabbing the bottle, I take a swig and choke down the strong taste.

"There ya go, good job." She takes the bottle back and downs a little herself, wiping her mouth off after. "Now, first of all, you're not a terrible person. People make mistakes, and let's be honest, although the last comment was unnecessary it also wasn't untrue. Even Sawyer knows that."

I shake my head. "That might be his reputation but he's never been like that with me. He's only ever been kind, and I treated him so horribly."

Julia coasts her hand up and down my back. "Don't beat yourself up so much, Grace, like Kayla said—people make mistakes. All you can do is apologize and ask for forgiveness."

"You're right. That's exactly what I'm gonna do. I'll bake him a special pie, an apology pie, then I'll take it to him." I glance at the clock, knowing if I start now it won't be too late and I can take it to him tonight.

"Can we help?" Kayla asks. "I'd love to learn how to make a pie."

A smile spreads across my lips, my heart dancing in excitement. "I'd love to show y'all, come on."

We head into the kitchen and I turn on music, which is something I always do when baking, then I teach my two best friends how to make a pie. I put extra special care into this one though, hoping it will be enough for Sawyer to forgive me.

CHAPTER 13

Sawyer

"Another one, Jack," I bellow, waving my shot glass at the bartender.

Instead of going back to the gym and throwing my bad mood around at my friends, I decided to come to Badass Jack's. The local waterin' hole is the perfect atmosphere to drown my anger and that's exactly what I have been doing.

Jack walks over to my end of the bar, bringing me another shot of whiskey. The moment it hits the counter I throw it back and relish in the burn.

"You wanna talk about it, kid?"

I shake my head then regret it when the room spins. I'm fucked up. And the worst part is, I can still feel the tightness in my chest.

"You know what, Jack?"

"What, SEAL boy?"

I ignore the *'SEAL boy'* comment from the former badass Marine. "When people tell you that doing the right thing feels good, they're fuckin' lying."

The older man grunts, amused.

"It's the damn truth. I did something that would have made my mom proud, but the thanks I got for it was a swift kick to the balls. And let me tell you something else," I continue, shaking my drunk-ass finger at him. "The women you have to watch out for are the sweet-looking blonde ones who smell like cupcakes and make delicious pies. I'm telling you, they don't look like they could hurt a fly but they'll take your ass down hard."

Talking about it gets me all fired up again.

"I mean, who gives a shit about cupcakes and delicious pies anyway?"

The older man shrugs. "I like pies. How good we talkin' here?"

I stare him dead in the eye. "Real good. Dangerous good. So good that it can rip you to pieces and stomp on you good."

Jack chuckles. "Shit, that does sound dangerous; I ain't never had no pie like that."

I grunt, and am about to continue my drunk tirade when something warm presses up against me. Looking over, my gaze collides with a great pair of fake tits. I already know who it is before my eyes lift to her face that's caked with makeup.

"All by yourself tonight, Sawyer?" Jenny asks, laying her hand on my thigh.

"What do you want?"

"You," she whispers in a sultry voice, her fingers finding my cock that's standing to attention behind my jeans.

That goes to show just how drunk I am. Not even her annoying voice can kill my hard-on.

My eyes move over her, and I pay attention to how different she is from a cupcake. Her eyes are blue and don't cause a shift in my chest. Her brown hair with a hint of red is the complete opposite of the golden wavy hair that feels like silk. And most of all, she doesn't smell like a cupcake.

Grabbing her wrist, I stop her traveling hand and yank her against me. "One night. You hear me, Jenny? One fucking night and that's it. If you want more than that then get the hell out of here."

She smiles, revealing her lipstick on her teeth. "I'm a one night kind of girl, Sawyer."

I don't waste time thinking about it. Standing, I throw my money on the counter and catch Jack shaking his head before I let her drag my drunk-ass out of the bar.

Any second thoughts that try surfacing I shove back down, praying this will kill the need I have for sweet little blonde cupcakes who don't want anything to do with me.

Grace

The night is quiet and peaceful as I walk to Sawyer's apartment building, my nervous fingers gripping the pie tightly that I made for him.

Hopefully he's not upset that I'm stopping by like this without calling first.

I just couldn't wait until morning. I've been absolutely heartsick since seeing him earlier at the diner. I've been running through my mind what to say; hoping my apology and this pie will be enough.

As I come up to the complex, an elderly lady walks out. Her smile is kind as she holds the door open for me. Thanking her, I walk in and make my way toward the apartment number Julia and Kayla gave me.

My pulse begins to race, anxiety plaguing me as I reach his door. Taking a deep breath, I raise my hand to knock when a loud moan stops my fist midair.

"Sawyer, that feels so good."

My heart plummets straight to my stomach. All the air leaves my lungs in a painful rush as I grab on to the wall next to me, feeling close to collapsing from the pain infiltrating my chest.

"Grace?"

My head snaps to the left and I find Cade striding toward me, his eyes dark with concern.

"What's wrong? Are you—"

I lift a finger to my lips; tears spilling down my cheeks as I plead for him to be quiet.

Frowning, he comes to a stop and that's when that god awful sound happens again.

"Yes! Fuck me, harder!"

My eyes close, stomach violently twisting.

A harsh curse leaves Cade, knocking me out of my painful stupor. Unable to listen to any more, I shove the pie at him and get the hell out of there. When I make it outside, I head left, trying to pull in deep breaths through the sobs trapped in my chest.

Calm down, Grace. You don't have a right to feel this way.

My heart doesn't listen to my head and those imprisoned sobs break free, tumbling past my lips.

"Grace, wait!" Cade calls, running out of the building. He catches up to me, grabbing my arm. "Let me give you a ride home." His voice is soft, a complete contradiction to how it normally is.

Wiping my tears, I nod then follow him over to his truck. He's still holding the pie as he opens the door for me. A pie I shouldn't have bothered making.

Once I'm situated, he closes the door and climbs in on his side. I rattle off the directions to my house then rest my forehead against my window, the cool glass offering no reprieve to the pain scorching me from the inside out.

I shouldn't feel this heartbroken, this…betrayed. We were nothin' more than friends, but for some reason those are the only emotions I'm feeling at the moment.

Cade clears his throat, breaking the heavy silence. "Sorry you had to hear that, Grace."

"Don't be. It's no one's fault," I whisper. Actually, it's a lie. It's my fault. Had I not pushed him away none of this would have happened.

He grunts. "I doubt that. Most of the time, if there's a fuck-up, it's Sawyer's fault. Trust me, I've known him a long time, his egotistical pride can fuck with his judgment."

Is that why he did this? Because of pride? Did he have to choose her of all people?

I know exactly whose snooty voice that was. How can I forget when I've been on the receiving end of it many times as she's hurtled insults at me. Jenny has always been nothin' but a nasty bitch to me.

Anger begins creepin' in, overriding the hurt. "Is it terrible of me to say I hope his dick falls off?" I blurt out, before I can think better of it.

I'm about to apologize for the outburst, knowing it's a cruel thing to say, especially to his best friend, but I don't get the chance before a laugh barrels out of Cade. It's low and rusty, the simple act foreign when it comes to him. Eventually it softens into a smile, and boy what a smile it is. Who knew he was hiding that behind that hard mask of his.

The beauty vanishes in an instant when he catches me watching him. Clearing his throat, he shifts uncomfortably. "No. It's not awful. I, for one, would find it funny as hell."

I chuckle but it's halfhearted, because the truth is, even if it did happen, it wouldn't make me feel better. It wouldn't change how hurt I am. "You know, normally I'm a girl who always tries to see the glass half-full, but life just really sucks sometimes."

"It sure fucking does," he agrees, his tone hard once again.

I have a feeling if anyone can understand the kind of pain I've endured over the last few years it's Cade. Hidden in his dark eyes, you can see it, a void, a loss, something that's impossible to fill. I know mine is, without my mama that hole will never be filled.

"It's good you still try to see the glass half-full, Grace," he speaks again. "Whatever you do, don't lose that, because once you do there's nothing left." His gaze remains straight ahead but that ever-present pain is there, making my heart ache for whatever happened to him.

When he pulls into my driveway, I take my seat belt off and crawl over to his side, wrapping my arms around his neck. Every muscle in his body stiffens but I don't let go because sometimes a hug can go a long way.

"My mama always used to say that God never gives you more than you can handle. I personally think that's a giant load of crap."

The slightest chuckle vibrates his chest.

"But she was a real smart lady, so I try to stick with that mantra."

"Sounds like she was," he says, his tone softer.

Feeling myself close to tears again, I pull back and offer him a small smile before exiting the truck. "Thank you for giving me a ride home. It was awful nice of you."

"No problem. Do you want your pie back?"

I shake my head. "He should still have it."

"Did you want me to throw it in his face?" he asks, seeming rather hopeful I say yes.

"That's all right, but thanks for offerin'." Before leaving him, I say one more thing. "You should smile more often, Cade. It suits you."

Closing the truck door, I run into my house and head straight to bed. In the quiet dark is when I really let my tears flow, those awful moans filling my heart and mind until the sun breaks the next morning.

CHAPTER 14

Sawyer

I come awake slowly and wonder why it feels like I've been run over by a truck. My eyes drift open then slam back shut, a sharp pain spearing my head.

Groaning, I roll over and hit something. My eyes spring open again and I find a naked chick next to me, one that has regret burning within my blood. It all comes rushing back to me in a flash.

Oh shit!

I shoot out of bed like a fucking rocket, crashing into the wall and it rouses the biggest mistake I've ever made.

Jenny sits up with a sleepy smile, dropping the sheet to her waist. "Why are you getting up so early? Come back to bed."

I shake my head then regret it when the room spins, tilting beneath my feet.

Shit, not a good idea.

"One night, Jenny, remember?" I croak, my throat feeling like sandpaper. "It's time for you to go."

Ignoring her sleepy glare, I grab my jeans from the floor and throw them on before walking out. I head into the bathroom to wash up, then make my way into the kitchen, needing some coffee.

Cade sits at the table, his disapproving eyes on me as I reach for a mug from the cupboard above my head.

"Save it. I'm not in the fucking mood," I grumble, not wanting to hear whatever lecture he's thinking. I already know what an idiot I am for bringing that crazy bitch back here. Cooper warned me how many damn times, but did I listen? Nope. I let my wounded pride, and drunk ass make a stupid decision.

After filling my cup, I take a hefty sip but the hot contents spew from my mouth when I spot a pie on my counter. A pie I'd know anywhere.

My gaze shifts to Cade, eyes wide. "What the fuck is that?" I ask, pointing at the pie.

"Read the note that's attached to it."

Stepping forward, I rip off the folded paper, dread curdling in my gut when I see whom it's addressed to.

Sexy Sawyer,

This is a brand new pie I created just for you. It's called Forgiveness Pie. I'm hoping, after you eat it, you will forgive me for being so terrible. I'm sorry I hurt your feelings. You mean an awful lot to me, and I don't want to lose your friendship.

Please forgive me.

Love,
Grace

I swallow thickly, the sudden knot in my throat excruciating. "Please tell me she gave this to you at the diner?"

I can tell by his expression that's not the case. "When I got back last night from the gym I found her outside our door about to knock until she heard you fucking someone's brains out."

"Fuck!" I drop my head into my hands, shame and guilt snaking through my chest, gripping my heart into a tight vise.

Jesus, I think I'm going to be sick.

A scoff yanks me from my torment. Looking up, I find Jenny reading the note, her lips curled in disgust. "Seriously? She's pathetic."

Anger swells in my veins, not just at her but also myself. Grabbing her by the wrist, I jerk her closer to me, ripping the note out of her hand. "What did I tell you about saying shit when it comes to her?"

Her eyes grow wide, throat bobbing nervously.

"It's time for you to leave." I drag her to the door and thrust her out into the hallway, pointing my finger at her. "Stay away from Grace and keep your mouth shut." My warning is loud and clear before I slam the door in her face.

She drops her fist on it, giving one solid pound. "You're a real asshole, Sawyer?"

Yeah, I am. Especially for hurting a girl who is far better than the likes of me. I walk back into the kitchen only to have Cade start in on me.

"It's bad enough you fuck up, but with her? What part of what Cooper said didn't sink in?"

"Are you really giving me shit about this? You, of all people?"

I'll admit I fucked up but he is the last person to judge me considering the torture he inflicts upon himself over Faith.

"I'm the one who drove her home last night and listened to her cry, so I can say whatever the fuck I want to you."

My anger deflates when I hear she was crying. "I have to fix this."

"Good luck. However, she did say last night she hopes your dick falls off," he relays, looking rather amused. "Why don't you hand that to her on a silver platter? That might help."

Grunting, I head to my room to change and think of a way to fix it without having to cut my dick off. I can't lose her friendship. I can't lose whatever we almost had.

Hours later, I pull up to the diner and still have no clue how I'm going to make this right. My stomach is in fucking knots thinking about how much I hurt her, just like so many others have.

I walk up to the door and find Kayla and Julia as they exit the diner. They come to a hard stop at my approach.

"Hey," I greet them, waiting for the blast I deserve.

"Sawyer," Julia replies quietly, disappointment strong in her voice.

It makes me feel even more like shit.

Kayla, however, has no problem telling me exactly how she's feeling. "Well hello, douchebag."

Julia gives her a slight elbow but I ignore it, knowing I deserve it.

"How is she?" I ask, my eyes remaining on Julia, since she's probably the only person who will give me an answer at the moment.

"She's sad," she answers honestly. "Especially after Jenny came here and was so cruel."

I tense. "What do you mean?"

Kayla is the one to answer. "That stupid whore came walking in here earlier to rub it in Grace's face that the two of you shared her pie this morning, after fucking each other's brains out."

An unrelenting fury takes hold of me, my blood pumping violently. "That's not true. She's lying."

"We know that," Julia says. "I think Grace does too, but it didn't stop it from hurting her."

"I fucked up. I know that. I'll fix it."

"It's not going to be easy, Sawyer," she whispers, her voice growing thick with tears. "It takes a lot for Grace to trust someone and she trusted you easier than anyone else."

The truth of her words hit me like a painful blow to the chest. I swear I've never felt this much fucking guilt in all my life.

"I know but I swear to you, I'm going to fix this. I won't stop until I make it right again."

She offers me a sad smile and gives my shoulder a squeeze before walking past me to Kayla's car.

Taking a deep breath, I step forward and brace myself for what awaits me behind the diner door.

CHAPTER 15

Grace

My heart is heavy as I wipe down the table that Julia and Kayla just left. I'm thankful for their company this morning and even more thankful they were here when Jenny walked in, spewing all her nasty hate. I'm not in any shape to fight with her. Not today.

I head for the kitchen, shoving my towel in my apron and run straight into a brick wall, the breath knocking from me on a whoosh.

Strong arms come around me, holding me steady while my hands clutch a soft T-shirt. A familiar scent penetrates my senses, making my heavy heart skip a beat. I know without looking who the brick wall is. With my stomach in knots, I slowly lift my gaze and connect with a pair of intense green eyes.

"Hi, Cupcake."

A storm of emotions plagues me at the sound of Sawyer's deep, smooth baritone. His usual upbeat persona nowhere in sight.

"Hi," I reply quietly.

Neither of us makes an effort to move from our embrace. Even though I shouldn't, I can't help but want to soak in the safety of his arms and find myself zeroing in on his perfect lips.

Lips that were just on Jenny's.

The reminder is like a bucket of cold water. I tear my gaze away from his handsome face and move to step back but he tightens his hold on me.

"Can we talk?" His soft voice contradicts his fierce expression.

I nod, knowing we can't avoid having this conversation. "Yeah, I can take a quick break. Come on."

We head into the back where Mac stands at the grill, filling orders.

"Mind if I take a break?" I ask.

He shoots a cold look Sawyer's way before his eyes shift back to me, softening with affection. "Not at all, darlin'. Take as much time as you need. Shelly will be all right on her own for a bit."

"Thanks." I lead Sawyer out back and open the big steel door, needing the fresh air. My attention is focused on the sunny sky since I'm too nervous to look at the man behind me.

"Has the dog come back?" he asks, breaking the heavy silence.

"Not yet. I've been checkin' every night. I'm worried about him."

When he doesn't say anything else, I glance over my shoulder and find him watching me, so many emotions etched across his face.

I hate myself a little more for noticing how good he looks today. Instead of the usual jeans he always wears, he's sporting black athletic pants and a red T-shirt that stretches across his broad shoulders. A black backwards hat covers his unruly hair, the sleep-mussed strands poking out beneath it, hitting the sharp angles of his handsome face.

My eyes lift back to his and I find him wearin' a sly grin.

Busted!

Clearing my throat, I look down at the ground, paying special attention to how dirty my white shoes are. "I'm assuming you got my pie?"

"Yeah, I did," his voice is quiet, thick with regret. Or maybe that's just wishful thinking on my part.

"Did you eat any of it yet?" Dread tightens my stomach as I think about Jenny's mean comment this morning.

"No, I didn't," he answers, his tone hard—angry. "That bitch lied to you, Grace."

My head snaps up, surprise infiltrating my chest. It's not long before I realize he must have run into Julia and Kayla outside.

Nodding, I return my attention to my feet again, hating the awkwardness between us. I decide it's time to get this over with. "I'm really sorry for what I said yesterday, Sawyer. I let my humiliation run my mouth. I didn't mean it."

"You don't need to apologize, Cupcake. I'm the one who's sorry; I was an asshole. I showed up here yesterday, pissed off because you were ignoring me, and I let it bruise my ego. Even though I have a really big one, I still don't like it to take a beating."

My lips twitch with a small smile but it fades quickly with what he says next.

"It didn't mean anything, Grace."

I put my hand up to stop him from going further. "You don't need to explain anything to me. We're nothin' more than friends."

"Bullshit! What I feel for you is a lot more than a fucking friend and we both know it."

My eyes snap to his, all the anger from last night returning with a vengeance. "Are you really sayin' you care for me more than a friend, after you just shoved your dick in someone else, Sawyer Evans?"

"I know I fucked up and I regret it more than you'll ever know. I still don't understand how it happened."

I scoff, the words the worst cliché I've ever heard.

"It's true, damn it." He starts pacin' back and forth, jaw flexing. "One minute I'm at Badass Jack's, drinking my face off, spewing shit to Jack about delicious pies that can kick your ass and blonde chicks who smell like cupcakes. Then the next thing I know that bitch walks in, comes on to me, and I start comparing her to cupcakes. She is the complete opposite, by the way," he adds, feeling the need to throw that into his tirade. "I was so pissed off at you that I let it fuck with my judgment and it's something I'll regret for the rest of my life."

The explanation should make me feel better but it doesn't. "That's the thing, Sawyer. She's the complete opposite of me," I choke out, my tears beginning to slip free. "She's your type, I'm not and I'm not ever gonna be."

"She is not my fucking type. I like fucking cupcakes!"

The ridiculous words elicit a small laugh from me but it quickly trails into a sob. I drop my head into my hands, unable to keep my composure any longer.

He comes to stand in front of me, his warm fingers encircling my wrists. "Look at me, Grace," he demands, pulling my hands away. "It—didn't—mean—anything. I know you don't understand that, but it's the truth. She means nothing to me and never will."

I peer up into his green eyes that shine with regret and sincerity. I desperately want to believe him, a part of me does, but the pain from last night is too fresh.

"I'm sorry she came in here this morning," he adds. "She was mad at me and took it out on you."

I sniffle and wipe my wet cheek. "Don't worry about it. Kayla put her in her place."

"Yeah?"

I nod. "She told her if she didn't leave she was gonna rip off her fake boobs and beat the shit out of her with them."

A husky laugh barrels from his chest. "That girl is really hard not to like. Even when she's calling me a douchebag."

I wince, imagining just how bad she laid into him. She was furious about the whole situation. "I'm sorry. She's upset and just being a good friend to me."

He frames my face between his large hands, resting his forehead against mine in an intimate gesture. "I'm going to be one of those people again, Grace. I know it's going to take time for you to trust me, but I'll make this up to you. I'll make things right between us or I'll die trying."

I swallow thickly, the ache in my throat preventing me from saying anything more. My wounded heart is too scared to believe in him.

His gaze drops to my mouth, eyes darkening.

"Sawyer Evans, if you put those lips anywhere near mine, after you just had them on someone else, I will punch you in the throat."

A half-laugh, half-groan rips from his chest. His arms encircle my waist, yanking me against his hard body. There's no mistaking the erection against my stomach and it sends my body into a heated frenzy.

His torture doesn't stop there. Ever so softly, he drags his nose across the side of my cheek, his lips almost brushing but not quite. Goose bumps whisper along my skin, my breathing turning quick and shallow as he stops just shy of my ear.

"I won't kiss you until you ask me to, Cupcake. And I promise you, one day you will, because I know you feel this, too," he murmurs, eliciting a shiver down my spine. "This heat—fire, the unrelenting need building between us. I know it's not just me who feels it."

"Grace?" Shelly's voice breaks our heavy moment.

I suck in a startled breath and jump back from Sawyer, banging my head against the door like a doofus.

"Oh crap! I'm so sorry," Shelly sputters, giving us her back. "I didn't mean to interrupt you but I'm having problems with the register. Whenever you're done, can you help me?"

"Of course. I'll be right there."

"Thanks." She scurries away, leaving us in tense silence.

"I should get going." The words are nothing but a mumble as I sidestep him, my shoulder brushing his.

"Grace?"

Stopping, I take a deep breath and turn back to him.

His eyes hold mine, determination burning within. "I'm going to prove to you how much I like cupcakes."

Unable to stop it, a small smile dances across my lips. "Bye, Sexy Sawyer."

I walk away, feeling his eyes upon me with every step I take. There's a little more hope in my heart when it comes to fixing our friendship and right now, having him in my life as a friend is what I care about most.

CHAPTER 16

Grace

That evening, I finish closing up by walking the trash outside when a loud whimpering snags my attention. My heart stills, praying it's the dog I've been searching for. I pause and listen carefully, trying to decipher where it's coming from.

"Here, boy," I call gently, my eyes scanning over the dark alley.

The whimper turns into a keening cry, sounding painful.

Dropping the garbage bags, I move around the large metal bin and find the chocolate Lab lying on his side, his leg twisted at an odd angle.

I drop down next to him, my heart breaking at the sight of small bloody wounds on his nose. It looks as if his skin has been rubbed raw. "What on earth happened to you?"

His response is another whimper and it has agony striking my chest.

"It's okay, don't cry. I'll get help." Since Mac has left already, I dig my cell out of my purse and scroll through my contacts with shaking fingers, stopping on Sawyer's name.

He answers on the second ring. "Cupcake, what a coincidence. I was just going to call you."

"Sawyer," I choke out, my voice trembling as bad as my hand.

"Grace? What's wrong?"

"It's Chuckie; he's hurt real bad. He needs a doctor, and I don't know how to get him there. He can't walk."

"Where are you?"

"I'm behind the diner."

"I'll be right there."

"Thank you." Hanging up, I put a gentle hand on the dog's body. "It's all right, boy, Sawyer's comin'; he'll help us." I bury my face into his neck, stale cigarette smoke filling my nostrils as I hold him close.

It's not long before an engine roars down the back alley. Headlights blind us as Sawyer puts the truck in park and jumps out.

Chuckie startles, his cryin' turning frantic at Sawyer's quick approach.

"It's okay, he won't hurt you," I soothe.

Sawyer kneels down beside me, observing the dog's wounds.

"He's hurt real bad," I tell him on a sob. "I think his leg is broken, and somethin' is wrong with his nose."

He drapes a comforting arm around my shoulder and pulls me in close. "It'll be okay, Grace. We'll help him."

I lean into him, thankful for his calm composure because the thought of losing Chuckie kills a small part of me. It will be another blow to my heart that I'm not sure I can handle.

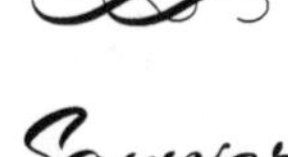

Sawyer

We sit in the waiting room at the animal hospital, waiting for word about the dog. Grace sits next to me, steadily wiping her tear-stained cheeks.

"Do you think someone did that to him, Sawyer?" she asks, her sad voice ripping apart my chest.

"Yeah."

I don't just *think*, I know, and I want to beat the shit out of the person who did it. Not only for the violence they inflicted upon the dog but for also making my cupcake cry…

My Cupcake?

Jesus, I'm fucking losing it.

Her jaw clenches, emotional brown eyes narrowing in fury. "When I find out who did this, oh boy are they gonna be sorry," she seethes, punching a tiny fist into her open hand.

"Easy there, Rocky Balboa; let's wait to see what the vet says first."

As soon as the words leave my mouth, the man in question walks into the waiting room.

"Grace Morgan?"

We both stand to greet him.

"I'm Dr. Richards," he says, extending his hand first to Grace then me. "You can come in now and see Chuckie."

My hand moves to Grace's lower back as we follow the doctor into the exam room. The moment we enter she flees to Chuckie's side where he lies on the examination table with a cast on his leg and a bandage covering his nose.

She buries her face in his neck, her shoulders shaking as she cries.

The doctor gives her a moment before asking his first question. "The nurse told me Chuckie is not your dog; is that correct?"

She straightens and faces him. "He wasn't before but he is now."

He nods. "I'm gad to hear that because if you don't take him home I'll be forced to call ASPCA to come pick him up. By the looks of things it seems Chuckie has been abused for quite some time. The X-rays show previous broken bones that were not treated properly. To be honest, I'm surprised he was able to walk at all."

The information has a small sob fleeing her. Unable to hold back any longer, I walk over and gather her into my arms.

"What about his nose?" she asks. "What are those wounds?"

"Cigarette burns."

Her eyes close, face pinching in devastation. "Why would someone do this?"

"Unfortunately it's something I see too often in my profession," he tells her regretfully.

She shakes her head, an angry breath escaping her. "Can I take him home now?"

"Absolutely, but he needs to come back in three weeks time to get his cast off. I'll also provide you with medication to help manage his pain. Lauren will give it to you when you take care of the bill."

Her shoulders slightly tense, probably because it never crossed her mind, but she recovers quickly. "I'll do that now, thank you for helpin' him."

"It was my pleasure. Thank you for bringing him."

Once the doctor leaves the room, she peers up at me, uncertainty shining in her emotional eyes. "I should pick up a bowl and some food, too. I don't know what's good. I've never had a dog before."

"It's not hard, Cupcake; I'll help you. Come on."

We head to the supply section and I grab everything he will need, including some dog treats, a bone, and even a bed. As the nurse rings up the items, I catch Grace staring at the price each time it flashes on the screen, her teeth worrying into her lip.

"All righty, is that everything?"

Grace nods.

"It will be $850 please."

"$850?" she sputters, choking out the price.

I pass the lady my credit card but Grace throws my hand away.

"No!" She leans in closer to the nurse, lowering her voice. "Do y'all have a payment plan or anythin'?"

"I got this," I tell her.

"No, Sawyer. I mean it, this isn't your responsibility."

Grabbing her arm, I excuse us and drag her stubborn ass over to a quiet corner. "Listen, it's not a problem for me to pay, it is, however, a problem for you."

"I'll figure it out. I can ask Mac for an advance and pick up some extra shifts."

"Why would you do that when I am telling you I can afford it!"

"Because I can't accept this from you, Sawyer," she says, voice softening. "I didn't call you just so you can get stuck with the bill."

"I know you didn't, that's not what this is about. I have the money so I am paying for it and that's fucking final!"

The ultimatum strikes a chord, her eyes narrowing and chin lifting.

Taking a breath, I reel in my frustration and decide to handle this a little more delicately. "I want to do this. Please, Grace. Let me help you."

The plea works, her shoulders slumping in defeat. "Oh, all right. But I'm paying you back," she says, pointing her delicate finger at me.

Grunting, I head back to the register, refusing to argue further. After paying for everything we load up the dog and head to her place. Chuckie is asleep when we pull onto the driveway. I carry the heavy fucker inside, surprised by his weight.

"Bring him this way. He'll sleep in my room with me."

Lucky little bastard.

I get my feet moving and follow her into the master bedroom—her bedroom. I come to a hard stop, taking in the wrought iron headboard. My dick roars to life as I think about all the shit we could do with those bars.

"Sawyer?"

My attention yanks to Grace where she stares at me. "Yeah?"

"I asked if you could lay him down here," she says, pointing to the ground by her feet.

"Right."

Get your shit together, Evans.

When I lay him down on the dog bed, Grace covers him with a blanket before settling beside him.

"Cupcake, he doesn't need that. His fur is a blanket."

"It's not just for him. It's for me, too."

The information has a scowl forming on my face. "You're sleeping on the floor?"

"Yeah, just until he's more comfortable bein' here."

"You should be in your own bed, Grace. You need sleep, too."

"I'll be fine," she says, curling around the dog.

I decide to drop to it, knowing the argument is pointless. "I'll be back. I'm going to go get the rest of the stuff from the truck."

"Thank you," she says, her voice soft as she pets the dog.

I head outside, grabbing the remainder of the supplies and bring them into the kitchen. After dishing the dog some food, I grab his water bowl to fill and spot an oversized picture that hangs on the fridge of Grace and whom I'm assuming is her mother, since the woman looks just like her.

Grace holds up a freshly baked pie, her mother's arms wrapped around her neck, a first place ribbon attached to the picture. Both of them beam with pride and even though I have seen Grace smile and laugh, I've never seen her look as happy as she does in this picture.

Placing the water bowl on the floor, I head back into the bedroom, coming to an abrupt halt at the sight I'm met with. Grace kneels on the floor, her beautiful ass pointed straight into the air as she hugs the dog. She's changed into a pair of sleep shorts that mold to her like second skin, tempting me in ways I've never imagined.

My hands clench as I fight the urge to touch it, caress it.

Spank it.

"Everythin's gonna be okay, Chuckie. We're gonna be each other's family now. I promise to take really good care of you."

Her words yank me back into the moment, hitting me like a punch to the gut. I clear my throat, alerting her of my presence.

She spins around with a startled gasp.

I flash her a smile that dies the moment she climbs to her feet and I get a full look at her sleep wear.

I swear she's trying to fucking torture me.

Her matching tank top is just as tight as her shorts. Her nipples poke through the stretchy fabric, making my mouth water for a taste. That overpowering need only intensifies as my eyes travel down the length of her, taking in her toned legs that are half covered by gray wool knitted socks that come up to her thighs. They're cute and sexy as hell, just like the woman herself. Images of what they would feel like wrapped around my back as I drive into her emerge quickly.

A blush stains her cheeks at my blatant eye fuck.

"Nice socks, Cupcake." I compliment her with a smile, not the least bit ashamed.

"Thanks," she says, shifting from foot to foot. "Kayla and Julia bought me a few pairs for my birthday a while back. They're called Alpine thigh-highs and they're from

Grace and Lace; they're my favorite. I wear them as slippers sometimes and…" Her ramble comes to an end and she lets out a frustrated breath. "Never mind, you don't care."

If she only knew how much I cared. I'd sit here and listen to her talk about her fucking grocery list if it meant I could be in the same room with her. I'm that far gone over this girl.

"Thank you again, Sawyer, for coming when I called," she adds quietly, eyes cast down to the floor. "I don't know what I would have done without you."

Walking over, I tilt her chin up, bringing those warm amber eyes to mine. "You don't need to thank me, Grace. I told you, anytime you need me, I'll come."

She offers me a nervous smile. "I promise to pay you back soon. Maybe I can—"

I cover her mouth with my hand. "We're not going to talk about this anymore."

Anger sparks in her eyes but I don't let her argue and reel her in close, her soft body pressing into mine in all the right places. "You need to learn how to accept help from people, Cupcake."

She licks those pretty pink lips of hers, tempting me further. "I don't like acceptin' help from people, because you never know what they're gonna expect in return."

My lust fades at the pain in her eyes. "You don't owe me anything, Grace. Except for pie. I want my own special pie, one that's as amazing as I am."

She smiles like I hoped for her to, a sweet giggle escaping her. The sound of it washes over me, drifting through the air like one of my favorite songs.

"Well, now that I can do, Sexy Sawyer."

My hand lifts to her face, caressing the soft skin of her cheek. She gazes up at me, her eyes storming with unrelenting need. The same one I have roaring in my veins. Before I can think better of it, I lean in, bringing my lips to hers, just a feather of a touch.

Her mouth parts on a gasp, breath racing across my lips.

I remain still, because even though I fucking ache to kiss her, I promised her I wouldn't until she asked. She wants it, I can see it, but she's not ready and that's my fault. I still have a lot to make up for.

My nose skims her delicate cheek as I bring my mouth to her ear. "I'm going to leave now, Cupcake, because if I don't I'm going to end up doing all sorts of things to you that you're not ready for…at least not yet. I'll help take care of Chuckie while you're at work, okay?"

"Okay," she whispers.

My hands squeeze her hips, digging into the soft flesh as I fight to hold onto my control. "One day soon I'm going to have you, and when I do I'm going to fuck you with nothing on but these socks you're wearing."

"Sawyer," my name falls past her lips on a breathless whimper.

I put an end to our torture and press a hard kiss to her forehead then walk out, keeping my promise to her, but it's the hardest promise I've ever had to keep.

CHAPTER 17

Grace

A strand of hair escapes my ponytail, falling into my face as I wipe down one of the many dirty tables we have after the crazy dinner rush.

"Grace, darlin', phone's for you," Mac calls from the kitchen.

Frowning, I look over my shoulder at him. "Me?"

"Yeah, want me to ask who?"

"That's all right, I'm comin'." I carry back the stack of dirty dishes with me and deposit them in the sink before grabbing the phone. "Hello?"

"Grace, it's Cooper."

"Hi, Cooper," I greet him in surprise, curious as to why he would be calling me, especially at work.

"I'm sorry to bother you, but can you come down to the station and see me?"

Uneasiness skitters down my spine, a bad feeling forming in the pit of my stomach. "Is everything all right?"

A beat of silence passes before he speaks. "If it's okay with you, I'd like to wait until you get here to talk about it."

This doesn't sound good at all.

"I can come pick you up," he offers.

I shake my head then remember he can't see me. "No, it's only a block away. I'll be there soon."

"Thanks."

I hang up, my hand visibly shaking.

"Everything okay, darlin'?" Mac asks.

"It was Cooper. He wants me to come down to the station."

"Did he say why?"

"No. He wants to wait and tell me in person."

Worry darkens his expression, mirroring my own. "Do you want a ride?"

"No, it's fine. If Sawyer comes in before I get back can you let him know where I am?"

"You bet. Make sure to call and let me know what's going on."

"I will." Grabbing my coat, I deliver him a quick kiss on the cheek then head out the door, givin' speed walking a whole new meaning. My mind reels as I try to figure out what on earth this could be about. By the time I arrive at the police station, I'm a bundle of nerves.

Cooper awaits me at the front desk, his somber expression worrying me further.

"Thanks for coming in" he says, putting a comforting hand on my shoulder.

"You're scaring me, Coop, what's goin' on?"

"Come with me, there's someone here to see you."

I follow him into his office, feeling completely baffled. My feet come to a screeching halt when I see who's waiting for me. "Detective Ramirez?" I say, choking out his name in disbelief.

The detective who was in charge of my mother's case stands.

"Hello, Grace."

"What are you doing here?"

"Why don't you have a seat," Cooper says, gently coaxing me into a chair.

The regret on both of their faces has my heart hammering in my ears.

"I have some upsetting news," Detective Ramirez starts. "Miguel Sanchez was released from prison a week ago."

Every muscle inside of my body freezes, icy terror flooding my blood. "How can that be? He was given a life sentence."

"Yes, he was but he appealed and was granted a retrial."

I blink, swearing I misheard him.

He begins to explain things, things I can't understand because I feel like I can't breathe. The walls close in on me, threatening to swallow me whole.

"He wasn't allowed to leave town, Grace, but he did and we can't find him."

"Oh god!" I fall out of the chair onto my knees, fear gripping my chest into an iron fist. Grabbing the garbage can next to the desk, I empty everything from my stomach into the small metal bin.

Cooper kneels beside me, putting his hand on my back, but I can't feel its warmth. I feel nothing but the panic thrashing through my veins.

He's coming for me.

The terrifying thought sends me fleeing. I run out of Cooper's office, ignoring him and the detective as they try calling me back. The front doors barrel open as I charge through them, my body colliding with something solid.

Strong arms grab my shoulders, trying to steady me. I look up and find Sawyer yelling at me. I see his mouth moving but hear nothing. All I can hear is my thundering heart.

Fear and desperation have me ripping from his grasp and running faster than I thought myself capable. Right now, I only have one instinct and that's survival.

Two and a half years before

"All rise," the bailiff bellows.

I stand amongst the silent courtroom, my fingers gripping the bench before me as I await the verdict. My uncle stands next to me, looking bored, like he'd rather be anywhere else than here.

I now know why Mama never stayed in contact with her only family. He's mean and vindictive, and I don't think I've seen him at his worst. There's only one person on this earth I hate more than him… My eyes shift to Miguel Sanchez. A member of the Blood Ties, a gang that he killed my mother for.

Tears build behind my eyes as I think about every awful thing he and his brother did to her. The only thing that brings me a small measure of peace is knowing his brother is dead. He was delivered the fate he deserved while awaiting trial.

There's so much hatred in Miguel's eyes as he stares back at me that fear begins crawling up my throat.

"Mr. Foreman, has the jury reached a verdict?" the judge asks.

I bring my attention over to the jury who holds the fate of this monster's life in their hands.

"Yes, Your Honor."

"Please read that verdict before the court."

"We, the jury, find the defendant, Miguel Sanchez, guilty on all charges."

My eyes close, a breath of relief escaping my chest.

Detective Ramirez pulls me into a hug. "Justice has been served."

I nod, tears of victory spilling down my cheeks.

A loud commotion to my left breaks us apart. Looking over, I see Miguel pull away from the escorting officers and charge at me, his hands cuffed in front of him. Fear immobilizes me, a scream of terror shoving from my throat.

Detective Ramirez jumps over the bench and tackles him to the ground before he can reach me. Two more officers jump in to help restrain him, his body thrashing violently.

"You're going to pay for my brother's death, you little bitch," he rages in a fit of fury. "When I get out of here I'm going to kill you, just like I did your dirty mother. Do you hear me, whore?"

The truth is there in his eyes, rattling around inside my terrified heart. I know with every fiber of my being if he ever escapes I will suffer the same horrific fate as my mother…

I barrel into my house, almost throwing the door off the hinges. Chuckie barks until he sees it's me then follows me into my room, my quick feet never faltering.

"We need to leave. We can't stay here anymore." I swing open my closet door and grab my suitcase, throwing every piece of clothing I own into it.

"Grace? Where are you?" Sawyer bellows. Seconds later, he storms into my room, looking furious. "What the hell is going on?"

"I don't have time to explain, I have to go," I choke out, continuing to pack.

"Where?"

I don't respond and he grabs hold of my shoulders, pinning me in place. "Talk to me"

"I can't! I need to get out of here before he finds me." When he doesn't release me, I hit him in the chest, fighting his firm grip.

"Stop!" He locks his arms around me and takes me to the ground.

I finally give up, sobs shattering my chest. "He's going to kill me."

He hugs me closer, burying his face in my hair. "Calm down, baby, I don't know who you're talking about, but I swear, no one is going to hurt you."

"You're wrong," I cry. "He's comin' and he's gonna finish what he started."

"Who? Talk to me, Grace. I can help you."

"The man who murdered my mother," I choke out, unable to say his name out loud. "He's comin' for me. Just like he said he would and he's gonna kill me." My face drops into his chest, gut-wrenching sobs ripping from my throat once again.

"Look at me!" he demands, forcing my gaze back to his. "I won't let anyone hurt you. Do you hear me? No one will fucking touch you."

"I'm so scared," I confess quietly.

"Don't be. I'll protect you, Grace. Trust me." The fierce determination reflecting back at me brings a small measure of peace to my terrified heart.

I nod because, at the moment, he's the only one I trust.

He lifts me into his arms and stands, laying me out on the bed before following down next to me. His hard body curls around mine, bringing the safety I so desperately need.

It isn't long before exhaustion grips me. It's so strong there's no fighting it, and I let it take me, knowing as long as I'm in Sawyer's arms, I'll be okay.

CHAPTER 18

Sawyer

Grace is fast asleep, my shirt clutched firmly in her hand. I've never seen fear like this in all of my life and I've watched grown men shit themselves before their death was delivered.

He's going to kill me, Sawyer.

My teeth grind so hard I'm surprised my jaw doesn't snap. The rage coiling through my body is powerful and I intend to unleash it on the very person who caused her so much terror.

I meant every word I said; no one will lay a fucking hand on her.

A soft whimper snags my attention. At the end of the bed, the dog stares at her, his face resting next to her feet.

I get it, buddy, she makes me feel the same way.

A heavy knock on the door penetrates the air. Grace doesn't even flinch, her face soft with sleep. I carefully pry my shirt from her small fist then grab the yellow blanket from the end of the bed and cover her with it. The dog crawls up the mattress, resting his head on her thigh.

"Take care of her until I get back," I order.

The banging starts again as I walk out of the room. "Grace, open up!"

Cooper.

Charging for the door, I fling it open to find Coop and a middle-aged man in a suit that I've never seen before, standing behind it.

"What the fuck is going on?" I ask, my eyes trained on Cooper.

Without responding, he walks in with suit on his heels.

My attention shifts to him next. "And who the fuck are you?"

"Easy, Sawyer," Cooper says, trying to calm me.

It does the opposite, shattering my control. "Don't you tell me to take it easy when Grace fled from your fucking station, crying her fucking eyes out. So someone better fucking answer me right the fuck now!"

Suit grunts. "Let me guess…military? Probably a SEAL."

I tense, sizing him up. "Who wants to know?"

Cooper finally introduces us. "Sawyer, this is Detective Ramirez with MPD. He handled Grace's mother's case."

I point my finger at him. "So you're the fucker who made her cry?"

He grunts again. "Definitely a SEAL. You know, the way you arrogant pricks throw the F-bomb around gets old real quick."

I reach for him but Cooper intercepts me.

"I'm going to throw a lot more around than the F-bomb, asshole, if you don't start talking and keep your goddamn insults to yourself."

"Jesus, Sawyer, will you calm down?"

"Then start talking!"

"Where's Grace?" he asks.

"Sleeping, which is where she's staying for now."

Coop expels a heavy breath, pinching the bridge of his nose. It's something he often does when he's stressed. "How much did she tell you?"

"All she could manage during her hysterics was that the asshole who killed her mother is out of prison, and she thinks he's coming for her." I direct my attention to suit and see his expression filled with regret. "How does someone, who gets life in prison, get out in three years?"

I expect another insult but instead, I finally get answers. "The DNA evidence is being retracted. The forensic scientist, who testified, was found dead two weeks ago. He left a suicide note saying that the DNA did, in fact, not match Miguel Sanchez and that he was paid off to say it was him. Sanchez's attorney was able to get him a re-trial. The moment he was granted bail he fled, and now we have no clue where he is."

My mind reels with this entire clusterfuck.

"My guess, though, is Grace isn't all that far off with her fear."

"Are you saying she is in danger?"

He nods. "I was there when he made the threat. He blames her for his brother's death."

"Unfuckingbelievable!" My feet eat up the carpet as I pace back and forth, fury burning in my gut.

"Sawyer?" Grace's vulnerable voice cuts through the air, stopping me in my tracks.

Turning, I see her leaning against the wall with Chuckie sitting at her feet. She's changed into her black shorts and tank top, wearing an open, thin sweater over top. The socks she wore the other night reach the top of her slender thighs. Even with sleep tumbled hair and swollen red eyes, she's the most beautiful thing I've ever seen.

"Hey, baby." I pull her into my arms, feeling the need to hold her.

She returns my embrace, hugging me tight.

"Did we wake you?" I ask.

She shakes her head then turns and looks at Cooper and the detective. "I'm sorry I ran out on y'all earlier. I was just really scared; I still am."

"No need to apologize, Grace," the detective says. "I know this is a lot to take in."

"I don't understand how this happened," she whispers, her voice broken.

Cooper points over to the couch. "Why don't we sit down and Detective Ramirez can explain everything."

I lead her over to the couch and take a seat first, pulling her down on my lap. She relaxes back into my chest, fitting against me perfectly.

There are questions in Detective Ramirez's eyes as he watches us but he's smart enough not to ask them. It's obvious he's protective of her but that changes nothing, he's still on my shit list for the moment.

As gently as possible, he fills Grace in on everything he told me about the DNA and the forensic scientist who has been found dead.

"Wait," Grace breaks in, sitting up. "What do you mean he lied? That's impossible, I saw Miguel with my own eyes, he hit me for crying out loud, and his brother almost raped me. What about my testimony, doesn't that mean anything?"

My blood burns with rage, from hearing what those bastards did to her.

"I don't believe the forensic scientist committed suicide. I think someone killed him and I'm in the middle of trying to prove it."

"I can't believe this," Grace mumbles, sounding defeated.

"I know it's frustrating—"

"This is a lot more than frustrating, Detective, this is downright bullshit."

I'm pretty sure this is the first time I've ever heard her swear, and I'm not going to lie, I'm proud of my Cupcake. Sometimes, swearing can help you let off steam and make you feel a little fucking better.

My proud moment deflates when she speaks again. "You were there," she continues, voice soft. "You heard his threat that day. He admitted to raping and killing my mother in front of everyone, then said he was going to make me pay. Screw what that forensic scientist said, what about that?"

"I don't know. It doesn't make sense that the judge granted him bail. Something is going on, and I promise to find out what it is and put that bastard back behind bars where he belongs."

"Good, because you have to. My mama deserves justice." Her words finish on a sob and she drops her face into her hands.

Sitting up, I wrap my arms around her and press a kiss to her shoulder. "She'll get justice, baby. I promise."

Even if it's delivered by my hands.

The conversation comes to an end when Grace's front door flies open. Kayla barrels in, leading Julia, Jaxson, and Cade.

"You have got to be shittin' me," Cooper says, glaring at Kayla. "Did you need to tell the whole fucking world?"

Her eyes narrow right back at him. "We're her friends, you idiot. We should all be here for her."

The girls yank Grace from me, wrapping her in a hug. I wait patiently for them to give her back but they end up pulling her down between them on the couch.

I find it unfair since *I* had her first. Instead of calling them out, I decide to act like a mature adult and stand to join Jaxson and Cade. The three of us share a silent exchange, the promise of vengeance passing between us.

"Sorry, Grace," Cooper says. "I was worried about you when you ran out of the station, so I called Kayla, thinking you could use a friend. I didn't expect her to bring the whole damn world with her."

"Oh give it up, Coop, you're such a drama queen," Kayla fires back.

If shit weren't so serious right now, I'd laugh at the tight expression on Cooper's face. He looks close to strangling his little spitfire.

"Don't worry, Grace, everything is going to be okay," Julia says. "You can come stay with Jaxson and me. He would never let anything happen to you. He can kick anyone's ass. Isn't that right, Jax?" She directs her attention to her husband, awaiting his answer.

"You know it, baby."

The urge to roll my eyes like a fuckin' chick is strong. "That won't be necessary. I'll be staying with Grace."

Her shoulders tense, eyes snapping to me.

What did she think would happen when I said I would take care of her?

She breaks our connection, her fingers twisting nervously in her lap. "I appreciate all the offers but I don't want anyone gettin' hurt over this," she whispers, shifting her attention to the detective. "Is there somewhere I can go? Like witness protection or somethin'?"

"Don't even think about it!"

The outburst has the room falling to a tense silence.

I point at her. "Kitchen, now!"

Her eyes narrow but she follows the order.

Kayla breaks the tension as we head into the kitchen. "Well, drama queen, should we finish our fight while they have theirs?"

The room breaks into muffled chuckles.

"You're pushing it, Kayla."

His aggravation doesn't deter her in the least. "Oh come on, Coop, you know you love me."

Conversation picks back up in the living room, giving us the privacy we need.

I focus on Grace as she leans against the wall, arms crossed. "What the hell are you thinking? What part of 'I'll take care of you' did you not get?"

"Listen, Sawyer, I appreciate it, more than you know. But we don't know how long it will take for the police to find him. You can't put your whole life on hold worryin' about me and my problems. And if something ever happened to you, because of this, I'd never forgive myself." The last of her words trail off on a choked whisper.

My temper fades as I step into her personal space, my hand moving to the smooth surface of her cheek. "Cupcake, how many times do I have to tell you, I'm a badass motherfucker."

Her lips twitch with a smile and she shakes her head.

"I'm serious, Grace, I'm trained for this shit. I can protect you."

"I don't doubt that for a second. Believe me, I don't feel safer with anyone more than you."

Both pride and relief fills my chest to hear her say that.

"But again, we don't know how long it will take to find him."

"I don't give a fuck how long it takes. I told you I take care of what's mine, so that's what I'm going to do."

She huffs out a frustrated breath.

I gather her into my arms and rest my forehead against hers. "Tell me you get me, cupcake. I swear, no one will protect you better than I will."

She gazes back at me, tears slipping down her cheeks. "I get you."

It's exactly what I needed to hear. From this moment forward, she's mine to protect and I don't plan on ever letting her go.

CHAPTER 19

Grace

I walk into the kitchen the next morning with Chuckie trailing behind me, and find Sawyer sittin' at the table with a sandwich in front of him. The sight of him this early in the morning brings warmth to my heavy heart.

"A sandwich for breakfast, Sawyer?" I ask, lifting a brow at him.

"Nothing beats a peanut butter and jelly sandwich."

I hold out my hand for his plate.

He covers the sandwich, hugging it closer to him. "Get your own sandwich, woman."

Giggling, I snatch the plate from him. "I'm not gonna eat it, silly." Walking over to the stove, I pull my frying pan out, then start buttering each side of the bread.

"What are you doing? You heard me when I said it was peanut butter and jelly, right?"

"Trust me, you're gonna love this." After buttering it, I sprinkle cinnamon and sugar on it then place it in the pan.

Sawyer drops his head in his hands, acting as if I just ruined his whole breakfast.

Whatever, he'll see.

While the bread is grillin', I fill Chuckie's dish. I'm bent over at the waist, scooping his food out of the massive bag when a deep groan fills the air. I peek over my shoulder to find Sawyer staring directly at my ass. The hungry look in his eyes has my pulse kick starting.

I clear my throat, forcing his eyes up to mine.

He flashes me one of his panty droppin' smiles, not the least bit apologetic.

I shake my head.

"What?" he asks, mock innocence coating his tone.

"Don't you 'what' me, Sawyer Evans, you know what I'm shakin' my head at."

"You can't expect me not to stare at your ass in those small shorts, Grace, that's just impossible not to do. And those fucking socks… Jesus."

"What's wrong with my socks?" I ask, insulted.

"Baby, there isn't a thing wrong with them, that's the problem."

"You have got to be kiddin' me. I have a feeling it doesn't take much to get you worked up, Evans."

"Not when it comes to you, Cupcake."

Rolling my eyes, I move back to finish his sandwich. It's not that I don't want to believe him, because I do, desperately. But I have a hard time when I'm still hearing

Jenny's moans in my head.

Don't think about her, Grace, I scold myself.

Once the sandwich is done, I cut it in half and watch the peanut butter and jelly ooze out. I bring the plate over to Sawyer then turn to grab myself something but he snags my wrist, halting me in my tracks. I look down at him, finding all his earlier amusement gone.

"How did you sleep last night?" he asks.

"No worse than I usually do."

It's a lie. I slept horribly, only because I knew he was down the hall. The temptation to flee my bed and join him was strong. I wanted to be held by him, wrapped in his protective arms and feel safe.

"How about you?" I ask.

His response is a grunt.

"Is the spare bed uncomfortable?" The last thing I want is for him to be getting no sleep when he's already doing so much for me by being here.

"The bed is fine, Cupcake. It just would have been better if you were in it with me," he says, gracing me with a sexy wink.

Heat invades my cheeks, hating how close his thoughts are to mine. "Be quiet and eat your breakfast of champions."

His chuckle sounds behind me as I grab a banana from the counter before taking the seat across from him. I watch him eye the sandwich before he finally takes a bite.

A deep groan rips from his chest. "Marry me," he says with a mouth full.

I take a triumphant bite of my banana. "Told ya."

"That you did, Cupcake." His smile fades, a look passing over his face that I can't decipher. "I want to take you to the gun range today to teach you how to shoot."

My eyes flare in surprise, the entire thought giving me anxiety. "I don't think so, Sawyer. I hate guns. I don't like any kind of violence."

"This isn't violence, it's self-defense," he argues. "Look, I don't plan on leaving your side until that fucker is back behind bars, but anything can happen, and I will feel a lot better knowing you can at least shoot a gun if you need to."

He makes a good point. The last thing I want is to ever be vulnerable and helpless again, especially to that monster.

"Okay," I relent. "I guess it's not a bad idea."

"Good. We'll head out after we eat."

"I need to stop by the diner at some point today; I have to talk to Mac about my schedule."

"You can't work right now."

I rear back at his bold statement. "I have no choice. I need the money."

He shrugs. "Don't worry about that. I have more than enough to help out."

I gape at him, flabbergasted by the outrageous comment. "I'll pretend you didn't just say that."

His eyes narrow and I feel an argument brewin' but I don't give him one. I refuse to fight about this.

My hands press on the table as I climb to my feet. "I'm gonna go ahead and get dressed. I'll be ready soon."

Without another word, I walk away, feeling his disapproving gaze on my back like a lingering caress. Even when frustrated with the man, he still makes me hot and bothered. It's incredibly unfair.

The amount of guns that line the walls are intimidating. My eyes are wide as I take in the impressive selection while I stand next to Sawyer at the counter. He grabs us ear protection and safety glasses, handing me mine before leading me out back into an open space.

I slip my headset on and take in the black piece of paper that hangs before me. The white outline of a human body makes me feel like I'm in one of those CSI episodes.

A tap on my shoulder startles me. I spin around to find Sawyer wearing a smirk, amusement dancing in those sexy green eyes of his. He slips my ear protection off and hangs them around my neck. "Baby, you don't need these on until you shoot. Otherwise you can't hear me."

"Sorry," I mumble, feeling embarrassed.

His cocky grin softens into a heart-stealing smile. "It's not a big deal."

Maybe not to him because he's not the one who looked like an ass.

He opens the steel case that he brought with us and pulls out two nifty looking guns. As much as I hate weapons, I have to admit he looks damn good holdin' one.

While he locks and loads, my eyes wander over him, taking in what I've come to realize is his standard worn jeans that hang in all the right places and basic T-shirt molding to his lean, muscular frame. There's nothing outstanding about the apparel except for the man wearing them.

The sound of a throat being cleared has my eyes yanking to his.

"Whenever you're done looking, Cupcake, I'm ready."

My eyes narrow, hoping to hide the blush heating my cheeks. "I'd be careful how smug you are, Evans, considering you're puttin' a gun in my hands."

Chuckling, he turns his black hat backwards then puts his own glasses on.

Sweet Jesus, it just got a whole lot hotter in here.

He places the gun in my hand and it takes everything in me not to recoil at the cold hard feel of the deadly weapon.

"All right, turn around." He grabs onto my shoulders and turns me himself. "Spread your legs shoulder-width apart."

I follow his instruction.

"Wider." Grabbing my hips, he kicks my feet further apart.

Oh man, that was so hot.

"All right, now hold up the gun."

I raise it.

"Forward, baby. You're going to shoot the goddamn roof off holding it like that," he says, laughing.

"Stop making fun of me. You act like I should be an expert or somethin'. It's not like I've ever done this before."

"I'm not making fun of you," he argues.

"Yes, you are."

"All right, I am."

I elbow him in the stomach, which only makes him chuckle more.

Sexy jerk.

"Okay, no more. I promise. Now hold your arms in front of you, and I'll reposition your hands."

I raise the gun again, this time directly in front of me.

Sawyer crowds my back, his hard body covering mine as he begins explaining things but I hear nothing. The heat of his body and his warm breath tickling my ear short-circuits my brain. My pulse skips as pleasure races over my hot skin.

For a girl who's never had an orgasm before, I'm pretty sure I'm about to finally know what it feels like.

"Grace!" Sawyer's warning growl yanks me back to the moment. His fingers dig into my hips as he pulls me back against him, his erection nudging my bottom.

Oh god.

"Be careful, Cupcake. My control is really fucking thin when it comes to you. Keep it up and I'll bend you over right here and fuck you within an inch of your life."

My chest rises and falls with heated breaths, the war within my body strong.

He ends up stepping back, a curse fleeing past his lips.

I grab on to the wall to steady myself. My head twists to the side, eyes meeting his over my shoulder. The hunger in his gaze mirrors my own.

I've never felt like this with someone before, never felt this strong of a pull. My body craves to feel his skin upon mine. The urge to know what it's like to be at the receiving end of his touch, even for just a night, has heat exploding through my body.

"Get into position again," he orders, voice gruff.

I comply, my knees feeling weak.

Instead of coming up behind me, he stands to the side and adjusts my hands to where they need to be. "It's important to keep your arms locked tight, do not loosen your stance."

I nod, but don't feel very confident, my hands visibly shaking with nerves.

"You got this." After the vote of confidence, he puts on his ear protection then he reaches over and slips mine in place. Resting his hand on my back, he gives me the go-ahead.

I remain frozen, unable to move. My entire body begins trembling as bad as my hands and it's not long before tears form in my eyes. It's a ridiculous reaction but for some reason I'm terrified to pull the trigger.

Sawyer presses a kiss to my temple then moves in behind me, wrapping his arms around me. He locks up our stances and places his finger over the trigger with mine then does what I couldn't do on my own.

The first shot we fire off, I flinch. The second is a little less jolting. Sawyer keeps our stances locked, his finger never faltering as he squeezes off five additional shots before he steps back to reload.

This time when he hands it to me, I take it with a little more confidence. He remains behind me but doesn't help. I aim at the target, focusing on the white outline and picture Miguel. The memory of dark, malicious eyes that stole my mother's last breath has all my pent-up anger bubbling to the surface. It gives me the push I need to pull the trigger.

The first shot, I stumble back but regain my footing quickly and lock my stance up tighter. I continue firing off consecutively, hitting my target each time until the clip is empty.

I stare at the black paper, a little surprised at how good that felt. My lips lift into a smile and I turn around to see a matching one on Sawyer's face.

"Did you see that? I shot that shit up."

His laughter fills the air as I launch myself at him.

"I can't believe I just did that," I say, hugging him tight.

"You did good, Grace. I'm proud of you."

His praise has my throat growing tight. "Thank you for teachin' me this. It makes me feel a little safer."

He pulls me in closer, his arms banded tight around me. "You are safe. I'll never let anything happen to you."

For the first time in three years, I feel a small measure of peace; one I haven't felt since my mother was ripped away from me.

CHAPTER 20

Grace

Sawyer and I have a nice dinner at the diner. Once the supper rush clears, I head into the back and speak with Mac privately about my schedule. He tells me not to worry about it and says he wants me to make the pies from home then deliver them to the diner in the morning.

My eyes narrow, suspicion rearing its head. "Sawyer put you up to this, didn't he?"

I can tell by his expression that I hit the nail on the head. "Now don't go getting all mad, you stubborn girl. Sawyer may have brought it up to me, but I had already thought about it and it's my decision."

I shake my head. "I can't, Mac. I appreciate what you're trying to do, but I can't accept paychecks when I'm not workin', it's not right."

"You're still working, darlin', you're just doing it from home."

"My pies ain't worth what you're trying to pay me."

"The hell they aren't," he counters. "Listen, you're going to accept this, Grace. I need you to worry about yourself right now. I can't have anything happen to you, it would break my heart."

My throat tightens at the concern in his eyes.

He steps forward, wrapping me in one of his famous bear hugs. "You have people who love and care about you, darlin', let us help you."

"I love you too, but what are you gonna do for help?"

"Don't worry about me. Shelly is doing better now, and Ruby said she would come help out. I also have another interview tomorrow."

"I hope they catch him soon," I whisper. "Then my life can get back to normal."

"I hope the son of a bitch comes in here," he seethes. "I'll fry the motherfucker's ass right there on my grill."

I chuckle at the image, my arms hugging him tighter. "Thanks for everythin', Mac. One of the best things that ever happened to me was meeting you."

"Me too, girl. You're like the daughter I never had."

His sweet words have me blubberin' like a fool. Oftentimes, I've found myself wondering how different my life would be if Mac had been my father.

"Now go on and get out of here," he says, stepping back, his own eyes red with emotion. "I'll see you tomorrow when you bring in the pies."

Nodding, I wipe the remainder of my tears then walk out of the kitchen, coming to a hard stop when I find that bitch Jenny with Sawyer. They seem to be in a heated conversation but it's hard to tell since Sawyer's back is to me.

Jenny glares over his shoulder at me, a smug smile lifting her lips.

My blood heats with jealousy, a sick feeling forming in my gut.

Sawyer turns around, finding me by the kitchen door that I've become glued to. "You ready to go?" he asks, walking away from her without a second thought.

It should make me feel better, but it doesn't. All I can hear are her stupid moans from weeks ago.

"Yep!" I walk out the door, my feet quick as I leave him behind. By the time I reach his locked truck, I'm fighting to dispel the anger gripping me.

His gaze is on me as he walks over but I avoid eye contact. Once he hits the locks, I climb up into the truck, slamming my door.

Silence fills the truck as Sawyer pulls away, heading back to my house.

"Did you get everything worked out with Mac?" he asks, side glancing me.

"Yup."

"Is he giving you some time off?"

"Yup." My answer is just as short and clipped as my last, my attention anchored ahead of me as I stare out the window.

"Is there a goddamn problem, Grace?"

"Nope."

He grunts, knowin' I'm full of it, but thankfully he leaves it alone.

I feel bad for taking my anger out on him. I'm more mad at Jenny. She's the one who's always so darn mean to me, but Sawyer hurt me more and it's a pain I'm having a hard time letting go of. Just thinking about the night they shared makes my stomach churn.

When we pull onto my driveway, I hop out of the truck and hurry into the house. Chuckie greets me like always; his wet kisses bringing a small reprieve to my hurting heart.

Sawyer charges in seconds later, his expression tight with anger as he slams the door behind him. "You want to tell me what has you so pissed off so we can get it the fuck out of the way?"

I stare up at him, and consider telling him everything. How angry it makes me feel to see them together, how much it still hurts to know he was with her, but I know it's pointless because what's been done is done. It can't be taken back, no matter how much I wish it could.

Shaking my head, I stand. "I don't wanna talk about it. I just want to go to bed."

He doesn't stop me as I head into my bedroom and close the door.

In the quiet dark, the silence taunts me more and I end up lying awake, wishing for what could have been.

CHAPTER 21

Sawyer

A clanging noise pulls me from my restless sleep. Glancing at the clock, I see it's three in the morning.

What the hell is she doing in the kitchen at this time of night?

I debate whether or not to go check on her, unsure if it's safe to do so. She was so pissed off at me tonight for god knows what. I've endlessly racked my brain trying to figure it out but I can't. I'm at a loss over what I did wrong.

When I hear more banging around, I give up and decide to go find out. It's time to sort this shit out because I do not like fighting with her. Not unless there's makeup sex involved but I have a feeling I'm not anywhere close to that with her.

I throw on my jeans from earlier, not bothering with the button and almost forgo a shirt too but then remember the scars that mark my body. She hasn't seen them yet and now is not the time to reveal them to her.

My strides are purposeful as I make my way to the kitchen, but I pull up short when I find her pacing angrily, a wooden spoon clutched in her hand as she grabs everything she needs to bake a pie. The dog's head moves from side to side as he sits in the corner, following her every move.

"Oh my god, really?" she says dramatically, talking to the air in front of her. "You like my boobs? Well thank you, they're fake, just like me."

What the hell?

My mouth splits into a grin while I watch my Cupcake mimic who I'm assuming is that bitch Jenny. It takes every ounce of willpower I possess not to burst out laughing.

So this is what she's mad about—Jenny. Well now I feel like shit. Obviously, she misinterpreted what happened between us earlier.

As she bangs things around, my eyes zone in on her sweet ass in her tiny shorts but my appreciation is short-lived because her crazy ass talking brings my attention back to the rest of her.

"And I'm gonna put ice cream in it because she's a cold bitch; a cold, fake bitch. I'm gonna call it Cold, Fake Bitch Pie."

Unable to contain myself any longer, I sneak up behind her, stopping just a couple feet away and lean in close. "You should just call it Jealousy Pie."

I realize my mistake too late.

A startled scream rips from her as she spins with a bag of flour in her hands. She throws it at me, dousing me in the shit then whacks me in the head with a wooden spoon.

"Ow, fuck!" I rip the utensil out of her hand and grab her shoulders, giving her a small shake. "Grace, calm down, it's me."

Her eyes widen further, recognition finally dawning on her. "Oh my god, Sawyer," she breathes. "I'm so sorry. I thought you were a robber. Are you all right?"

I stare back at her pale face, feeling bad that I scared her, but the guilt is soon masked by the ridiculousness of the situation and it isn't long before we both break into laughter.

"I'm so embarrassed right now." She takes a seat at the table, her hands moving to her pink cheeks. "You must think I'm a complete loon. I swear I don't always talk to myself."

Chuckling, I take the chair next to her and sit down but my amusement fades when she looks away from me. I grab her chin, forcing her eyes to mine. Behind the embarrassment lies hurt.

"That's why you were so mad at me earlier?" I ask. "Because of Jenny?"

She remains silent, her eyes dropping to her lap, telling me what she can't say.

"Talk to me, Grace."

"I just don't like her; she's said and done some real awful things to me, Sawyer, and it hurts to see her hang off you like that." She shrugs, tears glistening in her eyes. "It's a reminder of what I heard that night and it's somethin' I've been trying really hard to forget."

Guilt burns inside of me, mixing with the regret and anger I have at myself for fucking up the way I did. My hand hooks behind her neck, reeling her in close, my forehead resting on hers as I stare into her eyes. "I need you to hear me. What happened with her is something I will regret for the rest of my life. She means absolutely nothing to me. She never has and never will. What we exchanged when you saw us talking wasn't fucking pleasant. Understand?"

She swallows thickly, her lips pressing together as she tries to hold in her tears.

Dipping my head, I run my nose along her soft cheek, bringing my mouth to her ear. "Tell me you hear me, baby. I need you to believe me, Grace."

"I believe you," she whispers.

I pull back, peering into her heavy-lidded gaze and know that if I made my move on her now she wouldn't turn me away. I want to; I ache for her like I have never ached for another. But I want her to fully trust me again and she doesn't, not yet but she will.

"What are you doing up?" I ask. "Other than playing charades with yourself."

An embarrassed smile curves her perfect mouth. "I couldn't sleep, so I thought I would get an early start on the pies for the diner."

"You need to sleep."

"Sleep doesn't come easy for me. There was a time when I trained myself to wake up every few hours so I wouldn't be caught off guard, and I still haven't found a way to get off that schedule."

"Why? What were you so afraid of?" I ask, knowing this is the part of her life she has kept hidden from everyone, including Julia and Kayla.

She remains silent but the secret in her eyes screams to be let out.

"Tell me what happened, Grace."

She licks her lips, her entire body beginning to tremble. "I'm sorry, but I just can't talk about it, not right now."

I want to push the matter but decide it's better to back off. "All right, if you're not going to go back to bed then can I help you?"

She quirks a disbelieving brow at me. "You want to help me make a pie?"

"Sure, why not?"

I'm pretty much willing to do anything just to be around her. And if I'm being honest, I really have no intentions of helping; I just plan to eat as she makes it. But she doesn't need to know that.

"Okay. Come on then." Standing, she grabs the ice cream and puts it back in the freezer. She turns back to me, looking a little sheepish. "We'll make a different pie now."

I smirk. "Good idea, baby. That bitch doesn't deserve her own pie."

"Agreed." She chuckles. "I originally intended to just do a lemon meringue and apple pie so let's just stick with that. Can you grab me the lemons please?"

Opening the fridge, I bend down, my eyes wandering over the array of food she has stocked in here. "Which ones do you want, the green or yellow ones?"

When she doesn't answer, I look over my shoulder and see her biting back a smile.

"Yellow. The green ones are limes," she replies, barely containing her laughter.

This is exactly why I eat out so much.

I hand her the yellow ones then go see what she has in one of the mixing bowls. Whatever it is, it looks good, like whip cream or something. I stick my finger in to taste test.

Grace gasps in horror and slaps my shoulder. "Sawyer, you can't do that!"

"Why?" I ask, sucking the sweetness off my finger.

Oh fuck that's good.

"It's unsanitary, that's why. Now I have to make a whole new bowl."

I shrug. "No one will know."

"They won't but I will." She pulls out another bowl and starts remaking it.

Leaning over, I see what's in the other bowl. This shit looks good, too. I grab an apple slice that's coated in some gooey sweetness.

"Sawyer!" Grace slaps me again, harder than last time. "Ugh! Go sit, now!"

I chuckle at her pissed off face and follow the order. Fine, I'll just watch her while she makes the shit, then I can stare at her ass.

She stomps over, tossing the bowls down before me. "You may as well finish them now, since I have to make new ones."

"Why thanks, Cupcake."

She shakes her head, but I don't miss the twitch of her lips.

For the rest of the night I watch her work. We talk, I make her laugh, which is starting to become my favorite thing to do, and I soon realize I'm in very serious shit. Because doing something so simple with her, ends up being one of the best nights of my life.

CHAPTER 22

Sawyer

The smell of freshly baked pies invades my senses as we walk into the diner early the next morning. I tried to convince Grace to tell Mac she dropped the pies and give them to me instead but she wouldn't go for it.

"Have a seat and I'll get you some coffee." She disappears into the back, taking her delicious pies with her.

Grumbling, I sit at the end of the counter so I'm out of the way and continue to sulk. That's until she walks back out with a pretty smile on her face, bringing me a cup of coffee with two sugars and one cream, just the way I like it.

"Nice to know you've been paying close attention to me, Cupcake."

She gives me one of her famous eye rolls. "In your dreams, Evans."

If she only knew what she does in my dreams, her porcelain cheeks would turn that pretty shade of pink.

"Hang tight. I'm gonna help Mac get things goin' until Ruby gets here. She's running a few minutes late."

I nod and watch her walk to the other end of the counter, my eyes zeroing in on her perky ass hugged by tight black leggings that leave nothing to the imagination. Her long wavy hair is swept up in a pretty mess on top of her head, a few stray pieces kissing the side of her face. She wears those damn thigh high socks again but a different color. These ones are burgundy and are just as hot over leggings as they are without.

One day I am going to feel those socks hugging my hips while I drive into her over and over…

The bell over the door jingles, yanking me from the fantasy. "Well if it isn't my favorite waitress."

I spin in my chair to see some preppy dickhead strolling up to the counter like he owns the damn place. He leans over the top, getting much too close to my Cupcake.

"Oh hi, Blake." Grace gives him a shy smile, a blush staining her cheeks.

Who's this jackass?

He whispers something to her I can't hear, dragging a giggle from her.

I don't fucking think so, pretty boy.

I push to my feet and start over to them.

"I've only been gone two days," Grace says, still giggling.

"Well it's two days too long for me not to see your sweet face."

This motherfucker is about to meet my fist.

I stop next to him, leaning against the counter.

His smirk fades when he looks over to find me glaring at him.

Grace clears her throat. "Sawyer, this is Blake Carson, he's a doctor at the hospital here. Blake, this is my friend, Sawyer."

Friend? Did she just say 'friend'?

Dr. Dick barely acknowledges me with a nod. "Hey."

I don't return his greeting, my eyes narrowing further.

"Anyway," Grace says, trying to break the awkward tension, "I'm not going to be around the diner for the next little while."

The douche frowns. "Is everything all right?"

"Everything is fine," I answer before she can.

The guy finally turns to me, looking as annoyed as I feel. "I don't recognize you. Are you from around here?"

I'll show this nosy fucker where I'm from.

"Sawyer is a friend of Jaxson's from the Navy," Grace rushes to say. "He just moved here not long ago."

He grunts. "I should have known."

I straighten at the comment. "What the fuck does that mean?"

"Sawyer!" Grace scolds under her breath.

Instead of answering me, the asshole turns to Grace again and grabs her hand. "Is there anything I can do to help?"

He's one ballsy motherfucker. I rip Grace's hand out from under his. "If you don't want to lose your hand, I suggest you keep it to yourself."

"Sawyer, stop it!" she scolds again. "I'm sorry, Blake, he's normally not this rude."

Rude? If she thinks this is rude, she hasn't seen nothing yet.

"Like I tell Julia, don't apologize," he grinds out, pushing from the counter. "I hope everything works out for you, Grace. I'll see you around." Without another word, he walks out empty-handed.

Ha! He didn't even get his coffee.

Grace glares at me, looking good and pissed. "What the hell is the matter with you?"

"Me?" I ask incredulously.

"Yes, you!"

Before I can speak further, Ruby walks in. She comes to an abrupt halt, noticing the tension. "Oh hey, guys. Everything all right?"

"Yup, everything is fucking great," I answer cheerfully, a little *too cheerfully*.

Grace shakes her head, grabbing her purse. "Whatever, let's go. I'll see you tomorrow, Rubes," she says, storming her sexy, pissed off ass out the door.

I follow her out, my hot blood pumping in anger.

She starts in on me again as we drive to her house. "Why were you so rude?"

"Because the guy is an asshole."

"You don't even know him. He is actually very nice."

"He's fucking nice all right because he wants in your panties!"

"Oh my gosh. You are ridiculous. He does not."

"Come on, Grace, you are not that fucking naïve. '*Well if it isn't my favorite waitress…two days too long to see your sweet face,*'" I mimic the prick.

She bursts into laughter, finding it funny. I, however, find none of it amusing.

"So he's a flirt big deal? He's like that with everyone. You of all people should understand that."

"We are not talking about me. We are talking about Dr. Fucking Sissy," I bellow. "And what the fuck was with 'this is my friend' bullshit?"

She gapes back at me like I've lost my damn mind. "How am I supposed to introduce you?"

Well… I don't know but not like that.

I remain silent, since I don't have a good answer.

"I don't see why you care anyway," she mumbles under her breath.

I point over at her. "Don't ask me why I care. You know why."

Her eyes narrow. "It doesn't feel nice, does it, Sawyer?"

No, it doesn't.

"Imagine if you heard him screwing me against the door."

My stomach churns at the image. Just thinking about it makes me want to find pretty boy and strangle him.

Well fuck!

She lifts her chin, driving home her point.

"I told you, we are not talking about me!"

"Of course not." She turns to look out her window, ignoring me the rest of the way home.

Well fine, because I don't want to talk to her right now either.

When we pull up to the house, I'm surprised to find Julia and Jaxson parked out front. "What are they doing here?"

"Julia is picking up a dress I borrowed," she explains, jumping out of the truck.

The rest of us climb out at the same time.

"Hey," Julia greets us, the smile on her face fading as she picks up on the silent tension. "Everything okay?"

"No, it's not," Grace answers truthfully. "Sawyer is acting like an idiot."

Jaxson chuckles. "What did he do now?"

"He was incredibly rude to Blake this morning at the diner."

Jaxson tenses, the smugness vanishing from his face. "Who cares, that guy is an asshole."

"Ha! See, that's what I said."

Julia shakes her head. "Jaxson, he is not. You don't even know him."

"I know enough, the guy needs to keep his hands to himself."

"Again, that's exactly what I said," I say, getting all riled up again as I think about it. "You should have seen the prick."

I tell him the whole story, mimicking the fucker, which the girls find hilarious.

What's so funny about this?

Jaxson gets just as fired up as I am. "Yep, I fucking believe it. What kind of bedside manner is that for a doctor to have? He should be reported."

"Good fucking idea!" I agree.

The girls gape at us then burst into another fit of laughter.

"You guys are ridiculous," Grace says. "Come on, Julia. We are not gonna waste our time arguin' about something so insane."

They walk away, leaving Jaxson and I alone and pissed off.

The only *insane* person is Dr. Sissy, especially if he ever puts his hands on her again.

CHAPTER 23

Sawyer

That evening, I sit in the living room watching a movie while Grace bangs around in the kitchen, making pies. Since the clusterfuck at the diner earlier this morning, we've been doing our own thing, pretty much ignoring each other all day.

I miss her. I miss hanging out with her and making her laugh. But I'm still annoyed about Dr. Sissy, and my ego is too big to apologize first.

I'm surprised when she enters the room a few minutes later holding a slice of pie. "Are you done pouting?" she asks, a hint of a smile tugging at her pretty lips.

"I don't fucking pout."

"Yes, you do, but that's okay because I brought a peace offerin'." She dances the pie in front of me, all cute and sexy like.

"What kind is it?" I ask, refusing to give in too easily.

"I thought I would take your advice and call it *Jealousy Pie*."

My eyes narrow as she laughs, not finding her the least bit cute. Actually, that's a lie, I always find her cute, even when I'm mad.

"I'm kiddin', it's coconut cream," she says.

I love coconut and find myself unable to say no. "Okay, Cupcake, apology accepted." I smirk, taking the pie from her.

"I said it was a peace offerin', not an apology. I'm not apologizing for you being ridiculous." She dismisses me by lying down on the floor in front of the TV, curling herself around the dog. "How's my baby?" she coos, making kissy noises at him.

Lucky little bastard.

I've come to the decision that I need to move a little quicker. After today, it's obvious she's doesn't understand that she is mine.

I shove a spoonful of pie into my mouth and want to groan over how good it is. By the time I inhale it, I'm in a much better mood.

"What are ya watchin'?" she asks, staring at the TV.

"Paranormal Activity."

"What's it about?"

"It's a horror movie. You might get scared, so you better come sit up here with me."

She scoffs. "I don't get scared of horror movies. I think they're silly. Besides, Chuckie will save me, won't you, boy?" she says, kissing the dog's face.

I've never wished to be a dog so fucking bad in all my life.

Time passes as we watch most of the movie together. Me on the couch while

Grace remains on the floor with the dog. I've caught her jump a few times and now she's staring at the screen as if that damn demon is going to come out of it.

"He's inside her, ain't he? Oh no, that boyfriend is in big trouble."

She's been making comments like this throughout the whole movie. It's a good thing I find her hot, otherwise I'd never watch a movie with her again.

"Oh no, buddy, don't go down there."

Knowing what's about to happen, I get on the floor and move up silently behind her. As soon as the chick throws the guy at the camera, I grab her hips.

Her scream pierces the air and she jumps so high I swear she almost hits the fucking roof. The dog barks and hobbles out of the room.

"Sawyer, you asshole!" She spins around and starts punching the shit out of me.

I block her tiny blows, laughing my ass off.

"What the hell is wrong with you? You could give someone a heart attack doin' that. Ugh!" She climbs to her feet angrily.

"Oh come on, it was a joke, Ms. 'I think horror movies are silly not scary.'"

She delivers another pathetic kick to my ribs, making me laugh some more.

"I ain't scared of horror movies. Anyone would have jumped when someone does that to them, including you, ya jackass." She stomps off to her room, her hips swaying with every angry step she takes.

I have to admit, she's cute when she's mad. Composing myself, I lock up then head to bed. "Night, Cupcake," I call, walking past her room.

"Shut up!"

Her angry retort has me chuckling.

After brushing my teeth, I strip down to my underwear and climb into bed. With my hands behind my head, I think about the pretty girl across the hall from me, like I do every night. I picture her curled up on her side, face peaceful as she sleeps, the strap of her tank top slipping down her shoulder as my lips… I groan, my cock hardening.

I don't know how much longer I can hold off. I need that girl like my next breath and not just her body but her. I want it all.

My thoughts stall when I hear her shuffling around in her room. "What was that?" I hear her whisper to the dog.

I bite back a smile. *Not scared, my ass.*

I hear another gasp, then more shuffling. Moments later, her tiny footsteps make their way to my room.

"Sawyer?" she whispers from the door.

"What?"

"You awake?"

I roll my eyes like a fuckin' chick. "I am now."

"Did you hear that noise?"

"What noise?"

I can't wait to hear this.

"I dunno, it sounded like it was comin' from the wall though."

You have got to be shittin' me.

"Nope, never heard anything like that, Cupcake."

She checks behind her and gasps again. "See, did ya hear that?"

"Grace, there's nothing there. Believe me, if there were noises I would hear them."

"Can I sleep with you?"

Her innocent question has my dick roaring to life.

Easy, Evans.

"Yeah, you can sleep—"

She leaps from the door onto the bed, almost nailing me in the balls.

"Jesus, woman, what the hell are you doing?"

"I'm sorry, I didn't want something to grab my feet from under the bed," she says then pushes my shoulder. "Move, I wanna sleep between you and the wall."

"Why does that matter?"

"Because if something comes to grab us, it will take you first."

Instead of being insulted, I laugh my ass off.

She can't hold back either, her laughter mingling with mine but hers is a little more hysterical. "God, Sawyer, I'm serious, I'm so darn scared right now. I've never been this scared of a movie before. I keep thinking some invisible demon is gonna grab my foot and drag me from my bed."

"Don't worry, Cupcake, I'll kick any motherfucker's ass if they try to drag you from this bed."

"Sorry, but not even you can keep me safe from a demon."

I grunt, the hell I can't.

Rising up on her knees, she leans over me, her silky hair sweeping across my bare chest and cupcake smell invading my senses. "Chuckie, come here, boy," she calls, not having any idea what she's doing to my dick right now.

The dog comes limping in.

"Come to the end of the bed, baby, I'll help you up."

"What the hell are you doing?" I ask. "That dog isn't sleeping up here."

Her head snaps toward me. "Why not?"

"Because there isn't any room."

"I'll curl up and he can sleep at the end of the bed by my feet."

"He has a bed, Grace, why are you having him sleep up here?"

"Because he might be scared."

"He isn't scared. I'm serious, he stays on the floor."

"Geez, you're grouchy."

Yeah, well, having a constant hard cock does that to me.

She leans over further, petting the dog. "Sorry, boy, Sawyer's bein' a grump. You stay here and I'll keep checkin' on ya."

My palm twitches at the way her ass is pointed in the air and I just can't fucking resist. Slowly, I rise up and slap it.

Another scream leaves her.

I grab her shirt before she careens off the bed.

"Sawyer, you stupid jerk!" She starts slapping the shit out of me again. "You know what, forget it, I'm outta here."

My arms wrap around her waist before she can make her escape, pulling her down next to me.

"I mean it. Let go!" she demands, struggling against me.

"I'm sorry. I'll stop."

Her body stills. "Promise?"

"Scout's honor."

She scoffs. "I'm sure you were no boy scout, Sawyer Evans."

She's got that right.

I bring her in closer, her back to my front. She's tense at first but eventually relaxes into me, her body fitting against mine perfectly.

"I want to talk to you about something," I start.

She turns in my arms to face me, concern filling her warm eyes. "What's wrong?"

"Nothing," I rush to assure her. "I just forgot that I booked a flight home this weekend to see my family. My parents are going away over Thanksgiving, so I promised my mom I would come home early to see them. It's only for a few nights."

"No problem," she says. "I'm sure I can stay with Cooper and Kayla or even Jaxson and Julia."

"No. I want you to come with me."

Shock flares in her eyes. "Oh no. Really, it's fine. You go ahead. Don't worry about me. Like I said, I can—"

I cover her mouth with my hand, cutting off her ramble. "I'm asking you because I want you to come with me, not because I feel obligated. I'm not going without you."

She pulls my hand away. "Don't be ridiculous. Of course you're going."

"Does that mean you're coming with me?"

She shakes her head. "I appreciate the offer, but I can't. I don't have the money and—"

"I'll pay for your flight."

She opens her mouth to argue but I don't let her.

"Don't start this not accepting bullshit. I'm asking you to come so I'll fucking pay for it."

Her eyes narrow. "It's not just about that. I have Chuckie to think about, too. I can't leave him."

"I'll talk to Jaxson. I'm sure he and Julia will take him. It's only for a couple days. Besides, the dog will love it out there with that big yard."

Her expression softens and I can see her wheels spinning. She's close to caving.

"If you say no I'll have to cancel, and that will make my mom cry. You don't want to be responsible for making my mom cry, do you?"

"I definitely don't want to make your mom cry," she says with a smile but it doesn't last. "Are you sure? Maybe you should ask your parents first?"

"I'm sure, and I already spoke to my mom about it. She was ecstatic. So no more excuses, okay?"

"All right," she relents on a sigh. Comfortable silence falls upon us before she breaks it a few moments later. "Guess what?" she whispers.

"Why are you whispering?"

Another moment of silence.

"I don't know," she says on one of her sweet giggles.

My mouth breaks into a grin. "What, Cupcake?"

"I've never been on a plane before."

Shock courses through me at the confession. How the hell has she gone her whole life never taking a plane?

The internal thought has a different question surfacing. "How old are you?" I ask.

"How old do you think I am?"

I shrug. "Twenty-four."

"I'm twenty-one."

"Holy shit, really?"

"What's that supposed to mean?" she asks, sounding insulted.

"Nothing bad, I'm just surprised. I always assumed you were Julia's age."

"Well, how old are you?"

"How old do you think I am?" I mimic her words back.

"Hmm…" She shrugs. "I dunno…forty?"

I grunt, knowing she's fucking with me. Especially by the way she laughs her ass off.

"I'm just kiddin'," she teases. "I'm gonna guess twenty-five."

"Close, twenty-six," I tell her. "Now back to this flying business. How did you get here if you didn't fly?"

That pain she keeps buried surfaces in her warm amber eyes. "I took a bus."

Questions burn inside of me but I refrain from asking them, not wanting to bring up bad memories for her. "You can sleep tonight, Grace, I got you," I promise her.

She dips her head, burying her face in my chest. I make sure to stay awake until she falls asleep, vowing to extract vengeance on anyone who dares to ever try and hurt her again.

CHAPTER 24

Grace

I come awake, wrapped in the most amazing warmth. My eyes drift open and I find sunlight streaming through the blinds. Realization strikes me that I slept all night. For the first time in three years I did not wake up once.

A peaceful smile dances across my lips and my eyes close once again as I snuggle closer to that warmth until my leg comes in contact with something hard.

A loud, tortured groan fills the air.

I quickly realize I'm practically on top of Sawyer, my leg resting right over his erection.

Yikes!

I shoot upright, throwing myself into the wall at the other side of the bed.

He grins over at me, looking wide awake. "Morning, Cupcake."

"Mornin'," I croak out.

Before I can stop them, my eyes shift lower, taking in his half naked body. I didn't think I could find this man sexier than I already do, but I was so wrong. His shoulders are broad, torso long and lean, every line hard and profound. His abs alone are a work of art. He bears a tattoo on his left pectoral, a symbol of an eagle. The words, *U.S. Navy SEALs,* then under it reads, *SEAL Team 3.*

My gaze continues its discovery, taking in the white sheet that lies low across his hips, doing nothing to shield his erection. And what an impressive erection it is.

"How did you sleep?" he asks, yanking me from my dirty thoughts.

"Very good," I tell him honestly. "I didn't wake up once and that's the first time in years."

He gazes back at me, his expression somber. "Maybe this should be our sleeping arrangement from now on then."

"Maybe it should," I whisper, feeling our relationship shift within this one moment. My lips twitch with a smile. "Except in my bed, so Chuckie can sleep on it, too."

He grunts, obviously not keen on the idea.

"We should get going soon," I say. "I need to get the pies over to Mac."

The longer I'm in this bed with him, the stronger the temptation.

He nods. "After the diner we'll go pick up anything you need for our trip on Friday."

I still can't believe I'm going to meet his family this weekend. I'm both excited and terrified at the prospect.

I begin making a mental list of everything I'm going to need but my thoughts come to a halt when Sawyer sits up. A gasp parts my lips, pain striking me all the way to the core as I stare in horror at the mangled skin of his back.

His shoulders tense, as if he's just realized what he's revealed but he remains still, allowing me to see what he has always kept hidden.

This is what Julia was talking about, and I finally understand the pain I witnessed in her eyes that day. Large jagged scars run crisscross, taking up the entire expanse of his back. It looks like someone took a knife to him or a whip. I don't know which, and like Julia, I don't want to. I don't think I could handle knowing what exactly was used to harm him this way.

Buried within those horrendous scars is a tattoo across his shoulder blades. In black script the words stand out, bringing beauty to the horror.

You will not break me, for I am unbreakable.
I will live with integrity, fight with honor, and die for what's right.

My watery eyes lift to his, and I find him watching me over his shoulder. "Sawyer." His name falls from me on a choked whisper, my trembling hand resting across my aching heart.

Sliding closer, I reach out, tracing the words of his tattoo, words that will forever be ingrained into my heart whenever I think of him. When my fingertips dance over the final letter, I can't hold in my pain any longer. I cover my mouth as a sob tumbles past my lips.

Sawyer reaches for me, pulling me onto his lap so I'm straddling him.

I hug him close, crying into his neck. "I'm so sorry someone hurt you."

"Don't cry for me, Cupcake. I survived and I'm stronger for it."

My heart not only breaks for him, but for all of them. It just goes to show how cruel the world can really be. I lift my head, resting my hand against his hard jaw. "This world is full of awful people, isn't it?"

"Yeah, baby, it is but it's also filled with some of the best." His fingers squeeze my hips, driving his point home.

"It sure is," I agree, dancing my fingers across his lips.

His heated green eyes hold mine, something powerful passing between us, reeling us into a world of our own.

Leaning in, I tentatively press my lips against his jaw, trailing them toward his mouth. They hover just above his, the need for so much more filling the space between us.

"Ask me, Grace," he says, voice rough as he cups my bottom to bring me closer. "Just say the word."

My mouth opens to do just that, to tell him I want it—want him—but before I get the chance, my doorbell rings.

Both of us still, my disappointed heart plummeting.

"What—the—fuck?"

The look on Sawyer's face is so comical that I burst into laughter.

"There's nothing funny about this."

"I disagree. Your face is hilarious," I tell him, continuing to laugh.

He grunts, not sharing in my amusement. "It's probably Cade. I asked him to bring some stuff by for me."

I move to climb off him but his arms tighten around me, keeping me in place. "We're going to pick this up soon, Grace. No more denying us what we both want."

I nod because he's right. It's time to give into this pull between us. The problem is, I'm scared. He has such a hold on my heart that I fear when he actually touches me I'll be lost to him forever.

CHAPTER 25

Grace

I drag my suitcase out of my closet and begin packing, starting with the essentials. Each item that gets tossed in has me getting more excited.

As anxious as I am for this trip, I can't wait to meet Sawyer's family, to get a glimpse into the lives of the people who raised him to be the amazing man he is today. Next to Mac, he's the best I've ever known. Even his big ego can't overshadow his honorable heart… The thought has a smile cracking my lips.

I go in search of him, wondering when he plans to start his packing, only to come up short when I find him in the living room. He sits on the couch, reading one of my books. A very sexy book.

Oh god.

His head lifts, gaze meeting mine, and the knowing smirk stealing his face has my cheeks heating furiously. "So, my little Cupcake reads porn. Who knew?"

Humiliation threatens to swallow me whole. "It's a romance novel," I grind out.

"No, it's not, this shit is porn, baby. Old school porn, but it's still porn all the same."

"Give it to me!" I storm up to him but he jumps to his feet, holding the book over his head. "I mean it, Sawyer. I'm not messin' around."

He chuckles, finding the threat amusing. Opening the book over his head, he begins reading from the page he was on. "He thrusts his cock inside—"

"That's it!" I launch myself at his hard body, trying to swipe the book from his hands but my efforts prove pointless.

He spins me around, bringing my back to his front, his arms pinning me in place. "Tell me, Grace, how wet does your pussy get when you're reading this shit?" His dirty words in my ear have shivers dancing along my skin but my humiliation overshadows it.

"Stop it, you're embarrassin' me," I whisper.

"Don't be embarrassed, baby. I think it's hot. Do you touch yourself while reading it?"

"No!" I grind out.

He chuckles. "I don't believe you. There is no way you don't get yourself off reading this shit."

"I'm not lying! I've never even had an orgasm before." I regret the words as soon as they leave my big mouth.

He tenses, his arms easing their hold on me. Turning around, I rip the book from his hands and avoid eye contact as he gapes at me.

"What the hell did you just say?"

"You heard me," I mumble, my gaze remaining on the floor.

"Are you a virgin?"

It's obvious the thought is appalling to him. Looking up, I glare at him. "I'm not a virgin, you asshole. For your information, I've had sex three and a half times."

Oh god, shut up, Grace.

Utter disbelief fills his expression. "How the fuck do you have sex three and a half times? That's not even possible." Chuckling, he shakes his head. "Wait, hold that thought, first things first—clearly the losers you were with didn't know how to get you off. All right, fine. But are you telling me you haven't been able to get yourself off?"

I didn't think it would be possible for me to get any more embarrassed than I already am, but I was so wrong. "What's the matter with you? You don't ask people personal questions like this."

"I'm not asking 'people,' I'm asking you."

"Well, it's none of your business," I grumble, hating this conversation more and more every second.

Realization soon dawns on him, his knowing eyes seeing right through me. "Holy shit! You've never touched yourself, have you?"

"Would you stop it?" I snap. "You know what? Forget it, I'm out of here." I stomp off but don't make it far.

"Not so fast, Cupcake." He pulls me against him, his back crowding mine once again. "I'm sorry. I didn't mean to be an asshole. I'm just shocked as hell right now."

"It's not that big of a deal."

"On the contrary, Grace, I think it's a very big fucking deal that someone as beautiful as you has yet to experience that kind of pleasure. It's an abomination."

I clear my throat, feeling uncomfortable with what I'm about to say. "I'm not sure I can; I think there's something wrong with me."

His fingers grip my hips, a deep noise yanking from his throat. "Believe me, baby, there's nothing wrong with you."

The room grows hot, air thickening with that ever-present pull between us.

"Let me show you, Grace," he whispers, his lips grazing my ear. "Let me touch you. Just touch, nothing else. I promise."

My pulse races, the longing I've had buried for this man climbing its way to the surface, threatening to consume me, body and soul. I can't say no and I don't want to either. Not anymore.

I nod, too nervous to speak.

His tongue darts out, tasting the shell of my ear. "Say it," he demands. "I need to hear you say it."

I lick my lips, my mouth dry. "I want you to touch me."

He spins me around and claims my mouth in a ruthless kiss, rocking the ground beneath my feet.

Oh god.

His lips are warm and firm, dominating and demanding. The moment his tongue thrusts inside, I'm lost to him. "You taste even fucking better than I remember," he growls.

I want to tell him the same thing, but all I can manage are incoherent noises, my senses reeling with all the feelings this man evokes in me.

I fist his shirt, trying to get closer. His hands slip to my bottom, cupping the supple flesh and lifting me off my feet. My legs lock around his waist and arms around his neck. The belt that holds the denim low on his hips nudges the very place I crave to feel him.

Moaning, I grind myself against the cold metal, trying to relieve the fierce ache.

Sawyer moves to the couch, never breaking contact as he stretches us out, his hard body covering mine. He pulls back, allowing me oxygen, and trails his heated lips down my neck. My fingers sift through his mussed hair; back arching as his lip descends.

He cups my breast through my thin tank top, his fingers squeezing the tight nipple poking through.

"Sawyer," his name pours from me on a moan and I raise my hips, coming in contact with his erection.

"Jesus, Grace, I've waited so fucking long to touch you." He pushes up, one knee pressing into the couch between my legs as he reaches for the edge of my shirt. "Lift your arms." The order is gruff, fueled by lust.

I sit up just enough for him to remove my top then drop down to my back again. His eyes are fixated on my bra. My plain white cotton one with cherries on it.

Seriously? Out of all the dang bras I own, did I have to be wearing this one?

I clear my throat, yanking his attention back to my face. "If I had known we were gonna be doin' this I would have worn something different."

His lips kick up in an amused smirk. "The bra is more than fine, baby. Sexy as fuck actually since it's on you, but it doesn't matter either way. Because it's coming off."

My breath stalls in anticipation as his warm hand travels up my stomach, leaving a path of heat in its wake. With a deft flick of his fingers, he opens the front clasp, baring me to his stare.

The cool air whispers over my heated flesh, making my nipples pebble beneath his hungry gaze. I get the urge to cover myself, insecurity rearing its ugly head.

A noise that can only be described as animalistic erupts from his throat. "So fucking pretty." Leaning down, he closes his hot mouth over my aching nipple, obliterating any insecurity I have.

"Oh!" My back arches, pleasure racing through my blood as his tongue lashes me with fiery licks. His fingers grip my other nipple, the pull so strong I feel it between my legs. I thrash beneath him, wild for more. "Sawyer," I beg, my mind reeling with something I can't understand.

Reaching between us, he cups me through my shorts, exerting pressure where I need it most. "You're ready for my touch, aren't you, Grace?"

Oh boy, am I ever.

"Tell me, baby. Tell me you're ready."

"I'm ready," I pant breathlessly. "I'm really, really ready."

Chuckling, he removes my shorts along with my underwear.

Sheer dominance fills his expression, his eyes storming with something I can't name. "Fucking perfect." By the way he gazes down at me, it's impossible not to believe him, and for the first time in a long time, I feel beautiful. I feel like I'm enough.

His hand dances up the inside of my thigh, sending shivers up my skin. I bite my bottom lip to stifle a moan and let my legs fall open, yearning for his touch. When his fingers delve into my wet heat I practically fly off the couch.

"Aw, yeah," he groans. "You're fuckin' soaked." His hard body comes back over top of mine, pinning me in place as he inserts a single finger inside. "And so damn tight."

A gasp flees me on a rush, the beautiful invasion knocking the breath from my lungs.

"Feels good, doesn't it?"

"Yes."

"Just wait until it's my cock invading this tight little pussy. It's going to be so good, you'll fucking beg for more."

I don't doubt it. That arrogant mouth of his already has me close to begging.

He braces one hand on the couch behind my head and rises up, leaving a gap between us. "Watch, baby, look at the way my fingers fuck this sweet pussy."

My eyes become riveted to the erotic sight between my legs, watching his fingers disappear inside of me.

"I'm going to show you how to do this one day, show you how to pleasure yourself."

"That's okay, you can just do it," I pant, my breath racing past my lips. "I think you will be better at it anyway."

His chuckle trails into a groan. "Oh, I'll always be better. But sometimes I won't be around when you need it, and you should never go without pleasure, baby." Flicking his wrist, he curls his fingers inside of me, sending a foreign sensation to form low in my belly.

"Sawyer," I breathe his name, unable to explain what I need, what my body is trying to grasp.

"Get ready, baby, because I'm going to make you come so goddamn hard you'll never forget this."

Oh god!

I can feel it; I'm so close, teetering on the edge of destruction, but the pleasure remains just out of reach.

"Let go, Grace."

I shake my head. "I can't."

"Look at me!"

My eyes snap open at his harsh command, dominance radiating in his expression.

"Give into it, I got you." Leaning down, he takes a sensitive nipple into his mouth, gripping it between his teeth. The erotic sting shoots to my throbbing clit and sends me flying.

My cries echo through the room as I catapult to another universe, one where nothing exists but divine oblivion.

"That a girl, come all over my fingers," he groans.

I drown in the sensations claiming my body, wave after wave of pleasure thrashing through me.

The moment I begin to drift back to reality, Sawyer crawls down my body. "We're not done yet." I have no time to comprehend what that means before his mouth descends on my hot center.

A heated cry rips from my throat and my back bows off the couch. His large hand splays across my lower stomach, holding my hips in place while his tongue devours me.

My fingers grip his hair in a tight hold. I'm unsure if I want to push him away or pull him closer, a war battling within my body. In the end, I opt for more pleasure and my knees fall open, granting him access.

He groans his approval, his skillful tongue inflicting a sweet torture. He eats me like he can't get enough; taking my body to highs I never knew possible. It doesn't take long before another orgasm claims me, this one just as intense as the last.

Eventually, I become limp and sated, basking in my post-orgasmic bliss.

Sawyer crawls back up my body, his lips cherishing every patch of bare skin he passes until his handsome face appears before mine. "Told you there wasn't a damn thing wrong with you."

"Mmmhmm," I mumble, unable to form words at the moment.

"Wait until you see what I can do with my dick."

Laughter spills past my lips. His arrogance knows no bounds but after what he just did to me, he has every right to be.

His mouth takes mine in a searing kiss. Moaning, I slide my hands under his shirt and up his back, feeling every deep groove of his jagged scars. My heart becomes heavy as I remember what lies beneath his clothes every day.

Sensing my sad thoughts, Sawyer pulls his mouth away and climbs to his feet. He reaches for the throw on the back of the couch and covers me with it before lifting me into his arms. I cling to his neck, my head resting on his shoulder as he carries me into my bedroom.

After lying me down, he surprises me when he turns to walk away. Reaching out, I snag his arm, bringing his eyes back to mine. "Don't leave," I say, peering up at him. "Sleep with me tonight."

His expression softens and he trails a finger down my cheek. "I'm just locking up, I'll be right back."

I watch him walk away, my eyes closing as I take pleasure in my blissful state. A recipe for a new pie takes hold, the ingredients slamming into me with the perfect idea—

Chocolate covered graham crust
Whipping cream
Bananas
Raspberries…

"What's going on inside that pretty head of yours, Cupcake?"

My eyes snap open to see Sawyer standing over me, looking rather amused, and I realize I'm smiling like a fool.

"I'm creatin' a pie," I tell him.

"Oh yeah, and what's this one called?" he asks, crawling in next to me. I don't miss the fact that he stays on top of the blankets rather than getting beneath them.

I turn on my side to face him and shrug. "Not sure yet. Grace's First O Pie, Orgasm Pie, Pie Of Pleasure…"

"Sawyer is Fucking Amazing Pie."

Giggling, I roll my eyes. "Nah, I don't like that one."

His smirk spreads into a full smile that has my heart skipping a beat. "Is it going to be good?"

"Oh, it's goin' to be delicious. No—it's gonna be explosive."

A husky laugh barrels out of him, a contagious one that elicits one of my own. He throws an arm over me and drops a kiss my head. The simple gesture has warmth spreading through my chest.

He peers down at me, amusement bright in his eyes. "You have to tell me how the hell you've had sex exactly three and a half times. Because I have to tell you, Cupcake, that number confuses the fuck out of me."

"Because the fourth time we never finished." The quiet confession leaves a bad taste in my mouth as the horrible memory begins poking through the dark recesses of my mind.

"What happened, Grace?"

I gaze up at him, hating to have to tell him but know there's no avoiding it. If only I could learn to shut my big trap…

"Wait," he speaks again, holding a hand up. "Does the prick live here? Because if he does, maybe you shouldn't tell me."

A frown pulls at my face. "No. Why would that matter?"

"Because the thought of someone else touching you drives me fucking insane, and if it turns out that you see him often, the poor bastard might find himself with some serious injuries."

My brow quirks. "Says the man who has taken many women to his bed."

"That was my old ways, baby, I'm a new man now."

I scoff playfully because the truth of the matter is, I believe him. The past is the past and I'm really hoping that we will be each other's future. The hope is both terrifying and exhilarating.

"Enough stalling. Tell me what happened."

A heavy sigh escapes the tightness of my chest. "I was dating Adam when I lost Mama but he moved away for college right after it happened and we didn't stay in touch." I pause, remembering how much I needed him but he left without a second thought. "Anyway, we ended up reconnecting a short time later and a moment of weakness had me losing my virginity to him." The confession rolls off my tongue with regret, especially when I think about why I went to see him in the first place.

"Is he a douchebag? Do I need to kick his ass?" Sawyer asks.

My lips lift in a halfhearted smile. "He's definitely a douchebag, but no, you don't need to kick his ass." Sighing, I continue the dreadful story. "One of the times we were together that weekend his roommate walked in and tried to join us."

Sawyer tenses, eyes flaring in both shock and anger.

"I know, believe me. It caught me off guard too, but it turns out it was their plan from the beginning. He set me up," I tell him on a whisper, the betrayal still feeling fresh years later. "I never thought he would do something like that. I thought I could trust him, but turns out I never could."

"He's a fucking idiot," Sawyer says, his voice tight with anger. His expression softens as he reaches out to caress my cheek. "But his loss is my greatest treasure."

His words send my heart into a tailspin, healing the ache in my chest. I lean into his touch, wishing I could convey just how much he has made my lonely life better these past few months.

Our moment is interrupted when my phone dings with a text. Turning over, I grab it off the nightstand and see it's from Mac.

Mac: *Night, darlin'. Just wanted to let you know I'm thinking about you. I'll see you in the morning.*

My already bursting heart swells in my chest. He has been sending these sweet messages lately; I think the big lug misses seeing me around the diner so much.

I send a quick reply back, telling him I love him too and I'll see him in the morning. After, I keep the phone in my hand and turn back to find Sawyer watching me, his gaze questioning.

"That was my boyfriend," I tell him. "He's comin' over so you better leave before he gets here." No matter how hard I try to keep a straight face I can't and end up laughing the entire time.

"You're the worst liar," he says, not nearly as amused as I am about the joke.

"I know. I've always been bad at it," I tell him, feeling no shame. Once my laughter dies down, I realize he's still on top of the blankets, fully clothed. "You plan on sleeping like that?" I ask, gesturing at him.

"Yep."

I frown. "Why?"

"It's for the best right now, trust me." His voice is husky, lust still lingering in his green eyes.

Guilt plagues me, hating that he's left wanting. Holding his gaze, I bring my hand to his hard stomach, inching it up his shirt. I don't make it far before he grabs my wrist, the act so fast it startles me.

"No." The one word is gritted between clenched teeth, his restraint apparent.

"Sawyer," I start, hating to see him like this.

"I meant what I said, Grace, tonight is just for you. Getting to touch you is all I wanted." Before I can argue, he pulls me in close, dropping a kiss on my head. "Sleep."

I curl into his hard chest and breathe in his scent, letting peace, safety, and another emotion I'm a little scared to name wash over me. Even though I'm relaxed, sleep evades me, my mind reeling from everything that transpired between us tonight.

It's not long before I feel Sawyer's breathing become deep and even. Lifting my chin, I find his eyes closed and face soft with sleep, and that warmness in my chest grows even stronger.

I reach for my phone that lies next to me and send a group text to Kayla and Julia.

Me: *Well, girls, it finally happened…*blush**

My phone flashes a moment later.

J: *OMG! No way!*

K: *SHUT UP! YOU SLEPT WITH SAWYER?*

Me: *NO! Uh…he just gave me one…two, actually. ;)*

K: *WHOO HOO! That a boy Sawyer! See, I told you that cocky mouth of his would prove useful. Wait…he used his mouth, right?*

J: *LOL! ?*

I snicker quietly.

***Me:** Yes! *Blushing again**

"Don't forget to tell them I used my fingers, too."

Yelping, I throw my phone across the bed, realizing Sawyer is still awake. "Oh—my—god." I groan and cover my hot cheeks with my hands. "What are you doin' awake? I thought you were sleeping."

"Nope," he relays all too happily, "just resting and it's a good thing I was. Look what I would have missed. I can't wait until you tell them about my big dick when the time comes."

Humiliation burns inside of me as his laughter fills the room. This is by far the most embarrassing moment of my life. I tuck my head back in his chest, praying for sleep to take me. My wish is I'll wake up and the last three minutes never happened. It was all just a bad dream.

Sadly, that wish never came true.

CHAPTER 26

Sawyer

We board the plane the following morning, my ass dragging after the sleepless night I had. Grace's attention is riveted on our surroundings, a look of wonderment splashed across her face.

"Oh my gosh, Sawyer, isn't this so darn excitin'?" She flashes me a smile over her shoulder, her enthusiasm palpable.

"Yeah, baby, really exciting."

Actually, I don't find any of it exciting. I've flown a thousand times before. However, I can't deny that watching my Cupcake burst at the seams over something so small makes me pretty damn happy.

She continues down the aisle, almost bulldozing people down in her haste, until I grab her arm at row ten. "These are our seats."

"Oh sorry," she says, glancing up at me sheepishly. "Can I sit by the window or do you want to?"

"Go ahead, I prefer the aisle anyway."

After flashing another one of her bright smiles, she crawls over to her seat, giving me a great view of her ass in those damn yoga pants. My control is thin, bordering on the edge of destruction. Now that I've got to touch and taste her, it's all I can think about. I need more, I need *her*. This weekend I plan to do exactly that, I will take her in ways she's never imagined, by the time I am done with her, there will be no questions about who she belongs to.

Once she's situated, I take my seat and send my mom a quick text to let her know what time we will be arriving. She was shocked as hell when I asked if I could bring Grace with me but also elated. I've never brought a girl home and even though I explained Grace's situation to her, she knew that me bringing her was more than that.

Pocketing my phone, I shift my attention over to Grace and find her checking everything out. From playing with her TV to rummaging in the seat pocket in front of her and even looking out the window at the wing next to us. I've never seen someone so fucking intrigued by an airplane before. You'd think she was on a rocket ship. It amuses the hell out of me.

The flight attendant comes on, telling us to buckle our seat belts and watch the safety video. Grace follows the instructions, staring transfixed at the video that no one ever pays attention to. Her excitement quickly transforms to fear when they talk about what to do in case of an emergency.

"You okay, Cupcake?" I ask.

She nods but I don't miss the hard swallow she takes.

I reach for her hand, curling my fingers around hers. "Don't worry. It's the safest form of transportation. Everything will be fine." Resting my head back, I shift in my seat, trying to get comfortable but it's impossible to do when you have no fucking leg room.

The plane rolls forward, starting down the runway. Once it's in position the pilot punches the gas, picking up speed for takeoff. The nose of the plane lifts, transitioning from ground to air. There's minor turbulence and it sends Grace over the edge.

Gasping, her hand darts out, slamming into my chest.

"It's okay. This is normal," I tell her.

She doesn't acknowledge me, her face ashen and eyes wide with fear as she stares straight ahead. I shift to move closer but her fingers tighten on my chest, nails clawing into me.

"Don't move, Sawyer. I'm serious, you're big and your weight might mess somethin' up."

I pull her hand away, and lean in to nuzzle her throat. Her body is still stiff but she angles her head, allowing me to have more. I taste her skin, my lips soothing and coaxing and it isn't long before I feel her relax.

"You good?" I ask, lips brushing the shell of her ear.

"I will be if you keep doing that."

Little does she know, I never plan to stop.

CHAPTER 27

Grace

Nerves begin to override my excitement as we leave the airport in our rental and head for Sawyer's parents' house. My attention is riveted out the window on the Rocky Mountains as I find myself completely in awe of their beauty.

"How far is the drive?" I ask.

"About an hour. I grew up in a small town just outside of Denver, on an acreage."

"You're a country boy, Evans?" I ask, my brow lifting in surprise as I look over at him. "I would have never guessed. Do you own a cowboy hat, too?" I snicker.

He grunts. "Not that kind of country, baby. You'll see."

My curiosity piques at the vague response. "Tell me more about your family."

"What else do you want to know?"

"How long have your parents been married? What do your sisters do for a living?"

"It's going on thirty years for my parents. My youngest sister, Sam, graduates this year from high school, with honors," he adds proudly. "And my middle sister, Jesse, is your age—she's in the fashion industry and makes clothes. She's even thinking about opening her own store."

"Wow," I say, impressed. "They sound like wonderful people. I sure hope they like me." My gaze reverts out the window again, my anxiety kicking up another notch. I value Sawyer's friendship and the thought of his family's disapproval absolutely terrifies me.

He takes my hand in his, the warmth of his touch bringing my attention back to him. "They're going to love you, Grace, just like everyone does. And if they don't, I'll kick their asses."

I roll my eyes but a smile cracks my lips. "You can't kick someone's ass for not liking me, Sawyer."

"The hell I can't. I'll kick anyone's ass who hurts my Cupcake's feelings."

Laughter tumbles from me at the ridiculous statement, but I can't deny the flip my tummy does. I really like it when he says things like that. I haven't had someone care about my feelings in a long time.

Resting my head back on the seat, I keep my eyes on him, admiring the way his body fills the massive SUV. Where my seat is pushed forward, his is all the way back to accommodate his long legs. His dirty blond hair wisps out the side of his black hat and makes my fingers itch to touch it again.

Unable to stop myself, I reach over and rip it off his head.

"Hey! What the hell are you doing, woman?"

Giggling, I push to my knees and lean over to wrap my arms around his neck, making sure not to obstruct his vision of the road, and give him a big loud smooch on the cheek. "Thank you for bringin' me here, Sexy Sawyer."

"You're welcome." His voice is gruff, thick with need, one I feel all the way to my core.

Feeling bold, I rest my forehead on the side of his and dance my lips across his stubbly jaw, bringing them to his ear. I take a sharp nip like he always does to me, hoping it elicits the same reaction that I get.

It does.

His low growl fills the truck, the sound of it hitting me right between the legs. "Grace, you need to get back in your seat or I'm going to pull over and fuck you right here. I don't give a shit who drives by."

I can hear the strain in his voice; hear how close he is to snapping. As much as I'd love to see just how far he can be pushed I don't want my first time with him on the side of the road. So I'm smart enough to listen but not before giving him one more kiss, right below the ear.

The sound he makes in his throat has me giggling as I take my seat again.

"There's nothing funny about how hard you make my dick, Cupcake."

"Calm down, I was just teasin', ya grump."

He reaches over and laces his fingers with mine. "Tease away, baby, because I have big plans for you this weekend."

Anticipation has my heart skipping a beat. I'd be lyin' if I said I wasn't curious what those plans are. More make out sessions? Or will we both cross that line of no going back? In my opinion, I think we already have but I'm ready to take that next step with him. I've come to care very deeply for Sawyer, more than I've ever cared about another before. It's a little scary, especially for my heart, but I refuse to let fear ruin something that could potentially be everything I've been searching for.

The rest of the drive is mainly quiet with our thoughts, the silence saying more than we could. Eventually, we pull up to a wrought iron gate in the middle of nowhere. Sawyer lowers his window and enters a bunch of numbers into the keypad that has the gate opening.

I frown, wondering where the heck we are. Until we drive down the long paved road that leads to one of the biggest houses I've ever seen. "You're rich!" I shriek, looking over at him incredulously.

"No. My parents are."

"Why wouldn't you tell me this?"

His eyes narrow. "Because I knew you would make a big fucking deal about it."

"Because I don't fit in here, Sawyer."

"Fuck that! You belong wherever I do."

I shake my head, betrayal thickening my throat. "I can't believe you kept this from me, that you would let me find out this way."

"It's not a big deal, Grace. It's just money."

Easy for him to say, he fits in anywhere, I do not. Feeling close to tears, I turn my face away, fearing for the impending disaster when his family meets me and realize I'm far from fitting in.

Once the SUV comes to a stop, he reaches for me. "Come on, baby, don't be upset." He pulls on my arm until I'm straddling him, remorse shining in his eyes.

"This doesn't change anything. Yes, my parents have money, but my dad worked his ass off to have all of this. They're good people, which you will soon see, and they're going to love you, I promise."

"You should have told me. I shouldn't have found out like this."

"You're right, I'm sorry. I really wanted you to come with me, and I didn't think you would if you knew."

I probably wouldn't have.

His hand lifts, fingers grazing the side of my cheek. "Forgive me?"

I nod. "Just don't keep things from me, it ain't right."

"I promise, Cupcake, never again. Now let's kiss and make up."

Smiling, I wrap my arms around his neck and seal my mouth over his for a toe-curling kiss but that's where my control ends. His hand fists my hair, angling my head so he can devour me.

I shift on top of him, his erection nudging me where I crave him most. A growl erupts from his throat as he cups my bottom. My breath races, hips rocking faster as I drown in all the feelings this man evokes in me. I'm so caught up in them that I forget where we are. Until a loud bang on the window yanks me back into reality.

Gasping, I fly off Sawyer, landing back in my seat.

A girl, whom I'm assuming is one of his sisters, has her face plastered against his window. "What are you doing in there, big brother?"

Even though I'm incredibly embarrassed at the moment, I can't help but laugh at the way her nose is squished against the glass.

Sawyer glowers at her, not finding her as funny as I do. She gives him a sweet smile and waves, her fingers dancing in the air.

It elicits another giggle from me but it fades quickly when I look out my window and see Sawyer's entire family standing outside waiting to greet us. My stomach plummets, knowing they all witnessed us making out.

Oh god. They probably think I'm such a whore.

Sawyer blows out a frustrated breath, oblivious to my torment. "Come on, let's get this over with so I can get you alone." He climbs out and is attacked by his sister. She throws her arms around his neck, kissing his cheek. Sawyer hugs her back, lifting her off her feet as he rounds the truck.

"You can do this, Grace. Pull yourself together," I mumble. By the time I work up enough courage to open my door, Sawyer is there, offering me his hand.

I accept it, thankful to have something to hold onto.

"Grace, this annoying pest is my youngest sister, Sam," he says, introducing the girl who clings to him. She's stunning, just like her brother. With long blonde hair and big green eyes, but a shade lighter than Sawyer's.

She gives me a radiant smile, then surprises me by wrapping me in a hug. "Nice to meet you, Grace. Sorry for interrupting, but I've been awaiting my brother's arrival impatiently."

"That's all right. Sorry you had to interrupt anythin'," I whisper, still feeling mortified.

"I love your accent," she says.

Accent?

Before I can ponder that, a loud squeal comes from the front steps, and another beautiful girl comes bounding down the stairs. She launches herself at Sawyer but rather than hug and kiss him like Sam just did, she hooks him in a headlock. At least she tries to, but Sawyer ends up flipping her upside down.

"Put me down, you brute!"

He ignores the demand and turns to me. "And this one here is Jesse. She thinks she's tough, so I'm constantly having to prove her wrong."

She extends her hand to me as she hangs upside down. "Hi, Grace, nice to meet you."

"It's nice to meet you, too."

She drops her hand and squints up at Sawyer, a mischievous smile curling her lips. "She's pretty. How did you land someone like her with your ugly mug?"

I cover my mouth as a snicker escapes me, but Sawyer grunts, unamused.

"All right, let me up now, all the blood is rushing to my head," she says, slapping his arm.

"Nah, I think I'll keep you like this for a little while longer."

Her eyes narrow. "If you don't let me up, I'll tell Grace about the time you were ten and cried because—"

Sawyer rights her quickly, cupping a hand over her mouth.

I raise a questioning brow at him.

"She's fuckin' lying."

"Sawyer Evans, watch your language!"

My attention pulls left, taking in the beautiful blonde woman who descends the steps gracefully. Her warm smile contradicts her scolding tone, love dancing in her eyes as she approaches her son.

"My boy is finally home." Rising up on her tiptoes, she cups his face between her hands, forcing him to bend down, then rains a million kisses all over his face. "I" *smooch* "have" *smooch* "missed" *smooch* "you" *smooch* "so" *smooch* "much" *smooch.*

Jesse rolls her eyes in my direction. "He is such a momma's boy."

"Hey, Mom," Sawyer grumbles, clearly embarrassed by the affection but he's kind enough not to push her away.

After she finishes showering him with love, she turns her kind smile on me. "And you must be Grace."

Returning her smile, I extend my hand, trying to hide my nerves. "Yes, ma'am. It's nice to meet you, Mrs. Evans."

Instead of taking my hand, she wraps me in a gentle hug. "Please, call me Catherine. I am so happy you're joining us this weekend."

"Thank you for having me."

My eyes meet Sawyer's over her shoulder and he gives me a knowin' smirk. Guilt and shame strike me as I realize just how judgmental I was of these nice people only minutes ago, all because of their money. I expected them to be stuck-up and materialistic. Catherine Evans might have money to flaunt herself, but she doesn't. Her designer jeans and a soft pink, thin cashmere sweater, is simple yet stunning on her.

She steps back, her hands remaining on my shoulders. "You are so pretty. Isn't she pretty, John?" she says, turning to the attractive man behind her who only now begins descending the steps.

"She sure is." He's almost as tall as Sawyer, with the same lean, muscular build and a headful of dirty blond hair. With dark green eyes and a charming smile, there is no doubt that Sawyer is the spittin' image of his father. "Nice to meet you, Grace. I'm

John, Sawyer's father," he says, his large hand engulfing my small one.

"Nice to meet you, John. Thank you for having me."

"Like Catherine said, we're glad you could join us." His attention shifts to Sawyer and that's when all easiness vanishes. The love that was in the air since we've been here is now replaced with tension. "Sawyer," he acknowledges him.

"Dad."

Catherine's eyes dim, and the girls shift uncomfortably. Sawyer told me he and his father didn't see eye-to-eye but I didn't realize it was this bad.

Catherine flashes me the best smile she can muster. "Why don't we go inside? We can have a drink and visit before I start supper."

"We'll be there in a minute," Sawyer says. "I'm going to take our stuff to the guesthouse first."

"You aren't staying here with us?" Catherine asks, seeming disappointed.

"I offered Sawyer the guest house, Mom," Jesse says. "To give them more privacy.

Guilt rears inside of me to hear she's giving up her home for us. "Don't leave on our account," I tell her. "I'm fine to sleep anywhere. Honest."

"No. Jesse will sleep at the main house," Sawyer says, his tone brooking no further argument.

I turn on him, unbelieving how rude he's being. "Why on earth would you kick your sister out of her house? It's unnecessary. Like I said, I'm fine to sleep anywhere."

"We're taking the guesthouse!" he fires back.

My eyes narrow and I open my mouth to argue back but the sound of muffled chuckles keeps me from my tirade. His family watches on, looking more than amused by our bickerin'.

Jesse slings her arm around my shoulders, starting us up the stairs. "Oh, Grace, I have a feeling you and I are going to be great friends."

CHAPTER 28

Grace

The visit with Sawyer's family was really nice. I had a great time getting to know them all. They are some of the nicest and funniest people I've ever met, which shouldn't surprise me since they are a part of Sawyer.

It's obvious his sisters are thrilled to have him back, even if it's for a few days. They might tease and banter with one another, but they look at him as if he's their hero. As beautiful as this family's interaction is to see, it also makes me miss my mama. Our family may have been small, but our bond was strong.

The tension between Sawyer and his father was present for most of the hour and you can tell it upset the rest of the family. The more I get to know John, the more I have no doubt that looks are not the only similarities between he and Sawyer. They have the same personality, which makes me wonder if that's why they butt heads so much.

When things became a bit too tense to ignore anymore Sawyer took our luggage to the guesthouse while I joined Catherine in the kitchen. It's a dream kitchen if I ever did see one—wide-open with lots of counter space and more than enough cupboards. The triple wall ovens are what do it for me though. The amount of pies I could bake up in this kitchen has my fingers twitching and ingredients emerging.

"Here, honey, take this and have a seat," Catherine says, handing me a glass of wine.

"Are you sure I can't help with somethin'?"

"I just want your company, nothing else."

Smiling, I hop up on the stool at the granite island where she begins shredding lettuce. "You have a real beautiful home, especially this kitchen," I say, still in awe of my surroundings.

"Thank you. Sawyer tells me you're a baker and create some incredible pies."

"I don't know how incredible they are but I do love baking and people seem to really enjoy them. Now my mama, she could make a pie like nobody's business. From breakfast, lunch to dinner, she could create a masterpiece out of anythin'." I pause, a little surprised by how easy it was for me to tell her that. Usually, I don't talk about my mother for fear I'll break down into a blubberin' mess, but right now I find myself happy to share this information about her.

Catherine reaches across the counter, placing her hand over mine, her expression soft. "I'm really sorry to hear about what happened to your mama, Grace. Sounds like she was an exceptional woman."

My heart warms with her kind words. "Thank you. I miss her very much."

"I'm glad to know my boy has been there for you. He'll take good care of you."

I had wondered how much Sawyer told her, obviously the whole story. My biggest worry was she'd be upset for me, knowing her son would be in danger for protecting me but right now I see no resentment from her, only kindness.

"I think Sawyer is a real wonderful person," I tell her quietly. "He has come to mean an awful lot to me."

"My son is a good man…with a big ego."

"He is," I agree, unable to stop the giggle that escapes me.

"He comes by it honestly, he gets it from his father," she says, her smile fading. "But I promise you, his heart is much bigger than his ego."

"And I know that, too."

"You have my permission to take him down a notch whenever he needs it and I am sure he needs it often."

"Trust me I try, but sometimes he can be awfully stubborn."

"Who can be stubborn?"

My eyes shift to find Sawyer has entered the kitchen, my heart skipping a beat at the sight of him. He has changed into a pair of loose jeans and a faded green shirt that stretches across his perfectly sculpted body, complementing the color of his eyes.

"See something you like, Cupcake?"

Heat invades my cheeks as I realize I've been caught ogglin' him in front of his mother. My eyes narrow at his smug smile. "In your dreams, Evans. I was just noticin' a small dirt mark on your pants is all. I'm surprised your giant head can even fit in this kitchen."

Catherine's laughter fills the kitchen. "That a girl."

Sawyer only seems further amused as he strides toward me, slinging an arm around my neck. "That's okay, baby, I check you out, too."

I give him a playful elbow to the ribs.

"What were you ladies talking about when I walked in?" he asks, reaching over to stick his fingers in the salad bowl.

"We were talking about Grace's pies," Catherine tells him, slapping his hand away before it can make contact.

"You braggin' about your pies, Cupcake? And you tell me that I have a big head."

"Your mom is the one who brought it up. Sounds like you were the one *braggin'*, shockingly, it wasn't about yourself this time."

He chuckles, not the least bit fazed and drops a kiss on my lips. The simple act has my heart exploding. His mom pretends not to notice but there's no denying the smile that steals her face as she cuts vegetables.

"Listen. I just got a text from a friend," he says. "He asked if I would come play hockey tonight. They're short a player and it's the rival team. What do you think? You up for it?"

"Works for me."

"Good. Jesse's going to come, too. Her boyfriend also plays. She'll sit with you."

"Sounds fun."

I've never been to a hockey game before and the chance to watch Sawyer do something that was such a big part of who he was growing up is not something I want to miss.

His attention moves to his mother. "Any chance you know where my equipment is?"

She shrugs, avoiding eye contact with him. "You will have to ask your father."

I have a feeling she knows exactly where it is but Sawyer will have to talk to his father to find out. Something he seems less than thrilled about.

A short time later we sit around the dinner table, awkward tension filling the room. Whatever happened when Sawyer asked his father about his hockey equipment seems to have put them both in a foul mood. However, Catherine and his sisters keep conversation flowing, doing their best to make the situation better.

"You best bring your A-game tonight, big brother," Jesse says, "sounds like this team is a tough one to beat."

"I'm not worried." He leans back in his chair, glancing over at me with a sexy smirk. "Wait until you see me in action, Cupcake. I'm a damn legend around here."

Before I can take him down a notch, John grunts, making the table fall silent.

Sawyer tenses next to me, his attention shifting to his father who refuses to look at him. "You have something you want to say, Dad?"

My anxious heart kicks up, worried for the confrontation that I am sure is about to ensue.

John finally acknowledges him, his animosity as prominent as Sawyer's.

"John," Catherine warns.

"No, Mom, let him say whatever the fuck he needs to say. Maybe if he gets it off his chest, we can all finally move on."

"Sawyer, watch your mouth!" Catherine scolds.

Sawyer ignores the warning, his anger prominent. "C'mon, old man, just spit it out."

"You want to know what my damn problem is?" John asks, his voice rising.

"Daddy, stop, you promised," Sam cuts in, on the verge of tears.

Oh gosh, this is so bad.

"Yeah, I wanna fuckin' know."

"Language!" Catherine snaps but both men ignore her.

"I'll tell you what my goddamn problem is," his father bellows. "You're not a legend, you could have been but you threw it all away. You had talent and gave it all up to be…to be—"

"A hero," I blurt out before I can stop myself.

Silence falls over the table, all eyes pinning on me.

Oh lord, Grace, what have you done?

My eyes drop to my plate as I push on, knowing I can't back out now. "I don't know about any of you, but for me, a man who fights for his country is much more honorable than being a legend." When silence continues to greet my ears, I brave the chance to look up and find everyone still starin' at me. "Uh, no disrespect to any hockey players. I'm sure they all mean well, too."

Catherine and his sisters smile at me while Sawyer slings an arm around my neck. "You hear that, old man? I'm a fucking hero."

"Sawyer Evans, I swear to God, if the F-Bomb falls from your mouth one more time, I'm going to shove an entire bar of soap down your throat."

Hearing his mother threaten to wash his mouth out has me bursting into laughter. Thankfully, his sisters do too and it somewhat eases the tension.

Jesse takes advantage of the easy moment and changes the subject. "Grace, how about we get ready for the game together? I'd love to show you some of the clothes I've designed."

"I'd like that."

Conversation flows again, but there's no denying the lingering animosity. Sawyer's hand reaches for mine under the table and has me lookin' up at him. The grateful look he shoots me has my heart leaping in my chest.

Smiling, I squeeze his hand, knowing there isn't anything I wouldn't do for him, even defending his honor to his father.

CHAPTER 29

Grace

After supper, I follow Jesse upstairs to her design room and I'm impressed with what I find. Three large racks of outfits sit in the center while mannequins and body forms are placed throughout with the beginnings of more creations.

"Wow, Jesse. These are amazin'," I say, completely in awe of her talent as I swipe through the mounds of clothes.

"Thanks. I love what I do. One day I'm going to open my own boutique."

"I think that's a wonderful idea, it'd be a shame not to share this talent with the rest of the world."

She beams at the compliment.

"Would you like to wear an outfit to the game?"

"Really?" I ask excitedly.

"Of course."

"I'd love to. Thank you so much."

Sam walks into the room to join us. "Looks like my sister found her next victim."

Jesse throws a bunched up ball of fabric at her. "Says the girl who is always asking me to make her something."

"True," she admits on a giggle.

As Jessie selects an outfit for me, Sam watches me, a knowing smile on her face. "My brother likes you a lot."

"You think so?" I ask, hope flaring inside my chest.

"I know so," Jesse says, cutting in. "I've never seen him so taken with a girl, and not just because he's never brought one home before. I can tell by the way he looks at you."

"I agree," Sam says. "He has it bad."

My heart dances with excitement to hear them say that. "I like him a lot, too."

"I'm glad he found someone like you," Sam speaks again, more quiet this time. "Someone who will look out for him. He may come across arrogant and tough, but I know what happened to him and his friends in Iraq has left more scars than just the ones that mar his skin."

Pain lances through me, the same one reflecting in her voice as I think about the mangled skin of his back. "I'll watch out for him," I promise.

"We know. You proved that tonight when you stood up to my dad. Which was totally badass by the way."

"Definitely," Jesse agrees. "Here, give these a try." She hands me a pair of black leggings and a cherry red cashmere sweater.

I accept the items and walk behind the dressing screen, taking off my top first.

"What size are your feet?" she asks.

"Usually a seven and a half."

"Perfect." I hear her rummage around before she passes over a pair of black thigh-high boots. Thankfully, ones without a heel. "These are mine but you can borrow them."

"Thank you."

"So how did you and my brother meet?" Sam asks.

"Through our mutual friends, Jaxson and Julia."

"Ah yes, we've met Jaxson. A little more sociable than Cade but not much," she snickers, though it quickly trails off. "How's he doing?"

"Cade?" I ask.

"Yeah."

I shrug then remember she can't see me. "Good, I guess. Like you said he doesn't talk much."

She sighs. "No he doesn't. He never has."

"Why is that?" I ask, the question burning inside of me not for the first time.

Jesse is the one to answer. "Let's just say he's had a rough life. He lost his younger sister tragically. I'll let Sawyer give you the details, but when I say it was tragic, it was absolutely devastating."

My heart breaks to hear that, but I'm also not surprised. I knew something awful had to have happened by the pain lurkin' in his eyes. A pain I know all too well.

"All right, get your pretty ass out here and let's see my creation," Jesse says.

Smilin', I finish zipping up the last boot and step out from behind the screen. Low whistles come from Jesse and Sam as they look me over from head to toe.

"Yeah? Does it suit me?" I ask.

"See for yourself." Jesse steps aside, revealing a full length mirror behind her.

I stare at my reflection, loving what I see. The outfit is trendy yet casual. The sweater is a great contrast against my skin color and complements my blonde hair. The black leggings feel like butter and hug my body in all the right places, especially my behind. The boots are different and something I usually wouldn't wear but I have to admit they are badass and I love them.

"Thank you, Jesse. I feel beautiful."

"Well duh, that's all you, silly, not me," she says, warming my heart. "But you're welcome. When everyone is fawning over you tonight at the game just make sure you tell them where you got it from."

"I definitely will."

"Good. Now let's finish dolling up."

She grabs her cosmetic bag and not only does her makeup but mine as well. She does a wonderful job once again, the shades of eye shadow and lip gloss she chooses enhance my ensemble. I must say, she really has a knack for this fashion thing.

While she does her finishing touches, I ask if there's a bathroom close by.

Sam points to the left. "Third door on the right."

"Thanks, I'll be right back." I head down the long hallway, admiring the family pictures hanging on the walls. Many are of Sawyer playing various sports throughout the years, and the transformation from boy to man is incredible, especially when I reach the photo of him dressed in his Naval uniform.

The second door I come upon is half-open and I find John inside, standing at his desk. He's bent over a set of blueprints, his expression hard in concentration.

I hesitate for only a second before lifting my hand and gently knocking.

His head snaps up, eyes flaring in surprise. "Grace."

"Hi." I wave nervously. "Do you have a moment?"

"Of course, come in." He takes in my outfit as I enter and smiles. "I see my daughter got ahold of you to play dress up."

I laugh but it cracks from my nerves. "She did. It was very kind of her. She's good at what she does."

"Yes, she is," he agrees, pride strong in his voice.

An awkward silence quickly settles over us.

"I just wanted to apologize for interruptin' you at the dinner table. I meant no disrespect."

He waves away my apology. "If anyone should apologize, it's me. Clearly, my boy and I have some issues, and it shouldn't have been brought up at the table like that. I hope you can forgive me."

"Already forgiven," I tell him. Instead of leaving it at that and walking out, I open my big trap again. "I hope I'm not out of line here but I just want you to know that Sawyer is an amazing man. The best I've ever known and you should be so proud. My own father wants nothin' to do with me and I think it's really sad for you two to let anythin' wreck your relationship. Believe me, it takes only a second to have the people we love ripped away from us."

The stark pain that enters his eyes makes me feel horrible. I really need to learn when to shut up and mind my own business.

"Anyway… I just thought you should know that." After a lame wave, I walk away only to have him call me back. I turn around to find him walking up to me. My heart bangs inside my chest, fearing he's gonna tell me to pack my bags and get out of his house. I wouldn't blame him. However, he doesn't do that. Instead, he surprises me by pulling me into his arms, giving me a warm hug.

I tense, stunned for only a second before I wrap my arms around his waist and return his embrace.

"I'm glad to know my boy has been there for you, Grace. You're a good girl, and that father of yours is a damn idiot. Any man would be lucky to have you as their daughter. I want you to know you're always welcome in my home."

My heart swells in my chest, emotion thickening my throat. "Thank you," I choke out on a whisper.

He drops a kiss on my head; another thing that reminds me of Sawyer, then walks out the door, leaving me alone in his office, his kind words lingering in my heart. It amazes me how fast this family has accepted me and made me feel a part of it.

Eventually, my feet put me in motion again, sending me in the direction of the bathroom, but before I can reach it I'm yanked into a room on my right.

A startled gasp escapes me when I'm lifted off my feet and pinned against the wall. It's not long before I register the feel of Sawyer's hard body. I lock my legs around his waist, my breath catching at the feel of his erection between my parted thighs.

The room is fairly dark, only the cast of moonlight creating a soft glow dancing across the handsome face before me. The emotions reflecting in his intense green eyes as he gazes back at me has my pulse kicking up.

"Sawyer?" I ask, wondering if everything's okay.

Instead of answering, he dips his head, bringing his mouth upon mine. His lips are like a heated caress, coaxing mine into a timeless dance that I'll remember for the rest of my life. Never have I been kissed like this before. Every one we have shared prior to this has always been passionate and urgent. But this one? This one is different. It's on a whole other spectrum and any kiss previous to this has been obliterated.

By the time he pulls back, I'm breathless, drunk on his intoxicating taste. I inhale several deep breaths but keep my eyes closed, basking in the moment for as long as I can. When I can no longer avoid it, I open my eyes and get lost in his green irises.

"Hi," I croak out, not knowing what else to say.

He flashes me a cocky smirk. "Hi, Cupcake."

"Why are you hiding behind doors and preying on innocent women?"

"I'm only preying on one woman, baby." He leans in again, pressing his lips to the base of my neck.

My head falls back, giving him all the access he needs. "Tell me about her," I say, trying to be sexy but my voice comes out ridiculously breathless.

"She's beautiful," he murmurs, his hot breath a contradiction to the goose bumps he's eliciting across my skin, "she makes the best pies in the world, and she smells like cupcakes." His words are followed by a sharp nip to my delicate skin.

A shiver racks my body, dancing all the way to the tips of my toes. "Mmmm. She sounds yummy."

He chuckles but it trails into a groan. "Oh, baby, she's fucking delicious." Driving the point home, his hips surge forward, his erection hitting where I want him most. "And she wears sexy fuck-me boots. Jesus, where did you find these and why haven't I seen them before?"

"They're your sister's."

His muscles tense before he drops his head on my shoulder. "Well, that just killed the fantasy I was having."

"You asked. Next time, keep quiet and use your mouth for other things," I tease.

Lifting his head, his heated gaze penetrates mine. "Is that what you want, Grace? For me to bury my mouth in your pussy again?"

"Yes, among other things," I whisper boldly.

Groaning, he grinds his cock harder against me. "Me too, baby." Keeping one hand on my bottom, he moves the other one between us and slips it into my pants, fingers sneaking beneath my panties and delving into my wet heat.

A harsh whimper parts my lips, his skillful touch dousing gasoline to the flames claiming my body.

"Fucking soaked," he growls, inserting two fingers inside me.

I cry out, my senses reeling at the pleasure racing through my blood.

"This hungry pussy is going to feel so good wrapped around my dick, baby. It's all I've thought about."

"Me, too," I admit shamelessly.

"Tonight, Grace. Tonight I'm going to have you, and I'm going to make you come so many times you will think you're dying from pleasure." His fingers curl inside of me, stroking that hidden spot within.

"Oh god." My head falls back against the wall as an army of sensations implodes across my body.

"Lift your shirt for me, baby, my hands are a little busy at the moment," he says with a dirty grin.

I eagerly do what he says, exposing my black lace bra. Thank goodness it's not the cherry one again.

"Now, pull it down so I can suck on your pretty tits."

Moaning, I flick the front clasp, letting my breasts tumble free.

A low growl rumbles from his chest before he sucks an aching nipple into his mouth.

"Yes!" I spear my hands into his disheveled hair, holding him captive. My hips begin riding his hand, trying to reach the impeding orgasm building inside of me.

"That a girl, fuck my fingers," he urges me on, tempting a side of me that I never knew I had.

The need for release is so strong it's almost painful. "Sawyer, please?" I beg, knowing he has what it takes to put me out of this sweet misery.

His teeth sink into my hard nipple the same time his thumb brushes my throbbing clit and it sends me over the precious edge I've been teetering on.

His mouth covers mine, inhaling my cries as I sob out the intensity of my orgasm. Eventually, my body becomes limp, my breathing erratic as I try to recover from his soul-shattering touch. Soft, warm lips brush across my cheek, delivering a heart-warming kiss.

Opening my eyes, I look into Sawyer's, something strong and beautiful passing between us.

"Grace? Did you get lost, silly girl?" Jesse's voice penetrates our moment, yanking me back to reality.

Panic grips me as I try to think of a way out of this.

"She's busy," Sawyer yells behind the closed door.

Gasping, I slap his shoulder, absolutely mortified.

There's a brief moment of silence before she speaks again. "Ew, I'll be downstairs whenever you're done."

My eyes narrow. "What are you thinkin'? Now she knows we were up to no good."

"On the contrary, Cupcake. I think what we were up to is very good."

I shake my head, but a smile twitches my lips. "You're incorrigible, Evans, but also cute."

He grunts. "I am not cute. There are a lot of things you can say about me—sexy, charming, handsome—but there is nothing fucking cute about me."

"Yep, you're all those things…and cute," I tell him, delivering a quick kiss across his lips. Reaching for my open bra, I snap it back in place.

"Screw hockey, let's stay home and fuck all night."

"As appealing as that sounds, I'm sure your friends want to see you, and I'll bet you want to see them, too."

"I want you more."

The admission has warmth invading my chest. "I want you, too," I whisper, my hand moving to his jaw. "But I also want to see you on the ice. I want a glimpse at the legend in action."

It was the right thing to say. "Fine. We'll go," he relents, but doesn't sound happy about it. "But tonight, Grace. When this is all over—you're mine." The promise in his dark voice has a shiver of pleasure skipping down my spine.

Little does he know, I'm already his.

After a brief kiss on my lips he places me on my feet, taking his hard, warm body with him. "Go ahead. I need a minute to calm down."

Turning, I reach for the door but come up short when he calls out to me.

I glance at him over my shoulder.

"You're the best person I've ever met, too."

His words take a moment to register, but it doesn't take long before I realize he heard my conversation with his father. Thankfully, he doesn't seem mad, if the grin tilting his lips is anything to go by.

Smiling, I walk out, and decide maybe not minding my own business isn't such a bad thing after all.

CHAPTER 30

Grace

Fascination renders me speechless as I follow Jesse into the arena. The stands are packed with fans from both teams, their excitement palpable.

"Hockey is a big deal in this town," Jesse says with a smile, sensing my thoughts. She leads me up to the bleachers where a friend of hers saved us seats. She and the pretty brunette greet each other with a hug before she introduces me. "Grace, this is my best friend, Maggie. Mags, meet Grace, Sawyer's girlfriend I was telling you about."

I'm not a hundred percent on the term 'girlfriend,' but I don't correct her, because to be honest, I like the title.

"Hi, Grace, it's nice to meet you," Maggie greets me, extending her hand.

"Nice to meet you, too."

"So, tell me how you managed to snag Colorado's most eligible bachelor? Especially one who turns green at the word *commitment.*"

I shift uncomfortably, not knowing how to answer that.

"What do you mean how? Look at her," Jesse says, saving me from having to answer.

The implied compliment warms my heart.

Maggie nods. "True, she's pretty, but we all know it takes more than that to capture Sawyer. After all, he is the biggest manwhore in the state."

Having Sawyer labeled as a *manwhore* is no surprise, but it still turns my stomach to hear it.

Jesse's eyes narrow at her best friend. "People can change, Mags, especially when the right person comes along."

The awkward conversation comes to an end when the crowd breaks into cheers, going wild as the hockey players take the ice. Their excitement bleeds onto me, the arena charged with an energy I've never felt before. It's incredible.

My eyes search for Sawyer amongst his team but other than height differences they all pretty much look the same from this distance.

"There," Jesse says, pointing him out to me. "Number eleven."

He glides across the ice with incredible grace and agility for his size. His green eyes scan the crowd until they land on me and just like that, the noisy arena falls to a silence, everyone around me fading away. It's as if we are the only two people here.

He graces me with one of his panty droppin' smiles then shows off by skatin' backwards, flashing me a wink through the glass. A ridiculous smile steals my lips. He may be one cocky son of a gun, but he is the sexiest one I've ever laid eyes on.

"Damn, you weren't kidding, he does have it bad," Maggie says to Jesse.

"Told ya," she replies smugly.

A high-pitched giggle penetrates the moment, Sawyer's name falling in the mix of it. Jesse and I turn to see three girls seated together, their bleached blonde hair and bright makeup reminding me of Malibu Barbie. The one in the middle points at Sawyer, a hungry look in her eyes that has jealousy rearing its ugly head.

"You have got to be kidding me," Jesse growls.

"Nope," Maggie says, "she's been up there gushing and waiting for your brother's arrival since I got here."

"Who is she?" I ask, fearing the answer.

"Stephanie Taylor," Jesse bites out, "she's the town bicycle, and the biggest bitch you'll ever meet. Pretend she isn't here."

I nod, knowing her type…she's a Jenny. I shove aside the instant hatred I feel and do what Jesse says, pretend she isn't here. The two girls explain the rules of the game to me but I find it all very confusing. I'm hoping to pick up on it as I watch.

All the players take a seat on the bench except for five of them, one of those five bein' Sawyer. He skates to center ice where the ref is standing, facing off his opponent. An almost hushed silence falls over the crowd just before the ref blows the whistle and drops the puck. Sawyer gains control and then the battle is on.

Anticipation thrums through my veins as I watch every player from the other team skate after him. Sawyer maneuvers around them, easily dodging their greedy sticks. His first shot is from a distance, the puck lifting from the ice and sailing through the air, finding its way in the top corner of the net.

My mouth drops as the crowd erupts into applause with the first goal. Eventually, I join in, jumpin' up and down excitedly. Jesse and Maggie laugh at my excitement but I don't care, I'm so darn proud of Sawyer.

His four teammates skate up to him with their arms in the air, congratulating him by either hitting gloves or punchin' him in the arm. Afterward, he skates past the glass, pointing directly at me with an arrogant smile and sexy wink. It makes my heart leap, my smile growing even bigger.

"Oh my god, it's almost sickening to watch," Maggie teases. Rather than feel embarrassed, I beam with happiness.

"Who's the girl you brought, Jesse?" a snooty voice asks behind us.

Jesse turns, directing a glare at bicycle bitch. "Oh her?" she asks innocently, jerking her thumb at me. "She's Sawyer's girlfriend." The news is delivered with a sickeningly sweet smile.

Town bicycle scoffs.

I hate those scoffs.

"Nice try but we all know your brother doesn't date, especially ones like her," she says, flicking a disdainful look my way.

Well, now, what the hell does that mean?

Jesse speaks before I can. "Actually, he does date, just not whores. That's why you never knew that."

Maggie bursts into laughter while I bite back a smile of my own. Bicycle girl's eyes narrow but she keeps her mouth shut. I turn back to the game, bringing my attention to Sawyer again. I refuse to let her ruin my night.

Eventually she becomes nothing more than an afterthought, the intense game keeping my attention the entire time. Sawyer wasn't lying when he said he was good, he's far beyond that. He dominates the ice yet plays well with the rest of his team, never hogging the puck. You'd never know these guys don't always play together. It's fascinating to watch.

They end up winning the game 8–4, Sawyer scorin' five of those goals. Once the players clear the ice, Jesse and I wait outside the glass doors that lead to the dressing rooms. Several minutes pass before Sawyer walks out of the change room with his hockey bag slung over his shoulder, freshly showered.

My heart does its usual leap at the sight of him. Four others follow him out, laughing at something he says. As if sensing my eyes on him, his gaze shifts, penetrating mine. His mouth splits into a crooked grin and he picks up pace, blowing through the double doors.

Dropping his bag, he strides over and picks me up off my feet, claiming my lips in a toe-curling kiss, right in front of everyone. The show of possession and declaration has my heart soaring.

Eventually, he pulls back, his face hovering before mine with a devilish grin. "Hey, Cupcake."

"Hey yourself, Sexy Sawyer."

"Didn't I tell you I was something, baby?"

"You sure did. You were amazin'."

"Damn straight I was."

I giggle, refusing to give him heck since he deserves to be a little cocky right now.

"Are you going to introduce us or keep staring at her like a fool?" a deep voice booms next to us, interrupting our moment.

Sawyer places me back on my feet then takes my hand, linking our fingers together. "This is Grace. Grace, these are my lifelong hockey friends—Jake, Austin, Mike, and Cam," he says, pointing out each one.

"It's nice to meet y'all."

Cam lifts a brow, amusement dancing in his eyes. "She's a southerner, Evans? Who knew that's what it took to keep your dick in one woman."

Sawyer shoves him back a step. "Shut up, asshole. Don't say shit like that in front of her."

"Calm down. I was just screwing around."

Jesse chooses that moment to walk over with her boyfriend, Cory, and introduce us. He's as attractive as the rest of the guys and by the way he looks at her it's obvious he's smitten.

"We're heading out," she says, looking at Sawyer. "We have plans with Mags and Danny."

He nods. "I'll see you tomorrow."

She kisses his cheek, then gives me a hug and walks out.

Once they're out of sight, Jake knocks Sawyer in the shoulder. "You coming for a victory beer?"

"I don't think so."

"Come on. We haven't seen your ass for two years and you're not even going to come have a beer with us?"

"Why don't we go for a bit, Sawyer," I intervene, not wanting him to refuse on my account.

He gazes down at me, indecision battling in his gaze. “You sure?”

“Absolutely.” I nod.

“All right. We’ll meet you guys there,” he relents. “Overtime?”

“The one and only,” Cam says, clapping him on the back. “See you there.”

They walk out of the lobby, leaving us alone.

Sawyer pulls me against him, his hard body engulfing mine. “I want to be alone with you so fucking bad. Say the word and we’ll ditch their asses.”

I push to my tiptoes, winding my arms around his neck. “I want to be alone with you too, but it’s important for you to spend time with your friends. Besides, we have all night.”

His hands drop to my bottom, giving it a generous squeeze. “All night is nowhere near long enough for what I plan to do to you.”

Anticipation builds low in my tummy for what I’m sure will be an unforgettable night.

The double doors to the dressing room slam open, startling me. An incredibly attractive guy comes strolling out, his icy glare trained on Sawyer. Sawyer’s eyes are just as hard, his body suddenly stiff. The tension bouncing between them is undeniable, stifling the air until good-lookin’ angry dude walks out.

“Whoa, what was that about?” I ask, looking back at Sawyer.

“Just someone I don’t get along with.”

I have a feeling it’s a lot more than that but I don’t push the matter since it’s not my business.

“Come on, let’s get out of here,” he says, tugging on my hand. “I want to get this over with so we can be alone.”

There’s a pep in my step as I follow him out of the arena. Tonight, our relationship will change forever and I for one cannot wait to finally know what it feels like to be all his, body and soul.

CHAPTER 31

Grace

My enthusiasm is short lived when almost an hour later I'm sitting by myself in the crowded pub, feeling incredibly uncomfortable and a little hurt. Sawyer's at the pool table with a crowd gathered around him, everyone excited that the town's golden boy is back home.

In all fairness he did try to bring me with him to play pool but I had been waiting for my drink to come and one of the guy's girlfriends, who was somewhat friendly, said she would stay and keep me company. She did so, awkwardly, for about five minutes then saw a friend of hers. She told me she would be right back, that was almost an hour ago.

So now I sit here alone, wishing I wasn't such a chicken to just go stand next to Sawyer but I find all the people vying for his attention a little intimidating, especially for a girl who is nervous around crowds to begin with.

To make matters worse, the town bicycle bitch, has been front and center, hanging off Sawyer every chance she gets. He doesn't flirt back or show interest, but he doesn't push her away either. Which is just as bad in my opinion.

"Now, why is the prettiest girl in the whole bar sitting all alone in a dark corner?" a deep voice breaks me out of my self-pityin' thoughts.

Looking up, I find the guy who was glaring daggers earlier with Sawyer, holding two shots in his hand and wearin' a lazy grin on his handsome face.

He takes the chair across from me, without waiting to be invited. "What's your name, sweetness?"

My eyes narrow, suspicion rearin' its head. "It ain't '*sweetness,*'" I tell him, feeling annoyed.

He quirks a brow, looking rather amused. "All right, what is it then?"

"Grace," I mumble.

He gives me a crooked grin, one that I know so well. "A sweet name for a sweet-looking girl."

I roll my eyes at the lame line.

"And sassy," he adds. "Just the way I like them."

"Settle down over there, Romeo, because this sweet and sassy girl is taken, which you already know since you saw me with Sawyer in the lobby at the arena."

Surprise, and something that looks a lot like admiration, flashes in his eyes. He rests back in his chair, crossing his arms over his broad chest. "Well, that's just it, I did see you with him earlier, but for the last forty-five minutes I've been watching you from across the bar, sitting here all alone. So, I figured maybe I misinterpreted you two earlier, because if you were my girl I wouldn't leave you alone for a fucking second."

The truth of his words sting. My eyes drop to the table and I shrug. "He's been gone a long time and his friends want to catch up."

He grunts. "Whatever you say, sweetness. Why don't you have a shot with me?" he suggests, pushing one of his shot glasses over to me.

"I'm not drinkin' that. How do I know you didn't put somethin' in it?"

He rears back, insulted. "Are you serious? Look at me! I don't need to put shit in a girl's drink, I can get any chick I want."

The incredulous look on his face has me bursting into laughter.

A handsome smile plays at the corners of his mouth. "You were fucking with me, weren't you?"

"No, I wasn't," I reply honestly, continuing to laugh. "But your face was pretty darn funny."

He chuckles, his husky tone infectious.

I have to admit he is one good-lookin' dude, with dark hair and warm chocolate eyes that complement his bronzed skin. He has a hard, lean body, not quite as muscular as Sawyer's but still one that any female would notice.

"Well, I guess I know now why you and Sawyer don't get along," I say.

His easiness vanishes. "Oh, yeah? Enlighten me."

"Because you're both exactly alike."

He grunts. "I am nothing like that asshole."

"Yes, you are. You're both sexy, charming buggers, with the biggest egos I've ever seen."

He flashes me another lopsided grin. "You think I'm sexy?"

I roll my eyes. "See? That's so somethin' Sawyer would say too, you also missed the big ego part."

"First of all, that asshole's ego is way bigger than mine," he says, pointing at me, "and secondly, the reason why I hate him is because he fucked my girlfriend a couple of years ago when he came back for a visit."

I wince at the information. I must say, no matter how big of a manwhore Sawyer was, I'm surprised to hear he would do somethin' like that.

"Well...that wasn't very nice of him. Or your girlfriend for that matter," I mumble, not knowing what else to say.

He cracks into laughter, finding something funny in what I just said. "I have to admit, sweetness, you are just as cute as your accent."

I throw my hands up in frustration. "Why on earth do y'all keep sayin' I have an accent?"

"Because here 'we ain't talk like this,'" he says, mockin' me.

My eyes narrow. "First off, buddy, that's not an accent, it's just how I speak. It's how my mama always spoke, too. And secondly, it's not nice to make fun of people."

"I wasn't making fun of you," he says, exasperated. "I just said it was cute, and it is. Actually, I think it's sexy as hell." His tone drops, a husky undertone to it.

I have to admit, this guy might just give Sawyer a run for his money in the flirtin' department. It's a good thing I know better and am immune to it.

"So, that's why you came over here? You saw an opportunity and thought you would get back at Sawyer?"

"Honestly?"

I nod.

"Yes, at first it was. I see my ex hanging all over him, and even though I could give a shit about her anymore, it still pisses me off because, like you said, I have a big fucking ego."

"Your girlfriend is here?" I ask, surprised.

"Ex," he corrects firmly.

"Who?" I ask, my eyes scanning the large crowd.

"Her name is Stephanie."

"Town bicycle?" I shriek, my stomach plummeting.

Ugh! I hate hearin' that.

"I guess that means you've met her?"

"Just briefly. She really didn't seem all that nice. If you ask me, it was a blessin' in disguise. You're way better off without her."

"She's a total bitch, but it still doesn't make me any less pissed at Sawyer."

I nod, because I can understand that.

"But to finish your earlier question, yes, my original intention coming over here was payback, but not anymore. Now I think you're pretty cool, and I just want you to have a shot with me and maybe a conversation, since your asshole boyfriend is too busy."

He makes a valid point. "All right, I'll have this shot with you, on one condition."

"What's that?"

"You have to tell me your name, keep your sweetness comments to yourself, and don't call my boyfriend an asshole."

"That's three," he says.

"Fine, then on three conditions."

"All right, no more sweetness, or asshole, and the name is Jase." He grabs his shot glass, holding it up.

Grabbing mine, I do the same, tilting it in his direction.

"To sweet southern girls."

"How about to men with big egos?" I return.

A chuckle rumbles from his chest. "That works, too." He tosses his shot back, looking like he's done this many times before.

I follow suit, but the nasty liquid barely makes it down my throat. Fire erupts, shredding my vocal chords. "Oh god!" I sputter, coughin', "What the hell was that?"

His laugh explodes through the bar, finding my amateur ass funny. "Suck on this, it'll help." He leans across the table and shoves a lime between my lips. "Haven't you ever done tequila before?"

I shake my head, his face blurring before me.

His eyes move to something behind me, his easy demeanor changing in an instant. That's when the energy in the room shifts, a dark presence looming at my back. I already know who it is before I even turn around.

Sawyer glares down at us, fury dominating his expression. Bicycle bitch stands not far behind him, a snotty smirk on her face.

"Having fun?" he asks, his voice dangerously hard.

"Actually, we're having a great time, aren't we, Grace?"

I shoot Jase a warning look, not appreciating his smart mouth at the moment.

"I don't know what the fuck you're up to, Crawford, but you better get away from her before I wipe that smirk off your face with my fist."

I push to my feet, feeling both annoyed and embarrassed. "Cut the crap, Sawyer, we were just talkin'."

"Stay out of this, Grace."

"You are actin' like a fool," I fire back.

"She's right, Evans," Jase says, speaking again instead of keeping his trap shut. "If anyone should be mad right now, it's her. You're the one who left her sitting here by herself. Can't expect someone not to come along and keep her sweet ass company."

Sawyer reaches for him and it sends Jase to his feet. They shove one another, knocking chairs over in their haste. Friends quickly jump in to keep them apart but Sawyer fights against them, his anger overriding his common sense.

"Outside!" Sawyer orders, pointing at Jase over Cam's shoulder. "We're going to finish this once and for all."

"No, you're not. Let it go, Sawyer," I yell.

When he refuses to even acknowledge me, I decide I've had enough.

"Fine. Do what you want, but I'm not standin' here and watchin' this shit for another second." Swiping my purse and jacket from the chair, I turn to Jase and the friends I met earlier tonight. "It was nice meeting y'all," I say, not wanting to be rude. My eyes move to bicycle bitch last, teeth grinding at the smug look on her face. "Except for you!" Spinning on my heel, I fight my way through the heavy crowd, apologizing as I knock into people's shoulders.

"Nice meeting you, Grace. Call me," Jase yells at my retreating back.

I roll my eyes and hear Sawyer go after him again, but I don't stop. I am so done with his arrogant ass. How dare he ignore me all night then get mad because I'm having a conversation with someone.

The frigid air hits my heated face as I push outside, giving me a small reprieve. I have no idea where to go so I pick a direction and start walkin'.

Sawyer crashes out the door soon after me. "Grace! Get your ass back here, right now."

Ignoring him, I pick up the pace, my boots tearing up the cement, the clicking of my heels matching the furious rhythm of my heartbeat.

His growl sounds behind me, too close for comfort, and before I'm able to anticipate it he lifts me off my feet, tossing me over his shoulder.

"What the hell are you doin'? Put me down right now, Sawyer Evans," I demand, squirming against his hold.

A sharp slap is delivered across my ass. "Stay still," he growls.

I tense, my mouth dropping open at his audacity. "Did you just spank me?"

That's it!

My fists pound his back as I demand to be put down. It does me little good. He opens his truck door and tosses me inside. I swipe my tangled hair out of my face and glare up at him. "I'm not going anywhere with you!"

My hands shove against his chest but he pins me back into my seat, his furious expression hovering before mine. "Do not fuck with me right now. We're leaving and we're doing it together."

I swallow hard, the fury raging in his eyes keeping me in place. The slam of my door has me flinching. Grinding my teeth, I throw on my seatbelt and turn to face my window.

Once he climbs in on his side, the truck roars to life and he punches the gas, peeling away from the curb like a maniac.

"Slow down! You're actin' like an idiot," I yell.

"And whose fault is that?"

"Yours. You're the one overreacting!"

"Bullshit," he bellows. "What the fuck do you think you were doing with him?"

"I was having a conversation with the only person in the whole damn bar that would pay any attention to me. *A conversation*...that's it!"

"Oh really, that's why, when I walked up, that motherfucker was shoving a lime between your lips?"

"I had never done tequila before so he shoved the lime in my mouth because I was gaggin' the nasty shit up."

"You shouldn't have been doing any shots with him period," he bellows, pointing his finger in my face. "Never again, Grace. Do you hear me?"

I slap his finger away, my anger boiling over and exploding like dynamite. "How dare you tell me who I can talk to or have a drink with when you ignored me all damn night."

"I tried to bring you with me. You're the one who said you were going to sit with Amanda and wait for your drink."

"Yeah, and she left me five minutes later. I also didn't think you would leave me all damn night."

"I figured you would have come join me if you were alone."

"Well, maybe you would have noticed me by myself if bicycle bitch didn't soak up all your attention."

He rears back, confused. "Who the fuck is bicycle bitch?"

"Jase's ex girlfriend that *you* slept with."

He tenses, his hand gripping the steering wheel tighter.

"I can't believe you did that to someone, Sawyer. You should be ashamed of yourself. It's no wonder he doesn't like you very much. I wouldn't either if you had sex with my girlfriend...err boyfriend...oh, you know what I mean."

"Let's get one thing straight. I did not pay any attention to that bitch tonight," he says. "And secondly, that shit was a misunderstanding and he needs to get the fuck over it already."

I lift a brow. "A misunderstanding?"

"I didn't know they were still dating! She told me they broke up."

I scoff at the poor excuse.

"Why are you so protective over some asshole you don't even know?"

"I am not protecting him. I'm just sayin' I understand why he doesn't like you. You were a complete jerk with the way you came at us like that. You didn't even stop to ask me what was goin' on, you just shot your mouth off and started a fight."

"I didn't need to ask. I could see what was going on."

"Well, it's nice to know you noticed me after forty-five minutes!"

"What do you want from me, Grace? I tried to bring you with me and you said no. You could have joined us when Amanda left you."

"Why should I be the one to join you? I'm your guest. Do you think it's fun for me to be around a crowd of girls you've slept with while they hang off you?"

"That's not what happened!"

I bite my tongue, refusing to argue anymore. It's obvious our view on what happened tonight is not one and the same. By the time he pulls up in front of the guesthouse, I'm close to tears.

When he puts the tuck in park, I turn to face him, my heart breaking at the distance between us. "Why did you even bring me there?"

"You're the one who said I should go and let's face it, I was not going to leave you behind."

His words hit me like a slap in the face, the realization hitting me that he only brought me along because he felt obligated.

"That did not come out right," he says. "That's not what I meant."

"Save it. I don't give a shit what you meant." I hurry into the house, refusing to spend another moment in his presence.

"Grace, get the fuck back here, we are not done talking."

"I have nothing more to say to you!" My feet are quick as I charge inside, heading straight to the master bedroom. Both of our suitcases sit by the bedroom door. Grabbing Sawyer's, I toss it out into the hall just as he comes charging into the house. I close the door and lock it before he can enter.

He bangs on the wood. "Open this door right now!"

Not in this lifetime, bucko!

I throw myself on the bed and cover my head with a pillow, trying to block out his stupidity and mask the tears I can no longer keep in.

How did this night turn so awful?

Sawyer, that's how. The darn jerk!

More pounding sounds on the door. "Grace, I mean it, if you don't open this fucking door, I will break it down."

When I make no effort to move he does exactly that. The loud crash has me sitting up in a panic. I flip around to find the door off its hinges, lying on the ground. I blink several times, disbelief coursing through me as I climb to my feet.

"What the hell are ya doin'? You just broke your sister's door, ya idiot!" I swing my pillow at him, furiously hitting him in the head, chest, anywhere I can reach.

His arms lift to block my blows but I show no mercy. "That's enough! Give me that fucking thing." He manages to grab the pillow, tugging it hard enough that it sends me crashing against his chest. The moment my body collides with his, his arms band around me and his mouth descends, stealing my lips like a greedy thief. The act catches me off guard for only a moment before my fingers wind in his hair, anchoring him in place.

He cups my bottom, lifting me off my feet. My legs wrap around his waist and arms around his neck as he pins me against the hard wall. His tongue thrusts in, assaulting mine in a blaze of fury. I can taste his anger, desperation and need, the same one imploding through my body at this very moment. My tears join that mix, falling even harder in my attempt to make things right between us again.

He breaks the connection, his chest heaving to the same frantic rhythm as mine. "Tell me this is okay. Tell me, Grace, that you need me just as fucking bad as I need you."

"I need you so much right now. I can't wait any longer." My words are thick with tears, coming out more vulnerable than I want them to.

"You are fucking mine," he bites out the claim, his fierce eyes holding mine. "Do you hear me, Grace? Mine and only mine." His hips surge forward, his hard cock grinding against the spot I ache for him the most. "Say it! I want to hear you say it."

"And what about you, Sawyer?" I whisper. "Are you mine?"

The fury raging in his eyes eases with something else, something softer. "Yeah, baby, I'm yours. You own all of me, Grace. You owned me before I even knew you."

My breath seizes in my chest, making it hard to breathe. His words don't make sense, but I believe them wholeheartedly because I feel the exact same way.

"Just like I own your ass, every sweet fucking inch of it." His hips keep me pinned in place as he reaches for the bottom of my sweater. I raise my arms and it barely clears my head before he moves to my bra, unlatching the front clasp. My breasts tumble into his waiting hands, the touch branding my skin.

I grip his shirt, dragging it up his back. "Take this off, I want to feel your body against mine."

Groaning, he pulls away just enough to rid himself of the material. His hard, naked chest collides with mine, the contact stealing my breath and warming me to the depths of my soul.

He buries his face in my neck, his breath hot on my fevered flesh. "Jesus, I've never felt anything softer than your skin."

My hands roam across his strong, sculpted back, feeling the puckered skin of his scars, ones that don't belong on a man as honorable as him. I relish in the feel of our bodies so close but it's not enough. I want more.

I want it all.

As if sensing my thoughts, he places me back on my feet, his mouth descending lower, tasting my skin as he drops to his knees before me. He continues undressing me by removing my boots then brings his efforts to my pants, his fingers slipping beneath my waistband. He drops a hot open-mouthed kiss on my stomach before sliding the snug material down my legs, leaving me in nothing else but my black lace panties.

A low growl rumbles from his chest, his eyes fixated on the apex of my thighs. His hot breath hits the lace of my panties, creating a mass of sensations to explode through my body. My fingers drive into his hair, trying to bring his mouth against me.

He resists against my greedy effort and looks up at me with a smirk. "You want my mouth don't you, baby? Want my tongue buried deep in your pussy again?"

His erotic words have me moaning and thrusting my hips toward his face.

"Answer me, Grace."

"Yes, I want it, I want it so badly," I admit shamelessly, my words nothing more than a whisper.

"And I'm going to give it to you, baby, because I want that, too. I want the scent and taste of your sweet pussy all over my face." He slips his fingers beneath the center of my panties, running them through my wet slit.

My lips part on a gasp as pleasure ravages my body.

"Always so fucking wet for me." He groans. "I hope you're ready, Grace, because tonight I am going to kiss, taste, and fuck every inch of your body. I'm going to bring you so much pleasure you'll be screaming for it."

I don't doubt it. I already feel like screamin'.

Grabbing the side of my panties, he tears them from my body and buries his mouth in my hot flesh.

"Oh god!" My knees buckle but Sawyer catches me, his hands grabbing the back of my thighs. He throws them over his shoulders, my back bracing against the wall as he devours me.

Every fiery lick of his tongue and brush of his lips takes me higher, threatening to send me over the edge of destruction. When he adds a finger, there's no prolonging it. A cry of pleasure shoves from my throat as my orgasm claims me. I drown in it, letting it swallow me heart and soul.

He trails his lips along the inside of my thigh, his mouth continuing to love me as I fight to get my bearings. In a quick move, he removes my legs from his shoulders, wrapping them around his waist before pushing to his feet.

My arms curl around his neck, our eyes seeking one another's in the darkness. No words are needed in this moment, our silence and gazes say it all, our relationship is about to change forever. My back meets the cool mattress, his hard body covering mine.

Skin to skin, heart to heart.

Our mouths align in heated bliss, his desire matching my own. His hand caresses my flesh, cupping the heavy weight of my breast and teasing my puckered nipple. It has a new ache igniting between my legs again.

My hips lift, connecting with his jean-clad erection. He pushes up on one arm and reaches between us to undo his belt. I move to help him, my hands urgent. Once we get his jeans unzipped and lowered, I take him into my hand, my fingers curling around his shaft.

"Fuck!" He pushes forward, pumping his smooth cock into my grip. "I'm trying so hard not to rush this, but I'm not sure I can't. I need you so fucking bad."

"Then take me," I say, without hesitation. "I want you, Sawyer. I'm ready for this."

He rests his forehead on mine, his eyes penetrating. "I'm clean. I've always used a condom before but if you're okay with it, I don't want to use one with you. I want nothing between us when I take you."

"I'm more than okay with it." I want to feel all of him too and I want a part of him that no one else has ever had.

He hooks an arm under one of my knees, opening me further to align himself. His lips meet my forehead for one more act of tenderness before he drives deep inside of me with one quick thrust, stealing the air from my lungs.

My lips part on a gasp, both in pain and ecstasy.

"Aw, fuck!" he groans. "So tight."

My arms lock around his shoulders as I bury my face into his neck.

He stills, his body tense. "Shit, you okay? Did I hurt you?"

I pull back to look at him, hating the guilt in his eyes. "A little but it's the most beautiful pain I've ever felt." To reassure him, I wrap one leg around his back and lift my hips for more.

He gives it to me, delivering slow, hard strokes.

"Yes." Moaning, I arch my back, my fingers digging into his powerful shoulders as he completes me like never before.

"Goddamn, you're perfect."

My eyes close as I drown in this man. Everything about him engulfs me—his scent, his taste, the way his hard body feels beneath my touch. It's the most perfect thing I've ever felt.

"Look at me, Grace." His harsh demand has my eyes snapping back open. "Do you feel this, baby? Feel how perfect this is?" he asks, speaking my thoughts. "No one is ever going to take this from us, do you hear me? I will never let anyone take you from me. You—are—mine!" The possession in his words leaves no part of me unclaimed. "I want to hear you say it," he demands, driving into me harder.

"I'm yours," I whisper, my breath racing.

"That's right, baby, every part of you belongs to me."

He has no idea what hearing those words do to me, how much they mean to me. After three long, painful years—I finally do belong to someone and it's even better that someone is Sawyer. I don't know for how long but it doesn't matter. Because belonging to someone, even if only for a short time, means everything to someone who has no one.

My hand lifts to his face, fingers tracing his full lips. "And you belong to me," I tell him, my throat burning with emotion. My words probably don't affect him the same way his do me, but I still want him to know, need him to know, how much I care about him.

His fierce expression softens as he stills deep inside of me. "Yeah, baby, we belong to each other."

Before I can stop it, a lone tear trickles from the corner of my eye.

Sawyer catches it with his lips, kissing it away. "Everything is going to be okay now, Grace, because as long as we have this, nothing and no one else matters."

Hooking a hand behind his neck, I bring his lips upon mine. The kiss turns from a slow burn to a heated frenzy. He renews his efforts, his hips pumping harder and faster. By the flex of his jaw I can tell he's still holding back.

My hand moves to his SEAL tattoo, directly over his thrumming heart. "I meant it when I said I want all of you," I tell him quietly. "You don't need to hold back anymore."

I don't care what intensity he takes me at, as long as it's all of him.

Indecision battles in his fierce eyes before he succumbs to the ravenous hunger we both feel. "Grab on to the headboard."

I comply with the demand, grabbing onto one of the thin iron rods behind me. He places his hand just above mine then his other under my knee. My breath races in anticipation as his fierce eyes hold mine. Without warning, he unleashes, pounding inside of me without abandon.

It's raw, powerful, and indescribable.

Screams of pleasure rip from my throat, my fingers gripping the pole harder to anchor myself.

"Is this what you wanted, Grace?" he growls. "My cock fucking you until you're screaming for mercy."

"Yes," I moan, surprised that I can even manage the one word.

My orgasm builds, but I try to hold it at bay, not wanting this to be over yet.

Sawyer senses it. "I'm nowhere near done with you, Cupcake, so let it take you because there's still much more to come." He reaches a hand between our sweat-slicked bodies, his finger teasing my clit as his thrusts never falter.

The orgasm crashes into me like a freight train, lights exploding behind my eyes. My screams of pleasure bounce off the walls, echoing through the room.

"Fucking beautiful!" Those are the last words he speaks before succumbing to his own pleasure, his face burying into my neck. I hold him close, his thumping heart drumming against mine as we lie in a sweaty, tangled mess. It's minutes later that he withdraws from my body, both of us groaning at the disconnection.

I sit up with the intention to head to the bathroom but Sawyer stops me, his arm banding around my waist. "Don't leave me."

My heart aches at the vulnerability in his voice. I turn on my side to face him and he pulls me in close, our lips only a breath away from one another as we gaze into each other's eyes.

"Are we okay?" he asks, bringing up tonight's earlier events.

"I don't know, are we?"

He continues to watch me, waiting for a better answer.

"We were just talkin', Sawyer."

"I don't care. I didn't fucking like it."

My eyes narrow, my forgotten anger coming back. "Well get over it. He was the only one who spoke to me, I was not going to turn away the only company I had."

"You had me."

"No I didn't. Everyone else in that bar had you. I sat by myself for most of the night, Sawyer. Something you would have noticed if you hadn't been so preoccupied with bicycle bitch."

"I did not pay her any attention."

"You might not have flirted back with her but you never pushed her away either, and to me that's just as bad." My throat begins to ache as I remember how awful it was to watch her hang off him. "You really hurt my feelin's tonight," I whisper, emotion thickening my voice.

His hard expression softens, remorse reflecting in his green eyes. "I'm sorry, Cupcake, you're right, I should have checked on you instead of assuming you would have joined us. This dating thing is new to me and I'm not used to worrying about anyone else but myself. Make no mistake though, Grace, I was caught up with *friends*, not that bitch. Not any girl for that matter. You're the only one I care about."

"Is that what we are, Sawyer, dating?" I ask softly, wanting to finally label whatever this is.

He brings his hand up, cupping the side of my face. "We're more than that, baby, way fucking more."

Happiness blooms inside of me, my hurt feelings evaporating. Grabbing his wrist, I turn my face to the side, brushing my lips across his palm. "Good."

"Now that we have that out of the way." With lightning speed, he flips me to my back and comes over top of me again. "Let's make up."

"Didn't we just do that?" I laugh.

"Yeah, but that was for our earlier fight, now we have to make up for this one." His head dips as he sucks one of my nipples into his mouth.

I moan and decide if this is what's goin' to happen every time we fight, then we just may need to do it more often.

CHAPTER 32

Sawyer

"Sawyer, wake up! You're never gonna believe this." Grace's excitement pulls me from the best sleep of my life.

Groaning, I roll over and glance at the clock to see it's only eight a.m. *What the hell is she doing awake so early?* I fucked her most of the night and she's up already?

Just the thought of how we spent the last several hours has my cock hardening again. I'm pretty sure I'll never have enough of her. If I thought I was addicted to her before, that's nothing compared to what I feel now.

When the sound of the front door squeaks open, I climb out of bed, wondering what the hell she's up to. I throw on my jeans from the night before but don't bother with the button, because now that she woke my ass up, I plan to be back inside her.

A blast of cold air hits me when I walk out of the room, the front door left wide open. Once I get a view of outside, I stop dead in my tracks at the sight before me.

It's cold and snowing like a motherfucker, but there's my Cupcake, face tilted up to the foggy gray sky, her arms raised out at her sides, palms up, catching the heavy, fat flakes in the palms of her hands. She wears nothing but my shirt from the night before, and my sister's winter boots that go up to her bare knees.

Eventually she becomes aware of my presence and brings her eyes to mine, giving me the biggest smile I've ever seen on her. It's like a blow to my chest, the force of it almost knocking me on my ass.

"Isn't it beautiful?" she whispers, a look of wonderment splashed across her pretty face.

"Yeah, it is." My shoulder rests against the doorjamb as I watch her soak in something that's so simple to me yet extraordinary for her. The white, sparkling flakes begin to coat her long, wavy hair and fall to her eyelashes, proving she's the most beautiful thing I've ever seen.

Realization strikes deep—that the sad girl I met a few months ago has a smile now that radiates true happiness, one I've never gotten to experience until now. I decide this very moment I will spend the rest of my life making sure she smiles like this every day.

She crosses her arms over herself with a shiver. "Holy shit it's cold out here." She laughs, jumping up and down.

"Damn straight it is. Now get your pretty ass in here and get in the shower, we have plans."

Confusion pinches her face. "Where are we goin'?"

"It's a surprise."

Another beautiful smile steals her lips. She runs into the house, launching herself at me, her cold body curling around mine. "You have a surprise for me, Sexy Sawyer?" she asks.

"Yeah, it's in my pants." Her smile falters and she slaps at me playfully.

"I'm kidding."

"What is it? Tell me," she demands impatiently.

"Soon," I promise, heading to the shower. I plan to make this a day she never forgets.

An hour later, I pull up to the rink for the second time since coming home. This place meant everything to me growing up and I want Grace to experience it in a different way than she did last night. In a way she will never experience again.

"You have another hockey game?" she asks, a hint of disappointment in her voice.

"Not exactly." I leave her with the cryptic answer and climb out of the truck to grab my hockey bag out of the back.

She walks around to meet me, curiosity bright in her gaze. "You're torturing me here, Evans."

Chuckling, I take her hand in mine and lead her through the side door.

Joe, the rink attendant, is waiting for us as we enter. "There's our golden boy," he greets, slapping me on the back.

"Good to see you, Joe. Thanks for doing this."

"You bet, kid. This her?" he asks, shifting his attention to Grace.

She smiles back at him, having no idea what's going on.

"It is. Grace, this is Joe Paletti, he's been in charge of this place for as long as I've worn skates."

She extends her hand to him. "Nice to meet you, Joe."

"You too, honey. You all can go on back. You have an hour before anyone else comes in."

I thank him again then lead her into the rink, taking her into the player box.

"Are you gonna tell me what's goin' on?" she asks.

I drop my hockey bag and pull out my sister's figure skates. "We're skating, baby."

The biggest smile takes over her face and she claps excitedly. "I was hopin' you were gonna say that."

When she told me she had never skated before I knew I had to rectify the situation immediately. It's an abomination. Some of the best times of my life were spent on the ice.

"We get the whole place to ourselves?" she asks, sounding in complete awe as she takes in our surroundings.

"Yep, the rink doesn't open for another hour."

"How did you manage that?"

"I told you, Cupcake, I'm a legend around these parts."

She rolls her eyes playfully before taking a seat on the bench and toeing her boots off.

I help her with her skates, making sure they are tied tight. I'm barely finished with the last skate when she stands, moving for the ice.

"Aren't you going to wait for me?" I ask, biting back a smile.

"I'm good. I'll just hold on to the wall until you come out." Her arms go out at her sides, trying to balance herself as she steps onto the ice.

Her laughter fills the place as I get my own skates on. Standing, I walk to the opening and take my first stride onto the cold, hard surface, a sense of peace washing over me.

Grace is only a quarter of the way from where she started. She's bent over at the waist, her ass up as she tries to balance herself. She looks fucking ridiculous but cute as hell.

Chuckling, I glide over and lay a smack across her ass.

With a yelp, she grabs onto the wall and glares up at me as I skate backwards, passing her for a second time.

"Your stance is good, Cupcake. Just stick your ass up a little higher."

"Quit bein' a show-off and help me."

Showing mercy, I take both of her hands in mine. "Stand up straight."

Once she does, I begin skating backwards again, pulling her along with me.

"Whoa, whoa, whoa." She laughs, acting like we're going fast when we're really creeping at a snail's pace. Eventually, she relaxes and I pick up speed. The smile on her face lights up the whole damn arena, sending a weird sensation through my chest. I bring us to a stop, my arms going around her waist.

"What's wrong? Why are we stoppin'?" she asks, looking up at me, her nose pink from the cold.

Reaching down, I cup her backside and hoist her up.

Another squeal leaves her, her arms clinging to my neck. "Oh lord, don't you drop me, Sawyer."

"Wrap your legs around my waist, baby. Just watch your blades, I have enough scars on my back."

Her amusement vanishes, not taking it for the joke it was meant for. "I'll be careful," she promises.

When her knees grip my hips, I start gliding across the ice, keeping my pace steady. Her body is tense, fingers digging into my shoulders.

"Relax, Grace, I got you."

Her teeth sink into her bottom lip. "What if I fall?"

"I'd never let you fall."

Her smile returns, a powerful one that punches me in the chest. She releases her grip on my shoulders and raises her arms out at her sides, closing her eyes. "Faster," she whispers.

I quicken my strides and the faster I go, the bigger her smile becomes and it's a sight to behold. Her expression is soft and sweet, hair whispering across her face from our speed. In this moment, as I hold her warm body against mine, I know without a doubt that God made this beautiful girl just for me.

For the next hour, I go back and forth from carrying her to teaching her how to skate. We laugh, have some major hot make out sessions, but most importantly we have fun. All too soon, Joe is peeking in, letting me know our time is up.

"Sorry, Cupcake, that's our cue," I say regretfully, skating one final lap with her in my arms.

"Thank you, Sexy Sawyer, for bringin' me here. It's a memory I'll cherish forever."

"You deserve to be happy like this, Grace, always."

She rests her forehead against mine. "You make me happy."

I'm not going to lie about how fucking awesome that makes me feel. This arena holds some of the best memories of my life, but this one, by far, will always be my favorite.

CHAPTER 33

Sawyer

We share another awesome meal at my parents' table, my mother's home cooking is something I've missed. Grace tells my family about our skating session, her face still lit with excitement.

When there's a break in conversation, Jesse switches the subject, opening her big mouth about last night. "I heard you had quite the evening at Overtime, care to fill us all in?" she asks, shooting me an amused glance.

My mother's expression pinches in concern. "What happened?"

"Nothing." I glare at Jesse, warning her to keep her mouth shut.

Of course, Sam speaks up, ratting me out. "It seems Sawyer is all sorts of possessive over Grace. He didn't like Jase Crawford talking to her last night."

My glare swings her way, promising retribution on her tattletale ass.

"Sawyer Evans, you better not have been fighting," my mom scolds.

"Leave the boy alone, Catherine. That kid needs to be taken down a notch, he's a hothead just like his old man."

All of our gazes pull to my dad, shock coursing through me and everyone else that he just stood up for me. He refuses to acknowledge it though and keeps his eyes on his plate as he continues to eat.

Eventually, my mom breaks the silence. "Well, I know another father and son with the same problem, and there's no excuse for fighting."

"There was no fight, Mom," I assure her. "The girls are just stirring shit up."

It's obvious she doesn't believe me but she lets it go. The rest of our dinner is spent talking about Grace and her pies as she shares her secrets with my mom and sisters. After dessert, I excuse us, wanting to be alone with her, but my dad stops me and asks for my help with something in the attic.

I hesitate, knowing damn well if he needed help with something he wouldn't ask me. In the end, my curiosity gets the best of me and I reluctantly agree.

The air is thick with awkward tension as we climb the stairs.

"I heard you played quite the game last night," he says.

I shrug. "Not bad, considering I haven't played in a few years."

He nods and things fall silent again. Once we reach the attic, he takes me to the far back corner where I find an entire shrine dedicated to all my hockey years. All the medals I ever won, every pair of skates I've ever had, old jerseys, newspaper articles, and even pictures hang on the wall.

"I can't believe you have all this," I say, surprise strong in my voice.

"These are memories to keep and be proud of. And who knows, if you ever have a boy maybe this stuff could be passed down to him."

My eyes shift to his, shock rendering me speechless at the mention of kids.

He clears his throat and shifts nervously. "Listen, son, I know things haven't been good between us for a while, and I know most of that is my fault. I just…I worked my ass off, Sawyer, to give you all this," he says, gesturing to my hockey shit.

"Dad…" I trail off the warning, not wanting to fight about this anymore.

"Just hear me out."

I cross my arms over my chest and let him finish.

"I worked really hard for my kids to have a good life, so they could be the best they could be, and most importantly, so I could keep them safe. Then one day, my biggest fear came crashing down on me, all because my only son, the one who was going to be something great, tells me he wants to join the Navy and fight for his country."

Guilt flares in my gut but my answer still hasn't changed and never will. "I don't know what to tell you, Dad. I lived a good life and still do. I appreciate everything you've done for me. I love hockey and I always will but at the end of the day it wasn't something I wanted to do for the rest of my life. I'm sorry if that disappoints you—"

"No, son, you're not understanding what I'm saying. I'm not disappointed; I was upset because I was scared. I didn't want to lose you; it's something that this family would have never been able to overcome. That day we got the call about you and Cade…" He pauses, his voice cracking. "It almost broke us all."

My chest constricts, hating to think about all they went through after getting that call.

"I guess what I'm trying to say is, I finally understand why you did it, and that's mostly thanks to that girl you brought here. Your mom told me some of what's going on, and I'm damn proud of you for stepping in to help her. I'm glad you're trained to protect her, and well…I'm just goddamn proud of you, kid."

His approval is something I've longed to hear for years. He's always been my role model and when our relationship took a hit it was harder on me than I care to admit. "Thanks, Dad," I finally manage, my voice gruff.

He pulls me in for a hug, something he hasn't done since the day I told him I was joining the Navy. After a few hard claps, he steps back but keeps hold of my shoulders. "Now, I want you to listen to me. I know we can both be arrogant sons of bitches, because of our crazy good looks."

I chuckle, knowing it's true.

"But that girl you brought here is special, just like your mom is to me. Do you understand what I'm telling you?"

"Yeah, I do. I care about her a lot."

"You more than care and we both know it."

He's right.

"Whatever you do, don't let her go. You hold onto her tight and you fight for her every step of the way."

"Trust me, she's mine. Forever."

A proud smile takes over his face. "Good. Now go tell your mom I made up with you so she will talk to me again."

Chuckling, I turn to walk away but he pulls back for one more hug. "I love you,

Sawyer."

"I love you too, Dad."

The cold air bites my face as Grace and I trek through the snow, heading back to the guesthouse. She walks next to me with a knowing smile on her face. "I'm happy you and your dad worked out your differences."

"Yeah and it's all thanks to this nosy little blonde chick who smells like cupcakes."

"Those damn chicks who smell like cupcakes. Where do they get off?" she teases, the melody of her soft giggle floating through the night.

I grunt but can't deny that I'm grateful for her and her meddling ass.

She comes to a stop and bends down, scooping up a handful of snow. There's a gleam in her eyes as her hands clap the white powder, trying to form a ball.

"I wouldn't start that shit if I were you, Cupcake," I warn her. "I'm the king of snowball fights, and you do not want to fu—" My words are cut off when a big pile of snow hits me in the face.

It's the most pathetic attempt at a snowball I've ever seen but she still finds it amusing and laughs her ass off. "You were saying?" she says, the sass in her tone turning my cock hard.

"Just remember, baby, you were warned."

Knowing what's about to come, she turns and bolts. I find it funny as hell that she actually thinks she has a chance to escape. It takes me no time at all to catch up to her, my body colliding with hers as I take her to the ground. I accept the brunt of our fall before flipping her beneath me.

She screams in laughter, squirming to get away. "Get off me, it's freezin'."

"This isn't freezing, Cupcake. *This* is freezing." Taking a huge pile of snow, I shove it beneath her jacket, spreading it all over her bare stomach.

"Please stop!" she pleads. "I'm sorry, I won't do it again, I promise."

My smirk spreads as she begs for mercy. "You want up?"

"Yes!"

"Then say, Sawyer has a big dick."

She tenses beneath me and bursts into laughter. "No way. I ain't sayin' that."

"All right…" I reach for more snow.

"No, stop. Okay, I'll say it." She licks those pretty lips of hers, pink marring her cheeks. "'Sawyer has a big dick.'" Her words are followed by an eye roll.

"Good girl." Leaning down, I nuzzle her neck, tasting her skin, my teeth grazing the column of her throat. "Now say, I want Sawyer to fuck me."

A moan parts her lips but she pushes against my chest. "Stop bein' a sexy jerk and let me up."

"You know what you have to say." To drive the point home, I thrust against the apex of her thighs, my cock aching to be inside of her.

The sexiest whimper leaves her, her back arching. "I want you to fuck me."

A growl erupts from my chest, the words putting me in motion. I sweep her up from the ground, my strides fast as I race back to the house.

Her laughter fills the air as she clings to my neck.

"This shit isn't funny, Cupcake. I've been dying to get my cock inside you all day."

"You're lucky to get anything from me after you shoved snow up my shirt."

"Don't worry, we're going to hit the hot tub to warm up."

"Hot tub?" She frowns. "But I didn't bring a swimsuit."

"You don't need one."

"Oh, yes, I do. I'm not gettin' in that hot tub naked. Your family could see."

"No, they can't. They're five acres away."

"Doesn't matter. Your sisters could come over or even your parents. No way, I'm serious, Sawyer. It's not happening."

"Fine, you can borrow one from my sister." She doesn't need to know that shit will be coming off either way.

Once we get into the house, she calls my sister to ask if she can borrow a swimsuit even though I told her she doesn't need to. She then proceeds to tell me I have to wear one too or we won't be able to resist each other. She's fucking crazy if she thinks I'll be able to resist her at all, swimsuit or not. However, I comply then head out to remove the top and check the chemicals before climbing in. I rest my head back on a groan, eyes closing at the soothing hot water.

"Holy moly, it's freezin' out here."

My eyes spring open, every muscle in my body tensing at the sight of Grace in a tiny black bikini.

She dances her way over to the hot tub, her arms wrapped around herself to ward off the chill but it does nothing to cover her tight body. Her hair is up in a knot, displaying her slender neck and my mouth waters for a taste.

"My feet are about to get frostbite," she chuckles, stepping into the steaming water. "Oh, that stings." Her attention drifts to me at my silence, her eyes widening when she sees me moving for her. "Hey now, stop lookin' at me like that."

"Like what?" I ask, reaching for her.

"Oh no you don't, Sawyer. I mean it, I have already been busted by your family makin' out with you once. I do not want it to happen again."

I grab her around the waist and haul her over onto my lap, my lips brushing against her ear. "Come on, baby, I'm not going to let anyone see this." My hand molds over one of her breasts, kneading the soft flesh. "Just let me touch you, then we'll go inside where I'll fuck you properly."

Her response is a whimper as she grinds against my raging hard-on.

"Is that a yes?" I ask, pinching her tight little nipple through the thin wet fabric.

"Yes," she moans, her response breathless.

I tug the string at the back of her neck and her top falls away, revealing perfection. My hands mold over the wet mounds, her hard tits scraping against the palm of my hands.

"Oh god!" Her head drops back on my shoulder, her hot breath racing across my jaw.

"Such pretty tits," I growl, licking the shell of her ear. "I swear they were made for my hands. Just like the rest of you." My fingers coast down her stomach, slipping beneath her swim bottoms.

"Sawyer," she pants, need edging her voice.

I pass over the swollen nub before inserting two fingers deep inside of her.

A whimper purges from her delicate throat, her body trembling against me.

"After I make you come on my hand, I'm going to have this tight pussy dripping all over my cock."

Moaning, she brings one of her arms up to wrap around my neck. I kiss the side of her face, my lips brushing her damp cheek as my fingers stroke deep inside of her. Her hips pick up the rhythm, matching the harsh breaths breaching her lips.

"That's it, baby, fuck my fingers."

"I'm going to come," she cries out the warning.

I work her faster, plunging in and out of her hot depth while my other hand lays a slap to her tit. The resounding smack fills the air and pushes her over the edge.

Her cries echo through the night, feeding the need I have clawing inside of me. She relaxes against me, her breathing labored as she fights to catch her breath.

Turning my head, I press my lips against her temple then pick her up and climb out of the hot water. My arm is snug around her waist as I grab our towels and walk us into the house.

Her lips skim across my jaw to my ear, tongue darting out to taunt the beast I carefully try to keep locked up. I enter the living room and flick on the fireplace then grab the blanket that's draped over the back of the couch, spreading it out on the floor.

I'm about to take her to her back but her hold on me tightens. "I want to be on top this time," she says.

Her boldness surprises me yet pleases me at the same time.

She clears her throat, a blush staining her cheeks. "I mean, if that's all right with you."

I chuckle, unable to help myself. "I fucking love that idea, baby."

She smiles, causing that monumental shift in my chest and pushes me to my back, her knees straddling either side of my hips.

"Damn, Cupcake, look at you being all forceful. I like it."

"I have a feeling you like me any way I am, as long as I'm naked."

Little does she know, I love her all the time, naked or otherwise. But I decide to keep that to myself for now.

She comes over me, giving me a taste of her lips that has my cock screaming to be inside of her. My hands mold to her ass as her mouth descends, kissing its way down my chest. The few scars she comes upon are given extra attention, her expression pinching with sadness.

I lift her chin, forcing her gaze to mine. "No being sad when we're about to fuck, Cupcake. It's my number one rule."

Her lips twitch with a smile. "You have rules?"

"Yep. And that's rule number one."

"What's rule number two?" she asks with a note of seduction in her voice, her tongue darting out to taste my skin.

"Rule number two is time to speed this up."

She chuckles, enjoying the fact that she's driving me wild. "All right, no more teasin'." She sits up and undoes my board shorts. Once my cock is free she grips it in a tight fist, making my head swim with pleasure.

My fingers pull the tie of her swim bottoms, baring her slick wet pussy. I grip her hips and line her up, the head of my cock breaching her tight heat.

Our groans fill the air as she takes me inch by inch.

My jaw flexes as I fight to restrain myself from plunging inside of her. Once she's fully seated, I give her time to adjust, letting her set the pace. Her hips move, motions slow and unsure. I cup her perfect tits, my fingers teasing her sweet little nipples.

"Oh god, that feels so good," she whimpers, picking up rhythm.

"That's it, baby, ride me. Show me how much you want it." I unlatch the clip from her hair, freeing the golden locks from its confines. It tumbles past her shoulders, framing her pretty face. The firelight flickers along her flawless skin, making her glow like the angel she is. "Jesus, you're a fucking sight right now."

Her teeth sink into her bottom lip, a shy smile stealing her mouth.

Unable to restrain myself any longer, I thrust up, driving my cock deeper inside of her. She gasps, her nails biting into my skin.

I still, teeth grinding. "This okay, Grace?"

"Yes. Do it again and don't stop."

Growling, I plunge myself inside of her, taking her the way I've been dying to. Her pussy grips me as I fuck her hard and fast, her cries fueling me further.

"Sawyer…" She lets my name trail off but the warning is loud and clear.

"Let me have it, baby. I want to feel you soak my cock."

Her head falls back on her shoulders, screams of pleasure ripping from her throat as her orgasm claims her. It's the hottest damn sight I've ever seen. Fire spreads through my veins, seconds before I spill myself inside of her, filling her with everything I have.

She drops down on me; the rapid beat of her heart thumping against mine. My arms hug her close until our breathing returns to normal. Eventually, she lifts her head, giving me one of her sweet smiles. "That was fun."

I grunt. "That was more than fun, Cupcake. That was fucking incredible, explosive, awesome…take your pick."

"All of the above."

"Agreed."

She presses against my chest as she lifts herself off my cock. The missing heat of her body makes me want to weep like a pussy. She reaches for one of the towels next to us and wraps it around her before standing.

"Where the hell are you going?" I ask.

"To clean up, Mr. Nosy."

"You don't need to clean up. I'm just going to get you dirty again anyway."

She shakes her head, a smile playing at her lips as she walks to the bathroom.

The least she could have done is walk there naked and give me a damn show.

CHAPTER 34

Grace

Locking door the behind me, I face the mirror, hardly recognizing myself. My lips are swollen from his kisses, cheeks flushed and eyes glowing with every powerful emotion invading my heart. I look pretty, happy, which is exactly how I feel.

I use the private moment to absorb this feeling, to really soak in everything this man makes me feel. Afterward, I make sure to freshen up quickly then walk back out.

I come to a stop before rounding the corner, taking the opportunity to watch him unaware. He sits up against the couch, a blanket wrapped loosely around his hips as he stares into the roaring flames of the fire.

His eyes shift to where I stand, a cocky smirk lifting his perfect lips. "You going to come join me or just stand there and check me out all night?"

"How did you know I was here?" I ask, stepping out from the corner I was tucked in.

"Because I know everything, especially when you're near."

Charming bugger.

He opens the blanket for me to join him. Smiling, I take my place on his lap, straddling him so we're face-to-face.

"Get rid of this thing." He rips the towel from my body and shares his blanket with me, folding it under my arms before hugging me close, chest to chest, heart to heart.

I wrap my arms around his neck, our faces only inches from one another. "Let's stay here and never go back."

"Why?" he asks, peering back at me.

"Because here is happy and safe. Here it's just you and me, where nothing can take you away from me," I admit, feeling an ache build in my throat. "I've barely thought about him since we've been here, Sawyer. I'm scared what awaits us back home."

Regardless of his hard expression, he reaches up, cupping the side of my face in a tender gesture. "I'll tell you what awaits us when we go back, Cupcake. Our friends, Chuckie, Mac. Wherever we are, I promise we will always be safe and happy. I meant it when I said I wouldn't let anyone fuck with this, Grace. No one will ever take this from us. Okay?"

I nod, feeling bad for not thinking about everyone else, because I do need them. Especially Chuckie.

"I promise we'll come back," he says, his thumb stroking my cheek. "Maybe next time I'll even teach you how to play hockey."

I cringe at the thought. I couldn't even stand up on those dang skates, I'd hate to think what I would do with all that equipment on. "Do you miss playing?" I ask, remembering how at home he looked on the ice.

"Sometimes, but not enough that I regret my decision of walking away."

"What made you decide to leave it behind and join the Navy?"

"9/11," he answers, no hesitation. "I was in high school when it happened, but I'll never forget the impact it had on me. Members of the military came to the school, trying to recruit seniors. Listening to them speak made me realize that everything I thought was important really wasn't."

I think that catastrophic event was a big wake-up call for many of us. I remember Mama cryin' for days over it.

"Cade and I spoke about it after they left," he continues, "he told me he had always planned to join the military after school but he was mostly interested in the Navy. That day I went home and researched it, especially the SEALs, and I knew right away that's what I wanted to do, too. I called Cade and told him I was in. We made the pact that after high school we would go together, and we did. Much to my father's disappointment, as you know."

I smile, thinking about him and Cade at a younger age. "How long have you and Cade been friends?"

His easy smile returns. "Since the second grade. We were the most unlikely duo. I was a kid from a good family who had money, and Cade, well…let's just say he was the opposite. One day after school, three older kids were picking on him at the playground, so I walked up and beat the shit out of all three of them," he tells me. "I saved his life. After that he followed me around everywhere I went. No matter what I did, I couldn't get rid of him, so I thought, ah, what the hell, I'll be his friend."

I blink at him, the story so disbelieving that I burst into a fit of laughter. "You're lyin'."

"I am not! You should have seen me, baby, I kicked major ass."

I shake my head, continuing to laugh.

"Fine, it was actually the other way around," he admits on a grumble. "Don't judge, Cupcake, I was small for my age, believe it or not. I didn't get all this until closer to junior high."

I have a hard time picturing Sawyer small for his age, considerin' what a giant he is now. "So you're the one who followed Cade around until he became your friend?" I ask, amusement lacing my words.

"Wouldn't you? The guy kicked the shit out of all three of those assholes for trying to steal my new Pumas. I decided right there that he was going to be my friend, and I was going to bring him everywhere I went," he tells me. "At first he tried to act like he didn't want to be my friend, but of course it didn't take long before he realized I wasn't going anywhere. In the end, he gave in, and we have been best friends ever since."

I wrap my arms around his neck, my cheeks aching from smiling so much. "That's a great friendship story. I'm glad y'all met, and he was able to save your Pumas for you."

"Me too, baby. My mom had just bought those for me, she would have kicked my ass."

I doubt Catherine would have laid a hand on him, even now it's clear to see she has a soft spot for her only son. What Jesse mentioned earlier tonight about Cade's past comes flooding back.

"Can I ask you somethin'?"

"Anything."

"How did Cade's sister die?"

His expression turns to stone, a steel of armor slamming down around him.

"Sorry, I shouldn't have asked," I whisper, feeling guilty for the pain that's in his eyes.

He shakes his head. "No, it's fine. I'll tell you but I'm warning you, it's not easy to hear. And don't ever mention it around Cade. He never speaks about it and it will send him into a rage you don't want to witness."

I nod and swallow hard, bracing myself for what I'm about to hear.

"His sister was eight years younger than him and worshiped the ground he walked on. He took care of her since his mom was always high as a fucking kite, especially after his dad died."

My heart pinches, thinking about how much responsibility Cade shouldered as a young child.

"At one time she hooked up with a real crazy son of a bitch. He lived in a commune and called himself a prophet. Cade knew the guy wasn't right in the head but he didn't realize how bad, until it was too late."

Lead sinks into the pit of my stomach, fear rippling through me for what he's about to tell me.

"The bastard raped and killed his little sister when she was only seven years old."

"No!" The one word purges from my mouth as bile restricts my throat, my heart shattering into a thousand pieces. An image of what happened to my mama emerges but in her place is a sweet innocent little girl. I shake my head, too horrified to comprehend it.

"Cade walked in on it."

Horror washes over me as I think about how awful that must have been for him. Just like it was for me with Mama. "Please tell me the man went to prison," I say, hoping some sort of justice was served.

Sawyer gazes back at me, rage darkening his green eyes. "No. Cade drove a fucking bullet through his skull and sent him to hell where he belongs."

I can't say I'm sad to hear that. I always felt Miguel deserved the death penalty. Jail was letting him off too easily, especially now that he's out.

"Cade has had some really shitty luck. It's shaped him to be the hard bastard he's turned into, and I can't say I blame him. What happened to his sister is the very reason why he will never step foot into a church. Even though the asshole was no prophet let alone a person of God, Cade associates the two."

I guess I can understand that, as horrible as it is, there have been times in the last few years when I have questioned my faith also.

"It's one of the reasons it shocked the hell out of Jaxson and me when he fell for a preacher's daughter."

"He did?" I ask, not expecting to hear that.

"Yep. He met her when we were in Iraq. She was there with her church. She was the rescue mission we went against orders for and ended up walking into a fucking ambush, which was how we ended up spending a week in hell."

I remember Julia telling me about the rescue mission, but I didn't realize the girl was someone Cade cared about.

Reaching up, I cup the side of his cheek. "I'm sorry, I hate that you guys were hurt."

"It was the worst week of my life but I don't regret it. I'd live it all over again if it meant saving Faith and Anna."

Because that's the kind of man he is—honorable, loving, and strong. The words tattooed on his back make even more sense now. "That's what your tattoo means."

He nods, confirming my statement.

To know he lived through that kind of hell yet still has no regrets makes me admire him all that much more. There are so many things in my life that I regret and wish I could change.

"If you could go back and change one moment in your life, what would it be?"

I expect him to say that horrific week in Iraq, when such cruelty was inflicted upon them, but he doesn't. Instead he says something that I will remember for the rest of my life.

"It would be to find you sooner, because I would have never let anyone hurt you." His words are strong and sure, his green irises holding mine.

My breath hitches, tears clouding my vision. Resting my forehead on his, I close my eyes, trying to hold in my emotion but it's no use. "Your moment should be that week in Iraq."

"I'd live through every painful lash again if it meant keeping you safe."

A sob pours from my lips, a million emotions banging around inside of me.

Sawyer takes me to my back, covering me with his hard warm body. "Everything is going to be good now, Grace, you'll see."

I hug him close, unable to believe how lucky I am to have met him. "You're the best thing that's ever happened to me, Sawyer," I say instead.

He pulls back to look at me, his expression soft. "Same here, Cupcake… I'm the best thing that's ever happened to me, too."

I frown, his words taking a moment to sink in.

He bursts into laughter, thinking he's so dang funny.

Sniffling, I slap his shoulder but can't deny the smile taking over my sad lips. "Leave it to you to ruin another romantic moment, Sawyer Evans."

"Don't worry, baby, I'm going to make it up to you…right now."

His lips descend as he makes good on his promise, claiming what will always be his for as long as my heart is beating.

CHAPTER 35

Sawyer

Leaving my parents' house was harder than usual. Not only did my mom and sisters cry but so did Grace. She loved my family as much as they did her. I'm glad I brought her along and that we had this time away together but now it's time to deal with everything going on here. Time to eliminate the threat once and for all.

Jaxson is pushing Julia on the swing when we pull up to the house. Chuckie runs circles around their feet, barking like crazy while Jaxson looks pissed, his hands waving around heatedly as he talks with Julia.

"My baby!" Grace cries, fleeing my truck before I can even come to a complete stop. Chuckie meets her halfway. She falls to her knees, hugging and kissing him as if it's been three years and not three days.

Shutting off the truck, I climb out and make my way over to them.

"Thank you so much for watching him," Grace says, giving both Jaxson and Julia a hug.

"Anytime." Julia smiles. "He was very well-behaved. Did you have a good time with Sawyer's family?"

Grace turns to me, beaming with happiness. "The best."

I toss her a wink then glance over at Jaxson to see him still looking pissed off. "What's wrong with you?"

"Wanna know what's wrong with me?"

I remain silent since it's a rhetorical question.

"*She,*" he says, jerking a thumb at Julia, "and Susan, are allowing Anna to bring her boyfriend overnight to my house for Thanks-fucking-giving!"

Well, that explains his current mood.

Julia's back straightens, her eyes narrowing on her husband. "Excuse me, Jaxson, but it's *our* house and if her parents are okay with it, then we will be, too."

"There's no way Bill is okay with this," he argues.

"It's not like they're sleeping in the same room for heaven's sake."

"You're damn right they won't be!" His attention shifts back to me and he points his finger at my chest. "I'll tell you what I'm going to do. I'm going to rig that fucker's door shut. I'll be alerted immediately if anyone goes in or out of that room."

"What happens if he needs to use the bathroom?" Grace asks.

"He can piss out the fucking window!"

Both Grace and Julia break into muffled chuckles.

"This is not funny!"

Julia rolls her eyes, not the least bit fazed by her husband's tantrum. "Give it a rest, you're being ridiculous, and if you're not careful you will push Anna away."

He dismisses the warning with a grunt and brings his furious eyes back to me. "Guess what else she did?"

I'm scared to ask, especially by the nervous look on Julia's face.

"She invited Ray Jennings for dinner, too."

My shocked gaze yanks to Julia. "Why?"

The man is the father of the bastard who tried to kill her, he's also the most arrogant prick I've ever met. Why she would even consider inviting him is beyond me.

She lifts her chin but there's no denying the tears forming in her eyes. "Because he has no family, and no one should be alone on Thanksgiving. Including him. But it doesn't matter because he turned down the offer," she bites her trembling lip, her voice cracking with emotion, "I was only trying to be nice."

Well, shit! Now I feel like an asshole and so does Jaxson if the guilt on his expression is anything to go by.

Grace puts an arm around Julia's shoulders, hugging her close. "I think it was awful nice of you to ask him. I agree, no one should be alone on Thanksgivin'… Right, guys?" she adds, directing a hard glare our way.

"Yep," I agree quickly, not wanting my Cupcake mad at me.

"Come here, Jules." Jaxson pulls her against his chest. Well, as close as he can considering her stomach has expanded quite a bit. "I'm sorry. Thanksgiving will be good, I promise." He kisses her forehead, trying to smooth things over.

She lifts her head from his chest, looking at Grace. "Dinner is on the Sunday. I'm hoping y'all will come, too?"

"We would love to. I'll bring dessert."

"That would be great." She smiles, her earlier hurt feelings fading.

Soon after we say our goodbyes and head home. Once there, Grace starts dinner while I unpack, making sure to move the remainder of my shit from the spare room into her bedroom. As I'm hanging up shirts in the closet, something from the top shelf tumbles out, falling at my feet. Picking it up, I see it's a sketchbook. I open it to the first page and am shocked by what I reveal.

What the hell is this?

My steps are slow as I walk over to the bed and take a seat, admiring a sketch of a bakery. There's a lot of detail, right down to the soft yellow walls and pink tables. Pictures of uniforms are glued to the pages and a menu has been created, all with Grace's recipes.

At the top of the page is written, *A Slice of Hope with a Sprinkle of Grace.*

"Sawyer, do you know where—" Grace comes to a hard stop just inside the room. "Where did you get that?" she whispers, her face paling.

"I was hanging my clothes in the closet and it fell out."

She remains silent, her eyes riveted to the book. She doesn't seem mad just…embarrassed maybe?

"What is this?" I ask.

Shaking her head, she pulls herself together and reaches for it. "Nothin', it's stupid."

"It's not stupid. Tell me what it is."

She gazes down at the drawing, her fingers dancing along the sketch. "Remember when I told you that Mama and I were headed out of town that day for a bakin' contest?"

I nod.

"The prize money was for $20,000. It was going to be enough with the savings we had to start up this bakery. It was our dream for as long as I can remember…" She pauses, sadness adopting her expression. "But it never happened because she was taken from me." Her eyes lift to mine, tears pooling in their depths. "She worked her butt off her whole life for us to have this and they took it all away within an instant."

My chest constricts at the unfairness of it all. At how much not only she has suffered but her mother. When I get my hands on that piece of shit he's as good as dead.

She wipes a stray tear away and points to the top of the page. "Her name was Hope. We wanted something with both our names, so that's what we came up with. A couple years ago, when I was missin' her, I decided to draw it out. I picked our uniforms and even designed a menu, just for fun." She looks up at me, a shy smile stealing her sad lips. "You think I'm crazy, don't you?"

Reaching out, I pull her down on my lap. "No, I think you're incredible."

She rests her forehead against mine, pressing the softest kiss to my lips.

My hand hooks her neck, reeling her in for more. For the rest of the night we stay in bed, and I do everything in my power to ease the pain that she always carries. I might not be able to change her past but I sure as hell can change her future and I intend to do exactly that.

CHAPTER 36

Grace

The blare of a cell phone pulls me from a deep slumber. My eyes flutter open and I stretch, feeling every glorious muscle in my body from the hours spent in Sawyer's arms. His warm, naked chest shifts beneath my cheek as he reaches over to answer it.

"Yeah?" His gravelly voice has me burrowing into him, but soon I feel his body tense. "Is he all right?"

The concern in his tone has me shooting upright. I glance at the clock to see it's one in the morning and realize a phone call at this time can't be good.

"We're on our way," he says, hanging up.

"What is it, what's wrong?"

He cups the side of my face, regret burning in his eyes. "It's Mac, Cupcake. We need to go to the hospital."

I flee from the bed, scrambling to get my clothes on. My mind races with all the horrible things that could have happened to him.

Car accident? No, it's a heart attack, I know it. I told him that greasy food he's always eatin' was going to catch up to him. I charge for my dresser to grab my purse and run full force into Sawyer.

He grabs my arms, giving me a little shake. "Grace, are you even listening to me?"

My heart was pounding so loud I didn't realize he was talking to me. "Please tell me he's all right?" I choke out.

He pulls me against him, enfolding me in his strong arms. "I don't know all the details yet, baby. Cooper is going to fill us in at the hospital, but he said Mac is stable."

Stable... My thundering heart begins to settle.

Sawyer frames my face between his hands, lifting my eyes to his. "Everything will be okay, Grace. I promise."

I nod.

"Come on, let's go." He laces his fingers with mine, offering me the strength I need, and pulls me out the door.

We arrive at the hospital quickly and rush through the emergency doors, hand-in-hand. I immediately spot Cooper by the nurses' station. He looks terrible, his hair is a mess, his uniform and face covered in somethin' that looks an awful lot like soot. His head lifts at our approach, revealing a horrible gash on his forehead.

"Cooper, are you all right?" I ask, hurrying over to him, my arms wrapping around his waist.

He hugs me back but it's strained. "Yeah don't worry about me, I'm fine."

"What the heck is goin' on? Where's Mac?" I ask, steppin' back to look up at him.

My heart plummets at the remorse in his eyes. It's now I realize that whatever has happened is much worse than I originally thought. I have a feeling this has nothin' to do with a heart attack and everythin' to do with me.

Miguel.

"No," I whisper, shakin' my head. "He's here, isn't he? He's found me." My words sound distant to my ears, like an echo in a tunnel, my entire body vibrating in fear.

"I think so, yes."

Sawyer wraps his arms around me, giving me the stability I need. I soak in his warmth and fight hard against the panic threatening to take me.

"What did he do to Mac? Tell me he's okay."

"He's going to be all right but he's pretty banged up. He was at the diner, closing up, when someone struck him from behind. His face was pushed into the floor so he never got a look at the guy, but the attacker was demanding to know where you lived. He beat Mac repeatedly when he wouldn't give him any information."

My breath hitches as I stifle a sob, my heart shattering into a million pieces.

"That's not all."

My watery eyes snap to his, terror gripping my chest like a tight vise.

"He set the diner on fire and left Mac to burn."

"No!" My knees buckle, an agonized sob tumbling past my lips.

Sawyer lifts me into his arms and walks us into the waiting room, taking a seat in a chair. I bury my face into his neck, tears of sorrow staining my cheeks. "This is all my fault. I knew it was only gonna be a matter of time before he found me."

He grabs my face between his hands, forcing my eyes to his. "This isn't your fault, Grace, none of it. Do you hear me?"

Despite his words my eyes drift closed, guilt threatening to claim me.

"Look at me, baby."

I follow the order, his face blurry before me.

"The good thing about all this is now we know where he is and that's going to make it a hell of a lot easier to catch him."

"How bad are Mac's injuries?" I ask, looking over at Cooper.

"Apart from aggravation of the smoke, the majority of his injuries are from the assault. I was on my way home shortly after the fire was set. I was able to get to him in time."

"And the diner?" I ask, my breath stalling in hope.

He shakes his head. "I'm sorry, Grace, but it's gone...all of it."

Devastation consumes me as I cover my face and cry into my hands. *Everything...he lost everything because of me.*

Sawyer's arms tighten around me. "It's all right, baby. Mac's okay, and that's what's most important."

Sniffling, I wipe my wet cheeks with the back of my hand. "I want to see him."

"I've arranged that. They're only allowing family in to see him but I explained that you were the closest to a relative he has."

"Thank you."

"You need to be prepared though. He's in bad shape."

I don't think anything will prepare me for this but I will be brave for Mac's sake.

Climbing to my feet, I follow Cooper and continue to lean on Sawyer for support.

An older nurse steps out of the room as we approach. She gives me a sad but kind smile. "Are you Grace?"

"Yes, ma'am."

"He's expecting you, just not too long, all right? He needs his rest."

"I understand."

Sawyer drops a kiss on top of my head. "I'll wait right here for you."

Nodding, I reach for the door and take a deep breath, bracing myself for what's on the other side of it and enter quietly, The room is fairly dark, only a soft glow from the bathroom light, but it's not enough to conceal the horror in front of me. Bile inches up my throat as I take in Mac's battered face.

The door clicks shut, drawing his attention to me. "There's my darlin'," he croaks painfully, "you bring me any pie?" His attempt to lighten this horrific moment has my heart crumbling.

Tears stream down my face as I rush to his side. I hug him gently, making sure to be mindful of his wounds. "I'm so sorry, Mac. So sorry this happened to you."

"Hey now, none of that, you crazy girl. This isn't your fault, Grace."

I shake my head, disagreeing with him. "You should have told him where I was."

"Hell no! Look at me."

I lift my head and peer into his swollen face.

"Nothing would have made me tell him where you were—nothing. I'd die before I ever gave you up to him."

Hearing that only has me crying harder. "You lost everythin'—all of it because of me."

"No. If I would have lost you, then I would have lost everything."

My wounded heart warms from his kind words.

"The diner is just that, Grace. It's just a building. I had planned to shut that place down and retire a while ago. But I never did, because two years ago a beautiful, sad, broken girl walked in, asking for a cup of tea and messed with my heart like no other. When I found out she needed a job and made the best pies this world has to offer, there was no way I was gonna let her go."

A smile lifts my trembling lips, his confession meaning so much to me.

"The point is, Grace, I'm more than okay to retire. I kept it as long as I did for you."

I hug him again, making sure my arms are gentle. "I love you, Mac. I don't know what I would ever do without ya."

"I love you too, kid," he replies gruffly. "Don't worry about me. Thanks to the sheriff, I'm gonna be just fine. You worry about yourself. Stay safe and don't leave Sawyer's side. I like that cocky son of a gun, he's good for you, and I know he'll protect you."

"I like him, too," I whisper.

He grunts. "I think you more than like him."

I nod. "You're right, I do."

The nurse walks in, interrupting our moment. "I'm sorry but it's time for some more pain medicine for our big tough guy here, then he needs to rest."

"Just give us another moment, sweetness, we're almost done here," Mac says, flashing the nurse a wink from his swollen eye.

She blushes, clearly flustered. "All right, I'll be back in *one* minute."

When she backs out of the door, I look at Mac, quirking a brow at him.

His puffy face gives me a sly grin. "She's a looker, ain't she?"

"She is. I think she has a crush on you."

"You can't blame her for that, I'm one good-lookin' son of a bitch...even messed up like this."

I chuckle, wiping the remainder of my tears. "You are."

He gazes back at me, his expression softening. "I expect you to come back every day with some pie and grace me with your sweet face, all right?"

"I will." Lifting my fingers to my lips, I press a kiss to them then lay them gently across his battered cheek. "I love you, Mac."

"I love you too, darlin'. Remember what I said...don't leave Sawyer's side."

"I won't." Pushing to my feet, I head to the door but turn back to Mac one more time, blowing him another kiss before walking out into the hall.

Sawyer is waiting for me like he promised. He gathers me in his arms once again, knowing what I need. "You okay, Cupcake?"

I shake my head. There's no sense in lying. This isn't okay and it isn't going to be. Not until Mac is out of here and Miguel is caught.

Bending down, he sweeps my legs out from under me, cradling me into his arms. I hug him close, thankful for his support.

"I'm taking her home now, call me with any news," he says to Cooper.

"Will do. Take care, Grace."

"Bye, Cooper." I rest my head on Sawyer's shoulder as he walks us out of the hospital, feeling too defeated and tired to hold it up anymore.

"Don't worry, baby, he's going to fucking pay for this. I promise."

I hope he's right. I pray Miguel pays for every horrible thing he has done. He deserves no mercy and come judgment day, may justice be served.

CHAPTER 37

Grace

The stress and heartbreak brought the nightmare back full force, sucking me into its black abyss. There's no fighting it, no stopping it, and I'm forced to relive the night I finally escaped the evil I had lived with after my mother's death.

The click of my bedroom door pulls me awake. Before I can fully open my eyes, his heavy weight settles over top of me, his hand slamming over my mouth. "Don't you make a fucking sound."

Panic thrashes through my veins, his beer-stench breath sending bile surging up my throat. I don't obey his demand and fight with everything I have, hitting him in the chest. It earns me a blow, the back of his hand connecting with my cheek. The crack is so loud it rings in my ears. My vision blurs and my lungs scream for air.

"You've been a bad girl, Grace. I know you fucked him. I could smell him on you when you got back."

He's talking about the weekend I spent with Adam. Not wanting to make him angrier, I lie and shake my head beneath his hand.

He grasps my hair in a painful grip, forcing my eyes to his bloodshot ones. "Don't lie to me. You're a whore, just like your mother was."

My blood heats at the insult, mixing with the dread coursing through me.

He settles himself between my legs and the feel of his erection takes my hysteria to a whole other level. I fight back even harder, refusing to let him make me a victim any longer but I am no match for his strength.

"Consider this payment for everything I have done for you, you ungrateful little bitch." He pushes up with all of his weight on the hand covering my mouth, crushing my jaw.

Defeat settles over me, drowning me into a pit of despair.

"Grace, wake the fuck up!"

I crash out of the nightmare and shoot upright, a scream ripping from my throat. My body is covered in a cold sweat and tears soak my cheeks.

Sawyer's face appears before me, his green eyes filled with concern. "Jesus, are you all right?"

"I'm so sorry." They're the only words I can manage at the moment, my throat raw from screaming.

"Who the fuck is Earl?" he asks.

The mention of his name has a sob bursting from my mouth. I climb onto Sawyer's lap, my arms wrapping around his neck as I absorb the feel of his body; wanting to replace the one I just felt crushing me moments ago.

He holds me close, his hand coasting up my back. Once I manage to compose myself, he pulls back to look at me, his eyes hard and determined. "It's time, Grace. I want to know who the fuck he is and what he did to you."

I promised myself to never speak of that man again; to pretend he never existed but there's no use. He will always plague me, just like Miguel.

Gazing back at Sawyer, I finally decide to open up and for the first time in my life, I tell another soul what I went through after I lost my mother.

Sawyer

Rage has me wound tight, every muscle in my body coiled and restricted. The fear in Grace's eyes is a damn good indication that whatever I'm about to hear is only going to drive this overwhelming fury higher.

"He hated me," she whispers. "He just…hated me so much, and I don't know why."

I shove aside my emotions for the time being and bring her to lie down with me, holding her close. "Who is he?"

"My uncle," she answers. "Since my father wasn't on my birth certificate I didn't have a legal guardian after Mama passed away. I knew she had a brother, but she rarely spoke about him, she said they never got along. I eventually understood why but not before it was too late…"

She pauses, collecting herself.

"A couple of days after the murder, he came to the police station. He was nice and seemed to genuinely care about what happened to Mama. He told me he hated how his relationship with her turned out and wanted to help me. He offered for me to come stay with him in Virginia. Since I didn't have any other options, I accepted."

She pushes up on her elbow, lifting her eyes to mine, revealing what looks a hell of a lot like shame.

"You have to understand, Sawyer, I had no one, no other family. Not even my friends' parents offered to take me in."

"Hey." I cup her cold cheek, my fingers grazing her soft skin. "You don't have to justify anything to me, Cupcake. You've done nothing wrong. I just want to know what happened."

Her eyes drift shut and she takes a hard swallow before continuing. "The first six months weren't that bad, but I quickly realized he was not at all who he portrayed to be. He drank excessively and never held down a job. Yet he was buying things for himself, including a new truck, and I never understood where he was getting the money from since we rarely had food in the house."

Her jaw ticks, the first sign of anger peeking through her despair.

"When I started questioning it he became angry and defensive and that's when living with him became unbearable. He'd hit my shoulder with his, hard enough to leave a mark, or stick his foot out when I walked by to trip me. He always claimed it was an accident but the hate in his eyes told me otherwise. Once the trial was over, I got a job so I could make enough money to leave. I stayed away as often as I could but it wasn't often enough." Her words trail off on the saddest whisper.

I brush a piece of hair off her shoulder, hoping to offer a small measure of comfort.

"One night we got into a fight about having a funeral for Mama. We had both agreed to wait until after the trial to have one, but he kept prolongin' it. Well, that night he told me he wasn't payin' for a funeral. He said he'd already paid for her to be cremated and that was enough."

Who doesn't give their own sister a fucking funeral?

"I asked him about the money from her life insurance, said we could use that. That's when I found out he spent it. All of it, Sawyer, that's where the new truck came from, all the new shit he had bought, he spent all of her money that was supposed to be for me."

My muscles tense, jaw flexing so hard I fear it's about to snap.

"It didn't take me long to realize that's the only reason why he asked me to come live with him. He wanted any money there was. That night I tore out of the house and purchased a bus ticket to go see Adam. Only, when I got there he wasn't the person I remembered and well…you know how that turned out."

I do, and to know he did that to her when she needed him most only pisses me off more.

"After that, I truly felt like I had no one. I ended up going back to Earl's to pack my stuff and leave for good. I had a little bit of money hidden in my room. Not much but enough to take care of myself for a few weeks until I could find another job. Only, when I got back, my room was in disarray and the money I had been saving was gone. He took it all. I was furious and told him so, and I paid the price dearly for it."

Those last few words have fear boiling in my gut. "What does that mean?"

"He hit me," she whispers. "He backhanded me so hard I fell to the ground and he didn't stop. He took off his belt and whipped me repeatedly." Her eyes lift to mine, tears streaming down her cheeks. "He hit me so much, Sawyer, I couldn't walk for days."

I pull her into my arms, fighting to breathe through the fiery rage pounding in my veins. All I see is red, dark and rich, his blood that I will shed when I extract my revenge.

"I stayed in bed until I was well enough and knew I couldn't stay. I couldn't wait for more money. But the night before I could make my escape he took his volatile feelings for me to another level."

I have a feeling I know what level she's about to tell me but I pray I'm wrong.

"His girlfriend, Candy, was sleeping over. She was a drunk like him, but nicer and she was a good distraction. Usually she kept him away from me, but not that night." She pauses, her entire body beginning to tremble.

"What did he do, Grace?" I ask, my voice tight.

Her breath hitches, tears of sorrow once again staining her cheeks. "He came into my room and forced himself on me," she cries. "He told me it was payment for takin' me in. I fought with everythin' I had, but I couldn't get him off of me, I was still weak from the beating he gave me."

Fire races through my blood, fury barreling through me at the thought of him touching her. "He raped you?" My voice doesn't even sound like mine. Cold, hard—detached.

She shakes her head, sending relief through my fiery chest.

"His girlfriend woke up and called for him. It gave me the chance I needed. The moment he snuck back out of my room, I packed everything I owned and climbed out my window, never looking back. I took a bus with the intention to go see my father but I chickened out, fearing for his rejection. I knew my heart wouldn't be able to handle another blow. Not at that time."

Can't say I blame her. I'm surprised her heart handled all she had been through up until that point.

"I ended up meetin' a really nice, old lady on the bus. She told me about Sunset Bay and how beautiful it was. Since it was close to Charleston, I decided to check it out until I had the courage to face my father. It was then I stumbled upon the diner and met Mac…my angel." The softest smile steals her sad lips but my emotions are too all over the place to share in her one salvation she found.

She should have been protected but instead was betrayed.

"Want to know the worst of it all?" she whispers.

I gaze back into her defeated eyes, wondering how much worse it could get.

"I left without her," she chokes out.

My brows bunch in confusion. "Without who?"

"Mama. He took her ashes from me, just to be cruel, and I don't know where he hid her. I wasn't able to search again before leaving that night. I just left her there," she cries, her expression twisting with guilt. "I can't believe I left her with him."

I hold her close as she breaks into another sob. "Don't you dare blame yourself for that, Grace. You did the right thing by leaving. I'll get her back for you, I promise."

Right after I make the son of a bitch pay.

She bolts upright, her eyes wide with fear. "No, you can't! You can't go anywhere near him or he'll know where I am. He will find me."

"Whoa, baby, calm down," I say, reaching for her.

"No!" She slaps my hand away. "I mean it, Sawyer. Promise me that you won't ever go near him. That you won't tell a soul about this."

"I promise." The lie flows seamlessly from my lips, guilt following soon after because I won't be keeping that promise. Vengeance will be extracted and no mercy will be shown.

"You must think I'm so weak," she whispers brokenly.

I pull her down and roll over top of her, my chest covering hers. "No. You're the strongest woman I've ever met. You survived all of this, Grace, and look at the person you are. You're beautiful…" I lean in, pressing a kiss to the corner of her eye. "Kind…" My lips skim across her damp cheek to the spot I crave most. "And so damn sweet." The last word leaves me on a growl right before I capture her pretty pink lips with mine.

Her fingers wind in my hair, holding me there, the taste of her tears flooding my tongue.

Slowing the kiss, I rest my forehead on hers. "I know you're scared right now, but I swear, I'll never let anything bad happen to you again. You're not alone anymore. You have me."

She trails her fingers across my jaw, a trembling smile dancing across her lips. "You're my angel too, Sawyer. Just like Mac."

My eyes narrow. "But a badass angel, right?"

I'm rewarded with one of her sweet giggles. "Very badass and sexy," she adds.

"Damn straight."

Her smile fades, her expression turning somber. "Thank you for always bein' here for me."

"You don't have to thank me, Cupcake. I told you, I take care of what's mine. I'm not going anywhere."

She curls a hand around the back of my neck and pulls me down for another kiss. I happily oblige her, vowing so much more to her in that moment than she could ever know.

CHAPTER 38

Sawyer

I pull up to Jaxson and Julia's house the next day, parking next to Cade's truck. Grace gazes out her window, her shoulders slumped in defeat. I hate seeing her like this. I want my Cupcake happy again.

"You ready, baby?"

She turns toward me, faking a smile for my benefit and nods.

Climbing out of the truck, I walk around and help her down. Once on her feet, I curl an arm around her waist and pull her against me, my fingertips brushing the soft skin of her cheek. "You okay?"

She peers up at me, the answer to my question reflecting in her sad eyes. Instead of answering, she stretches up on her tiptoes and brushes a kiss on my lips. "I am now."

Growling, I cup her ass and lift her into my arms. Her legs curl around my waist and arms around my neck. My mouth descends, tongue parting her lips for more. She gives me the access I crave, her fingers driving in my hair as I inhale all of her, the sweet taste of her settling deep within my chest.

Eventually, I break the kiss, my forehead resting against hers. "If a kiss makes you happy, then just say the word and my mouth will never leave yours again."

A more genuine smile teases her lips. "As long as I'm yours. I'll always be happy."

This girl is fucking perfect.

"You're mine, Grace. Never doubt that." I seal the words with another kiss, keeping this one brief, then lower her to her feet. "Let's go. The sooner I speak with Jaxson and Cade the sooner I will have you to myself again."

Her giggle penetrates the air as I drag her behind me.

Julia opens the door, greeting us with a smile. "Hey, guys, come in," she says, stepping aside for us to enter.

Grace walks in first, pulling her into a hug. "Hi, Julia."

I follow in after her and wrap my arms around both of them, squeezing them until they're laughing.

"Where's your spaz of a husband?" I ask.

"In the kitchen. Go do your man talk. I'm taking Grace up to the baby's room." She smiles at Grace. "We bought the baby furniture yesterday."

"Oh my gosh. That's so darn excitin'."

They bound up the stairs, leaving me in the privacy I need. I head for the kitchen; that buried rage I've been managing to keep within threatening to explode.

"Hey," Jaxson greets me, both he and Cade nodding as I take a seat.

"Hey."

"So what's up?" Jaxson asks.

"I need a favor."

"Shoot."

"I need you to get an address from Cooper for me."

Suspicion dominates his expression. "Whose?"

"Earl Morgan. He's Grace's uncle. He lives in Virginia but I can't find his address for some reason."

He leans back in his chair, crossing his arms over his chest. "Why don't you just ask Grace?"

"Because she can't know about this."

His eyes dart to Cade before returning to me. "I'm not getting shit for you until you tell me more."

I figured it wouldn't be that easy.

"Look. He has something that belongs to her. I need to get it back and he needs to pay for a few things."

"What kind of things?" Cade asks.

I shake my head. "I can't tell you guys, I promised Grace. But trust me when I say the son of a bitch needs to pay for what he did to her."

"What makes you think Cooper has his address?" Jaxson asks.

"He told us at the gym that he saw the case file and she lived with an uncle in Virginia. I know he either has it or can get it for me."

There's a moment of silence before he lets out a heavy breath. "What's your plan? I don't want Coop getting in shit over this."

"I'm not going to kill him if that's what you're asking me but he has to pay, Jaxson."

"I'll go with you," Cade says, backing me up like I knew he would.

I nod my thanks at him then look back at Jaxson, cocking a brow. "You going to help me or not?" I'll be shocked if he doesn't. We made a pact on the battlefield and it followed us out of war.

"I'll get the address from Coop and come with you, too."

"Thanks. Whatever happens, don't take no for an answer. We need that address," I say, and decide to tell him just how much rides on this. "He has her mom's ashes. We need to get them back."

"I'll get it," he promises.

"Good. And don't tell Julia any of this either. Grace can't know."

"Fuck me! That's just perfect. Ask me to lie to my wife."

"I'm not telling you to lie to her. I'm just telling you to withhold the information for now. She'll forgive you."

Hopefully, Grace forgives me too, but even if she's angry it will be worth it if it means giving her back the one person she loves most.

CHAPTER 39

Sawyer

Nights go by with no more news and it's making me antsy as hell. I want this fucker to show himself already. To make his move so I can finally end this once and for all.

My attention is pulled away from the television when Grace steps out of the bathroom in nothing but a towel, freshly showered and holding her cell phone up to her ear.

"Mac, I told ya, I ain't bringin' you sausage pie to the hospital. I'm sorry but the doctor said your cholesterol is high, so that's the worst thing for you right now."

My cock hardens as she walks past the living room into the kitchen. Standing, I follow in after her and see the dog whining at the back door. I walk over to let him out but the moment she bends down to grab something out of the dishwasher, my dick has me changing directions.

I come up behind her, grabbing her hips. She lets out a squawk and steadies herself against the counter, shooting me a dirty look over her shoulder.

"No, sorry. I tripped," she says, relaying the lie to Mac over the phone. She shoves me back then moves to the sink, thinking this will keep me away.

Silly, Cupcake.

I come up behind her once again, my hands going around her waist as my lips press against the base of her neck that's still damp with water. A low growl erupts from my throat when her cupcake scent impales my senses.

"No, that was Sawyer, believe it or not. He gets like that when he's hungry," she says, elbowing me.

I'm fucking hungry all right. My hand drops to the front of her leg, trailing up her silky thigh.

A shiver claims her body and I know I have her right where I want her. "Ah, hmmm."

I chuckle as she tries to form words.

The dog's whining gets louder but I ignore it.

Sorry, buddy, but my cock is in much more need at the moment.

"Mac, I'll call you right back, okay? Love you, too. Bye." Hanging up, she rests back against me, giving me more access to slip my hand under her towel. "You could have waited until I was off the phone," she scolds but it trails into a moan when I tease the inside of her thigh, right next to her sweet spot.

"If you walk around here like this there's no fucking way I'm keeping my hands to myself."

The whimper she releases has my hand inching even closer, ready to inflict the best kind of pleasure. That's until something out in the backyard snags my attention, freezing my hand in its place. Every muscle in my body tenses as I stare out into the dark, waiting to see it again.

"Sawyer?" Grace whispers, picking up on my sudden change of mood.

I remain still and silent, my eyes trained on the back corner of the yard and it's then I see the subtle shift again amongst the trees.

Adrenaline surges through my veins, knowing the time has finally come. Slowly, I turn Grace around to face me, pulling her in close. The dog's whining kicks up another notch and he starts clawing at the door.

I finally realize he's known all along, and I'm pissed at myself for letting my emotions get in the way.

Grace fists my shirt, her body trembling. "What's going on, Sawyer?"

"Don't make any sudden moves."

"Oh god, someone's out there, aren't they?"

I hug her closer, wishing I could erase her fear. "Listen to me. Everything is going to be fine but I need you to do exactly what I tell you to. Understand?"

She nods against my chest, her breathing coming in short, hard pants.

I dip my head, resting my lips at her temple while keeping my eyes trained outside. "I want you to walk out of here slowly and go into your room to call Cooper. Do you remember where I put the gun?"

"Yes," she answers shakily.

"Keep it with you and don't open the door for any reason until I tell you to. If someone comes in there, Grace, you shoot first and ask questions later, do you understand?"

"I can't do this," she chokes out.

"Yes, you can. I got you. I promise."

"Please be careful," she whispers, tears thick in her voice.

"Don't worry about me, baby. I'm good. Now go, but walk naturally. I don't want to tip him off."

Giving her a gentle push, I don't look behind me and pray she does what I said. I flick on the tap, letting the water run then reach down with one hand and open the cupboard, grabbing the gun I have strapped there. Once in my hand, I shut off the light, blanketing the kitchen into darkness.

It's then I spot the motherfucker just as he takes a step back into the bush. I inch toward the door, my hard eyes never leaving that spot. The house behind him turns on their backlight, sending him bolting across the yard.

"Fuck!" I take off out the door, my feet pounding the hard ground. The dog barks and follows me out, catching up to him faster than me but just misses his ankle as he hops the fence.

Picking up speed, I leap over the dog then jump over the rickety wood right after him. Sirens explode through the air and brakes screech to a halt in front of the house. Cooper flies out of the passenger side of the squad car and intercepts the asshole, taking him down.

The guy bellows in rage, thrashing around as he's cuffed.

I tuck the gun behind me and start over to them, fury pumping through my body with unrelenting force. "Is it him?" I bite out the question, already knowing the answer.

Cooper hauls the bastard to his feet and confiscates a large knife from him. The thought of what he planned to do with it sends me over the edge.

My anger spins into a spool of rage and I charge at him. "You fucked with the wrong girl, motherfucker."

"Shit! Grab him!" Cooper orders to the deputy as he tries to turn Miguel out of harm's way but there's no stopping me.

My fists are quick, striking out hard and fast, knocking him from Cooper's hold. I follow him to the ground, delivering blow after blow. Hands grab at me, but I don't let them slow me down, relishing in the tiny bones I feel crushing beneath my fist.

A force hits me from the side, the impact penetrating the roaring in my ears. Cooper pins me down while the deputy pulls the bastard to his feet again, his face mangled and soaked with blood.

"What the hell are you thinking?" Cooper bellows.

"It's the least he deserves," I snap, my lungs heaving in fury. "For Grace, for her mom, and for Mac."

"He will pay, Sawyer, but not this way. Let the law handle it."

"He came onto my fucking property to hurt her! He's lucky he's not dead."

"Justice will be served. I'll make sure of it."

The only justice he deserves is death.

"Are you good now? Can I let you up?"

I nod.

He releases me and I climb to my feet.

"How did you get here so fast?" I ask.

"A neighbor called before Grace did. The people behind her said they saw someone hop the fence into her yard."

"And you didn't think to call and give me a heads-up?"

His eyes narrow. "I did and you never picked up."

I pat my pockets, realizing I don't have my phone on me.

Shit!

"Sawyer?"

The soft sound of Grace's voice has me spinning around. She stands at the front door, arms crossed over herself, her terrified eyes fixated on Miguel.

"Grace, get back in the house, now!"

A roar penetrates the same moment Miguel manages to break out of the deputy's hold, his hands cuffed behind him. "You bitch. I'm going to kill you!"

Cooper and I move at the same time but I'm faster. I take him to the ground once again, pulling my gun from behind me and shoving it under his chin. "You will never get to her because I will always be here, waiting to drive this bullet through your fucking skull."

The son of a bitch actually smiles, his bloodstained teeth gleaming at me. "Do it. I dare you. Come on, shoot me."

It's so damn tempting. He'd finally get the fate he deserves.

Cooper's hand rests on my shoulder. "He's not worth it, Sawyer."

Miguel's grin spreads as I hesitate. "I'm going to fuck her like I did her mother, then I'm going to cut her up into—"

Taking the butt of my gun, I coldcock the motherfucker, refusing to let him finish the threat.

"Damn it, Sawyer!" Cooper snaps, pulling me off him.

I turn on him, my body vibrating with restraint. "Get him out of my fucking sight before I change my mind and shoot him."

"What the hell do you think I'm trying to do? Get in the house and go take care of Grace. I got this."

My eyes shift back to Grace where she still stands by the door, her face pale with fear. The terror and anguish that bleed from her puts me in motion. She snaps out of her fear when she sees me moving for her. She bounds down the steps, leaping into my arms with a sob.

"It's okay, baby. It's over now," I say quietly, carrying her into the house. "He won't ever hurt you again."

It's a promise I intend to keep for as long as I live.

CHAPTER 40

Grace

That night sleep evades me, too many emotions banging around inside of my wounded soul. The police were here for hours, questioning Sawyer and collecting all the evidence they could from the scene. By the time they left, my stomach was a giant knot and I was emotionally spent, yet here I still lie, staring up at the dark ceiling hours later.

Glancing at the clock, I see it's just past three. I finally give up and climb out of bed, careful not to wake Sawyer. After slipping on my Alpine thigh-highs and grabbing my thin cardigan, I head into the kitchen to start on the pies I'm going to bring to Julia's for Thanksgiving. Music fills the silence when I flick on the old radio that sits on my counter, hoping the soft melody will be able to calm me.

I've never felt so many conflicting feelings as I do in this moment. Fear and anger tear through me at seeing Miguel again after all these years, the despicable monster who stole my mother's life and took away the only loving family I had. Yet relief is there, battling with all the other emotions, glad to know that Detective Rodriguez has him and is taking him back to Florida. But most of all…I feel lost.

What happens now? Where do I go from here?

The diner is gone, Mac is still in the hospital because of all this, and Sawyer…our relationship is the one thing that scares me most right now. Will he leave? There's really no reason for him to stay here anymore. Yet, the thought of not being with him every day and feeling his arms around me every night as I drift off to sleep leaves me with a panic I can't bear to think about.

It's something I should be used to. I have been on my own for a long time now, but since Sawyer's been here I'm reminded what it feels like to not be alone anymore. To fall asleep in someone's arms then wake up to their dashing smile. It's even better when that someone is Sawyer and the thought of not feeling him next to me anymore when I sleep kills a small part of me.

Sighing, I blink back the tears threatening to fall and begin rolling out my dough. One of my all-time favorite songs "With or Without You" by U2 quietly filters through the air, dancing along my skin. I begin humming to the tune and it isn't long before I feel someone at my back, a tingle of awareness tickling my spine. It's the same feelin' I always get when Sawyer is near, a warmth that floods every part of my body, especially my heart.

"It's just me, Cupcake, don't beat me with that rolling pin," he teases, bringing a smile to my face as he crowds my back, his arms bringing me the comfort I so desperately need. "Couldn't sleep?" he asks, his deep, gravelly voice whispering in my ear and eliciting goose bumps across my heated flesh.

I shake my head.

Bringing his hands to my shoulders, he turns me around to face him, my gaze colliding with his strong chest. One that's decorated with a tattoo of his honor, flawed with scars, and the one place my cheek loves to sleep against.

He curls his fingers under my chin, forcing my eyes to his. "Talk to me, Grace."

Unable to voice what I'm feeling at the moment, I drop my sweater to the floor and remove my tank top, baring myself to him from the waist up.

His sharp intake of breath penetrates the air, seconds before he snakes an arm around my lower back and brings me flush against his hard chest. I gaze up into his handsome face, my pulse skipping. When he leans down, my eyes close and I wait with bated breath for that first touch of his lips, but it never comes. Instead of kissing me like I expect him to, he lifts me slightly off the ground until my feet land on top of his.

Every muscle in my body stills and my eyes spring back open to see his lips kicked up in a sexy smirk.

"No judging, Cupcake, I'm not the best dancer, but for you, I'll try."

My heart tumbles in my chest when his feet start shifting from side to side. In my kitchen, he dances with me to one of my all-time favorite songs, giving me the one moment I always wished I got to experience with my father. A man who never wanted me.

This moment is so much better.

I press my lips against his strong, steady heartbeat before I rest my cheek there. Once again, I close my eyes and soak in everything about this moment, knowing it will be one I will cherish forever. I absorb the feel of just him and me, skin to skin, our scents mingling in the air between us. It's as if we are in our own world, one no one can be a part of but us. It's beautiful, safe, and the most perfect thing I have ever felt. It's one I want to stay in for the rest of my life.

The last thought has my earlier turmoil resurfacing, and I become anxious once again for the unknown. Gatherin' my courage, I keep my cheek against his steady heartbeat and ask the one question I fear the most. "What happens now, Sawyer?"

He stills at my whispered question. His hands travel up my back to cup either side of my face as he brings my gaze to his. "What do you want to happen?"

"I'm not sure but I know I don't want you to go." I lick my sudden dry lips before revealing to him the one thing I am sure of. "I'm in love with you."

His eyes widen, a heavy silence descending upon us.

Oh god, what did I just do?

My heart bangs inside of my chest, fearing I just messed this up. Instead of back-tracking like I want to, I swallow nervously and decide to just let it all out. "I'm sorry if you don't want to hear those words, but I won't take them back because I mean them. I love everythin' about you. I love how you can make me laugh, even if there's nothing to smile about. I love the way you touch me, whether it's slow and gentle or fast and urgent. Heck, I love you even when you're arrogant and cocky. I never know if I want to slap or kiss that sexy face of yours."

His lips twitch, giving me the courage to continue.

"But most of all…I love this," I whisper, placing another kiss directly over his heart. "I love how you make me feel when I'm with you—safe and important—like for the first time, since my mama died, maybe I matter to someone again."

Hot tears begin spilling down my cheeks as I terrifyingly pour my heart out to him.

"I love you with my whole heart and nothin' or no one will ever change that. And now that the danger is over, the thought of you not bein' here anymore, of not feeling you against me as I sleep, it scares me to death." I bite my lip to stifle the sob wanting to slip free and wait for him to say something, my terrified heart pounding in anticipation.

Leaning down, he presses a kiss to the corner of my eye, catching my flow of tears before trailing his warm lips across my damp cheek, stopping just before my ear. "I have to tell you something, Cupcake, and I hope you're going to be able to handle it."

Defeat settles over me, heavy and hard, my eyes closing in despair.

"I loved you first." The whispered words graze my ear and yank me from my devastation.

"Huh?" I blurt out, unsure if I just heard him right.

His handsome face appears before me, wearing that trademark sexy smirk of his. "I said, I loved you first."

A breath of relief escapes the confines of my chest, a sob of joy tumbling past my lips.

His expression sobers as his fingertips stroke my wet cheek. "I don't know when it happened, Grace, but I'm pretty sure I loved you before I even met you. From the first moment I inhaled your sweet cupcake scent, I knew you were mine. You don't just matter to me, baby, you fucking belong to me, every inch of you. There's no going back now."

Warmth, happiness, and love explode through my chest as a huge smile takes over my face. Jumping up, I wrap my arms around his neck and kiss the ever-lovin' hell out of him.

"I love you, I love you, I love you!" I mumble against his lips. Saying those words feels so freeing and so darn right.

"I love you too, baby." He crushes me against his chest and takes control of the kiss, his mouth dominating mine. An explosion of heat whips through my body and I claw to get closer, needing more. Groaning, he severs the contact of our mouths, trailing his lips down the side of my neck.

"Sawyer, I need you so bad."

"Tell me what you want and I'll give it to you."

As soon as the words leave his mouth, I push against his chest and drop to my knees before him, my face coming in direct line with his erection. I slip my fingers in his waistband and peer up at him through heavy-lidded eyes. "I want to know what you taste like."

His jaw flexes, lust glowing wildly in his green irises. He threads his fingers through my hair, winding the thick strands around his fist. "Then take it, it's all fucking yours."

I push his underwear down just enough to free his erection. With both hands, I grasp his smooth, hard cock and stroke firmly from base to tip.

A hiss escapes his clenched teeth, his hips surging forward to pump himself into my hand. A pearly white liquid forms on the tip, making my mouth water. Leaning in, I take a long, leisurely lick, loving the erotic taste of him.

A groan shreds his throat, the rough sound encouraging me further. This time when I lean in, I take all of him into my mouth, my lips closing around his shaft as I take him as deep as I can go, my hand stroking where my mouth can't reach.

"That's it, baby, take all of me." His fingers tighten in my hair, creating a delicious sting that increases the pulse between my legs.

Hollowing my cheeks, I suck my way back to the top and give him a show, swirling my tongue around the tip of him.

With a growl, he takes control and begins thrusting his cock in and out of my mouth. I give into it freely, humming my approval, loving the wild look in his eyes.

"Jesus, you're a sight right now. The way your pretty lips look wrapped around my cock while I fuck your mouth, Grace, it beats out every fucking fantasy I had."

I moan from his dirty words, my panties becoming insanely wet. When he thrusts again, hitting the back of my throat, I grab his hips to keep him there and swallow.

An animalistic sound erupts from his chest seconds before he pulls himself away and hauls me to my feet.

"Why did you…" My question falls flat at the raw expression on his face.

Spinning me around, he brings my back against his hard chest and cups both of my breasts, his thumbs tormenting my aching nipples.

Moaning, I drop my head back to his shoulder, relishing in the sensations he evokes within my body.

"As much as I love your mouth, Cupcake, I want to come inside your tight pussy."

A shiver of anticipation dances down my spine as he coasts his hand down my stomach, slipping it into my shorts. His two fingers delve into my wet slit, teasing my throbbing clit.

"You want it too, don't you?" he growls, his lips brushing my ear. "Want my cock buried deep in your pussy."

Lord, I love it when he talks like this to me, his voice thick with lust and tight with restraint.

"Yes," I respond, my breath racing past my lips.

"How do you want it, baby? Fast and hard or slow and deep?"

"All of it. As long as it's you, I don't care."

"It will always be me. Forever, Grace, you belong to me."

"Forever," I agree.

Disappointment crushes me when he removes his fingers from between my legs. Before I can beg for his touch, he grabs each one of my wrists and braces my hands on the kitchen table before me, forcing me to bend over.

"Keep them there."

The authority in his voice has a shiver wracking my body.

His lips press against my shoulder then continues their way down my back, leaving goose bumps in their wake. His hands mold over the lace cupping my bottom as he kneels behind me.

"Your ass was made for my hands, Grace. Just like the rest of you." He grips the material at my hips and shreds them from my body in one hard pull, leaving me in nothing but my Alpine thigh-highs.

A gasp parts my lips, trailing into a heated moan. The air whispering across my bare flesh only serves to drive my need higher.

Sawyer turns, situating himself between my legs, his mouth only a breath away from where I ache. Using two fingers, he spreads me open for his viewing. "Look how pretty your clit is."

"Sawyer," I whimper, my body trembling in need.

"Tell me what you want, Grace."

"Lick me, touch me, just…do somethin', please," I beg, desperate for him to put me out of this sweet misery.

He buries his mouth against me, his tongue lapping at my throbbing flesh. A keening cry pours from my lips, my knees buckling at the pleasure whipping through me.

Sawyer cups my bottom to keep me upright, his tongue wreaking the most beautiful havoc. My hips have a mind of their own and I begin grinding against his mouth in greedy desperation, feeling my impending orgasm.

He groans his approval, the vibration of it rocking me to my core. When his hands move from my bottom to my breasts, fingers teasing my aching nipples, I shatter. I sob out my orgasm, soaring to an incredible world that only Sawyer can send me. Time becomes nothing more than an afterthought as I drift back to reality.

I drop down on the table, arms braced so I don't melt into a puddle right here on the floor. He shifts out from under me then his bare hard chest is covering my back as he comes up behind me again. His fingers grasp my chin and he turns my face to the side, his lips claiming mine in a heart-stealing kiss.

"See how fucking good you taste? I could eat you for hours, baby, and never tire of it."

Moaning, I grind back against him, my pussy craving another part of him.

"I'm finally going to fuck you with nothing on but these sexy socks and I'm going to enjoy every minute of it," his voice is rough in my ear, the promise of more sending a shiver down my spine. "Straighten your arms," he commands.

I obey, my breath racing as I wait with anticipation.

He kicks my legs apart, widening my stance. His fingers dig into the flesh of my hips seconds before he plunges inside of me with one quick thrust.

The beautiful invasion has his name ripping from my throat.

"So tight," he groans, his voice gruff with pleasure. "You good, Grace?"

"Yes. Don't stop!" I beg breathlessly.

He gives me what I want, fucking me hard and fast, every stroke more perfect than the last. My fingers grip the table tighter, it bangs against the wall from his force. The carnal way he takes me is raw and wild, the most perfect thing I have ever felt. Heat coils low in my tummy, my inner walls gripping his relentless cock.

"You're close. I can feel it, baby. Give it to me." His hand lands across my bare ass with a resounding smack and the sharp, erotic sting sends me propelling over the edge for a second time.

My senses reel as the most incredible sensations ravage my body. If not for the table I'd be down on my knees. Sawyer stills inside of me and follows, his sweat soaked chest melding to my back. His lips find my shoulder, raining gentle kisses along my damp skin. The tender act brings a smile to my face, a complete contradiction to the savage way he just took me. Both are equally beautiful.

"Was that too much?" he asks, concern edging his gruff voice.

I shake my head. "It was perfect."

He drops his forehead against my back. "That's because you're perfect."

I smile, my heart melting to the same temperature as my body.

After cleaning up, he pulls his underwear back in place then lifts me into his strong arms. My head rests on his shoulder as he carries me to bed and that's where I stay for the rest of the night. If I'm really lucky, it's where I'll be forever.

CHAPTER 41

Grace

"I can't believe you did this," I shriek, feeling aghast as I stare down at the three pies on my lap, a single slice missing from each of them, all thanks to Sawyer. I'm absolutely horrified to show up at Thanksgiving dinner with these.

My annoyance only rises when he glances over at me from the driver's seat, a look of mock innocence resting on his ridiculously handsome face. "I like how you immediately blame me for the missing slices," he says. "How do you know it wasn't that dog of yours? That little bastard is a pig, he's constantly trying to swipe food from somewhere."

"Yes, I'm sure Chuckie cut a perfect triangle from each pie. Did he wash the knife after, too?" I ask, gazing at him for the fool he is.

He chuckles, his husky laugh filling the truck.

"It's not funny! I'm mortified that I'm bringing half eaten pies to Thanksgiving dinner."

"Oh, come on. You act like I ate the whole damn pie, when all I did was take a sliver of each."

"A sliver? A sliver?" I screech. "Sawyer, a quarter of each pie is missin'."

He shrugs. "You were in the shower and I got hungry."

I shake my head. "You are unbelievable."

"Whatever. You're *my* woman, which means I get exclusive rights to all of you, including your pies. These assholes are lucky I'm willing to share any of it with them."

My mouth drops open and I gape at him for his audacity. I'm about to tell him exactly where he can shove his exclusive rights when he looks over at me with a dirty grin, flashing me an equally sexy wink.

I bite back a smile, my irritation fading. "What am I gonna do with you, Sawyer Evans?"

"I have a few ideas." By the hungry look in his eyes, I know exactly where his thoughts are. That one look alone has my body humming. "I'm serious, Cupcake, that classy-ass dress of yours has me wanting to do all sorts of dirty things to you."

I glance down at myself, taking in the simple chocolate brown baby-doll dress with cream polka dots. It falls about mid-thigh and my cream dress extender gives the bottom edge some peekaboo lace. If Sawyer thinks this is sexy, just wait until he gets a look at what's beneath it.

The thought has an idea forming—the perfect revenge for eatin' my pies. Smiling, I decide to wait until we get to Julia's; otherwise, we are liable to cause an accident.

"Well, you look pretty darn good yourself, Sexy Sawyer."

He looks good every day but especially today. He's a little dressier than usual, wearin' a nicer pair of faded jeans, and a white fitted tee with a jade green button-down shirt over top that's been left undone. The long sleeves are rolled a quarter of the way up, showing off his cut forearms and bronzed skin.

It's ridiculous how hot this man is.

"If you don't stop looking at me like that, baby, I'm going to pull this bad boy over and fuck you right here on the side of the road."

My eyes dart away and heat invades my cheeks for getting busted. Dang it. His aviators hid his knowing eyes from me.

Clearing my throat, I ignore his comment and change the topic. "Is it all right if we don't stay too terribly late this evening? I want to stop by the hospital and spend some time with Mac. I hate that he's spending Thanksgivin' on his own."

"Yeah, Cupcake. Don't worry, I'll make sure you see him tonight."

This man does so many wonderful things to my heart.

"I forgot to tell you that Kayla texted me this morning. We're going shopping on Tuesday for our bridesmaid dresses. Are you still going out of town with Jaxson and Cade that day?"

"Yeah. We're leaving early in the morning but we'll be back later that night."

"Works out perfect then," I say, smiling over at him. "Where are y'all goin' anyway?"

There's a brief moment of silence before he answers. "Just picking up something."

My head tilts at his vague answer. There's a subtle shift in his demeanor but it's so quick that I begin to think I imagined it. Before I can think more about it we pull up to Jaxson and Julia's and the moment is forgotten, an almost gleeful smile forming on my lips.

Time for payback.

Just as Sawyer parks the truck, I put the box of pies down next to me and rise up on my knees, facing him. "Hey, Sexy Sawyer?"

"Yeah, baby?" he says, distracted as he removes his sunglasses.

"I just wanted to show you somethin'."

He finally looks over at me and that's when I lift my dress, bunching the material at my hips as I reveal my cream lace panties and matching garter belt that's clipped to my stockings.

His swift inhale penetrates the truck, a hungry expression adorning his face that is both comical and knee weakening. His deer in headlights look has me bursting into laughter.

When he reaches for me, I lean back, pressing against my door. "Uh-uh," I tsk, waving my finger at him mockingly. "No touching. Just like you weren't supposed to touch my pies." With a sassy smile, I pull the handle behind me and jump out of the truck, taking my box of pies with me.

"Grace!" His desperate protest is cut off by the slam of my door.

I hurry up the front steps when I hear him exit the truck, knowing if he catches up to me there is no way I'll be able to resist his touch and we will be later than we already are.

"Grace," he whispers heatedly, "I mean it, you get the fuck back here, right now."

A snicker escapes me as I finish making my way up the stairs.

I lift my hand to knock but Julia ends up opening the door first. "Oh, hey, Grace. I knew I heard someone pull up. Thought maybe you were Grams."

"Nope, just Sawyer and me."

She smiles. "Well, just as exciting. Come in."

Stepping inside, I shift the box of pies under my arm and pull her in for a hug. "Happy Thanksgiving. You look so darn beautiful," I say, loving the burgundy maternity dress she's wearing.

A warm smile rests on her face. "Thank you. So do you." She moves to close the door but swings it back open, peeking her head outside. "Sawyer, what the heck are you doing? Are you coming or not?"

I turn and find Sawyer still standing by the truck, his narrowed eyes promising retribution.

Oh, boy, I'm in trouble.

"I'll be there in a minute. Forgot something in my truck," he mumbles.

I have a feeling I know exactly why he isn't coming in yet.

Thankfully, Julia has no clue. Shrugging, she closes the door. "Come in, everyone is in the kitchen. We're just waiting on Cade and Grams."

She reaches for the box under my arm, her hand halting when she sees the half eaten pies.

My cheeks heat with embarrassment. "I'm so sorry, Julia. Sawyer ate a piece of each pie while I was in the shower. I didn't have enough time to make more before we left."

She chuckles, not seeming the least bit surprised. "Don't worry about it. This is still plenty for everyone. Come on."

I follow her into the kitchen to find a few people already sitting at the kitchen table that has been beautifully decorated for the occasion.

Both Kayla and Katelyn stand to greet me, Kayla hugging me first then Katelyn.

"Happy Thanksgiving, ladies," I say, hugging them back.

Katelyn is another person who has been so nice and acceptin' of me. From the time I moved here she has gone out of her way to make me feel welcome, even giving me deals at her salon. She knows what it's like to move to a small town you didn't grow up in. Over time, she's become more than my esthetician, she's become a good friend.

"Hi, Grace," a sweet, young voice greets me.

I peek around Katelyn to see Anna walking over to me. "Anna, hi." I pull her in for a hug, too. "Don't you look as pretty as ever."

"Thank you." She smiles shyly, running her hands down her dress nervously.

Her boyfriend, Logan, sits at the kitchen table, a scowling Jaxson across from him, glaring daggers at the poor kid.

"Hi, Logan, nice to see you again," I say, giving him a small wave.

"You, too." He seems calm and cool, despite Jaxson's hard unrelenting gaze.

"Jaxson! Give it a rest already," Julia snaps.

He grunts but finally shifts his attention from Logan over to me, acknowledging me with a nod. "Hey, Grace. Glad you could come."

"Thanks, me too."

Cooper approaches me next, his expression soft as he enfolds me in a hug. "Happy Thanksgiving, Grace."

The gesture catches me by surprise but more than anything, it completely warms my heart.

"Happy Thankgivin', Cooper," I whisper, hugging him tight. Coop and I have always had a good relationship but since everything with Miguel I feel like it's become stronger. He's done a lot to protect me, watch out for me like he does for the rest of this town and it means a lot to me.

"Hey, get your hands off my Cupcake!" Sawyer teases, striding into the kitchen.

Giggling, I step back from Cooper and start unloading the pies while he and Sawyer exchange a handshake.

Sawyer continues his greetings, heading for Anna next. "There's our girl." Slinging an arm around her shoulders, he playfully ruffles up her hair. "Lookin' good, kid."

She glares up at him, smoothing the mess he just made. "Why must you always mess my hair? Don't you know that's a sin when it comes to us girls?"

"Should I go mess with your boyfriend instead?" he asks, a cocky smirk resting on his face.

"All right, that's enough," Julia breaks in. "Leave poor Anna alone."

"Yeah, leave me alone," she says, throwing a playful jab to his ribs.

Chuckling, he dodges her attempt and walks over to greet everyone else.

I finish displaying most of my pies on the kitchen island then open the freezer for the ice cream and that's when I feel a hard body move up behind me, crowding my back.

Sawyer's fingers dig into the soft flesh of my hips, his erection pressing into my bottom. "You're going to pay for that little stunt you pulled, Cupcake. I'm going to spank your ass so good, baby, you won't be able to sit down without feeling me."

A shiver skips down my spine, my breath racing as I remember feeling his hand last night when he had me bent over the kitchen table.

"Guys, they're here. Come help please," Julia calls out, penetrating our moment.

Sawyer leans in, his jaw brushing mine as he gives my ear a sharp nip.

If not for the cold air from the freezer, I would melt to the floor right here, right now.

He steps back, giving me the reprieve my overheated body needs before following the others out of the kitchen. Pulling myself together, I close the freezer door and turn around to see that Katelyn, Anna, and Logan are the only ones left with me.

"What's goin' on? Where did everyone go?"

Katelyn flashes me a knowing smile. "Why don't you go see for yourself?"

Frowning, I walk out of the kitchen only to come to a cold, hard stop when I see Sawyer, Jaxson, and Cooper carrying Mac through the door in his wheelchair.

"Mac?" I whisper, blinking in disbelief.

His eyes snap to mine, his battered face splitting into a grin. "Well, hey there, darlin', you mind an old man joinin' you for some turkey dinner?"

The laugh that escapes me tumbles into a sob. Rushing forward, I fall to my knees before him, burying my face into his chest. He wraps his arms around me but they lack their usual strength.

"I can't believe you're here," I cry. "I thought you weren't getting out for another week?"

"I am. I have to go back after dinner but the sheriff here pulled some strings and got me out for the evening. I couldn't pass up Miss Julia's invitation, not when it meant spending Thanksgiving with my girl."

His girl.

Such simple words mean so much, especially when my own father doesn't even want me.

"I'm so glad you're here," I whisper.

"Me too, darlin'. Me too."

Leaning back, I swipe my wet cheeks and see Cade walk in. It isn't long before I realize he must have brought him here. I face everyone, my heart melting at their generosity. "Thank you all for being so thoughtful."

Julia wipes away her own emotion. "It's our pleasure, Grace, but I'm afraid we can't take all the credit. It was actually Sawyer's idea to surprise you."

My blurry eyes shift to Sawyer, to where he stands leaning against the railing, lookin' rather proud of himself.

I should have known this was all him—the sweet, sexy, arrogant son of a gun.

Kayla clears her throat, breaking the sudden silence invading the room. "Why don't we head into the kitchen and, well…oh hell, let's just leave these two alone for a minute."

My eyes never leave Sawyer's as everyone exits the room. Slowly, I start forward. His eyes travel the length of my body, heat darkening his green irises. I have no doubt he's thinkin' about what I have beneath this dress.

Smiling, I push up on my tiptoes, wrapping my arms around his neck. He hugs me close, his hard body crushing mine as he lightly lifts me off my feet. Unable to put into words what he means to me, I decide to show him. My lips land on his, deep and passionate, the warmth in my heart spreading right to the tips of my fingers and toes.

By the time I pull back, we're both breathless.

My hands rest against his hard jaw, my feet continuing to dangle off the floor as I peer into his handsome face. "I love you, Sawyer. Thank you for bringin' Mac here today. It means more to me than you'll ever know."

"Anything for my Cupcake."

I didn't think it was possible to love this man any more than I already do, but I was very wrong.

"Does this mean I'm forgiven for eating your pie?" he asks hopefully.

"Oh, yes, you're more than forgiven. In fact, I'm gonna make you your very own special pie. One that no one else can eat but you."

"Good, and I want you to deliver it wearing nothing but what you have on under here." His hand slips between us, traveling up the inside of my thigh and grasping one of the straps that are clipped to my stocking.

"Does this mean you're not gonna spank me tonight after all?" I ask, surprised I can even form a coherent word at the moment.

His eyes hold mine. "That depends."

"On?"

"You." His hand moves to my backside, cupping one cheek, squeezing the supple flesh. "Do you want me to spank this pretty ass, Grace?"

"Yes," I breathe. "I liked it when you did it to me last night." The confession falls shamelessly past my lips, my need for him growing by the second.

Growling, his mouth claims mine once again, his lips hot and eager. My fingers drive into his hair, gripping and urgent. I forget everyone else but him, drowning in this perfect world that only he and I create.

In a quick move, he withdraws his hand from under my dress and places me back on my feet. My heavy eyes open, mind spinning. I'm about to ask why he stopped when Julia breezes past my back.

"Don't mind me. Just grabbing the door."

Feeling mortified, I push away from Sawyer and smooth my hands down my dress, making myself presentable.

Goodness, I didn't even hear anyone knock.

Julia is nice enough not to acknowledge our inappropriate behavior and swings the door open to reveal Grams.

"Hi, my sweet Julia," Grams greets her, kissing each one of her cheeks before bending down to press one to her tummy. "And how's my darling great grandbaby today?"

Julia's smile glows with her happiness. "The baby is great. Hungry though, the smell of turkey cooking all day has been torture."

"I'll bet it has," she snickers, patting her shoulder.

"Hi, Grams," I greet her with a smile. "Happy Thanksgivin'."

"Oh, Grace, my dear. You look beautiful." She links her elderly arm with mine and gives me a kiss on the cheek. "How are you doing, sweetheart?"

"I'm doin' well. Thank you."

Her gaze shifts to Sawyer behind me and she practically beams with excitement. "Sawyer, you sly devil." She lugs me behind her as she marches up to him. Her hand tangles in his shirt and she forces him to bend down so she can kiss his cheek.

He soaks up every bit of her attention, even kissing her cheek in return.

Such a charmer.

"I hope you've been taking good care of our sweet Grace here," she says, flashing me a kind smile.

"You bet. Her butt has been in good hands."

My eyes narrow, not missing his double meaning.

By Grams's snicker, it seems she doesn't either. "Oh, I'll just bet it has."

Julia saves me from further embarrassment. "All right, Grams, let's take you into the kitchen so you can say the rest of your hellos."

I flash her a grateful look and follow them into the kitchen, but not before delivering Sawyer a punch to the arm, silently scolding him. He graces me with a wink, not the least bit apologetic.

The good-lookin' bugger.

I walk over to the table and stand next to Mac, my hand moving to his shoulder. When he looks up at me, I smile, my heart filled with love.

He grasps my hand, his fingers wrapping around mine, no words needed.

Grams continues her rounds with Cade, dropping a kiss on his cheek.

He visibly tenses but tries to hide it.

"Oh, you!" she scolds, smacking his shoulder. "You should be used to this by now. My goodness, I think you're worse than what my Jaxson used to be."

All of us bite back a chuckle.

Cade's hard expression, however, never wavers but he does grumble her a greeting.

She moves for Cooper next. "And how's the handsome sheriff of Sunset Bay?"

He stands from his chair, leaning down to accept her affection. "I'm doing good, Miss Margaret. Happy Thanksgiving."

"Same to you, honey. Now, we need to talk. I have a message for you from Miss Gladys. She wants you to come to the home tomorrow to investigate some shady things that have been going on."

"What's wrong now?" he asks, not sounding all that concerned as he takes his seat once again.

"Well, she's pretty sure someone from the home has been stealing her cigarettes and..." she bends down to whisper in his ear, "underwear."

Anna chokes on her drink, hearing Grams loud and clear like the rest of us.

Kayla pats her on the back, but her attention remains on her husband. "This sounds serious, Coop. You better go over there. It sounds like Sunset Bay could have a panty raider on their hands. Your mad investigating skills might be the only thing that catches him."

All of us burst into a fit of laughter except for Cooper. He glares at Kayla, not appreciating the commentary. She blows him a kiss, unaffected by his icy glare.

Snickering, Grams pats his shoulder one last time before heading over to Jaxson. "And last but not least, my favorite boy, the father of my great grandbaby. Come here, honey, and give me some love." She wraps her arms around his waist, hugging him longer than everyone else.

He accepts it graciously, embracing her back. "Happy Thanksgiving, Grams."

Julia watches them with a soft smile, tears forming in her eyes. She waves her hand in front of her face, reining in her emotion, then moves for the oven. "All right, everyone go on and take your seat. The turkey is ready."

While chairs scrape across the floor, I push Mac closer to the table and fix him a plate, making sure to cut everything up. By the time I'm done, I look up and find one empty seat between Sawyer and Cade.

Sawyer pats it, a sly grin on his face. "Saved you a seat, Cupcake."

My heart pitter-patters in my chest. Smiling, I move in next to him, pressing a kiss to his cheek. "Thank you." Leaning over on my other side, I bravely give one to Cade also, catching him off guard.

"What was that for?" he grumbles.

"For pickin' Mac up and bringin' him here. Thank you."

He shifts in his seat, uncomfortable with the praise but nods in my direction. "You're welcome."

I find that small acknowledgment a great feat.

"Who's going to say grace?" Grams asks.

The moment the question leaves her mouth, Cade's demeanor changes, his entire body stiffening.

Jaxson clears his throat, interrupting the awkward silence. "You know what, Grams? We're going to skip that tonight."

"No, we're not. It's fine!" Cade grinds out.

It's obviously not *fine*. I can literally feel the tension rolling off him in waves.

Jaxson shakes his head and tries refusing again but Cade shoots him a look, keeping him quiet. It's then that Katelyn speaks up and offers to say grace.

Everyone bows their heads, except Cade.

I side-glance him, my heart breaking at the pain on his face. Every word Katelyn breathes only seems to add to his agony. He looks like he's about to be physically sick.

Reaching beneath the table, I grab his hand, hoping to offer him some sort of comfort. I sense him look over at me but I keep my head down, not wantin' to make him feel even more uncomfortable than he already does.

Once Katelyn finishes, I release his hand and begin fixin' my plate. My head turns in Sawyer's direction and I find him watchin' me with an expression I can't decipher. It's obvious he saw me.

I swallow thickly; worried I overstepped, but the moment the thought arises it vanishes. His face dips next to mine, lips at my ear. "Do you have any idea how much I love you?"

Warmth blooms across my chest, the biggest smile spreading across my face. "I love you, too," I whisper, brushing my nose across his stubbly jaw before pressing my lips there.

"Katelyn, honey," Grams speaks. "Julia tells me your uncle is going to be the senior pastor at the Peace Hill Baptist Church. You must be excited to have family moving close by."

"I am, especially for my cousin. She and I are very close and I haven't seen her for quite some time."

"Isn't Peace Hills the abandoned church?" Jaxson asks.

"It is but my uncle plans to fix it up. His goal is to have it functioning by spring. He and my cousin have big plans for that place, especially the youth in this town," she says, her excitement palpable.

"Well, I think it's great," Julia says. "I'll help any way I can, at least until Annabelle is born…"

Everyone stops mid bite, all eyes shooting to her.

"What did you just say?" Kayla asks.

A beautiful smile transforms her face. Reaching over, she grabs Jaxson's hand. "Jax and I found out we're having a girl and we've decided to name her Annabelle, after my mother. Annabelle Margaret," she says.

Loud squeals penetrate the air as all of us girls push out of our seats and run over to hug her. "Oh my gosh, this is so excitin'," I say, my heart exploding with happiness.

Grams does nothing but blubber, her reaction making my own throat feel tight.

Eventually, she moves to Jaxson, cupping his face between her well-worn hands. "You did good, I'm so proud of you." She plants a million kisses on his face, acting as if he purposely made it a girl.

"I can't wait to babysit," Anna says as we all take our seats again.

Sawyer watches Jaxson from across the table, amusement dancing in his eyes.

"What the hell are you looking at?" Jaxson asks.

"You're having a girl and she's going to grow up to be hot, just like Julia."

Everyone finds the comment funny, except Jaxson. His eyes narrow into an icy glare. If looks could kill, Sawyer would be ten feet under by now.

Cooper reaches over and slaps him on the back. "Don't worry, buddy, just send her to school sporting a mullet and you'll never have to worry about any guy going near her."

"Cooper!" Kayla gasps, slapping his shoulder.

I shake my head but can't hide my smile.

As more jokes get tossed around, my eyes move to every single person at the table, a feeling of contentment settling over my heart. For the first time since my mama passed away, I realize I've found more than really good friends, I've found a family.

When my gaze lands on the man next to me, I know without a doubt that I am exactly where I'm meant to be.

CHAPTER 42

Sawyer

Once we finish dinner, us guys stand from the table, deciding to head upstairs to Jaxson's office while the girls talk nursery colors.

Jaxson claps Logan on the shoulder. "You come too."

"Jaxson!" Both Anna and Julia warn nervously.

"What? I'm being nice and including him."

By the look Anna shoots him, she's doubtful.

"It's fine, Anna," Logan tells her, pushing to his feet.

"See, it's fine," Jaxson says.

Anna glares at him, pointing her finger. "Be nice!"

"I'm always nice."

I smirk at the lie and follow out after him, all the others trailing behind me except for Mac, he stays with Grace.

Cooper is close to my side as we climb the stairs, his questioning gaze burning into the side of my face. It's been this way all night and I have no doubt it's because of the address Jaxson has asked for. I hate that I even had to put him in the position but one way or another, I'm getting that damn address.

As we enter the office, Jaxson grasps Logan's shoulders and pushes him into a chair. "Have a seat, Logan, let's get to know each other better."

Logan rests back in the chair, looking nothing but relaxed.

Jaxson walks around his desk and enters some numbers on a pin pad. The sound of a lock releases and that's when he pulls out his gun, sitting it on the desk in front of the kid.

Logan peers up at him, unimpressed. "Save your little scare tactics. They aren't necessary."

The kid has some balls; I'll give him that. Or he's stupid. I haven't decided yet.

"My gun isn't scary, Logan. You know what's scary?" Jaxson asks but doesn't give him a chance to respond. "*Me* and all the different ways I've been trained to kill, and I have…many times."

"Don't you think I know that?" he snaps, his eyes narrowing. "I'm fucking thankful every day that you're trained for that shit, otherwise Anna wouldn't be here right now. I'm serious, you can save your breath. I'm not the bad guy. I'm the one who loves her and will do everything in my power to make sure no one ever hurts her again!"

A heavy silence settles over the room, the two of them locked in a hard stare.

"Okay, time to break this up," I say, deciding it's time to intervene. "Sorry,

Jaxson, but I like the kid. Knowing he loves her and is protecting her is good enough for me, and it should be for you, too."

Jaxson returns his attention back to Logan, his expression a little less threatening. "You really love her?"

Logan nods, no hesitation.

"Fine, but just so you know, I have your fucking door rigged," he adds, pointing his finger at him. "I will be alerted if anyone goes in or out of that room tonight. If you want to keep your dick intact, you will keep your hands to yourself."

He grunts. "You don't need to worry about that."

The answer appeases Jaxson enough that he finally backs off.

"Now that we have that settled," Cooper says, his attention shifting to me. "Let's move on to another topic. Like where the three of you are going on Tuesday."

"What do you want to know?" I ask, facing him head on.

"I want to know that I didn't make a mistake giving Jaxson that address. I want your word, Sawyer, that you're not going to do something stupid."

"I have it under control."

"Do you?"

"Look, my biggest priority is getting back what belongs to her."

And to beat the fuck out of the guy, but I decide to keep that part to myself.

"That's the only reason why I'm giving you the address," he says. "That girl has been through enough, and I'm sure I don't even know the half of it. But I'm warning you, Sawyer, if you lose control like you did with Miguel, or worse, I won't be able to get you off the hook so easily again."

"I said I can handle it!"

"Jaxson and I will be there," Cade says, inserting himself into the conversation. "We won't let him go too far."

"*Too far*?" Coop repeats. "Well that makes me feel so much fucking better."

"Sometimes people have to pay for what they've done," he says, his expression hard. He understands that better than anyone.

"Well, this is enough heavy shit for me, boys," I say, clapping Logan on the shoulder. "I'm taking my woman home." I shake Jaxson's hand then do the same with Cade. "You okay to take Mac or do you want Grace and me to do it?"

He waves me off. "I got him. I promised to stop and get him some junk food to hide in his room."

I'm not surprised he roped Cade in, he's been trying to do the same with me but no way am I getting in shit from my Cupcake.

I walk up to Cooper next, and extend him the same handshake as the others. "Thanks, Coop. You did the right thing."

"Don't make me regret it."

My response is a single nod before I walk out. The plan is not to kill him, death would be too good for him, but I do plan to make him suffer. He will pay for what he's done.

The sound of Grace's sweet laugh washes over me as I reach the bottom of the stairs, fueling the warmth within my chest that I always get when it comes to her. When I make it to the kitchen, I see she's laughing over something Mac says, her smile lighting up the whole damn room. I lean against the wall, arms crossed over my chest and watch her, wondering how anyone could hurt someone as kind as her.

Feeling the weight of my stare, she looks over at me, her pretty whiskey eyes punching me in the chest. She watches me with that smile of hers, a smile I will ensure she has for the rest of her life.

"Everythin' okay?" she asks, her soft twang snapping me out of my thoughts.

"Yeah, Cupcake, I'm good. You ready to go?"

"Sure am." Her attention shifts to Mac. "You gonna come with us?"

"Nah. You go on," he declines. "Cade said he would take me."

I bite back a chuckle, knowing what a sneaky bastard he's being.

"All right, if you're sure." Leaning over, she gives him a peck on the cheek. "We'll come by tomorrow and check on you."

"Sounds good, darlin'. I'll see you then."

We start our goodbyes to everyone else. I make sure to mess Anna's hair before pulling her in for a hug. "Don't worry, kid. We only roughed him up a little bit."

Her body stiffens. "Oh god."

"I'm kidding, he's fine. You picked a good one," I tell her.

She smiles up at me, her arms hugging me tight. "Thanks. So did you."

She doesn't have to tell me, I already know.

Julia sees us out, she and Grace yakking for another few minutes at the door about their plans Tuesday. It takes every bit of control I possess not to haul Grace over my shoulder and charge out of there.

By the time we make it outside, my body is coiled tight; the need I've kept buried all night surfacing.

"That was such a great dinner, wasn't it?" Grace says, having no idea where my thoughts are. "The news of Jax and Julia's baby being a girl still has me feeling emotional. They are gonna make great parents. And let's not forget…"

Everything else she says pretty much falls on deaf ears, my eyes dropping to her ass as I remember what she has on beneath that classy fucking dress. My dick throbs violently, the need to feel her tight, wet—

"What do you think?"

I snap back to reality, having no idea what she just said and right now, I don't really care. The moment she reaches for my truck door, I grab her hips, my chest crowding her back.

Her sharp breath penetrates the humid air, my stiff cock pressing against her backside, hard enough that she braces her hands on the door.

"I'll tell you what I think, Cupcake. I think it's time you pay up for that little stunt you pulled earlier."

Her breath races, shoulders rising and falling.

My face dips next to hers, lips brushing the shell of her ear. "Here's what's going to happen, you're going to get into the truck and do exactly what I tell you to, understand?"

"Yes." Her response is breathless, anticipation edging her voice. She wants this as much as I do.

I open the door and help her up, the rise of her dress teasing me with another peek. Groaning, I climb in on my side and start the truck up before looking over at Grace. "Lean back against the door, baby, and bend your knee. I want your legs spread wide for me."

She follows the order eagerly while I pull away from the house. When I look back at her, she's already in position, the glow of my dashboard illuminating everything I want.

"Pull up your dress and show me what's mine."

Her hands coast up her creamy thighs, moving painstakingly slow until the material is bunched at her hips. My eyes are riveted to the cream lace that barely covers what I know is the sweetest, tightest pussy I've ever had the pleasure of fucking.

I wrap a hand around her ankle and drag her closer to me. She braces back on her elbows, her breathing rapid, breasts rising and falling, calling to every primal instinct I posses.

I snake a hand between her legs, running my knuckle along the damp center. "Did you wear this for me tonight, Grace?"

"Yes," she moans. "Everything I wear is for you."

"That's right, baby. Because you're mine." I rip one of the straps that's attached to her panties before moving to the next one.

"God, Sawyer, as hot as this is, I only have one of these things and they aren't cheap ya know."

"Don't worry, Cupcake. I'll replace it. I'm going to buy you one in every fucking color."

Her soft giggle trails into a moan when I slip a finger beneath the lace and run it through her slick pussy. Her hips lift, seeking more.

"Always so ready for me," I growl.

My foot is heavy on the gas, eyes on the road as I stroke her clit, my cock hardening further as my finger moves to her entrance, hovering over the hole, never breaching just teasing.

She grows restless, her body shifting to move closer. "Sawyer, please…"

"It's not very nice when people tease you, is it, Grace?"

"No, it's not," she moans. "Just like it wasn't nice of you to eat my pies that I worked so hard on."

I still, my gaze darting over to her; her face is flushed, eyes wild with need but there is no denying the truth of her words.

"Okay, Cupcake, you're right. I guess we'll just have to punish each other." I enter a single finger inside of her, just up to my knuckle, her pussy gripping, begging for more.

She wiggles her hips, seating herself fully on it.

"Fuck, you want it bad."

"So bad," she confesses shamelessly, driving me to the brink of insanity.

Thankfully, it's not long after I pull onto her driveway. I reluctantly withdraw my hand and put the truck in park, leaving it running. "Come here, baby."

She sits up and crawls over to straddle me, her knees encasing my hips. Our mouths meet in a heated frenzy, the sweet taste of her exploding on my tongue. My hand snakes up her back, unzipping her dress until it's bunched at her waist. Her heavy tits tumble into my waiting hands, my fingers tormenting her hard nipples.

"Oh god," the two words rush past her lips on a heavy breath.

My mouth descends, closing over one peaked tip as my fingers roll and pinch the other, feeling the nub harden further.

She grinds down on my hard cock. Wanting—needing.

As bad as I want to drive up into her right now, I have other plans first. My hands grip her hips, stilling her movements. "Easy, Cupcake, not so fast."

"Yes, fast. I want fast and hard."

I groan, her eagerness making my dick weep. "Soon, baby, but first, I'm going to show you something."

She pulls back, her swollen pink lips wet and parted. "What's that?"

My eyes hold hers as I take her soft hands in mine and bring them to her chest, molding them over her breasts.

Her eyes flare for a fraction of a second, uncertainty peeking back at me. "I'm not so sure about this."

"Don't be nervous. It's just me. I want you to experience pleasure by your hands."

Curiosity reflects in her heavy-lidded eyes. She wants it too, she just doesn't know how but she's about to learn.

Leaning in, I lick the seam of her lips, coaxing and tasting. She sighs softly and opens for me. My hands curl around hers, encouraging her to squeeze the generous mounds. Her body slightly tenses.

"Relax, baby. Pretend it's only my hands," I murmur.

She complies, her expression softening with pleasure. I drag her fingers along her tight little nipples, letting her feel their reaction. A sexy moan spills past her lips, colliding against my mouth.

"Good girl. Now pinch them like I do. Make them hurt."

She follows the order, her subtle gasp filling the thick air between us.

"Feels good. Doesn't it?"

"Yes," she whispers, her eyes closed and voice breathless.

Taking one of her hands, I bring it down between us, pushing it under her dress.

She tenses again.

"Don't think about it, Grace. Just feel. Give yourself the pleasure you deserve." My voice is gentle, words coaxing as I slip her hand into her panties, pressing her fingers between her wet folds.

"Oh," she cries out, her eyes closing once again as we pass over her clit.

I remove my hand and lift her skirt past her hips, my eyes riveted as her fingers shift beneath the lace. Growling, I shred the panties from her body, leaving nothing hidden to my view. I watch while she continues to tease her slick clit, my cock aching for contact.

I rest my seat back further, removing my shirt first then unbuckle my belt and unzip my pants to free my cock. A small noise escapes her when I start stroking myself, her eyes anchored on my every move and fingers stilling on her pussy.

"You like watching my hand fuck my cock, Grace?"

"Yes," she whispers.

"From the first day I laid eyes on you, this is what I had to do, to ease the aching need I had for you."

"Sawyer," my name falls past her lips on a heated moan, her fingers moving again as she watches me jerk off.

It's the hottest damn thing I've ever seen.

Unable to withhold any longer, I join my free hand with hers, slipping my fingers into her snug hole while she plays with her clit.

A keening cry flees her, echoing around us. The faster I fuck her pussy with my fingers, the faster her own hand moves, her hips bucking, matching my thrusts.

"I'm going to come," she whimpers.

"Give into it, baby, so I can fill your greedy pussy with my cock."

The filthy words send her careening over the edge, her cries of pleasure penetrating the stifling air and rushing through my veins. I don't give her time to recover before I replace my hand with my cock, driving up inside of her tight, wet heat.

She grabs onto my shoulders for support, her head falling back in ecstasy.

My teeth grind as the aftershocks of her orgasm grips me.

"God, I love feeling you inside of me," she moans.

"Me too, baby. It's where I'm meant to be." My fingers tighten on her hips, eyes holding hers. "Do you still want me to fuck you hard and fast, Grace?"

"Yes."

There's no hesitation in that word, only need, the same one I have roaring in my veins. It was all I needed to hear. My hips are relentless as I pound up inside of her, fucking her harder than I ever have before.

Her nails bite into my shoulders, tits bouncing enticingly only inches from my face. It isn't long before I feel her tighten around me again with another orgasm. "Give it to me, baby." Rearing my hand back, I deliver a sharp slap, hard enough that the sound of it echoes through the air.

Her head falls back on a scream as she shatters for a second time. I stare transfixed at her pretty face, watching her drown in pleasure. That alone is enough to make me follow along with her. Fire erupts through my body, searing my veins as I come hard, filling her with every last drop.

She falls forward, her forehead resting on my shoulder as we both fight for air.

"Jesus, Grace," I murmur. I'm not really sure what else there is to say.

She lifts her head, her warm gaze penetrating mine and glowing with satisfaction. A small smile steals her lips as her hands frame my jaw. "Wanna know somethin', Sexy Sawyer?"

"What, Cupcake?"

"I'm madly in love with you."

The biggest grin breaks out across my face, mirroring the one shining back at me. My hand cups the back of her neck and I reel her in for a kiss.

"I love you too, baby," I whisper against her lips. "And I'm glad I found someone who loves me as much as I love myself."

"Actually, you found someone who loves you more. Who knew that was even possible?"

I chuckle, loving the sass that falls past her mouth. Definitely a far cry from the shy girl I met so many months ago.

After laying one more hard kiss on her lips, I pull her dress back in place then carry her into the house and take her to bed, wrapping her in my arms. A place I intend to keep her for the rest of my life.

CHAPTER 43

Sawyer

The closer we get to our destination, the rage I've fought hard to bury over the past few days surfaces, threatening to swallow me whole.

He hated me. He hated me so much, and I don't know why.

I grip the steering wheel tighter as Grace's sad, trembling voice replays in my head.

"What's the plan?" Jaxson says. "How do you want to play this?"

"We go in there and do whatever it takes to get what belongs to Grace," I tell him.

"What if he doesn't have the ashes?" Cade asks. "He could have gotten rid of them."

"For his sake, that better not be the case." My voice is hard, the threat ringing through the air.

"You need to rein it in, Evans," Jaxson warns. "I have no problem handing someone a beating, but right now you look like you're ready to commit murder, and if I get my ass thrown in jail Jules will fucking kill me."

"I'm not going to kill him." The words are weak even to my own ears. "My first priority is to get what belongs to Grace, but after that, he will pay for what he did to her."

I haven't given them details on what exactly happened. It's not my place, but they know he hurt her, took something that means everything to her and for that, he will pay greatly.

"You know, Anna brought up an idea to me the other night for the gym that I think we should talk about," Jaxson says.

My gaze briefly meets his in the rearview mirror. "I'm listening."

"She thinks we should give self-defense classes."

"For women?"

He nods. "She even mentioned a kids' program, as well. We could teach them the dangers of talking to strangers and what to do if they were ever in a situation of being abducted. Cooper thought it was a great idea, too. He said Victim Services are always looking for classes in the area but have a hard time finding any. Our main goal will still be a place for fighters to train but on the side, this could work."

"I agree," Cade says. "Especially the children's program. Although, Evans or Coop will have to run it. You and I will scare the shit out of little kids."

Jaxson grunts his agreement on that statement.

"I'm in," I tell him.

"Good. I'll have Cooper get us in touch with Victim Services. Once we open we can run a class for the girls. I'd love nothing more than to teach Jules how to kick some serious ass."

I can understand that. How different things could have been for her months ago with that whack job Wyatt if she had known how to defend herself. Even Grace, what she faced at the diner weeks ago with those high school punks, what could have happened had I not shown up. Or even worse, what happened to her and her mother all those years ago.

The thought has my muscles coiling tight again.

By the time we arrive at our destination, my body is humming, words of rage whispering in my ear. It only escalates when I spot the pimped out silver truck that's parked in the driveway of the run-down house, the same truck he no doubt bought with Grace's money.

Reaching over, I open my glove compartment and grab my gun.

"What the fuck do you need that for?" Jaxson asks. "I thought we agreed no body bags."

I glance behind me, quirking a brow. "Are you going to tell me that you're not packing?"

"Of course I am. That's why you don't need it. Put it back."

"I could kill him with my bare hands if I wanted to and we both know it. This is just for a little fun," I tell him, then reach under my seat for the metal baseball bat I have stashed there. I hand it over to Cade with a smile. "Hold this please."

He takes it without question.

"Jesus," Jaxson mutters.

It's on the tip of my tongue to ask when the hell he became the voice of reason. However, I decide that's a conversation for later. Right now, I have bigger things to take care of.

We all jump out of the truck at the same time. A neighbor walks out to get her paper and takes one look at us before running back inside. I assume the bat Cade is holding is a pretty good indication we aren't here for a friendly visit.

After we climb the stairs, I knock. When there's no answer, I bang again, my fist heavy and relentless on the door. Eventually, there's movement on the other side.

"Hold on!" The door swings open, revealing an old man who looks like he hasn't showered in a week and smells like it, too. His graying hair is a greasy mess and bloodshot eyes sunken on his pale face. "What the hell do you want?" he rasps, sizing up the three of us.

"You Earl Morgan?" I ask, wanting to be sure.

"Yeah, who the fuck are you?"

"I'm a friend of Grace's."

His beady eyes narrow into tiny slits. "Listen, like I told the other guy. I don't know where that whore is and I don't fuckin' care."

My foot meets the door, hitting him square in the face. The force of it sends him backwards, his head snapping back as I charge in after him. I send another blow, knocking him to the ground.

Jaxson and Cade follow me inside, closing the door behind them.

I grip the bastard's throat as I keep him pinned to the cold tile floor and pull my gun, jamming the steel against his forehead.

"Earl, what's going on?" A woman walks in, coming to a hard stop. Her wide, terrified eyes are smudged with yesterday's makeup.

"Call the police," Earl wheezes, my fingers keeping their pressure.

She reaches for the phone but Cade intercepts her, shaking his head.

"Why don't we call the police?" I say. "We can tell them all about the time you beat my girl with a belt and tried to force your dick inside of her."

"Earl, what's he talking about?" she asks, every word trembling past her mouth.

"Nothing, Candy. Just shut up!"

"Nothing?" I press the gun harder into his skull, making him howl in pain as my finger hovers over the tempting trigger. "It's something all right and you're going to fucking pay for what you did."

"Look, I don't know what she told you, but she's lying. I didn't touch her."

My composure shatters and I send the butt of my gun across his face, not once but three times, splitting his cheek open. Satisfaction fills me at the way his blood spatters across my face. I shove the gun into his groin, making him cry out again. "I should blow your dick off right now for what you did." My finger shakes with restraint, the urge to pull the trigger is strong.

"Evans, remember what we came here for," Jaxson says, his voice penetrating the rage roaring in my ears. "Let's get it and get out of here."

I shove aside the urge to shed more blood and lean in closer. "You have something that belongs to my girl and I want it back."

"I don't have anything of hers."

"You have her mother's ashes and I'm not leaving until I get them."

He peers back at me, knowledge embedded in his eyes. "I—I got rid of them."

"Wrong answer." Grabbing his hand, I twist it in a quick move that has a sickening crack echoing through the air, the tiny bones shattering between my crushing fingers.

His howl lingers, tears mixing with the blood smeared on his face.

"Next, it will be your other one, then your arms and legs. I will break every fucking bone in your body until you give me what I want."

"Jesus, Earl, just give it to him," Candy sobs.

When he makes no move to do so, I reach for his other hand.

"No, wait! I'll get it for you."

I grip the front of his dirty white shirt and yank him to his feet. He struggles to stay upright, cradling his broke hand to his chest. I turn him around and press the barrel of my pistol into the back of his head. "You have seconds to get me what I want or I blow your brains all over this house."

He moves down the hallway, leading us into the small kitchen that reeks of old food and dirty dishes. His feet come to a hard stop just in front of one of the counters.

"It's up there," he grinds out, nodding to the top cupboard. "Top shelf."

My eyes shift to Jaxson and he steps forward to retrieve it. "It's here," he says, pulling down a cream marble urn that has her name scripted across it in gold letters.

Something shifts inside of my chest as I stare back at the name of the woman who gave life to the girl I love. A woman who Grace misses with her whole heart. This entire time she's been shoved in the back of a cupboard and kept from the only family who loves her.

"There, you have it. Now get the fuck out of my house."

Hate boils in my blood, merging with the deep-seated anger burning inside of me.

My foot strikes out, kicking him in the back of the knee. The sound of his bone shattering penetrates the air, mixing with his painful scream as he crumbles to the floor.

Dropping next to him, I grab his hair and yank his head back. "I've decided I'm going to let you live…for now. But I can change my mind at any moment. So know this, if you so much as even breathe my woman's name, even think about her, I will come back here and I will destroy what's left of your miserable existence. Do you understand?"

"Yes!" The word is delivered through clenched teeth, his breathing labored.

I release him with a shove, his face smacking into the cupboard. He curls into a ball and cries like a fucking baby, his busted knee twisted at an odd angle. I feel no remorse. He will never shed more tears than Grace has and for that, he deserves so much more.

"Come on. Let's get out of here," Jaxson says, clapping me on the back.

I follow him out of the kitchen, finding Cade in the same place we left him.

A fearful Candy continues to cry, her arms wrapped protectively around herself. She lifts her head, remorse reflecting in her emotional eyes. "I didn't know," she chokes out. "If I knew I would have tried to help her."

"It doesn't matter anymore. All that matters is it will never happen again by anyone or I will kill them. Remind your boyfriend that."

Without another word, I walk out the front door, the fresh air doing nothing to ease the burning fury barreling through my chest. My head turns to the side and I come face-to-face with the silver truck.

I reach for Cade's shoulder, stopping him from going further. "Give me the bat."

He does as I say. The cool metal is heavy in my hand as I walk forward.

"Evans," Jaxson warns. "Let's not draw more attention to ourselves than we already have."

I twist back to face him. "He stole every fucking penny that was left to her and bought this truck. He's not keeping it." I hop up on the hood and start in on the windshield, relishing in the glass that rains around me. After I'm done, I move to the side windows.

Cade and Jaxson both join me, grabbing a crow bar and a hammer that lie on the driveway. It takes us less than a minute to completely demolish it. By the time we leave, I finally feel a small sense of justice.

Silence fills the truck as we start the six-hour drive home, the event that just took place replaying in my head. The back of my neck tingles, something Earl said niggling at me.

"What do you think he meant when he said he told the last guy who went there he didn't know where Grace was?" I ask.

Jaxson shrugs. "I assumed he was talking about Miguel. It would make sense that he found out she lived with him and checked there first."

"Yeah, maybe," I murmur.

"You don't think so?" Cade asks.

"I don't know. Something doesn't feel right."

Jaxson claps me on the shoulder. "Relax, man. She's good. I just got a text from Jules and they're having a blast dress shopping."

I nod but still don't feel confident. I can't seem to kick this feeling in my gut, a feeling I'm usually never wrong about.

CHAPTER 44

Grace

We had a very successful day of shopping and are now having dinner at Giovanni's, a quaint little Italian restaurant with some of the best food in town. I've had a great time with my friends but I've missed Sawyer terribly. It's the first time we have been apart in weeks. The cocky bugger has really left his mark on me. I'm counting down the minutes to kiss his handsome face.

"I'm so in love with the dresses," Kayla says, her smile reaching from ear to ear as she pours us all another glass of wine.

"It really is stunning," Julia agrees, "but nothing compares to yours, which is exactly how it's supposed to be."

"Cheers to that." Kayla raises her drink for a toast that we all share in.

"The whole wedding is going to be beautiful," I say, bringing my glass to my lips for a generous sip.

"Thank you, you girls are the best bridesmaids a girl could ask for. I just wish Katelyn could have joined us today."

Me too. It was a shame she had to cancel last minute. One of the pipes exploded at her salon and made quite the mess, Kayla offered to reschedule so we could all help her but she refused. We sent her pictures throughout the day though and she loved what we chose.

The sound of a text message dinging through the air has us all reaching for our phones. It turns out to be from Julia's, a blush staining her cheeks as she reads it.

"Let me guess, the Hulk is sexting you right now," Kayla says.

The smile on her face says it all. I can't judge, I've received a few from Sawyer myself today.

Julia types in a quick reply then tucks the phone back into her purse and brings her attention to me. "Jax says they're almost home."

"They sure travelled far," I muse, taking another sip of wine. "Do you know where they went?"

"No, but I didn't ask either."

"They went to Virginia," Kayla says.

Every muscle in my body freezes, my blood running cold as she names the one place I try to forget. "How do you know?" The question is barely above a whisper, the words thick in my throat.

"I overheard Coop talking to Jaxson about it. Whatever brought them there has Cooper stressed right out." Her answer voices my biggest fear.

My eyes close, betrayal washing over me.

"Grace? Are you all right?" Julia asks, putting a warm hand on my shoulder.

I shake my head, tears burning the back of my eyes. "I'm sorry, I have to go."

I push to my feet, ready to flee but Kayla grabs my wrist. "Whoa. Hold up. What's going on?"

"I promise to tell you everything later, but I can't right now. Please understand."

When she sees me close to tears, she releases my wrist. "All right. Can I at least give you a ride home?"

"No, it's fine. Stay here and enjoy the rest of your dinner. I'll call you both later." Without another word, I run out of the restaurant, my boots stomping the pavement as I start my walk home. A million emotions plague me but one overrides them all—betrayal.

I can't believe he did this to me.

I pull out my phone and dial his cell, my hand shaking with anger as I hold it up to my ear.

He answers on the third ring. "Cupcake. We're almost home." His cheerful greeting rips through my tortured heart.

"Y'all sure drove far for one day. Where did you say you were goin' again?" No matter how hard I try, there's no keeping the anger out of my voice.

Silence fills the line as he realizes I know.

"You lied to me!"

"I didn't lie."

"Yes, you did! You promised, Sawyer. You promised you wouldn't ever go there, that you wouldn't tell a soul. How could you betray me like this?" My voice cracks along with my heart.

"We'll talk about this when I get home."

"I don't think so, buster, you are not comin' back to my house, you can sleep at your own damn place tonight!"

"Goddamn it, Grace, listen to me!"

I hang up, refusing to hear him out. Not right now. I'm too angry, too…hurt.

Within seconds, my phone rings. I turn it on silent and toss it back in my purse. The streetlights begin to blur from the tears tracking down my cheeks, my emotions ripping through me faster than I can fight off. By the time I enter the house, I'm a blubbering mess.

Locking the door behind me, I drop my purse down on the bench and unzip my boots. Once I toe them off, I still, a frown pinching my face when Chuckie doesn't come to greet me like usual.

"Chuckie?" I call out.

His low whimper sounds from my room.

I start down the hall, a familiar feelin' tugging at me, one that has alarm bells banging inside of my chest. My steps slow, becoming more cautious as I reach my room and push open the door. I flick on the light and find Chuckie hiding under my bed, his sweet head poking out from beneath it.

"Hey, you. What's wrong?"

His whimpering becomes louder as he crawls out, limping his way over to me. I start toward him, concern plaguing me. The moment I reach him, I catch movement to my left, a dark figure emerging from my closet.

A scream rips from my throat, fear fueling my speed as I charge from my room. I don't make it far before a force knocks into me from behind, tackling me to the ground in my living room. My face hits the side of my coffee table, the impact splitting my cheek open. Pain explodes through my head as I'm flipped to my back.

A man with black hair and hauntingly familiar dark eyes straddles me, his hand wrapping around my throat, pinning me where I lie. "Ah, Grace, we finally meet. You have no idea how long I've waited for this moment."

A loud snarl penetrates the air seconds before Chuckie attacks him, sinking his teeth into his neck. The intruder howls in pain and sends Chuckie flying across the room. He lands on his back, his yelp infiltrating my terrified heart. When the man pulls a gun, it stops beating altogether.

"No!" I reach for his arm the same time the deadly weapon fires off, a bullet penetrating my dog.

An agonized scream pours from my mouth, a sob shattering my chest. I claw the huge gash on the side of his neck in retaliation, my fingers gripping the raw flesh.

He falls to the side, cupping the bloody wound.

I roll over and push to my feet only to have him snag my ankle, ripping my foot out from beneath me. I face plant onto the floor and the metallic taste of blood fills my mouth.

"You bitch!" He delivers a few heart-stopping blows before flipping me to face him again, jamming the barrel of his gun against my forehead. His eyes are wild and furious. "I'm going to make this as painful as possible."

"Why are you doing this?" I sob, confused as to who this man is and why he wants to hurt me.

"You haven't figured it out yet? Come on, Grace. I thought you were smarter than this. I look exactly like my brothers."

My heart stops, body going still beneath his. I peer up into his haunting eyes and finally realize why they are so familiar. "Miguel's brother?" I whisper.

"You guessed it. Another brother that no one knows about. I grew up in Missouri, with my whore of a mother who got knocked up by the same man who fathered my brothers."

My mind spins with what he reveals.

"I had just finished high school when my brother found me and asked me to come to Florida to be a family with him and Emilio." A distant look enters his crazy eyes as he takes a trip down memory lane but fury quickly enters them once again. "But then you had to go and fuck it all up. Emilio is dead because of you," he screams. "And now, Miguel is back in prison, after all of my hard work of getting him out!"

Everything becomes achingly clear. "It was you. You killed the forensic scientist."

"You're damn right I did. The plan was three years in the making. Judge Robinson was such an easy target. Get some drinks into that guy and put some pussy in front of him and I got all the pictures I needed to blackmail him. It was fucking brilliant. Until you had to go and fuck it all up," he rages, his expression hardening. "You keep taking my family from me!"

I gape up at him, my eyes widening at the irony of his statement. "I took your family from you? Your brothers murdered the only family I had!" Tears of sorrow track down my cheeks as I'm forced to relive that fateful day. "My beautiful, kind mother was raped and stabbed thirty-seven times by your fucking family!" I scream, anger replacing my hurt. "Emilio deserved to die and so does Miguel. I hope they both rot in hell."

His hand wraps around my throat, cutting off my air supply. "The only person who's going to burn in hell is you, bitch! Right along with your mother."

I struggle beneath his gripping hold, clawing at his hands as I fight for air. Darkness hovers within my vision but it fades when a loud knock sounds upon my door.

"Grace, baby, open up!"

Sawyer.

My mouth opens to scream but his hand slams over top of it with brutal force. "Shut up. Or I swear to God I will drive a bullet through his fucking skull."

Just the thought has a gut-wrenching sob ripping from me.

"Grace, I mean it. I'm not going anywhere until you hear me out."

Miguel's brother stares down at me, indecision battling in his calculating eyes. "Get rid of him," he orders. "Or he's dead. Got it?"

I nod, my eyes closing on a silent prayer that I can find a way out of this.

I bite back a cry when I'm pulled to my feet by my hair. He yanks me back against him, his mouth pointed at my ear. "Not one wrong move." He pushes me ahead of him, his gun pressing into the back of my head.

My forehead rests on the door, fingers gripping the handle. "Sawyer?" His name falls on a sob before I can stop it.

"Grace, baby, please don't cry," he pleads, remorse thick in his voice. "Let me in. Give me a chance to explain."

I shake my head, wishing I'd never gotten angry with him in the first place. It all seems so stupid now. I swallow back my fear and pull myself together while I think of a way out of this. "You need to go."

"I'm not leaving until you hear me out!"

The gun presses harder into my head, turning the cold blood in my veins to ice.

"Please. Just go back to Cooper's. We can talk about what happened with Kayla in the morning."

Silence greets me beyond the door, giving me a small measure of hope that he catches on.

"Fine, tomorrow. But I want you to know I'm not going anywhere. This is far from over." His shoes pound the cement steps with his descent. Seconds later, the sound of his truck roars to life, sending a heavy dose of fear in me.

Where's he going?

Before I can think about it, I'm yanked backwards by my hair and backhanded across the face, the force of it knocking me to the ground. I don't even have time to get my bearings before the bastard is on top of me again, his crushing weight pinning me to the floor.

Beads of sweat dot his forehead, his face pale as blood spills from the gash in his neck. "Time for you to suffer the same fate as your mother, just like Miguel wanted." He sets the gun next to my head, his fingers wrapping around my throat while his other hand moves to the V-neck of my thin sweater. "After I'm done fucking you, I'm going stab you thirty-eight times instead of the thirty-seven your mom got. The last one will be for Emilio."

An uncontrollable rage grips me, overriding my fear. I fight back with every bit of strength I possess, refusing to be his victim.

Never again!

My fingernails gouge his face, drawing more blood. "Get off of me!"

His hand tightens around my throat, cruelly robbing me of air. He's strong, so strong, but I don't give up.

I will never give up.

An enraged roar penetrates the blood rushing in my ears. One minute his weight is crushing me, his hand roughly grabbing at my clothes, then the next I feel nothing, my hands only hitting air.

"Motherfucker!"

Rolling to the side, I see Sawyer on top of him, his expression savage as he delivers blow after blow, his fists fast and deadly.

I open my mouth to speak but find I can't, my throat on fire as I try to inhale the air my lungs so desperately crave.

Sawyer pulls a gun out from behind him, shoving it under his chin. "Give me one good reason why I shouldn't blow your fucking brains out right now."

Oh God.

"Don't!" I choke out.

He ignores me, his arm shaking with restraint. "Who the fuck are you?"

The man's beaten and bloody face splits into a gory smile. "I'm the guy who's going to chop your girlfriend into a million—"

His words die when Sawyer rears back and knocks him out with the butt of his gun. I sit stunned, my body trembling violently as I try to process the last few minutes.

Sawyer's head turns, his eyes meeting mine and thunderous expression softening. "Jesus, Grace, are you okay?" he asks, approaching me cautiously.

I meet him halfway, a sob tearing from my throat as he pulls me into his arms. "Thank God you came," I cry against his chest, my fingers gripping his shirt. "I tried to fight but I couldn't get him off."

"It's okay, baby. You did good." Pulling back, he cradles my face, his eyes assessing my injuries, jaw clenching in fury. "I'm so fucking sorry. I shouldn't have left you."

"No. It's not your fault. I don't even know how he got in. He was hiding in my closet when I got home, and Chuckie—" I gasp, rememberin' the bullet that struck him. Pushing away from Sawyer, I crawl across the room, rushing to his side where I find him lying in a pool of his own blood. Another sob flees me, mixing with relief when I see his belly rising and falling, his breathing labored. "Sawyer, we have to get him help. Hurry!"

He kneels next to me, placing the gun at my side as he removes his shirt and balls it up, pressing it against Chuckie's wound. "Hold this here. I'm going to get more towels. Police and ambulance are already on their way," he says, walking into my kitchen.

I bury my face into Chuckie's neck, my tears falling into his soft fur. "It's okay, boy, just hold on."

Police sirens pierce the air, announcing help's arrival. I push to my feet with the intention to open the door for them but Sawyer's warning shout stops me cold.

"Get down!"

Turning, I see Miguel's brother conscious, his gun pointed directly at me.

"Fuck!"

It happens so fast—I hear the blast just as Sawyer slams into me, taking me to the ground.

The breath gets knocked out of my lungs in one painful swoosh. His hard body covers me as he grabs the gun next to us and shoots Miguel's brother in the head.

Deafening silence falls around us, my ears aching from the loud shots.

Sawyer rolls off me with a groan and that's when I see I'm covered in blood. My hands frantically search myself, trying to see where I was hit. It doesn't take me long before I realize it's not my blood. Sawyer clutches his shoulder, blood pouring between his fingers.

"Sawyer!" I sit up in a panic, my hand going over his, helping apply pressure. "Oh god, oh no."

My door busts open, five uniformed officers charging in, guns drawn. One of them is Cooper, his concerned eyes taking in Sawyer and me.

"Get paramedics in here now!" He drops to my side and removes my hands from Sawyer's gaping wound. "What the hell happened?"

"The fucker shot me," Sawyer explains through gritted teeth.

"Because you threw yourself in front of his bullet, ya idiot! What were you thinkin'?" I yell, even though what I really want to do is kiss the hell out of him.

"I was saving your sweet ass, Cupcake." He sucks in a sharp breath when Cooper adds more pressure to his wound.

"Did the bullet go through?" Cooper asks.

He shakes his head, his jaw locked tight.

"Oh god! I'm so sorry," I cry, resting my forehead on his. "I love you so much. Please don't die."

"I'm not going to die, baby, it just hurts like a motherfucker."

The paramedics enter and force me to the side while they work on Sawyer. Cooper orders for Chuckie to get help too and be taken to the animal hospital. He offers to go deal with it so I can stay with Sawyer. My heart breaks, hating that they're both suffering because they saved me.

The rest of the night happens in a blur. All of our friends wait with me at the hospital, their concern as great as my own as Sawyer enters surgery to have the bullet removed. I feel numb, time becoming nothing more than an afterthought as I think about all that happened tonight.

Kayla and Julia sit on either side of me, their arms wrapped around my shoulders as tears continue to stream down my face.

"Can I get you anything?" Kayla asks. "Some tea maybe?"

I shake my head, emotion robbing me of speech. The thought of anything in my mouth right now has me feeling nauseous. I excuse myself to use the restroom, needing a moment to collect my thoughts but on the way I find Cade down one of the hallways, pacing relentlessly.

His head shoots up, concerned eyes meeting mine, and his usual hard expression softens. Well, soft for Cade. Both of our worry and pain is apparent, written all over our faces and passing back and forth in the silent exchange between us.

Stepping forward, I wrap my arms around his waist, burying my face in his chest.

He tenses only for a brief second before hugging me back. "He's going to be okay, Grace. I've been trying to get rid of the fucker since I was eight years old, he's not going anywhere."

For the first time tonight, I smile, rememberin' Sawyer's story about the two of them. I pray he's right, because if not, if I lose Sawyer too, I won't survive it.

CHAPTER 45

Grace

The distant sound of a door clicking shut pulls me from sleep and all last night's events come flooding back with a vengeance. My eyes spring open and I sit up quickly, wincing at the tightness in my muscles but my pain fades when I lay eyes on Sawyer. He sits up in his hospital bed, a sexy smile on his handsome face.

"Hey, Cupcake."

The sound of his voice and sight of his smirk has my heavy heart swelling in my chest. I get up from my chair next to his bed and come to sit beside him, my hand moving to the side of his face. "Hey. How are you feeling?"

"Like I've been shot," he says, amusement dancing in his eyes, but I find none of it funny. His smirk fades as he pulls my hand from the side of his face and kisses the inside of my wrist. "I'm okay, Grace. Doctors say I'll be good as new in a few weeks."

"Thank God for that," I whisper.

His eyes wander over my bruised face, expression hardening.

"It looks worse than it feels."

"You shouldn't have a single fucking mark marring you," he grits out. "It shouldn't have happened."

"You're right. It shouldn't have but it could have been so much worse if you wouldn't have shown up," I tell him. "You saved my life, Sawyer."

Hooking a hand behind my neck, he reels me in close. "I'll always save you, Cupcake."

My eyes close, lips pressing against his, the contact penetrating my soul and wrapping around it like a peaceful blanket. It terrifies me to think how close I came to never feeling this again.

Eventually, I pull back, resting my forehead on his. "Was someone just here?" I ask, remembering the sound of the door closing.

"Yeah it was Cade. He brought something by for me. Said they tried to make you leave last night to get rest but you wouldn't go."

"I'm not leavin' without you. Except to go check on Chuckie. But then I'll be coming right back."

He smirks. "How's he doing?"

"Healing, like you," I say, feeling grateful for that.

"Good."

"Do you need anything?" I ask.

"Just you, baby."

I swallow past the lump in my throat, my heart warming and breaking at the same time. "I'm so sorry I got mad at you," I choke out sadly, speaking out the biggest regret I have from last night. "I was just hurt. You promised me you wouldn't ever go there."

"I know, but I had to. I couldn't let him get away with hurting you like that. He had to pay for what he did."

"Please tell me you didn't kill him."

As much as I hate Earl, the last thing I need is to lose Sawyer to a federal prison.

"I didn't kill him. I just roughed him up a bit…and I might have fucked up his truck," he adds, with a sly grin.

"You didn't." I laugh, a matching smile forming on my face.

"Yeah, baby. I smashed the fucking thing to pieces."

A small level of satisfaction fills me to hear that. That truck was his pride and joy, a vehicle he never deserved and used Mama's hard-earned money for.

"I have something for you," he tells me, an expression adopting his face that I can't quite name.

"What?"

He points over at the table beside him.

My gaze follows his finger, and I gasp, my breath completely seizing my lungs as I find the one thing I thought I would never see again—my mama.

Sawyer picks up the pearl urn and passes it to me. "This belongs to you. I hoped, after I showed you this, you would forgive me for breaking my promise."

My hand trembles as I take the urn from him. After all these years, I finally have my mama back. The knowledge has a sob tumbling past my lips. I hug her to my chest and cry.

Sawyer drags his fingers across my tear-soaked cheek in a sweet gesture. "Everything's going to be okay now, Grace. We'll give her a nice funeral like she deserves, and you can bury her ashes, spread them, or keep them. Whatever you want to do. We will do it."

I shake my head, unbelieving how lucky I am to have found this man. I believe with all my heart, that Mama sent me here to Sunset Bay, not only to meet the bestest friends that I have ever had, but to find Sawyer. The only person who has reminded me what it feels like to love and be loved again. It's something I will cherish for the rest of my life.

CHAPTER 46

Grace

Christmas morning

My eyes sweep open, the sound of a strong and steady heart beating beneath my cheek as I come awake, wrapped in the most amazing warmth. Once my mind clears and I become more alert, I remember what day it is and shoot up with excitement rushing through my veins.

I'm about to jump out of bed but Sawyer grabs me around the waist and hauls me back against him. His hard, warm body curls around mine as his lips press against the side of my neck, traveling upwards.

"Where the hell do you think you're going, Cupcake?" he asks, the words whispering in my ear before his teeth sink into the tender flesh.

Shivers rack my body but I fight against the temptation and pry myself from his arms, fleeing from bed.

"Get back here, woman, I'm not done with you."

I look back at him with a smile, my heart skipping at how ridiculously handsome he is. "Hold that thought. I'm going to get your Christmas presents. Be right back."

"I want you as my present!"

His words follow me out the door, making me laugh as I descend the stairs of our new house. I walk into the living room where my beautiful tree is and grab Chuckie's stocking then Sawyer's presents. Surprise fills me when I still see no gifts under the tree for me.

Where is he hiding it?

Shoving the thought aside, I walk up the stairs with my arms full, feeling nervous for him to open what I got him. I wasn't able to afford much because I still don't have a job, which is mostly Sawyer's fault. He made me promise I wouldn't work until after the holidays, since we were so busy with finding a new house and moving. As much as I loved and appreciated Mac letting me stay in his rental, I couldn't live there anymore, not after everything that happened there that fateful night.

Detective Ramirez called a week ago with the news that Miguel has been sentenced to life in prison with no chance of parole. He was not only convicted for my mother's death, but also for the part he played in the forensic scientist's murder. The judge who let him out confessed about the blackmail; he is also facing charges of his own now.

It was the closure I so desperately needed to put this all behind me. Now I can move forward with the one man who has stolen my heart like no other. The thought has me walking back into our room with a smile on my face.

Sawyer is sitting up in bed, his arms crossed over his strong chest and a scowl on his face. "Why aren't you naked yet?"

Smiling, I ignore his poutin' and kneel on the floor to give Chuckie his stocking. "Merry Christmas, my sweet, precious boy. This is for bein' the best dog a girl could ever have."

He licks my cheek with his big sloppy tongue then chows down on all the treats I have stashed inside.

Standing, I find Sawyer still glaring at me. "Don't worry, I got somethin' for my other special guy, too." I climb onto the bed next to him and lay the biggest present on his lap first. "Hurry up and open it."

"I told you not to get me anything," he grumbles.

"And I told you I was going to anyway, so quit your fussin' and open it already."

He grunts but begins unwrapping it. My teeth sink into my bottom lip, butterflies flocking in my tummy, but they fade when he gets the biggest smile on his face. "No way. This is awesome." He holds up his hockey jersey that I had framed.

"Really?"

"Yeah. How did you get it?"

"I had your mom mail it. I did a pretty good job at hidin' it from you, didn't I?"

"Yeah, baby, really good. I had no idea."

"Open this one next." I pass him the second present, keeping the small one for last.

He tears apart the wrapping paper, revealing the black scrapbook. He opens the book, flipping through all the pages of his hockey years. Every picture that was ever taken, to all the newspaper clippings his dad kept. When he reaches the very last page, he reads the words I had scripted on it.

Silver Creek's Hockey Legend
#11 Sawyer Evans

His eyes lift to mine, a sexy smirk curling his lips.

"Do ya like it?" I ask.

"Yeah, baby. I love it. Thank you."

He leans over to kiss me but I stop him, putting my hand over his mouth. "Hold that thought, lover boy. I got one more I need you to open before distracting me with your sexy kisses."

He grunts but accepts the gift I hand him.

Heat creeps up my neck and into my cheeks as he reaches into the gift bag that's stuffed with tissue paper. This present is probably the boldest thing I've ever done but havin' Julia and Kayla with me made it a little easier.

When he pulls out the framed photo, he sucks in a sharp breath, his eyes turning to liquid fire.

My blush deepens as he stares fixated at the 8 x 10 boudoir photo of me in his hockey jersey. "Hope you don't mind I wore your jersey before framin' it," I say lamely.

A strained laugh rumbles from his chest. "I don't mind one fucking bit. Hell, I say we take it out of the frame and make that your choice of pajamas from now on."

"I don't think so," I say, giggling. Though, I can't deny how much I love sleeping in his clothes, especially his shirts.

"Turn it over," I tell him gently.

He does so and reads the words I wrote for him.

Sexy Sawyer,
You may be a legend in Silver Creek, but you will always be a hero to me.
I love you more than words can express.
Love, your Cupcake

He looks up at me, his fierce eyes making my heart dance in my chest. "I love it, Grace, almost as much as I love you."

Smiling, I crawl over and straddle him, his erection straining beneath my bottom. "Good, because I mean every word." I lean in, pressing my lips gently against his.

He hooks a hand behind my neck and yanks me in for a crushing kiss that sets my soul on fire. My tongue slides against his as I give myself to him and this beautiful moment.

"Sawyer?" I breathe, my lungs craving oxygen but my heart craving his touch more.

His mouth never misses a beat, continuing its delicious assault. "Yeah, baby?"

"Where's my present?"

The kiss comes to a stop as he pulls back to look at me, his mouth splitting into a huge grin before he busts into laughter. I join in, having no shame. I wanna know where he's hidin' my dang present.

He slaps himself in the forehead, feigning ignorance. "Damn, Cupcake, I knew I forgot something."

I shake my head, knowin' he's full of it.

His smile never falters. "Get dressed and I'll take you to it."

"It's not here?" I ask, my curiosity piquing.

"Nope."

"Scared you weren't goin' to be able to hide it from me, Sexy Sawyer?"

"Yeah, something like that," he says evasively. "Now go on and get dressed, time's wasting."

I leap off the bed and dash into my closet.

"Nothing fancy," he says. "Just throw on something comfortable."

I slide on a pair of the softest leggings I own and choose my long sage green sweater that drapes off my shoulder. A Christmas gift from Julia and Kayla. It's my favorite sweater and reminds me of the color of Sawyer's eyes.

By the time I walk out of the closet, Sawyer is dressed too, wearing black athletic pants and a white T-shirt that looks anything but plain on him. How the man can make sweats look so damn hot is beyond me.

"Keep looking at me like that, Grace, and we won't be going anywhere."

My eyes shoot up to his face, cheeks heating for getting busted once again. I swear, I can never catch a break with him.

He flashes me a wink, his lips kicking up in a sly smirk.

Sexy son of a gun.

I leave Chuckie chewing on one of the smoked bones and follow Sawyer out the door. Anticipation dances through my belly as we pull out of my driveway.

"How long is the drive?" I ask, practically bouncing in my seat.

"Not long."

"Give me a hint."

"No."

I glare back at him, my lips puckering in a pout. "You're mean."

"You're hot," he fires back, making me laugh.

I decide to give up and look out my window, my excitement palpable. It quickly fades though when I realize we are headed toward main street and my heart plummets straight to my stomach. I haven't been down here since the fire, unable to bear seeing the diner as nothing but ash. Sawyer knows this; surely he wouldn't take me this way?

It seems he would. The moment we turn down the street, I close my eyes and keep my head turned away. Dread twists my stomach when I feel the truck come to a stop.

"Why are you stopping here?" I whisper, hurt edging my voice. I don't have to open my eyes to know exactly where he has parked.

He reaches across the truck, his hand wrapping around my cold fingers. "Grace, baby, look at me."

I shake my head, suddenly feeling like I swallowed razor blades. "I don't want to be here, Sawyer. I'm not ready. I want to leave."

I hear him release a pained breath seconds before his door opens and he steps out. My aching heart bangs against my rib cage as he comes around and opens my door. He takes my hand once again, forcing me out of the truck.

I finally open my eyes but look only at him, knowing the destruction is at my back. "Why are you doin' this?"

He gazes down at me, guilt flashing in his eyes. "Don't you trust me, Grace?"

I trust him with my whole heart but I'm not ready for this. Not today.

He reaches out, his fingers skimming across my cheek. "Please. Just give me a chance."

I find myself unable to refuse him. Leaning into his touch, I nod.

He takes my hand in his and pulls me around the front of the truck. I keep my head down, eyes on my boots as we start across the street; coming to a stop just before the one place I've dreaded seeing. My heart thunders, roaring in my ears.

"Merry Christmas, Cupcake. I hope you like it."

A frown pinches my face as I wonder what on earth he's talkin' about. My head lifts, lips parting on a gasp as all the air gets sucked out of my lungs. I stand motionless, riveted to the sight before me. The beautiful soft pink Victorian-styled building with white scalloped trim is something I've seen a thousand times before but only in my dreams. Across the large windows, in white script reads:

A Slice of Hope with a Sprinkle of Grace

"Sawyer," his name falls on a choked whisper. "What have you done?"

Instead of answering, he lifts my hand to his mouth, brushing his lips across my fingers. "Come on. Let me show you inside."

My feet move mechanically as he leads me to the door, my mind scrambling to catch up with my heart. Every step that brings me closer to a dream I've had for so long has more tears beginning to fall.

Once he has the door unlocked, he opens it and pulls me inside. My hand flies to my mouth, heart melting. It's the exact replica of my drawing, from the soft yellow walls to the baby pink tables and chairs. I tug from his hand to explore further inside.

My fingers dance along one of the tables, a watery laugh escaping me at the cupcake that's been painted on the top. I look over at him, his face blurry but I don't miss his dashing smile.

"I know this is your thing, but I had to add a little something of me in here."

I shake my head, unbelieving any of this. "How?" I ask. "How on earth did you do this? Only eight weeks ago the diner was here."

"My dad."

My eyes widen. "Your father?"

He nods. "After the fire I told him about your drawing. I asked if he could get it done by Christmas and he said he'd make it happen. He called in every favor he had owed to him and brought a crew down here. We busted our asses but we pulled it off."

I gape back at him in utter disbelief. "*This* is where you have been disappearing to? Not the gym?"

His response is a sly smile.

"This had to have cost a fortune, Sawyer," I say, guilt mixing with the warmth in my heart.

"It doesn't matter."

"It does."

"The hell it does! It's my Christmas gift, and I can spend however much I want on it."

My chin drops to my chest, my flowing tears falling faster. A war battles within me, wondering how I am supposed to accept the most beautiful gift anyone has ever given to me.

Sawyer comes to stand before me, his hands cupping my wet cheeks as he lifts my gaze to his. "This is something you've wanted your whole life, Grace, and I get to be lucky enough to give it to you. Take it and live it."

"I don't deserve this."

"You more than deserve it, baby, and so does your mother." Before I can register the last part of his sentence, he turns me to the side and there I find my favorite picture of her, beautiful and smiling.

In Loving Memory Of Hope Morgan

The image is enlarged, taking up half the wall and is so crystal clear it looks like she's really here, sharing in this moment with me. My feet move on their own accord, my tearful eyes riveted on my beautiful mother. The woman who taught me how to love, how to bake…my best friend. Upon reaching the wall, my hand lifts, fingers touching her face as I recall how soft her skin was, her sugary scent even invading my senses.

The sob I've been holding in pours out of me, shattering my chest and echoing through the bakery. I drop my forehead on her shoulder and cry out at the unfairness of it all. That she doesn't get to be here to live our dream like we always wanted.

Sawyer walks up behind me, his large body covering my back as his arms come around me.

"I miss her so much," I cry.

"I know, baby." His lips press against my neck, arms pulling me back closer to him. "But now her memory will be kept alive through this bakery and a piece of her will be shared with everyone who comes in here and eats the pies that the two of you created. You're still going to share this with her, Grace, just in a different way." His words wrap around my heavy heart, creating a blanket of peace that I so desperately needed.

I turn to face him, wrapping my arms around his waist as I peer up at him with all the love I feel in my heart. "You have no idea what you've given me. Not just this bakery but so much more." My hands slide under the back of his shirt, his hot skin warming my soul further. "The day you came into the diner to walk me home, that huge gaping hole in my heart got a little smaller, and now, it barely exists. I love her and miss her every day but since you came into my life, it doesn't hurt as much. You make it better…you make everything better."

His hand lifts to my cheek, the familiar gesture saying so much more than words could. "I have a confession, Cupcake."

I remain silent, a little nervous for what he's about to say.

"That day when I came in to walk you home, remember when I said I just wanted to get to know you because our friends were married."

"Yeah…"

"Well I lied. I planned the whole time to get you in my bed and never let you go."

I burst into laughter; shaking my head at the fact he can make me laugh even at a time like this. "You're incorrigible, Sawyer Evans."

"Yeah, but you love me."

I peer up at him, my smile fading. "I do. So much."

"Good, then I need you to do something for me."

"Name it," I say without hesitation. There isn't one thing I wouldn't do for this man.

He drops to one knee before me, making my breath stall in my lungs. "Marry me."

My jaw drops, hands going on either side of my face as I stare down at him in shock. "Are you serious right now? Because if this is a joke and you're messin' with me, I'm going to hurt you."

He rears back, shocked by my outburst. "Of course I'm serious. Look." He reaches in a pocket and pulls out a small black velvet box. The moment he flips it open the entire world falls away except for what rests inside. A pink diamond sits on a platinum band, accented by smaller yellow stones on either side of it. It's the most stunning piece of jewelry I have ever seen.

"Grace? Are you listening to me?"

My eyes shift from the ring to Sawyer, and I quickly realize he's been talking to me but I haven't heard a word of it.

"What the hell could you possibly be thinking about at a time like this?" he asks, sounding thoroughly amused.

Sniffling, I wipe my wet cheeks with the back of my hand. "That my Christmas presents to you suck."

Laughter barrels out of him, the husky sound of it washing over me and feeding my happy soul. He climbs to his feet, pulling me into his arms once again. "Your gifts were perfect, baby. But the best one you will give me today is if you say *yes* right now." He leans his forehead against mine, adding to the moment. "You once told me that everyone should belong to someone. I'm asking you, Grace, to belong to me for the rest of your life."

The beautiful words feed a part of me, a part that has only and will only ever belong to him.

He brushes his lips against mine, my tears mingling with the touch. "Say yes."

"Yes, I'll marry you."

He slides the ring on my finger, making me the happiest girl in the whole world.

"It's perfect," I whisper.

"I tried to get them to make the diamond into a cupcake but they told me they couldn't do it. Can you fucking believe that? Who can't make a diamond look like a cupcake?"

The ridiculous statement has me bursting into laughter but it's cut off when he lifts me off my feet and steals my lips in a searing kiss. Moaning, I match him stroke for stroke and lose myself in this perfect world we create together.

His hands cup my bottom, hoisting me up higher. "I need you, Grace. Right fucking now."

"Yes!" The permission flows freely past my lips, my need mirroring his.

My legs wrap around his waist as he blows through the set of doors that lead into the kitchen. He sets me down on the stainless steel island, the cold metal a shock to my heated blood.

"This is so unsanitary," I say, not caring nearly as much as I should.

"Fuck sanitary. Nothing matters right now but the two of us."

He's right. Nothing else will ever matter more than our love for one another.

Our mouths barely miss a beat as we remove our clothes in record time. The moment he enters me, my entire world tilts on its axis.

Every single time.

My head falls back on a cry, pleasure whipping through my senses. "God, Sawyer," I whimper, wishing I could put into words how he completes me, body and soul.

"It's so good, baby, isn't it?"

"So good," I agree.

"That's because it's us, Grace. You and me, forever."

"Forever," I repeat, my heart soaring with the knowledge.

His thrusts are hard, deep, and soul shattering. I will never have enough of this, never have enough of him. He feeds my heart and body like no other and I will cherish this love with him, always.

He reaches between us, his fingers circling my slick nub as he pounds into me.

My inner muscles grip him with my impending orgasm but I hold back, not wanting to go alone. I grip his shoulders, feeling every one of his muscles strain beneath my fingertips.

"Come with me," I whisper.

Our gazes lock, seizing the moment as we find our pleasure together. We cling to each other, our sweat-soaked bodies anchored to one another the same way our souls are. Tears sting my eyes at the beauty we create together, a love I never knew existed until he came along.

"Thank you," I whisper, my lips brushing his ear. "Thank you for making this the best Christmas I've ever had."

He pulls back slightly, his green eyes reeling me in like always. "I promise to always make you happy, Grace."

I smile back at him, my hand resting against his hard jaw. "You already do."

Our moment is interrupted when someone bangs on the bakery door. I jump, startled by the unexpected guest. Sawyer, however, doesn't seem the least bit surprised.

"Good thing I locked that shit."

"Who is it?" I ask, quickly throwing my clothes back on while he throws his shirt over his head.

"Come see," he says, a sly grin stealing his lips.

What has he done now?

Excitement grips me as I follow him out front only to come to a hard stop, another gasp fleeing past my lips at the sight of his family standing outside of the glass doors. "Oh my gosh, are you serious right now?"

Jesse and Sam wave to me as I run to the door and let them in. Both girls pull me in for a group hug. "Merry Christmas, our sweet little southern sister."

"Merry Christmas to you, too. I can't believe y'all are here."

"There's no way we were going to miss the big reveal," Sam says.

They move to Sawyer next, almost bulldozing him down in their excited haste.

A gentle hand lands on my shoulder and I turn around to find Catherine, a warm smile resting on her face. "Merry Christmas, Grace," she says, pulling me in for a hug.

"Merry Christmas. I'm so glad y'all came."

"Us too, honey."

John walks over to greet me next, looking rather proud of himself. "Well, what do you think?" he asks, spreading his arms wide. "I did good, didn't I?"

Like father, like son.

I wrap my arms around his waist, embracing him like the others. "You sure did. It's magical. Thank you so much."

He hugs me tight, practically squeezing the breath out of me. "It was my pleasure, Grace. You're a good girl, you deserve this."

"Don't be taking all the credit, old man. It's still my Christmas gift," Sawyer says, walking over to us.

"Yeah, yeah, yeah," John grumbles but pulls him in for a hard hug, too. "You did good, boy. I'm proud of you."

"Thanks, Dad."

Catherine smiles back at them with tears in her eyes, her love for the two of them written all over her face.

"Ready for one more present?" Jesse asks, handing me the black garment bag she carried in with her.

"Another one?"

"Yep. This is from Sam and me. Go on and open it."

Her enthusiasm sparks my own and I waste no time tearing into it. My mouth drops when I pull out the three waitress uniforms, the exact same ones I cut out of a magazine and added to my sketchbook. There's a pastel yellow, pink, and purple, all of them having scallop-edged white aprons attached to the puffy skirts.

"These are amazin'," I whisper, completely enraptured by their stunning detail.

"They all have adjustable backs, for a one size fits all," Jesse explains, turning the dresses over. "These are just to get you started but I promise I have more coming."

"They're perfect, thank you."

"You're welcome. I'm glad I could contribute to making your dream come true."

"We all are," Catherine says.

Everyone's love and generosity is absolutely breathtaking and I am so lucky to be a part of this family.

A commotion near the door draws my attention and my heart explodes once again when I see all my friends entering with food in their arms. Julia and Jaxson lead the way, followed closely by Kayla and Cooper. Cade helps Mac hobble in on his crutches and Katelyn enters in last with Grams on her arm.

Kayla lifts the casserole dish she holds, her smile as big as my own. "We thought we would christen your new place with Christmas breakfast."

"Too late, we already did that," Sawyer says, a cocky grin on his face.

"Sawyer!" Catherine scolds, sounding as appalled as I feel.

However, everyone else explodes into laughter, finding him as funny as he does himself.

I, on the other hand, do not. Embarrassment heats my face and I nail him in the arm, but it doesn't faze him in the least.

Once the girls put their dishes down, we do a group hug and wish each other a Merry Christmas. Sawyer's mom and sisters welcome Cade with opens arms, embracing him also.

"It's so beautiful in here, Grace," Julia says softly.

"It's incredible, isn't it? I can't believe Sawyer and his family did this for me."

"We can't take all the credit, Cupcake," Sawyer cuts in. "There's one more person who contributed to this."

"Oh?" I ask curiously.

He tips his head to the person behind me and I turn around to find Mac, watching me with a bashful smile.

"It's his land, baby. He signed it over to you."

My hand covers my heart as I peer back at the man who has become like a father to me. "You own this land?"

"Not anymore, it's yours now."

"I should have known you had something to do with this." Walking over, I wrap my arms around him and bury my face in his chest. "I love you so much, Mac."

He gathers me close. "I love you too, darlin'. What do you think about an old man workin' for you?"

My head lifts from his chest and I peer up at him in surprise. "You want to work here with me?"

"Why not? This way I can keep an eye on my girl, and make sure she's being taken care of."

I smile, warmth invading my chest like always when he calls me his girl. "I would love for you to be here with me." Stretching up on my tiptoes, I frame his face between my hands and kiss his worn cheek.

"Uh, Grace?" Kayla says. "What the hell is that?"

I turn around to see her pointing to the ring on my finger.

Catherine gasps, her eyes bugging out of her head. "Oh my god."

"Um..." I glance over at Sawyer for help.

"*That,*" he says, walking over to sling an arm around my shoulders, "is my woman's engagement ring. I asked Grace to marry me this morning, and of course, she said yes."

Chaos breaks out over the room as everyone runs over to congratulate us. All the girls examine my ring, their happiness mirroring my own.

Eventually, I turn around to find Mac standing in the same spot I left him, watching me with a smile. "So my darlin's getting married."

"I am." I walk over to him, hugging his waist again. "What do you think about walkin' me down the aisle?"

His grin spreads and eyes turn glassy. "Well, that would make me damn proud, girl...damn proud."

Realizing the room has fallen silent, I twist around and see everyone looking at the photo of my mother. Mac and I walk over to join them. Catherine sidesteps to make room for me. She puts an arm around my shoulders while Julia takes my hand in hers. Sawyer comes up behind me, his hard body warming my back.

We share a moment of silence for my mother, her stunning smile that I often think about lighting up the whole room.

"She was really beautiful, Grace," Jesse says softly.

"Thank you. I wish you all could have met her. She was so special."

"I have no doubt," Catherine says, giving my shoulder a squeeze. "She had to be to raise someone as wonderful as you."

Her words mean so much to me but not even I hold a candle to my mother. She was one of a kind and someone I strive to be like every day of my life.

Kayla clears her throat. "We should eat before the food gets cold."

Looking over, I see her blinking back tears. It's then I notice all the girls are misty eyed, all affected by a woman they never knew yet truly understand just how special she was.

Everyone heads back into the kitchen but I remain where I am, not ready to follow just yet.

Sawyer stays with me, his arms remaining around my waist as he pulls me back against his chest. "She will live on forever, baby. Through you and through our kids."

Warmth spreads through my chest as I think about having his children. Turning in his arms, I gaze up at him with a smile. "Are you sayin' you wanna have babies with me one day, Sexy Sawyer?"

"Hell yeah. Do you have any idea how good-looking our kids are going to be?"

I walked right into that one.

I burst into laughter and lift to the tips of my toes, trying to plant a kiss on his mouth but I still can't reach. His arms tighten around me and he lifts me off my feet, bringing me in direct contact with what I crave.

My lips brush his in a heated caress. "I love you. Thank you for makin' this the best day of my life."

He rests his forehead against mine. "Anything for you, Cupcake." After one more heart-stopping kiss, he places me back on my feet. "Come on, baby, let's eat."

His fingers link with mine as we start for the kitchen, but I stop at the door, gesturing him to go ahead of me. "I'll be right there."

"You sure?"

I nod.

He hesitates for another second then disappears behind the doors, giving me the privacy I need.

I turn to my mother's picture, her beautiful smiling face lighting up my soul. "It'll always be our dream, Mama, and I promise to make you proud." Kissing two of my fingers, I press them to her lips. "I love you…forever."

EPILOGUE

Grace

Four months later

Pride surges through my chest as my friends and I sit in the new gym, all of us feeling proud for everything our men have accomplished. It's everything I expected and more. Top-of-the-line exercise equipment sits off to the right, weights in the far back corner to the left while the sparring ring sits before us in the very center.

SEAL Extreme has something for everyone. Whether you want to work out, take a self-defense class, or train. The three of us girls are here along with Katelyn and her cousin for the guys to test out their new self-defense class. Faith is as sweet as Katelyn said she was and I know she is going to fit in great with us.

"We need to hurry up and get this show on the road," Kayla says. "I'm having baby withdrawals. I need to hold my goddaughter."

"I miss her, too," Julia says. "And it's only been an hour."

"You probably miss her because that husband of yours is always hogging her. He never shares," Kayla pouts, making me and everyone else laugh.

It's true, he does hog her but it's so beautiful to see. That sweet baby girl has her daddy wrapped around her tiny finger.

"Who's at the bakery for you, Grace?" Katelyn asks.

"Just Mac at the moment. I'm heading back over there right after I'm done here. I have an interview with a girl from the high school today."

The bakery has done better than I ever thought it would and I couldn't be happier, but it's beyond Mac and me. We need more staff and we need it quickly.

"I'm not sure what kind of help you're needing, but I'd be more than happy to lend a hand," Faith says. "At the moment, my evenings and weekends are free."

My heart warms at her kind offer. "Thank you, Faith. I appreciate it. Why don't you come by after and we can talk?"

"I'd love to."

"And you know you have our help if you need it," Kayla says.

"I do, thank you."

They have helped out a lot and I appreciate it very much but they have their own jobs and lives. It's time I hire on more waitresses.

Our conversation ends when the office door opens at the other end of the gym and out walks Sawyer and Jaxson with Cade following close behind. My eyes sweep over the man I'm madly in love with, that ever-present pull between us stronger than ever. His eyes meet mine and he flashes me that sexy wink that has my body temperature rising. We made love just this morning and already I want him again.

"Oh my god," the words are nothing more than a choked whisper, coming from the left of me.

I look over at Faith, all the color from her face draining.

"What is it, what's wrong?" Katelyn asks, looking as worried as the rest of us.

Faith pushes to her feet, trying to hide her face. "I have to go. I have to get out of here."

"What? Why?"

Sawyer comes to a hard stop, his eyes widening on Faith. "Holy shit."

Kayla, Julia, and I share a look, wondering what the heck is going on.

Faith doesn't notice Sawyer's reaction, her head cast down and feet on the move. Cade steps out from behind Sawyer and Jaxson, walking right into Faith's hasty exit.

The two collide accidentally, Faith slamming into Cade's hard chest.

"Whoa." He grabs her shoulders to steady her.

"I'm so sorry, I…" Her words die in her throat as she looks up at Cade with tears streaming down her face, her lips parting in a subtle gasp.

Complete and utter shock adopts Cade's face for all of one second before his expression turns hard, even harder than usual. "What the fuck are you doing here?" His harsh tone makes her flinch.

She rips from his grasp, a sob falling past her as she runs out of the gym.

"Faith, wait!" Katelyn calls. She glares over at Cade before following her cousin out the door.

"Jax, what's going on?" Julia asks, walking over to him.

When he makes no effort to answer, I ask Sawyer next but he remains tight-lipped, his eyes only on Cade.

Katelyn eventually walks back in, tears trickling down her cheeks as she stares at Cade. "It was you," she chokes out. "You're the ones who pulled her out of hell."

Oh god.

It all suddenly becomes clear, Katelyn's cousin, Faith, is the girl they all lived through that torturous week to save.

Turn the page for a letter from the author.

Dear Reader,

Thank you for reading my second novel in the Men Of Honor Series. I hope you enjoyed Sawyer and Grace. My love for the movie *Waitress* was my inspiration for Grace's pie creations and I had so much fun writing her character. Although most things in this book are fictional, one detail wasn't, and that is Grace and Lace. If you loved Grace's Alpine thigh-highs then definitely check them out.

Thank you,
K.C. Lynn

Resisting Temptation

Men of Honor Series

K.C. LYNN

Resisting Temptation

Published by K.C. Lynn

Second Edition

Cover Art by: Vanilla Lily Designs
Editing: Wild Rose Editing
Formatting: BB eBooks

Dedication

Dedicated to my Cupcakes. Thank you so much for the overwhelming support you are constantly showing me. You all mean so much to me. XO!

PROLOGUE

Cade

Fifteen years old

Adrenaline hammers in my veins as I lie in bed, remembering the fight I got into earlier tonight with Clay Rogers. It's the last time I allow myself to be dragged to a preppy jock party. Rogers is lucky all he got was a broken nose and a busted mouth. Maybe next time he will think twice about opening his fucking trap about my family.

I know my father was an abusive alcoholic and my mom a junkie. He did not need to remind me. I've never forgotten where I come from. How can I when I live the hell every day? My old man may be dead now but I carry his DNA. The same darkness that lived inside of him lurks in me, hidden in the darkest parts of my soul. Despite that, I will never become him, or my mother for that matter.

No, not Mother…Maria. She doesn't deserve to be called *Mother.*

There are times when I think she's worse than he was. He would beat me to the point I would be bedridden for days, and she never gave a shit. She was never strong enough to stand up to him.

The best thing that ever happened to our family was when the asshole drank himself stupid and wrapped his truck around a tree. I thought she would straighten out after that and start being the mother she was always supposed to be, but it never happened.

Until recently, she rarely worked, she was always too busy latching herself to whatever loser would provide her next fix, leaving me to fend for my little sister.

Mia is the only reason I'm still here. A sacrifice I will make until the day I die.

As if my thoughts summoned her, she appears in the doorway, my gaze barely making out her tiny figure in the dark. "Hey, squirt. What are you still doing awake?"

"Can I sleep with you again?"

It's the fourth night this week. Usually, I don't even hear her come in; I just wake up with her plastered against my chest or back. It's unlike her and getting to be a little unnerving. However, I could never deny her.

"Yeah, come on."

I move back as she crawls her tiny body up beside my big one. I'm bigger than most kids my age; it's the only thing I'm grateful that I inherited from my old man. Mia is the complete opposite though. For a seven-year-old she is smaller than most. She's also sweet, innocent, and untainted. There isn't an ounce of darkness inside of her. We're polar opposites yet she's the best part of my family. She means everything to me.

Guilt fills my chest, for not being able to do more to get us both out of here and away from Maria. My mother says things are going to be better because of this new guy she's seeing, the one who's going to help her get on a new path, *God's path.*

Yeah right.

The guy is a fucking nut job, and Maria is even crazier if she thinks we are going to have anything to do with him. I overheard them talking about us going to live out on his compound that's out in the middle of nowhere. The place is isolated and completely fucked up. I thought he was Amish or something, but Maria says he's not. I don't know what his deal is but I do know my sister and I are having no part of it.

Mia curls up next to me, holding her stuffed pink rabbit that she carries with her everywhere. I won it for her at the fair last year and it's the best five bucks I ever spent.

She peers up at me with big brown eyes, her white hair bow that she wears every night to bed flopping to the side.

"Talk to me, kid. What's wrong?"

She shrugs. "Just couldn't sleep."

"You sure that's all? You've been coming in here a lot lately."

"I'm sure."

I don't believe her but I also don't push. She'll tell me when she's ready. We're close like that.

Things are quiet for a few minutes, and I think she's fallen asleep but she proves me wrong when she speaks again, her voice barely above a whisper. "Cade, do you believe in God?"

The question catches me off guard and the alcohol that was fogging my brain moments ago begins to clear. I take a second to think about how to answer then decide on the truth. "I don't know. I don't think much about it. There are times when I think maybe there is and other times I don't."

What kind of God lets my sweet, little sister get stuck in a hellhole like this? It's one thing to throw me into it, but not Mia. She deserves all the happiness the world has to offer, not a mother like Maria.

"Why?" I ask, looking down at her.

"Mr. Charles says he's special and that God speaks to him. He said we must follow God's orders or we don't get to go to heaven."

I knew it. A crazy, fucking head case.

"He's full of shit, Mia, okay? The guy is crazy."

Something I should have known, since Maria is shacked up with him.

"Mom's making me go to church out there tomorrow morning. Will you come with me?"

I blow out a heavy breath and think of a way to let her down gently.

"Please, Cade," she begs. "I—I really don't like him much."

I tense at the fear edging her voice. "Why? Did he say or do something to make you upset?"

If he did I will fuck him up.

It takes her a moment to answer. "No. I just don't like him, and Mom is making me go out there tomorrow by myself, because she has to work. Please come with me."

I look down at my sister's wide, hopeful eyes and know I can't let her down. "Don't worry, I'll come."

And I'm going to have a little talk with that asshole about the shit he's been spewing. I'll also be letting him know that we will never be a part of his messed-up life. Ours is screwed up enough.

"Thanks, Cade. I knew I could count on you." She throws her tiny arm around my waist and buries her head in my bare chest.

"No problem, kid."

Silence fills the air once again and my eyes drift shut, sleep tugging at me, until she speaks again. "Do you think I'm a good enough girl to go to heaven when I die?" she whispers.

My eyes spring back open, body tensing.

I swear, this asshole is going to get a serious beating when I'm through with him.

"Yeah, Mia, if anyone gets to go to heaven, it's you."

She snuggles deeper into me, seeming satisfied with that answer. "I love you, Cade."

"I love you, too. Don't worry about tomorrow. I'll be there and everything will be fine."

She nods against my chest and that's the last I hear from her.

I allow myself to fall into a deep slumber but not before I hear her whisper two little words.

"I'm sorry."

There's a nasty taste in my mouth and a serious pounding behind my eyes when I wake up the next morning. Groaning, I turn over and stop abruptly when I remember Mia is next to me. Only when I look down she is nowhere in sight. I glance at the clock and see it's ten in the morning already.

Shit!

I shoot up in a panic and throw on my clothes from the night before then head into the kitchen. There I find Maria pouring herself a cup of coffee, looking worse than I feel.

"Where's Mia?" I ask.

She ignores my question and dumps the contents of her purse all over the counter until she finds what she's looking for. Grabbing a bottle, she shakes out a couple of aspirin and throws them into her mouth before taking a sip of her coffee.

"Where the fuck is Mia?" I ask again, my patience wearing.

She winces, her eyes narrowing. "Stop shouting. Charles picked her up about an hour ago, to take her to church with him at the compound."

My earlier panic comes flooding back with a vengeance. "What the hell are you thinking letting that psycho take her anywhere?"

She tosses me an annoyed look. "She has been alone with him before. She's fine."

"She begged me to go with her, told me that she hated him."

"Oh, stop it, Cade. You're being ridiculous. Besides, Charles didn't want you to bring her. He doesn't think you will fit in there."

"That's because the guy is a fucking lunatic!"

Please, Cade. I don't want to be there by myself, I really don't like him much.

My gut clenches when I think about how scared she sounded. Suddenly, I'm plagued with the feeling that something is very wrong.

I walk up to Maria and stick my hand out. "Give me the keys to your car, now."

"No, I have to go to work soon. And watch your tone when you're talking to me. Charles is right; I should send you to a boot camp. You have no respect for me."

That darkness I keep locked inside begins clawing its way to the surface. I take a threatening step forward, backing her into the counter. "You don't want to screw with me right now, Maria. Give me the keys to your car."

She swallows nervously, but makes no move to hand them over.

"Now!" I slam my fist down, making her jump.

She tosses me the keys. "She's fine, Cade, you'll see."

"She better be. Otherwise he won't be the only one to pay."

"If you think anyone in that compound is going to let you in when you look like you're about to commit murder, you better think again. Everyone is very loyal to him."

"Thanks for the tip." Walking away, I head into her room and ransack the closet until I find the gun my father kept there. The same one he used to pretend was loaded while he held it to my head and pulled the trigger as part of a sick game.

"What on earth do you think you're doing?"

Ignoring her, I charge out of the house, jumping into our rusted out, piece of shit car and peel away. My dread grows with each passing mile, fury colliding with an unspeakable force.

She has to be okay; she would have told me if something was going on, right?

The more I mull over that question, the more I fear I'm wrong.

It takes all of fifteen minutes for me to arrive at the compound. I spot a cluster of vehicles in the distance, trailing behind each other in a long line as they leave the entry of a big, black gate. When I see the gates beginning to close, I step on the gas, sending the car racing forward, and make it just in the nick of time.

I drive down a dusty street, briefly registering the wooden-made houses. A couple of women who are dressed like they're from another century stand on their front lawn, eyeing me fearfully. My foot presses harder on the gas when I spot the church up ahead on the right-hand side. I come to a screeching halt just outside of it and climb out with my gun in hand.

"You can't be here, you must leave now," a young female voice says.

Turning around, I rear back, almost falling on my ass when I see the girl looks to be about my age but has a large pregnant stomach.

What—the—fuck.

It doesn't take me long to realize this place is even more fucked-up than I thought. My fear for Mia grows, twisting my stomach into a tight knot.

"Where's my sister?" It's obvious she knows whom I'm talking about but she keeps her mouth shut. I point my gun at her, the cold metal heavy in my hand. "Tell me where she is or I will drive a fucking bullet through your head."

The last thing I want to do is take anyone's life but if it comes down to that in order to protect my sister, I won't think twice about it.

"Just tell him, Helga," another girl says, fear edging her voice as she sidles up next to her.

"You cannot change what is God's will," Helga finally speaks. "God spoke to Charles about your sister, she is where she needs to be."

Her words have my panic reaching a whole new level. Flicking the safety off, I shoot the ground right next to her feet.

Both girls scream and jump back.

"Fuck you and your god. Tell me where my sister is, right now!" My arm begins to shake with restraint, my finger hovering over the trigger.

"She's in the back of the church, in his sacred room," the younger one blurts out.

Without a second thought, I race up the church steps, watching as another girl charges through the door ahead of me. I fight to keep up with her as she races down one of the hallways, stopping at the last door on the right. "Father Charles, there's trouble!"

I shove her out of the way and attempt to enter the room, but it's locked. "Mia!" I shout, my fist heavy as I pound on the door. "Are you in there?"

The sound of muffled curses and shuffling penetrates the roaring in my ears. Then I hear something that has my chest constricting with despair—small, quiet sobs.

My sister's.

Backing up, I kick the door open and charge inside, but the sight that I'm met with has my feet stopping in their tracks. My legs threaten to crumble beneath me as bile surges up my throat. I blink several times, thinking what I'm seeing isn't real.

It can't be real.

My sister is tied to a bed, wearing a white dress that's hiked up to her hips, baring her most private part. Two men hold towels that are soaked with blood. Fear is written all over their faces as they stare at me and my gun. My gaze lands on Charles S. Winston, the guy whose pants are still undone, the center of them stained crimson.

"Now just stay where you are, son," he warns, holding up his hand. "This is God's will and you cannot change what he wants."

The darkness that I've always kept hidden unleashes with a vengeance and I welcome it, letting it swallow me whole. "You sick motherfucker!" I charge at him, my body colliding with his as I take him to the ground.

My gun flies out of my hand on impact but I don't let that stop me, my fists raining down on his face, heavy and hard. Rage fuels my violence, consuming me right down to my black heart.

Hands quickly grapple me, yanking me off and locking my arms behind my back. It gives the asshole an opportunity to strike back. I don't feel his hits though; I feel nothing but the fury surging through my veins.

Eventually, I manage to rip out of the arms that hold me and land beside my gun. I reach for it and when I see the asshole move toward my sister, I don't hesitate. The blast is deafening, echoing through the room as the bullet finds its way into the center of his skull.

As he crumbles to the floor, I push to my feet. By the time I point the gun at the other two, they are already scrambling out the door.

"Cade." My sister's weak sobs have me pushing forward. Only then do I see just how badly she's hurt, her small body lying in a pool of blood.

"Oh shit." The two words are choked through the restriction of my throat. I quickly fish my cell phone out of my pocket and dial 9-1-1, rattling off my location. The lady begs me to stay on the line but I hang up, wanting to give all my attention to my sister.

Untying her wrists, I climb on the bed behind her, pulling her between my legs as I cradle the top half of her tiny body to my chest. Her labored breathing tells me things are bad.

"Why didn't you tell me?" I grit past the fire erupting in my throat.

"I'm so sorry," she sobs. "He said he'd kill you if I ever told."

She was scared for me; she kept the secret to protect me. Guilt strikes me hard and fast, mixing with all the other painful emotions pulsing through my body.

"I'm scared," she cries.

"Don't be, kid, everything is going to be okay. I promise." Leaning down, I press a kiss to her clammy forehead and watch as hot tears spill onto her pale face, mixing with her own. Only then do I realize they are mine. A foreign emotion for me. I haven't cried since before my dad died.

No matter how tightly I hold her, wishing her to be okay, it never happens.

That day, before the ambulance had even arrived, my sister died in my arms. And the moment she took her last breath was the exact moment ice froze over my heart. It was the same day I stopped living and only existed.

CHAPTER 1

Cade

Ten years later—Iraq

The hard earth crunches beneath my boots as I trudge through the trees and dry patches of grass, making my way to the location I have been coming to for the past few nights in hopes *she's* there again. A woman who has invaded my every thought and penetrated walls that I thought were impenetrable.

A woman I've never even met.

I'm alerted of her presence before I even see her, the beautiful sound of her voice drifting through the air like a harmonic melody, hitting me like a powerful blow to the chest.

As I come up to the wide, grassy clearing, I finally spot her, and once again the beautiful sight of her rocks me to my fucking core. She sits cross-legged and leans against a tree, strumming her guitar and singing what sounds like country. It's music I would never listen to but if I knew I'd always hear it from her, I'd gladly listen to it every day of my life.

Long red hair cascades down her back and frames her slender shoulders, catching certain rays of the sun. My eyes travel south and I see she's not wearing her usual sundress. Instead she wears a white tank top and jean shorts that show off her smooth legs and scuffed-up cowgirl boots. The way the sun has started to set casts a glow on her that doesn't even make her look real. It makes her look like something that people try to fill your head with, but I know is bullshit—an angel. But if I did believe in angels, I'd swear this girl is one.

Three nights ago, I left camp and went for a walk, needing to be alone. On that walk, only a few short minutes from base, a sweet, soft laugh had caught my attention. Following the sound, I had come up to this clearing and found her with a bunch of Iraqi kids. She was chasing after them while playing a game.

The moment my gaze landed on her, something happened inside my chest, something that I haven't felt in years, and I have no idea why. Sure, she's beautiful, but I've seen lots of beautiful women. I've fucked most of them, too. Yet something about this girl had me staying out of sight and watching her until she left. She was all I thought about that entire night and the next day, which really pissed me off.

The next evening I came back, hoping to catch another glimpse of her, wanting to reassure myself that I was being an idiot and that she was not what I made her out to be. Instead of getting the reassurance I wanted, that same feeling came back, except this time it was even more powerful because she had a guitar and was singing. The sound of her voice rooted me to my spot and seized my lungs. If it were possible, it would have knocked me on my ass. I had never heard anything like it.

That night I sat for two hours and listened to her sing shit that I would never usually listen to. I felt like an asshole for spying on her, but I was unable to leave. I'm still trying to figure out how, after ten years of being completely numb, some beautiful, redheaded country girl evokes something inside of me that no one else ever has. It's far from warmth, because I'm incapable of feeling that, but it's still something.

In the midst of these foreign feelings, I've been wondering what the hell she is doing in a place like this. Even though most troops have been evacuated and the war declared over, it's still dangerous, and the insurgency is ongoing. It's actually been getting a lot worse lately, which is why I'm here.

So what drives someone like her to be here?

My attention shifts across the field, to where I find a young boy walking toward her. The woman is clearly expecting him and is even happy to see him, if her smile is anything to go by. A smile that causes that weird sensation in my chest. An emotion I can't quite name.

The boy approaches her shyly and hands her a single white flower. Her smile brightens as she accepts it, and she even gives him a kiss on the cheek.

Lucky little fucker.

She sits back down and opens her arms to him. Turning, he sits on her lap and she places the guitar in his hands. Her arms go around him as she helps him strum the guitar. The biggest smile lights up the kid's face and they both begin to sing a song.

Finding myself unable to walk away once again, I take a seat by the tree I have been sitting at for the past three nights and soak in everything about her, wondering why she has such a hold on me.

Faith

My voice is soft as I sing "Hallelujah" with Aadil, the sweet boy I met days ago, my heart warming at the infectious smile on his face. I'm pretty sure he loves music as much as I do. We have been practicing this song ever since he found me in this field, singing it almost a week ago. His English is not the best but he's gotten much better at following along with me.

I came to Iraq on a missions trip with my church a few weeks ago and it has changed my life forever. I've met some of the most special people in my time here, one of them being this little boy.

The day I spotted him in the trees listening to me, he had a look of wonderment splashed across his young face. He was timid when I first approached him but warmed up to me quickly. From there, I completely lost my heart to him, and every evening since he has come to this spot to be with me. The other day he even brought a bunch of his friends with him and we had a wonderful time playing games.

It bothers Beth, the missions' leader, that I leave camp, so I tried to have Aadil come to us, but for some reason he's scared of being seen with me. The fear in his eyes troubled me and I didn't want to pressure him so I promised to meet him here every night until the day I leave. When that final day arrives, I don't know how I will deal with it. He has come to mean an awful lot to me and I don't look forward to saying goodbye.

After we finish the song, Aadil turns to me, looking rather proud of himself. "I did better."

"Yes, you did. Have you been practicing without me?"

He nods. "Only in here though," he replies, tapping his temple.

"Well I can tell, you did wonderful, Aadil. I'm very proud of you."

He beams at my praise. I'm just about to suggest another song but am interrupted by an angry bellow. My attention shifts across the field where I see a furious man storming toward us, hollering in Arabic.

Aadil gasps. "Oh no. My father." Pure fear washes over his face as he quickly stands.

I promptly follow suit, placing my hands on his small, trembling shoulders, hoping to offer reassurance. Though, I'd be lying if I said I wasn't terrified right now too, my heart thunders in my chest at the threatening approach of the man.

Aadil begins apologizing profusely in Arabic, but his father will hear none of it. It doesn't take me long to realize he's angry that Aadil is with me.

Praying he understands English, I swallow back my fear and raise my hands, calmly telling him I mean no harm.

"Shut up, bitch!"

I guess he understands English.

Once he gets within arm's reach, he raises his hand to strike out at Aadil.

"No!" I lock my arms around Aadil's small body and turn us around, bracing myself for the powerful blow I'm about to receive, but it never comes.

After a few tension-filled seconds, I look over my shoulder to find a tall, dark, and very threatening man behind me. An American soldier.

His fingers grip Aadil's father's wrist in the air, preventing it from landing on me. The lethal expression on his face has fear skipping down my spine. Thankfully, I'm not the one he's angry at.

"Mind your own business, Soldier," Aadil's father seethes, clearly having no sense like any sane person would when it comes to this man. "You don't know who you're fucking with."

The soldier shoves Aadil's father, hard enough that he lands on his back with a hard thud. "I don't care who you are. Leave now or I will rip out your fucking spine."

Whoa!

By the lethal look of this soldier, I have no doubt he will do it. If Aadil's father has any sense at all he will heed the warning. Thankfully, it seems he does. He climbs to his feet, his furious eyes moving from the soldier to Aadil. He yells something at him in Arabic that has the little boy flinching in fear.

I hug him closer, trying to offer as much comfort as I can.

His father drags his furious gaze from him back to the soldier. "This isn't over. You have made a very grave mistake," he threatens before storming back off the way he came.

The soldier doesn't seem the least bit concerned, his cold, hard expression remaining on him until the very second Aadil's father disappears into the trees.

A relieved breath escapes my chest, my rapid pulse beginning to slow. I'm about to thank the American but Aadil's quiet sniffles stop me cold. Dropping down on my knees before him, I cup his small, scared face between my shaking hands. "Are you all right, Aadil?"

"No. I have to go home."

Panic seizes my chest, fearing what will happen to him when he leaves here and faces his father alone. "I don't think that's a good idea. He is very angry right now. Why don't you stay with me for a little while longer and give him some time to calm down?"

Though, I have a feeling no amount of time is going to calm that man down.

He shakes his head, shutting down the suggestion right away. "The longer I wait, the worse it will be."

The remark sends my heart plummeting, drowning in a pool of fear. "Aadil, I'm scared for you. Come back to camp with me and we will figure out a way to help you."

"I will be okay, I promise. I will go to Ommah."

His mother.

He throws his arms around my neck and presses a kiss to my cheek. Emotion clogs my throat, tears welling in my eyes as I hug him back tightly.

"Please come back so I know you're okay," I plead on a whisper.

"I will when I can. I promise." He breaks our embrace then glances up at the soldier timidly. "Thank you, mister." The words fall from him quietly before he takes off running in the same direction his father left.

I watch until he disappears in the trees, feeling absolutely terrified for him. Climbing to my feet, I turn to the soldier and swallow nervously, licking my sudden dry lips, his presence still giving off a threatening vibe.

"Thank you," I speak, barely managing the two words. "I'm not sure how you found us, but I'm glad you did. He was—"

"What the hell is wrong with you, lady?"

I flinch from his harsh tone, caught off guard by his anger toward me. "I beg your pardon?"

"I said, what the fuck is wrong with you? Don't you know there was a war here between them and us only a few months ago? It's dangerous, especially for people like you."

People like me?

"And here you are, without a care in the world, strumming your damn guitar while off in fucking la-la land."

"Hey!" I clap my hands in front of his face, cutting off his rude tirade. "First off, buster, I know exactly how dangerous this place can be. My camp is only a few minutes from here, and I am always careful—"

"Careful?" he bellows. "You call jumping in front of a guy's fist careful? Jesus, I'd like to see what you think is safe."

"What did you expect me to do? I wasn't going to stand by and let him hit Aadil. Besides, who are you to bark at me? You—you…pompous ass!" Turning on my heel, I stomp away only to have my fiery temper get the best of me. Midstep, I spin back around and charge back over to him, my head craning all the way back as I match him glare for glare.

In the midst of my anger, I notice he smells really darn good.

The mean, delicious-smelling jerk.

Refusing to let his large size and cold expression intimidate me, I square my shoulders and jam my finger into his hard chest. "I'll have you know, I am not some dumb girl who sits around and strums her guitar in 'la-la land.' So before you judge someone you don't even know, *buddy*, you might want to choose your words more carefully next time. And when someone says *thank you*, you say *you're welcome.* Not cuss and shout at them. So…yeah! That's all I have to say."

Feeling a little better after putting him in his place, I turn back around, and head for my guitar. Before I'm able to make it there though my boot sinks into a pothole and throws me off balance. My arms flail and a sharp sting slices through my ankle. I land painfully on my butt, a heavy oomph shoving from my chest.

Oh, God, that did not just happen.

Heat invades my face, my cheeks turning the same shade as my hair as I feel the rude, sexy soldier at my back. He's probably laughing his butt off right now but my wounded ego prevents me from checking.

With as much dignity as I can muster, I push off the rough ground to stand, but as soon as I put weight on my tender ankle, it gives out on me again. Sucking in a sharp breath, I drop back to the ground.

"Easy there, Firecracker," the jerk says as he approaches. He drops down in front of me, and I expect to see amusement on his face, but am surprised when I find the same hard expression he's had this entire time.

"I'm fine. I just need a minute," I mumble.

He grunts at the lie and reaches for my booted foot.

I scoot back, my pride refusing to let him help me. "I said I'm fine. Go get back to whatever it is you were doing before showing up here and yelling at me."

His jaw flexes, teeth grinding. "Look, I'm sorry for yelling at you, all right?" he snaps, not sounding the least bit apologetic. "Now let me look at your damn ankle to make sure it's not broken."

My mouth drops open at his audacity. "What kind of apology is that?"

"The only one you're going to get from me. Now give me your damn foot!"

I'm too blown away by his rude behavior to evade him a second time. His hand is quick as it grabs my boot and carefully brings it over to him. Teeth grinding, I look away as he pulls off my boot. His large warm hand is like a heated caress on my bare calf, the soft touch a contradiction to the hard man before me. It causes a gasp to part my lips, my traitorous body feeling something it absolutely shouldn't be feeling.

His eyes lift to mine, a subtle warmth entering the dark irises. He breaks our connection quickly and clears his throat before mumbling off another apology, thinking the gasp that came from me was due to pain.

While he examines my ankle, I find my gaze drawn to him, eyes roaming in appreciation. Despite his terrible attitude, there is no denying how incredibly attractive he is. His dark mussed hair is a little longer than I would expect a soldier to have but it complements his warm skin tone and eyes that are framed with thick, black lashes. Lashes any woman would envy.

His white muscle tank shows off his lean sculpted muscles while also displaying a tribal pattern of black ink woven up both arms. The design reaches all the way up past his shoulders and ends at his collarbone. Everything about him is darkly beautiful and reminds me of a fallen angel.

At the sound of his throat being cleared, my eyes snap to his, face flaming when I realize I've been busted checking him out.

Get a grip, Faith!

He gently probes my ankle with his thumbs. "Does that hurt?"

I shake my head, worried what my voice will portray.

"It's not broken but will probably be tender for a while."

He releases my foot and I instantly miss the warmth of his hand.

"I'm sure it's fine," I say, avoiding eye contact. "I'm just going to sit here and move it around for a few minutes before trying to walk again."

When he makes no move to leave, I spare him a glance and find him staring at my chest, his eyes even harder and colder than they were before.

Looking down, I realize he's glaring at the cross hanging around my neck. I clutch the heavy metal nervously, confused by the sudden anger.

His eyes drift back to mine, and for a brief second I swear I see pain resonate on his face. But it's so quick I begin to think I imagined it.

Things between us become even more awkward. "Well, thank you for looking at my ankle. Take care." I wince at my pathetic attempt of trying to part ways.

He grunts, not seeming the least bit offended. "Nice try, Red. I'm not leaving you here by yourself after what just happened with that asshole."

I can't deny the way my pulse skips at the nickname. "You don't have to do that. I'm sure he's not coming back. He was only here for Aadil."

The thought has my stomach clenching in fear for the young boy.

"What are you even doing here?" he asks.

My gaze meets his, head tilting inquisitively.

"In Iraq," he elaborates.

"I'm on a missions trip with my church."

Again, something hard flashes in his eyes, but before I can even question it he looks away.

"What about you?" I ask. "Was Aadil's father right, are you a soldier?"

"Something like that," he replies, not offering anything more.

"How did you know we were in trouble?"

"I was out for a walk."

"Is your base close by?"

He responds with a single nod.

"Anyone ever tell you that you're a real chatterbox?"

He doesn't smile like I hoped he would.

Oookay…

It's a good thing the guy is so good-looking, because he doesn't have much going for him in the personality department. I should be offended, or even scared from the vibes he throws off, but instead I'm finding myself intrigued with this very dark soldier.

"What's your name?" I ask, wanting to find out as much about him as I can before he leaves. When he doesn't offer an answer, I push. "Come on. It's only two words. It's the perfect question for your vocabulary."

He watches me unamused, not finding me as funny as I find myself. I start to think he's not going to answer but he surprises me a moment later. "Cade Walker."

Figures, even his name is sexy.

"It suits you," I say as a compliment. Instead of saying *thank you* he continues to stare at me.

Seriously, what is it with this guy?

"Well, it's nice to meet you, Cade Walker. My name is Faith Williams."

A laugh barrels out of his chest, but there's nothing funny-sounding about it. "Of course it is."

I flinch from his harsh tone. "Is there a problem with my name?"

When he doesn't answer, I try to draw my own conclusion, remembering the way he glared at the cross around my neck.

"You have something against God, Cade Walker?"

"Can't have a problem with something you don't believe in."

I'm not offended by his answer, I respect everyone's beliefs, but I'd be lying if I said I wasn't saddened by it. He clearly has a lot more problems with God than just not believing in him.

"Your ankle doing better?" he asks, changing the subject and climbing to his feet.

The dismissal is apparent, and I find myself disappointed about not getting to talk to him more, though, I'm not sure why since he hasn't been all that much fun to be around.

"Yeah. It's good." Just as I'm about to push to stand, he offers me his hand. I gaze up at him, surprised by the thoughtful gesture. His usual hard gaze is a little softer as he waits for me to accept it. This man's moods give me serious whiplash.

Reaching up, I put my small hand into his big one, and again I'm struck with that same feeling I had when he touched my leg. It's a feeling that is foreign to me, but I like it, a lot.

Once he pulls me up, I get a whiff of his clean, masculine scent and it takes every ounce of willpower I have not to lean into him.

I am seriously losing it.

He releases my hand quickly, clearly not having the same problem that I am at our close proximity. I try not to let that offend me too much.

"Well, thanks again…for everything." I begin limping to my guitar, feeling his hard eyes boring into my back.

"Hey, Red!"

I ignore the tiny shivers at the nickname from his deep voice and turn back around to face him.

"Make sure you don't come back here. Especially by yourself."

Again, I find myself wondering why he cares. "Sorry, but I plan to come back here every night until I see Aadil. This is the only place he knows where to find me."

His expression tightens with anger. "You can't be here by yourself, it's too dangerous. Why can't you understand that?"

Instead of getting upset by his surly reply, I flash him a bright smile. "Well then, maybe I'll see you again after all, Cade Walker."

Leaning down, I pick up my guitar and feel him watch me with every step I take.

I have a feeling tonight will not be the last I see of Cade Walker. At least I'm hoping it's not.

CHAPTER 2

Cade

The next night, I head back to that same spot, berating myself the entire way. I swore I would not go near her again, she's not my business, but I have no doubt she will be back for that kid, and the thought of something happening to her makes my gut churn, dread twisting my insides.

At least that's what I keep telling myself why I'm coming back. No way is it because I can't get the sexy redhead out of my mind. If I thought the woman was beautiful from afar, that's nothing compared to how she looked up close.

She had creamy flawless skin with the exception of a small dusting of freckles across her perfectly shaped nose. Her emerald eyes are pronounced, complimented by dark red hair that cascaded down her slender shoulders. She was absolutely perfect except for one thing…one very big thing.

My teeth grind as I think about that fucking necklace around her neck. It pisses me off that after knowing everything I do about her, and what she believes, I still want her. It's because I've never met another girl quite like her. Definitely not one that has ever intrigued me as much.

Beneath that soft, pretty exterior lies a spitfire. When I gave her shit about being there she dished it right back and it only made my cock harder. To top it off, I caught her openly staring at me while I examined her ankle, and the blush that stained her cheeks when I busted her… It took every ounce of control I had to restrain myself from ripping her clothes off and finding out just how far that pink color went.

My thoughts trail off when I come up to the clearing and spot her sitting against the tree again, her head tilted back as she strums her guitar. The sun has started to set, casting a glow on her that makes her look as innocent as I know she is.

With no other choice I start toward her, because now that I have met her, if I stayed back in the trees I'd be even more of a pervert than I was before.

Her eyes are closed when I reach her, but she knows I'm here. "Nice to have you back, Cade Walker."

My cock jumps at the sound of my name falling past her lips.

She opens her eyes, her emerald irises punching me in the chest as she graces me with a beautiful smile.

I push away the warm feeling that tries worming its way into my chest and sit down next to her, but not too close. This chick has proven to be fucking dangerous.

"Don't get too excited, Red, you didn't leave me much choice, since I knew you would be by yourself again."

She's not put off in the least by my shitty attitude, her smile never wavering. "*It's nice to see you too, Faith,*" she mocks.

I grunt, completely unamused by her sarcasm. "I take it the kid hasn't come back?" I ask, changing the subject.

She shakes her head, sadness taking over her expression. "I'm hoping he comes tonight. I'm very worried about him."

I decide to keep my mouth shut and not add my thoughts on the matter. There are many reasons why the kid might not come back, none of which will make her feel better.

Silence settles between us, her eyes burning into the side of my face as I look straight ahead.

"You don't dress like a soldier," she says.

I lie back on the dead grass, my arms crossing behind my head. "I never said I was."

"But you said—"

"I said 'something like that'."

She pauses for a moment. "So what are you then? Special operations? CIA? The Navy? A Marine?"

I quirk a brow at her.

"My grandfather was a Marine. I don't know much but I know a little."

"I'm surprised he's okay with his granddaughter traveling to a place like this."

She shrugs. "He was concerned and so was my father, even though it's his church I'm with."

My head snaps to her so fast I get whiplash. "Your father is a minister?" The question comes out hard and unforgiving, my voice thick with the rage I feel.

She tilts her head, studying me. "He's a pastor, yes."

Dread twists my stomach into a giant knot. Is she not as innocent as I thought? Has he done things to her? Unfathomable things?

My jaw locks at the thought, rage thrashing viciously through my veins.

"I'm curious, Cade Walker. How does an honorable man who fights for his country not believe in God?"

"Don't paint me in a good light because of my career choice. There's nothing honorable about me."

She studies me harder. "I find that hard to believe for a man who risks his life for the sake of his country."

I shake my head at how naïve she is. "I'm the perfect person for the job. I have no family, I'm not scared to die, and I have no problem killing people who deserve it."

"You have no family?" she asks quietly.

There's no denying the sorrow in her voice. I don't need her pity, there's nothing sad about it.

"No."

"What about your father?"

"He's dead."

"I'm so sorry," she whispers.

"Don't be, I'm not."

She continues to stare at me but I keep my gaze on the sky above. "What about your mother?" she asks carefully.

"Don't know and don't care."

"What about—"

"That's enough questions!" I snap then immediately regret it when she flinches.

"I'm sorry. I didn't mean to pry."

Instead of acknowledging the apology, I switch the subject back to her. "Tell me, Red, what is it with you and music?"

The question has her relaxing and a smile gracing her pretty face again. Leaning back against the tree, she softly begins reciting words to a poem, "Music speaks what cannot be expressed. It soothes the mind and gives it rest. It heals the heart and makes it whole. It flows from heaven to heal the soul."[1] She glances down at me. "You see, Cade, just as I need oxygen to survive, God and music keep my soul alive."

All of it was okay, until the God part. A part of me actually feels sorry for her, with how delusional she is. But I know it's not her fault and has to do with what her father has pushed on her. Bile creeps up my throat, thinking what else he has forced on her. I quickly push away the disturbing thought, unable to bear thinking about it.

"I have to admit, you're pretty good at it," I tell her, getting back to the music topic. "Why aren't you singing for a living?"

"Because I don't think I would love it as much as I do if I did it for money. But I'm curious, Cade, when have you ever heard me sing?"

Well, shit! I just busted myself there.

I don't respond, knowing there's no way of digging myself out of it.

A soft giggle parts her lips. "Don't worry, Walker, your secret is safe with me."

I side-glance her and consider wiping that smug look off her face by flipping her over and sinking into what I bet would be the sweetest, tightest pussy I've ever felt.

"I love all music," she says, pulling me from the perverted thought. "Elvis is one of my favorite artists, same with Johnny Cash and the Beatles. I love country, oldies, and rock and roll. Every song has a story; it comes from someone's heart and soul. I'm actually pretty good at pegging people for their genre of music," she adds proudly.

"Yeah? Let's see if you can pick out mine."

She accepts the challenge and digs into her guitar case for her iPhone before climbing to her feet.

"You brought your iPhone with you to Iraq?" I ask, staring up at her.

"Of course. I use it to listen to music and take pictures." She scrolls through what I'm assuming is her playlist, a smile lighting up her pretty face when she finds what she's looking for. "This is what I picture you listening to."

Twisted Sisters's "We're Not Gonna Take It" blares from her phone. It's a good song choice and is pretty bang on for something I would listen to. What's even funnier though is the way her red hair swings through the air as she head bangs to the beat. After a thirty-second show of rocking out to the lyrics, she throws her head back and laughs, the sound infiltrating the air and penetrating my chest.

When she brings her head forward and looks at me, her smile vanishes and her mouth drops. "Is that a smile I see on your face, Cade Walker?"

I quickly realize there's a small lift to the edge of my mouth.

She clutches her chest as if she's about to have a heart attack and drops to the ground dramatically. "Be still my heart, the man does have a sense of humor in there somewhere." More laughter spills from her at my glare as she finds herself fucking hilarious.

"Take it easy, Red. I was just thinking about how ridiculous you looked."

Ridiculously cute, but I keep that to myself.

Instead of being offended, she rolls closer to me, her face not far from mine. "I'd gladly look ridiculous every day if I knew it would bring a smile to your handsome face, Walker."

My cock hardens, eyes drawing to her full, kissable lips. It takes every ounce of willpower I possess to stop myself from tasting her. I don't even deserve to breathe the same air as this chick, let alone kiss her.

A smile dances across her lips. She knows exactly where my thoughts are. "Do you have a girlfriend, Cade Walker?"

What is it with her saying my whole name, and why do I like it so much? "I don't do girlfriends, Red. I fuck."

My truthful answer doesn't faze her like I expected it to. "Mmmmm," she responds quietly before lying down beside me, too close for comfort. It does things to me. Makes me feel things I don't understand, and I hate it.

"And here I am still waiting for my first kiss."

I tense, my head twisting in her direction. "Are you trying to tell me that you have never kissed a guy before?"

"Of course I have," she responds with a giggle.

Why does hearing that piss me off?

"But I haven't had *the kiss.*"

What the hell does that mean?

She turns to me with a smile and must see the confusion on my face. "You know…*the kiss.* The one you feel through your whole body as soon as your lips touch theirs and everything that is going on around you falls away. You could be in the busiest, noisiest place but everything becomes silent and time stands still. It's as if, in that moment, you're the only two people on the planet. It's that one kiss you will remember for the rest of your life and you will never have another one like it unless it's with that same person because it was *the kiss.*"

I blink back at her, wondering if she's serious. I quickly realize she is. The chick might be pretty but she is also fucking delusional.

"Sorry to disappoint you, Red, but you're going to be waiting your entire life because there is no such thing."

She looks back at me. "You haven't had yours yet either, huh, Walker?"

I refrain from rolling my eyes like a chick. "Believe me, there is no such thing. That crap stems from the same shit as love. It's all fucking make believe."

"You don't believe in love?"

The look I shoot her has her bursting into laughter.

"Well, speak for yourself, Cade, I will have that kiss one day, and I also plan to fall in love."

I grunt. "Good luck with that."

"Why, thank you, but I won't need it. As much as I'd love to stay and tell you all the reasons why, I'm afraid it will have to wait until tomorrow because it's time for me to go back to camp."

Rolling over, she lifts her guitar and puts it back in the case. My eyes drop to her ass as she bends over, hoping her dress rises just a little higher so I can get a peek at what she's wearing beneath it. Unfortunately, it doesn't happen.

Climbing to her feet, she looks across the field, her expression solemn once again. "Hopefully, Aadil comes tomorrow night."

I have a feeling the kid isn't coming back but, again, I decide to keep that to myself.

Her smile returns when she looks down at me. "Either way, I hope to see you again tomorrow night, Cade Walker." She blows me a kiss and sashays her sweet country ass across the field.

I watch her walk away and already miss the sound of her voice and sight of her smile.

What the fuck is happening to me?

CHAPTER 3

Faith

My fingers strum the guitar as I sit in my usual spot against the tree, wondering what's taking Cade so long. Usually, he's here by now. The thought that something might have happened to him has my heart plummeting to my stomach, which isn't good since I've already been a distraught mess over Aadil.

Please, God, let them both be all right.

For the past week Cade has met me here every night at the same time. I've enjoyed every moment with him, but last night was my favorite of all the nights so far. He asked me to sing for him, which I did, and I ended up singing for almost the entire two hours we were together. I made sure to pick songs that I thought he would like, and he genuinely seemed content to listen to me. I've had people tell me I have a nice voice before, but something about the way he watched me made me feel different.

It made me feel special.

Usually our evenings are spent with me doing most of the talking but he has opened up a bit more with me. He finally shared that he's a SEAL and told me a little bit about his training. He also told me about his friends, Sawyer and Jaxson, who sound more like brothers to him. It made me happy since I know he doesn't have family. I can only imagine how lonely it must get to always be alone. To have no one to come home to or anyone to tell you that they love and miss you.

Cade Walker is like no man I've ever met before. He's sexy, cynical, brooding, but most of all, mysterious. Even though I am grateful for the little he has shared with me, I find myself craving to know more. Like what has made him into the man he is today. A man who's strong and silent, one who never smiles, and doesn't believe in God. But more than anything, I want to know what made him into a man who thinks so little of himself.

Don't paint me in a good light because of my career choice. There's nothing honorable about me.

That one remark ripped through my heart and has been plaguing it ever since. It makes me want to strip him bare and learn every dark place he has inside of him. I want to know his every flaw then I want to tell him how perfect he is because, obviously, no one has ever told him before.

The man can pretend all he wants but I know what lies beneath that hard exterior. Not only is he a man who fights for his country, but look at the way he stood up for Aadil and me. Or how he has come here every night because he worries about my safety. Although, I have been hoping it's more than that. Hoping that maybe he feels the same connection I am, because boy am I feeling a connection. I have never felt this way about anyone before. Especially someone I barely know and someone who detests the very things I live for, God and love.

I don't do girlfriends, Red. I fuck.

My stomach tightens in response as his vulgar remark echoes through my mind. It's something that has happened often since meeting him. He makes my body feel things I have yet to want with anyone else.

I'm probably the only twenty-two-year-old virgin on this planet and it's not because of my faith or religion. It's because I haven't met anyone who I feel a strong enough connection with yet. Until him.

I know it's crazy to feel that now, but I can't seem to help it. There are times in life where I believe some things happen for a reason, that we are meant to meet certain people, and I strongly believe Cade is one of them. How else can I explain these feelings he evokes within me?

It kills me to think that the day will soon come when we won't be having these nights together anymore, but what's even more upsetting is to know I will most likely never see him again after this. I've thought about asking him for his contact information, but I don't want him thinking I'm some crazy stalker and, if I'm being honest, I'm a little scared of his rejection. It would be a blow to my pride that I'm not sure I'm ready to deal with.

Although, with the way things are going tonight, I may not even get the chance to say goodbye. I glance at my phone once more to see another thirty minutes has passed. Again I fear something has happened to him. But as soon as the thought emerges, I spot him across the field, walking toward me.

Thank God.

Relief swamps me as I climb to my feet, and I don't hesitate running toward him, meeting him halfway. My body slams into his, my arms wrapping around his neck as I hug him tight.

He tenses, clearly uncomfortable with my affection, but I'm too relieved to care.

"Everything all right, Red?" he asks, sounding both confused and worried.

"It is now. I was so scared something happened to you," I murmur, "you're never late."

Silence descends upon us seconds before his strong arms come around me, pulling me in close to him. My heart falters in surprise, but more than anything, pleasure erupts through my body. His warmth embraces me as I breathe in deep, loving the smell of his clean, masculine scent.

"Sorry, things ran late today. We're getting close to wrapping up what we came to do."

His response slams me back into reality and disappointment crushes my heart, but I try to push it aside, not wanting to ruin what may be our last night together.

After one more deep inhale, I step back and paste a smile on my face that I don't feel. "Well, I'm glad you're here now because I brought a surprise for you." Grabbing his hand, I lead him back to my guitar, trying to ignore the tingles that shoot up my arm just from the small contact.

"You brought me something?" he asks, sounding irritated by the fact.

"Actually, I brought it for both of us." I pull him down beside me and dig around my case until I find what I'm looking for. "Ta da!" I hold up the chocolate bar and dance it in front of his face.

He gazes back at me, clearly unimpressed.

"Hello? Do you see what I have here, Walker? Chocolate with caramel. It's my very last one. I thought I would be nice and share it with you. That goes to show how much I like you, because I do not share my chocolate with just anyone."

This still does not seem to impress him.

"Sheesh, you're a hard guy to please. I thought you would go crazy over this. How long have you been away from American food? It's only been a few weeks for me, and I already miss some of my favorites."

"It hasn't been that long, and chocolate isn't something I miss. Now if it were a steak you had, that would be a different story." He lies back like he always does, his arms crossing behind his head. His hard, lean body stretched out like this has my mouth watering.

I hurriedly open the chocolate bar before I do something impulsive, like jump him or take a bite out of him. The thought has a small snicker escaping me.

He looks at me questioningly, wondering what's so funny.

I get ahold of myself and clear my throat. "Well, sorry to disappoint you but that will never happen because I don't eat meat. I'm a vegetarian."

"What?" he asks, looking a little shell-shocked. "How the hell do you survive without meat?"

I'm used to hearing this comment from people, especially men. "I survive quite easily, and a lot healthier than most, I might add. Animals are our friends and I refuse to eat them. Want to hear the story on how I became a vegetarian?"

His response is another blank stare.

"Good. I planned to tell you anyway. So here it goes, when I was seven I had a friend who owned a cattle farm. They had the sweetest cow named Hank, and we had quite the bond. He always recognized my parents' vehicle when we drove up and he always waited for me at the fence. Honestly, I usually spent more time with him than my friend. He was nicer than she was, if you get my drift."

He quirks a brow at me so I take that as confirmation he does.

"Anyway, one day I came over and Hank was gone. When they told me what happened to him, I cried for three days straight and swore I would never touch meat again. All through my childhood I begged my parents to buy a farm so I could have cows, pigs, and chickens—ones I would never let anyone eat. Unfortunately, it fell on deaf ears, but at least they never forced me to eat meat again."

He blinks at me, silence descending. "That's what cows are meant for, Red."

My eyes narrow. "No, they're not! That's it, no chocolate for you now, mister!"

His lips lift slightly and my heart skips a beat.

Oh man, I can only imagine how sexy he would look with a full smile. I will make it my mission to see it before he leaves.

Raising the chocolate bar to my lips, I take my first bite. My eyes fall closed, a moan purging from my throat at the orgasmic explosion in my mouth. A low growl penetrates the air and pulls me out of my chocolate-loving bliss, my eyes snapping open. My pulse kick-starts at the dark expression on Cade's face.

Embarrassed, I swallow my bite then offer him some.

He stares at my outstretched hand. "That's all right, Red. You can have it."

"I don't mind. I brought it for both of us to enjoy."

"Believe me, I enjoy watching you eat it," he growls.

Whoa.

His fierce gaze never wavers from mine, taking my breath away and making me ache for things I've never felt.

Before I can think of a clever response, he breaks our connection by looking away and changes the subject. "When do you go back to wherever it is you're from?"

I wrap my chocolate bar up for later then lie down on my side next to him, propping my head up on my hand. "Is that your way of asking me where I'm from, Walker? You know, in case you ever want to look me up?"

He gives me his usual hard look, making me giggle. When I realize he isn't going to respond, I decide to give in. "I'm here for another week. Then I go back to Montana. Where are you from?" I ask bravely.

"I'm originally from Colorado but I live in California. Not that I'm ever home."

"Do you go on missions often?"

"Yep. Just the way I like it."

"Are you going on another one after this?"

He nods.

"And you're leaving soon?" The sadness that falls with that question is undeniable.

He looks over at me, the same regret I'm feeling in his eyes. Or maybe that's just wishful thinking on my part.

"Yeah. Probably in the next day or two."

Nodding, I swallow back my disappointment and try to lighten the mood. "Poor guy," I sigh. "You're going to be so lost without me."

"Is that so?"

"Yep. Who's going to sing for you when you're gone? Or show you how to rock out to your music? Admit it, Walker, you're going to miss me when I'm gone." Sitting up, I start slapping my knees and clapping my hands in rhythm, breaking out into the song "When I'm Gone" by Anna Kendrick.

When I finish the little demo, the sound of crickets fills the night, his hard expression never wavering.

"It's from *Pitch Perfect*? You know, the movie?"

He shakes his head, having no idea what I'm talking about.

"Seriously, Walker? It came out to theaters months ago. It's an epic movie. You must watch it when you go home."

His noncommittal grunt doesn't sound promising. "I'll take your word for it, Red."

I shrug, whatever, his loss.

"But you're right though," he adds quietly, avoiding eye contact. "I will miss you and your voice."

My heart falters, warmth spreading through me at the unexpected confession

"I'm going to miss you too, Cade…a lot," my admission falls on a whisper. I can tell things are getting too intense for him, so I quickly lighten things up again. "I mean, next week is going to be so lonely sitting here and talking to myself…oh wait, I already do that."

The second the words leave my mouth, something incredible happens. Not only does my joke elicit the biggest smile I have yet to see from him, but also, a rusty laugh rumbles from deep within his chest. It's the most beautiful sound that has ever fallen upon my ears. It literally robs me of breath.

When his eyes meet mine, the symphony stops abruptly. "Why the hell are you looking at me like that?"

My hand rests against my stuttering heart as I answer honestly. "Because you, Cade Walker, have the most beautiful laugh I've ever heard."

He shifts uncomfortably. "There is nothing fucking beautiful about me, Red. Never again associate that word with me in the same sentence. And it was more a quiet chuckle than a laugh."

It definitely was not, but instead of saying that, I try to put his wounded male ego at ease. "Okay, sorry, what I meant to say was, your almost quiet chuckle is badass."

"That's better."

His lips twitch as another giggle falls from me.

Since he seems in a better mood than usual, I decide to broach the one thing I've been dying to know about him. "Can I ask you something?"

"You can ask, but I can't promise you I will answer."

I think about that response then nod. "Fair enough." Clearing my throat, I shift nervously, praying I don't upset him. "Well, I was just wondering…why don't you believe in God?"

Every muscle in his body stiffens, that shield of armor locking down around him, banishing any amusement he had.

Before he can misunderstand what I'm asking, I rush to explain. "You don't have to tell me if you don't want to. I'm not judging, I swear. I'm just curious what makes you disbelieve in him so much."

The sound of nature fills the night as I wait patiently while he decides if he's going to answer or not. To my surprise, he does. "I just don't. I'm the kind of guy who doesn't believe in shit that can't be explained."

"Some of the best things in life are the unexplainable."

"Come on, Red. Look around you. If there was a great and powerful God, like so many of you believe, do you really think we would live in a fucked-up world like this?"

I shrug. "I believe we were put on this earth with free will. Why is it his job to fix the mess that others have made? So many people wait for God to change the bad in the world, but I strongly believe it's him who's waiting for us to change it."

"Fuck that!" he snaps. "That's your old man talking with whatever shit he's brainwashed you with."

I try not to let that comment offend me. "I agree that the world we live in can be very ugly, but I also believe the beautiful parts outweigh the bad. My father always says—"

"Your father is the worst kind of fucking people out there," he bellows, making me flinch. "It's people like him who made up the illusion of God so others would follow him. So he can fucking control them."

That misperception and insult has my blood heating. "My father is a pastor, Cade."

"So!" he cuts me off again. "You think that makes him a good person? A fucking minister raped and killed my seven-year-old sister because it was supposedly God's will!"

Oh my god.

My heart plummets straight to my stomach and bile inches up my throat. The pain in his eyes strikes me to my core, rocking the very foundation of who I am.

"Fuck!" He climbs to his feet, furious for what he revealed.

"Cade, wait. Please don't go." I reach for his hand but he pulls away from me.

"Are you happy now, Faith?"

I flinch at the way he sneers my name.

"Happy to finally know why I don't believe in God? It's people like your father that should be locked up from society. Then the world would be a better place!"

I shake my head, tears forming in my eyes. "That's not true. My father is a good man. I don't know who hurt your sister, but I can assure you he was no man of God."

"Save your preaching for someone who gives a shit. For your sake, Red, I hope one day you wake up and join reality. The sooner you realize there is no God, the better off you will be."

Before I can get another word in, he storms off, leaving me alone and shattered.

I sit stunned, trying to absorb what just happened.

Tears stream down my cheeks, my heart breaking for the little girl who never got a chance at life, for the little boy who lost his sister, and for the man who clearly still hurts so much over it. And even more, I regret asking the question, for forcing him to live through it again and knowing that this is the way our time together has ended.

A sob tumbles past my lips, knowing I'll never see him again. Why does it feel like I just lost something I never even had?

CHAPTER 4

Cade

I head up the familiar trail I didn't think I would ever walk on again, my steps quicker than usual, hoping I will catch her before the dreary sky dumps the impending rain we're all expecting.

Watch her not even be here. It would serve me right after the way I lost it on her last night. Guilt constricts my chest at the memory and so does a good dose of disbelief. I still can't believe I told her about my sister.

What is it about her that fucks with my judgment?

I know I shouldn't come back, but after finding the kid I have to let her know he's okay. And if I'm being honest, I also want to see her one more time.

One last time.

Jaxson, Sawyer, and I leave tomorrow, and for some reason, the thought of never seeing her again has panic ripping apart my chest. It's a feeling I haven't felt in years.

It pisses me off that after years of nothing but numbness some redheaded, country girl had to come along and fuck with my dark world. A girl who stands for everything I loathe, yet her smile is all I see every time I close my eyes. One whose presence I constantly ache to be around, when usually, I yearn for nothing but solitude. Whose voice I crave to hear, when all I ever want is silence. A girl I have no business feeling any of this shit for because I will only ruin her. She lives in a world of light, and I was long ago swallowed by darkness.

Last night when she ran up to me the way she did, throwing herself at me out of fear because she was worried about me, I had no idea what to do with that. How to feel. Other than Sawyer and Jaxson, I have no one in my life who cares if I live or die. Which is exactly how I've always liked it. Even though her affection took me by surprise and made me uncomfortable, it also shifted something within my chest. Something I didn't think I was capable of feeling anymore.

Then I had to go and ruin it by yelling at her and telling her that her dad should be locked up and away from society.

Jesus, I still can't believe I said that. Even if I do hate the guy for what he stands for, I shouldn't have said that to her. The pain in her eyes is all I've seen since leaving her and it's killing me.

Just tell her about the kid, say your piece, and get the fuck out of there.

The moment I come upon her, my feet stop, anchoring in place at the heartbreaking sight before me. She looks nothing like the girl I've come to see this past week. Instead of strumming her guitar with her beautiful smile, she sits back against the tree with her arms wrapped around her knees, head turned away from me. I don't have to see her face to know she's crying, the gentle shake of her shoulders is a pretty good indication. My guilt climbs to a whole new level. This is a damn good reminder why it's best to stay away from her. All I will ever cause her is pain and that is not something I can live with.

A gust of wind kicks up as I start for her, my heavy boots alerting her of my presence. Her head snaps in my direction, her wet, green eyes colliding with mine and making my chest tighten painfully.

She wipes her wet cheeks with the back of her hand. "I'm surprised to see you. I thought you left."

I take the spot next to her. "I leave tomorrow, but I wanted to come tell you that I found the kid."

Her back straightens, hope igniting in her eyes. "You found Aadil? Is he okay?"

"He seemed to be. I found him at his mother's workplace." I decide not to share that the *workplace* is a local bar and whorehouse, knowing it will only make her more worried. "He said he would try to come tomorrow night and see you."

"Good. I'm glad he's all right. I was going to search for him tomorrow if he didn't come tonight."

Panic hammers through my blood at the thought of her traipsing around here unprotected. "Don't do it, Red. You could end up making things worse for the both of you if you go looking for him. Just stay here. He'll come to you when he can."

She gazes at me, her sad eyes doing shit to my chest that I didn't think was possible up until a week ago. "Thank you for coming and telling me."

I nod then look away, her tear-stained cheeks too much to bear. Another gust of wind kicks up, reminding me I don't have much time with her. I try to find the right words for an apology and the goodbye I'm dreading but she ends up beating me to it.

"I'm sorry about yesterday, Cade," she whispers. "I did not intend for our conversation to end up the way it did. I shouldn't have pried."

My attention remains on the trees that surround us. "It's fine. It's a sensitive subject for me, but I shouldn't have exploded on you the way I did."

It's a shitty apology but I've never been one to apologize for anything.

"I'm also really sorry about your sister," she adds quietly.

My teeth grind, an unbearable pain slicing through my chest. "I don't want to talk about it, Red. Just let it go."

Before either of us can say more, a loud crack of thunder sounds through the air and the sky opens up. Fast and heavy rainfall immediately soaks us.

"I guess that's our cue." Standing, I turn back to her and offer my hand.

She places her soft one in mine and allows me to pull her up. Her white dress is already soaked through and plastered against her body like second skin.

I curse my dick for noticing.

She peers up at me through the rain, her seductive green eyes burning with a need that matches my own. A longing that I can't give her, no matter how much I want to.

Before I do something really stupid, I close the distance between us, dipping my face close to her. "Be safe, Red." After planting a hard kiss on her forehead, I turn around and get the fuck out of there.

The entire time I walk away from her, I have an ache in my chest I haven't felt since I was fifteen years old. One I am not sure will ever go away.

CHAPTER 5

Faith

I can't believe I'm doing this.

I swipe my soaking wet hair out of my face and fight my way through the heavy rainfall as I search for Cade's camp. I have no idea if I'm going the right way. I can only guess based on the little information he has shared with me and the direction he always came from.

My teeth chatter, making me wish I had gone back to camp for dry clothes and an umbrella first. This is the craziest and definitely the boldest thing I've ever done but I can't let him leave, not like this. Ever since he walked away, I haven't been able to get this sick feeling out of the pit of my stomach. The feeling that I'm making a huge mistake by letting him go.

I know what kind of man he is and his beliefs, and know he does not do more than one night. But something tells me that having one night with him will be better than not having him at all.

I'm shocked he even came to find me. I was so sure I'd never see him again after our altercation last night. I sat in that field, crying as I remembered our nights together and the regret I felt about how it all ended. Then I lifted my head and there he was, my dark angel. That has to be a sign, right?

Yes, I know it. It's a knowledge I feel all the way down to my bones. Now I just have to find him.

As soon as the thought emerges, I come up on a camp. Hope ignites in me at the American flag that stands tall. A chain-link fence lines acres of land that resides a cluster of small buildings, while a helicopter and tank sit off in the distance.

I begin walking around the fence, wondering if there is even a way in, when I slam into a brick wall.

"Shit!" Hands grab my shoulders, helping steady me.

I look up into the face of a very attractive man that's as soaked as I am.

His gaze sweeps down my body in appreciation, right down to my cowgirl boots. My face heats as I'm reminded that the dress I'm wearing is white and it's plastered to my body. I'm certain I cannot get more embarrassed than I am in this moment.

"Well, what do we have here?" he muses, a smirk taking over his face. "You lost, Country?"

It takes me a moment to find my voice. "I'm looking for Cade Walker. Do you know him by chance?"

Recognition flashes in his dark green eyes before suspicion takes its place. His gaze dips to the heavy metal cross that's hanging around my neck. "How do you know Cade?" he asks.

"Umm, well, the last week we have been meeting in the evenings and—"

"Whoa, wait!" His hand lifts, stopping me midsentence. "You're the one he's been seeing every night?"

"Yes," I say hesitantly, worried I'm getting him into trouble.

"Un-fucking-believable." He chuckles, shaking his head. "Yeah, Country, I know him. I tell you what, see that building over there?"

I nod at where he points.

"Go to the third door on the right. That's his room." He leads me over to an opening in the gate, pulling the metal back to allow me in.

"Thank you."

"Tell him Sawyer will take care of the admiral."

My gaze snaps to his again, realizing he's one of the friends Cade always spoke about. I smile, my worry easing knowing I haven't gotten him into any trouble.

He tosses me a charming wink then continues on his way, leaving me to take off in the direction he pointed to. Once I make it to the door, I take a deep breath, gathering all the courage I can muster then knock. Butterflies flock in my tummy, my insides twisting into a nervous mess.

What am I going to say?

Hey. I know we don't know each other that well but I have this crazy attraction to you, and I want to lose my virginity to you.

Oh god, what am I thinking? This is such a bad idea. A bad, bad idea.

The longer it takes for him to answer, the more I seriously consider making a run for it. However, the thought flees me when the door swings open a moment later, revealing a shirtless Cade.

Holy mother of pearl.

He wears nothing but a pair of black athletic pants and a towel draped around his neck that catches drops of water from his rain-soaked hair. I briefly take in swirling black ink that wraps around the most powerful body I have ever seen, just before my eyes land on metal. My mouth drops as I stare at his nipple rings.

"Faith?" His surprised voice has my gaze snapping up to his. I'm knocked out of the trance when he yanks me into the room. He peeks out the door, looking back and forth before closing it and turning toward me. "What the hell are you doing here?"

I open my mouth then quickly close it, unsure how to start. My feet begin tearing up the floor as I pace the small room before I eventually turn to him again. "Honestly, I don't know. I don't know what I'm doing."

He blinks at me like I've lost my mind, and I'm not so sure he's wrong.

Shaking my head, I square my shoulders and take a leap of faith. "Ever since you walked away from me tonight, I feel like I lost something I never even had. I know that sounds crazy. I can't explain it. I think about you constantly, Cade, and feel things I've never felt before." Tears begin to burn my throat but I push through it, knowing I'll regret it if I don't get this out. "I want one night with you. A night to remember forever with no promises attached. I know we barely know each other and this is probably really creeping you out right now. So feel free to stop me and—"

My babbling turns into a surprised gasp when I'm lifted off my feet and pinned against the wall. I barely have time to register what's happened before his mouth lands on mine, fast and furious.

It takes me no time to respond, an intense need sweeping over me. My knees hug his hips, fingers rushing through his hair and gripping the wet strands.

When his tongue parts my lips, slipping in, I'm completely lost to him, my entire life changing. Warmth explodes through my body, spreading right to the tips of my fingers and toes. My heart skips a beat as time preciously comes to a standstill. Our tongues dance together in perfect harmony, and even though it's all new, it feels like we have been doing it our whole lives.

It feels right.

At this exact moment, I know without a doubt, that I am having "*the kiss*." The one I've been waiting for my whole life.

A kiss I will remember forever.

Minutes, seconds, hours. I have no idea how much time passes before he pulls back.

My eyes flutter open, colliding with a desire that matches my own.

"Do you hear that, Walker?" I whisper, breathless from all the air he just stole from me.

His eyes narrow in confusion. "Hear what?"

"Silence," I answer with a smile.

It doesn't take him long to catch on. "That's because it is silent, Red. We are the only two people here."

Laughter shoves from my throat while a small smile tugs at his lips.

"Don't ruin the moment, just go with it," I tease, brushing my lips against his once again.

Growling, he grips my wet hair with one hand, wrapping it in a fist as he ends my control and takes over, completely dominating my mouth in a way I've only ever dreamed about.

I shamelessly grind myself against him, desperately craving more, but all too soon he pulls away again.

His eyes penetrate mine, restraint blazing in their depths. "What are we doing, Red?" The torment in his voice has my heart pinching in my chest.

"I'm hoping we're about to do something that I haven't been able to stop thinking about since meeting you."

His jaw flexes, a war battling within him. "Have you ever done this before, Faith?"

The question has heat invading my cheeks. I shake my head, my answer only escalating whatever fight he has going on inside of him.

"I meant what I said, Cade. I know where you stand. I don't expect any promises, if that's what you're worried about then don't be."

"You should," he says. "You should expect promises. Why would you want to give yourself to some asshole who can't give them to you?"

"Because it's you," I tell him, knowing that probably doesn't make any sense to him but it does to me. "If one night is all I can have from you, then I will take it. Because I know having you for one night will be better than not having you at all."

He shakes his head before dropping it to my shoulder.

Holding him close, I kiss the side of his face and keep my lips close to his ear. "Tell me that you don't feel this, Cade. Tell me you don't want this just as much as me."

"That's not it. I want you more than my next fucking breath."

"Then take me. I'm right here."

He shakes his head again.

"What are you so afraid of?"

He tenses, every muscle straining beneath my fingertips. "I'm not scared."

"Then what is it? Talk to me, please."

"I don't know how to fucking do this, all right!" he snaps, bringing his turbulent gaze to mine. "I told you I fuck, that's all I know, and you deserve more than that, you deserve more than me."

My heart clenches at his tortured admission. "I don't want you to be someone you're not. I just want you, no matter what way that is."

Silence hangs thick in the air, his tormented eyes peering into mine, and I finally realize this isn't going to happen.

Swallowing back my disappointment, I gently rest my forehead on his. "It's okay," I whisper, unsure if my reassurance is for him or me. "I want you more than you will ever know, but I won't push. The last thing I want is for you to regret any of this in the morning. It would kill me." My voice cracks with emotion, despite my best effort.

"It's not me who's going to regret this in the morning, Faith. It's you."

I remain silent, not knowing what else I can say to make him realize how much I want this, how much I want him.

"Fuck it!" The words leave him in a heated rush.

Before I can even understand what that means, he tosses me on the small single bed, his hard body following down on top as he takes my mouth in a soul-shattering kiss.

Victory washes over me, desire seeping into my blood once more as I wrap myself around his powerful body.

His greedy lips trail down my neck, leaving a path of fire in their wake. "Say it again, Red," he murmurs against my skin. "Tell me you're sure about this."

"I'm sure. I've never wanted anyone as much as I want you."

He sits up, making sure to keep his weight off me, and pulls down the top of my dress, revealing my simple white lace bra. Something passes over his face, an emotion I can't quite decipher. That's until he grabs the heavy cross lying on my chest.

His fingers curl around it, jaw locking. "Is it okay if I take this off?"

I nod, hating the mix of anger and agony in his gaze.

He slips it over my head then leans over, placing it on the nightstand. As he does, my lips brush his shoulder, tasting his skin. Then our mouths are one again, the connection obliterating any hesitancies over what will happen next.

"I know I don't deserve this," he says, "but I'm going to be selfish and take it. Because I've been dying to kiss, taste, and fuck every inch of you since I found you singing in that field a week ago."

It pleases me to know he has felt this too, this raw need and unexplainable connection.

He drops to kneel on the floor before me, grabbing my hips to drag me to the edge of the bed. "Sit up." The demand is thick with arousal.

I follow the order, my body quivering in anticipation. With my legs dangling on either side of him, he reaches around behind me, and with a deft flick of his fingers my bra falls loose, the straps slipping down my arms and baring me from the waist up. My nipples instantly tighten, straining for his touch.

His gaze devours me, making it impossible for any insecurity to take hold. "You're perfect." Leaning in, his hot mouth latches to one aching nipple.

My head falls back, a cry of pleasure purging from my throat.

He takes his time, moving between each tortured bud and giving them the attention they yearn for. The ache between my legs becomes unbearable and I lift my hips, grinding against his stomach.

His mouth descends, coasting lower, lips cherishing every inch of skin he passes until reaching the fabric of my dress that's bunched at my waist. He wastes no time removing it, leaving me in nothing but my white panties.

His knuckle grazes the center of the damp lace, causing heat to explode through me like wildfire. "Fucking soaked." Grabbing the string of lace at my hips, he shreds my panties in one swift pull.

"Oh god. That was so hot," I moan, the admission leaving me before I can stop it.

A soft chuckle rumbles from his chest, but the beautiful, foreign sound quickly turns into a growl as his eyes focus on my most intimate part. I've have never been this exposed to anyone before in my life, and yet, I feel no insecurity. I can't, not when he's looking at me the way he is.

"I have to admit, Red. I'm surprised as hell to see you're waxed, but I'm glad you are. Because I want nothing in my way when I taste this sweet pussy of yours."

My face flames but my hips rise involuntarily, my body clearly wanting what he's offering.

"You should take your clothes off, too," I suggest, wanting to see all of him. Every glorious part.

"Don't worry, baby, we'll get there. But first we need to make sure this pussy is nice and ready for my cock." Taking two fingers, he runs them through my wet flesh, making them slick with my arousal before inserting one inside of me before quickly following with the other.

I cry out at the snug invasion, my legs instinctively clamping around his arm.

"So tight," he groans, his voice as rough as sandpaper. "Ease up a little, baby." Prying my legs apart, he slowly pumps his fingers in and out, sending an army of sensations to explode through my body. "Do you have any idea how good it's going to feel to have this wrapped around my cock?"

Good heavens, for a guy who doesn't usually talk he sure seems to have a lot to say now.

A knowing smirk tilts his lips. "You like it when I talk dirty to you, Faith?"

"Yes," I pant out breathlessly. "If I would have known this is what it took to get you to talk to me, I would have suggested it sooner."

My response takes him by surprise. Shaking his head, he lets out a half-chuckle, half-groan. "I swear, Red, that smart mouth of yours is going to get you into trouble one day."

Before I can think of another witty reply, his fingers speed up, banishing any coherent thoughts I have. Moaning, I raise my hips, meeting him thrust for thrust.

"That's it, baby. Fuck my fingers."

My breathing kicks up, body reaching for that mind-numbing pleasure as a foreign feeling takes residence inside of me.

"Cade?" His name comes out as a question, asking him for something I don't quite understand.

"I got you." Keeping rhythm, he leans down and runs his tongue along my wet slit.

A wail of pleasure leaves me, my back arching off the bed as my body explodes with the best sensations.

He splays a large hand over my belly to hold me in place, his tongue devouring me in the most intimate way.

I wind my fingers tightly in his damp hair, hips lifting in greedy desperation. His groan of approval vibrates against my throbbing clit, bringing me to teeter on the edge of destruction.

"Give it to me, baby, come all over my face." No sooner as the words leave his mouth do I fall apart, my entire world tilting on its axis, as I become overwhelmed with the most intense pleasure I've ever felt. His sweet torture is relentless, until he has taken every bit of pleasure I'm capable of.

Time becomes nothing more than an afterthought as I float back down to reality. When my eyes open, they collide with Cade's. They are the darkest I've ever seen, storming with so many emotions as he climbs to his feet.

Sitting up to my knees, my face becomes level with his chest. I wrap my arms around his waist, bringing us skin to skin. An unexpected bolt of electricity shoots through my body, both of us groaning at the contact. I hold him close, pressing a kiss right over his heart, its strong, steady beat playing a beautiful rhythm against my lips.

My eyes sweep up, meeting his. "It's my turn to do some exploring, Walker."

His jaw locks, gaze turning to liquid fire. My hand moves to rest on his abdomen, his muscles twitching beneath my palm. When I reach the dark, swirling lines of the tattoo that starts at his hip, I begin following the beautiful design with my finger, tracing it until I reach his ribs. There, in the intricate lines of black ink, is something that looks like a piece ribbon and in the center of it is the name *Mia* in script.

"Your sister?" I ask, looking up at him again.

His response is a single nod, but there is no denying the grief twisting his face.

Feeling the need to offer comfort, I place a soft kiss over her name before moving on quickly, not wanting anything to ruin this moment. My lips create a path of warmth until I reach a nipple ring.

I finger the piece of metal, fascinated. "Did it hurt?"

He shakes his head, his gaze darkening as I play with the hoop. When my nail catches it by accident, snagging it, he groans.

My hand stills. "Did that hurt or feel good?"

"Good, baby. Really fucking good."

Feeling emboldened by the heat in his eyes, I lean in and flick the ring with my tongue, grazing his nipple before giving it another generous tug. Something that can only be described as animalistic rumbles from his chest.

In a swift move, I'm taken to my back again, his weight settling over top and erection pressing against the one spot I crave to feel him most.

"I wasn't done yet," I complain, though it's halfhearted.

"Too bad."

"You got all the time you wanted to explore me," I counter.

"I could spend a lifetime exploring your body and it still wouldn't be long enough."

His words send my heart into a tailspin. I can immediately tell he regrets letting that out.

Shaking his head, he mumbles something I can't quite catch then reaches over for his wallet that's on the small stand beside his bed and pulls out a condom.

His eyes come back to mine as he hesitates. "If you want to back out, now is the time to say so."

I hold his gaze, not feeling an ounce of uncertainty. "I'm not changing my mind, Cade. I want you. I want this." Cupping the back of his neck, I bring his mouth upon mine, sealing the words with a kiss.

Our tongues tangle, dueling in a fevered pitch of give and take. I run my hands down his powerful body until I reach the waistband of his pants. Pushing the black material down, his erection springs free. I grasp his smooth, hard flesh in a firm grip, a small gasp escaping me when I feel how large he is.

Groaning, he pulls his mouth away and looks between our bodies where I'm stroking him. He pumps himself into my hand, a small bit of moisture spilling from the tip. My thumb swipes over the pearly fluid.

"Shit!" The curse leaves him on a hiss and he pulls away from my efforts. Getting to his knees, he rips open the foil packet and sheathes himself in record time before moving back over me, bracing himself on his elbows. I feel his hard length on the inside of my thigh, my heart racing in anticipation for what we are about to do.

"You ready, baby?"

I nod without hesitation.

Leaning down, he presses his lips to mine, soft and gentle before rising up on one arm and grasping his cock with the other. He runs the tip of it through my wet flesh, eliciting a whimper when he grazes the sensitive bundle of nerves. Once slick with my arousal, he slowly slides inside.

I gasp at the tight invasion, burying my face into his neck.

"Fuck!" he grits between clenched teeth. "Try to relax, Red."

I let my legs fall open and try to breathe through the agony and pleasure. Cade's arms shake with restraint, sweat beginning to dot his forehead as he slowly rocks back and forth until he's fully seated inside of me.

"You okay?"

"Yes," I reply truthfully. "It's getting a little better."

"Good. Because you feel fucking amazing." His lips brush a kiss along my cheek. The unfamiliar tenderness from him has warmth exploding through my heart.

Eventually, my hips lift to meet his. At my silent assurance, he begins thrusting with sure, steady strokes. Our gazes never waver as his beautiful, powerful body moves inside of me with absolute perfection. A moment I wish I could capture in a bottle and keep forever.

I finally realize why I hadn't done this until now, because it was always meant to be with him. I know with every fiber of my being that I was meant to meet Cade Walker, even if it was only for this short moment in time. And no matter who or what comes after this, I will cherish this moment with him for the rest of my life.

My hand lifts, fingers tracing his rough, scratchy jaw all the way across his lips. His eyes fall closed, breaking contact with mine just before he tucks his face in my neck. "What the fuck are you doing to me, Red?" The words bleed from his soul.

My arms come around him, holding him close as I turn my mouth to his ear.

"This is one of those beautiful things I was telling you about that life has to offer us. Don't fight it, Cade, for once just let yourself feel."

He aligns his mouth with mine in a powerful kiss, his strokes becoming a little harder and a little faster. Slight shock waves begin to flutter low in my tummy, my leg curling around his lower back as my body accepts all of him.

"That's it, baby. Take it. I can feel how close you are again."

He changes the angle of his thrusts, hitting a certain spot inside of me, one I didn't even know existed.

The soft whimper of his name is the only warning I'm able to manage before I fall over the edge once again, traveling to a place that's indescribable. A place where only pleasure lives and he and I exist.

A growl rips from his chest right before he allows himself his own release and to see him let go is absolutely breathtaking.

His forehead comes back to mine as we fight to catch our breaths, our hearts beating against the other's, merging even further than they were seconds before.

The softest smile claims my lips. "I knew you liked me, Walker."

He grunts. "*Like* is a fucking understatement."

A small giggle leaves my mouth but it trails into a moan when he pulls out of me. I turn on my side to face him, my leg draping over his since there isn't much room. "How on earth do you sleep on this? It's so small, especially for a big guy like you."

"This bed is paradise compared to where I normally sleep while on a mission."

I can only imagine the places he has been, the things he's had to endure. It makes me sad to think about.

Silence settles as I am left wondering what happens now. Should I be leaving already? I'm not ready to go, I don't think I ever will be, but I told him I knew the deal and wouldn't push for more…

With that last thought, I swallow past the sudden lump lodged in my throat and manage words. "I should get going." The weak attempt is pathetic even to my own ears.

Something that looks an awful lot like panic flashes in his eyes before his arm shoots out and wraps around my waist, pulling me snug against him. "Not yet. Stay for a few hours and sleep. I'll set my alarm and make sure you're out of here before anyone gets up."

Relief floods my chest, thankful he isn't ready for me to leave yet either. "I didn't take you for the cuddling type, Walker," I tease, hoping to lighten the moment.

He doesn't return my smile. "I'm not but you always seem to be the exception."

The admission has my heart skipping a beat. I move in closer, resting my head on his shoulder.

"You doing okay?" he asks, concern edging his voice.

"I'm more than okay," I assure him, my hand moving to his stubbly jaw. "It was perfect, *you're* perfect."

He grunts. "I'm far from perfect."

"You're perfect in my eyes," I tell him honestly.

"That's because you have only known me a week."

"Are you telling me that you get more charming than this? Because, if that's the case, you might just melt my panties right off."

His eyes narrow. "You really do have a mouth on you, Red."

"Thanks, I'm proud of it."

The response only earns me another grunt.

"I forgot to tell you that Sawyer said he would take care of the admiral."

His body tenses. "Sawyer?" he repeats in surprise.

"Yeah. I ran into him when I happened upon the base. He told me where I could find you."

By his stoic expression, I'm unable to gauge his feelings on that.

"I hope that was okay?" I ask, suddenly feeling unsure.

"It's fine," he assures me. "I'm just never going to fucking hear the end of this is all. The guy is a pain in my ass."

"I thought he was your best friend?"

"He is. But he's still a pain in the ass."

I refrain from rolling my eyes. "You probably think anyone who talks to you is a pain in your ass."

"Pretty much."

"Are you trying to tell me that I'm a pain in your ass?"

His eyes shift back to mine with an intensity that steals my breath. "You do a lot of things to me, Red, but a pain in my ass isn't one of them."

I'm not sure who is more shocked by his admission—him or me.

I seize the moment and coast my hand up his chest, sliding it over his nipple rings. "I'm surprised you're allowed to have these, being in the Navy."

"We're not but what they don't know doesn't exist. I got them before I joined."

My hand continues its path, gliding across the grooves of his hard, powerful body until I reach the tattoo on his ribs. I lightly trail my fingertips over his sister's name. "Why a ribbon?"

I curse my curiosity when misery flashes in his eyes. I'm just about to apologize when he surprises me by answering.

"Because she slept with a white ribbon in her hair every night for as long as I can remember." The gruffness of his voice laced with pain has my throat burning.

Swallowing thickly, I lean over, my lips pressing to his, lingering in the softest touch. He doesn't acknowledge my sympathy and instead tucks me back into his side. "Get some sleep, Red, before I end up doing things to you that you're not ready for."

I can't deny the delicious shiver that claims my body at the thought, but he's right, as much as I would love to spend every moment with him inside me, I'm not sure my body could handle it right now.

I snuggle in closer and rest my cheek against his steady heartbeat, committing the strong rhythm to memory. It isn't long before I feel him slip into a deep sleep.

Hours pass but to no avail am I able to do the same. I haven't wanted to miss a second of this time with him. When I can no longer stall, I quietly slip out from under his arm, careful not to wake him, and begin dressing.

After slipping my necklace back on, I sit back down on the edge of the bed and reach for the pen and paper that lies on the small nightstand, beginning to write my goodbye.

Thank you for giving me what will always be the best night of my life. I am so thankful our paths crossed and I got the chance to meet you. I said I didn't expect any promises and I mean that. But here is my number in case you ever make your way to Montana, or maybe you can just send me a text to let me know that you are safe. Because even though you don't think so, there is someone out there who loves you and cares what happens to you. No matter how much time passes, that will never change. I will always be thinking of you, Cade Walker.

Take care,
Love, Faith

Tears stream down my cheeks as I write down my cell number. When the grief becomes too much to hold in any longer, I drop the pen and bury my face in my hands, making sure to keep my sobs silent.

Once I gather some composure, I spot the anklet my papa bought me for graduation. The rhinestone music note is one of my favorite pieces of jewelry. Bringing my knee up, I unclasp the small, dainty chain then place it on the piece of paper, leaving it so he will have something to remember me by.

Afterward, I turn to Cade and watch him for a few moments. His face is soft with sleep, and for the first time I get to see what he looks like unguarded.

Struggling to keep my emotions in check, I lean over and give him a gentle kiss, only a feather of a touch. "Stay safe, Cade Walker. I'll remember you forever."

With a heavy heart, I pull myself together and reluctantly walk out the door. It takes everything in me to continue putting one foot in front of the other as I traipse through the dark and back to my own camp. I'm so caught up in my grief that I don't realize something is wrong before it's too late.

"Faith, run!" Beth's scream pierces through the night just as a gun fires off and I'm grabbed from behind.

Fear grips my chest as a hand slams over my mouth with brutal force. Chaos erupts around me, orders being shouted as I struggle against the steel hold banded around my body. I'm spun around only to be backhanded across the face.

The powerful blow sends me to the ground, my vision blurring from pain. I land next to Beth's lifeless body and realize the gunshot I heard moments ago killed her. An agonized sob rips from my throat as terror washes over me.

A fist grabs a handful of my hair and brutally yanks my head up. There, in the black of the night, my gaze lands on a sobbing Aadil. He struggles against a man who holds him back, his face bruised and marred as he begs for me to be released. The sound of his grief has agony ripping through my already tortured heart.

Heavy black boots appear in my line of vision, blocking the small boy from my sight. Crouching down, Aadil's father comes into view, a sinister smile on his face. "It's payback time, bitch."

Before I am able to fully comprehend just how much trouble I'm in, he raises his fist, slamming it into my face. Aadil's cry is the last thing I hear before darkness takes me.

CHAPTER 6

Cade

"You may as well talk to us, man, you know I'm not going to let up about this."

My eyes narrow on Sawyer from across the table as we sit having a drink in the small village before we go wheels up. Since watching Faith walk out the door in the middle of the night, I've had this excruciating pain in my chest, which only escalated when I read her note and found the bracelet she left me.

Pretending to be asleep when she left was a coward move and I know it, but I couldn't bring myself to say goodbye. For the first time in my life, I wanted to make promises, even though I'd never be able to keep them. I'm incapable of it and she deserves better.

I feel like a dirty bastard for taking what was offered to me last night, tainting her innocence with myself, but I can't regret it. It was the best night of my pathetic existence.

I stayed up all night, battling with my decision to walk away. By morning I was so overloaded with emotions that I gratefully packed up my shit and couldn't wait to get the fuck out of here. Except once I walked out of my room and ran into Drake as he walked out of his, he had a smug smile on his face and asked why I hadn't shared.

I didn't find it funny. Just the thought was enough to shatter my composure. I struck out, my fist connecting with his face. It took both Sawyer and Jaxson to hold me back. The admiral walked out and was none too happy about it. He ordered them to take me away until I calmed down. That's how we ended up here.

The place is more of a whorehouse than anything. It's close to Army bases and caters to the soldiers. The only reason I agreed to come is because Aadil's mom works here, something I kept from Faith. I'm hoping I will either see him or be able to get him a message to go see Faith tonight. I have no doubt she will be back in that clearing waiting for him…alone. Just the thought has panic constricting my chest.

Sawyer and Jaxson continue to stare at me, waiting for an explanation that I refuse to give them.

"Fine," Sawyer says, relaxing back into his chair. "At least tell us how the fuck you stumbled upon this girl. Because I have to tell you, man, after running into her last night she definitely doesn't seem like your type, especially with that cross hanging around her neck."

My jaw locks, hating that he even ran into her. She's something I've kept from the both of them this past week. Not because I'm embarrassed by her but because I wanted her to myself. This past week has been one of the best and it's something I don't want to share with anyone else.

I'm just about to tell him to mind his own fucking business when the bar door slams open and the kid I've been waiting to see comes rushing in. His face is a mess of tears and bruises. It instantly puts me on alert, my back straightening.

He runs toward me, shouting in Arabic. It's a language I can usually understand but I'm having a hard time understanding anything he's saying through his hysterics. Sawyer and Jaxson watch confused as the scene unfolds, not understanding that I know him.

"Please hurry!" he stresses, switching languages and pulling on my arm. "You have to help her. He took her and they're hurting her right now."

The few English words have my blood running cold. I grab the small boy by the shoulders, giving him a firm shake. "Who do they have?"

"Faith," he sobs. "My dad took her in the middle of the night. They shot her friend."

Terror seizes my chest, making it impossible to breathe. It's a fear I've only ever felt one other time, and it's one I never wanted to feel again. Amongst that fear though, lies the darkness that I've kept locked away since that awful morning ten years ago, threatening to claim me once again.

My fingers grip the boy's upper arms, desperation taking hold of me. "Take me to her. Show me where she is."

He nods. Despite his willingness, there's a hesitancy in his eyes, one I shouldn't ignore but all I can think about is getting to her.

Jaxson convinces me to go back to camp first for reinforcements. Only, the admiral refuses to let us go due to the other mission he has lined up for us. Instead, he says he will notify the proper authorities. It's a very grave mistake on his part.

For the first time since joining the Navy, I disobey orders. The three of us leave his office, making a decision to walk away from the one thing we thought we would do for the rest of our lives. Instead of going on the mission that was assigned to us, we lead one of our own, gathering up all the weapons we can manage.

Determination fuels every step I take as I follow Aadil. I have only one goal in mind, and that's to find her and kill every fucking person who dared to hurt her. Only the closer we are led to our destination, the more we realize something isn't right, but by then it is too late.

The ambush comes out of nowhere, bullets spraying the desert ground. There are at least thirty of them and only three of us. We manage to kill over half before they get the better of us.

The last thing I see and hear before darkness takes me is the kid crying out an apology. "I'm sorry. He said he would kill her if I didn't do it."

That day my life irrevocably changed for the second time. I, along with the two men I consider brothers, managed to live through what would be the worst week of our lives. The only thing I regret was not realizing the setup sooner. Because if I had to live through it all over again, to save the only girl who ever mattered to me other than my sister, I would do it again in a fucking heartbeat.

CHAPTER 7

Faith

Two years later

A horn blares from outside, alerting me that my cousin Katelyn has arrived. Scooping my water bottle up from the kitchen table, I forgo a jacket and head out my front door.

The morning sun dances along my skin, instantly warming me from the inside out. I love the weather here in South Carolina. It's much warmer than what I am used to in Montana, though I'm sure I will miss the snow at Christmas.

After locking up behind me, I dash down my front steps and round the house to find my cousin waiting in her little Honda Civic. Her bright smile triggers one of my own. As soon as I climb in her car, she wraps me in a hug.

"Hey," she whispers.

"Hey." My throat burns with emotion as I hug her back. I've missed her so much. I'm glad that my father got the transfer and fate has reunited us once again.

Eventually, she leans back, gracing me with another smile. "You ready for this? I'm so excited I can barely contain it."

I must admit I'm excited too but also nervous. She convinced me to take this self-defense class with her that her friends' husbands are doing as sort of a test run. It's free and sounds like fun, even if a little intimidating, but I'm pushing down my anxiety and going for it. If there is one thing I've come to learn, protecting yourself when you are most vulnerable can mean everything.

"Is what I'm wearing okay?" I ask.

She takes in my usual workout gear, yoga shorts and matching tank, before giving me a nod of approval. "You look perfect. Like always."

My heart warms at the compliment. The two of us may be cousins but we look nothing alike. I have dark red hair and she has dark brown. My skin tone is barely sun-kissed, hers is golden. Where my eyes are green, hers are a chocolate brown. She looks like an Amazonian and I look like, well…the opposite.

As she pulls out of my driveway, I throw my long hair over my shoulder and begin braiding it to keep it out of my face.

"I still can't believe you're here," she says. "That we are once again living in the same town. It still hasn't sunk in yet."

"I know. It hasn't for me either."

Katelyn and I grew up in a small town in Montana. We were practically neighbors our whole lives until her brother, Kolan, moved her here with him. Not that I blame him. He wanted to get them both away from their parents. My aunt and uncle are horrible, vile human beings, nothing like the loving parents I was blessed with.

"How are you settling in here?" she asks, breaking into my wayward thoughts. "Are you liking living on your own again?"

I nod. "I do. It's taking some getting used to but I need the space. My parents and Papa, however, don't quite feel the same. They are finding it difficult, but I try to see them almost every day. They know how important it is for me to do this. I feel like, for the first time in two years, I'm finally getting my life back."

She reaches over and covers my hand. "Things are going to be great here, Faith, a fresh start for you. My friends are going to love you and you will love them. You will fit in with us perfectly."

"Thanks. I'm excited to meet them. From everything you have told me, they sound wonderful."

"They are. You'll see. Their men are great too, a little growly but they warm up once you get to know them."

I smile, feeling both anxious and excited again.

"How is the church coming along? I feel terrible I haven't been there to help out as much as I'd like to."

I brush off her guilt with a wave of my hand. "Don't be. You're a businesswoman and have your own things to worry about. Dad and I are getting along just fine; we will hopefully be finished in a couple of weeks. We've had a lot of youth helping out too which is great for me since I'm able to convince them to sign up for the programs I have coming."

"What about the troublemaker? Is he still showing up to do his community service?"

I think about the angry fifteen-year-old boy who reminds me so much of someone else I met a couple of years ago. Someone I try not to think about on a daily basis.

"The troublemaker's name is Christopher, and yes, he still comes, not that he has any choice in the matter." I rest back against my seat, letting out a defeated sigh. "I feel bad for him, Katelyn. He's a good kid; he's just got a chip on his shoulder. I've tried reaching out but he acts like he would rather eat nails than associate with me."

"You can't help everyone, Faith, but I know if anyone can reach him, it'll be you."

I smile over at her. "Thanks."

"Did Cooper ever tell you what he did to get community service?" she asks, talking about the sheriff who brought him in to work for us.

"Not really. He did check in the other day though and asked how he was doing. He agreed that Christopher was a good kid, just needed some guidance. Cooper seems like a great guy. I'm glad he cared enough to check in."

"Coop is the best. He watches over everyone in this town, but especially Kayla's friends. He has done a lot for me."

Hearing about all the amazing people Katelyn has met since moving here makes me really happy. She didn't have it easy growing up, even when making friends, something I've never understood. She's one of the most likable people you could ever meet.

"We're here," she announces, parking in front of the tall brick building that's just off main street. It's one of the few areas I haven't been yet. I've been so busy with getting settled at my new place and helping at the church that I haven't had time to venture out much. "Let's go kick some ass," she says, fist bumping me before climbing out of the car.

"I'm surprised you don't already know how to kick some ass, considering that brother of yours."

"Kolan would rather beat people up for me than have me do it myself."

I can definitely see that. Kolan is a fighter, a natural born scrapper, and is as protective as they come. He's had to be with the bad hand they were dealt in the parent department.

I'm just about to ask how he's doing but as soon as we walk in the gym doors we come face-to-face with all of her friends.

They immediately get up from their spots on the floor and make a beeline for Katelyn, pulling her in for a hug. I shift uncomfortably and probably have the most awkward smile on my face.

A brunette girl with bright aquamarine eyes is the first to bring her attention to me. She extends her hand, a warm smile on her face. "You must be Faith. It's great to finally meet you. I'm Julia."

"Nice to meet you, Julia. Thanks for allowing me to join you today."

"Of course. Any friend of Katelyn's is a friend of ours."

The kind reception has some of my nerves subsiding.

Katelyn slings an arm around my shoulders and begins pointing out the other girls. "And these beauties are Kayla and Grace."

"Hi." I give them a small wave and get a friendly greeting in return. After introductions, we make our way back over to the mat where the girls were sitting when we first arrived.

"The place looks amazing," Katelyn says, eyeing the gym in appreciation.

I have to agree. It's pretty incredible. I've always been a person who enjoys exercising but more recently, I have a newfound love for running outdoors. It's something my therapist, Dr. Mathews, from back home recommended to help with the anxiety I've become plagued with since Iraq. It's helped immensely.

The last two years have been a long and painful process, but with my faith in God, the love of my family, and the help of Dr. Mathews, I'm almost my old self again…except that missing piece of my heart.

"Isn't it great?" Julia agrees, pulling me from my thoughts. "I'm really proud of all the guys. It's a great venture and I have no doubt they will turn this place into a success."

"Speaking of ventures," Katelyn pauses, clearing her throat. "I would love for you girls to come to Centennial Park Saturday morning. I'm teaching my first outdoor yoga class and I'm hoping for a great turnout."

"Count me in," Kayla says, while Grace and Julia confirm their attendance as well.

I forgo chiming in since I already told her I would come, too. It will be my first time ever doing yoga.

"Thanks, guys. I appreciate it. Feel free to bring Annabelle if you want," she says to Julia, talking about her newborn baby.

"Thanks but I'm sure Jaxson will be more than willing to hang out with her for a few hours by himself."

"Of course he will," Kayla grumbles. "The man is such a hog."

Grace chuckles while Julia delivers a radiant smile, clearly not having a problem with that like Kayla seems to. Before anyone can say more, a door at the other end of the gym opens and out walks two men with a third trailing behind them.

My gaze becomes riveted to the one with light sandy brown hair who seems to only have eyes for Grace. The arrogant smirk he flashes her strikes a familiarity inside of me, though I can't think of a single reason why. My head tilts the closer he comes and when recognition finally dawns, it slams into me like a freight train, knocking all the air in my lungs.

It can't be.

Despite my disbelief, painful memories from two years ago emerge with a vengeance. Blood rushes in my ears, my heart hammering so loud it's all I can hear.

"Oh my god," the words are choked out before I can stop them.

A cold sweat breaks out across my skin as I feel the walls around me begin to close in. Tears blur my vision as I climb to my feet on shaking legs.

"Faith? What is it, what's wrong?" Katelyn asks worriedly, snagging my wrist.

"I'm sorry. I have to go. I have to get out of here." Without another word, I pull from her grasp and run for the door, practically stumbling over my own feet as I keep my hair shielding my face from the men moving forward. Before I'm able to reach my destination, I slam into a brick wall, the impact jarring.

"Whoa." Big, warm hands grab my shoulders to steady me.

"I'm so sorry, I—" My apology trails into a gasp when I look up through blurry eyes and stare into the face of the one man I never thought I would see again. The same one I find in my dreams almost every night.

With tears rolling down my cheeks, I watch as shock dominates Cade's face, his fingers digging into my slender shoulders just before his expression turns to stone. "What the fuck are you doing here?"

I flinch from his harsh tone and feel my heart shatter all over again. A small sob slips past my throat as I pull from him and continue my hasty exit out the door. The moment I'm met with fresh air, I slow, bracing my hands on my knees as I try to take in the breaths my lungs are so desperately grasping for, the panic attack hovering just at the edge.

No, please. Not here. Not now.

Straightening, I look around, trying to get my bearings on which direction I need to take.

That's when Katelyn comes barreling out the door. She comes to a hard stop when her eyes meet mine, seeing the devastation I'm unable to hide. Her sad expression mirrors the grief suffocating me. "Faith, talk to me. What's going on?"

"It's him!" I sob. "It's all of them."

Her eyes narrow in confusion.

"Iraq!"

It takes a solid minute before realization dawns on her. "Oh my god," the words are barely a whisper, shock gripping her soft expression before regret fills it. "I'm so sorry. I had no idea. Never did I think the three of them were the ones…" She trails off, unable to bring herself to say it, unable to say the same words I can't speak myself.

I begin backing away, needing to get out of here. "I can't stay here. I have to go."

"Of course, just let me grab my keys—"

"No, stay. Please, I just need to be by myself right now."

Hurt replaces her shock.

"I'm so sorry. Please understand."

She nods but the pain is written all over her face.

"I'll call you later." In fear of someone else walking out, I spin on my heels and start running, faster than I ever have before.

Tears blur my vision as I run toward the one place I've loved going since moving here. The bright sun pours down on me but my body is plagued with too many emotions to feel any of its warmth. They rush through my veins and crawl up my throat, trying to suffocate me as memories from two years ago play through my head. Good ones, bad ones, they all hit me at once…

The unsuspecting smile of a beautiful but dark man who captured my attention. The evenings of singing to him in the sunset. His hands and mouth exploring my body as I explored his. A man whose eyes held me captive and made me feel like the most beautiful woman in the world as he moved inside of me, not only claiming my body but also my heart. The same man who's shown me the only loving touch I would know for the last two years, and maybe the rest of my life.

Then come the ugly memories. The ones of rough, unwanted hands that delivered not only pain to my body but shame to my soul. Ones that tore at my clothes and took what was not offered to them. The sound of a little boy's screams as he begged them to stop while he was forced to watch me be violated in the worst way.

This is what bitches are for, boy. Fucking, not singing. We will make a man out of you yet.

A sob of agony rips from my throat, and I push myself harder and faster. The burn in my legs and lungs not enough to quiet the evil running through my head.

"Do you still believe in your God, female?" he asks, holding my cross necklace over my beaten and naked body. When I don't answer him, he sends another blow to my already battered face. "Answer me!"

"Yes," I choke out through the blood that pools in my mouth. The sounds of a little boy's broken sobs fill the air and rip through my wounded heart.

"You are a stupid, stupid woman. I will teach you who the real God is. And before you leave this earth, you will call me Allah."

This disgusting person may have stolen my body and tortured my soul but he will not take my faith. Not ever.

I stare defiantly into his malevolent dark eyes, my fear long forgotten. "Over my dead body."

He responds with a malicious smile. "So be it, bitch."

Spotting the crystal blue waves in the near distance, I race toward the beautiful, deserted beach. As soon as my feet hit the sand, I slow only enough to toe off my running shoes and ankle socks before rushing into the ice-cold ocean. Once I'm far enough out, I dive in headfirst and let the fresh water steal my breath and cleanse my soul.

My lungs begin to burn so much it's almost unbearable but it does the trick. The dirty, ugly memories begin to wash away, but instead of being replaced with beautiful ones of the man who once held my heart, it holds the one of a man who was severely tortured and beaten, all because of me. The same man who saved my life then refused to ever see me again. The worst part is, I still don't know if it's because he blames me or because he can't bear to look at me after knowing what they did to me.

CHAPTER 8

Cade

Emotions I have fought hard to keep buried explode like a volcano as I try to process what just happened. Shock anchors me to my spot; disbelief hammering through my veins as I stare at the door the beautiful redhead just ran out of. The girl that has haunted every one of my thoughts for the last two years.

"Jesus, Walker. Did you need to be so harsh?" Sawyer's heated remark yanks me back to reality. "She's clearly just as surprised as we are."

The memory of the pain that struck her emerald eyes at my cold reception has pain searing my chest.

Katelyn walks back inside, her face pale and eyes filled with tears as she looks at the three of us. "It was you. You're the ones who pulled her out."

Collective gasps fall from the girls as they finally understand what just ensued, filling the deafening silence of the room.

"I never said their names," Katelyn chokes out, looking at her friends. "I always just referred to Jaxson and Sawyer as your husbands. I knew Navy SEALs pulled her out, but I would have never thought for a moment…" She trails off before bringing her attention over at me. By the look she sends me, I have no doubt she knows everything that happened between Faith and me. "How dare you," she spits, as angry with me as I am with myself. "How dare you speak to her like that. She didn't know. None of us did."

I swallow the burn in my throat and don't bother responding, knowing nothing I say will make up for the way I reacted.

"I can't believe this is happening," she cries. "This is supposed to be a fresh start for her."

All the girls surround her in comfort.

"Where is she now?" I ask, surprised to hear how gruff my voice is.

Her attention comes back to me, anger replacing her sorrow. "She said she needed to be alone, so I gave her space to do that."

"Do you know where?" Julia asks quietly.

"I'm guessing the beach, she goes there a lot."

My feet are moving before she even finishes.

"Hey!" She jumps in front of me, blocking my way. "Where the hell do you think you're going?"

"To look for her."

"No way!" She pokes her finger in my chest, hard enough that I'm surprised it doesn't snap off. "You stay away from my cousin. Do you hear me? You have caused her enough pain."

Annoyance sparks in my blood as I rein in my temper. She's out of her fucking mind if she thinks she can stop me from seeing Faith.

"Katelyn," Julia starts timidly, "maybe Cade should be the one to talk to her. She shouldn't be by herself right now and clearly they have a lot of things they need to discuss."

When she doesn't budge, Grace puts a comforting hand on her shoulder. "He won't hurt her."

"He already has!"

I push aside the guilt that threatens to claim me. "You think I don't know that? Why do you think I've stayed away from her?"

Despite the anger in her eyes, her expression softens. Without waiting another second, I sidestep her and walk out the door, climbing into my truck. I bring it to life, the engine roaring seconds before I pull away.

I crank my music, trying to block out the memories threatening to surface, but it doesn't work. The sweet soft sound of her voice overshadows the harsh beat filling my truck as I remember all the nights she would sing to me. The way her smile would warm every cold, dark place inside of me, her cries of pleasure as I sank into the warmest body I've ever felt, a body that was later violated and taken against her will.

Rage seeps into my hot blood, a memory taking over, bringing forth a nightmare I constantly try to forget…

Anchored by the chains that shackle me to the wall, my broken body hangs limp. For the first time since captivity, I can feel the warmth of the blood that soaks my back and chest, the paralysis of the drugs finally wearing off. The agony that comes with it is nothing compared to the fear of what Faith could be enduring right now. I haven't seen her, have no idea what they are doing to her. The thought that she could be suffering half as much as us fuels a desperation I've never felt.

I will not give up until I get her out of here.

I look over at my best friends, guilt spearing my chest when I see they are just as bad off as I am. "You got feeling again?" I ask, speaking through the pain.

"Yeah," Jaxson answers.

Sawyer nods his heavy head.

Before I can talk some sort of game plan, the sound of a boy's cries pierce the desolate air, followed by heavy boot falls. Our cell door opens, two of them entering and dragging the small boy with them.

"Which one is it?" one asks Aadil, speaking Arabic. "Which one does the bitch belong to?"

I tense, every muscle straining beneath my skin.

"I will not tell you no more," he says, barely managing the words through his grief.

The asshole raises his hand, a loud crack filling the air as he delivers a blow to the young boy's face. "Tell me!" he roars. "Your father wants me to bring him!"

Aadil doesn't even look at me, his sobs driving the fury inside of me.

"I'm right here, motherfucker." The words come out sounding as weak as I feel.

His eyes snap to mine. He tosses the boy aside and strides up to me, leaning down to get in my face. "The bitch belongs to you, yes?"

My jaw clenches as I remain silent, refusing to confirm it for a second time.

A taunting smirk appears on his face. "She's a fiery one, Soldier."

Rage surges through my body with unspeakable force. "If you hurt her in any way, I will cut out your fucking heart."

"Too late," he replies smugly. "Don't worry, she's still alive. But we had to show our boy here what it means to be a man."

The boy's despair tells me it's true.

"She put up such a fight," he gloats, "but in the end it was not enough. We fucked her so hard she—"

I don't let him finish; my fury fuels a strength I didn't know I still possessed. Kicking my legs up from under me, I wrap them around the fucker's neck, and with a quick twist I hear the sickening crack before I let his dead body fall limp to the ground before me.

The other guard runs out, shouting for the others. Within seconds, the sound of pounding boots on the hard cement echoes down the hall.

"Shit!" The curse comes from Sawyer.

The young boy peers back at me, his eyes wide as he takes in the lifeless body. "I'm going to help her," he promises. "I will try to get you guys out of here."

Before he can say more, chaos erupts, our cell filling with what has to be at least twelve of the bastards. They all have their whips, chains, and any other torture devices they possess.

In silence, I take every lash of the whip, slice of their dagger, and blow that breaks my bones. No matter how badly my body wants to give up, I refuse. I will fight until I get her out of here, and when I do, I will fucking kill every single one of them.

My time will come and their blood will be shed.

I come back to the present as I pull up to the beach, parking just shy of the sand. My head drops back against my seat while I take a moment to collect my thoughts and emotions, my mind and body further tortured from the lingering nightmare.

Why the hell did this have to happen now? Fighting to keep my distance when she was all the way on the other side of the country was hard enough, but now that she's in the same town… I don't know how I will do it. How I'll coexist. She's the only person to ever penetrate my dead heart, now it will never lay dormant.

Letting go of a heavy breath, I climb out of the truck and start my walk across the beach, my eyes scanning the distance. I come across a pair of running shoes and socks, but find no sign of her. It isn't long before something in the ocean catches my attention. It's then she emerges from the water like some fucking angel, a goddess.

She doesn't notice me as she wrings her long, red hair out over her shoulder. Instead of walking out like I expect her to, she remains standing in the water, letting the waves crash against her ankles. Her head falls back on her shoulders, face tilted up to the clear blue sky, basking in the warmth of the sun.

By the way the sunlight hits her, I'd swear it's only shining for her. It takes me back to that first week in Iraq. The sunset would cast a similar glow as she strummed her guitar.

I fight like hell to push away the old feelings and emotions bubbling to the surface, but the moment she brings her head forward, her green eyes collide with mine, hitting me like a blow to the chest. The impact is so powerful it makes it hard to even pull in a full breath.

Her eyes widen, mouth parting in shock as she stares back at me. The hurt and uncertainty in her gaze drives this ever-present guilt deeper into my gut.

I start toward her first, only to eventually have her meet me halfway. She peers up at me in silence, her sad, innocent eyes holding mine. I have to clench my hands at my sides to stop myself from reaching out.

"I'm sorry. You caught me by surprise." The apology sounds shitty even to my own ears.

Her chin lifts in indignation. "Do you think I was expecting to see you?"

"No. Like I said, I'm sorry."

Her stiff shoulders deflate, gaze dropping as she sinks her toes into the sand. "So I guess this means you don't live in California anymore."

"No. Jaxson is from here. Sawyer and I came to see him about a year ago and the opportunity of owning the gym was offered to the three of us so we accepted."

"You're not in the Navy anymore?" she asks, her voice sounding sadder than it did a minute ago.

"No."

She nods. "My father was offered the job of senior pastor at Peace Hill Church. He took it so we could be close to Katelyn and Kolan."

"Yeah. I'm figuring that out."

She mumbles something under her breath, still avoiding eye contact with me.

My jaw tightens, annoyance creeping in with all the other emotions dominating me. A slight breeze kicks up, eliciting goose bumps across her smooth, wet skin. I remember what that skin felt and tasted like. It's a night I'll never forget.

"Come on. I'll drive you home," I tell her.

"That's okay. I need to dry off and the sun will do that on my walk home."

"I'm not letting you go alone, Faith. Grab your things and I'll take you."

Fire flashes in her eyes. "I said I'll walk!"

"And I said I'm driving you!" I drive a hand through my hair in frustration, fighting to rein in my temper. "Look, it's not a big deal, just let me drive you home or at least take you back to Katelyn…please," I add, remembering the few times she lectured me on my manners.

It does the trick, her eyes soften before she drops her gaze again and nods. "All right."

After grabbing her socks and shoes, she follows me to the truck but keeps her distance. It bothers me more than I care to admit. I open the passenger door, waiting for her to climb in but she hesitates.

"I'm going to get your seat all wet."

"It's doesn't matter, Red, it's leather."

Her eyes dart to mine as the nickname slips. Something passes between us, that ever-present pull as strong as ever. Breaking eye contact, she finally climbs in. As I walk around the truck, I use the moment to collect myself.

"Back to Katelyn at the gym?" I ask once inside.

She keeps her gaze out the window. "No. Home please."

I don't like to think of her going home alone but figure it's probably not best to argue about that right now. She rattles off her address and that's all she says the entire drive home. Usually, I seek comfort in silence but not with her, not like this. It's driving me fucking crazy.

When I park in front of the single family home, I'm plagued with questions, ones

I forgo asking. The less I know the easier it will be.

Despite the pep talk, panic strikes when she reaches for the door handle and climbs out. "Thanks for the ride," she mumbles.

Say something, you shithead.

"Faith, wait. I just want to say—"

She throws a hand up, stopping me from going further. "Please don't. You don't have to say anything. I promise to try and avoid anywhere you may be from now on."

A scowl forms on my face, her words striking a chord. "What the fuck does that mean?"

"It means I got your message loud and clear two years ago."

It's the perfect moment for me to explain, to tell her why I stayed away, but I can't bring myself to do it. I can't revisit that time with her. Not now and maybe not ever.

"You don't need to worry about that. It's a small town and we're going to run into each other eventually. You don't have to stay away because of me."

She looks away, swallowing thickly.

"Besides, I don't go to many places other than the gym, so it shouldn't happen often anyway."

Shit, that did not come out right at all.

She shakes her head, a bitter laugh escaping her. "Duly noted."

"I didn't mean it like that."

She refuses to listen, slamming the door before I can say anything further and walking away, taking the only part of me that exists with her.

CHAPTER 9

Faith

Hours later, when I can no longer take the silence and loneliness, I head to the church to see my father. I decide to walk rather than drive, hoping more fresh air will soothe my conflicted heart. As much as I appreciated Katelyn's offer to come over for the day, I need my dad.

I'm close with both my parents and my papa who has lived with us since my grandma passed away, but I am closest with my dad. Joshua Williams is the very best man I know. His patience and calm demeanor always anchors me, and with the chaos I'm feeling, I need that more than ever.

My mind hasn't stopped spinning from the events that took place earlier, something Katelyn still feels bad about but she shouldn't. None of us could have ever expected this. Not once did I ever tell her names, especially Cade's. I told her all about the man who had captured my heart before the devastation but speaking his name had hurt too much.

I'm surprised he came to find me at the beach. My heart had turned over in my chest when I emerged from the water and found him waiting for me. Wearing black athletic pants, a white muscle tank, and a pair of aviators, he stood strong and beautiful. He looked exactly how I remembered him; except for the black beanie. That was new.

All the feelings I had kept buried unleashed with a vengeance. I wanted to throw my arms around him and tell him how much I missed him, but after his reception at the gym, I knew my greeting wouldn't be reciprocated. In all fairness, it's a lot to take in but it doesn't stop it from hurting. He's all I've thought about, all I've dreamt about to keep the nightmares at bay.

He disappeared without so much as a goodbye. I never even had the chance to thank him for saving my life. Though, if he's still angry I can't blame him. He and both his friends lived through a week of hell in that cell, all in order to protect me. I don't think I will ever be able to forgive myself for that, so how can I expect him to forgive me?

The depressive thought trails off when the church comes into view. Feeling close to tears, I speed up, taking the stairs two at a time then enter through the wooden stained glass doors.

My father walks out of his office at the same time, carrying a large box, the melody he whistles echoing through the silent church. He comes to a hard stop when he spots me, his smile infectious. "Hey, sweetheart. How was…" The question drops when he sees the pain written all over my face. Dropping the box, he starts toward me. "Faith, honey, what's wrong?"

I waste no time rushing into his arms, barely restraining the burdening grief. "I just need you to hold me, Dad."

His soothing arms hug me closer, delivering the comfort I so desperately seek. It has me taking in my first full breath since chaos ensued. Eventually, he pulls back but keeps an arm around my shoulders as he ushers me over to one of the dusty pews. "Talk to me, my girl. What's the matter?"

I look up at him, peering into his patient green eyes. "You're never going to believe it."

"Try me."

"Remember how Katelyn was taking me to the gym this morning for that self-defense class?"

He nods.

"Well, the men who own it are the same men who rescued me in Iraq."

His eyes go wide, shock and disbelief flashing in their depths. "Whoa," he breathes out.

"Yeah. Two of them are her friends' husbands and the third one was *him*," I whisper sadly. There's no need to elaborate, he knows exactly who I'm talking about.

"That must have been quite the shock on all of you."

"You can say that."

"How did you handle it?"

"Not well." I pause, thinking about how to explain it to him but have no words and end up shaking my head. "It was such a nightmare, Dad."

"I'm sure it wasn't easy on any of you."

"No, it wasn't, and seeing Cade after all this time…" My voice cracks as my emotion gets the best of me.

My father shifts, clearing his throat, and I fear this conversation is about to take an awkward turn. "You know, I never asked you much about him because I knew it hurt you too much to talk about. I know you met him before everything happened, and that you were quite taken with him, but…just how close did you two become?"

As uncomfortable at this conversation is, I stare right back into his knowing eyes, letting him see the truth.

He lets go of a long exhale, dropping back in the seat. "Oh boy."

"I'm sorry," I start quietly. "I know you probably wanted me to wait until I was married, but—"

He puts his hand up, cutting me off. "No, that isn't necessarily true. I think, like most dads, I really hoped that, married or not, you would never, ever do that."

I toss him a look, my brow quirking.

It drags a chuckle from him. "I know it's unrealistic of me to think that but I can't help it, you're my girl."

My heart warms, bringing along a smile with it.

"I also know that I can trust you to make the right decisions for yourself. You're a good girl, Faith, the best I've ever known."

His kind words have a tear slipping free that he ends up wiping away with his thumb.

"So let me ask you a question, do you regret it?"

"No, and I never could," I tell him truthfully. "Not only is he the only man I've ever felt this deeply for, but he also showed me what it was like to be touched in a way that wasn't cruel or forceful." My breath hitches as my tears flow faster. "I thank God every day that I got to experience a loving touch like his before what was taken from me."

A mixture of anger and devastation masks my father's expression before he pulls me into his arms once again. The sob I've been keeping in breaks free, my tears soaking his shirt.

"Everything is going to be okay now, Faith. This is a new beginning for all of us, but especially you."

"I thought so, but now with Cade being here… I just don't know, Dad."

"Did you ever stop to think that maybe he's supposed to be a part of that future? Because if you ask me, honey, it seems this could be the work of God bringing you two together again."

Pulling back, I wipe my cheeks with the back of my hand. "I don't know about that. He can barely stand to look at me." Speaking the words brings on a fresh wave of pain.

"No way. I refuse to believe it. How can anyone have a hard time looking at you?"

I roll my eyes, knowing the man is biased.

His chuckle fills the air before he drops a kiss on my forehead.

I lift my chin, peering up at him somberly as I voice my biggest fear. "I'm not sure if it's because he blames me or because he can't stand to know what they did to me."

Sympathy flashes in his eyes. "Oh, Faith. If he's as smart as I think he is, then I'll bet it isn't either of those things. None of what happened is your fault, and you have nothing to be ashamed about."

Logically, I know this. It took many long sessions with Dr. Mathews to accept that, however, sometimes I still can't help but feel guilty when I think about all the people who were hurt or killed as part of my capture. Beth, Cade, his friends, and most of all, Aadil…

I squeeze my eyes shut and try to block the memory from resurfacing, knowing I'm not in any condition right now to deal with it.

"You were really taken with this man, weren't you?"

I look back up at my father. "If I thought it was possible to fall in love with someone in a week then I would tell you I loved him."

"Anything is possible. I knew I loved your mother right away. I also knew I would make her my wife. Thankfully, it didn't take me long to convince her of the same thing."

His proud smile brings one of my own. "Yeah, thankfully. Otherwise, you would never have gotten to experience what it's like to have the perfect child."

It drags another laugh out of him like I hoped it would. "You are most definitely right about that."

I smile back at him, my heart feeling lighter for the first time today.

"Everything will work out, Faith, you'll see. Sometimes God knows what's right for us before we do. In the meantime, focus on your goals and dreams for what we have in store here. The rest will fall into place, and like I always say…have *faith.*" Giving my hand one more squeeze, he kisses my cheek then picks up his box and heads to do whatever it was he was doing when I arrived.

I remain sitting for a little while longer, using the opportunity to send a prayer above, not only for me but also for all of us involved. May we all find the peace we deserve.

The sound of a throat being cleared breaks my attention. Turning, I find Christopher, the fifteen-year-old boy, standing behind me. His usual brooding expression softens when he realizes I've been crying.

"Sorry," he apologizes quietly. "You didn't hear me come in. I just need to know what you want me to do."

"No problem." Pulling myself together, I stand and force the best smile I can manage. "Let me find out what my dad needs done."

As soon as the words leave my mouth, my father walks back in. "Oh, hi, Christopher."

Christopher barely acknowledges his greeting but my father takes no offense.

"What would you like Christopher and me to do?" I ask.

Christopher stiffens, probably recoiling at the thought of us doing anything together.

Thankfully, my father gets the hint, knowing I've been trying to reach out to him for some time now. "The entrance is ready to be painted, if you guys could start on that so I can keep working in my office that would be great."

"Sounds good," I tell him, happy to get this opportunity to be alone with Christopher.

Christopher, on the other hand, seems less enthused, but he follows my lead, remaining silent as he helps set up. Once we have all the materials, I grab an old stereo to plug in, knowing he enjoys music while he works.

"Look, you don't have to help me," he says, finally speaking. "I can manage on my own."

"I'm sure you can but together we will get it done faster. Besides, I've had a bad morning and could use the distraction."

He grunts. "Yeah, I'll just bet you know how 'bad' life can be."

I try not to let that remark sting but a bitter laugh escapes me anyway. "Oh, Christopher, you have no idea."

The weight of his stare burns into the side of my face but I don't look over or elaborate more. Bending down, I turn on the radio, putting it to the station I've been hearing him listen to lately and let the music fill the silence as we begin to paint.

When Coldplay's "Viva La Vida" comes on a few minutes later, I begin to hum along, eventually singing some of the words. It's then I feel Christopher's gaze on me once again. This time, I make eye contact and find him watching me in disbelief.

"A church girl like you knows Coldplay?" he asks doubtfully.

I don't let his "church girl" comment offend me. "Of course. I know all genres of music. I am the queen of music," I brag proudly.

He grunts, not believing me.

"It's true. Name any band and I'll tell you everything about them."

After a long pause, he finally decides to give in and play along. "Fine. Metallica."

"Metallica is a heavy metal band that was formed in 1981. The members consist of James Hetfield, Lars Ulrich, Kirk Hammett, and Robert Trujillo. 'The Unforgiven' is my favorite song of theirs. They've won nine Grammy Awards and have had five albums debut at number one." I pause, a smug smile stealing my lips at his shocked expression. "Shall I keep going or do you have another for me?"

His eyes narrow at the challenge. "Guns N' Roses."

"Hmmm," I muse, tapping my lip with my finger as I pretend to think hard about it.

He smirks when he thinks he has stumped me.

"Guns N' Roses is a rock band that started in 1985. The members are Axl Rose, Slash, Izzy Stradlin, Duff Mckagan, and Steven Adler. Today, Axl Rose is the only remaining original band member. My favorite song of theirs is 'Paradise City'. They have sold over one hundred million copies worldwide." I flash him another smug smile. "Next."

His mouth drops, eyes wide. "Holy shit. You're like a walking, talking, breathing music dictionary."

My proud smile wavers. "Hey, watch your mouth when you're in here. It's disrespectful to swear in church."

He grumbles an apology.

"Besides, I told you, I love music. I have since I was a small girl. I love all genres, though my favorite is country and oldies. Like Johnny Cash, Elvis Presley, and the Beatles."

He quirks a brow.

"No dissing the legends or you and me are going to have some problems."

He grunts, not fearing me in the least.

"Have you ever listened to any of their songs?"

The look he shoots me says it all.

"I tell you what. I'll give you a list of my favorites and I want you to give them a chance. If you don't like them, then okay. But I have a feeling you know good music when you hear it."

"Yeah, maybe," he says noncommittally. His mood suddenly takes a turn and he becomes quiet and withdrawn again.

I change the subject since I'm not quite ready for him to go back to ignoring me again. "Listen, once the church opens I'll be starting up a Friday night youth group. I'd really like it if you would consider joining us."

A harsh laugh escapes him. "I don't think so."

"Why not?"

He stops his current task and turns to me, a scowl on his face. "Why are you doing this?"

"Doing what?"

"Why are you being nice to me?"

The question knocks me off-kilter. "Why wouldn't I be?"

"Because in the entire year I've lived here, no one else ever has."

My heart literally breaks to hear that.

"They only see what they think they know."

"And what is that?" I ask quietly, a little nervous to hear the answer.

"That I'm the bad guy. That when anything bad happens in this town or the school, they always blame me."

"Are you trying to tell me that you're here because you were blamed for something you didn't do?"

If that turns out to be the case, I need to talk to Cooper.

"Oh no. I punched that guy out but he deserved it. I'm tired of the people in this town running their mouths because I don't have the money they do or because of who I come from."

I tread carefully with my next question, wanting him to continue talking to me. "Who do you come from?"

"You haven't heard about my old man yet?" he says, sounding surprised. "Well that explains why you're being so nice to me. Just wait, you'll hear it all soon and then you'll treat me just like the others."

I shake my head. "I don't care about any of that."

"Whatever," he says, not believing me.

"It's true."

"Look, forget I said anything, all right? Let's just get back to work so I can get out of here."

My shoulders deflate, hating the conversation is over. "Okay, but can I just say one thing?"

"What?" he grits, refusing eye contact.

"I don't care who you come from or how much money you have. Everyone is welcome in this church. And I know you probably don't think I understand how crappy life can be but you're very wrong. I understand more than you will ever know. So if you ever want to talk, or if you need anything, you can come to me. You can trust me, Christopher. I'll never turn my back on you."

He remains quiet but his jaw tightens as he reins in whatever emotions he's feeling. Sighing, I pick up my paintbrush and continue where I left off, allowing him the silence he so desperately wants.

One day I will get him to trust me. I plan to make it my mission from here on out.

CHAPTER 10

Cade

With a clipboard in hand, I walk across the gym only to be pulled aside by an annoying chick who is pretending she doesn't know how to use the equipment.

"Can you tell me if I am doing this right?" she asks, her voice sounding like nails on a chalkboard. She bends over the weight bench with her ass in the air, doing tricep kickbacks.

"Yeah," I reply dryly, barely sparing her a glance before continuing to the front counter. Her offended scoff is loud and clear behind me but I couldn't care less.

This is becoming a problem, something the guys and I need to talk about. Half the women coming in here are just looking to get laid, mainly choosing me since the others are taken. Well, they are barking up the wrong fucking tree. Because unless they have green eyes, red hair, and flawless skin with a light dusting of freckles, my dick doesn't want it.

Stupid dick.

It's been two very long years since I have felt a woman. I've had plenty of opportunities, and at times I've come close to taking them, needing to get her out of my head, but the thought of touching another, especially after everything Faith went through, turns my stomach into fucking knots.

Now that I know she's here, it drives that feeling home even more. It's going to be me, my right hand, and the vision of the night that I got to know what perfection felt like for a long time to come. At least until my dick starts cooperating again.

My thoughts come to a halt when Evans charges through the door like his ass is on fire. "Are Cooper and Jaxson here yet?" he asks, sounding mildly out of breath.

"No. Are they supposed to be?"

"Yeah, I just sent them a text."

Moments later, Cooper walks through the door. "All right, Evans, what the hell is so important that I had to leave work for in a hurry?"

"Trust me, you'll be glad you did."

Jaxson walks in not long after and I literally have to do a double take, blinking at the sight before me. Annabelle is decked out in all pink and strapped to his chest as he carries a diaper bag in one hand. I've never seen my friend look so out of place in my life.

"What the hell is going on, Evans? If you dragged me in here for something stupid I'm going to kick your ass."

Silence fills the air as the three of us stare at him.

"What the fuck are you all looking at?"

Sawyer, of course, says what we're all thinking. "You look fucking ridiculous."

The truthful statement elicits chuckles from us all, except Jaxson. His eyes narrow as he grumbles out something unintelligible.

"Don't worry, Annabelle," Sawyer coos, bravely walking up to her, "you don't look ridiculous, just your dad does. You are pretty, just like your mom."

Jaxson shoves him back a step. "Get away from my kid."

Cooper uses the opportunity to break in, asking what we're all wondering. "All right, Evans, out with it. Why the hell did you bring us here?"

His mouth splits into a cheesy grin. "You guys are never going to believe what I stumbled upon. Follow me." His gaze meets mine. "You too."

"We can't all leave the gym," I tell him.

"Sure we can. Holly is here."

We look over at the terrible receptionist we hired a month ago, allowing the high school student two months for work experience. She snaps her gum and gives us a smile before continuing to file her nails.

My gaze darts back to Evans as I give him a doubtful look.

"She'll be fine, we aren't going to be gone that long. Trust me, you aren't going to want to miss this."

Curious over what he's harping on about, I reluctantly follow him and the others out the door. He leads us down the street, stopping directly across from the park where there's a group of women doing yoga in the open field.

His arms spread wide at the view. "See, what did I tell you. Beautiful, right?"

You've got to be shitting me.

I reach over to slap him across the head, but my hand halts midair when my gaze lands on red hair. The air in my lungs seize as I take in the one girl I've been craving to see again.

Sawyer claps Jaxson and me on the back before taking a spot on the bench. "Have a seat, boys, and let's enjoy the view of our beautiful women in tight-as-fuck clothing while their bodies bend in every position known to man."

Despite the fact that Faith is not my woman, I drop down next to him, unable to look away.

Is she someone else's woman?

My blood pumps violently at the thought, a reaction I shouldn't feel.

I glare over at Sawyer, pissed at him for bringing me here when I've had a hard enough time trying to keep my thoughts straight the last few days.

He's not offended in the least; a smug smile takes over his face. "You're welcome."

I nail him in the shoulder. "You're an asshole."

"Whatever, don't act like you aren't happy I dragged you here," he replies, before reaching over to rip my beanie off my head. "What the hell is with you wearing this thing? It's eighty-five degrees out for fuck's sake."

I yank it out of his hand and put it back on without answering the question, mainly because I don't have an answer. I've grown attached to the damn thing for some reason. If I don't wear it, I feel like I'm walking around without pants on or something. I can't fucking explain it but it bugs the hell out of me.

"At least go buy a summer one if you want to wear it so bad. I'm sweating my balls off just looking at you."

My eyes narrow in annoyance. "Who the fuck are you, the fashion police? Why don't you shut up and go put on one of your woman's waitress uniforms and bake a pie, *sexy fucking Sawyer.*"

Jaxson and Cooper break into muffled chuckles while Evans grins, not the least bit offended. "You should see what I do in that bakery to my woman when everyone is gone and she's wearing her sexy dress uniform."

I barely refrain from rolling my eyes. "Spare me."

I swear, all the guy does is stop in at that bakery, day in and out, to fuck the poor girl to death.

Laughter draws my attention across the street, the sound of Faith's floating above the others. The sweet, soft melody, along with the beautiful smile on her face, hits me like a powerful blow to the chest. She still effects me so strongly, everything about her is perfect.

"Hey, what kind of snacks do you have in that diaper bag?" Sawyer asks, reaching for the bag next to Jaxson. "I'm hungry."

Jaxson slaps his hand away, shooting him a hard look.

"What? Chicks pack food in those things all the time for their kids. Julia probably has tons of shit in here."

"She's five weeks old, you idiot. She only takes formula."

Sawyer rears back at his hostility. "Well, how the hell am I supposed to know that, daddy fucking daycare? Jesus, you're in a real mood today. What the hell crawled up your ass?"

"It's because he hasn't gotten laid in five weeks," Coop divulges, a small smirk taking over his face.

Jaxson's hard eyes move from Sawyer to Cooper, not appreciating his response.

"Well that explains it," Sawyer says. "How much longer do you have to wait? I think my dick would fall off if I had to go that long without Grace."

I shake my head. The guy doesn't know when to shut up.

"She sees the doctor in a few days. Three to be exact," Jaxson mumbles, pressing a kiss to his daughter's head.

The conversation ceases when the sound of a speedy motor cuts through the air as a little old lady on a motorized cart comes racing toward us, the front basket filled with groceries. She slams on her brakes so hard she skids to a stop in front of the bench, her eyes spitting venom at us all.

"Perverts," she snaps, but only shakes her finger at Cooper. "Why am I not surprised to see you involved in this, *Sheriff*? You should be ashamed of yourself."

Sawyer straightens, shoulders squaring. "Hey! Those are our women out there and we can perv on them if we want to."

I cannot believe he just fucking said that. My eyes close as I refrain from nailing him in the shoulder again.

"Don't worry, Mrs. Haywood," Cooper responds calmly, "we're just waiting for the girls. I promised Kayla I would take her out for lunch today."

Her icy glare moves among each one of us, her chin lifting. "Well, you should wait in your vehicles." She harrumphs before speeding away, burning rubber in her wake.

I have to admit that thing packs some power behind it.

"Well, isn't she in a real fucking twist," Sawyer grunts, looking over at Coop. "She sure seems to have a real problem with you, *Sheriff*," he sneers the name, mocking the elderly woman.

"She busted me pissing in her rose bushes when I was like fourteen years old and she still hasn't gotten over it."

"I remember that. She even called your mom," Jaxson chuckles.

The conversation takes a turn when the sound of a high-pitched squeal penetrates the air. "Oh my goodness, my baby girl is here." Julia runs across the street, all the girls following just as quickly behind her.

All of them but one.

Faith hangs back hesitantly, her eyes meeting mine briefly until she turns away and begins packing up. It makes me feel like complete shit.

Julia takes Annabelle from Jaxson, raining kisses all over the baby's face. "How's Mommy's sweet girl?" she coos then passes her to Katelyn's outstretched hands.

While each girl takes a turn, Jaxson pulls Julia in for a long kiss, practically mauling her like he hasn't gotten any in weeks.

"What are y'all doing here?" Grace asks.

"Sawyer texted us when he spotted you girls," Cooper responds, having no qualms about ratting him out.

Grace shakes her head, a knowing smile teasing her lips. "Why am I not surprised to hear this was your idea, Sawyer?"

"Because you know me so well, baby." He lifts her off the ground, throwing her over his shoulder.

Her surprised squeal pierces the air. "Sawyer Evans, put me down right now, you're embarrassin' me!"

"Sorry, Cupcake, but I have plans for you before you head back to the bakery," he says, moving for his truck down the street.

"See you later, Grace." Kayla laughs, tossing her a parting wave.

She waves back, embarrassed.

Before getting too far, Sawyer turns back, his eyes shifting to Faith across the street before coming back to me. "Don't be an asshole, Walker."

It's on the tip of my tongue to tell him to mind his own fucking business, but he continues on his merry way.

It doesn't take long before I realize it's suddenly quiet. I look over at the group to see everyone shift uncomfortably while Katelyn glares at me, her feelings apparent. "I'll see you guys later. Thanks for coming today."

They all bid her a soft goodbye as she walks back to Faith across the street, their eyes moving to me expectantly soon after.

"I'm going, I'm going," I grumble, my feet starting forward. I planned on talking to her, I just don't need a crowd while doing it.

Faith is kneeling on the ground, back turned to me as she helps Katelyn pack everything up. It isn't long before her back straightens, sensing my approach. Her eyes meet mine over her shoulder, surprise gripping her pretty face. She whispers something to Katelyn before climbing to her feet and facing me.

Katelyn quickly follows suit, taking a protective step in front of her.

I find it quite amusing but also comforting. I'm glad Faith has someone looking out for her.

"Hey, Red."

"Hi," she whispers, an edge of surprise in her voice at the use of her nickname.

"Do you have a minute?"

She nods. "Sure."

We both look over at Katelyn when she makes no effort to leave.

Faith places a reassuring hand on her shoulder. "I'll meet you at the car, okay?"

"You sure?" she asks, refusing to take her furious eyes off me.

"Yes. I'm sure."

She hesitates for only a second before picking up her bag and walking away but not before knocking me in the shoulder on her way past. A frustrated huff leaves her when I don't budge.

I cock a brow at Faith. "I get the feeling she's starting to like me."

The joke elicits a smile like I hoped it would. The sight of it lights up every dark place inside of me. I'm fucking pathetic.

"I'm sorry, she's a little protective."

"Don't be. I'm glad she is."

Her smile fades, silence descending as her eyes drop to her feet.

I move in closer, lifting her gaze back to mine. "Don't."

"Don't what?" she asks, her voice barely above a whisper.

"Don't look away from me. I hate it."

Her tongue darts out to lick her dry lips, the innocent act wreaking havoc on my cock. "What did you want to talk to me about?"

"Why didn't you come over with everyone else?"

"I wasn't sure I would be welcome, so I thought it was best to stay where I was."

Guilt grips my chest in an unforgiving vice. "You're always welcome, Red."

"Am I?" she asks, no longer having a hard time holding my gaze.

"Yeah. Always."

Her gaze moves over my shoulder, looking in the distance as she crosses her arms over herself.

A heavy breath escapes the confines of my chest before I tread on. "Look, us running into each other again has been a lot to take in, for the both of us, but I meant what I said, you don't have to stay away. I want you to be friends with the girls. They're nice and they'll be good to you."

I'm proud of myself for not fucking up the words like I did last time.

Her gaze comes back to mine, eyes searching. Whatever she finds has her tense shoulders relaxing. "All right, thank you."

I nod, before clearing my throat and broaching the next subject with her. "Since it didn't happen the other day, I would like it if you came to the gym for the next self-defense class."

She seems surprised by the request. "Will you be the one teaching it?"

"No. I won't be teaching any of them, unless something happens where I have to. As you know, I'm not really big on people."

She feigns shock. "You, not big on people, really?" A teasing smile plays at the edge of her lips, reminding me of what a smart-ass she can be.

"Yeah, it seems Sawyer thinks I'll scare the women away."

The softest laugh escapes her, the sound of it causing that shift again.

I really fucking hate that…kind of.

"That's only because you don't let anyone see the real you. If you did, then no one would be afraid of you." Her gaze strays from mine once more, clearly not meaning to have said that out loud. "I should probably get going," she whispers. "Katelyn is waiting."

She plays with her braid over her shoulder nervously and it's then my eyes drop to her chest, every muscle in my body stiffening at the small tattoo resting above the swell of her left breast. Reaching out, I trace the small music note. The name *Aadil* is written through it in script with the word *Honorable* beneath it.

Her breath hitches at my touch, eyes shooting up to mine. The sight of tears forming in the emerald irises is almost enough to bring me to my knees.

"I got it done shortly after I got back home," she explains, her voice a choked whisper. "I wanted something to honor him by and keep him close to my heart. I researched his name and found out it means honorable. It's perfect for him." A single tear slips down her cheek.

My jaw locks as I fight the emotion building in my chest. I pull her into me, dropping a hard kiss on top of her head. "Be safe, Red."

Without another word, I walk away before I end up doing something I can't take back.

CHAPTER 11

Faith

At least a half dozen youth walk among the church, all of them helping to put the finishing touches in place so we can be ready for opening in just a few short weeks. It warms my heart how many have volunteered their time here, most of them are as excited as we are, especially for the Friday night youth group I am putting together.

Things are finally starting to fall in place.

Christopher comes rushing in just then, looking frazzled and out of breath. He tows a young girl behind him, his eyes scanning the crowd until they land on me. He hurries over, dragging the little girl behind him.

"Hey," I greet him. "Is everything okay?"

"Yeah, but I need to have my sister with me today. I can't leave her at my house." There's something in his tone, something that isn't usually there. A worry that only adds to my own.

I look down at the sweet little girl who hides behind her brother. She's dressed in clothes much too small for her and wears big thick black glasses that take up half of her face. Despite the size of them, they do nothing to deflect from her bright blue eyes and adorable face. She peeks around him, flashing me a darling smile that I can't help but return.

"It's no problem at all," I say, looking back up at him. "I told you everyone is welcome in this church, and that includes your sister."

"Thanks. I promise she won't cause any problems. She'll quietly sit in a corner with a book until I'm done."

His sister looks up at him, scowling as she shoves her glasses up higher on her face. Obviously, she's bothered to be cast aside.

"I have a better idea," I say, treading lightly. "I was planning to go visit my friend's bakery for a slice of pie that is supposed to be the best in this world. Would it be okay if I brought your sister along so I have some company?"

Excitement lights up the little girl's face. "Oh tan I, Twistiphwor? Pwease?"

Christopher glances down at his sister, looking unsure. It's clear he's very protective of her.

"It's only down the street," I add, hoping to reassure him. "I promise we won't stay long."

"All right. Just…don't be gone with her for too long, okay?"

"I promise."

"Yay!" The little girl hugs his leg excitedly. "Tanks, Twistiphwor."

He nods down at her. "You be good for Faith, all right?"

"Pwomise." She comes to stand next to me, reaching for my hand and wrapping her tiny fingers around it. It completely warms my heart. She clearly doesn't have the same trust issues as her brother does. "I'm weady whenever you are, Miss Faif."

"Perfect. There are just two important things I need to know before we go."

She peers up at me expectantly.

"Are you allergic to anything?"

She glances at her brother who shakes his head.

"Good. And the next one, what's your name?"

Christopher is the one to answer. "It's Ruth Jean."

Her small face pinches in distaste. I have to admit it's unique, just like the little girl herself.

"Well hello, Ruth Jean, as you know my name is Faith and I am so very happy you are going to keep me company over some pie."

She beams up at me. "Tanks for invitin' me."

After one last wave goodbye to her brother, we walk outside into the bright sunshine and start walking toward Grace's bakery that's only a block away.

"Tell me a little about yourself, Ruth Jean."

"I'm six yeaws owd and in gwade one. I have the wost name in the wold betause my mama named me after my gwandma. I tan't say wots of wods wight, as you tan pwobably tell. I don't have many fwiends, but dat's otay betause dey're mean anyway and I have Twistiphwor. He's my best fwiend and I wuv him a whole wot." She looks up at me happily; as if she didn't just list all the things she sees wrong about herself, except for her brother.

"Well, I can understand you just fine, and I think there is nothing wrong with your name. It's refreshing and unique." She looks at me doubtfully, but I ignore it and continue. "I also think it's pretty special that you love your brother, he seems like a great big brother."

"He's de best. Now yowr tourn."

I smile and start the same way she did. "Well, I am twenty-four years old, almost twenty-five, my birthday is in a few weeks. I love music, singing, and dancing. I'm an only child. I always wanted a brother or a sister but my mom couldn't have any more children after me."

"Why not?"

I shrug. "I'm not really sure. I guess God intended it to be just me for my parents."

"It's pwobably betause yow're special."

Warmth invades my chest at how beautiful this young girl's heart is. "Has anyone ever told you how incredibly sweet you are, Ruth Jean?"

She thinks about it for a moment, tapping her chin before answering. "Nope! Well, maybe Twistiphwor. When odder kids tease me he tells me I'm pwetty, and says not to wisten to dem."

Hearing that no one besides Christopher has told her that has me curious about her parents. "I bet your mom and dad think you're special, too."

I regret the words immediately when her shoulders slump and sadness grips her face. "No. Mama weft Twistiphwor and me when I was just a baby betause she didn't want us no more. And my dad…he's not vewy nice. Espesially to Twistiphwor."

The admission has my heart sinking into the pit of my stomach, especially to hear the father isn't nice to Christopher. Before I can question her further, her face lights up as she points ahead at the pink and white Victorian, gingerbread-styled bakery, A Slice of Hope with a Sprinkle of Grace.

"Is dat it?"

"It is," I tell her with a smile.

"Wow, it's amazin'."

I have to agree. I also think it represents Grace perfectly.

We walk through the doors to find only a few patrons sitting with their coffee and pie.

Grace is clearing tables, a friendly smile taking over her face when she spots us. "Faith, hi," she greets kindly, embracing me with a warm hug. "I'm so happy you finally came in."

"So am I." Once she steps back, I point down to Ruth Jean. "This is my friend, Ruth Jean. Ruth Jean, meet Grace."

Grace kneels down to shake her hand. "Well, hi, Ruth Jean. It's a pleasure to meet you."

"You too, Gwace. I wike your name, and I weally wike your dwess."

"Why thank you, I like your name, too."

By the expression on Ruth Jean's face it's clear she doesn't believe her. But I push on before she can go into all the reasons why she doesn't like her name. "We thought we would come and try some of the world's best pie."

Grace stands, a soft blush staining her cheeks. "I don't know about the world's best, but my mama sure had some amazin' recipes. Come in and have a seat. Your timing is perfect, the lunch rush just left." She leads us to one of the tables. "I'll bring y'all the special of the day. Do you like chocolate and raspberries?"

We both nod.

"How about sweet tea?"

"Yes, ma'am," Ruth Jean answers.

"Perfect, hang tight. I'll be right back."

"Thanks, Grace."

Ruth Jean's eyes wander among the bakery, a look of wonderment on her face. "It's so pwetty in here. It kinda weminds me of de tandy house in Hansel and Gwetel. Do you know dat stowy?"

"I do, it's one of my favorites. And you're right, it does look like that."

"I wonder who dat is," she says, pointing to the large canvas behind the counter. The photo of a younger Grace and a beautiful woman, who I assume is her late mother, takes up most of the wall. They both smile brightly, holding up a first place ribbon. Above the picture reads, *In Loving Memory of Hope Morgan.*

Katelyn told me about the tragic way Grace lost her mother. My heart broke for her but it was quickly replaced with warmth when I heard Sawyer had this bakery built in her memory. I think it's incredibly special.

"That is Grace and her mother. She passed away," I tell her regretfully.

"Das sad."

I nod. "It is."

"Sometimes, I weally miss my mom, even though I don't wemember her."

My curiosity piques once again but I refrain from asking, knowing Christopher wouldn't appreciate it. I need to gain his trust and let him be the one to tell me, hopefully that will be soon.

Grace returns shortly with our order. "Here you are. It's on the house."

"Oh no. That's okay, Grace. I'll pay for it."

She waves away my objection. "Nonsense. Consider it a welcome gift. I hope you like it. This is one of my favorite recipes from my mama, it's called Grace's First Kiss Pie."

Ruth Jean giggles at the name, which makes Grace and me do the same. Our moment is interrupted when an older man pokes his head out from the kitchen, calling for Grace.

"Excuse me a moment."

At my nod, she heads back into the kitchen, leaving Ruth Jean and me to devour our pies and it's exactly what we do. I must agree with all the hype, this is the best pie I've ever had, and my mother is no slouch in the kitchen.

The bell above the door jingles, alerting someone's arrival, and it's then a warm feeling invades, sliding over every inch of me. I don't have to look to know who it is. Only one person has that affect on me.

In my peripheral vision, I see Sawyer and Cade, Sawyer's laughter filling the bakery when Cade shoves him for whatever comment he just made. My attention immediately anchors on Cade as I become pulled in by that force, the one I seem to have no control over. I take in everything about him. From his loose, black athletic pants to his fitted white muscle tank that stretches across his lean, muscular form in all the right places, showcasing many of the tattoos he bears. His messy, dark hair peeks out from beneath a black beanie, my fingers remembering the way the strands felt between them the night we…

I let that thought trail off, my cheeks flushing with heat. He looks just as strong and beautiful as always, and for the second time in two years, feelings begin to warm inside of me. Ones I never thought I would feel again.

Both men falter when they spot me. Sawyer's easy smile returns, but as usual, Cade's expression is hard to read. I swallow nervously and hope he meant what he said the other day and that he's okay with me being here.

They start over to our table, both of them eyeing Ruth Jean with curiosity.

"How's it going, Country?" Sawyer greets me with an easiness that has me relaxing a little more. "Good to see you again."

"You, too." My gaze swings to Cade where I find him scowling at Sawyer. "Hey." My acknowledgement comes out barely a whisper but it catches his attention.

His expression softens as he looks down at me. "Hey, Red."

My heart trips in my chest to hear my nickname fall past his lips, a nickname only he uses.

"Who's this pretty little girl?" Sawyer asks, looking down at Ruth Jean.

Guilt plagues me for getting so caught up in my emotions that I forgot my manners.

"This lovely girl is my friend, Ruth Jean. Ruth Jean, this is my…" I pause, knowing *friends* isn't the right word, "um, Sawyer and Cade."

Oh God!

My eyes close when I realize how that sounded, wishing the ground would swallow me whole. Thankfully, no one calls notice to it.

"How's it going, Ruth Jean?" Sawyer asks.

I bite back a smile at the expression on her small face as she stares up at both men, her head craned all the way back, eyes wide and mouth open.

"Your name is…unique…" Sawyer adds, flashing her his most charming smile.

Ruth Jean finally snaps out of her stunned state and pushes her glasses up on her nose. "It's a tewwible name. I didn't choose it."

Sawyer seems not only amused by the response but also surprised. He recovers quickly though. "Ah, don't worry about it," he says, chucking her under the chin. "Your pretty face makes up for it."

The compliment has her beaming. "Tanks, mister." Her gaze moves to Cade next and her newfound confidence crumbles as fear takes over her expression, her loud gulp filling the silence.

He doesn't offer her a smile, which I didn't expect him to, but he gives her a small nod. "Hey, kid."

"Hi." The one word comes out shaky.

He shifts uncomfortably when she continues to stare at him.

Sawyer takes pity on him, breaking the awkward moment. "So what do you think of my woman's pies? Pretty darn good, aren't they?"

"Gwace is yowr woman?" she asks in surprise.

He stands a little taller, a proud grin spreading across his mouth. "She sure is."

"So is dis pie named after you? Was you her fwirst tiss?"

Sawyer's easy grin vanishes, a scowl forming on his face. "I'm the only one who matters, kid." His gaze scans the diner. "Where is my Cupcake anyway?"

"Right here," Grace announces cheerfully as she walks out from the back, oblivious to the topic of conversation at the moment.

Sawyer becomes a man on a mission. He wastes no time striding over to her, picking her up off her feet and laying one heck of a kiss on her.

Ruth Jean giggles and I do as well. Cade, on the other hand, shakes his head.

By the time Sawyer pulls away, Grace's cheeks are bright pink. "Well, hello, Sexy Sawyer. What was that for?"

His scowl returns. "Why are you serving people your First Kiss Pie?"

"Because it's the special of the day, and both Ruth Jean and Faith like chocolate."

"Well, you need to rename that shiii…crap"—he catches himself—"to Sawyer Is My Only Kiss Pie."

She rolls her eyes at him. "Stop bein' ridiculous and put me down."

He grunts, unhappy with her reply but complies with her demand.

She grabs a takeout bag from the counter and hands it to Cade. "Here ya go. There's something in there for Jaxson, too."

"Why are you giving it to him?" Sawyer asks, affronted.

"Because if I give it to you, you will eat it all and not share," she responds sweetly, tapping his cheek.

"We've had this talk before, Cupcake. You're *my* woman, so these are *my* pies. I don't have to share if I don't want to."

Both Ruth Jean and I muffle our giggles while Grace shakes her head, but she too can't hide her smile. She lifts to her toes to kiss his cheek.

Smiling, I look over at Cade to find him watching me, his fierce gaze taking my breath away. It's a look I remember well and one I see often in my dreams—the good ones, not my nightmares. Something passes between us, something powerful and consuming.

It's broken a moment later though when Sawyer punches him in the arm. "Come on, man, we need to get back before the fighters come in."

He makes no move to leave, his eyes remaining on me as Sawyer says his goodbye to Ruth Jean. It's then he raises his hand, ever so carefully, and to my surprise, grazes my cheek, his knuckles skimming the soft skin.

A sharp breath infiltrates my lungs, my pulse hammering at the warm but subtle contact. I desperately get the urge to lean into the warmth of his hand, but all too quickly he moves it away, his jaw locking, as if he only just realizes what he did.

"I'll see you around, Red."

"Bye," I whisper, the one word coming out shaky.

His attention moves to Ruth Jean next, bidding her a parting nod, then just like that he and Sawyer are gone.

My hand rests over my cheek where his knuckles just grazed, still feeling the warmth of his touch. Grace offers me a sad smile and it's then I shake myself of the moment.

"Are you ready?" I ask Ruth Jean. "We should head back to church. Christopher should be almost finished."

Nodding, she stands and turns to Grace. "Tank you for de dewicious pie, Miss Gwace. It was de best I eva had."

"You are very welcome, Ruth Jean. I hope you will come see me again sometime."

"You bet I will."

Once again, I offer to pay but Grace refuses. It's then Ruth Jean and I make our exit and start back to the church.

"Dose guys were huge," she says, making a dramatic gesture with her hands. "Especially dat one with all the tattoos, he doesn't seem all that fwiendwy."

I smile. "Cade is just quiet is all. He warms up once you get to know him."

"How do you know him?" she asks, looking up at me curiously.

"I met him a few years ago when I was on a missions trip with my church. He and Sawyer were both Navy SEALs. Do you know what that is?"

She shakes her head.

"Do you know what a soldier is?"

"Yeah, dey awe good guys who help save people and fight for Amewica."

"That's right. Navy SEALs are very similar, except they are trained a little differently, and do different missions. He…he saved my life from some very bad men," I tell her, the words trailing on a whisper.

"He did?"

I nod. "Along with Sawyer and another friend of theirs, Jaxson. He was the one Grace mentioned."

"So he's a good guy den?"

"One of the best," I say, meaning it.

"Well, he wooked weally stwong."

A sad smile touches my lips. "Ruth Jean, he's the strongest man I've ever known." My heavy heart must show in my expression because she reaches for my hand and gives it a squeeze. The entire gesture has my throat burning.

"Twistiphwor is the stwongest guy I've ever known. He never wets anyone huwt me, not even my dad."

The comment snaps me back to the here and now and has dread sinking into the pit of my stomach. Before I can ask what she means by that, the church comes into view, sending her forward.

Without any other choice, I jog to catch up to her. She takes the stairs two at a time, running inside. There we find Christopher off in the corner, sweeping up the floor, though his eyes are glued to Alissa Malone. The fifteen-year-old girl whose parents are members of the church. His attention is anchored on her, eyes mesmerized when she laughs at something one of the girls say.

"Twistphwor!" Ruth Jean runs up to him, yanking his attention our way. He drops the broom, opening his arms for his little sister as she jumps into them. He doesn't notice when Alissa turns and watches him.

"Did you have fun with Faith?" he asks.

"It was de best. Gwace is so nice and her pie is dewicious. Den we ran into dese big guys, one wooked stary but Faif says he's a good guy. He saved her wife from bad guys a wong time ago."

Christopher looks over at me with questions in his eyes, but thankfully doesn't ask any. I've had enough revisiting that part of my life for one day.

"Listen," he says, stepping closer, "I don't have any money on me right now, but I'll pay you back for however much the pie was when—"

I cut him off before he can go any further. "Absolutely not. I never expected that. Besides, my friend Grace gave it to us on the house."

He looks at me doubtfully but doesn't push the subject anymore. "Well, thanks for taking her. I really appreciate it." He places her back down on her feet so he can pick up his bag. "Can you say thank you, Ruth Jean?"

She launches herself at me, wrapping her arms around my waist. "Tanks so much, Faif. I'm gwad to have another fwiend."

"Me too, Ruth Jean. You're welcome to come with your brother anytime. I would love your company again." I look back up at Christopher. "Can I give you guys a ride home?"

He shakes his head. "We're fine. But thanks anyway."

I want to push the idea, especially after what Ruth Jean just said. I want to see where they live and find out more about their home life, but knowing Christopher and how closed off he is, I must tread carefully.

"All right then, I guess I'll see you soon."

Nodding, he takes Ruth Jean's hand and heads toward the door, but not before glancing at Alissa one more time before walking out.

Smiling, I follow them outside. "Her name is Alissa," I tell him.

His eyes shoot to mine, knowing he's been busted. "So? I don't care."

I shrug. "Just thought you may want to know."

"Well I don't."

"Okay," I reply easily, but we both know he's not fooling anyone.

Shaking his head, he kneels down so Ruth Jean can jump on his back before descending the stairs. My heart swells at seeing the tough-looking boy be so gentle with his sister.

Ruth Jean gives me one more parting wave before they disappear down the street. It's not long after that a sudden feeling of panic plagues me, and I'm left to wonder what kind of home they are going to. I decide I'm going to find out and soon, because I will not stand by and watch another child be destroyed if I can do something about it.

Not ever again.

CHAPTER 12

Cade

The summer morning is cooler than usual so I take the opportunity to run outside at a nearby park. Its trails are remote and often not filled with many people. I made sure to leave a little earlier than usual to avoid running into anyone, but of course, as luck would have it, someone is already here. And who does that someone have to be? The one girl who invades my every waking thought. Faith is kneeled down, her back to me as she ties her shoes.

Unwanted anticipation hammers through my blood. I want to kick myself for the reaction.

Once she finishes with her shoes, she stands and sticks her earbuds in. My gaze travels down her long lithe body that's hugged by black spandex, and I have to curse my dick at the attention it takes.

She turns around, startling for only a second before surprise takes over her pretty face. She recovers quickly, flashing me a sassy smile. "First the bakery now here? If I didn't know any better, Walker, I'd think you're following me."

"I moved here first, remember, Red?"

Amusement dances across her face, her eyes seeing more than I want her to.

"I didn't know you run?" I say, changing the subject.

Her smile slips. "I started after Iraq, it's been a big part of my healing process," she admits softly.

The moment becomes heavy, my chest pulling tight as I think about what she had to heal from.

She visibly shakes herself of the moment, her smile returning once again. "I've actually become quite fast, if I do say so myself. What do you say, Walker? Think you can keep up?"

I cock a brow, wondering if she's serious.

"I'll take that as a yes." Without another word, she pushes off, starting a slow jog.

I give her a few seconds of glory before catching up to her, making sure to stay just slightly ahead of her.

She accepts the challenge eagerly, and picks up speed. I have to admit she's quick, but not anywhere close to my quick. I pass her again, a smirk taking over as I bait her.

"Don't get too cocky, Walker. My legs are much shorter than yours, which means I'm working harder than you."

I spare her a glance over my shoulder. It has her pushing herself harder and faster. She's damn persistent, I'll give her that.

A light sheen of sweat dots her skin, giving it a glowing effect, and it reminds me of another time I made her look like that, except it was much more fun than this.

Jesus, I need to get laid. If only my dick would work for anyone else.

"Your shoe is untied," she gasps.

I shoot her a look. No way does she think I'm that stupid.

When I don't fall for her pathetic attempt, she shoves my shoulder, trying to make me falter, but I don't budge. She laughs, finding herself fucking hilarious, and I can't deny what the beautiful sound does to me.

When her breathing becomes too heavy and her wheezing can no longer be ignored, I take pity on her and slow my pace. "Take it easy, Red, before I have to pick you up and revive you."

"Well, when you put it that way…" Stopping abruptly, she falls to the ground dramatically, lying amongst the lush, green grass.

I stare at her unimpressed, not finding her funny. Okay, maybe a little funny, but I'll never let her know that.

When she realizes I'm not coming to her rescue, she lifts up, resting back on her elbows. "Hello, aren't you going to revive me, or were you just being a tease?"

My dick throbs at her sassy mouth, my fists clenching as I fight to restrain myself from kissing the smug look off her pretty face. "Be careful, Faith. You're playing with fire."

Her smile falters, heat igniting in her emerald eyes that matches my own. "Maybe I like the heat."

Fuck, she is going to kill me. Despite the effect she has on me, I keep my scowl in place.

She rolls her eyes, climbing to her feet. "All right, calm down, Mr. Oh-so-serious." She starts forward only to gasp and flinch, grabbing her ankle.

"What is it?" I ask, hurrying over to her. The moment I reach her, she takes off like a fucking rocket.

"Sucker!" she calls out behind her, laughing her ass off.

I drop my head back on my shoulders, wanting to slap myself for being stupid enough to fall for that shit. She runs all the way back to our starting point before I finally catch back up.

Her smile is as sassy as the girl herself. "I win. Man, you're slow."

My hard eyes only make her laugh harder.

"You have to admit, Walker, it was a good one."

"I didn't take you for a cheater."

She shrugs. "A girl's got to do what a girl's got to do."

Grunting, I begin stretching next to her, making sure to keep a safe distance since my control is already close to shattering.

That's when our private time is interrupted. "Looks like my bad morning is about to take a turn for the better," a deep voice booms out of nowhere.

My head turns left and there I find some asshole who looks oddly familiar jogging over to us. By the way he eyes Red, I want to knock him on his ass.

Faith smiles politely, but I don't miss the subtle apprehension in her shoulders. "Hi, Dr. Carson."

Oh yeah, Dr. Fucking Sissy, who Sawyer and Jaxson are always griping about. I knew I recognized him from somewhere.

"Call me Blake, remember?" he replies with a flirtatious wink.

I try to keep myself impassive and continue stretching, but what I really want to do is knock this motherfucker on his ass.

"Looks like I'm a little late. Too bad, we could have finally had that date I've been asking you on."

A jealous rage ignites beneath my skin, searing my veins.

Faith glances over at me, looking as uncomfortable as I am furious.

"How about Friday night? I'm off at seven."

I finally look over at him, amazed by the balls he has. For all he knows Faith could be mine. She is mine!

Faith's eyes move to me again, this time a small smile playing at the corner of her lips. I give her a look, letting her know exactly what will happen if she pushes me. I have no right to feel like this, but I can't control it. I've never been able to control my emotions when it comes to her.

"Sorry, Blake, but I already have plans."

I can't help but wonder whom with. Probably Katelyn. As far as I know, she doesn't hang out with anyone else…I don't think.

Fuck! I hate this. I hate not knowing. I hate that she isn't mine, no matter how much I want her to be.

"Maybe another time then," the loser says, trying to hide his disappointment.

"Maybe." She nods noncommittally. "Well, I better get going. I'm helping at the church today before I have lunch with friends. Take care, Doctor, er, Blake." Her eyes move to mine, a more genuine smile claiming her lips. "I'll see you around, Cade Walker." She jogs out of the park, every stride taking her further and further away.

The asshole eventually turns to me, his stupid smile diminishing when he sees the look on my face. "You have got to be shitting me. You, too? Why is it every time someone new comes here, they belong to one of you assholes?"

I decide to let the "asshole" comment slide just this once.

"Or is she yours?" he asks, smirking at my silence. "That's what I thought. May the best man win."

He starts forward only to be yanked back by me, my fingers squeezing the back of his neck.

"Hey. What the hell do you think you're doing? Get off me, man."

I lean down close, my hard face only inches from his. "Stay the hell away from her or you'll fucking regret it." I release him with a shove then make my exit, hoping he heeds the warning.

On my run back to the gym, I realize my resolve is slipping. All the reasons I thought it was best to stay away from her are starting to not matter anymore. It's dangerous because these feelings could very well destroy us both.

CHAPTER 13

Faith

At the bakery, Katelyn and I sit with Julia and Grace, waiting for Kayla to arrive for our lunch date. I crack a smile when the girls share a laugh but I have no idea what was just said because my mind is elsewhere, my thoughts on the man I haven't stopped thinking about since I left him this morning.

Katelyn notices my distraction. She curls an arm around my shoulders, pulling me in close. "Talk to us. What is going on in this pretty head of yours?"

I consider lying, not wanting to ruin our lunch, but by the look on all of their faces it would be pointless. "I ran into Cade this morning," I start softly.

Katelyn's body tenses next to me. "What did he do?"

"Nothing." I rush to say. "Actually, we ended up running together and…it was nice. Really nice." My shoulders deflate on a soft sigh. "I guess I'm just feeling off-kilter since seeing him again after all this time."

Julia reaches for my hand, offering a sympathetic smile. "You all have been through a lot. It's just going to take some time."

She and Grace peer back at me, patience and understanding reflecting in their gazes. I decide now is a good time to say to them what I have been wanting to say.

"I feel like I owe you girls an apology."

"What on earth do you have to apologize for?" Grace asks.

"For what Sawyer and Jaxson went through because of me," I whisper, a burning sensation erupting in my throat.

Katelyn puts her hand on my leg under the table for support as I fight to rein in the guilt I've felt for so long.

"Oh, Faith, no," Julia says, her voice sounding as sad as mine. "We don't blame you at all. Listen, I still don't know the full extent of what happened. Jaxson has only shared very little with me, but I know enough. As hard as it is for me to say this, I'm glad Jaxson was there for you. If they hadn't been, then they wouldn't have been able to save Anna either. God only knows where you both would be now."

My back straightens to hear the name of the young girl I've often wondered about over the last two years. "You've seen Anna?" I ask, tears instantly welling in my eyes.

Julia nods, a small smile taking over her face. "She visits us often and has become a big part of all our lives. She's doing really well and even has a boyfriend she cares very deeply for."

The information has my composure breaking. I cover my face and sob into my hands, feeling so grateful to hear she's doing well. She endured so much at such a young age, she deserves peace.

Comforting arms surround me, all the girls consoling. Quickly, I pull myself together and look up at them to see they're a blubbering mess like me.

"I'm sorry, you guys," I apologize, wiping my wet cheeks. "I didn't mean to turn this into a cry fest."

"Don't be sorry," Grace says gently. "It's completely understandable, but I think it's important you know something."

"What's that?" I ask, holding her gaze.

"Sawyer has always said if he had to do it all over again in order to save you and Anna, he would. He doesn't regret a second of the decision he made that day."

The admission has a fresh wave of tears forming.

"Nobody blames you, so please don't blame yourself."

It's hard not to, especially knowing the horrendous torture they all endured, but hearing that Sawyer said those words mean more than she could ever know.

Just then Kayla comes rushing into the bakery, looking flustered. "Sorry I'm late. I had to—" She comes to a stop when she sees the lot of us with tears in our eyes. "Should I come back?"

I shake my head. "No, of course not. Please sit down. We were just having a heart-to-heart and the girls were comforting me."

She takes the seat between Grace and Julia. "Well that's because our little Grace here," she coos, squeezing Grace's cheeks together, "just loves getting all sentimental."

Grace slaps her hand away with a laugh. "Stop."

"Anyway, as I was saying when I walked in, sorry I'm late, I had to drop something off for Coop at the station. And as usual the guy had to be looking all sexy, so I had to get my fill before leaving."

Laughter fills our table and just like that we fall into easy conversation, mainly discussing the details of Kayla and Cooper's upcoming wedding. It's not long before I realize that the five of us are going to become very good friends.

That night, I'm just about to head upstairs to get ready for bed when a knock sounds at my door. I glance at the kitchen clock and wonder who could be coming by this late. Taking a few steps closer, I look out the peephole to see it's Sawyer. Surprised, I quickly unlock the door and open it.

"Sawyer, hi," I greet him, my surprise evident.

"Hey, Country. I hope it's not too late."

"Not at all." I lie.

I'm probably the only single twenty-four-year-old who goes to bed at nine thirty.

"I was hoping I could talk to you for a moment before I pick up Grace from the bakery."

"Sure." I wrap my cardigan around me and step out onto the porch, using the opportunity for some fresh air. "Can I get you something to drink?"

"No, thanks. This won't take long." He pauses, an awkward silence filling the evening air.

I start to feel nervous, wondering why he's here.

"Grace told me about your guys' conversation today at lunch," he starts.

"Oh." The one word is all I can seem to manage, my eyes casting down as I begin to feel even more uncomfortable.

"I know this isn't easy to talk about, and I probably should have come sooner to see you, but..." He trails off, running his fingers through his hair as he tries to find the words he wants to say. "I just want you to know I don't blame you. Everything that happened wasn't your fault."

My heart immediately swells with his kind words. "I appreciate you saying that, but we all know you guys wouldn't have gotten hurt if you hadn't come after me."

"Maybe, maybe not." He shrugs. "Who knows what would have happened in the next mission. That was part of our job; we walked in never knowing but always fought like hell to come out alive. The difference with that mission is it's one we chose on our own, and it's a decision none of us regret." His gaze shines bright with sincerity.

"Are you so sure none of you regret it?"

Confusion slips over his expression. "Yeah. Why?"

I don't elaborate, but I don't need to, my thoughts are written all over my face.

He shakes his head. "No. He doesn't regret it at all."

"He refused to see me once we were transported to that hospital. He couldn't even look me in the eye after, Sawyer." My breath hitches as I struggle to hold in my pain. "If it's not that then it's because he can't stand to know what they did to me, and I'm not sure which one is worse." The last of my words choke off on a sob.

A harsh curse leaves him seconds before he pulls me into his arms. I'm surprised by the gesture but also find it comforting.

Once I finally compose myself, he takes hold of my shoulders and steps back, looking me in the face. "Listen, I've known him most of my life. He's gone through some really terrible shit and it's fucked him up."

"I know about his sister," I whisper sadly.

Shock registers on his face. "You know about Mia?"

I nod. "Not much, but he told me about her one of the evenings we spent together in Iraq. He told me the man who killed her was a minister."

"Wow," he says, sounding dumbstruck. "I can't believe he told you."

"Unfortunately, it turned into quite the argument, especially when it came to my father being a pastor."

"It wasn't a minister who killed his sister."

Every muscle in my body stills. "What? But he said—"

"The guy was some sick asshole his mother shacked up with. He ran a polygamy commune and preached he was one of God's prophets."

"Oh my god," I whisper, not having any other words.

"That's what I'm trying to say, Country. He's fucked in the head; his logic is different than ours. You can't take to heart the shit he does."

"His perception might be misguided but he's a good person," I say, feeling the need to stand up for him.

A grin cracks his lips. "You don't need to tell me that. He's my best friend, fucked up and all."

I smile back at him, seeing how much he truly cares about Cade despite his poor choice of words. A guy thing I guess.

He glances down at his watch. "I should get going. Grace will be finishing soon."

I nod. "Thank you for coming by. It means a lot."

"Hang in there, Country. I have a feeling things will start falling into place for all of us."

I hope he's right. We all deserve to find peace.

"If you need anything, don't hesitate to ask."

"Thanks," I whisper, feeling a weight being lifted off my chest.

"I'll see you around."

"Bye." After a small wave, I walk back inside, lock up, and head to bed.

In the quiet of my bedroom, I think about my conversation with Sawyer and can't help but hope he's right. That maybe Cade doesn't blame me at all. Maybe, just maybe, he's missed me as much as I have missed him.

CHAPTER 14

Cade

The mother of all nightmares grips me, taking me prisoner and drowning me in its black abyss.

Heavy boots tread down the hall toward us, the air reeking of impending death. Only, if everything goes as planned, it will be their blood shed, not ours. Thanks to the boy's mother's prior visit, we might just get out of this place alive.

"Where are you taking me?" The sound of Faith's terrified voice has fire spreading through my chest.

Despite the effect, I remain slack, appearing weak. It's no hard feat. They did a real number on me after I broke that motherfucker's neck. What they don't know though, is what I have always kept buried inside, a deadly monster within just waiting to be unleashed.

The moment I hear our cell door open, I'm unable to hold back and look up to finally see the girl I've been fighting for all week. My lungs seize at the battered sight of her, rage festering and fueling, threatening to erupt sooner than the plan allows. Several guards surround her along with the boy's father, his smirk fueling the rage.

Her gaze lands on mine, pain like I've never seen washing over her face. "Cade" My name falls on a cry as she runs toward me, dropping to her knees. She runs her hands along my blood-soaked body, an agonized sob ripping from her chest before she wraps her arms around my neck. "Oh god, I'm so sorry. I'm so sorry, Cade."

My chest heaves at the feel of her trembling body against my broken one. I run my nose across her swollen cheek, bringing my mouth to her ear. "Be ready, Red. We're getting the fuck out of here." The warning is barely a whisper.

She leans back, hope lighting her emerald eyes seconds before a stark pain enters them once again. "They killed Aadil," she cries, informing me what I already know about the boy. "He tried to save me and they killed him."

I'm just about to tell her everything will be okay but I don't get the chance. A guard grabs her by the hair, ripping her away from me.

"Let go of me!" She fights against him, but it's to no avail. I helplessly watch as she's spun around and backhanded. The blow is so hard it knocks her to the ground.

An enraged roar rips from my chest, every muscle protruding from my skin as I fight against the chains shackling me to the wall. "I'm going to fucking kill you. Every single one of you motherfuckers are dead!"

Sawyer murmurs a warning next to me but I refuse to hear it. All sense is gone.

The kid's father laughs. "Is that so, Soldier?" Walking up to me, he gets in my face, his taunting smirk making my fists clench. "I can't wait until you see what I have in store for you. I am going to fucking break you."

My dead stare never wavers. "You can't break something that's already broken."

Faith's sob penetrates the room while a flicker of surprise flashes in the man's eyes before he quickly masks it.

"We're not soldiers, you fucking idiot. How many times do we have to tell you assholes that? We're N-a-v-y S-E-A-L-s."

My eyes close at Sawyer's taunt, as he tries to deflect the attention off me. It works. The bastard straightens, walking toward him with the club he has in his hand. Small metal spikes poke out from the end. He sends it into Sawyer's chest, ripping the flesh from his body. Warm, wet blood spills onto my face but Sawyer barely makes a sound, his breathing harsh and labored.

"Navy SEALs. Soldiers," the man spits out. "They're all the same—you all live and breathe your honor. Well, boys, we're going to see just what it will take for you to break your so-called honor." He turns to the men behind him. "Set her up!"

Dread tightens my gut as two guards set Faith on her knees. Defiance rages in her eyes, chin lifting as the man walks up to her.

"We're going to have some fun with this man you seem so smitten with. Maybe you can show him some of the new tricks we have taught you." He straightens, looking over at me. "Did you know, Soldier, that many of us have fucked her? Tied her to a bed and fucked her while she begged us not to."

Fury spreads through my veins like wildfire, the monster rising to the surface, whispering words of rage as they all laugh.

Faith's head hangs in shame, her shoulders trembling with sobs. It makes me feel fucking helpless. Once again, I wasn't able to stop it. The pain that thought brings on is brutal and heart stopping.

"Keep it together, man," Sawyer breathes, barely able to manage the words.

I conjure up all the different ways I am going to kill these bastards. I'm going to gut every single one of them and bathe in their fucking blood.

"Akram. Get the soldier," he orders.

The one referred to as Akram walks up to me with keys in his hands. His gaze nervously meets mine, trepidation prominent. It should be. He's about to meet his death.

He unshackles me from the wall, but keeps my wrists chained in front of me. I'm dragged closer to Faith and set up the same way, on my knees before her. I'm unable to look at her, her terrified sobs already making it hard for me to focus.

"Now!" It's the only warning I get before pain explodes through my body, flesh flying with every blow as the spikes gouge what's left of my back.

"Stop!" Faith's desperate cry rips through the air, causing me more pain than any physical blow could. "Please stop hurting him."

The beating doesn't stop until the asshole finally tires out. My ears ring from the excruciating agony but I try to breathe through it and get my bearings again.

Distantly, I hear orders being shouted before Jaxson is standing before me, his hands still locked in front of him as a guard stands behind him.

"Tell me, Soldier," the kid's father starts, speaking to Jaxson. "Would you ever turn on a fellow brother?"

Jaxson remains silent, his jaw clenching. Our eyes connect, knowing the time to strike is coming. The guard behind him sends a blow to his back, knocking him to his knees. He barely makes a sound, his expression tight with pain.

"Answer him!" the guard orders, pulling him back up to his feet.

Jaxson shakes his head. "No."

"No? There's nothing that would make you kill this man in front of you? What if it was to save this woman here? His woman."

Jaxson shakes his head again, eliciting a smirk from the bastard.

"We will see. Give it to him."

The guard places a dagger in his hand, making my painful body tense in surprise. Anticipation hums through me, vengeance just in reach.

"Don't get too excited and fill that head of yours with any ideas," he says, pulling a knife and holding it to Faith's throat. "Now, let's just see how loyal and honorable you are. I want you to end this so-called broken soldier's life. If you don't, we will take this woman again. We will make you all watch her beg until the exact moment I end her life."

"Don't do it," Faith sobs. "Please don't hurt him, I don't care what they do to me."

My tortured soul bleeds like the rest of me to hear her say that. I don't know whether I want to rage at her or fucking kiss her for it.

"Shut up, bitch!" He backhands her again.

My body vibrates, the beast threatening to appear any moment. "Do it!" I order Jaxson, unsure of what he's waiting for. "Just fucking do it already!"

"No! Don't do it!" Faith cries.

The asshole cranks back to hit her again and it's then Jaxson makes his move. The dagger leaves his hand, sailing through midair and driving into the center of the bastard's forehead.

The monster within unleashes with a vengeance and it's more powerful than I remember. It blinds me, nothing but rage consuming me as it possesses me with a strength I didn't even know I was capable of. All I see, taste, and feel is blood of the enemy, and I fucking relish in it.

I'm so blinded by hate that I move to the kid's father where he lies on the floor, cold and dead with the dagger sticking out of his head.

It's not enough.

Every taunt he delivered about hurting Faith, taking what's mine, and killing the kid fuels the vengeance burning in my blood. Ripping the dagger out from his forehead, I use it, gutting him from the inside out until every one of his organs are nothing more than a mangled mess on the floor.

When someone grabs my arm, I spin around with the dagger in hand, ready to shed more blood until I come face-to-face with an angel.

"Stop! It's me, it's just me," Faith says, holding her hands up protectively in front of her, horror etched on her face. "You can stop. They're dead now."

The dagger falls from my hand, clattering to the floor. I reach for her the same time she lunges at me. I sweep her off her feet and cradle her in my arms, holding and protecting her the way she deserves.

Jaxson finishes unlocking Sawyer, both of them quickly turning around to help only to find a bloodbath. The look on their faces are ones I will never forget, the moment they finally realize just what evil I possess inside. It's a cold reminder of why I can never have this woman I hold in my arms.

CHAPTER 15

Faith

Nerves dance in my belly as I walk to the gym to see Cade. I'm hoping he doesn't mind me stopping by unannounced like this but it can't wait. I need to see him.

Earlier today, Christopher told me he needed to find a job and I immediately thought of the gym. It would be good for him to be around men like Cade, Sawyer, and Jaxson. Men who haven't always had it easy and know how hard life can be. I'm hoping they can help Christopher deal with whatever is troubling him and getting him into so many fights. Maybe even help him find a different way to release this aggression he has.

The moment I walk inside, I find Sawyer by the ring, talking to a fighter. His eyes briefly flash with surprise before he gives me a genuine smile and makes his way over to me. "Hey, Country, good to see you."

His friendly greeting eases some of my nerves. Ever since our talk the other night, I feel much more comfortable being around him and Jaxson. "Hey. Is Cade around? There's something I want to ask him."

"Yeah. He's in the office getting prepped to spar with one of our guys."

"Oh, well if he's busy I can come back."

"No, it's fine. Go on down, it's the last door on the left."

"Are you sure?" I ask, not wanting to intrude.

He gives me a gentle push. "Yes, I'm sure. Go."

Chuckling, I head in the direction he sent me in and find Jaxson spotting one of the fighters. He nods my way in greeting and I return a wave.

Reaching the office door, I see it slightly ajar. I knock lightly, slowly pushing it open. The sight I'm met with stops me in my tracks and has a painful gasp leaving my throat.

Cade stands shirtless with his back to me, his mangled torso on full display. The sight of his scars has pain slicing through me, it's instant and heart-stopping.

He turns at the sound of my agony, our eyes colliding as my breathing becomes labored. The panic attack hits me strong and fast, black spots dancing in my vision.

Cade lunges for me, catching me just as my knees give out. He sits me on a couch next to the door, his hands framing my face as he shouts at me, but I can't hear a single thing. I slip out of reality and into the past. Images of that awful day slam into me, imprisoning me where I sit.

Finding him chained to the wall, his beaten and broken body raw and blood-soaked. His eyes wild and crazed from the torture he had to endure.

You can't break something that's already broken.

"Faith! Snap the fuck out of it!" His harsh demand penetrates the roaring in my ears and snaps me back to reality.

My hands cover my ears, trying to silence the most agonizing sound piercing through the room, and that's when I realize it's coming from me. My throat raw from screaming.

Jaxson and Sawyer charge into the room, shock and concern gripping their faces as they watch me struggle to breathe.

"Out, now!" Cade shoves them back a step and slams the door in their faces before coming back to me, his warm hands framing my wet cheeks as he rests his forehead on mine. "Come on, Red, breathe, baby. You're okay, everything is okay."

I take in lungfuls of air, the soothing sound of his voice slowing my hammering heart.

"That's it, baby, deep breaths."

I stare into his warm eyes, my hands gripping his shoulders to feel his warmth. To feel him here with me, but amongst what I seek, I feel the scars. The awful horrendous marks that mar his skin all because of me.

"Oh god, I'm so sorry," I sob, wrapping my arms around his neck. "Please forgive me."

His body tenses seconds before he pulls back, confusion masking his expression. "What are you talking about? Forgive you for what?"

"For the scars. For everything that happened to you." My breath catches, emotion thick in my voice. "I understand now and I don't blame you for never wanting to see me again."

His jaw clenches, teeth grinding. "Do you really think that's why I stayed away? You think I blame you?" The last of his words are choked out.

"How can you not? It's my fault. You're all scarred for life because of me."

He shakes his head, jaw locking down even harder. "That's not true. It's not your fault. None of us blame you. I swear, Red, that's not why I stayed away."

"Then why?" I ask, needing to know. "Why did you just walk away? Is it…" I pause, swallowing thickly as I try to find the strength to ask the question I'm terrified to hear the answer to. "Is it because of what they did to me?"

His expression turns from disbelief to outrage. "Fuck no. Are you serious right now? How can you even think that?"

"Because you left me without so much as a goodbye!" I cry.

Guilt flashes in his eyes but I don't let him speak, not yet.

"You couldn't even look at me. You refused to see me. I've thought about you for the last two years, ached to know that you were okay, and you never even tried to contact me. I could have been dead for all you know. What am I supposed to think?"

An array of emotions washes over his face, every single one of them infiltrating my heart. When he remains silent, I shake my head and begin to stand, needing to get out of here, but he doesn't let me.

He grabs my arms, forcing me to sit back down. "No, you're not fucking going anywhere. Look at me!"

My eyes snap to his at the command, the hard intensity in his eyes making my heart skip in my chest.

"You lived at 216 Maple Drive in Great Falls, Montana, with your mom, dad, and grandfather. You drove a red truck and had a dog named Badger that went almost everywhere with you. Shortly after you arrived home you started seeing a therapist named Dr. Alex Mathews. You taught music lessons at your father's church three days a week and volunteered at a homeless shelter every Sunday night."

All I can do is gape at him, his words leaving me speechless.

Big, warm hands slide up my arms, cupping my neck just under my jaw. "You think I never thought about you, Red? That I didn't know whether you lived or died? I knew everything about you for the first nine months you arrived home, and then I stopped because the ache in my fucking chest, at not being able to be near you, was too much. But don't think, for one moment, that I stopped thinking about you. I have thought about you every fucking second of my life since walking away from you."

Tears roll down my cheeks, spilling onto his wrists where he still holds my face between his hands. "Then why did you stay away?" I ask, feeling even more confused now.

"Because I'd only hurt you," he says, grief adopting his face. "You saw what I did to them. The way I gutted those motherfuckers from the inside out without a second thought. That's what's inside of me, Faith, what's always lived beneath the surface."

"And thank God for that," I choke out. "Otherwise, we would have never gotten out of there alive."

"I don't regret killing them; I'd do it all over again. But when it takes over, I have no control. I almost killed you and you know it."

I shake my head. "No. You would have stopped. You *did* stop."

"That time I did, but what about the next time?"

"You will always stop," I say with absolute certainty.

"Are you so sure about that? Are you willing to bet your life on it? Because I'm not."

"I've never been more sure of anything."

He's about to argue, but I don't let him.

"We all have a darkness inside of us, Cade. Everyone does, it's a fact of life, but that's not always a bad thing. What's bad is when you have more dark than light. That's not you."

"You don't know me, Red."

"Yes, I do," I argue back. "I may not have had a long time to get to know you, but if there is one thing I know without a doubt it's that you are a good man. One of the best I've ever known." My hand moves to the side of his face, fingers fanning his jaw.

"He took you to get back at me," he grits between clenched teeth, his breathing turning heavy with anger. "They did that shit to you to hurt me, and it did. Far more than any physical blow that marks my body."

Leaning in closer, I rest my forehead against his, our mouths only a breath away from one another. "You saved my life. I would be dead right now if it wasn't for you."

"I'd do it all over again if I had to. I would take every fucking blow they delivered if it meant saving you."

My eyes close, heart near bursting. "Did you mean what you said down there?"

"About what?"

"That you're broken."

"What do you think?" he asks, evading the question.

"I think you believe that, but you're wrong. You may be damaged, Cade, but not broken."

"No, Red, damaged means it can be fixed and put back together again, broken—it can't, and that's me."

A choked sob breaches my lips. I'm not sure which one of us moves first, but suddenly our mouths become one. His growl and my cry of longing twine together as we get swept up in a storm of passion. My fingers spear into his soft hair, knocking his beanie from his head as I hold him captive to me, giving him no chance at escape. Not that he's pulling away. Oh no. His mouth is hot and demanding, ravishing mine with an intensity that steals my breath.

"I've missed you so much," I breathe against his mouth.

"Me too, baby. I fucking thought about you every second of every day."

Hearing those words does so much for my damaged soul.

His greedy lips descend down the column of my throat, tasting the sensitive skin. I tilt my head to the side, giving him the access he seeks.

His hot, wet mouth finds my puckered nipple through the thin fabric of my sundress, sending warmth to gather between my thighs.

A feeling I haven't felt in years.

My hips begin rocking against his hard stomach, trying to find relief for the pulsing ache.

His hands slip under my dress, coasting up my smooth thighs. Fire soars through my body, a feeling I cling to, but the moment his fingers touch the center of my wet panties, I tense. Panic strikes my chest, as memories of the last time I was touched there try pushing their way through the dark recesses of my mind.

God. Not now.

I squeeze my eyes shut, trying to block them out but it's no use. They hold me prisoner, just like the nightmares.

Cade senses the change in me and swiftly removes his hand. His eyes pull to mine, the hunger that was there moments ago now gone.

Shame washes over me, invading my soul. "I'm so sorry," I whisper.

He opens his mouth to speak, but is interrupted when the door opens, a large man walking through it with an ice pack on his face. I jump back from Cade, feeling like we've been caught doing something inappropriate. No, not inappropriate, it was beautiful and perfect until I had to mess it up.

God, I have to get out of here.

"Shit. Sorry, Walker, I need the first aid kit," the guy apologizes. "I'll come back."

"No!" I protest, standing quickly. "It's all right, I was just leaving."

Just as I head for the door, Cade calls me back. "Faith, don't go."

I turn to him but am unable to look him in the eye. "I'm so sorry. I'll see you later."

Tears cloud my vision, humiliation burning deep as I continue out the door, moving as fast as I can. Sawyer runs out of the gym behind me, sympathy reflecting in his eyes at the tears streaming down my face. "Can I give you a ride home?"

I shake my head. "No, but thank you. I just… I have to get out of here."

He nods, respecting my wishes to be alone.

I end up walking around town aimlessly until I'm more composed then I head to my parents' house, wanting to see my mom and Papa.

On my walk there, I replay the kiss, still feeling the warmth of Cade's lips on mine. I think about the way my body came alive beneath his touch and the way my soul remembered it so well. It was perfect, and something I didn't think I would ever get to feel again.

So why did I have to ruin it?

I shake my head, frustrated with myself. When I turn down my parents' street, I find Katelyn's car parked outside their house. It brings a genuine smile to my face. I'll bet Papa is over the moon to see her.

Despite the fact that Papa George is from my father's side and Katelyn is from my mom's, he always treated her as if she was his own. In the days when we were children, and Katelyn would need to escape home, we would spend long days and nights at Papa and Grandma's ranch. We'd go on long adventure walks with Papa, then bake cookies with Grandma. Late at night we'd camp out in the backyard and tell ghost stories, only to have Papa sneak out and scare us. The man is a jokester and the complete opposite of my father. A former Marine and a pastor would be.

Papa George can be a hard-ass but not when it comes to Katelyn and me. If it wasn't for him, Katelyn wouldn't have her own shop and I wouldn't be as financially set as I am. After my grandma passed away, he sold the ranch and gave both of us a large sum of money. It's made my dreams of opening a music school possible. The reminder has a smile touching my lips.

The moment I enter the house, I hear Papa's boisterous voice. "I'm telling ya, that doctor is a moron and doesn't know what the hell he's talking about."

"Now, Dad, there's no need to swear," my mom reprimands softly.

I follow the voices into the kitchen, my mother's face lighting up when she sees me. "Faith, hi." She walks over, enveloping me in her arms.

"Hi, Mom." My greeting is sad, despite my failed attempt to hide my heavy heart.

She leans back, eyes filled with concern. I shake my head, letting her know I don't want to talk about it.

A soft sigh escapes her before she cups my face and presses a kiss to my forehead. "We'll talk later."

I nod.

"There's my Shortcake, get your ass over here and give me some love."

"Dad! Enough with the language already," my mom scolds again, to which Papa rolls his eyes. I don't know why she even bothers, it's just who the man is. It's the way he will always be.

I walk over to where he's sitting at the kitchen table and drop a kiss on his worn cheek. "Hey, Papa, how are you doing today?"

A frown takes over his face as he takes in my bloodshot eyes. The man doesn't miss anything. "Why the hell does it look like you've been cryin'?"

"I'm fine. Just tired is all."

Katelyn's disbelieving snort makes me out to be the liar I am. I toss a look her way that has her keeping quiet. For now.

"What are you griping about?" I ask Papa, hoping to change the subject as I take the seat across from him. "What doctor is a moron?"

Annoyance flashes in his eyes. "That damn Dr. Carson. He thinks he knows everything, but he doesn't."

"I think he knows more about the medical field than you do, Dad," my mom argues.

I look between him and my mom, concern taking root inside me. "What did he say?"

Papa straightens, his expression tightening in anger. "That asshole is trying to get your mother to change my diet. He says my cholesterol is too high."

"Is it?" I ask.

"That's what he's trying to get everyone to believe," he fires back, getting riled up. "What the hell did I ever do to him? He doesn't even know me."

Katelyn and I burst out laughing.

"Papa, I'm sure if your cholesterol wasn't high he wouldn't tell you that."

"Yeah," Katelyn adds, backing me up, "and that *asshole* is damn good-looking."

Both of us share another laugh at the look on Papa's face.

He jabs a finger in Katelyn's direction. "You stay away from him. He's bad news, I can tell."

She shrugs. "You don't have to worry about me. It's Faith he wants."

I glare at her for opening her big mouth.

She blows me a kiss my way, finishing it with a sweet smile.

Papa points his finger at me next. "Don't you go near him, Shortcake, I'm serious. He's bad news. He's probably trying to get to you so he can mess with my diet."

This time we all laugh, including my mom.

"I'm serious! If his lying know-it-all ass goes anywhere near you, I'll bring out my shotgun."

"Oh, Dad, give it a rest. I think it would be great for Faith to get out, and he does seem quite smitten with her."

I barely refrain from rolling my eyes at her not-so-subtle hint.

Papa on the other hand looks like he's about to explode, I lift a hand up, stopping whatever tirade he's about to start. "Don't worry, Papa. I have no plans to go out with him. He seems nice and all, but I'm too busy with trying to get the music school up and running."

And I'm in love with someone else...I think.

Papa nods, content with that answer. "You have a good head on your shoulders, Shortcake. Always have."

The man is so biased.

"Well, I should get back to the salon," Katelyn says before sending me a look. "Walk me to my car?"

"Of course."

She hugs my mom goodbye then leaves Papa with a big, loud, dramatic smooch on the cheek.

"I love you, kid. Be good and come back soon," he says.

"I'm always good. I'll see you at Sunday dinner."

"Make sure to bring Kolan this time," my mom calls to our backs as we walk out of the kitchen.

Kolan has never been big on family gatherings. The only people he's close to in this family, or shows any affection toward, is Katelyn and me.

When we step outside, Katelyn wastes no time prying. "Wanna talk about it?"

I shake my head, still feeling too raw.

She reaches for my hand, offering comfort anyway. "All right, I won't push. You know I'm here for you though, whenever you need to talk. Day or night."

"I know. Thank you."

"Let's go out tomorrow night," she suggests. "A good friend of mine just opened a piano bar. We could celebrate your birthday early."

Usually, I'm not one for bars, but I think a night out is exactly what I need.

"I'm in. Sounds like fun."

"Great! I'll pick you up at seven." She drops a goodbye kiss on my cheek then hops in her little Honda Civic and drives off.

I wait until her car disappears before heading back inside only to hear Papa all riled up again. "I'm serious, Linda. We shouldn't make any hasty decisions until I get a second opinion."

"Dad, you are not having bacon and that's final."

CHAPTER 16

Faith

After being thrown back into the haunting past earlier in the day, I'm plagued with a nightmare. There's no fighting it as it helplessly drowns me in a pit of despair.

"Faith, wake up. We have to get you out of here."

I stir at the sound of Aadil's terrified voice, my battered body screaming in protest. My face turns toward his as I peer back at him from swollen eyes. I reach out, tracing my fingertips across his wet cheek, the chains around my wrists allowing me only so much access.

"Everything's going to be okay," I soothe.

For the past week I have lied and told him this, not knowing what else to say. He's been forced to watch me be beaten and brutalized at the hands of his father and men. Every night he sneaks back in, kneels by my bed, and sobs beside me, constantly apologizing for his father's heinous actions and begging for forgiveness. No matter how much I tell him that it isn't his fault, he insists on taking the blame.

Most nights, when it's just him and I, we pray or sing. Reaching for any kind of peace to help us get through the desolation.

"No, it's not okay. I heard my father talking. They are going to take you to him and do something horrible. We have to get you out of here, Faith."

Confusion takes hold, penetrating the painful fog. "What are you talking about? Take me to who?"

Guilt masks his small face. "I'm sorry I never told you. My father made me do it. He said he would kill you if I didn't."

Fear grips my chest, making it difficult to breathe. "Made you do what? What happened, Aadil?"

"You're going to hate me," he sobs.

I run a hand through his thick dark hair, trying to comfort him. "I could never hate you."

"The soldier is here."

Every muscle in my body tenses, hope igniting within. "Cade is here?"

He nods then proceeds to tell me what his father made him do and how it's not just Cade here but his two best friends too. The hope vanishes, dread taking its place when I realize they have been here as long as me.

"My father is going to take you to them and do something horrible. We have to get you out of here." He pulls a key from his pocket, holding it up. "It won't be long before he knows it's gone. We have to move fast."

Determination sparks a newfound hope. If I can get out of here and make it back to

Cade's base, surely an army of them will come.

Aadil moves quickly, unlocking my wrists. I stifle a scream at the feel of blood rushing down my arms and back into my fingertips. My battered body screams in protest but I push through it, adrenaline fueling me with strength.

I take Aadil's hand in mine. "You have to come with me. You can't stay here."

"But what about the soldiers? I need to help them, too."

My eyes close, fear washing over me as I think about all three of them. "We will get them help but you must come with me. Your father and his men will hurt you if you don't."

He nods his agreement. "We will go through the kitchen and sneak out through the garden doors. My father and his men are in his study on the other side of the house, but they were coming for you soon, so we need to hurry."

He leads me to the door, opening it quietly before peeking his head out. When there's no sign of anyone, he tugs on my hand, pulling me down the long hallway. I glance over my shoulder every so often, praying no one emerges.

Just as we turn the corner, a maid walks out of one of the rooms. We both come to a stop, panic seizing my chest.

Her eyes widen. She scolds Aadil in Arabic, sounding as terrified as I feel. Aadil argues back with her, his tone pleading. The woman's eyes move to me, sympathy flashing in her gaze before she shakes her head and turns away.

Aadil looks at me over his shoulder. "It's okay, she won't tell."

A sigh of relief leaves me before we're moving again, weaving in and out of hallways. I'm just about to ask him how much farther when a sharp pain slices through my scalp and I'm yanked off my feet by my hair.

"Faith, no!" Aadil charges at the guard behind me, kicking and punching him. "Let her go!"

The man calls for help before backhanding Aadil so hard it sends him into the wall. Anger thrashes through my veins, replacing my panic. I manage to slip through his grip enough to sink my teeth into his forearm, the taste of his blood filling my mouth.

His howl of pain tears through the air. Turning around, I bring my knee up between his legs. Just then the sound of an alarm goes off, piercing the air around us.

Grabbing Aadil, I haul him to his feet. "Come on. We have to keep going."

He gains his footing, taking the lead once again. I lift my long nightgown, continuing to look behind me as I see the man climb to his feet, roaring in Arabic. Just as we reach the end of the hallway, Aadil's hand is ripped from mine and we're both grabbed.

"Faith!" He fights against the arms that hold him, reaching for my hand.

I struggle against my own restraint, fighting with every ounce of strength I possess but it's no use. The man slaps me, knocking me to the ground. Pain radiates through my head, sending black spots dancing in my vision.

"What the hell is going on?"

I struggle to my hands and knees, looking up to find Aadil's father.

He takes in the scene before him, his expression twisting with fury and betrayal. "You little bastard. You betray your own father for this whore?"

Aadil lifts his chin, fear nowhere in sight, only determination and strength. "I won't let you hurt her no more."

His courage fills my terrified heart, horror soon replacing it when his father hits him. I push to my feet when his father reaches inside his jacket, withdrawing a gun.

"No!" Terror slams into me, throwing me forward. Everything falls into slow motion, the gunshot loud and heart stopping.

Agony strikes my soul, sending me crumbling to my knees. I reach for Aadil, cradling his lifeless body in my arms as he bleeds out. My screams of despair slice through the air as my heart shatters and life is forever changed.

I shoot upright on a scream, my body soaked with sweat as I clutch my chest, trying to ease the pain penetrating my heart. My eyes wander around the dark room as reality sets in. Unable to remain upright, I drop back down and curl into a ball, my pillow muffling my sobs as I think about the innocent boy who lost his life, all in order to save mine.

CHAPTER 17

Cade

I pull up to the piano bar, parking in the last available stall before shutting my truck off and taking a minute before entering.

I shouldn't be here, I should stay far away, but when Sawyer told me they would be here for Faith's birthday, I couldn't refuse. My need to see her overrides common sense. I need to know that she's okay, because the pain that was on her face when she left me yesterday has been haunting me ever since.

Our entire encounter has been torturing me, especially knowing she thought I blamed her for everything. I didn't think I could feel any more guilt when it came to her but I was so wrong.

The memory of her sweet taste that I have never forgotten is settled deep into my chest. My hands remembered every beautiful curve as her body came alive under my touch. All of it was fucking perfect, even if it was stupid, up until my fingers touched her smooth, damp panties and she froze in fear. The shame and humiliation that darkened her expression has anger swelling in my veins.

They did that to her, they made a beautiful, innocent woman who should only know mind-blowing pleasure feel ashamed and scared.

The chime of a text pulls me from my tormented thoughts. Digging my phone out of my pocket, I see it's from Sawyer.

Pain in the ass: *Where are you? Get your ass here or I will fuck you up.*

Shaking my head, I don't bother responding and climb out of the truck. At the front entrance, the bouncer moves aside, not bothering carding me. An upbeat tempo and booming voice singing "Journey" assault my ears as I enter.

I do a scan of the dimly lit, upscale bar, looking for familiar faces. It isn't long before I spot Sawyer, his hand raised in the air as he waves me over.

The table is full, except for one empty chair. Cooper, Jaxson, and Sawyer all acknowledge me with a nod. While Kayla, Julia, and Grace give me a smile and a wave. Katelyn gives me her usual death glare, which I ignore, and Red has yet to turn around. I take the empty seat next to Sawyer, which is directly across from her.

It's Kayla who calls attention to me. "How's it going, Cade?"

Faith spins around in her chair, her beautiful green eyes widening in shock. She recovers quickly and offers me a small smile. It's the saddest smile I've ever seen. Immediately, I know something is wrong. Her eyes are tired and haunted. She looks like she hasn't slept in a week. Even then, she's still the most beautiful sight I've ever seen.

"Hi," she greets me softly, so soft that I barely hear her over the music.

"Hey, Red. Happy birthday."

"Thanks. It's not for another two weeks. We're celebrating a little early."

Everyone's gazes are on us, but I pay them no attention, only Faith.

Sawyer punches me in the arm, pulling my attention to him. "You got here pretty quick after my text. Scared the shit out of you, didn't I?"

Grace elbows him playfully. "Stop antagonizing him."

"Listen to your woman before I have to embarrass you in front of her."

His response is a smirk. "Not going to happen, Walker. We aren't in second grade anymore."

"Doesn't matter. I can still kick your ass and you know it."

Grace rolls her eyes at our pissing contest. "Both of you, stop. No one is kicking anyone's ass. You guys are best friends and you love each other."

Sawyer and Jaxson both burst into laughter. I, on the other hand, find nothing funny about that statement. I'm just about to tell her that I don't love this dickhead but before I can reply, the song finishes and the place erupts in applause.

"Thanks, everyone, you can never go wrong with 'Journey,' the guy at the piano says into the mic. "Okay, next up. I've been told by a good friend that someone here is celebrating her birthday tonight and that this someone can sing better than the best."

Red immediately stiffens, turning to Katelyn. "Please tell me you didn't."

"Sorry," she replies with a sweet smile, not looking the least bit apologetic.

"Faith Williams," the guy calls out, pointing directly at her. "Come on up here and show us what you've got. Katelyn says you're better than me, and I need to hear it for myself."

It's obviously the last thing she wants to do but since everyone is staring at her, she pastes a fake smile on her face and stands up. For the first time I get a look at her outfit and my dick roars to life. The strapless, cream lace dress hangs midthigh, tempting any red-blooded man. Add in the cowgirl boots and she's the country girl I've always remembered.

The only thing wrong with her outfit is the silver cross that hangs around her neck. It fucking baffles me she would still wear something like that after everything that has happened.

Everyone applauds as she climbs up the stage, encouraging her further. She waves nervously at everyone before sitting next to the guy at the piano, her face ghost white.

"I take it she doesn't like singing in front of crowds," Jaxson says, a hint of amusement lacing his voice.

Katelyn shrugs. "Not usually but she'll be fine once she starts. Tonight though, she seems off about something." She sends a pointed glare in my direction; obviously thinking it's my fault.

It could be but something tells me it has more to do than with our encounter yesterday. Something I plan to get to the bottom of later.

"I can't wait to hear her," Kayla says. "Especially if she's as good as you say."

They all have no idea what they're about to experience.

Red tucks a piece of hair behind her ear then leans into the mic. "Well, I'm going to have a little chit chat with my cousin when this is done."

Laughter floats through the air while Katelyn blows her a kiss.

Faith looks over at the guy beside her. “I’m not really sure what to sing.”

“Sing anything you want, sweetheart. Whatever your little heart desires.”

His “sweetheart” remark makes me want to rip his throat out.

Something passes over Faith’s face, a beautiful pain that I’ve witnessed before long ago. “This song is probably different than what usually gets played here but it is exactly what my heart is feeling at the moment. There’s a story behind it but I will keep it short.” She pauses briefly, clearing her throat. “Two years ago I went to Iraq on a missions trip with my church.”

My lungs seize, while Sawyer tenses next to me.

“During my time there, I was lucky enough to meet some of the most honorable, brave, and courageous men of my life.” Her eyes make brief contact with mine and the emotion shining in her gaze hits me like a punch to the throat. “One of them happened to be an eight-year-old boy, who I’m pretty sure loved music as much as me. One evening he came upon me playing my guitar. He was so in awe over this song that, from that moment on, he met me every night and I taught him how to play it.”

Her smile slips, and I watch her swallow thickly.

“He was an amazing boy who stole my heart. He’s also a boy who died trying to save my life.” Those words trail off on the saddest whisper, sending a collection of gasps through the bar.

I sense Jaxson and Sawyer looking at me but I don’t acknowledge them, unable to take my eyes off Faith.

“This song is dedicated to him.”

I know exactly which song it is before her fingers even start floating across the keys, playing the soft melody of “Hallelujah.”

“I love this song,” Grace whispers, her words thick with tears.

Faith’s voice is something I’ve never forgotten; once you hear it, it’s unforgettable. But when those first words fall past her lips, nothing could prepare me for the impact upon hearing it again. It’s life altering, changing the entire world as we know it.

Everyone in the bar falls silent, becoming as captivated as me.

“Holy shit!” Sawyer blurts. “She’s incredible.”

“Told ya,” Katelyn responds, smiling proudly.

“What is she doing here and not off in Hollywood?”

I’m the one who ends up answering. “She wouldn’t love it as much if she did it for a living.”

Katelyn’s eyes snap to mine, the hostility I’m usually faced with nowhere in sight.

My attention moves back to Faith as something in her voice changes, her soul releasing with every word she breathes. You can see the exact moment memories of her and the kid begin surfacing.

Her head falls back, sorrow washing over her face as she really lets go and shows everyone what she’s made of. Tears track down her cheeks, falling with every word, but not once does she allow the beauty of her voice to crack or falter.

I chance a look at the crowd and see everyone completely enthralled. Almost every girl in the place shares her emotion as they witness the pain she has inside of her.

I make eye contact with Jaxson and Sawyer, their expressions displaying exactly what I’m feeling.

When the song finishes, there’s complete silence throughout the entire bar, everyone speechless before it erupts into a standing ovation.

A shy smile graces her sad face, her eyes meeting mine. Before long she is standing from the piano and heading for the bathroom, escaping everyone's prying eyes.

Katelyn and I stand at the same time but Julia thankfully holds her back. "Let him go to her."

I don't wait for approval, my feet starting forward. My shoulders knock into others as I try to dodge the crowd. As I come upon the woman's restroom, I don't hesitate walking in and locking the door behind me.

Faith stands at the sink, her arms braced on the counter and head down. At hearing the lock click in place, she quickly wipes her face and pretends to fix her makeup in the mirror.

She turns to leave, only to come to an abrupt halt at the sight of me. "What are you doing in here?"

"I needed to see you. I need to know you're okay."

Grief grips her face, her breath hitching as she shakes her head, telling me what I already know.

She's not okay.

Without wasting another second, I take her into my arms, holding her close. "Talk to me, Red."

"I miss him so much," she cries. "I've been able to work past so many things that happened there, but I don't think I will ever be able to get over what happened to him. I can't let him go, Cade."

Her pain suffocates me, shredding my insides. I wish more than anything I could take this pain away, but I know better than anyone it will never go away.

"It shouldn't have happened." She sniffles. "He shouldn't have died because of me."

I step back, holding her sad face between my hands. "He didn't die because of you. He died because of his piece of shit father. None of it should have happened, Faith. The kid shouldn't have been born to that bastard, and you shouldn't have been taken. Unfortunately, this is the kind of world we live in. It sucks but you can't blame yourself."

She peers up at me, the despair in her emerald eyes calling to every part of me. Unable to hold back any longer, I lean down, slowly and softly pressing my lips to hers.

Her subtle gasp breaches my lips seconds before her fingers spear into my hair beneath my beanie, taking the moment so much further.

Groaning, I reach down and hoist her up, her ankles quickly locking behind my back. I pin her against the door, my cock growing hard at every hot stroke of her tongue. Her hips move, grinding against it.

"Please." The one word falls on a needy whimper.

Growling, I fuck her mouth the same way I want her body. My hands snake under her dress to cup her ass and bring her closer, the heat of her pussy burning me through my jeans as she thrusts against my hard covered cock.

Her breathing starts to change, telling me she's close. Unfortunately the entire moment comes to a stop when there's a pounding on the door.

Shit!

With a disappointed groan, I reluctantly pull back.

"No, please don't stop," she begs, reaching for me again.

"Someone's trying to get in here, Red."

Confusion masks her face before the pounding begins once again.

"Oh..." Her face is flushed, lips swollen. Pain still lingers in her eyes but amongst it lies need and desire.

"What do you want, baby? Tell me and I'll give it to you."

There isn't anything I wouldn't give her in this moment.

Her hand moves to the side of my face. "I want you to take me home. I can't be here right now, and I want to only be with you."

I don't think twice about it. "Okay, then we're out of here."

"I should probably say bye to the others." By her soft tone it's clearly the last thing she wants to do.

"You don't need to see anyone right now, Red. We'll go out back and I'll text Sawyer to tell Katelyn. She can bring your purse home with her."

She nods, seeming relieved by that suggestion.

Instead of putting her down, I unlock the door and walk out with her in my arms. She hides her face in my neck, trying to escape everyone's prying eyes. There are a couple of really pissed-off chicks but I give them a look, daring them to say anything. When they realize the girl in my arms is the same one who sang earlier, they keep any rude comments to themselves and clear a wide path for me.

Thankfully, the back entrance leads us right out to my truck. Rain pelts down on us as I step outside. I quickly deposit Faith in the passenger seat then close the door and head for my side.

I have no idea what the rest of the night holds for us but I do know it's going to change my very existence.

CHAPTER 18

Faith

Cade climbs into the truck and passes me his jacket that was left on the seat. I gladly accept it, loving the scent that comes with it. Next, he turns on the heat, directing the vents toward me. "Can you feel that?"

I nod, my heart warming at his thoughtfulness. I had no idea he would come tonight but I'm glad he did. He's exactly what I need after my awful nightmare. I have no idea what's about to happen next but I know I need him. To feel his arms around me, to feel…safe. If anyone can make me feel that, it's this man next to me.

He shoots Sawyer a text like he said he would then drives away. Guilt weighs down on me as I think about leaving everyone behind after they came for my birthday but my heart is too heavy to face them right now.

Comfortable silence fills the truck as we drive out of the city, heading onto back roads. I rest my head against my window, listening to the heavy rhythm of rainfall.

Minutes later, I feel the truck begin to slow. "What the fuck is someone doing walking on a back road this late at night in a rain storm?"

Straightening, I look out the rain-spattered windshield to see a person walking along the side of the road. Something about the stranger's set of shoulders and fumbled strides tugs at me. Cade slows down even more as we pass him and it's then I get a better look, a gasp fleeing me.

"Stop the truck!"

He slams on the brakes. "What's wrong?"

"I know him!" Without further explanation, I push open my door and jump out.

"Faith! What the hell are you doing? Get back here!" His furious order follows me out into the rain as I run toward the soaking wet boy.

"Christopher, are you all right?"

"Shit!" He turns away from me, shielding his face from my view. "I'm fine. I'm just going for a walk." If I hadn't already known something was wrong, I would by the tone in his voice, it's rough and weak.

I'm about to question him more, but Cade storms over to us, looking furious with me. "What the hell are you doing running out in the middle of the road like that?"

I ignore the angry question for now, knowing there's no time for that and bring my attention back to the boy before me. "Christopher, please look at me."

When he doesn't make any move to comply, I grab his face, forcing it toward mine. A sharp breath infiltrates my chest when I see his face is nothing but a swollen, bloody mess.

"Who did this to you?" I ask, the question barely making it past my throat.

"No one, I'm fine."

I grab onto his shoulders, refusing to let him escape me. "You are not fine. Talk to me, Christopher, please. I can help you."

He rips away from me. "What is with you, lady? Why can't you just leave me alone. I don't need your fucking help!"

Cade steps closer, his chest crowding my back. "Watch the way you talk to her, kid."

Christopher's sharp eyes narrow. "Fuck you. Who the hell are you?"

"Someone you don't want to piss off."

I press my hand to Cade's chest, telling him to ease off. It won't help anything and it's obvious Christopher's more than hurt.

I grasp Christopher's shoulders once again, my touch gentle. "You can trust me. Let me help you."

His teeth grind, his chest heaving as he struggles to hold in his emotion. "You can't help me," he finally replies. "No one can. I'm stuck with him until I'm old enough to get Ruth Jean and me the hell out of here." Despair twists his expression just as his first sob breaks from his chest.

I lock my arms around him as his knees crumble, falling with him into the wet dirt. My heart breaks at the sound of his grief.

"It's okay," I tell him soothingly, whispering the words into his ear. "It's going to be okay."

"Red, let's move this into the truck," Cade says. "It's not safe to be sitting here like this."

I look up at him, the rain hitting my face and mixing with my tears. After nodding in his direction, I lean back down to Christopher. "Come with me. Trust me to help you."

Silence descends for a few moments before he finally relents. He struggles to stand, favoring his left side as we walk to the truck. Cade opens the back door for us, Christopher climbing in first then me right after. I pass him Cade's jacket that I had covering me earlier but he refuses, pushing it back in my direction. "You take it."

I don't argue, knowing it's pointless.

Once Cade climbs in, he looks in the rearview mirror, waiting for instruction.

"We should go to the hospital," I say carefully.

"No hospital!"

"Christopher, you're hurt and need to be seen by a doctor."

"I'm serious, Faith. No doctors and no hospital or I'm out of here."

A sigh of defeat leaves me. "All right. We'll go to my house then."

Cade continues in the direction we were going, silence filling the truck for the remainder of the drive. I rub Christopher's back, hoping to comfort him. Especially before I have to ask the hard questions, ones I know he won't want to be forthcoming about.

After what his sister told me the other day, I have no doubt that his father is the one who did this to him. It angers me yet also makes me think about another helpless boy who suffered at the hands of his sadistic father. I will not let Christopher suffer the same fate as Aadil.

Once we arrive at my house, Cade parks on the driveway then opens the door to help Christopher down. It's not appreciated.

"I can do it myself," he grumbles, refusing to take Cade's outstretched hand.

Cade doesn't back down and reaches for his arm. "Forget your pride, kid, or you're going to feel like an ass when you fall."

Christopher's eyes narrow but he reluctantly accepts his help. Once he's on his feet, Cade reaches for me next, his hands spanning my waist as he lowers me to my feet.

He makes no move to back out of my personal space, his large body crowding mine as he glares down at me. "Don't ever run out on me like that again, especially in the middle of the road."

It's on the tip of my tongue to argue but I refrain. Now is not the time. At my nod, he backs out of my space. I take Christopher's arm and help him into the house before situating him on my sofa.

After wrapping a blanket around his shoulders, I kneel before him. "Let me look at you."

He pulls back from my touch. "I'm fine. I'll just take some aspirin if you have some."

I open my mouth to argue, refusing to let him fight me on this any longer but Cade steps in at that moment. "Red, why don't you go change and grab a first aid kit."

I reluctantly climb to my feet and walk upstairs to my bedroom to change. Afterward, I grab the first aid kit from the bathroom and some aspirin then make my way back downstairs.

The sight I'm met with has a sharp breath impaling my lungs. Christopher's shirt is lifted by Cade, revealing black and blue ribs and angry red welts across his skin. Christopher's eyes meet mine, the shame and despair reflecting back at me drives that ache deeper into my chest.

Blinking away my tears, I move quickly, handing Cade the first aid kit. I can't help but wonder why he would let Cade help him and not me but I decide it's not important. All that matters is he's letting one of us help him.

Eventually, I take the seat next to him and begin rubbing his back again, feeling like I need to do something. His tense muscles relax, accepting the comfort.

"I don't think they're broken," Cade says, talking about his ribs. "But they are pretty banged up. We need to wrap them and you'll be popping some aspirin for a few days."

Christopher nods and allows Cade to wrap them.

"Does your father do this to you often?" I ask, deciding to try and broach this subject a different way.

He shrugs. "It's better me than Ruth Jean."

The knowledge that he takes it to protect his sister has my heart breaking even more. "You need to tell someone, Christopher."

He shakes his head. "I can't."

"Yes, you can. We can call Cooper right now. I know he will help you."

"No! I told you no one can know."

"Why not?"

"Because they will put Ruth Jean and me in a foster home. They'll split us up and I can't let that happen. I'll never let them take my sister from me."

Unfortunately I can't argue with that. He's right. They probably would be split up.

"Where is Ruth Jean now?" I ask.

"She's with Mrs. Jenkins. An old lady who lives down the road from us. She watches her sometimes when my dad is in a bad way. She's senile but safe. I'm supposed to be picking her up soon, but I can't take her back home unless my dad is gone. Not tonight."

"Don't you have other family that can help you?"

"No, my grandparents died a long time ago and my mom left us when Ruth Jean was only two years old." Anger tightens his expression as he mentions his mother. I can't imagine what would make a mother leave her children, especially with a monster like his father.

"I only need to deal with this for a few more years. Once I turn eighteen, I'm taking Ruth Jean and getting the hell out of here. I'll go someplace where my dad will never find us."

"Christopher, you may not survive a few more years. Look at you."

"I'll be fine. Tonight was just a bad night. He wasn't even supposed to be home but he ended up bringing his loser friends over instead."

I balk at the confession. "You mean to tell me there were other people there and they didn't help you?"

He grunts. "Are you kidding? They joined in. Some of them are bigger assholes than my dad."

Cade has remained silent this entire time but there's no denying the cold fury in his expression. He's as outraged as I am. More than my anger though, is fear. I'm terrified what will happen to Christopher if he doesn't get help. That thought brings on an image of Aadil. One boy I wasn't able to help.

I won't let that happen. Not for a second time. Deep in my heart, I know what I need to do.

I turn toward him, looking him straight on. "Do you trust me?"

Weariness enters his eyes. "More than I trust anyone else I guess, why?"

"Because I want to call Cooper." He opens his mouth to protest, but I don't give him the chance. "Just hear me out. I promised you I wouldn't do anything you're not okay with and I mean that."

He expels a frustrated breath but nods.

"I want to call Cooper, not as a cop but as a friend. I want to ask him what our options are. I need to find out what I have to do in order to have you and Ruth Jean come live with me."

Utter silence fills the room, his expression becoming one of complete shock. I feel the heavy weight of Cade's disapproving eyes but I continue to ignore it.

"Why would you do that?" he asks, the question barely a whisper. "You don't even know us."

The vulnerability in his voice has me reaching for his hand. "I don't need to know you a long time to know that I care about you and your sister. You guys need a place to stay and I have one."

Cade clears his throat, breaking the moment. "Faith, can I talk to you for a minute in the kitchen?"

I glance over at him, seeing the disapproval I knew would be there. "In a moment." I turn back to Christopher and give his hand another light squeeze. "Please, let me help you. Let me do this."

Relief fills me when he finally nods. "If you're sure."

"I am." Leaning over, I hug him, making sure to be mindful of his injuries.

I'm surprised when he embraces me back. "Thanks, Faith."

"We'll figure this out." I pull back, following the promise up with a smile. "Go on and call Mrs. Jenkins. If you're sure you can trust her, ask if Ruth Jean can spend the night. I'll go into the kitchen and call Cooper to find out what we need to do."

At his agreement, I walk into the kitchen, feeling Cade close on my heels. Just as I make it to the sink, he grabs my arm and spins me around to face him.

"What the fuck are you thinking?" he asks under harsh undertones.

I lift my chin, refusing to back down. "Two kids need help and I can help them."

"Red, you're twenty-four years old. You're old enough to be the kid's sister not his mother."

"I'm not trying to be his mother. I'm trying to be someone he can rely on."

"You have your own shit going on right now. You shouldn't be taking on someone else's."

"What do you expect me to do? Let him go back there?"

"Of course not. But let Cooper handle this, let the state take care of them."

I shake my head. "You heard what he said, and we both know he's right. They'll more than likely be split up, and let's not forget that foster homes aren't always a safe place. Whereas, my home is."

"I get that you care for the kid but this isn't your problem."

"I'm making it my problem."

He glares down at me, clearly not liking that answer.

"Please understand. I have the chance to make someone's life better. I can't just walk away from that."

His disapproving expression softens, a small understanding entering his eyes. He pulls me into his arms, giving me the hug I so desperately need. The comforting moment comes to an end when Christopher rushes into the kitchen, pure fear written all over his battered face. "We have to go, now!"

"What's wrong?" I ask.

"My dad picked up Ruth Jean from Mrs. Jenkins an hour ago."

Fear barrels through me for the small girl.

"Let's go," Cade says, both he and Christopher already moving for the front door. "We can call Cooper on the way."

I'm left with no other choice but to follow.

Cooper thankfully answers on the first ring. He's angry to hear how we found Christopher but doesn't seem all that surprised. He promises to meet us at Christopher's house and cautions me for us all to wait in the truck for him. By the time I hang up, we're driving down the same back road we found Christopher on, Cade's speed making my heart jumpstart.

"This is our driveway." Christopher points.

Cade cuts the wheel hard, fishtailing into the long driveway that leads to a small rundown house with two motorcycles parked in front.

"Shit! Spike's still here."

I have no idea who *Spike* is but by the fear in Christopher's voice, I'd say the man is no better than his father.

Cade barely cuts the engine before he and Christopher are reaching for their door handles.

"Cooper told us to wait in the truck."

They ignore me and jump out anyway.

Despite my hesitance, I quickly follow, my heart thundering in my chest. I pray Ruth Jean is all right and we aren't too late.

Christopher takes the front steps two at a time until Cade grabs the back of his shirt, halting his quick pursuit. "It's important to keep calm. We'll get her out, all right?"

Christopher complies with a nod then opens the door, unveiling an overwhelming stench of smoke and beer. He walks in first with Cade close behind. When I move to step in next, Cade stops me. "You stay here."

I open my mouth to argue but don't get the chance.

"What the fuck are you doing back here?" Two men appear in the entryway. Decked out in biker leather and bandanas covering their greasy hair, they glare at Christopher. There is no denying which one his father is, the resemblance is unmistakable.

"I'm here for Ruth Jean," Christopher tells him, showing no fear.

His father's eyes cut to Cade then me, realization finally dawning. "Get the fuck out of here and take these assholes with you before I mess you up some more.."

The threat instills a deep seated anger inside of me, masking some of my worry.

"Twistiphwor," a small, terrified voice breaks into the moment.

I look past Cade to see Ruth Jean standing at the far corner of the living room, a stuffed animal clutched firmly in her trembling arms.

I take a step forward only to be held back by Cade again.

"Get back to your bed right now!" her father orders.

"No, Ruth Jean, don't," Christopher says. "Come over here to me. Everything will be all right, we're going to go stay with Faith."

She starts forward but comes to a quick stop when her father shouts at her. "Get back to your fucking room, now!"

"Twistiphwor, what do I do?" she asks on a fearful sob.

A heated curse flees from Cade before he finally takes matters into his own hands. "Christopher, go get your sister."

The moment Christopher makes his move all hell breaks loose. His father charges at him, but Cade is faster. In a quick move, he takes him to the ground face-first. That's when Spike goes after him, beer bottle raised.

"Cade, watch out!" I cry.

He knocks the bottle out of Spike's hand and grabs him by his throat, lifting him off his feet. Spike struggles for air, clawing at the hand that robs him of breath. Cade tosses him into the kitchen, as if the man is nothing more than a rag doll. Spike lands onto the table, breaking it on impact. Christopher's father is already stumbling back to his feet.

Fear snakes down my spine when he pulls a knife from his pocket.

"You fucked with the wrong person, asshole." He strikes out but again is no match for Cade. Cade handles him much the same way he did the first time, only there is a sickening crack as he breaks his arm, twisting it ruthlessly behind his back. The other man's painful howl penetrates the air.

"Now, Christopher! Get your sister and take her to the truck." Cade's demand snaps him into motion.

Ruth Jean runs for him at the same time, meeting him halfway as sobs rack her body. Due to his injuries, Christopher struggles to pick her up.

Despite Cade's original warning not to enter, I move quickly, kneeling before the small girl. "Hey, Ruth Jean."

"Hi, Faif," she sniffles.

"I know you're scared but everything is going to be okay, I promise. I'm going to carry you out since your brother is hurt. Okay?"

When she nods, I waste no time picking her up.

"You bitch. Put my kid down!"

Cade delivers another blow that has the man wailing in pain as the three of us run out of the house. Just as we make it to the truck, Cooper shows up, screeching to a halt with another squad vehicle parking behind him.

I get Ruth Jean and Christopher situated in the truck then run over to meet Cooper and the deputy. "It's a mess, Cooper," I explain, following him as he moves for the house, gun trained low. "They went after Christopher so Cade had to step in."

Another loud crash echoes from the house, followed by grunting. I'm praying it's not Cade.

"Go wait with the kids," Cooper orders before he and the deputy charge in the house.

I hurry into the truck and find Christopher holding a sobbing Ruth Jean on his lap. "I was so stared when I touldn't find you. I'm sowwy he huwt you again, Twistiphwor."

My heart aches at the guilt in her voice. Christopher's gaze remains straight ahead, his eyes turning glassy as he struggles to hold in his emotion.

I place my hand on her shoulder, hoping to offer reassurance. "Everything is going to be okay. I'm going to find a way to have you come stay with me. How do you feel about that?"

She lifts her head to look at me, her face pale and streaked with tears. "I wike dat idea. It's betta den hewre, huh, Twistiphwor."

Christopher swallows hard and nods. "Yeah, it will be better with Faith."

"Do you have enough wooms?" she asks.

"I do. I only have one extra bed right now, but once we get everything figured out we'll buy you your own. Okay?"

The smallest smile takes over her sad face. Unfortunately, it doesn't last long when Cooper and the deputy walk out with their father and Spike in handcuffs. Both men's faces look much worse than when we left them. Their father's eyes are on me as he's hauled past the truck, icy disdain filling their depths.

I pull my attention away to find Cade walking out of the house, his expression hard as stone but thankfully looking unscathed. Jumping out of the truck, I run toward him, launching myself into his arms.

"I was so scared for you," I tell him.

He hugs me closer, his arms banded tight around me. "I'm good, Red. I can take care of myself."

Pulling back, I rest my forehead against his.

"Are the kids okay?" he asks.

"They are, thanks to you." I reach up, tracing my thumb against his lips before pressing the softest kiss there, my mouth lingering. "Thank you for coming and helping."

A low growl rumbles from his chest as he deepens the kiss but makes it brief before placing me down to my feet. His eyes move to something over my head. I turn around to find Cooper walking over to us.

"I'm taking them in," he says. "I'll be able to hold them for at least forty-eight hours, since I can charge them with possession and a judge won't be in until Monday to post bail."

"Possession?" I ask.

He nods. "Both had cocaine on them. I'm not surprised. Spike has been brought up before on possession charges."

"Why has this not been looked into prior?" I ask, feeling irritated. "If his dad is hanging around these kind of people then why would no one check on the children?"

Guilt sparks in Cooper's eyes. "I did, many times, but I never found anything. I pushed Christopher for details but he didn't trust me."

"He doesn't trust anyone," I whisper sadly.

After seeing all this, I can't blame him.

"I beg to differ," Cooper says. "It's clear he trusts you."

"Not quite but I'm making progress. This is where I need your help. He's worried about being put into foster care and losing his sister. I want to have them live with me but I don't know what I need to do to make that happen. Will you help me?"

Surprise flashes in his eyes. "You sure about this decision?"

"Absolutely," I answer without hesitation. "He can't go anywhere else, Cooper, or he'll take Ruth Jean and run."

He lets go of a heavy breath, driving a hand through his hair. "Okay. Take the kids home with you tonight. I'll come in the morning and bring Vicki Jenson. She's the social worker from Children's Services. We can find out from her what steps you need to take. I know her well and will vouch for you."

"Thanks, I really appreciate it."

"You're welcome." He heads for his police cruiser just then before stopping by the truck to speak to Christopher. Whatever is said has Cooper reaching out to touch his shoulder. After closing the door, he brings his attention back to Cade and me. "Has he seen a doctor?" he asks, looking as angry as I feel.

"He refused but Cade checked him over, and I'll make sure to take him to a doctor after we finish with you tomorrow."

With a final nod in our direction, he climbs into his cruiser and drives off, leaving Cade and I to follow suit. Ruthie Jean's eyes are wide and anchored on Cade.

"You remember Cade from the bakery, right?"

She nods but says nothing and neither does Cade.

My gaze strays to Christopher just then. "Everything is good. Cooper is going to help us find a way for you to stay with me."

Some of the tension leaves his shoulders before he relaxes back into his seat and stares out his window. The ride home is mainly silent. Every now and then I glance in the back seat to find Ruth Jean watching Cade. Her eyes are no longer wide or fearful but more…thoughtful, as if she's perhaps studying him.

Once we arrive back home, I get the kids situated in the spare room. I offered for

Ruth Jean to sleep with me if she wanted but she side-glanced her brother before saying she wanted to be with him. She followed me when I grabbed extra blankets then whispered that she chose him because she needs to make sure he's okay.

My heart completely melts over the love these two have for each other. I'm glad they've always had one another since it's obvious they haven't had anyone else.

After tucking them in, I'm unable to hold back from pressing a kiss to Ruth Jean's forehead. She wraps her tiny arms around my neck, returning a kiss on my cheek.

When I look over at Christopher, his eyes narrow. "Don't even think about kissing my head."

Chuckling, I hold my hands up. "I promise. No kisses." I'm just about to walk out but he calls me back. Stopping, I turn back around.

"Thanks for everything," he whispers.

A soft smile takes over my lips. "You're welcome. Good night."

"Night."

Closing the door, I head back upstairs and find Cade sitting in the living room. "Good, you're still here."

He says nothing, his eyes sweeping my body from head to toe, igniting a current of heat to spark within. I'm quickly reminded just how differently this night was supposed to turn out for the two of us, it leaves me wondering where we stand.

My heart kicks up when he stands, every stride bringing him closer until he's standing just before me. He reaches up, his hand cradling my cheek. My eyes fall closed and I lean into the warmth of his touch.

"I'm going to stay here tonight."

My eyes spring open in surprise, hope warming my chest. "You don't have to," I whisper, but my protest is weak, because the truth is, I want him here.

"I know I don't." The few simple words evoke so much more than he knows. "I'll sleep on the couch."

The light in my heart dims. "That's not necessary. You can sleep in my bed with me." I consider elaborating but we both know what the invitation holds.

He shakes his head. "Not a good idea, Red."

The rejection stings but I do my best to hide it. "I understand. I'll go get you a pillow and blanket then."

Turning around, I take only one step before his arm locks around my waist, pulling me back against his hard body. A sharp breath impales my lungs at the feel of his erection against my bottom.

He leans down, bringing his lips to my ear. "I'm saying no because I can't trust myself to be in the same bed with you right now. Not tonight, but I'll be thinking of you, Red. You get me?"

I nod, unable to utter a single word.

"Good. Now go grab me that blanket before I do something I can't take back."

The moment he releases me, I move quickly up the stairs, the skin on my back burning from his touch. He waits at the bottom and I decide it's best to throw it down instead of getting too close, but I make sure to give him my best smile. "Good night, Cade Walker. I'll be thinking of you, too."

The tight look on his face has a chuckle escaping me. After blowing him a kiss, I head to my room, leaving my door slightly open just in case Ruth Jean or Christopher need me, then crawl into bed.

In the silence of my room, my mind races with what's to come, knowing my life is about to change irrevocably. I'd be lying if I said I wasn't nervous about taking in these two children but I also know it's right. Not just for them but me too. I think maybe I need them as much as they need me. Together, we will make it work.

Then there's Cade. There's no denying that our relationship has shifted but I also know my choice of taking in Ruth Jean and Christopher may have just deterred him from starting anything. If there was anything to start. I decide I will take that one step at a time just like I am with the kids. I'll leave it in God's hands and pray he will direct us all where we are meant to be.

CHAPTER 19

Cade

Sleep evades me hours later, my thoughts on the woman sleeping only a short distance away. Tonight did not turn out how I expected, but despite that, I'm glad we stumbled upon the kid when we did.

I think back to the way Faith was with him. How calm and patient she was, never giving up. And when the kid finally broke—she locked her arms around him in the pouring rain and held him.

I'm not surprised by it, I know what kind of person she is, what kind of person she always has been, but it still evoked feelings I couldn't understand. I grew up with a mother who acted like her kids were nothing but a nuisance, always choosing her next fix over us.

Faith barely knows these kids, and what does she do? She offers to take them in. I'm still conflicted about that decision but I also know it's not mine to make. It's hers, and no matter what, I'll be here for her if she needs me but beyond that… I can't situate myself with these kids.

I'm not someone who should be around children. Not with what I have constantly lurking inside of me. Yet, the thought of never touching Faith or kissing her again has my chest constricting.

The soft pitter-patter of little feet yanks me from my thoughts. I rise up on one arm and look over to see the young girl standing just inside the living room, watching me while hugging a stuffed animal to her chest. I wait for her to say something but all she does is stare at me.

"What do you need, kid?" I cringe at my hard tone then soften my voice, trying again. "You need a drink or something?"

She shakes her head.

"You want me to get Faith?"

Shakes her head again.

"You hungry?"

"No."

"Well, what do you want?"

She pushes her broken glasses up on her nose and licks her small lips. "Tan I sweep wif you?"

Panic strikes me hard and fast. No way!

"Don't you want to sleep with your brother?"

"Dat bed isn't vewy big. Twistiphwor is sowe, and I don't want to huwt him."

Well, this couch isn't very big either.

Why would she want to sleep with me anyway? It's apparent she's scared shitless of me. Not that I can blame her, especially after what I did to her old man tonight.

"What about Faith?" I suggest, grasping at straws.

"No tanks."

Before I can offer up another suggestion, she walks toward me.

Shit!

"Listen, kid, this couch isn't big enough."

"Dat's otay, I'm small," she says, crawling up beside me.

I press myself against the back of the sofa, trying to avoid contact. "Yeah, you are, but I'm big. Really big."

She looks over at me like I'm an idiot. "I know. I tan see dat."

Instead of taking a hint like most people would, she removes her glasses and folds the broken arms before placing them on the coffee table. Then she reaches down by my feet and pulls the blanket up over us, situating herself so she's facing me.

I remain still, my mind scrambling as I try to figure a way out of this.

"Why do you have eawings in yowr boobs?" she asks, staring at my nipple rings.

Is this kid for real?

"Guys don't have boobs," I tell her firmly.

"Yes, dey do, dey're just wittle ones."

"They're called nipples not boobs."

She shrugs. "Fine. Why do you have eawings in dem?"

Unsure of how to reply, I opt for the simple truth. "Because I wanted to."

Instead of questioning me further, she moves onto something else. "You tan't sweep eider, huh?"

I sure as hell can't now.

Knowing I'm not getting out of this anytime soon, I accept my fate for the next few hours and lie back down but make sure I push back into the cushions as far as I can.

And what does she do? She moves in closer to me.

Jesus, someone fucking help me.

She's quiet for only a moment before she starts back up again. "I have de wost name in de wowld, huh?" She peers up at me, expecting me to answer.

I shrug. "It's not that bad, I've heard worse."

I'm half-lying, her name is pretty bad. I don't know why the hell someone would call their kid Ruth Jean, but I have heard worse.

"Yeah wight, what is it?" she asks.

"Tonto Schluckenburger."

Her eyes grow wide before she covers her mouth and giggles. "Otay, dat may be wowse den mine."

I grunt. "It's definitely worse than yours."

He was in my third grade class, and I remember that poor kid was ridiculed to death. His parents should have had their asses kicked, not him.

"You have wots of muscles," she states, changing the subject again. "And you're pwetty stwong, too. You frew my dad's mean fwiend acwoss de woom to save Twistiphwor."

It all finally makes sense. Rather than being afraid at seeing what I did to those assholes tonight, she thinks I'm safe. Time for a reality check.

"I didn't save anyone, kid. I just did what needed to be done until the police got there."

"You saved Faif's wife."

My eyes shoot to hers in the dark. "How do you know about that?"

"She told me. She said yow're de stwongest man in de whole wowld."

I remain silent but can't deny the shift in my chest to know Red confided in her.

"I bet noding stares you," she whispers.

Little does she know, she and Red scare the shit out of me.

"You don't say vewy much."

"And you talk a lot."

She's not offended by my honesty. Peering up at me, she points to my head. "Why awe you still weawing a beanie, awe you told?"

Shit! I reach up and rip it off, not realizing I still had it on. "That's enough questions for tonight. You need to go to sleep. You guys have a big day ahead of you tomorrow."

The tiny sigh she releases is sad. "I hope evewyding will be otay. I don't want to go bat to my dad. He's so mean, especiawwy to Twistiphwor."

My chest pulls tight at her scared voice. "Don't worry, kid, that won't happen. Faith will make sure of it."

And so will I.

Nodding, she moves in closer, and within seconds she's asleep. Pulling the blanket higher up on her bare arm, I look down at her small, vulnerable form and a memory strikes me, one so painful that I quickly shove it away before it can pull me down into its black abyss.

A girl I will never forget, no matter how hard I try.

CHAPTER 20

Faith

My eyes flutter open, the early morning sun dripping in my bedroom window as memories from last night come flooding back. I glance at the clock to see it's barely six in the morning and decide to go check on the children before I take a shower.

I slip on a thin open sweater over my tank top then head down two flights of stairs to the third level. When I peek my head inside the room, I only find Christopher sound asleep, not Ruth Jean.

Frowning, I close the door and look around the TV room but don't see her on the couch either. I check the bathroom next only to find it empty. It's then panic begins taking hold.

Promptly, I head back up the stairs, hurrying to wake Cade and that's when I find her with him, sleeping curled up against his bare chest.

Relief swamps me just before my heart completely melts. The sight of Cade's tattooed arm wrapped protectively around her tiny body, their faces both soft with sleep, is a sight to behold.

Unable to resist, I grasp my hair with one hand then lean down and press a soft kiss to Ruth Jean's forehead then another to Cade's. Just as I turn to tiptoe away, a large, warm hand grabs the inside of my thigh, halting me.

I look back down to find Cade awake. "Hey." The greeting is nothing more than a faint whisper, my gaze drifting between him and Ruth Jean.

"She asked me why I have earrings in my boobs," he tells me, blankly.

I cover my mouth to muffle my laughter, imagining the look on his face.

"She talks a lot," he adds later.

Smiling, I take a seat on the edge of the coffee table across from them. "She has a lot to say, she's very intelligent." When he doesn't respond, I start to worry he's actually bothered by it. "I'm sorry, you could have woken me."

He shrugs. "It's fine. I'm not sure she would have slept anywhere else. She seemed hell-bent on torturing me."

"She feels safe with you."

His eyes lock with mine. "Yeah, because someone told her I am the strongest guy in the world and saved their life."

Busted.

I clear my throat, refusing to feel embarrassed for speaking the truth. "You are the strongest man I've ever met."

He watches silently, his expression softening. "You're the strong one, Red."

Warmth invades my chest, my throat growing tight with the hell we all endured. Reaching over, I take his hand that was on the side of my leg earlier. "I know you don't think I should do this but it's right, Cade. I feel it in my heart. These kids were brought into my life for a reason. I can't turn them away, and I don't want to either."

He links his fingers with mine. "I'm just worried about you. It's a lot to take on, especially by yourself."

"It will be an adjustment at first but I know my parents will be supportive, and Katelyn will, too."

He's silent for a long moment, his eyes drifting down to our joined hands. "I'll be here for you too, if you ever need me."

My heart falters in surprise. I want to tell him that I'll always need him but then think better of it.

"Just don't ask me to babysit. I'm not good at that but any other favor, I can handle."

Amusement tilts my lips. "Mmmm, what kind of favors are we talking about, Walker?"

Desire ignites in his eyes, sending a current of heat to ripple through me. "Don't say shit like that, Red, when I have a kid against my chest."

I bite my lip to mask my smile and drop to my knees before him, pressing a kiss to the inside of his palm. "All joking aside, thank you for staying last night. I hate to think what would have happened with their father if you hadn't been there."

He runs his fingers through my hair, cupping the side of my face. "There's a lot I can't help you with, but kicking someone's ass I can do no problem."

I lean into his touch, seeking his warmth.

"I should put my shirt back on before she wakes up," he says, talking about his scars.

"You have nothing to hide," I whisper. "You're still beautiful."

A scowl forms on his face. "What did I tell you about using that word in the same sentence as me?"

I'm about to correct myself when someone clears their throat. I look over my shoulder and find Christopher standing at the edge of the living room. I climb to my feet and hurry over to him, my heart breaking all over again at the sight of his battered face.

"Sorry to interrupt, I just couldn't find Ruth Jean."

I point over at Cade.

"Figures," he grunts, but doesn't seem all that upset.

"Really? I was surprised when I found her with him."

"Not me," he says, "All she talked about last night was how he kicked Dad's and Spike's asses. Then she proceeded to tell me about the time you told her he saved your life and that he is the strongest guy in the world. She told me no one could beat him up, and I had to listen to it until I fell asleep."

I chuckle when I hear Cade's grunt across the room. The easy moment vanishes when I notice Christopher flinch as he stretches. My hand moves to his bare shoulder, soothing over one welt. "Do you want some more aspirin?"

"No, I'm fine."

He doesn't look fine, but I don't push, deciding he can make his own decisions.

"Listen, I spent a lot of time thinking last night," he starts nervously. "I just want to be upfront with you and let you know that if something doesn't work out, and they don't let us stay here...I'm taking her and leaving. I won't go back there, and I won't let them ship us off anywhere else."

Before I can even utter a word, Cade speaks up. "That's not going to happen, kid. We'll make sure of it."

His assurance means a lot, making me feel less alone.

"He's right," I say, turning to Christopher. "I'll do whatever I have to. I promise."

He nods but still looks unsure. "Do you mind if I take a shower? We'll have to go back to the house at some point for some clothes."

The thought of ever going back to that house has my belly twisting into a giant knot. "Of course you can. Don't worry about the clothes. We'll figure all that out later. Come and I'll show you what will be your very own bathroom. Ruth Jean and I will share the one upstairs."

I take him back down and get him situated with fresh towels, soap, and shampoo. I also let him know we will go buy whatever usual brand he prefers later today.

"This is fine, Faith. I'm just happy I get to use soap that some asshole didn't shove a razor blade into."

I tense, a sharp pain infiltrating my chest. The thought of someone doing something like that to him has agony striking my soul.

I step into him, wrapping my arms around his waist. "Never again, Christopher," I whisper. "I promise. Never again will you suffer like that."

Feeling close to a blubbering mess, I leave the room without another word, closing the door behind me. Tears stream down my face as I head back up the stairs and find Cade in the kitchen. He stands at the sink, fully dressed. His eyes narrow in concern when he realizes I'm crying. "What is it?" he asks, moving for me. "What's wrong?"

It takes me a minute to find my words. "His father put razor blades in his soap," I choke out through a painful breath. "Razor blades, Cade. On purpose. To hurt him."

I cover my mouth as the first sob escapes.

A curse flees from Cade seconds before he pulls me into his arms.

"How could someone do that to their own child? How could someone do that to any child?"

"Because the world is filled with assholes, Red. People who don't deserve to fucking breathe let alone have children."

I lift my head from his chest, looking up at him through blurry vision. "Maybe, but I still believe there are more good than bad."

He doesn't respond, and I know that's mostly because he doesn't believe it.

The energy in the room suddenly shifts and I become intimately aware of how close we are, my soft body pressed against his hard one, my fists clenched tightly in his shirt.

My tongue darts out, licking my dry lips. His eyes drop, heat igniting.

"Kiss me." The softly spoken words are out before I can stop them.

Groaning, his arms tighten around my waist and he lifts me off my feet, bringing our mouths to align and become one. It's just as powerful as last night, his lips a heated caress, coaxing and demanding, devouring mine in a way that takes my breath away.

My arms lock around his neck, hands slipping beneath his beanie to grip his hair.

"Seriously, what's with the beanie all the time, Walker?" I ask in a beat of a breath, our mouths never faltering.

"I don't know. I've grown attached to the fucking thing and can't seem to stop wearing it."

I giggle at his truthful answer. "I like it. It suits you, and you look sexy in it."

His growl vibrates in his chest as hands slide down, cupping my bottom. "I think you're fucking sexy, Red, every damn part of you."

A whimper breaches my lips, my legs wrapping around his waist as I become completely lost in him and the feelings he evokes within me.

"Sowwy to intewupt, but I'm hungwy." The little voice slaps us back into reality.

"Shit!" Cade drops me to my feet and jumps back, putting distance between us.

It takes me a moment to get my bearings before I turn to Ruth Jean and paste a smile on my face.

She smiles back at me, not seeming the least bit bothered.

"Well good morning, Ruth Jean, did you have a good sleep?" I ask, walking over to kneel before her.

"I sure did." She gives me a quick hug and kiss on the cheek before making her way over to Cade, who is leaning against the kitchen table. "How about you, Big Guy?" she asks, grabbing the chair next to him. "Did you sweep good?"

"I slept all right, considering I had a kid glued to my chest."

"Well, I had no choice since dere was no woom on de touch," she tells him.

"I told you the couch wasn't big enough."

"I know dat. And I told you dat I was small. So it's good dat we both had a good sweep den."

I bite back a smile as Cade blinks down at her, not knowing what to say. Taking pity on him, I decide to cut in. "What would you like for breakfast, Ruth Jean?"

She shrugs, unsure.

"What do you normally have?" I ask.

"Sometimes Twistiphwor makes me baton and eggs, if we have any food."

I try not to think about them not having food or I will be a blubbering mess all over again. "Well unfortunately, I don't have any of that, I'm a vegetarian."

Just then Christopher walks into the kitchen. "You're a vegetarian?" he asks, taking a seat next to his sister.

I nod and open my mouth to say more but stop at the sight of Ruth Jean's face when she looks at Christopher, her expression pinched with sadness. Without a second thought, she hops off her seat and crawls up onto his lap, her tiny arms wrapping around his neck as she kisses his cheek.

"I wuv you, Twistiphwor," she whispers, her voice thick with tears. It triggers a fresh wave of mine but I turn around before anyone can see them, doing my damnedest to blink them back.

Christopher shifts, uncomfortable at her affection in front of us. "I love you, too."

Something flashes in Cade's eyes, something so painful that I know mine doesn't even come close to matching his. It makes me wonder if he's thinking about his sister, and I decide it's best for everyone to change the subject.

I clear my throat and decide to talk about the topic at hand. "Yes, I'm a vegetarian so I don't eat meat."

"Den what do you eat?"

"I eat lots of things. Fruits, veggies…I eat everything else, just not meat."

"Why?" she asks. There's no judgment in her tone, only curiosity.

"Because I think animals are our friends and I don't want to eat them."

"So awe we bad if we eat meat?"

"Not at all. This is a personal choice for me, and I do not judge if someone else wants to eat it. You are welcome to continue to eat meat, but it will have to be either when we go out or when you are at school because I won't cook it."

She shrugs. "Otay. Well, I'll twy not eating meat wif you. I wike animals, too."

I smile. "That's great, but if you decide you want to eat it again that's okay, too."

Christopher raises his hands out in front of him. "Sorry, but I am not giving that up, I'll die without it."

Cade grunts in agreement then takes a seat at the table.

"That's fine. Like I said though, I won't cook it but you are welcome to eat it anywhere else. We will go grocery shopping later today and make sure we get food that we all like."

"Twistiphwor, too?" Ruth Jean asks hopefully.

I frown, a little taken aback by the question. "Of course. We have to make sure we get things he likes, too."

She turns to look up at her brother. "Dat will be nice, won't it, Twistiphwor? Now you will get to eat too and you won't have to—"

"Ruth Jean!" he snaps under his breath, forcing her to be quiet.

She drops her head and mumbles an apology.

Guilt immediately passes over Christopher's face.

Sighing, I walk over and sit in the empty seat between Cade and Christopher, making sure to face the children. My hand reaches for Ruth Jean's, forcing her to look at me. Christopher avoids eye contact but I know it's because he's embarrassed.

"Things are going to be better here, Ruth Jean. I'm not saying I won't make mistakes, I probably will because this is new for me too, but we will find our way together. I promise, no one will ever hurt you or your brother again."

"If dey do, Tade will tick deir asses, wight?"

Christopher rolls his eyes while I try not to cringe at her language, despite how cute she is.

"You know it, kid," Cade says, speaking up.

I chance a look at him over my shoulder, quirking a brow.

He shrugs.

Smiling, I shake my head then shift my attention back to the children before me. "So it's settled. Starting today, the three of us are going to rebuild our lives together and for the better."

"De fwor of us you mean."

My heart stutters to a stop and Cade tenses behind me.

"Well, no, the three of us, Cade doesn't live here."

Her eyes widen, a sense of fear entering. "Why not?"

"Because we're just friends," I explain, hating the words as they leave my mouth. What I feel for him is so much more than that. "He only slept here because we all had a hard night."

Ruth Jean's eyes narrow suspiciously. "But I saw you guys tissing dis mowning, and fwiends don't tiss."

Well crap. How do I explain that?

"That isn't our business, Ruth Jean," Christopher says pointedly.

"Sowwy."

"Don't be sorry," I rush to say. "You have a right to know."

"So does dat mean we won't see you no mowe?" she asks, looking at Cade with sad eyes.

"You'll see me, kid. I just don't sleep here, but I'll be around."

It's no promise of forever but it's a small commitment. Friendship or more, I'll take this man anyway I can have him.

CHAPTER 21

Faith

At the church, I sort through my plans and ideas for my music school while Christopher finishes his last day of community service. It's been a week since my life irrevocably changed, and I welcomed two extraordinary children into my home. It's been a whirlwind with the three of us trying to get settled in and find a routine that works for us all but my heart couldn't be happier.

Things went much better with the social worker than I expected. After Christopher and Ruth Jean were honest about their life with their father, getting them removed from his custody was not hard, especially after the amount of drugs that were found in his house.

For me to get temporary guardianship was a little more of a process. At first, Vicki Jenson had reservations about the children staying with me. She worried I was too young to take on the responsibility, she didn't like that I was single, and that I did not have a job.

I resolved each one of her concerns, telling her about the music school I would open this summer and showing her proof of my savings. Thanks to my papa, I am more than financially capable to take care of the children. I even told her I didn't expect any money from the state. That's when she informed me it was the law and I would be getting it anyway. I've decided to put it aside for Christopher and Ruthie for when they are older.

Cooper also vouched for me and both the children were very vocal about where they wanted to stay. I also assured her my family would be a very big support system for us. I was right, they have been.

To say they were shocked when I told them I was taking in Ruth Jean and Christopher is a major understatement. However, they trust I know what I want and they have accepted Ruth Jean and Christopher into the family with open arms.

My support has not stopped at them. The love that has been pouring in from not only Katelyn but also my new friends is astounding. Grace, Julia, and Kayla have all called or come by to meet the kids, and told me if I needed anything they were here for me. Ruth Jean has even spent some time with Grace at her bakery, learning how to bake pies. She even created her very own and called it New Family Pie.

In cewebwation of awe new famiwy, she had said. It completely warmed my heart.

Then there's Cade. He's been amazing too, but also a little distant. He hasn't kissed me or touched me affectionately since the day he said goodbye to me on my porch, after Cooper and the social worker left. I try not to let that bother me though, because I knew when making this decision that the chance of us having anything more than friendship was probably not going to happen.

Despite that disappointment, he still checks in with me, texting me almost every day and asking how we are doing. It means a lot.

All in all, we are finding a good routine together. There are still many legal proceedings I need to go through, but things are moving in the direction we need. Even though I have only been granted temporary guardianship for the meantime, I have every intention of going for permanent.

"Looks like you still haven't learned your place, Dennison."

My head snaps to the left when I hear a commotion at the front entrance.

"My place? And where is that exactly, Hunter?"

Uh-oh!

I climb to my feet quickly, recognizing Christopher's furious voice.

"It isn't with her, so move along before I remind you just who you are and where you come from."

"Stop it, Ryan, this isn't your business." Alissa's panicked voice has me moving even faster.

"I'd like to see you try, asshole."

"Fine by me, and I'm going to do more damage than what your old man just did to you."

Despite my best effort, I'm not fast enough. Just as I make it into the front entrance, I see Christopher go at Ryan in a rage. Alissa jumps back with a scream as I lunge for both of them.

"That's enough. Both of you, stop!"

They ignore me, continuing to scuffle.

I grab the back of Christopher's shirt, dodging Ryan's fist while I try to pull him back.

"Stop it now, please."

Christopher pushes Ryan, sending him into the wall with a force stronger than I thought he was capable of. I press my hand on his chest to keep him back but Ryan isn't done. He doesn't see me as he spins around and throws a punch, a very solid one right to the side of my face.

Agony explodes across my cheek, ringing in my ears for seconds later.

"Oh shit!" Ryan curses, backing off immediately.

Alissa puts her arm around my shoulders to help me stay upright while Christopher rushes to my side. "Faith, are you okay?"

"I'm fine," I whisper painfully, pressing a hand to my throbbing cheek. My eyes water as I try to get my bearings.

Christopher's head snaps up, a furious snarl leaving him. "You're dead, Hunter!"

Before I have a chance to stop him, Christopher charges once again.

Thankfully, my father comes rushing in just then. "What on earth is going on in here?" he asks, ripping Christopher off Ryan.

"He punched Faith!" Christopher tells him.

"What?" My father rushes over to me. "Honey, are you all right?"

"I'm okay, Dad."

He pulls my hand away from my face, his eyes narrowing in fury before he turns to the boys, waiting for an explanation.

Ryan raises his hands. "It was an accident, I swear."

"It was," I quickly add. "He and Christopher were fighting, and I got in the middle of them."

"I don't care if it was an accident. There should have been no fighting at all. I want to know what went on right now!"

Alissa is the one to speak up. "Christopher and I were talking and Ryan didn't like it so he started a fight," she explains, giving Ryan a pointed glare.

"It didn't go quite like that," he lies.

"Yes, it did," I cut in.

From the little I heard, I know Ryan instigated it. He is also the one Christopher was busted fighting with before and now I know why.

"I heard what you said to Christopher. It was rude and uncalled for. If you can't respect him and this church, then I suggest you don't come back."

I feel the weight of Christopher's stare but don't look over at him, my attention remaining on Ryan.

Instead of being apologetic like he ought to, an arrogant smirk tilts his lips. "If anyone should leave it's him. My father's money is what's backing this church."

My blood starts to heat at the smug, little jerk, but before I can put him in his place, my dad does. "That doesn't change the fact that this is my church and everyone here is welcome, especially Christopher. If you can't respect that then my daughter is right, you won't be allowed back here."

I nod, proud of my dad for telling him like it is.

"I'll make sure to let my father know," he replies, starting toward the door. He tosses me one more smug look before leaving. "Sorry about your face."

Christopher starts for him again but Alissa and I hold him back.

"Don't. He's just trying to goad you."

Once Ryan's out of sight, my father ushers me into the church, forcing me to sit in a pew so he can examine my face better.

"I swear, Dad, I'm okay."

"It doesn't look okay," he replies heatedly.

I grab his hand gently. "It is, I promise."

He finally lets it go. "All right. How are things going with you and the kids? I haven't had a chance to ask since I saw you the other day. Did you get their bedrooms together?"

I nod. "Yes, Cade came and helped."

He not only came and bought them with us but he transported and helped us set up. Something flickers in my father's eyes, something I can't decipher. "You know, I would like to meet the man who saved my daughter's life. Maybe you could invite him over to one of our Sunday dinners?"

I barely refrain from cringing, thinking how destructive that could turn out. "I don't think that's a good idea, Dad."

"Why not?"

I shift nervously, unsure how to tell him about Cade's feelings on the very thing he is so passionate about. "Well, he's different than us. He…um, well…" I shake my head at my stammering and decide to just spill it. "He doesn't believe in God. Actually, he despises the very idea of him."

My father's expression remains stoic but I see the disappointment in his eyes.

Before he can say anything, I rush to explain further. "His seven-year-old sister was raped and murdered by a man who claimed he was a minister and said it was God's will."

He tenses at the information, an array of emotions passing over his expression but one overshadows them all…understanding. "Well, if anything was to make someone question their belief in God that would do it, wouldn't it?"

I nod and swallow thickly. "He hasn't had a very easy life, and I barely know the half of it."

A thoughtful moment of silence hangs between us before my father breaks it. "You know, Faith, the more I think about it, the more I realize us coming here was a very good thing. Not only for our family but for others, too. I have a very strong feeling everything is going to fall into place and turn out exactly how it was always meant to." With that, he presses a kiss to the top of my head then walks away.

I think about his parting words for only a few moments before collecting my own things and grabbing Christopher so we can go pick up Ruth Jean from the bakery.

Christopher apologizes relentlessly as we head out to my vehicle, his expression twisted with guilt.

"I know you are but don't be. It wasn't your fault."

"It is. I shouldn't have let him get to me, but I appreciate you having my back in there. No one ever does."

"I'll always have your back, Christopher. No matter what."

"Thanks," he mumbles uncomfortably before climbing into the SUV.

Once I close my door, I look over at him. "Now with that out of the way, I think we need to find something you like. Something you're into so you can make some friends."

He barrels out a laugh. "I don't need friends but thanks."

"Everyone needs at least one friend. Come on, there has to be something that interests you. Something you've always wanted to do?"

An emotion shudders over his face but it's so quick I wonder if I imagined it.

"Nope. Nothing."

I peer back at him, a knowing smile taking over my lips.

"Why are you looking at me like that?" he asks, leaning back.

"I was right about Alissa."

"You know nothing, we were just talking," he grumbles.

"Mhmm, okay."

"It's true!"

"All right."

He dismisses me, looking out the window.

"I just want to let you know I have her number if—"

"Faith! I'm serious, I'm not talking to you about girls, so let it go."

"Why not?" I ask, offended. "I am the perfect person to talk with since I am one."

He shakes his head. "Forget it, there's nothing to talk about. She just came over and said hi. We barely spoke before Ryan came over and started crap."

"Well, maybe next time you should approach her. Why don't you ask her out for some ice cream or something?"

He looks back at me like I'm a complete loser.

"What? What's wrong with ice cream?"

"Faith, I'm fifteen, not twelve."

"What does age have to do with it? I'm twenty-four and I love going for ice cream."

When he quirks a brow at me, I roll my eyes.

"Okay, fine then. What about asking her to a movie?"

"Right, and how am I supposed to get us there? My skateboard?"

"You guys can walk, it's a small town. Or I have no problem driving you."

The look he shoots me says he's clearly not on board with that idea.

"Look, just let it go. It doesn't matter anyway, she's better off without me."

"Says who?" I ask angrily.

"Says me and everyone else in this town."

"Well you and everyone else are wrong! Alissa would be lucky to have a chance with someone like you."

He shakes his head. "Whatever. Can we please just drop this?"

Sighing, I decide to let it go for now but I am not giving up on this. I know his feelings and I know Alissa's, too. I'm going to prove to him how one person can make the whole world seem brighter. How one person could be exactly what you ever needed.

That thought brings on an image of my own, the very man who changed my life in more ways than he could ever know.

CHAPTER 22

Cade

My phone vibrates in my pocket as I make my away across the busy gym. I pull it out to see Faith's number and can't deny the hope in my chest. It makes me feel like a pussy but it seems inevitable when it comes to this woman.

Hitting the answer button, I lift it to my ear. "What's up, Red?" I brace myself for that first sound of her soft voice, the melody always feeding the darkest parts of my soul.

I swear I'm worse than Evans now.

"Thank God I got ahold of you."

The panic in her voice has me freezing midstride. "What is it, what's wrong?"

"I'm stuck in traffic right now and there is no way I'm going to make it in time to pick up Ruth Jean from school. My mother is gone to a doctor's appointment with my papa and I can't get ahold of my father," she says, beginning to run out of breath. "Katelyn can't leave her shop and Christopher is hanging out with a friend at the skateboard park. He has no cell phone, which, by the way, I need to buy him one and—"

"Okay, take it easy," I cut in before she can give herself a heart attack. "I'll go get her."

Her sigh of relief fills the line. "Thank you. I really appreciate it. I know it's probably not easy for you to leave and—"

"It's fine, Jaxson and Sawyer are both here. I'll go get her and bring her back to the gym. Or do you want me to take her to your place?"

"The gym is fine. I shouldn't be long…well, I shouldn't say that, it's all depending if the grandpa in front of me decides to put the pedal to the metal rather than go for a Sunday stroll here. Come on, buddy, let's go. Some people have things to do."

I shake my head, knowing her fucking window probably isn't even open so it's not like the guy will hear her anyway. "Take your time, Red, it's fine."

"Okay, do you need directions?"

"Is there only one elementary school here?"

"Yes."

"Then no, I know where it is. I'm leaving now."

After she says thank you about another fifty times, I hang up and head to the school. It takes me only five minutes and I find a parking spot across the street, right outside the front doors. I hop out of my truck and lean against it so she can see me. When the bell rings, an explosion of little people come pouring out of the double doors.

Shit. There has to be hundreds of them. How am I supposed to spot her in all this chaos?

When minutes pass and the crowd dissipates, I worry I missed her somehow. Just as I'm about to go searching, a lone kid comes walking out of the doors with her head down, looking sad as hell. I quickly recognize her by the color of her hair.

"Hey, kid!" I shout to get her attention.

Her head snaps up, a huge smile breaking over her small face as she pushes her shitty, broken glasses up on her nose.

"Tade!" My name excitedly squeals from her lips as she runs to the crosswalk. She sticks her arm out, looking both ways before bolting across, coming straight for me.

When I realize she isn't slowing down, I reach out and catch her. She wraps her tiny arms around my neck as I scoop her up, planting a sloppy kiss on my cheek. I peer back at her vacantly but can't deny the sudden warmth that invades me. It's something both her and Red can only trigger.

"Hey, Big Guy. What awe you doing hewe?"

"Faith got stuck in traffic and asked if I could pick you up. I'm going to bring you back to the gym. That cool?"

"De toowest."

I grunt. "Whatever you say."

I open my truck door and she crawls across my seat to the passenger side, putting on her seat belt. On the drive back to the gym, she stares out her window and is quiet. *Really* quiet. I quickly remember how sad she looked walking out of the school.

"You okay, kid?"

She doesn't look over at me but nods before pushing her glasses up on her nose.

Faith needs to get on buying her some new ones.

"You don't look okay. What's wrong?"

Her small shoulders deflate on a sigh. "Henwy Winkleman was bugging me again today. Wike he awways does."

I tense at the information and wonder who the fuck this Henry Winkleman is.

"He's always so mean to me. Talls me names and tells me I'm ugwy. Today he pushed me down and—"

"He put his hands on you?" I bellow, anger swelling in my veins.

"Yeah and he frew wocks at me."

That little fucker is dead!

My fingers grip the wheel tighter as I try to calm the rage flowing through me. "Did you tell the teacher?"

"Yes, and she told him to stop but he never does, and it will just teep happening."

The hell it will.

"Don't worry, kid. Once we get to the gym, I'm going to show you exactly what to do if that little fu—kid comes at you again."

By the time I'm done with her, that little asshole won't know what hit him.

CHAPTER 23

Faith

I pull up to SEAL Extreme almost forty-five minutes later and hurry into the gym, feeling horrible about how long it took me. Just when I finally got past one accident, another occurred. Traffic was definitely not in my favor today.

Upon entering the gym, the sound of a little girl's laughter and an overly dramatic male's groan fills my ears.

In the sparring ring is Ruth Jean decked out in padded gear while Sawyer lies on the ground. Jaxson stands on one side of her, looking on amused, while Cade stands on the other side, looking proud. My heart does a little flip like always at my first glance of him.

"That was a good one, kid," Sawyer says, still groaning. "I surrender, I'm out."

"Oh no you don't, you bully!" Ruth Jean shakes her fist, giving Sawyer a tough face. "It ain't owver until I say it's owver!" She jumps, sailing through the air straight for him.

Sawyer quickly covers his crotch with one hand while he catches her midair with the other. "Hey, easy, girl. What did I tell you about making sure to be careful of a particular spot?" he scolds with no heat as he holds her in the air above his head.

"Tade says no mewcy!"

"That's right, Evans," Jaxson says, amusement coating his tone. "So stop being a pus—wimp and man up."

Sawyer glares over at him. "Why don't we trade spots then, assho—" he stops, catching himself. "And you can risk your di—parts. I need to keep mine in working order so I can—"

"I'm here!" I call out before Ruth Jean can hear any more of this conversation.

"Faif!" She squirms out of Sawyer's arms and flips over the ropes before racing over to me in all her gear.

I catch her with a smile. "Hey, sweet girl. I'm so sorry I wasn't at school waiting for you, I got stuck in traffic."

"It's otay. I was so happy Tade was dere."

"I'll bet you were."

My eyes find Cade, watching him as he jumps down from the ring, taking in his powerful body. Black athletic pants hang perfectly off his lean hips while a white muscle tank showcases the beauty of dark ink that's woven up his cut arms. Pieces of dark hair peek out from under his black beanie, and I immediately get the overwhelming urge to slip my hands beneath it to feel the silky strands.

The man is havoc on my hormones.

His usual blank expression turns harder the closer he gets to us. "What the hell happened to you?" he bellows, ripping my sunglasses off my face.

I quickly remember the black and blue shiner I'm sporting from Ryan the other day. "Oh, it's nothing. Just an accident."

He grasps my chin and turns my face to get a better look at it. "This does not look like an accident, it looks like someone hit you."

"Someone did," Ruth Jean pipes in heatedly. "Twistiphwor got into a fight wif a mean boy and de boy hit Faif."

The fury dominating Cade's face has me rushing out an explanation quickly.

"It's my fault. He was swinging to hit Christopher and I got in the middle of them."

"Why the hell would you get in the middle of them?"

My shoulders straighten at his disapproval. "I wasn't going to stand by and let them beat each other to a pulp."

His jaw flexes, teeth grinding.

I realize this is going to get ugly fast if I don't diffuse the situation. Reaching over, I grab his hand gently and try to ignore the tingles that shoot up my arm. "Really, Cade, I'm fine and Christopher feels awful about it."

He remains silent but his hard expression softens.

I take my glasses from him and slip them back on my face. "Thank you again for picking her up."

He nods. "I told you if you ever need anything you can call me."

"De guys was showin' me some stuff. Isn't dat wight, Big Guy?" Ruth Jean says with a wink.

Cade puts out his fist for a knuckle bump, which she returns. It has me wondering what I've missed in the hour they have been together.

"Well, little miss. How about some ice cream? Maybe even a trip to the park since Christopher is out for a while with a friend."

"Yes!" She looks up at Cade. "You gonna tome, too?"

I jump in quickly, saving him from having to disappoint her. "Cade has to work, but maybe another time, okay?"

Her face falls in disappointment. "Otay."

Cade clears his throat. "I can come for a bit."

Surprise renders me speechless. Ruth Jean squeals, launching her padded self at him. He catches her easily, not looking as uncomfortable as he usually does.

"Are you going to pay for it?" he asks her, keeping his usual hard expression.

"Shoure, tan you wend me some money?"

Laughter spills past my lips. "I'll lend you money, but first why don't you take off all that gear. You can't eat ice cream with your face covered like that."

Cade places her back to her feet and thankfully helps her out of it since I don't have a clue where I would start.

Afterward, she runs over to Sawyer and Jaxson to say goodbye. "See ya, guys. I'll be back anoder time so you betta be weady fwor me."

Jaxson gives her a fist bump like Cade did. "See you later, kid."

Sawyer picks her up by one leg, hanging her upside down. "You're the one who better be ready for me. Next time I'm not going to go so easy on you."

Ruth Jean punches at him, coming very close to his nether regions again.

He quickly rights her. "You're a dangerous one."

Still giggling, she gives him a friendly punch on the arm. "Bye."

"Bye, pretty girl."

She runs back to us, slipping her tiny hand into Cade's big one. "All wight, wet's go."

With a smile of my own, I wave goodbye to Jaxson and Sawyer as we head out the door.

Ruth Jean and I are the only ones to get an ice cream, which Cade ends up paying for no matter how much I try to refuse. After, we head to the park down the street in comfortable silence. It's the quietest I've ever heard Ruth Jean.

Feeling the weight of Cade's stare, I look over to find him watching me. His eyes are shielded from his aviators but his expression says everything.

"Jealous of my ice cream, Walker?" I ask with a smile.

A giggle escapes me when his nostrils flare. Unable to help myself, I slowly and precisely lick my ice cream, the creamy chocolate gliding over my tongue and burning along my tastes buds.

The low growl that erupts from his chest tickles my spine, racking my body with foreign sensations.

"I told ya, you should have gotten one, Big Guy," Ruth Jean says, thankfully completely oblivious to the tension.

Cade glances down at her. "I guess I should have listened."

"Yep!" she replies, finishing the last of her cone.

Once we reach the park, she races off toward the playground. "Make sure to stay where I can see you," I remind her, to which I get a wave over her shoulder.

Cade and I take a seat over on a bench that's close by, my shoulder touching his arm. "Want some?" I ask flirtatiously, holding my ice cream out to him.

"Careful how much you push me, Red. You're lucky we're in a park full of kids right now. That's about the only thing saving you at the moment."

"Maybe I don't want to be saved from you."

He doesn't miss the double meaning of my words, his expression turning somber. "You should be."

Sadness fills my heart, a heaviness blanketing us in the truth. He reaches up and lightly traces his fingers across my bruised cheek.

"It looks worse than it is," I tell him softly.

His hand threads into my hair at the side of my head, cupping my cheek. "I don't like seeing any marks on you, Red. Ever. Whether it's an accident or not."

It's something I can understand, because it devastates me to see his scars. Placing my hand over his, I lean into his warm touch and revel in the connection that's always between us. The one that has never strayed.

"There's something I've been wanting to ask you."

"Anything," he says without hesitation.

A small smile graces my lips at his quick response. "Now that Christopher is finished with his community service, I want him to have something to do, maybe even make some money since he won't accept any from me."

Any time I offer him money, he turns it away when I know he needs it.

"Is there anything at the gym he could help with? I don't want him going just anywhere and I think it would be good for him to be around the three of you."

"Why do you think we would be good for him?" he asks, sounding genuinely curious.

"Because I think all of you can relate a little to what he's going through. To know what it's like to make it through some rough times."

I lean over him, throwing my ice cream in the garbage, then wrap my arms around his neck, bringing my face only a mere inch from his.

"But most of all," I continue, "I think it would be great for him to be around strong, honorable men. Men who all lived through hell to save a girl they barely knew."

His arms come around me now, bringing me in close. "You were more than a girl I barely knew, Faith. So much more."

I swallow thickly, feeling tears sting my eyes. "You guys would have done it for a stranger and you know it."

"Of course, because it's what we were trained to do."

I shake my head. "You were all trained with your hands but not your hearts. It all starts here, Cade," I tell him quietly, placing my hand over his strong and steady heartbeat. "You, Cade Walker, have the most beautiful heart out of anyone I know. Even when you're moody and brooding," I add with a smile.

A scowl forms on his face but before he can reprimand me my lips land on his, silencing his protest with a kiss. He's caught off guard for only a brief second then he ends my control.

A growl shreds his throat as he tilts my head, his mouth dominating mine in a hunger I've craved since that night at the bar. Unfortunately, it ends too soon, him pulling away on a tortured groan. "We have to stop now before I get arrested for indecent actions in a park full of kids."

He's right but love that I affect him like this, that I can make him feel the same way he does me. I sit back down and rest back next to him. His arm slips over my shoulders, our fingers threading as we sit in comfortable silence. It's easy…right.

"I'm glad you came with us today. I missed you this past week," I tell him truthfully.

"Me too, Red. Always." That's all he says, but he doesn't need to say more because that one statement means everything right now. "I'll find something for the kid to do at the gym."

"Really?" I ask, looking up at him. "Are you sure? If you guys don't have anything I understand. I'll think of something else for him. I don't want you to do it just because I asked."

"Red, take a breath. I'm sure, and we'll pay him. It's all good."

"Thank you."

His attention moving to something over my shoulder and his entire body goes rigid.

"What's wrong?"

Without responding, he climbs to his feet quickly. "Ruth Jean, come here!"

Ruth Jean hops off the swing and makes her way over to us.

"Cade? What's going on?" I ask again.

When he nods to something behind me, I turn around, my heart plummeting straight to my stomach at the sight of Spike on his motorcycle parked across the street.

"Oh no."

"What's up, Big Guy?" Ruth Jean asks.

He takes her arm, bringing her in close to me. "Stay with Faith."

Before I can ask what he's going to do, he heads across the park. Ruth Jean watches him, a subtle gasp breaching her lips.

"Is dat Spite? Why is he hewe?"

The fear in her voice has me reaching down to pick her up.

"I don't know but don't be scared. Everything will be all right." I'm not sure who I am trying to reassure more, her or myself.

Spike flashes Cade a smirk that has an icy chill sliding down my spine. He starts up the bike then raises his hand, pointing it at Cade like it's a gun and pulls the trigger. Cade picks up speed, racing for him, but Spike takes off before he can catch him.

"Fuck!" He slows to a stop, his hands linking on top of his head in frustration. His strides are quick and furious as he comes back for us. He takes Ruth Jean from my arms then grabs my hand and leads us across the grass, back toward the gym.

"What do you think he was doing here?" I ask, trying to keep up with his quick steps. A million different reasons run through my head, none of them good.

Instead of answering my question, he asks one of his own. "Do you know where Christopher is right now?"

"He was going to the skateboard park with a friend but he should be home by now."

"Call the house and make sure he's there. Tell him to lock the doors and stay put until we get there."

"Is Twistiphwor in twouble?" Ruth Jean asks, her voice trembling with fear.

Cade rushes to reassure her. "No, kid, he's fine. I'm just being careful."

Pulling out my cell, I call Christopher, my fingers shaking with each number I dial. Relief fills me when he answers. I relay Cade's order, which leads to a million questions, but I tell him I will explain everything when we got home.

Cade takes us both to the house, refusing to let us go alone, then calls Cooper on the way over. Thirty minutes later, the three of us are at my kitchen table while Christopher and Ruth Jean watch TV downstairs. Tension blankets the room, most of it coming from Cade.

"I'll talk to him," Cooper promises.

"That's it?" Cade snaps, clearly wanting a better answer. "You'll talk to him?"

"I can't go and arrest the guy for being in a public place."

"We both know he was not there to enjoy the fucking scenery," Cade grinds out heatedly.

"I know. Which is why I will talk to him, give him a warning. I also suggest Faith files for a restraining order. That way, if he comes near them again, I'll be able to arrest him."

"A restraining order," I repeat. "Can I even do that when he hasn't done anything?"

"If you feel endangered, then yes, especially given the circumstances."

"While you're at it, we should put one on my dad, too," Christopher says, walking into the kitchen, obviously hearing the conversation.

"Why your father?" Cooper asks. "Have you seen him around?"

Christopher nods.

"What?" I shriek, having no knowledge of this. "When and why didn't you tell me?"

He shrugs. "I've only seen him twice and it was in public. He didn't do or say anything; he just glared at me like he always does. I thought it was by chance, but now knowing Spike was watching you guys at the park, I guess it wasn't. I'm sorry.."

Cade points at Cooper, practically vibrating in fury. "I want twenty-four hour police protection on them until those restraining orders go through."

"I don't have the manpower to do that, or the budget. I will have someone drive by to check on them routinely though and—"

"That's not enough!" Cade slams his fist on the table, making me jump.

"You know how this works, Walker," Cooper bites out, losing his patience. "You're letting your emotions screw with your head. I know Tommy, the asshole is all bark and no bite. Which is why he took off when you went after him at the park."

"Are you willing to bet their lives on it?" Cade asks.

"Of course not. We'll get the restraining order on them, and I'll personally make sure to check on them often but that's all I can do right now. I can't have someone with all three of them twenty-four seven and you know it."

"He's right, Cade," I say quietly, placing my hand on his arm. "He was probably trying to scare us. They haven't threatened me or the kids, if anything, he seemed more angry at you."

His attention shifts to me, anger and fear dueling in his hard eyes. "Remember what happened last time, when someone wanted to get revenge on me?"

The reminder has my blood running cold.

"Never again, Red," he grits. "You hear me? Never—again." His eyes move back to Cooper. "I'll stay."

"What are you going to do, Cade?" I ask. "You have to work, I have things I need to do at the church and the kids have school. You can't be with us all the time, we have to live our lives."

He shakes his head, but before he can argue I cup the side of his face, hoping to get through to him.

"I know you're worried, but I swear I'll protect them."

"Who's going to protect you?"

My heat warms and aches at the same time.

"Tan I tome in now?" Ruth Jean says, rubbing her eyes tiredly as she enters the kitchen.

I brave a smile. "Of course, come on."

I make room for her to come sit with me but she ducks under Cade's arm and crawls up on his lap. She leans into him, snuggling against his chest.

Cade curls an arm around her tiny body, pulling her in close. He remains silent, his eyes staring ahead at nothing.

I reach over and touch Ruth Jean's leg, using the opportunity to assure her. "Sheriff Cooper is going to deal with what happened today and make sure that your dad and Spike can't come anywhere near you or Christopher. So it's really important that if you see either of them anywhere, and we aren't with you, that you tell us right away, okay?"

She nods then looks up at Cade. "Awe you gonna stay wif us?" Her eyes are wide and hopeful.

“Yeah, kid, I’m staying.”

I drop my forehead on his shoulder, trying to hide my forming tears and pray that what happened today meant nothing. That Cooper is right and this is just a scare tactic, because if anything happens to any of them, I’d never survive it.

CHAPTER 24

Cade

Covered in sweat, my muscles burn from the few rounds I just had with Benson. A quick glance of the clock reveals that Christopher will be here soon to start his first shift. I jump down from the sparring ring and head into the change room for a shower.

The restraining order went into effect quickly like Cooper promised, and both of the assholes were served yesterday. I could have left Faith's last night but I didn't. Again, I spent another night on her couch, only a few feet away from her bedroom, wishing I was in there with her. Feeling her body against mine, her scent lingering on my skin. Instead, I remained crammed on that couch with the kid next to me, despite me continuing to tell her there isn't enough room for us both. I complain but the truth is…I don't mind it. Actually, I more than don't mind it, that's the problem. Attachments are being made.

I shouldn't spend another night there, but the thought of leaving, of walking away from the only thing that has breathed life back into my dead heart, brings on a panic I don't want to accept.

Pulling myself together, I turn off the shower and tie a towel around my waist before walking over to my locker.

Just then Jaxson walks in. "Hey."

"Hey."

"Benson's improving," he says with a smirk. "I thought he was going to hand you your ass there for a minute."

I grunt, knowing he's fucking with me. Benson is good but not that good.

"So how are things at Faith's, all quiet?" he asks, leaning a shoulder against the lockers.

"So far."

"You know we have your back if you need us, right? Evans and me—we'll follow you if you need to take matters into your own hands."

They've always had my back, which is how they ended up spending a week in hell with me. It's something I still feel like shit about and probably will never forgive myself for.

"Thanks, but I'm hoping it doesn't come to that."

He nods and is just about to leave before I speak again.

"Can I ask you something?"

He turns to face me, and must be able to sense where my heads at because he walks further in and takes a seat on the long wooden bench in front of me. "What's up?"

I tug at the back of my neck, unsure of how to ask him this without sounding like a pussy. "What changed your mind about Julia?"

His brows furrow. "What do you mean?"

Clearing my throat, I cross my arms over my chest. I do not like talking about shit, not with anyone, but if anybody knows about all the feelings I'm battling, it's him.

"What made you change your mind about finally giving in to what you wanted with her?"

Realization finally strikes. "A bunch of things, I guess." He shrugs, probably feeling just as uncomfortable as me. "For the longest time, I felt I wasn't good enough for her, and the truth of the matter is, I never will be. But I also know that no one will love her more than I do, and no one will protect her like I will. So I just try like hell every day to be worthy of her."

Silence hangs between us as I think about his answer. I guess that's part of the problem with Red. I'm hell-bent on protecting her but how do I protect her from myself? From what lurks inside?

"Listen, I'm not one to pry, you know that. That's Evans's thing."

I grunt in agreement. That asshole has no problem inserting his two cents.

"But if this is about Faith, which I think it is, then take it from me, Walker, the longer you keep resisting, the more time you're wasting. Time that you can't get back and time for someone else to step in."

The thought of her with anyone else makes me feel fucking violent. Ever since that day at the park, I've thought about Dr. Fucking Sissy and picture him touching her, kissing her, stepping in to help with the kids… I quickly shake myself of the thought before it can drag me under.

"And what about doing the right thing?" I ask, looking back over at him.

"Who says it's wrong?"

"You saw what I'm capable of, what I did to them down there in that cell. That's something I've always had hidden in me. I don't know how much control I have over it."

I don't have to elaborate what I'm talking about. It's a moment in our lives we will all never forget.

"We all have that in us, Walker. I don't want to even think about what I would have been capable of if Faith had been Julia and our positions were reversed. But the monster that we have inside of us," he continues, holding my stare, "it's also what makes us good at what we do. You have more control over it than you think you do. I know this because I know you. I've seen you at your worst, man, and I've seen you at your best. There are very few people in this world I would trust my family with…you're one of them."

I look back down at my feet, my thoughts conflicted after believing what I have for so long…

Jaxson pushes to his feet, dropping a hand on my shoulder. "Take it from someone who was in the same place as you are. If I could go back and claim Julia sooner, I would. You've already lost two years with her, don't let it be any more." He heads for the door but turns back around one last time. "Oh, and one more thing, the acreage down the road from our house is for sale."

My eyes narrow in confusion, wondering why he's telling me this.

"It's a decent size place, lots of room… Just in case you wanted to know." With a not-so-subtle smirk, he walks out, leaving me alone with my thoughts.

Turning back around, I continue to wallow in my turmoil, until I hear someone enter a moment later.

"Holy shit!"

I glance over my shoulder to find Christopher, his eyes wide with horror as he stares at my mangled back.

"What happened to you?" As soon as the question leaves him, he quickly shakes his head. "Sorry, never mind, it isn't my business."

I stand then, throwing my shirt over my head and shielding him from the sight. "It happened in Iraq."

"Faith?" he asks.

I nod, wondering just how much he knows, unsure of what Faith has told him.

His eyes narrow as he gets that hard look I know so well. "They hurt her, too?"

I remain silent but he sees the truth in my eyes.

"Are they dead?"

"Yes," I tell him.

The answer seems to appease him.

"So what am I going to be doing here?" he asks, dropping his gaze and kicking at the ground.

"You're going to come in every day after school for three hours. You'll clean the locker rooms and also make sure the equipment stays clean and sanitized."

He seems less than thrilled by it.

"If you do everything we ask, without any attitude, I'll let you into the ring for the last hour."

His gaze snaps up to mine, his eyes wide and hopeful. "You'll teach me how to fight?"

"If you want me to."

"Hell yeah, I do."

"There will be some conditions first."

"Like what?" he asks.

"This is a way for you to let out your aggression here and not out there," I tell him, voice firm. "All fighting stays in this gym and this gym only. I'm still pissed off about Faith's face."

Remorse enters his eyes. "I didn't mean for her to get hurt, I would never want that to happen to her."

"I know. There will be times in life where you will need to use your fists, I get that, but you have to pick and choose your battles. Having your feelings hurt because some asshole runs his mouth isn't one of them."

He nods. "I understand."

"Good."

"How did you learn to fight anyway," he asks when I turn around and begin throwing things in my locker.

"The Navy mostly, but I had to learn at a young age how to take care of myself."

"Why?" he asks.

I turn back around to face him. "I had an old man like yours. Thankfully, he died when I was young, but my mother still dated assholes."

He drops his head, kicking the floor again. "Well at least your mother stuck around."

"Take it from me, kid, sometimes you're better off without them." I slam my locker shut, hoping to end the conversation at that.

"Can I ask you something?"

Something in his tone has me nodding, despite my reluctance.

"What are you doing with Faith?" he asks, rushing on. "It's obvious you guys are more than friends, and it's even more obvious she cares a lot about you. So, I want to know what your intentions are with her."

My eyes narrow, suspicion rearing its ugly head. "What does it matter to you?"

Please don't tell me the kid has some kind of fucking crush on her.

He senses where my thoughts are. "Relax, it's nothing like that."

Thank fuck, because I'm not sure how I would deal with that.

"She's done a lot for my sister and me." He shrugs. "I don't want to see her get hurt. If anyone does hurt her, I'll kick their ass. Even if it's yours."

I have to give the kid credit; he has balls. Usually, I would tell any person who asked me this to mind their own fucking business, but since the kid is living with her and a part of her life now, I feel like it's fair for him to ask.

"The reason I'm dragging my ass is because I don't want to hurt her any more than you do."

"Then make sure you don't. It's not hard."

If only it were that easy but I have no way of explaining it to him. Not now, not ever.

"Look. I care about her," he says. "She's the only one who has ever given a shit about me, you know?"

I nod. "Yeah, kid, I know exactly what you mean." Walking over, I clap him on the shoulder. "Come on. I'll show you where you're going to start."

After taking him on a tour and introducing him to some of the fighters, I get him started in the public locker room then head into my office to do some paperwork.

An hour passes before I get up to check on him only to be stopped midstride.

"Tade!"

My attention shifts to the entrance where I find a little girl running toward me as fast as her legs can take her. She sounds like Ruth Jean but looks nothing like her.

I catch her as she catapults herself into my arms and hold her out at arm's length, looking her over. She wears brand new clothes and has on a new pair of glasses that actually fit her face and showcases the prettiest blue eyes I've ever seen. Her long, light brown hair is clean and cut nicely around her shoulders. But the new item of clothing I notice the most, the one thing that has something shifting in my chest, is the black beanie she's wearing on her head. A smaller version of mine.

"Who are you?" I ask, once some of the shock wears off.

"It's Wuf Jean, ya silwy. I got a mateover. And wook," she says, pointing to the beanie. "I asked Faif to get me a matching hat wike you. Now we awe twins!" she announces excitedly. "Do ya wike it?"

A long moment passes before I finally find my voice. "Yeah." I clear my throat when I hear how gruff it sounds. "You look good, kid. Like you always do, except now you have a killer smile to match."

That very smile I'm talking about spreads across her face before she throws her arms around my neck. "Tanks, Big Guy."

Unable to find my voice again, I hug her back, my eyes searching out Red over her shoulder. She watches us with a soft smile, one that affects me just as strongly as the kid's but in a different way.

"And guess what else?" Ruth Jean says, pulling my attention back to her.

"What?"

"I have a new name!" she tells me excitedly.

"Not a new name exactly," Faith rushes to explain. "We are keeping her original name because it's unique and was given specially just to her. But she does have another name she would like to be called by, from now on."

I quirk a brow at the child before me, waiting patiently.

"Woofie," she tells me with a big smile.

A scowl forms on my face, wondering how that's any better.

"Ruthie," Faith corrects her.

I let that sink in for a moment before nodding. "Cool. I like it, kid."

"Estuse me?" she says dramatically, cupping her ear.

My lips twitch in amusement. "I mean Ruthie."

"Dat's betta. Are ya staying de night again tonight?" she asks hopefully.

I glance back at Red and can tell she's wondering the same thing, but she quickly looks away, breaking eye contact.

"Yeah, I'm staying again."

It's a decision I made just at this moment, my conversation with Jaxson earlier still weighing on me.

Red smiles back at me. A smile that I will do my damnedest to see on her face every single day if I can help it.

CHAPTER 25

Faith

With our hands full of grocery bags, Ruthie and I struggle our way up the front steps of the house.

"It doesn't wook wike Tade is home yet," she says, disappointment edging her voice.

Home… How many feelings one word can evoke.

This may not be Cade's home but it sure has felt that way the last few days. We have breakfast together every morning, dinner together every night, then settle in for an evening of television together. The only way this situation could get any better is if he slept with me instead of that darn couch.

Every night, I crave to feel him next to me. Long to feel his heartbeat that I committed to memory that incredible night so long ago. I will broach the subject again soon, I just haven't wanted to pressure him. I only want him there if he wants that, too.

"I'm sure he'll be here soon," I tell her, offering a smile as I finally manage to unlock the door. Stepping inside, I come to a stop at the sound of someone singing "Perfect" by Hedley. The voice is so incredible, so moving that I become rooted to my spot.

"It's Twistiphwor," Ruthie says. "Isn't he amazing?"

I stare down at her in utter disbelief, completely rooted by shock and the talent I'm hearing. Every word he sings bleeds from his soul.

Dropping the grocery bags at my feet, I head downstairs toward his room, Ruthie following close behind. When I find his door is slightly ajar, I push it all the way open and find his back toward me. Headphones cover his ears, his hands pounding the air with rhythm in the same manner he would the drums. Once again I'm blown away by the lyrics that fall past his lips, every word embracing my soul like never before.

Just then, he turns around. "Shit!" He flings his headphones off, jumping back in surprise. "Jesus, you scared the shit out of me."

"You can sing," I whisper.

He shakes his head, his eyes dropping to the ground as he shifts from foot to foot.

I step forward, grasping his shoulders and forcing him to look at me. "Yes, you can, you're incredible. Why would you keep this from me?" Hurt edges the question as I wonder why he wouldn't trust me with this, especially when he knows this is my passion.

Ruthie ends up speaking for him. "He isn't awwowed to sing. My dad says music is fwor pussies."

"Ruth Jean!" he snaps, not appreciating her honesty.

"It's Woofie, wemember?" She glares back, her hands planted sternly on her hips.

I cut back in, eliminating any further argument between the two. "Christopher, you have to know what he said is nonsense. Some of the best musicians in the world are males."

"Just leave it alone, all right." He walks over to the dresser, depositing his headphones in the drawer.

"No. I will not drop this. You have an incredible talent. One that should be shared with the world."

He remains silent, keeping his back to me.

"How about an instrument? Do you play anything?" I ask.

Ruthie is the one to answer. "He had a guitar dat bewonged to my mom, but my dad bwoke it. He weally wants to wearn de dwums."

Christopher turns around and glares at her but she shrugs unapologetically.

God bless this child or I would be kept in the dark.

"Is that true? Do you want to learn to play the drums?" I ask, wanting to hear it from him.

"It doesn't matter."

"It does to me. If you love it this much you need to explore it. The possibilities with a voice like yours are endless."

"You act like I could have a career in this," he grumbles.

"That's exactly what I'm saying."

He shakes his head, refusing to realize how talented he is.

Just then an idea forms, bringing a smile to my face. "Sing with me."

He rears back at the suggestion. "What?"

"Sing with me. We can perform at the church. An opening for my music school."

"No way!"

"Why not?"

"Because I'll look like an idiot."

"No, you won't!" I reply heatedly, knowing this is coming from his father. "You have a gift, Christopher. Embrace it."

He shakes his head and is about to argue, but I slap my hand over his mouth and giggle at his scowling expression.

"Just think about it. You don't have to answer right now." Before he can argue further, I grab Ruthie by the hand and leave him alone with his thoughts. I'm not one for pushing but there is no way I will let him deny this. I heard his passion in every word he sang. He has so many possibilities within reach. I won't let him give up on them.

After dinner, the four of us sit downstairs in the living room and watch TV. It's become somewhat of our usual routine before bedtime. Cade and I sit on one couch with Ruthie sitting on his lap, snuggled into his chest. I'd be lying if I said I didn't desperately want to trade spots with her, but I have to admit they are adorable, especially with her wearing a princess nightie and her black beanie that matches his.

She hasn't taken it off since I bought it for her.

Christopher sits across from us in the recliner, his attention riveted to the television. A smile tugs at my lips as I think about what I walked in on earlier. I excitedly told Cade all about it over dinner, which annoyed Christopher to no end, but I couldn't help myself. I'm still in shock that he's always had this talent and kept it hidden.

Feeling the weight of my stare, his head turns in my direction, a scowl forming on his face. "Would you stop it already?"

"What?" I ask, feigning innocence.

"You know what."

"Can't I be excited about how talented you are?"

He shakes his head in frustration before turning back to the television.

"I wish I tould sing. I tan't even talk," Ruthie says, but doesn't really sound all that bothered about it.

Cade nudges her shoulder. "Don't worry, kid, I can't sing worth a sh—crap either."

She throws an arm around his neck, smiling up at him. "We awe a wot awike, Big Guy."

I smother a laugh at the way his brow lifts.

They are nothing alike—Ruthie is full of life, outgoing, always optimistic, and full of smiles while Cade is...well, the complete opposite, but still just as special.

"You have your own special gifts, too," I say, not wanting her to think she isn't talented because she doesn't have the same gift as her brother. "But if you want to learn how to play a musical instrument, when the church fully opens you can enroll in my class and be my first student."

"She isn't going anywhere near that place."

I tense at Cade's cold, hard tone, my eyes shooting to his. "What are you talking about? Of course she is. She starts Sunday school soon."

Panic strikes his face seconds before it tightens in anger. "Like hell she is."

The room falls to a dead silence.

My eyes narrow on him, not appreciating his tone with me.

Christopher clears his throat. "Come on, Ruthie, say good night and I'll read you a story."

She hesitates, looking between Cade and me.

I manage a reassuring smile for her benefit then kiss her goodnight before heading upstairs and out the back door, my body vibrating in anger. Seconds later, the door swings open behind me. I turn around, bracing myself for the argument that's coming, because no way am I backing down from this.

"I mean it, Faith, she isn't going anywhere near that fucking place."

"Yes, she is. It's a good place for her to meet other children and learn about the good things life has to offer."

"There is nothing fucking good about any of it," he bellows. "It's complete bullshit and I'm not going to let you force this on her."

"I'm not forcing anything, she wants to go. And it may be bullshit to you but it isn't to me."

His jaw flexes, expression hard as stone.

"Listen, I know this must be hard for you because of what happened to your sister, but you have to know—"

"Watch it, Faith! You don't know a damn thing about it, so don't talk about her—ever."

Hurt clogs my throat at the way he shoves aside my feelings so easily. "Fine. Then I'll say this. I'm Ruthie's legal guardian, which means this is my decision. God is a big part of my life. He always has been."

"Let's talk about that for a second," he says, crossing his arms over his broad chest. "I'd like to know how the fuck you could still believe in any of that bullshit, especially after everything that's happened to you."

My back straightens, pain striking my chest. "How can you ask me that?"

He steps closer, catching me off guard by grabbing the heavy metal cross hanging around my neck. His shoulders are rigid with tension and expression furious. I'm not even certain who I'm looking at right now.

"Your God is so fucking great, Faith? Then where the hell was he when those assholes were forcing their dicks inside of you."

His cruel, vulgar words strike me all the way down to my soul. Tears fill my eyes, blurring his angry face before me. "He sent me you," I choke out, barely managing the words.

He rears back as if I just slapped him. "You really believe that, don't you?"

"With all of my heart." My chin lifts, despite the tears rolling down my cheeks. "I thank God every day that I met you and got the chance to know what it felt like to be touched in a way that made me feel beautiful before I had my body stolen from me."

An array of turbulent emotions splash across his face.

"Without my faith in God, Cade, I don't think I would have survived what happened to me there. They stole so much from me, but I did not let them steal my faith, and I will be damned if I give it up now."

Unable to bear another second, I push past him and run into the house, heading straight to my room. I slam the door behind me and drop down on the bed, curling into a ball as the first sob escapes.

Any hope I had for a future with Cade dwindles, fading further and further away. I would do almost anything for him but I will not give up my faith for anyone, including him.

CHAPTER 26

Faith

I come awake with a pain in my chest, a heaviness making it almost impossible to breathe. Blinking my swollen, burning eyes, I glance over at the clock to see it's three in the morning. With my head pounding, I climb from bed and grab my long, thin cardigan to throw over my white nightgown before making my way downstairs for some aspirin.

When I see that Cade isn't on the couch, I realize he must have left. A fresh wave of tears erupt but I shove them aside and head into the kitchen. It's then I notice the porch light is still on. I walk to the back door to turn it off and stop midstride when I see Cade sitting on the steps, his head hanging in defeat.

Has he been out there this whole time?

My pain deepens at how lost and alone he looks. I tentatively step outside and fold my sweater over my chest at the slight breeze in the air. Every step I take is cautious and uncertain until I'm right behind him.

"Cade." His name whispers past my lips, my hand gently touching his shoulder. "Are you all right?"

He tenses beneath my touch but keeps his head down.

I walk around to stand in front of him. "Have you been out here this entire time?"

Again he doesn't answer me, silence filling the night air.

With a defeated sigh, I drop my hand and am just about to walk away when he reaches out, snagging my wrist. "Don't go." His words are choked, barely sounding like him. He pulls me in-between his legs, his arms curling around my waist as he tucks his face into my stomach. "I'm sorry, Red. So fucking sorry for what I said."

My fingers thread into his hair, heart shattering at the sound of his voice. "Please look at me," I plead softly.

There's a moment of hesitation before he finally lifts his face to mine. I suck in a sharp breath at his tortured expression.

"Oh, Cade," I whisper, my hand reaching out to touch his jaw. It kills me to see him like this, especially when he never allows himself to feel any emotion.

He sweeps my legs out from under me and brings me to straddle him, our faces only a breath from one another.

Leaning in, I rest my cheek against his, bringing my lips to his ear. "I know this is a hard topic for you, but you have to know I would never put Ruthie in danger."

"I know you wouldn't on purpose but this is something we will never agree on, Red. I just can't. The whole subject makes me fucking crazy."

"We don't have to agree but we have to respect each other about our beliefs."

"I know. I didn't mean to hurt you. I'm just so fucked up, I can't think straight when it comes to that shit."

My heart bleeds from his tortured words. "You're hurting and that's okay. There's nothing screwed up about that."

He shakes his head. "I don't deserve you, not any part of you." His face turns into my neck, lips grazing my sensitive skin.

I tilt my head, my pulse kick-starting as his large hands inch higher up on my bare thighs, his fingers possessively gripping my hips.

"I can't stay away," he rasps. "I need to be near you, all the fucking time, Red, or I feel like I can't breathe."

Warmth embraces my soul to know he needs me as badly as I need him. "I don't want you to stay away. I need you, too."

His face appears before mine, lips descending possessively. Our groans mingle in the air as we let go of our pain and let passion consume us. The taste of him floods my senses; it's dark and sinful yet beautiful. Just like the man himself.

A minor ache ignites between my legs and I grab hold of it, letting it wash away any insecurities I have. I won't stop this. Not this time.

My sweater slips partway down my shoulder, his greedy lips passing over the smooth skin before making their way across the swells of my breasts. It isn't long before I feel his fingers trace Aadil's name.

My eyes fall close, heart swelling with too many emotions to name. Cade senses it and moves on, continuing his beautiful assault. As his mouth moves lower, I sense his hesitancy.

"Don't stop," I plead. "I need you to touch me, Cade. I want you to touch me."

A groan vibrates deep in his throat before he lifts his face to mine, his hazel eyes burning with the same need I have racing through my blood. "Has anyone touched you since?" There's a hardness in his tone, one that wasn't there seconds ago.

I shake my head, the unwanted feeling of shame surfacing.

Relief passes over his hard face. "What about you, baby, have you touched yourself?"

Heat invades my cheeks, turning as red as my hair. "No. I haven't had any desire to be touched, until you. You're the only one I want to feel, and I desperately want you to erase the awful memories." My throat begins to burn as I try to get out the words that I have not yet expressed to anyone. "I hate that they were the last ones who touched me."

Fury adopts his face, his jaw locking down.

"I'm sorry, I didn't mean to make you angry."

His eyes briefly close as he tries to gather his composure. "Don't be sorry. You can tell me anything, no matter how hard it is to hear."

His hand travels up my throat to the back of my head before he brings me forward and gives me a long, deep kiss. One that reaches the very depths of my heart.

He rests his forehead against mine, his breathing heavy. "We're going to take this slow, Red. I'm going to touch you, baby, and make you feel good, but if I do something you're not ready for, you tell me, okay?"

"Yes," I comply softly.

His hands move to my shoulders before he slides the sleeves of my sweater all the way down my arms. My heart kicks up in anticipation when his fingers work the few small buttons on my nightgown between my breasts. He spreads the material apart, pushing the straps down my shoulders until it's bunched at my waist, baring me to his stare.

The soft evening breeze whispers across my heated skin, eliciting goose bumps. His fierce gaze becomes fixated on my exposed breasts, my nipples straining for his touch.

A low growl rumbles deep in his chest, the sound increasing the throbbing between my legs. "You're still so fucking perfect." He cups the heavy weight of my breasts, his rough palms gliding across my aching points before he takes a tortured bud into his mouth.

My head falls back on a cry, pleasure stealing my senses. I relish in it, cling to it. No fear, no past. Only us.

He spends as much time loving the other one, torturing me with his fiery tongue until I'm writhing and begging for more. My hands slip beneath his beanie and thread through his soft hair, holding him desperately close.

"You want more, baby?"

My response is a fiery whimper, my hips grinding against his.

He wastes no time coasting one hand down my stomach, his fingers skimming over my panties, stroking the center of the damp lace.

A heated gasp breaches my lips, my nails biting into his shoulders.

"This okay?" His eyes hold mine, searching for any hesitation.

"Yes, as long as it's your hands, your mouth, and your body, then everything and anything is okay," I tell him, meaning it.

"That's because you're mine, Red. You always have been, even when you were miles away, and every part of you has always known it."

I rest my forehead against his, the truth of his words causing mixed emotions to storm inside of me. "You're right. I have always known. I wish you would have, too." The last thing I want is to bring up the past, especially in this moment, but the words are out before I can stop them.

"Believe me, baby, I've always known, which is why I haven't touched anyone else in the past two years."

Every muscle in my body stiffens, shock freezing me in place. "You haven't been with anyone since me?" I can't help but feel a spark of hope.

He shakes his head, his sincere gaze burning into mine. "You're all I could think about, all I wanted. I swear, Red, you've ruined me for anyone else."

Joy explodes through my chest, the admission doing all sorts of beautiful things to my heart. I rest my forehead against his, cupping the side of his face. "You're all I want, too. You're the only one I want to touch me."

"Good, baby, because that's exactly what I'm going to do." He takes my mouth in another searing kiss, branding my soul like never before. His hand is slow and tentative, shifting to slip inside of my panties, his fingers gliding between my wet folds.

"Oh god." Pleasure whips through my senses, my head spinning as he grazes the spot that has slight shock waves rippling through me.

"Cade." I grip his shoulders, terrified for the feelings he's evoking.

"I got you, Red. Don't think. Just feel."

He makes it impossible to do anything else, his skilled fingers bringing me closer to the edge of destruction. My grip on his shoulders tightens as I begin grinding against his fingers that press against the perfect spot.

"That's it, baby, fuck my hand."

The dirty words have me aching for more. "More," I gasp. "I want to feel you inside me."

A noise of disappointment leaves his throat. "Not tonight, Red. We're going to stay right here and go no further than this, but trust me, I'm going to make you come just as hard." Just then he shifts his fingers, hitting the exact spot that shoves me into divine oblivion.

My body becomes overwhelmed with pleasure, lights exploding behind my eyes as I visit that beautiful place he took me to so long ago, a place I have been terrified I would never visit again. It erases some of the shame from my soul and replaces it with something beautiful. I absorb every breathtaking second of it until my body is completely spent.

Mind-numbing moments later, I collapse onto him, my head dropping to his shoulder as I try to comprehend what just happened. Realization hits that I was just touched again. Touched by the one man I have ached for, the one man who gave me the beautiful gift of sexual pleasure before evil was delivered.

It isn't long before I become overwhelmed with that knowledge and the first of many sobs shatter my chest. I'm unable to hold back, all of it pouring out of me at once.

Cade remains silent but his arms come around me, holding all my broken pieces together as he lets me release what I need to. His lips press to my shoulder, expressing more than words could. I soak in his warm embrace, releasing in the safety it brings me.

Minutes pass before I find my composure again. "Thank you," I whisper, keeping my face turned into his neck.

"I'm the one who should be saying that to you, Red." I'm surprised just how gruff his voice is, every word bleeding with emotion. "You're perfect and beautiful and you let me touch you. This pleasure is all you should know, it's all you should have ever known, and I swear to you, it's all you will know for the rest of your life. I'll never let anyone hurt you again."

His vow heals a little more of my wounded soul.

Moments later, he pulls my nightgown into place then wraps my sweater around me before standing with me in his arms. He takes a couple steps before stopping suddenly. "Shit! My hat."

He bends down with me still in his arms and swipes his beanie off the porch from where I knocked it off his head in the moment of passion.

"You have a serious obsession with that thing, Walker," I tease.

"I know. It's fucking scary and completely unhealthy."

The admission has a giggle slipping past my lips. I rest my head on his shoulder, loving the way I feel cherished as he carries me inside to bed.

When my back meets the cool mattress, I grip his shirt, refusing to let him go. "Please don't leave me. Sleep here. I want you next to me."

His face hovers inches above mine, his hazel eyes penetrating the darkness of my room. "I wasn't planning on going anywhere, Red." He pulls his shirt from his body, revealing nothing but absolute breathtaking perfection.

My eyes travel over him, remembering how all those hard lines felt beneath my hands.

"Keep looking at me like that, Faith, and I won't be able to sleep here."

My gaze pulls to his, cheeks heating for being busted, but I manage an abashed smile. "Sorry, Walker. Just can't help myself."

He grumbles something intangible before crawling in next to me and pulling me into the safety of his arms. My cheek rests against his strong heart, the remembered rhythm bringing peace to fall upon me. Despite the contentment between us there is no denying the tension in his body, his erection unmistakeable. I dance my fingers along his chest, trailing them down his stomach, my touch tentative until his hand stops mine.

"No."

I lift my chin, meeting his gaze in the shadows of my room. "You deserve to feel good too."

"Getting to touch you was more than enough for me. Tonight's been good, let's leave it at that." His hand lifts to my face, fingers grazing my cheek.

I have no words what this man does to me, the feelings he evokes. I turn my face into his touch, pressing a kiss before cuddling into him. "Good night, Cade."

"Night, Red."

Exhaustion settles over my satisfied body and it isn't long before I fall into a deep slumber.

CHAPTER 27

Cade

A tiny gasp pulls me from one of the best sleeps of my life. My eyes shoot open and there I find Faith's beautiful face soft with sleep. It's then I realize the sound didn't come from her. Looking over my shoulder, I find Ruthie standing right behind me, her face pale and eyes wide with tears.

"What is it?" I ask, terrified something's happened to her.

Faith awakens just then, lifting her head and clearing the sleep from her eyes. "Ruthie, honey. What's wrong?"

She lifts her finger, pointing at my back. "Who gave you all dem owies?"

Realization strikes that she's seeing my scars for the first time.

Tears tumble down her small cheeks, a sob falling with them. Unable to bear the sight, I reach over and pick her up, bringing her on my lap.

Faith struggles to hold back her own emotion and reaches over to rub her back. "Ruthie, remember when I told you how I met Cade?"

Ruthie lifts her head and nods.

"Well, that is how he got these scars, because he saved my life."

The guilt hanging in Faith's voice only adds to the turmoil locking in my chest.

Sniffling, Ruthie removes her glasses so she can wipe her wet cheeks. "I'm sowwy someone huwt you, Big Guy."

"Don't be sorry for me, kid. I'm glad I have them, because if I didn't Faith wouldn't be here right now."

My response was meant to soothe her but it has Faith breaking into tears too and the sight of them are just as torturous as the young girl's. I pull her against me, feeling unequipped to deal with this shit.

"I'm sowwy fwor you too, Faif. I'm gwad Tade saved you."

She has no idea how glad I am, too. The alternative thought is unbearable to think about.

The two embrace, putting us in a giant tangled web. I rest my head back, feeling a sudden sense of purpose. This right here has become everything, my entire world, and I'll stop at nothing to cherish it and protect it.

We spend a good amount of time together before Faith gets Ruthie ready for school. However, I'm the one to drive her, wanting a moment to speak to her about the very thing that had Faith and me fighting last night, the one thing I cannot change. No matter how much I wish I could.

I glance to my right and find her gazing out the window, looking lost in thought.

"You feeling better, kid?"

She nods. "Yeah, I'm betta now."

"Good. Listen, there's something I want to talk to you about."

As if sensing my internal battle, she turns toward me, giving me her full attention. "Shoure what's up?"

I take a moment to collect my thoughts, making sure to word everything correctly. "I want you to promise me that if someone ever does anything to you, or says anything to you that makes you feel uncomfortable, you'll tell me."

A moment of silence fills the truck as she watches me, her brows pinched in confusion. "Otay."

"This goes for anyone, Ruthie, no matter who it is or what they say to you, you always tell me if they make you upset. Whether it's a teacher, kid, parent, friend…anyone at that church." I try my damnedest to keep my tone even at that last one but don't succeed. The entire thought makes me dizzy with fear and fury. "Can you promise me that?" I ask, desperate to hear some reassurance.

"Yeah, shoure, Big Guy. I pwomise."

Relief settles over me, bringing a measure of peace with it. I feel her watch me but I let the topic drop. As much as I hate the idea of her going anywhere near that place, I have to respect Faith and her beliefs. I have to believe that Faith won't let her out of her sight or around any potential threat.

If anyone does mess with her in any way, it will be the greatest mistake of their lives.

CHAPTER 28

Cade

Jaxson, Sawyer, and I stand in the center of the ring, going over material for the next self-defense class, when Christopher comes charging into the gym like a bat out of hell.

He hops over some of the equipment before jumping into the ring with us. "You have to help me. I'm in serious shit!" He rests his hands on his knees, trying to catch his breath.

"What's going on?" If I find out he's been fighting again he really will be in serious shit.

"Alissa asked me to the school dance."

I wait to hear what happened next but he says nothing else. "Okay…"

"And like an idiot, I said yes."

Again, I wait to find out what the problem is, but once more he adds nothing else.

"I don't understand. What do you need help with?" I finally ask.

"I can't dance!"

I straighten, finally realizing where he's going with this. "Don't look at me, kid. That's not something I can help you with."

"You don't know how to dance?" he asks in disbelief.

"Do I look like the kind of guy who can dance?"

He looks at Jaxson next, all but practically begging.

"Sorry, man. I can't help you either."

He drops his head into his hands. "I'm so screwed. I'm just going to tell her I can't go. I don't know why I said yes in the first place."

Sawyer uses the moment to insert himself into the conversation. "All right, calm down. Let's not be hasty, I got this shit."

I brace myself for whatever idiotic thing he's going to do because I know damn well he can't dance either.

"Listen, I just recently discovered how to do this and it's really quite simple. There is nothing to it. You grab the chick and pull her in nice and close." He holds his arms up and out in front of him. "Now, depending how close you want to feel her, you can either hold her hand in your right one or you can put your arms around her waist, and hers around your neck. Personally, I say the latter, especially if you want to cop a feel."

I knew it. An idiot.

Christopher gapes at him. "I can't be that close to her. I'll get a boner."

Jaxson chuckles, and I have to admit the kid's honesty is amusing.

Sawyer wears a smug smirk. "Exactly, and if you're lucky enough she will stroke it for you later."

"Jesus, Evans, what the hell is wrong with you?" I ask, slapping him upside the head.

"What? It's not like he isn't old enough." His attention shifts back to Christopher. "How old are you anyway? Fifteen?"

Christopher clears his throat. "I just turned sixteen two days ago."

"What?" I bellow, completely in shock. "What the hell do you mean you turned sixteen two days ago? Does Faith know?"

"No," he grumbles, keeping his head down.

"Why wouldn't you say something?"

"Because I knew she would make it a big deal."

"Of course she would. It's your birthday."

"Look, I haven't celebrated it since I was ten years old, and even then it was in fucking secret, so just leave it alone." He jumps down from the ring, heading to the locker room.

A tense silence settles over the three of us. I glance over at Jaxson to see him looking just as pissed off as I am while Sawyer stares at me like I did something wrong.

"What the hell are you looking at?" I snap.

"And you tell me I don't know how to talk to the kid. At least I didn't make him storm off."

"No. Instead you told him to get some girl to give him a hand job, you stupid shit." I shake my head, still unbelieving he said that to him.

"Whatever. You heard him, he's sixteen. We had our first fuck by then."

"So? You do not say that shit to him. We want him to be better than us."

"What the hell is wrong with being us?" he asks affronted. "I think I am pretty cool, and that kid would be lucky to be anything like me. He would definitely get laid more that's for sure."

The expression on my face has him bursting into laughter. Now the fucker is just trying to piss me off and he's succeeding. I refuse to take the bait, I have bigger things to worry about right now.

"Are you guys good here?" I ask, looking at Jaxson. "I'm going to take him home."

Faith needs to talk to him, she's the only one who will be able to help him with this dance predicament he has found himself in.

Jaxson nods. "Yeah, man, go on. We're fine here."

"Thanks."

"Let me know if the kid needs any more advice," Sawyer throws out the parting comment, earning himself a punch in the shoulder.

After collecting the kid, we head home, my truck filled with awkward silence.

"Listen, I didn't mean to piss you off back there," I say, wanting to smooth things over. "I understand your reason for not saying anything but Faith has been good to you and it's really going to upset her that she missed your birthday. You and I both know she is going to feel guilty about it, and she deserves more than that."

"I know," he mumbles. "I didn't want to hurt her I just don't want it to be a big deal. She has already done enough for us she doesn't need to go out of her way any more."

"Let her be the one to decide that but she needs to know and she needs to hear it from you."

He nods. "I'll tell her when we get home."

"Good, and while you're at it, ask her to help you with the whole dance thing. I don't know why you didn't ask her to begin with."

He shoots me a look that has my lips lifting slightly.

"Okay, I know why you didn't but she's going to be the one who can help you with it. And if you like this girl you would be stupid to cancel and not go, otherwise, someone else will step in and take her."

"Yeah, probably that douche Ryan, and I already have a hard enough time not punching that asshole out."

"Remember what I said, pick and choose your battles."

"I know, I am."

The conversation ends as we pull up to the house, a place that is starting to feel like home. I follow Christopher inside and find Ruthie and Faith sitting on the couch in the living room, both looking upset.

"What's going on?" I walk over to them, worried that those bastards didn't follow the restraining order.

Ruthie briefly peeks up at me before dropping her gaze back down to the floor. Faith looks less than impressed, and if I didn't know any better, I'd say she's pissed at me.

"I received a call from Ruthie's principal today," she starts calmly. "Turns out she got into a fight with a boy named Henry Winkleman. She broke his nose."

Oh shit.

"I was just asking her how she learned to do something like that." She glares up at me, knowing exactly where she learned it.

Ruthie lifts her chin, her face pinched in anger. "He wipped my hat off and talled me names," she tells me. "I wawned him twice, just wike you said. He waughed and pushed me down."

That little fucker…

Faith rubs her back when her lip starts to quiver.

Ruthie takes a deep breath and steels her resolve. "So, I got up den did what you towd me to, and he didn't know what hit him," she says, shaking her fist in the air.

Good, that will teach the little bastard.

"Way to go, sis." Christopher sits next to her and throws an arm around her shoulders, looking proud.

It has Faith glaring daggers at me as she climbs to her feet. "Can I talk to you for a minute in the kitchen?" She starts out of the room without waiting for a response.

Ruthie gazes up at me anxiously. "I'm sowwy."

"Don't be, kid. You did good." I put my fist out for a knuckle bump then follow Faith's pissed-off ass into the kitchen. I also can't help but notice what a beautiful ass it is, her jean shorts mold perfectly to it, making my hands itch to—

"What the hell are you thinking?" she snaps on a harsh whisper, pulling me from my thoughts.

"I'm thinking the little fucker got what was coming to him."

"How could you teach her how to break his nose? What kind of example are you setting?"

My own temper flares. "First off, I didn't teach her how to break his nose. I taught her how to defend herself, which she did. That little jerk has been messing with her for a long time. You heard what she said, the kid pushed her down. He's a damn bully and needed to be put in his place. If his nose got broken then it's a good reminder for him not to fuck with her again."

"Don't you think I should have known this was going on? I had no idea she was being bullied. I was completely blindsided with that phone call, Cade. The principal was furious and not all that friendly."

"Then I'll kick his ass."

"It's a woman," she informs me.

"Then I'll teach you how to kick her ass!"

She expels a disbelieving laugh, shaking her head.

"She clearly isn't doing her job since this crap has been going on for a long time. The kid even threw rocks at her."

"Well why didn't you tell me? Why didn't any of you say anything?"

Before I can respond, Ruthie comes running in, upset. "Pwease don't get mad at him. It's not his fauwt."

Faith's expression softens before she walks over and kneels in front of her. "Oh, honey, it's okay. I'm not mad; I'm just upset I didn't know. I wish you guys would have told me what was happening. I could have handled the situation better with the principal."

"I didn't mean to bweak his nose, but he's so mean to me awl da time and he gets evewyone else to join in. All I want is to fit in and have fwiends." She covers her face and sobs into her hands.

Faith's expression is one of heartbreak whereas I'm too angry for that. I want to tear the little fucker apart for hurting her.

"Ruthie, baby, look at me." Faith clasps her tiny, wet face in her hands, forcing her eyes up. "Some people are born to stand out and you, sweet girl, are one of them. You are too special to be like everyone else."

The kid gives her a small smile, her confidence boosting just a little higher. Leave it to Faith to say the right thing.

"Why don't we have a small get-together? You can invite some kids who you want to be friends with. We can go to the park and for ice cream or even a movie."

Her smile grows. "I'd wike dat. Tanks, Faif." She wraps her arms around her neck, hugging her tight.

"You're welcome. As for this situation with Henry, I will talk with your principal and make sure this stops. You need to tell me if it doesn't, okay?"

She nods. "I will."

"Good. Go on and get cleaned up while I start supper."

As she runs up the stairs, Faith stands and turns to me, her expression regretful. Right when she opens her mouth to say something, I lift her off her feet then claim her mouth, silencing whatever she's about to say.

Moaning, she wraps her arms around my neck, kissing me with an intensity that matches my own. My groin stirs at the feel of her slender body against mine.

My lips slow their restless assault as I pull back, resting my forehead against hers. "No more being pissed at me, Red."

"Mmmm, I don't know, Walker," she muses with a smile, "if that's what you're going to do to me when I get upset, I may stay mad at you forever."

"It doesn't matter what mood you're in, I always want you." I wait for regret to wash over me, for saying that out loud, but it doesn't. There is no such thing as regret when it comes to this woman.

Her hand finds the side of my face. "Then maybe it's time for you to take me."

The thought has me blinded with need but I shove it aside, knowing my time will come and soon. I have already been putting things into place. A birthday surprise since that night at the piano bar got so messed up. Which brings me to ask, "You got plans Friday night?"

"Not yet, why?"

I clear my throat, suddenly feeling nervous for some stupid reason. "I was wondering if maybe you wanted to go out?"

A pretty smile steals her lips. "You asking me out on a date, Walker?"

"What if I am?"

"I thought you didn't date?" she teases, biting her bottom lip to keep from laughing. The action has my cock growing hard.

I sit her down on the kitchen table, bracing my hands on either side of her hips, my face only an inch from hers. "You should know by now, Red, that those rules don't apply to you. So, are you going to quit fucking with me and say yes or am I going to need to convince you?" My fingers graze her bare thigh, trailing closer and closer…

"Otay, all cweaned up. What's fwor suppa?" Ruthie asks, walking back in at the worst time.

My eyes close in disappointment, teeth grinding as I fight to rein in my need.

Giggling, Faith grabs my shirt in her fist, pulling me in closer and graces me with her perfect smile. "You never need to convince me, Walker. I'd follow you anywhere you asked me to." Giving me a quick, hard kiss, she hops down from the table, as if she didn't just tilt my world on its axis and swings Ruthie up into her arms. "How about we all go out for dinner tonight?"

"Yes!" Ruthie cheers.

Christopher walks in just then. "Uh, before we go can I talk to you for a minute?"

"Of course." Faith places Ruthie back down on her feet and gives him her sole focus.

He shifts from foot to foot, clearly nervous. When his gaze swings my way, I give him a nod in encouragement.

"It was my birthday two days ago," he blurts out.

Faith's sharp inhale penetrates the kitchen, her expression ridden with guilt. "Oh, Christopher, I'm so sorry." She pulls him in for a hug. "I had no idea."

"It's not a big deal. It's something we haven't celebrated for a long time."

This has her stepping back. "What do you mean?"

Ruthie is the one to respond. "Dad doesn't wet us cewebwate his bwirfday." Walking over, she wraps her arms around her brother's waist. "I'm sowwy I fowgot, Twistiphwor. I've had awot on my mind wately."

"It's okay, Ruthie. You know how I am about it, I don't care."

"Well that stops now," Faith says, anger thick in her voice. "We are going to have a big celebration. A party."

"No way!" Christopher rushes out. "Look, Faith, I don't want a big deal to be made out of it. That's why I didn't tell you. I'm sorry, but I just…I really don't like that kind of thing."

Her shoulders deflate. "Okay, I understand. Will you at least let me have a dinner for you with family and friends? Just something simple, I promise."

It's obvious the kid isn't keen on the idea but he gives in, unable to say no to her. It's another thing we have in common.

"Excellent. I will plan it for the following weekend."

He nods. "That's fine but there's something else I need to talk to you about."

"Okay," she replies slowly, bracing herself.

"Alissa asked me to the school dance and I said yes, but—"

He doesn't get to finish before Faith launches herself at him in excitement. "Oh my gosh, Christopher, this is amazing! I told you she liked you. Okay, we're going to get you a new outfit. I know Katelyn would love to come and give her expertise. She is the queen of fashion."

"Whoa, stop!" He grabs her shoulders, stilling her movements. "I've decided not to go."

"Why not?"

"Because I'm not a good dancer. As in…I can't. I don't know how."

She waves away his concern. "Don't worry about that, I'll show you. It's really easy."

He shakes his head. "I don't know, Faith. I just think it's better if I say no. Nothing good can come of this."

She grabs the kid's shoulders, her expression determined. "You listen to me, Christopher, plenty good will come from this. Alissa will be the luckiest girl there because you're taking her."

He opens his mouth to argue but she doesn't let him.

"You are going to that dance because both of you deserve to have a good time. Got it?"

I have to admit, I'm impressed by her stern tone. I didn't know she had it in her.

"Fine," he grumbles, "but no new outfit. It's just a dance and I'm not dressing up like some preppy jock."

"I'm not going to dress you up like a 'preppy jock' because that's not who you are. We are going to go buy a new *you* outfit. One that suits your personality and style, because you are perfect just the way you are."

He rolls his eyes but there is no denying the color that invades his face.

Faith rises up on her toes and plants a loud kiss on his cheek.

"Hey!" He glares at her, wiping his face. "Stop that."

She smiles, looking damn proud of herself. "I had to catch you off guard and do it quick, or else I wouldn't have gotten the chance."

Ruthie giggles while Christopher shakes his head, but I don't miss the slight twitch of his lips. "Whatever, we'll be in the truck." He takes his sister's hand and leads her to the front door.

"We'll be right behind you," Faith calls out.

At the final click of the door, she turns to me with a beaming smile and starts jumping up and down excitedly.

"Oh my god, Cade, this is so exciting. Oh man, Katelyn and I are going to spiff him up. Just you wait." She walks to the back door, bending over to slip on her sandals.

Her voice fades away as my attention drifts to her ass. My focus remains there as she moves around the kitchen, gathering her things.

When she stops at the entrance, I suddenly realize it's become quiet. I lift my gaze and find her watching me with a knowing smile.

"You coming, Walker, or do you need me to *convince you?*"

My hard expression has her bursting into a fit of laughter. It makes me want to haul her upstairs and fuck the sass right out of her. Before I can even consider the idea, she walks out the door, her laughter trailing behind her.

Come Friday she is mine and she won't be laughing then.

CHAPTER 29

Faith

The kids and I sit at the kitchen table, eating our giant bowls of ice cream while Cade is out back on a phone call. Despite how full I am from the pizza we devoured earlier, I've always been a sucker for dessert, something Ruthie knows exactly how to play on. It also helps that she has the sweetest face in the world and is impossible to say no to.

Just as I reach for more chocolate sauce, the doorbell rings. My hand pauses midair, my gaze moving to Christopher. "Are you expecting anyone?"

He shakes his head.

Standing, I walk to the door, both kids following suit. I peek through the peephole and my heart plummets straight to my stomach when I see a furious man and a little boy with a swollen nose standing on my front steps.

This can't be good.

Despite my nerves, I open the door and paste a friendly smile on my face. "Hello," I greet kindly, hoping to diffuse the situation as much as possible.

It doesn't work. Mr. Winkleman doesn't reciprocate the friendly greeting, his narrow eyes drifting down me in distaste. "You Faith Williams?"

"Uh-oh," Ruthie whispers shakily, cowering behind me.

I place my hand on her head, keeping my smile in place. "I am. And you must be—" The rest of my words are stuck in my throat when he enters my house, backing me up a few steps.

"I am not here for pleasantries, lady. I'm here to show you exactly what that kid," he seethes, pointing to Ruthie behind me, "did to mine, and I am not leaving here until my son gets an apology."

Christopher takes a step forward but I put my hand up to stop him.

"Look, Mr. Winkleman, I'm not sure what you were told, but I think they should both apologize to each other."

"My son is not apologizing for anything," he bellows, pointing his finger in my face. "The only one who will be apologizing is…" He trails off, his gaze shifting to something behind me.

I turn around to find Cade standing in the entrance between the living room and kitchen, his powerful body on full display as he wears his usual loose, black athletic pants and white muscle tank that's showcasing most of his tattoos. His hard expression and commanding presence add to the tension in the room.

"What's going on?" he asks, keeping his gaze trained on the angry man in front of me.

I swallow past my dry throat. "This is Mr. Winkleman and his son, Henry, who Ruthie had the altercation with at school today. He wants Ruthie to apologize and I am telling him I think they should both apologize."

"I told you my kid is not apologizing for anything." He steps into my personal space, crowding me with his angry presence.

Cade is in front of me in a flash, shoving the man back a step. "Back the fuck up."

Mr. Winkleman stumbles but gains his footing quickly. He straightens his shoulders but there's no denying the fear in his eyes as Cade towers over him.

"I want my kid to get the apology he deserves, and I expect full coverage on the medical expenses."

Judging by the expensive suit he wears, I'd say money is not an issue for him.

"She is not apologizing to him," Cade says, voice hard. "Your kid has had this coming for a long time. She defended herself."

"She broke his nose! The girl is an animal and should be locked in a cage."

I gasp, anger rushing to the surface hot and fast.

Christopher steps around me. "Hey, who the hell are you calling an animal, asshole?"

Cade holds him back with a hand on his shoulder. "Take your sister downstairs."

Christopher makes no move to oblige, glaring down Mr. Winkleman.

"Now!" Everyone jumps at Cade's bellow, including Henry and his father.

Christopher picks Ruthie up, and heads downstairs, though not before shooting Mr. Winkleman one more hard look.

Silence fills the room once we're alone, the air seeming to drop in temperature. My heart thunders in my chest when Cade takes a threatening step toward Mr. Winkleman. "Watch your mouth, Winkleman, or I will bust it in front of your kid."

Mr. Winkleman swallows nervously, retreating as Cade continues to crowd him.

"Now let's get one thing straight. My kid is not apologizing to yours."

Every muscle in my body stills when he claims Ruthie as his.

"I taught her to do what she did today because your son has been pushing her around. So I hope, for his sake, he learned his lesson. Because if he even so much as makes her shed one more goddamn tear, I will make sure she breaks a different part of his body, then after she's done kicking his ass I'm going to come to your house and kick your ass."

Henry shirks back, looking scared spit-less, and his father doesn't look much better.

"Now get the hell out of my house before I throw you out."

This time, Mr. Winkleman is smart enough to listen. He and Henry scurry out the door faster than they barged in.

Cade watches them until the expensive BMW disappears then he slams the door. "Asshole," he mutters. He turns around to find me watching him with a big, silly smile on my face. "What?"

Before I have a chance to say anything, Ruthie and Christopher come charging back in.

Ruthie catapults herself at Cade. He catches her easily, sweeping her up in his arms.

"Did ya mean it?" she asks, peering back at him hopefully.

His brows bunch in confusion. "Mean what?"

"You talled me your tid. Did you mean it?"

By his expression, I don't think he even realized he said it. He glances at Christopher then at me, his gaze lingering before it reverts to Ruthie. "Yeah, kid, I meant it."

"I knew you woved me!" She hugs him tight. "I wuv you too, Big Guy. A whole wot."

My heart explodes with warmth, the emotions adopting his face triggering something inside of me. A happiness I haven't felt in a really long time.

My watery gaze shifts to Christopher.

He steps back, holding his hands up in front of him. "Don't even think about kissing me again."

"Of course not." I sidestep him, as if to move past him, then make a swift turn and plant one right on his cheek.

"Come on, Faith," he growls. "What is it with you?"

Giggling, I ignore his grumbling and grab Ruthie from Cade. "Let's get you ready for bed, shall we?"

After she says her good nights to everyone, I take her upstairs and tuck her in. "You okay about Henry now?" I ask, knowing she was nervous about the altercation.

"Much betta tanks to Tade."

My smile matches hers. "Cade is always good at making things better."

I bend down to give her my usual kiss on the forehead and she wraps her arms around my neck, hugging me close. "I wuv you, Faif, and I wuv ouwr family."

I hug her back. "Me too, Ruthie, all of you are the best things that ever happened to me."

I mean every word. The last few weeks I have wondered how I ever lived without any of them before.

Giving her one last kiss, I walk out of her room and head back downstairs into the living room. Cade sits on the couch, hunched over the coffee table, typing on his laptop. When I see no sign of Christopher, I start toward him, each step bringing me closer to everything I have ever wanted.

His head lifts, eyes roaming. He braces himself seconds before I jump at him. My knees land on either side of his hips and my arms around his neck. Then I make my move, taking his mouth in a searing kiss and pouring everything I feel into it.

He immediately takes control. His mouth firm and demanding yet gentle. Our tongues slide together in perfect harmony, saying everything we haven't yet. What doesn't need to be spoken out loud.

He's my dark angel and the man I love with my whole heart.

Eventually, I pull back, resting my forehead against his.

"What was that for?" he asks, voice gruff.

"You sticking up for Ruthie like that makes me want to do all sorts of naughty things to you, Walker."

His hands move from my hips to my bottom, bringing me snug against his erection. "If that gets you hot, Red, I'll kick everyone's ass and let you watch."

Giggling, I rip his hat off his head, threading my fingers through his hair while his lips press to the column of my throat. "Everything you do makes me hot. Even when you're moody and brooding, I still think you're sexy."

"You're the sexy one, baby." His mouth descends lower, finding my puckered nipple through my thin tank top.

A moan escapes my throat, my hips grinding against his hardness.

Growling, he slips his hand inside my shorts and beneath my panties, his fingers delving.

I gasp and writher.

"So wet already," he croons.

"Always for you." My hips buck against his touch, seeking more. We haven't gone past this point but I'm ready to, I'm ready for him. "I want more, Cade, I want you."

A tortured groan rips from his throat. "I know, Red, me too, but not yet. I have plans in place for that and I'm not taking you on the fucking couch, but I'll give you more, baby, if you want it." He slides his finger to my aching entrance, hovering just on the outside as he waits for approval.

I bite my lip, nodding my permission. When his finger breaches, I gasp, my nails biting into his shoulder. He inserts the single finger all the way in, sending my senses into a heated frenzy.

"Jesus, you're tight…hot," he growls.

"Don't stop." I all but practically plead.

"Never."

His finger works me, pumping faster and faster.

"Cade," I whimper, riding his hand.

"Look at me, baby."

Our gazes lock, the moment becoming so much more. I watch his jaw flex, watch as he reins in his own need. Without thinking twice, I slide one hand down between us, my fingers slipping beneath his waistband.

"You don't have to do that, Red," he grits, his chest heaving as he restrains himself.

"I want to. Please let me touch you, too."

He assesses me carefully and when he finds no hesitation, I slide my hand all the way in, my fingers curling around his erection. It makes us both groan. I revel at the feel of him; so smooth, yet hard…

Feeling him this way brings no shame or ugly memories, only the good ones. The way he filled and stretched me that one night so long ago.

I stroke him from base to tip, keeping my grip firm. He pumps into my hand, a hiss escaping him.

His rhythm picks up, finger thrusting deeper and faster.

"Oh god, that feels so good." My forehead drops on his, my teeth biting my lip to stop from crying out.

"Just wait until it's my cock filling this tight, hot pussy of yours again."

The erotic words do so many things to me, make me feel so many beautiful things. "I want that. I need to feel you inside of me again."

"Soon, baby, I promise." He leans in, sealing the vow with a kiss.

A flutter ripples through me with my impending orgasm and I know I won't be able to hold off much longer. My hand moves quicker along his shaft. "Come with me," I whisper against his lips, our mouth still moving in sync.

Our pleasure erupts at the same time, our hot breaths mingling, moans colliding the same way our bodies crave to be one.

Eventually, I drop against his chest, searching for gravity.

He removes his hand from my shorts. "Sit back for a minute, baby."

When I oblige, he reaches behind him and pulls his shirt off. My eyes drift over his powerful chest as he begins wiping our hands clean. I take in every defined line and hard curve before focusing on the silver metal piercing his skin.

"Keep looking at me like that, Red, and I will not be able to stop myself from sinking into your tight, warm body."

Heat creeps into my cheeks for getting busted, and then the most amazing thing happens. He chuckles, bringing a full smile with it, and it's absolutely breathtaking. It softens his features and reminds me of the one time I got to see it before—back in Iraq. It vanishes quickly though when he sees me smiling at him like a fool.

"What?" he grumbles uncomfortably.

My hands frame his face before I lean in, pressing a soft kiss to his mouth. "You should smile more often, Walker, not only because it looks good on you but because it's good for your soul."

His warm eyes penetrate mine, making time come to a standstill. "You're good for my soul, Red."

My pulse skips, his precious words doing so many wonderful things to my heart. It's now, in this moment, that I'm ready to lay it all out, right here. Right now.

"I love you, Cade Walker."

His body tenses beneath mine, alarm flashing in his eyes.

It's exactly the reaction I expected. Before he can say anything, I continue. "Don't say anything. I didn't tell you so you would say it back, I told you because it's the truth and I don't want to keep it in anymore. If there is one thing I've learned in the last two years it's that life is too short for us to hold back the things we feel."

I pause and swallow thickly, emotion thickening my throat.

"When I was dragged down to that cell and thought I was going to watch you die in front of me, I knew then, with every part of my soul, that I loved you. And I meant what I said down there, Cade. I didn't care what they did to me, I would have died for you."

His expression tightens, his hazel irises darkening with guilt and anger. He frames my face firmly between his hands, pulling me in close, his chest heaving with whatever emotions he's holding back.

"Never again, Red," he chokes out. "You hear me? We will never be put in that position again. I will protect you until the day I take my last fucking breath."

It may not be *I love you*—not yet—but it does sound like forever and right now that is enough for me.

CHAPTER 30

Cade

Friday evening, I pull up to the house after dropping Ruthie off with Sawyer and Grace for the night and climb out of my truck, anticipation building with every step I take.

I never thought the day would come that I would be going on a date, but then again, I never thought I would meet someone like Faith. If anyone could get me to break all the rules, it's her.

Walking into the house, I find her in the kitchen talking on the phone to Katelyn. My cock jerks at the sight of her wearing a black, strapless dress that flows loosely from her body. Cream lace edges the bottom, teasing the tops of her slender thighs. I'm dying to feel those perfect legs wrapped around my hips.

Sensing my presence, she turns around, flashing me a smile that almost knocks me on my ass. A faint blush stains her cheeks, matching her deep red hair that is tousled in loose waves around her shoulders.

"Katelyn, I have to go. I'll see you tomorrow." She hangs up, placing the phone on the counter before turning back to face me.

Without a word, I stride forward and pull her into my arms. My lips seize hers, tongue parting for a taste. When her arms lock around my neck, I pick her up off the floor and set her on the counter, positioning myself between her legs. I pull back, only long enough to trail my lips down her slender throat, tasting her perfect skin.

"I was going to ask if what I was wearing is okay, but I will assume by your reaction that it is."

"You're perfect, Red. Always." My hand slides up her silky thigh, slipping beneath her dress until I reach the damp satin between her legs.

Her head drops back against the cupboard behind her, hips bucking to get closer. I decide right here and now I am going to make her come before we leave here. I need it as bad as she does.

"Oh shit!"

The curse has me swiftly removing my hand. Turning my head, I find Christopher behind me, covering his eyes.

Faith gasps in horror, her hands shoving against my chest as she rights her dress.

"Sorry. I uh…I just came back to grab my iPod, don't mind me. Carry on," he spews, bolting down the stairs.

I'd find it rather amusing if Faith didn't seem so upset. Her hands frame her red cheeks, expression horrified.

"Please tell me that didn't just happen." Without giving me a chance to respond, she jumps off the counter, pacing back and forth. "They are going to take him away from me. I can't lose them. Oh my god, what are we going to do?"

I intercept her babbling, grasping her shoulders. "Faith, calm down. It isn't that big of a deal."

"Of course it is. Look what he just walked in on. That's not okay, Cade."

"Why? It's not like he walked in on us fucking. My hand was up your dress, which he couldn't see since I was covering you."

She stares back at me, her eyes wide and anxious. "Go talk to him," she orders. "You need to explain things to him."

"Explain what? The kid is sixteen, he has a pretty good idea what was going on."

She drops her face in her hands on a groan.

Christopher hurries back up the stairs, avoiding eye contact with us as he heads for the door. "See ya."

"Christopher, wait!" Faith calls out.

He turns around, shifting nervously as she walks up to him.

She places her hand on his shoulder. "I'm sorry you walked in on that. It will never happen again."

She's wrong. It could very well happen again because if I think we're alone, I am not keeping my hands to myself.

"It isn't a big deal," he mumbles. "It's not like you were expecting me."

"Still, it shouldn't have happened," she pauses before cautiously continuing. "Do…Do you have any questions?"

The kid rears back, practically offended. "What? No!"

"Are you sure? Because, if you have any questions about sex, you can talk to me."

I wince, feeling sorry for the poor kid.

"Seriously, Faith? I don't need you to give me the sex talk, I'm sixteen years old."

"I just want you to know if you ever have any questions, you can come to me."

His horrified eyes shoot to mine, pleading for help.

"Let the kid go, Red." I dismiss him with a nod and he wastes no time bolting out the door faster than he came in.

Faith turns to face me, her expression soft with guilt. "I just made it worse, didn't I?"

Walking over, I pull her in my arms. "Don't worry about it."

"I just don't want to lose them."

"That would never happen. You're the best thing for them and everyone knows it."

By the smile she flashes me, it was clearly the right thing to say. "Where are you taking me, Walker? I want to get on with this date, and…other things."

My cock hardens at the seductive look she gives me. Growling, I lift her off the ground and over my shoulder, making her squeal in laughter as I head for the door.

"Wait, my purse!" she cries.

"You don't need it."

I continue out the door, carrying her out to the truck. After two long years, I am finally going to have the one woman I've been dying to feel again, and I know, just like last time, it will change my life forever.

It takes approximately thirty minutes to reach our destination. I pull off to the side of the highway and into the small opening that leads to a deserted beach.

Faith turns to me with a smile. "How did you know the beach is my favorite place?"

"I know everything about you, Red."

This is mostly true. However, after much deliberation on where I should take her, it was Julia and Grace that suggested here.

Out of the truck, I come around to help her down but she's already out and toeing off her cowgirl boots. Grabbing her hand, I lead her toward the deserted cove that I discovered days ago.

"You don't need anything from the truck?" she asks.

"Nope."

Thanks to Julia and Grace, the only thing I need from my truck is her present, which I will come back for later. I have to wait for the right time.

"Always so mysterious, Walker."

Little does she know my feelings for her have always been a mystery.

After trekking across half the beach, we round a rock, heading into a cove where Julia and Grace set up for us. I refrain from groaning when I see they went above and beyond what I asked.

Faith gasps as she takes in the scene before us. A large blanket is spread out with flower petals sprinkled all over it. A picnic basket sits in the center, a bouquet of flowers, and...champagne. Something I would never drink.

Red turns to me, beaming with happiness. "I can't believe you did this."

"As much as I'd like to take the credit, Julia and Grace helped."

A lot but I keep that to myself.

That information doesn't seem to bother her. She stretches up, brushing a kiss to my mouth before walking over to the blanket, sitting amongst the petals. She looks beautiful, right where she belongs. With me.

She picks up the bottle of champagne, quirking a brow at me. "I wonder if they packed beer for you."

"Doubtful," I answer, sitting across from her.

She opens the basket, unveiling our food and a six-pack. "Looks like you're wrong. There is also a note attached." Opening the piece of paper, she bursts into laughter then passes it to me. "I believe this is for you."

I take the paper and quickly recognize Sawyer's writing. *Have fun on your romantic date, pussy.*

Grunting, I crumble the paper in my hand and toss it in the picnic basket.

Asshole.

"This all looks so good and it's vegetarian. What are you going to eat?" she teases.

I forgo telling her that I had a late lunch and made sure to fill up because I knew what would be packed. I asked Grace specifically for it to be all vegetarian.

We waste no time starting on dinner and I have to admit for being vegetarian it's not bad. Faith does the majority of the talking, like usual, and I contently sit and listen. She rambles on about how excited she is for shopping with Christopher and Katelyn tomorrow. Ruthie has decided she would rather come hang with me in the gym, which suits me just fine.

After we finish, Faith throws out our garbage and clears a spot before crawling over to me. She situates herself over me, her knees hugging either side of my hips. My hands slip beneath her dress, cupping her perfect ass.

"Take off your shoes, Walker, stay a while," she murmurs, leaning in to press a kiss to my mouth. The soft touch has me wanting to throw her to her back and take her right now, but somehow, I manage to refrain.

"Not yet. I have to go back to the truck for a minute."

"Why?" she asks, her breath racing past her lips as she tempts me with all the things I want.

"Because I need to get your birthday present."

She stiffens in surprise and pulls back. "Present?"

"Yeah. I wanted to give it to you sooner but it took me a little while to find what I was looking for."

"What is it?" she asks excitedly.

"You would know by now if you would quit distracting me."

Giggling, she climbs off my lap. "Then by all means. You're a free man."

I'm far from free, she has a hold on me like no one else ever has or ever will.

After grabbing the gift from the backseat, I make it back to our spot only to find her standing at the edge of the water, a soft smile gracing her delicate face as she watches the waves crash over her feet. The setting sun casts a glow behind her that takes me back to that first week in Iraq. She's the picture of perfection, almost surreal and somehow, she's with me.

Sensing my gaze, she looks up and takes in the guitar case that I hold. I put it down on the blanket, my palms beginning to sweat like a nervous fucking teenager.

Mock curiosity adopts her face as she moves toward me. "Hmmm, what could be in here?" she asks, kneeling down beside it.

"Open it and find out."

I drop down across from her, my heart hammering wildly as she opens the case. I watch her reaction carefully, her smile completely vanishing as she stares down at the sleek, black acoustic guitar. Her fingers tremble as they brush over the handwritten signature.

"Cade?" she asks, my name falling on a shaky whisper.

"Yeah?"

"Why is Elvis's name on this guitar?"

"Because he signed it. He played it at some concert back in 1976 and—"

"Holy shit!"

I rear back, shocked those words just flew from her mouth.

"Is this real, Walker? Like, I mean, is this for real?" she asks with a note of hysteria in her voice.

"Damn straight it is."

I trust the guy who found it for me, if Jimmy says it's real, then it's real.

She mutters to herself in disbelief before looking back up at me, her eyes glassy. "How did you find this?"

"From an older Marine I met overseas. He's a collector and runs his own shop now. It took him some time but he found it and says it's legit."

Before I can anticipate the move, she launches herself at me, knocking me to my back and peppering kisses all over my face.

"Thank you! Thank you! Thank you!"

"I guess that means you like it."

"I more than like it. It's the most extraordinary, precious gift anyone has ever given me, Cade."

Pride fills my chest for being the one who gave it to her. "I have one more thing for you."

"Another one," she says, quirking a surprised brow. "You really know how to make a girl feel special, Walker."

"It's not really another present, it's more giving back something that belongs to you."

She peers down at me, perplexed.

"Hold out your hand," I tell her, reaching into my pocket.

Once she obliges, I lay the delicate chain in her palm. Her sharp breath penetrates the night air as she stares at the anklet she left me two years ago.

"Our belongings were sent to us while we were in the rehabilitation center," I tell her, my voice quiet. "I've been waiting for the right time to give it back to you."

When she says nothing, I take the anklet then rise up slightly to hook it around her slender ankle.

She stares down at it for a minute before swinging her emotional eyes up to mine. "I gave this to you so you would have something to remember me by."

I reach up and cup the side of her face, her tears slipping over my hand. "I never needed anything to remember you by, Red, I could have never forgotten you."

A small sob escapes her just before she drops down on top of me, resting her forehead on mine. "I love you."

The three words whisper across my lips with brutal reality and I tense without meaning to. The impact they carry are as strong as they were the first time she said them the other night. They have panic gripping my chest like a tight vice, making it difficult to take in a breath. I've only ever had one person say those words to me, and it was a little girl who didn't know any better. A little girl who died because I couldn't protect her.

"You don't believe me," she whispers sadly.

"It's not that."

"Then what is it?"

Her emerald eyes burn for answers, and before I can stop myself, I tell her the truth. I tell her my biggest fear. "It's not that I don't believe you, it's that I'm wondering when you're going to wake up and realize I'm not worthy of it."

She sucks in a sharp breath. "Never."

"All love comes with conditions, Red. Why do you think so many people divorce?"

"Not mine. I love unconditionally, and I think you're perfect, all of you."

"There is nothing close to perfect about me. You have to know that by now."

"That's just it. I see every single one of your flaws, and I value them as much as I value your strengths. You are perfect to me in every way. The good"—she presses a soft kiss to my lips—"the bad"—another one—"and I was going to say ugly but there is nothing ugly about you, Cade Walker," she adds with a smile.

Leave it to her to completely flip my world upside down. Having no words for what she does to me, I pull her down for a kiss that only lasts seconds before I make a request. "Sing for me."

"Now?" she asks, caught off guard.

"Yeah. Now. Play your new guitar and sing for me."

Her eyes bug out of her head. "Cade, that there"—she points to the instrument in question—"is not a guitar you play with. That is a guitar you hang and worship."

"You better play it. That's what I bought it for."

She shakes her head vehemently.

"Come on, Red, one song, baby. I want to hear you sing."

Her stubborn expression softens before she tosses a longing glance over at the guitar. "Fine, one song." She crawls over, her hands trembling as she picks it up. "I can't believe I'm about to play from the same guitar Elvis did," she murmurs, gazing down at it before lifting her gaze to mine. "This had to have cost you a fortune."

"You're worth every penny I spent."

A pretty smile dances across her lips. "What do you want me to sing, Walker?"

"I don't give a shit. I just want to hear your voice."

She takes a moment to think about it. "Okay. Here is one you will know and I think you'll like."

What she fails to realize is any song that falls past her beautiful lips I will love.

She scoots back, resting against the log behind her. I remain where I am, wanting full view. My groin stirs when she brings one of her knees up to rest the guitar on, obliviously showing me a glimpse of paradise.

The moment her fingers start strumming the chords gracefully, the most breathtaking expression takes over her face. I quickly recognize the tune "Free Fallin'" and once again she's right, I do like this song.

Her mouth opens, that life changing moment happening as the lyrics fall past her lips with grace and beauty. I'm completely riveted, drowning in every word she breathes.

I don't miss the innuendo of the beginning lyrics and neither does she if her wink is anything to go by.

Her head falls back, voice hitting that note, the one that makes your breath catch and changes everything you thought you knew about the world.

I'm unable to hold back a second longer and make my way toward her. Her gaze remains on the sky above, lost in the song. The moment my hand reaches her slender ankle, she falters and brings her head forward, eyes meeting mine.

"Don't stop, Red."

She finds her place again, our gazes never wavering. I slide my hand up her smooth leg, my mouth following its path. Her voice cracks the higher I get. I push her dress up to her hips as I reach the highest part on the inside of her thigh, the clean scent of her arousal penetrating my senses, my mouth watering for a taste.

A fiery moan purges past her lips, the lyrics falling silent.

"Keep going, Red," I murmur against her soft flesh.

"Forget the damn song, Cade." She shoves the guitar aside and threads her fingers in my hair, trying to yank my mouth to the sweet spot between her legs.

My lips twitch as I resist. "What's wrong, baby?"

"You know what. You're being mean," she grumbles, exerting more force. The sting to my scalp has me close to coming in my pants. I've never needed a woman the way I need her right now.

"Tell me what you want and I'll give it to you."

"I want your mouth on me. I want…"

Whatever else she was going to say falls on a gasp when I rip her panties from her hips and bury my mouth in her sweet pussy.

"Yes!" Her cry of pleasure fuels me, feeding the dark hunger I have raging in my soul.

Her legs spread further, hips bucking and fingers gripping. It drives me fucking wild to see her like this.

"Cade, I'm going to come." The warning is a heated whimper, shooting straight to my cock.

I growl against her flesh and insert one finger in her tight, hot entrance.

She shatters. Her legs clamp around my head, muffling the sound of her cries. My tongue is relentless until I've taken every last drop she has to give. Once I feel her relax, I kiss the inside of one thigh before trailing my lips higher until I'm in direct contact with her mouth.

She moans at the taste of herself, her fingers tugging at my shirt. I sit up to my knees, getting rid of it in record time. The moment it clears my head she's there, her arms wrapping around my waist, lips and tongue tasting my skin.

"You seriously have one fine body, Walker."

It's from all those nights that I tried working my body into exhaustion because I ached so fucking bad for her.

Her exploring takes her to the name scripted across my ribs, a name I often can't look at. It hurts too bad. She presses a kiss, the softest one, right over top then thankfully moves on.

Her hands reach for my belt before hesitating. She peeks up at me beneath her lashes, heat evident in her gaze but also something else, something vulnerable.

"I want to erase all the horrible memories, with you. I want to take you in my mouth, but…I've never done it before, at least not willingly." She visibly swallows, eyes casting down in shame.

Rage rushes through my veins hot and fast but I fight to keep it locked up, knowing my anger won't help her. My hand moves to the side of her face, lifting her eyes back to mine. "We can do it another time, Red. Why don't we just work on one thing right now?"

Tonight, I want to be inside of her.

"I don't want to wait, I just want all the bad memories gone, Cade, all of them." Before I can respond, she undoes my belt and releases me from the confines of my jeans, grasping my throbbing cock in her hand.

A hiss escapes my clenched teeth, every muscle in my body straining beneath my skin.

She peers up at me shyly. "Tell me if I do something wrong."

"There isn't much you can do wrong, baby. Just your breath this close to my cock is enough to make me explode."

It was clearly the right thing to say because she smiles, her confidence returning. I remain still when she leans in, tentatively taking me into her hot, wet mouth.

"Fuck me!" My head drops back on my shoulders, fire racing through my blood.

It's been a long time since I had a woman take me in her mouth. Faith may be slow and unsure but it's still the best fucking mouth I've ever had wrapped around me.

I take her hand that's on my hip, and wrap it around the base of my shaft, showing her a firm grip and stroking where her mouth can't reach. She catches on quickly, her mouth moving to the same rhythm.

"That's it, baby. Just like that," I coax, my voice rough. "Fuck that feels good."

She looks up at me, her emerald eyes blazing with heat and confidence. She takes it one step further, taking me all the way back to her throat before sucking her way to the tip.

It takes everything in me not to fuck her mouth like I want to. Instead, I reluctantly pull out.

"Did I do something wrong?" she asks.

"No, Red. It felt amazing but it's been a long time and I want to be inside of you."

Her arms wrap around my neck, zero hesitation in her eyes. "Then take me, Walker."

Growling, I claim her mouth the way she has claimed every part of me, especially the organ in my chest. I gently coax her to her back, unzipping her dress and sliding it down her body to reveal…perfection. Goose bumps break out across her flawless skin, her pink nipples straining and begging for my mouth.

"Jesus, Faith, you're perfect."

She smiles and lifts her hand for me. "So are you. Now come over here and warm me up."

My body blankets hers, both of us moaning at the skin-to-skin contact. It warms the deepest parts of me, parts I thought were cold and dead forever. My jeans still hang midthigh but I'm too impatient to stop, my lips exploring her soft skin before drawing one sweet nipple into my mouth.

She whimpers and raises her hips, begging for the very thing I crave.

I pull the condom from my back pocket but she stops me before opening it, her fingers wrapping around my wrist.

"No condom. I'm on the pill and I want just you, Cade. I need to feel all of you."

I throw the unopened packet behind me, making her laugh. I personally find nothing funny about how hard my dick is right now. My mouth descends, taking hers again as I come over top, my cock poising at her entrance.

I rise up enough to look down at her. "You ready, baby?"

"Yes," she whispers strongly, but I don't miss the anxiousness in her gaze.

My lips press to the corner of one eye. "Don't be scared, Red. I have you."

Slowly, I slide the tip of my cock into her and groan as her tight, hot pussy sucks me like a tight vice. My face drops into her neck, eyes closing as I try to find my control.

"Cade?" The fear in her voice has me completely stilling.

I lift my head to find her eyes squeezed shut, face pinched in agony. Her breathing is heavy, and I realize I'm close to losing her.

"Look at me, Red."

Her eyes snap open at the command, gaze as haunted as my soul.

"Jesus, do you want me to stop?"

Panic flashes across her face. "No, don't. I need you. Just…help me, please, I'm scared."

Her tormented plea guts me from the inside out.

Grinding my teeth, I roll to my back and bring her to straddle me. It has my cock seating even deeper inside her. She gasps at the unexpected act but I notice the panic fading a little further away. I sit up, bringing my face an inch from hers.

"This is your show, Red. We go as fast as you want or as slow as you want. If you want to stop, we stop. Okay?"

Her bottom lip trembles, breath hitching before she drops her forehead on mine, a quiet sob falling past her lips. "I'm so sorry, I'm ruining this."

"You're not ruining anything, baby. I've got you, I promise."

She nods against me, her tears dripping down my face.

I cup the side of her neck, my thumb grazing her cheek. "Who's inside you?"

"You," she whispers.

"Say my name."

"Cade."

My hand moves down to her shoulder, lips following until I cup the weight of her breast. Moaning, she rocks her hips, grinding down on me.

"And who does this body belong to?" I ask, pressing a kiss to the corner of her mouth.

"Me."

I smirk against her skin. "Good answer. Let me rephrase that question. Who is the only one allowed to touch you?" I pinch and roll her stiff nipple between my fingers.

"You," she gasps, pleasure lighting up her face.

"That's right, baby. Only me."

"Yes." She rocks faster, every glide of her hips submerging me further in fiery pleasure.

I fight to keep still, letting her set the pace.

"That's it, Red. Let it feel good, baby."

"Keep talking to me," she whispers. "I like hearing your voice while you're inside of me."

My hand hooks the back of her neck, pulling her forehead to mine. "Do you know how many times I've thought about this, Faith? How many times in the past two years I ached to feel your body around mine again?"

"Me too," she confesses. "I thought about it all the time. It was the best night of my life."

"Mine too, baby. Every time I stroked my cock I thought about you, wished it was your body."

She whimpers, half with pleasure, the other half emotion. "I missed you so much, thinking about that week with you was the only thing that helped me get through the nightmares."

Guilt threatens to choke me, but before it can drag me down she seals her mouth to mine and begins moving with a desperation that matches my own.

Unable to hold back, I carefully meet her thrust for thrust. Her head falls back, face awash with pleasure.

"Good, Faith?" I ask, needing reassurance.

"God yes, don't stop, it feels incredible."

Our bodies move in sync, learning each other again, remembering that night so long ago. The one night that changed my entire life.

I drop a hand between us, my flinger dipping between her wet folds where we are joined, knuckle stroking her clit. The touch was all she needed to send her over the edge.

Her cries of pleasure fill the night air around us, igniting the blood in my veins. I watch her face through it all, feeling something I've never felt before as I watch her know pleasure again. It isn't until I feel the last of her tremors that I let myself go.

After it's over, she wraps her arms around my neck, burying her face in my shoulder. I feel her tears just before I feel her body tremble against me.

Even though I expected it, it still rips through my chest like a cruel blade. I reach for the blanket next to us, covering her body before lying down with her in my arms, holding her as she releases what she needs to.

If I could go back and gut those motherfuckers all over again, I would.

Eventually her tears subside and she tilts her face up to mine, pressing her wet lips to my jaw. "I love you, Cade Walker. You heal my soul in so many ways."

"I wish your soul didn't need healing," I tell her honestly.

"It doesn't anymore, thanks to you."

I turn her to her back, my face hanging inches from hers. "You trust me, right? You know I won't let anything happen to you like that again."

"Yes. No other man makes me feel safer than you, not even my father or Papa."

I'd be lying if I said that didn't make me feel pretty fucking awesome. I may not be good at a lot of things but protecting her is something no one could out best me at.

"Speaking of my father…" She trails off, watching me carefully. "I've been thinking about Christopher's birthday dinner and who to invite. Of course I plan to invite our friends, but…obviously, I want my family there, too."

I tense, knowing where she's going with this, and feel like a complete dick when she notices the reaction, her expression turning sad.

"I want you to meet my father, Cade, and he wants to meet you, too. He's a good man, you'll see."

The thought of being in the same room with a man who preaches the very thing I loathe has my gut burning in fury.

"Can't you just give him a chance? For me, please?"

Well fuck. How am I supposed to say no when she asks me like that? I gaze into her hopeful eyes and blow out a resigned breath. "Yeah, baby. I'll meet him."

"Thank you. I promise you will like him."

I wouldn't be so sure about that…

"And you'll really like my papa, he's a lot like the three of you guys. He says the f-word a lot." She expels one of her cute little giggles.

"I'm sure we'll get along fine."

Her fingers fan my jaw, amusement fading. "Thank you for giving my father a chance."

"I'll give you anything you ask for, Red, if I'm capable of it."

"I want you," she tells me.

"You have me, baby. You have since the moment I found you in that field."

She tugs me down, sealing my mouth over hers once again. It's how we remain for the rest of the night. With her in my arms where she will always belong.

CHAPTER 31

Faith

Ruthie and I are in the kitchen getting ready to decorate Christopher's birthday cake for Saturday when Cade comes barging in the door a lot earlier than usual.

My heart skips a beat at the first glance of him, awareness seeping into every part of my body. It will never get old. After our night at the beach, the night I took back control of every aspect of my life, things have been absolutely perfect.

However, I fear that is about to change when I notice Cade does not look happy, even more unhappy than usual.

"Hey, Big Guy," Ruthie greets him, licking the spoon that's covered with chocolate cake mixture.

"Hey, kid," he replies before looking at me. "Where's Christopher?"

"Isn't he with you?"

He shakes his head. "He didn't show up at the gym and he's not answering his cell phone."

Fear grips my chest, every awful image plaguing me at what could have happened to him. Before I can go into complete panic mode, the front door flies open and Christopher storms in looking furious. He slams the door so hard I jump.

"Where the hell have you been?" Cade bellows out the question.

"Out," he replies, throwing his backpack across the living room.

The answer doesn't suffice for Cade. "What do you mean 'out?' You're supposed to be at the gym."

"Yeah, well, something came up."

"Then you call me, damn it, or at least pick up your phone. That's the reason we bought it for you."

"Fine, here!" Christopher reaches in his pocket and throws the phone at him.

I gape at his attitude, having no idea who this boy is in front of me right now.

"And you can take back the stupid outfit you bought me for the dance too," he says, his attention directed at me. "I'm not going anymore."

He heads for the stairs but I intercept him, grabbing his arm. "What do you mean you aren't going? Why not?"

"Because Alissa's mom isn't letting her go with me. She's making her go with that asshole Ryan."

"What?" I gasp, praying I misheard him. "But why?"

"What do you mean, why? Because it's me, Faith!"

Despite his anger, pain bleeds through every word. He's heart broken, I can see it all over his face.

"I told you this would happen, but you don't ever fucking listen to me!"

"Hey!" Cade bellows, pushing forward. "Watch the way you to talk to her."

"Whatever, I'm out of here." He bolts down the stairs, his door slamming seconds later.

I remain rooted to my spot, staring at the empty space before me and try to process what just happened. What he just said.

I startle when Cade touches my shoulder. Turning, I find him holding an upset Ruthie.

"Are you okay to stay here with her if I leave?" I ask.

His gaze searches mine, sensing where my thoughts are. "Yeah, we're good. Just don't make me have to come bail you out of jail because you were pulling hair, Red."

"No hair pulling, I promise."

Without another word, I grab my purse and flee the house. My turbulent emotions turn to anger on my drive over to Alissa's house. I desperately want Christopher to be wrong and find out it was just all a misunderstanding but judging by how upset he was, I don't think it is.

It takes me only minutes to arrive. I park on the street in front of the two-story home that my family was invited to for dinner when we first moved here. Walking up the front steps, I take a deep breath before knocking on the door.

Alissa's mother answers quickly, surprise flashing on her face. "Faith, hi," she greets anxiously, standing between the small open space so I can't see in.

"Hi, Helen, do you have a minute?"

She cuts a glance behind her, looking more nervous every second. "Sure, a quick one."

"Great, then I'll cut right to the chase. Christopher just came home really upset, he says you're not allowing Alissa to go to the dance with him and that you are making her go with Ryan. I'm hoping you're going to tell me he is mistaken."

Her face pinches in distaste, immediately telling me what I already suspected.

"Look, Faith, I think it's really noble that you have taken in those kids."

My blood starts to heat at the way she says 'those kids.'

"But he is not someone I want my daughter to associate with."

"Why not? Alissa would be very lucky to go with him."

"I know his father and—"

"He is nothing like his father," I counter.

"I would say he is, considering what he did to Ryan Hunter's face."

My teeth grind. "Ryan is the one who instigated that, not Christopher."

"That's what I keep telling her but she refuses to listen." Alissa's upset voice carries out of the house, breaking into the conversation. She appears behind Helen, her eyes red and swollen from crying.

"Alissa, go upstairs now," her mother orders. "We will talk about this later."

"No. I want to stay here and make sure you hear Faith out."

"It won't make a difference!" she spits angrily.

"Why?" I ask. "I'm telling you he's a good kid, he's just had a terrible start to life. You have no idea how excited he was to go to this dance with her. Can't you just give him a chance to prove you wrong?"

"I know all there is to know about those kids, Faith. Everyone does and they are nothing but trouble. Just look at what that little girl did to poor Henry Winkleman's nose."

"Henry is an asshole," I snap, losing my temper. "He has been bullying her since she moved here. She finally stood up for herself, and I'm not going to let you or anyone else judge her for that."

"That does not make it right for her to break his nose. Those kids are violent and out of control. I hope for their sake you make them come to church once it opens because they need it."

"They need it?" I screech, barely withholding a bitter laugh. "Lady, if anyone needs God it's you." I step closer, making her retreat. "You think because you go to church every Sunday that makes you a good Christian? Well, it doesn't. You have to practice what you preach and clearly you don't, or else you wouldn't keep your daughter from a really good boy who will treat her a hell of a lot better than Ryan Hunter."

She turns her nose up at me. "Well, I guess we will have to agree to disagree. We have lived here longer than you, Faith, and his drunk of a father—"

"For the last time, Christopher is nothing like that man. I am also happy to say your daughter is nothing like you—a stuck-up self-righteous bitch."

She rears back, shocked by the verbal lashing, but I'm too angry to care. I decide now is the time to leave or Cade really will end up having to bail me out of jail.

Shaking my head, I head down the stairs, two at a time. Before I can reach my car, Alissa calls my name, barreling out of the house after me.

Tears rush down her face before she throws her arms around me. "I'm so sorry she's acting like this, Faith. Things have not been great at my house lately."

I hug her back, my heart breaking for both her and Christopher. "Don't be, it's not your fault. I'm sorry she's making you go with Ryan."

"I'm not going with him," she tells me, wiping her wet cheeks. "If she doesn't let me go with Christopher then I'm not going at all. Can you," she pauses, visibly swallowing, "can you tell him how sorry I am and that I really wanted to go with him. I like him a lot, Faith."

I nod. "He likes you a lot too."

The admission only has her crying harder. I give her one last hug before she's ordered into the house by her mother.

By the time I make it back home, I'm a bundle of emotions. I walk in the door and find Ruthie and Cade in the living room. She sits on his lap, a box of pizza in front of them as they watch TV.

He sets her down next to him and stands. "Hey, Red."

"Hey." I offer him a soft smile but it's as sad as I feel.

He follows me into the kitchen, grasping my chin between his fingers. "No cat fight?"

"No, but I definitely used some very powerful language on her."

He smirks, finding the statement amusing.

"She's a real b-i-t-c-h," I spell out. "The woman wouldn't listen to reason and Alissa is just as heartbroken as Christopher is. You wouldn't believe the things she was saying about the kids, all because of who their father is."

I shake my head, feeling angry all over again.

"Come here." He pulls me into his strong arms, giving me comfort.

"Has he come up at all?" I ask, lifting my face to his.

"No."

"Do you still have his phone?"

"Yeah."

I step back and hold out my hand. "Can I have it? I'm going to go talk to him. Maybe Alissa will call."

"No way. He isn't getting it back for a few days."

"Why?"

"Because the little shit threw it at me, and he never picked up when I called him so he can be without it for a few days."

"Come on. Isn't that a little harsh? He was upset."

"So what, just because he gets upset doesn't mean he can throw fits and ignore phone calls. How was I to know something bad didn't happen to him?"

I nod. "You're right, and I will talk to him about that. Now give me the phone."

He stares down at my extended hand, making no move to comply. "I'm not giving it back, Red."

"Walker," I try to say his name in warning but what I really want to do is kiss his sexy, stubborn face.

"Red," he mocks in the same tone.

Giggling, I grab his shirt and try pulling him down for a kiss but he doesn't budge. After flashing me that sexy smirk, he pulls me against him and lays one heck of a kiss on me. By the time he pulls back I'm breathless. Hunger rages in his eyes, a promise for what tonight will hold when we close our bedroom door.

"We'll pick this up later," I tell him, heading for the stairs before my hormones get the best of me. Just as I reach the first step, I turn back, flashing him a smile. "Oh and thanks for giving me the phone back." I lift the phone I managed to sneak from his pocket during that toe-curling kiss.

Shock registers on his face before his eyes narrow in disapproval. "Your ass is mine tonight, Red."

I blow him a kiss then bolt down the stairs before he can snag it back. My amusement fades though when I reach Christopher's closed bedroom door.

Lifting my hand, I lightly knock.

"Come in."

I open it and find him lying on his bed, staring up at the ceiling. "Hey."

"Hey."

He doesn't make eye contact but he doesn't seem as angry either. I take that as a good sign and walk further inside, sitting at the edge of his bed. "I'm sorry Alissa's mother is being so awful."

He shrugs. "It's not your fault. Besides, it's for the best, Alissa's better off without me."

"No, she isn't," I reply sternly. "Don't let that woman make you feel like you are not good enough, Christopher, she is wrong. I know it and so does Alissa."

He finally looks over at me, the torment in his eyes making my heart pinch in my chest. "I'll never get away from him. Everyone will always see me as his son. It won't stop until I leave this place and go somewhere no one knows me."

The thought of him leaving has dread forming in the pit of my stomach. "Don't leave. Once everyone gets a chance to know the real you, Christopher, they'll see you are nothing like him, and if they don't, well…screw them. You didn't need them before and you don't need them now."

He watches me, his expression softening. "How do you do it? After everything that's happened to you. How can you not be bitter or angry? How do you just forgive people so easily all the time?"

The question catches me off guard and it takes me a moment to answer. "Do you know who Mother Theresa is?"

His brows bunch in confusion. "Wasn't she like a nun or something?"

I nod. "She was more than that though. She was a woman who dedicated her life to helping the sick and feeding the poor. She spent her entire life trying to make the world a better place. But not everyone thought her intentions were good. When I was younger, my grandmother read me a script by her that went like this:

"People are often unreasonable and self-centered. Forgive them anyway.
If you are kind, people may accuse you of ulterior motives. Be kind anyway.
If you are honest, people may cheat you. Be honest anyway.
If you find happiness, people may be jealous. Be happy anyway.
The good you do today may be forgotten tomorrow. Do good anyway.
Give the world the best you have and it may never be enough. Give your best anyway. For you see, in the end, it is between you and God. It was never between you and them anyway."

The words are as powerful to me now as they were all those years ago. I can tell Christopher is also impacted by them. His expression is somber as he soaks in the words.

"After Iraq happened, it was my faith in God and the support of my family that helped me begin to heal," I tell him. "Every morning I would begin my day by saying that quote. When I moved here it was for a fresh start, not just for me but for my entire family. I'd hoped that starting over somewhere new would help me lay to rest the remainder of my pain."

"Has it worked?" he asks.

I smile down at him. "Yeah, I've finally healed but not because I started over somewhere fresh. It's because of the people I found here. It's because of Cade and you and Ruthie… All three of you have healed my soul more than anything or anyone ever could have. Which is why I ask you not to leave me, because I need you, Christopher, just as much as you need me."

His gaze shifts to the ceiling but not before I see the emotion in his eyes. "I won't leave you."

"Good." I reach for his hand, giving it a squeeze. "For the record, Alissa is heartbroken."

His gaze snaps back to mine. "How do you know?"

"I went to her house and spoke to her mother."

The admission surprises him. "And you saw Alissa?"

"Yes. She was crying and fighting with Helen. She's very heartbroken and she told me to tell you how sorry she was that her mother is doing this. She said she likes you a lot."

His jaw locks, teeth grinding. "Yeah, well now that jerk Ryan is going to get to take her."

"No, he's not. She said if her mother doesn't let her go with you then she isn't going at all."

Relief flickers in his eyes, a heavy breath escaping him.

"Look, the best advice I can give you is this, if you like her as much as I think you do, then be patient and wait for her. Don't give up, Christopher. This is her mother, not her. I have faith that this will all work out in the end. No pun intended," I add with a smile.

"Let's hope you're right because she's the best thing that's ever happened to me," he pauses, looking over at me. "Besides you."

Warmth invades my chest, the admission meaning so much more than he can know.

"Here." I toss him back his phone. "Take this back in case she tries texting or calling. Now, you need to go apologize to Cade for throwing it at him and not answering his phone call."

He remains silent, guilt reflecting in his eyes.

"You can't do that again, Christopher. Cade was worried about you. I know things with your father and Spike have been quiet for weeks, and nothing will probably ever come of it, but we need to know you're always safe."

"I understand. I'm sorry, it won't happen again."

"Good. Now come on, let's go eat. Cade ordered pizza."

He climbs out of bed, following me from the room. Before we head upstairs though, he grabs my arm. "Hold up a sec."

I turn back, watching him shift from foot to foot nervously.

"I've been thinking a lot, and I decided that if you still want me to sing with you, I will."

Shock flares inside of me before elation takes over. "Really?"

He nods.

"What changed your mind?"

He shrugs. "It's the least I can do after everything you've done for me."

Just like that, my excitement deflates. "Oh, Christopher, you don't owe me anything. I don't want you to do it just for me. I want you to do it for yourself."

"I'm doing it for me too. I'm uncomfortable in front of people, especially since my father made sure I knew what a pussy I was for wanting to play music. It's something I want to take back, but I'm not singing any churchy stuff," he quickly adds. "I mean no disrespect, but that just isn't my genre."

"The thought never even crossed my mind. I actually have the perfect song picked out, and I think you will like it, especially when we make it our own."

He nods. "Okay then."

I return the gesture with a smile. "Okay."

He slings his arm around my shoulder as we head up the stairs. My heart sings with the newfound place we have found ourselves in. Walking into the living room, we find Cade and Ruthie on the couch, eating their pizza.

I bite back a smile at the glare Cade shoots me, his heated gaze promising retribution. I can't deny the rush of excitement that brings me.

"I'm sorry for not answering your call," Christopher tells him, taking a seat on the couch. "And I'm sorry for throwing the phone at you. It won't happen again."

Ruthie leaves Cade's lap to sit on Christopher's, her arms wrapping around his neck as she kisses his cheek. "Don't be sad, Twistiphwor, it's her woss."

"Thanks, Ruthie."

Cade, on the other hand, isn't ready to forget the whole thing. "If you don't answer your phone again, when we call, you won't have a phone at all."

Christopher tenses at the authority in his voice but holds back any attitude and nods.

"And next time, if you aren't going to be somewhere you are supposed to, you call."

"Hey, Walker," I chime in, wanting to avoid any further arguing. "It's all good. He said he was sorry and it won't happen again." Smiling, I tap his cheek and move to sit next to him but he ends up pulling me down on his lap, his fingers digging into my hips in warning.

It has a delicious shiver sliding down my spine. Reaching over, I take a drink of his coke, needing to cool down.

Christopher reaches for a slice of his own. "Thank god you ordered one with meat."

I barely refrain from rolling my eyes.

"Well, me and Faif wuv our veggie one, and we awe healfier fwor it," Ruthie says, nodding over at me.

"That's right."

Cade grunts.

"Don't listen to them, Ruthie. They are just jealous because they do not have the willpower that we do."

"I don't think so, Red," he counters. "I can stop anytime. I just don't want to."

I shift on his lap to face him. "Is that so?"

"Yep."

"Prove it then," I challenge. "If that's the case then let's see if you and Christopher can go one week without eating meat after today."

"Please, I've been gone on missions for months at a time. A week is nothing."

"Maybe, but you were never around it, so it never tempted you."

"I'll do it," Christopher adds. "I can handle a week."

"I guess we'll see."

"Yeah we will," Cade says, determination in his voice.

I hold back a smile, secretly thinking of my reward. There is no way I won't win this bet.

CHAPTER 32

Cade

That night, I head upstairs to take a shower and overhear Faith putting Ruthie to bed.

"Faif, can I ask you somefing?"

"Of course, you can ask me anything."

"Why doesn't Tade bewieve in God?"

I come to a hard stop just outside her bedroom door, remaining out of sight.

There's a long pause before Faith answers. "Well," she starts, "I don't really know all the details why. It's something Cade doesn't like to talk about, but it's important we respect everyone's beliefs even if it's not something we agree with."

"But what about heaven?" she asks.

"What about it?"

"When we die we go to heaven, but if Tade doesn't bewieve in God what happens to him? Does he still get to go to heaven?"

Pain infiltrates my chest, the question reminding me of someone else from my past.

"Yes, he will go to heaven," Faith says without hesitation.

"How?"

"Because even though Cade doesn't believe in God, God believes in him."

Her nonsense has a storm of turbulent emotions blazing through me. I don't know whether I want to rage or kiss the shit out of her.

"Sometimes, Ruthie, things happen in our lives that hurt us so much it can change the way we look at things. I believe you have to do something very horrible to not go to heaven. You have to be a bad person, and we both know Cade is not a bad person. He is one of the very best."

"Well dat's good to know. I was vewy worwied about dat. My heawt hwurt to even tink of him not getting to be wif God."

I hate knowing she was worried about this, that she was worried about me. This is the exact fucking reason why I don't want her being brought into this shit.

"Oh, Ruthie, you can talk to me anytime you feel afraid about something, but God is not someone you should ever fear. He loves us more than we are capable of even understanding. Like I said, you have to be a very awful person to not go to heaven. So no more worrying about that, okay?"

"Otay, I won't."

"Good. Good night, sweet girl, sleep well."

"Night, Faif."

I step back, remaining out of sight when I hear her walk toward the door. As soon as she closes it, I'm on her. She lets out a startled gasp that I inhale when I claim her mouth with my own. The sweet taste of her explodes on my tongue, rushing through my veins like a drug. My drug of choice.

Slipping my hands under her short, classy dress, I cup her perfect lace-covered ass before hoisting her up. Her legs wrap around my waist as I stumble to the bedroom, kicking the door shut before pinning her against it.

Her eyes open, need colliding with my own. "Were you just eavesdropping, Walker?" she asks, a sassy note to her breathless voice.

Instead of answering that question, I carry her into the bathroom.

"What are you doing?" she asks.

"I was on my way to have a shower and now you are, too." I place her on her feet in front of me then turn on the water, making it hot enough that steam clouds the room.

A sassy smile lifts her lips, her hands resting on her hips. "Is this about the phone?"

I reach behind my shoulders, pulling off my shirt. Her amusement fades, eyes darkening as they drift down my body. I move behind her, pulling her back against my front.

She moans at the feel of my cock pressing her backside.

My fingers slip beneath the straps of her dress, sliding them down her shoulders until it pools at her feet. It leaves her in only a pair of white, lace panties. I cup the weight of her perfect tits, rolling her tight, soft nipples between my thumb and forefinger.

Her head drops back on my chest, lolling to the side as I trail my lips down her throat.

"Yeah, baby, this is about the phone, it's also about your sassy mouth that taunts me all day long." I nip her ear sharply, drawing another moan from her.

"Then by all means, punish away."

"Trust me, I intend to." Grabbing the side of her panties, I tear them from her body in one swift pull.

"I really like it when you do that," she confesses breathlessly.

I grin at her honesty then shed my pants quickly, leaving them on the floor next to her dress before hauling her into the shower and under the hot spray.

She turns to face me, stepping in closer, her tongue darting out to flick one of my nipple rings. Pleasure pounds through my blood, my cock swelling as I fight to not unleash on her like I want to. I've buried myself in her every night since the beach, but I've been letting her take the lead and set the pace.

"Have I ever told you how much I like these things, Walker?" she asks softly. "They are sexy, just like you." Grazing the metal with her teeth, she tugs it hard enough, sending a bolt of electricity straight to my cock.

"Red," I growl. "Be careful, I only have so much restraint."

She peers up at me, heavy drops of water framing her dark lashes. "Then release it, Cade. I'm ready. There is no fear. Not with you. Let me have all of you."

The permission might be the sweetest words that have ever fallen past her lips. "Are you sure?" I ask. "Really think about what you're saying right now, Faith."

I don't want to fuck anything up after all the progress we have made. I'd die before I ever hurt her like that.

"I'm sure. I want you. All of you."

My hand grips her long wet hair, pulling her head back as I peer down into her pretty face. I watch for any sign of hesitation but find none, only need.

My mouth descends, tongue colliding with hers in the same way I plan to do to her body. Afterward, I spin her around, bringing her back to my front. "Brace your hands flat against the wall in front of you."

She eagerly complies.

Grasping her hips, I kick her feet wider apart. "Move your hands a little lower, baby."

She follows the order, grabbing on to the knobs that are sticking out of the wall, bringing her ass higher for my position.

"Good girl, now hold on." Bending my knees at just the right angle, I thrust deep into paradise.

Her cry of pleasure tears through the bathroom, echoing off the walls.

I still, buried right to the hilt. "You good, Red?"

"Yes, don't stop."

Groaning, I impale her with a ferocity I've never used on anyone. Fucking her harder than I have ever fucked another. The sound of her pleasure fuels me, making me feel like a fucking animal as she meets me pound for pound.

Hot water pours down on us, the humid air billowing around the enclosed space.

Leaning back, I watch my cock disappear, greedily filling every inch of her. "Damn, Red. You should see how pretty you look with my cock fucking your pussy."

The words have a fiery whimper leaving her.

Reaching above us, I grab the removable showerhead before bringing it down in front of her and placing it against her pussy.

"Oh god!"

"You like that, baby?"

"Yes." She whimpers. "It feels incredible, I can't hold off."

I tighten my other hand on her hip and quicken my thrusts. "Then don't, Red. Let go and bring me with you."

As soon as the words leave my mouth, her pussy locks down on me, sucking me greedily into its hot depths. I groan as my cock explodes, pulsing violently as I fuck us both through our orgasms.

Once I've taken everything she has to give me, I reattach the showerhead and pull out, practically toppling over. I brace my hand on the wall, fighting to get my bearings as the warm water pours over us once again.

"You okay, Red?" I ask, pressing a kiss to her shoulder. I'll never forgive myself if she's not.

"I'm scared if I move I will drop to the ground and never get up."

Smirking, I take that as a good sign then pull her to stand, keeping her close against me.

"Don't let me go," she mumbles.

"Never," I whisper in her ear, that one word meaning more than she knows.

After washing her body, I shut off the water and wrap a towel around me then her before lifting her into my arms. She rests her head on my shoulder, a contented sigh leaving her as I walk back into the bedroom.

Turning down the covers, I lay her on the soft mattress and notice her shiver, goose bumps breaking out across her porcelain skin.

"Do you want me to get you some clothes?"

"No. I want you to come warm me up."

I crawl in next to her, pulling her into my arms. She rolls onto her stomach, making a fist on my chest before propping her chin on it.

A lazy smile graces her pretty face as she peers back at me. "That was fun, Walker, we should do it again sometime."

Fun is the biggest fucking understatement of the century.

"Give me a few minutes, baby, and I'll gladly do it again."

She chuckles, dropping a kiss to my chest, right over my heart before bringing her eyes to mine. "So, I've been thinking…"

I tense when she trails off, worried the direction this conversation is about to take. "About?"

"Us," she whispers. "Since you're here all the time, maybe…maybe you should bring all your stuff over permanently."

I wait for panic to set in but it never comes. It's obvious it's the reaction she was expecting as well. My fingers sift through her wet hair, brushing it out of her face. "Yeah, maybe I should."

The most beautiful smile stretches across her face before she leans up, brushing a kiss on my lips. "I love you, Cade Walker."

I stare into her sincere eyes and desperately want to respond, but the thing is, it would be a lie. Because I don't think there is a word strong enough to describe just what I feel for her. So instead of responding with words, I decide to show her.

Flipping her over onto her back, I settle between her legs and slide into her slowly, stilling when I feel how swollen she is. "Too soon?"

She wraps her arms around my neck, lifting her hips. "No, it's perfect. You're perfect."

I'm far from it but she is the very definition.

This time, I take her slow and deep. Not at all the way I just had her. I make sure she knows how beautiful she is, my lips grazing her ear as I whisper all the words she deserves to hear.

Afterward, I hold her close as she drifts off to sleep and know there is no place on earth that is better than where I am now. No matter how much I don't deserve it—don't deserve her—I will never let her go.

This is my sense of heaven.

CHAPTER 33

Cade

Ruthie trails behind me as I walk in the front door of the house, and we find Christopher on the couch, quickly shoving something behind his back.

"Oh, it's you," he says, letting out a relieved breath as he pulls a fast food bag out from behind him. "I thought you were Faith."

Ruthie gasps. "What awe you doin'? It hasn't been a week yet."

Christopher glares at her. "I don't care, I can't do it anymore. I thought I was going to pass out at school today from starvation. I ate what she made me and it did nothing to fill me up."

I've been feeling the same way. It's been harder on me than I thought it would. Red was right, being around it makes it harder.

"Why don't you just tell her then?" I ask.

"Yeah, right, I'll never hear the end of it. She'll rub it in my face every chance she gets." He reaches into the bag and pulls out a couple of burgers, temptingly offering me one of them.

"Don't do it, Big Guy," Ruthie says, clearly seeing the conflicting battle on my face.

My mouth waters, stomach clenching in hunger. Fuck it! I take it from him then sit at the other end of the sofa and waste no time digging in.

We both groan at our first bites.

Ruthie lets out a disappointed sigh and shakes her head, making me feel like an asshole.

Christopher points his finger at her. "You better not rat us out."

"I won't have to, secwets always have a way of toming out," she says, taking the spot between us.

I grunt, knowing Faith filled her head with that shit.

"The only way she will find out is if—" Christopher stops midsentence when we hear a car door being shut in the distance. His eyes shoot to me, his panic reflecting mine. "I thought she wasn't supposed to be home for another hour?"

So did I.

We move quickly, shoving the empty wrappers out of sight. I hear her faint footsteps climb the stairs and realize I still have my burger in hand. Before I can think better of it, I pull the collar of Ruthie's top open and throw it down her shirt.

She squeals in laughter but I cup a hand over her mouth and pull her on my lap just as Red walks in.

"Hey, guys," she greets us in a rush. "I forgot a letter that I need to mail off. I'm just grabbing it then I'm on my way to the store. Do you guys need anything?" She halts abruptly when she sees us on the sofa. "Everything okay?"

I release my hand from around Ruthie's mouth, realizing how bad that looks. "Yeah."

Her gaze shifts over all three of us, eyes narrowing suspiciously. "What's that smell?"

"What smell?" Christopher asks, his voice practically squeaking.

"It smells like fast food. Like…meat."

Ruthie shakes with silent laughter. My arms hug her in warning but all it does is make her giggle out loud.

Faith cocks a hip and holds out her hand. "All right, let's see it, you guys. Where are you hiding it?"

Christopher looks over at me, waiting for me to take the reins.

"Just settle down, Red, we aren't hiding anything."

"Really?" She walks over and begins her search, lifting pillows and cushions.

My gaze drops to her delectable ass that is clad in a pair of tight jean shorts as she bends down and reaches under Christopher's cushion, pulling out the now-empty fast food bag.

"I had fries," he blurts out quickly…too quickly.

She quirks a brow. "And you felt the need to hide that under the cushion?"

He finally gives up the farce. "Come on, Faith, give me a break, I almost died at school today. I just can't do it. This no meat thing is going to screw with my growth."

"You didn't have to do it. You both are the ones who said you could." She pauses and looks over at me now, her gaze accusatory. "Where's yours?"

I don't have to answer because Ruthie's laughter says it all.

"You have got to be kidding me, Cade." She pries my arms away and lifts up her shirt, letting the half eaten burger fall to the floor. Christopher laughs at the mustard and ketchup that's smeared all over his sister's stomach.

Shit!

Faith shakes her head. "I cannot believe you guys." She picks up a giggling Ruthie and carries her into the kitchen.

Christopher and I share a chuckle as I swipe the burger off the floor and head into the kitchen.

Red has the removable nozzle pulled from the sink, using it to wash Ruthie.

"I'll clean her up," I say, feeling bad that she's upset.

"No, I'll do it," she snaps, turning on me. "I can't believe you would do this. What were you thinking?" She points at me, forgetting about the spraying nozzle, and soaks the shit out of my shirt and face.

Gasping, she drops the hose, realizing her mistake. Christopher walks in to see what the commotion is about and stops short when he sees my wet state. A noise draws my attention back to Faith, where I find her hand cupped over her mouth, muffling her laughter.

The moment I push forward, she grabs Ruthie, holding her out in front of her. "I'm so sorry, it was an accident, I swear."

I rip the kid from her arms and she takes off in the split second it takes me to hand Ruthie off to Christopher. It doesn't take me long to catch her, my arms hugging her waist as I lift her off her feet.

She kicks and fights against me as I drag her back into the kitchen. "Seriously, it was an accident, I didn't mean to."

I ignore the apology, pinning her between me and the sink.

The kids' watch with amusement as I turn the water on and pick up the small black nozzle.

"Cade, I'm serious. Don't you even think about it. I swear, I will…" Her words trail off on a gasp as I soak her face, hair, and the front of her shirt. "Oh my god, stop! Please!"

Not until she is drenched do I drop the nozzle and step back.

She remains leaned over the sink for a good long minute before reaching for the dishtowel, patting her face.

"Sorry, it was an accident," I mock, feeling amused.

She turns to me, eyes narrowed and reaches for the dish soap next to her.

"Uh-oh, you'we in twouble now, Big Guy."

Faith starts forward, a sassy smirk on her perfect mouth.

"Don't even think about it, Red. You're not going to like the consequences."

She doesn't heed the warning and shoots the fucking soap all over me.

"Oh shit!" Christopher curses, unable to contain his laughter.

The second she finishes, she drops the bottle and runs. I grab her wrist, but she slips out of my wet grip, feet pounding as she heads for the stairs. I take off after her, swiping the chocolate syrup off the counter in the process.

A scream leaves her when she sees me right on her heels, taking the stairs two at a time. She runs into her room, attempting to slam the door on me but isn't fast enough.

She tries escaping to the bathroom but I tackle her from behind, sending us both to the bed. I roll her thrashing body beneath me as she laughs hysterically then I douse her in the chocolate syrup, covering her chest and stomach.

"Okay! Okay! I plead the fifth," she cries.

Growling, I throw the bottle behind me then take her mouth in a fiery kiss, the heated contact shooting straight to my cock. Moaning, she lifts her hips, grinding against my anatomy that begs for any part of her.

"Estuse me, but dere is a vewy big mess in de titchen, and I am getting hungwy."

Reluctantly, I pull my mouth from Red's and look over at Ruthie who stands right next to the bed. I really do love the kid but she has the worst fucking timing.

"Where's your brother?" I ask, annoyed he wouldn't keep her with him.

"He's on de phone," she explains, having no idea how badly she is cramping my style right now.

"We're coming right now," Faith tells her.

Actually, we are not, but I sure fucking wish we were.

"Truce, Walker?" Faith asks, offering me her hand.

The chocolate resting on the swells of her breasts has my mouth watering. Somehow, I find my restraint, and take her hand, pulling her to her feet with me.

Christopher enters the room then, looking as white as ghost. "You're never going to believe this."

"What is it?" Faith asks, walking over to him.

"That was Alissa on the phone. Thanks to her dad, she's allowed to go to the dance with me tomorrow night."

"Oh my gosh, Christopher, that's so great!" Her enthusiasm fades when she realizes he isn't as excited as her. "What's the matter, isn't this what you wanted?"

"It is, but she's really upset. Turns out her mom and Ryan's dad are having an affair."

Faith gasps, her eyes practically bugging out of her head. "No way!"

He nods, his expression grim. "I guess that's why her mom was on Ryan's side. Her parents are separating and she's really hurting right now."

"Poor Alissa. I can only imagine."

"She asked if I would meet her. Can I?"

"Yes, of course. Do you need a ride?"

"No. I'm going to take my skateboard and meet her at the mall."

"How about money? Do you need some?"

"No. Cade paid me last week," he mumbles, getting uncomfortable, like always, at the offer.

"Okay, well not too late and text me when you're on your way home or if you want us to pick you up."

"I will. See ya." He walks out of the room, the front door closing seconds later with his departure.

Faith's eyes shift to me, sparking in anger. "That woman is something else," she seethes. "Tell me my kids need to go to church when she's out committing adultery. Ha! Let me tell you something else," she spits, pointing her finger at me as she walks her pissed off ass around the room, pulling the covers off the bed to wash them, "it's people like her that give Christians a bad name. Acting all high and mighty when she's spreading her legs…" Her words trail off when she remembers Ruthie is in the room.

The kid blinks at her patiently. "Go on."

I smirk, but Faith doesn't find it as amusing.

"No. I shouldn't have said that. We aren't going to waste another minute talking about someone who doesn't deserve our negative energy."

Leave it to Red to take the highroad.

"Since it's just the three of us, how about we go out for dinner, maybe get an ice cream after?"

"Yes!" she cheers.

"Great. Let me grab a quick shower while Cade cleans the kitchen," Faith adds, sending me a pointed look.

"Why do I have to clean it?"

"Because it's your fault it's a mess," she returns.

"The hell it is. You're the one who sprayed me first."

She walks up to me, jamming her finger into my chest. "And you are the one who lied to me about eating meat then proceeded to shove your half-eaten hamburger down a child's shirt."

She's got me there.

"Christopher is the one who bought them," I grumble, having no shame over ratting the kid out.

Smirking, she grabs my shirt in her small fist and pulls me down for a quick, hard kiss. "You are forgiven, after you clean the kitchen." Without another word, she walks her sassy ass into the bathroom.

I glance over at the kid and find her watching me with a smile.

"I told ya, secwets always have a way of toming out."

Grunting, I pick her up and put her on my shoulders. "Come on, you can help me clean up."

I will let Faith win this battle, but not the war. Tonight, she's mine.

CHAPTER 34

Cade

Music blares from the kitchen as I make my way down the stairs, an oldies song that is right up Faith's alley.

Walking in, I see her in the midst of prepping food for Christopher's birthday dinner, her hips swaying to the music as she sings along, her talent outshining the original artist.

I lean against the wall, admiring the way her hips shake. Feeling the weight of my stare, she turns around and flashes me that blinding smile before dancing over to me, continuing to sing along.

Once reaching me, she wraps her arms around my neck, her smile stretching when she feels how hard I am.

"Sing with me, Walker. I love Dusty Springfield. She has me 'Wishin' and Hopin'.'"

The blank expression I give her has her bursting into laughter.

I cut the beautiful sound off with a kiss, my hands moving to cup her bottom.

She moans against my mouth, spearing her fingers in my hair as she matches me stroke for stroke. I have no doubt that if I shoved my hand up her sundress and into her panties she would be wet and ready for me.

I start to wonder if I have enough time to make her come before the first guest arrives but as soon as the thought emerges, the front door flies open.

"I'm here, the party can start now."

I groan at the sound of Katelyn's cheerful voice.

She walks into the kitchen, carrying a large bowl with a present stacked on top. Her feet falter when she finds me and Red wrapped in each other's arms. "Oops, bad timing?" she asks, not looking the least bit apolegetic.

"Your timing is fine," Faith lies, stepping out of my arms. She takes the bowl from Katelyn, giving her a kiss on the cheek. "Thanks for bringing this."

"No problem. Where's the birthday boy?"

"He's walking Alissa here, they shouldn't be much longer."

"He walked to her house to pick her up?"

Faith nods, her wistful smile matching Katelyn's.

"That is so sweet. Every guy I've ever dated would never do something like that."

I'm unable to hold in my grunt as I take a seat at the table.

It earns me a glare from her. "Got something to say, Walker?"

"Yeah, maybe you should try dating a different kind of guy."

"You mean a real happy gem like yourself?" she asks, sweet innocence coating her tone.

Faith chooses that moment to intervene. "All right, you two, that's enough. Be nice to each other, especially tonight."

Despite what just happened, Katelyn and I have somewhat come to a silent agreement of sorts. We both have one thing in common, we care about Faith. She has lightened up on me since I have been staying here.

"I can't wait for you to meet Papa." Katelyn smirks, as if I should be concerned.

The grandfather I am not worried about. The father though is another story. I've been trying not to think about it, to do what I have to do for Faith but the thought of even being in the same room with him has dread gnawing at my gut. Hopefully for Faith's sake, I can put on a front long enough to last through the evening. For her, I will do my best.

"Tatewyn!" Ruthie comes running into the kitchen, excitedly launching herself at Katelyn.

She scoops her up, gathering her into her arms. "Hey there, beauty queen. Guess what Auntie Katelyn brought you?"

"What?"

She walks over to the counter where she left her purse and pulls out a bottle of pink sparkly nail polish.

"I wuv it, tank you." Ruthie beams, hugging her tight.

"You're welcome. I'll paint your nails tonight before bed."

The conversation comes to an end when the doorbell rings. Ruthie jumps out of her arms and runs to the door with Katelyn following close behind.

My attention shifts to Red where I find her struggling to reach something from the top cupboard, the top of her dress rising high enough for me to catch a small glimpse of pink, satin panties—ones that will be shredded later tonight.

She does a little hop, still trying to reach the damn thing when I finally climb to my feet and help her.

"What are you needing, Red?" I ask, crowding her back.

"The seasoning salt, please and thank you."

When I reach over her head, she turns around, slipping her hand beneath my shirt. She peeks up at me beneath her lashes as she dances her nails across my abs. The light sting shoots straight to my cock.

"Be careful, Faith. Or I'll be hauling your ass upstairs, company or not."

Her soft chuckle floats through the air, seconds before an entire crew comes walking in.

"Hey, Country, do you know this kid by chance?" Sawyer asks, carrying Ruthie upside down by one leg. The whole group is behind him. From Grace, Jaxson, Julia, Kayla, Cooper, and Katelyn, who holds a sleeping Annabelle.

Red sneaks around me and walks up to Sawyer, her hands on her hips as she pretends to assess Ruthie. "Hmm, I think I do know this little girl, she looks oddly familiar..."

"Ah what the hell, let's throw her in the garbage anyway," Sawyer says, making her squeal in laughter.

"Don't even tink about it. Or Tade will beat you up."

Evans lifts her higher, bringing her upside down face level with his. "Is that what this guy has been telling you? That he can beat me up? He's lying, kid, no one can beat me up."

I grunt as I walk over and rip her from him, turning her right side up. "Quit filling her head with lies."

His brow quirks. "Shall we prove it?"

"No one is proving anything," Faith says, suppressing a smile as she takes everyone's gifts from them.

Just then, Christopher and Alissa come walking in, holding hands.

"There's the handsome birthday boy," Katelyn announces, giving him a loud smacking kiss on the cheek. "Happy birthday."

"Thanks, Katelyn," he mumbles, the poor kid's face red with embarrassment.

Katelyn greets Alissa next, running her hands through her long wavy hair. "Your curl still looks great from last night."

"It does. Thank you again for doing my hair."

"Anytime."

"How was the dance, kid?" Sawyer asks Christopher. "Did you follow my advice?"

Panic flashes across Christopher's face.

"What advice?" Faith asks.

"Nothing!" Both Christopher and I answer at the same time.

"I'm going to take Alissa on a tour of the house," he says quickly, tugging on her hand and leading her down stairs.

"They are so cute," Julia gushes.

Sawyer leans over to Jaxson, an amused smirk on his face. "I'll bet his bedroom is the first and only room she'll see." His voice is low but not low enough because Faith hears the asshole.

"No, Christopher isn't like that, he's too young."

"He's sixteen, Country," Sawyer returns.

"Exactly." She looks at each of us guys when we remain quiet. "How old were you guys?"

Of course, Sawyer is stupid enough to answer, "Fifteen."

Faith gasps, her hands going to her cheeks. "Fifteen? You were just a baby."

"Baby my ass," Sawyer replies insulted. "You should have seen—"

"All right, that's enough!" Grace interrupts, slapping a hand over his mouth. "We don't need to finish this conversation."

I couldn't agree more which is why I carry Ruthie outside and fire up the grill. She ends up grabbing a kite to play with, running around in the backyard.

Everyone else takes a seat around the patio table. All the women fight with Katelyn to hold the baby while Faith grabs drinks. It isn't long before Christopher and Alissa come out to join us.

"What are you feeding us, Country?" Sawyer asks. "Am I going to starve?"

"No you will not starve. I am happy to tell you there will be steak for those who want it. My mother is bringing them. After all, it's Christopher's birthday and he has informed me that he will die if he doesn't eat meat at least once a day."

"True story," the kid says, making everyone chuckle, including Faith.

The back door swings open, revealing an older man with salt and pepper hair and the same green eyes as Faith. "Hey, there are my girls," he boasts, dropping a kiss on Katelyn's cheek before pulling Red in for a hug. "How's my Shortcake?"

"Good, Papa, but I'm having a hard time breathing with you squeezing me so tight."

After dropping a kiss on her forehead, he opens his arms for Ruthie as she dashes into them. "How's my other girl doin'?"

"Hi, Papa George."

He grabs her wrist, assessing her hand. "Let me take a look at this hook. I heard you gave that little shit a good slug."

"Papa…" Faith warns.

"What? Just praisin' the girl is all. She stuck up for herself. That's a good thing."

Before I can agree with him, two more people step outside, one of them putting me on alert the moment he comes into view.

"Papa Joshua!" Ruthie reaches for him eagerly, making my blood pump violently in my veins.

I turn my back on them, reaching for some measure of composure.

You can do this, Walker, pull yourself together.

"Papa George this is Cade."

I turn back around and extend my hand to the older man. "Nice to meet you."

He assesses me long and hard before finally taking my hand. "You sure are a big bastard, aren't you?"

Sawyer chuckles as Faith groans.

"You served and my Shortcake likes you," he says. "So you're already on my good list. Keep it that way. You don't want to be on my shit list."

"Papa!" Faith scolds.

"What? I'm just stating this upfront and he's not rattled by it. He's a hell of a lot better than that arrogant asshole, Dr. Carson."

I toss a glance at Red. "I am definitely better than the doctor."

She gives me a sexy smile, wrapping her arms around my waist. "No arguments on that one."

"Don't even get me started on Dr. Sissy," Sawyer mumbles, he and Jaxson getting all riled up at the mention of the man's name.

The older man laughs at the nickname. "Dr. Sissy, now that's a good one, but it should be, *Dr. Sissy, the liar*. That asshole tried getting people to believe my cholesterol was high then he tried to date my Shortcake. The lying prick has some nerve."

"Okay, Dad, let's not get started on this again," a woman breaks in, "and watch your mouth around the littles." She steps forward, a kind smile on her face as she gazes up at me. Her hair is long and dark red, the same as Faith's, but her eyes are brown rather than green. She also has the same delicate features and porcelain skin.

"Cade, this is my mother, Linda."

I extend my hand again but she ends up wrapping her arms around my waist instead, hugging my tensed body. I try my damnedest to relax but my discomfort is obvious. It's a habit I have been trying really hard to break. Other than Red and Ruthie, I don't like to be touched.

"I'm so happy to finally meet the men who saved my daughter's life," she says, her voice thick with emotion as she casts a look in Jaxson and Sawyer's direction too.

I don't get the chance to respond before the inevitable happens.

"All right, Linda, let the boy go now so I can properly meet him."

His voice has every muscle in my body tensing further. Faith's mother steps back, leaving me no choice but to face the father.

He isn't what I expected. He doesn't look anything like *him*, he even has the same green eyes as Red and his father, but that doesn't stop the hate I have in my soul for him, especially as I watch him hold Ruthie. One of the most precious things to me. I fight the urge to rip her away from him as images from that day so long ago try to resurface.

"Cade, this is my father, Joshua." Faith's introduction is soft and apprehensive.

The man extends his hand to me first. "I have to agree with my wife. It's a pleasure to finally meet the men who saved my daughter's life, especially you, Cade."

I stare down at his hand, finding myself frozen, unable to move as blood roars in my ears, whispering words of rage.

"Cade?" Faith says nervously.

It knocks me out of the red haze. Somehow, I find it in me to accept his gesture but I keep it brief. "Hi." If my expression is as hard as my voice then I know I'm not fooling anyone.

However, the man doesn't deter from it. He even manages to keep his smile in place.

Katelyn clears her throat, breaking the tension. "How about opening birthday presents since everyone is here now?"

"There isn't supposed to be gifts," Christopher says, shooting an accusatory look at Faith. "I told you dinner is enough."

"Well of course we brought you presents, silly," Kayla replies. "What kind of party would it be without them?"

Christopher grumbles out something intangible but gives in, starting with Jaxson and Julia's gift. Everyone gathers closer, including me, but I hang back a little farther, my composure fragile, especially when Ruthie continues to cling to the one man I wish wasn't here.

My gaze shifts to Faith where I find her watching me, pain and sadness in her eyes as she senses my turmoil.

It makes me feel like complete shit.

Shaking my head, I walk inside and head to the bathroom, needing a moment to pull myself together. I brace my hands on the counter, fingers gripping the sink as I look into the mirror. The reflection staring back at me is not one I have seen in a while, not since Red came back into my life. My eyes are cold and hard, reflecting the ice I have reforming around my heart. My skin cold and clammy, the color slowly draining as I feel like I might be physically sick.

"What the fuck is happening to me?" I splash cold water on my face and try to take deep breaths through the tightness in my chest.

Minutes later, when I'm a little calmer, I walk back outside to see the kid opening the last of his gifts.

Everyone spares me an awkward glance before refocusing their attention back to Christopher.

Red remains watching me, misplaced guilt pinching her expression. She walks over, wrapping her arms around my waist before pressing a kiss right over my raging heartbeat.

Figures. I'm the one hurting her but she's comforting me.

I hug her in close, needing to show her what I can't bring myself to say—I'm sorry.

"Holy crap, Katelyn?" Christopher spews, gaping at the tickets he holds. "You got me tickets to KISS?"

"Sure did," she says, a sense of pride in her voice. "A client of mine hooked me up and even got us backstage passes. I was able to get four; two of those are for Faith and me and the other one can go to whoever you want." She follows up the words by flashing a wink at Alissa.

"This is seriously awesome. Thank you, everyone. All of the gifts were unnecessary, but I appreciate them."

"There's still one more," Faith adds quietly, looking up at me with a knowing smile. The sight of it eases a little more of the rage battling inside me. "Cade and I got you something, too. It's in the garage. Come see." She leads him across the backyard, everyone following suit.

"I tan't wait until you see dis, Twistiphwor," Ruthie says, her excitement as palpable as Faith's. I've been worried she was going to squeal all week but to my surprise she managed to keep it a secret.

Once we reach the side door, Red stands behind Christopher, covering his eyes before leading him inside. "I love you, Christopher. Happy birthday." She removes her hands and everything in that moment changes.

His expression is complete shock as he takes in the now cleaned out garage that has been turned into a music studio, along with a set of brand new drums, a guitar, and a microphone.

"It's all yours," Faith tells him.

He opens his mouth but then closes it, unable to find words. Finally, he shakes his head and reaches for Faith, pulling her into a hug. "Thank you," he whispers gruffly, "just…thank you for everything you've done for my sister and me."

"You deserve it and so much more."

Everyone watches the personal moment, a few of the women growing emotional.

Christopher moves to me next, shaking my hand. "Thanks. Not just for this but for everything."

"You're welcome. Faith is right, you deserve it."

He doesn't waste a second longer checking out the equipment, everyone falling in step behind. I'm about to join them but think better of it when Faith's father passes me, brushing my shoulder as he continues to carry Ruthie in his arms. He hasn't put her down since he got here and I don't fucking like it.

Sawyer watches me from across the garage, knowing exactly where my thoughts are. I decide it's best to go back to the grill and continue dinner. Just as I'm putting on the last steak, Sawyer comes over, his knowing gaze burning into the side of my face.

"You need to chill out, Walker."

My teeth grind as I restrain myself from lashing out. "Don't worry about it, I'm fine."

"The hell you are," he snaps. "You're not fooling anyone; least of all him. You look like you're ready to commit murder. Pull yourself together before you ruin the kid's birthday."

He doesn't understand. This rage, this pain I have inside of me is emerging with a vengeance and it only gets worse as the hour passes.

I even take the seat on the opposite side of him at the table, trying to keep my distance but every time he opens his mouth to speak that deep-seated anger builds, eating away at my soul until there is nothing left, especially when he talks about the plans for that so-called cult he fucking runs. The rage turns into something else entirely with what he says next.

"There's a weekend bible camp next month from one of the other churches in the area. I thought Ruthie and I could attend and meet some of the other children," he says, speaking to Faith.

"Over my dead body." My voice comes out cold and hard.

An awkward silence falls over the table, Faith's eyes swinging to mine. "It's something we can discuss later," she says carefully, tossing me a warning look.

"There's nothing to discuss. She isn't going anywhere with him or any other pedophiles."

"Cade," Faith gasps, horror washing over her face.

Her father sits back, calmly dropping his napkin to his plate. "Listen, son. I mean no disrespect."

Every muscle in my body tightens at the word '*son*,' another voice sounding in my head.

Now, just stay where you are, son. This is God's will and you cannot change what he wants.

I shake my head, trying to rid myself of the evil voice. Sweat dots my skin as my blood flows like lava.

"I heard what happened to your sister, and I just want to say—"

"Oh shit," the curse flees from Sawyer as I jump to my feet, knocking the chair over in my haste.

"You shut the fuck up." I point at him, fighting the urge to reach across the table and strangle him. "You don't know a goddamn thing about her or me."

"Cade, stop it right now!" Faith cries. "You are out of line and scaring Ruthie."

I look over at the small girl who has come to mean so much to me, her eyes wide and filled with tears. Everyone else watches on, clearly uncomfortable.

With anger thick in my veins, I kick my chair out of the way and walk off before I can do something I can't take back.

The knowledge that I just lost everything important to me sears my chest but not enough to stop me. I should have known it would happen. It was never going to work because the one thing that is important to Faith is something I will never accept. I can't.

CHAPTER 35

Faith

Tears stream down my face as I drive to the gym, hoping that's where Cade went since he wasn't at his apartment. The rest of the night was a complete bust; there was no coming back from the damage he caused. I'm angry with him for ruining Christopher's party but more than anything, my heart bleeds for him.

I knew this would be hard on him, I knew he hadn't dealt with his sister's death but I didn't realize it was this bad. From the moment my father showed up, he became a man I didn't know or at least hadn't seen in a very long time. He was cold and angry…so angry.

More than anger though was pain. His eyes were haunted, skin pale. He looked like he was going to be sick. It's as if he was having symptoms of post-traumatic stress.

It killed me to see him suffer like that but I also ache for my father. He didn't deserve Cade's wrath. He handled it better than I expected, saying he understood, but I could tell he was hurt. I'm hurt by it, too. I hate that my family saw this side of him, because the man who walked out on us tonight is not the same one I have given my heart to. That I am certain of.

I think Katelyn knows it too, which is why when everyone left she told me to go find him and she would stay with the children. She knew I needed to be with him.

Relief fills me when I pull up to the gym and find his truck. Climbing out of my car, I walk up to the door and am glad to find it unlocked. With a deep breath, I step inside and find the place mostly encompassed in darkness except for the dim light in the far back corner. The sound of fast breaths and even faster punches assault my ears.

As I draw nearer to the light, the man I came for appears. Cade pummels a punching bag, his lethal body soaked with sweat as he aggressively takes out his violence. Noises fall from him that sound more animal than human. A beast, an angry monster. It's terrifying and heartbreaking at the same time.

"You shouldn't be here," he says, never faltering his blows. "You need to leave."

The cold rejection stings but I stand my ground, refusing to let him push me away. "No. We need to talk and I'm not going anywhere until we do."

His fierce blows come to a stop as he rests his heavy arms on the bag, his breathing ragged. When he finally looks up at me, I suck in a sharp breath at the tortured look on his face.

"Say what it is you need to say then get out."

I swallow past the hurt in my throat and lift my chin. "That's it, Cade? You're going to push me away, you're just going to push us all away?"

"It's the best for everyone. As long as you have a relationship with him, this isn't going to work."

"Why? You haven't even give him a chance."

"I don't want to give him a fucking chance," he bellows, pushing off the bag. "I hate him. Don't you get that? I hate everything he stands for."

"What about me?" I wail. "I stand for everything he does and you don't hate me."

He grinds his teeth, his shoulders rigid with fury.

"He did not hurt your sister, Cade."

It was the wrong thing to say. He storms toward me, his expression savage. "Don't you fucking talk about her."

"No! We are going to talk about her," I scream back. "I'm done skirting around this; you need to deal with it. You need to deal with her death!"

"You don't fucking know anything about it!"

"Then explain it to me," I cry. "Tell me what happened, let me help you."

"You can't help me," he roars. "No one can!"

The pain in his eyes has the most devastating sob exploding past my lips. Within seconds it's silenced by his mouth, our tongues colliding in a blaze of heartbreak and fury.

My fingers grip his sweaty hair, my own frustration pouring out of me. When I bite his lip, he snarls and lifts me off my feet.

My back meets the wall on impact, his hips pinning me in place as he reaches up my dress and tears my panties from my hips. I reach down for him, grabbing his erection in my hand, needing him, needing to be joined, to mask the pain he has inside of him.

He enters me in one hard motion. I cry out at the invasion, my fingers clawing his shoulders. My body accepts him as much as my heart, but when I peer into his cold eyes, the man I've come to love is no longer there. The brutal reality is devastating. A fresh wave of tears tumble down my cheeks, my hand moving to his jaw as he takes me like he never has before. Angry and rough.

"Please," I cry. "Please come back to me."

He shuts his eyes, closing himself off from me, then reaches between us, fingers delving to the bundle of nerves throbbing for release. Despite my conflicted heart, my body responds, a powerful orgasm washing over me. When my eyes reopen, still finding the cold hard shell of a man, my heart shatters.

Guilt flashes across his face before he pulls out of me, refusing to finish. He places me to my feet, pulls up his pants, then turns his back on me.

"Leave, Red, now."

I shake my head even though he can't see me. "Please, don't do this to us. I love you. I just want—"

"I said *leave now*!" He spins around, his voice thundering throughout the gym.

I gaze back at him and realize I'm not going to reach him. Not tonight, and maybe not ever.

"Okay, I'll go, and I won't come back," I tell him, meaning every word. "The sad reality is, Cade, I love you more than anyone in this world and I will until the day I die, but I can't make you love me."

Something flashes in his eyes just then, something that gives me a little glimpse of the man I fell in love with but it's not enough.

“You aren’t capable of loving anyone until you deal with her death.” Unable to stay a second longer, I run from the building, knowing I just left my heart bleeding on that floor in front of him.

That night, as I cry myself to sleep, I pray. I pray for my broken heart, but most of all, I pray for Cade, that he will seek peace and find his way back to me.

CHAPTER 36

Cade

Monday rolls around and I am in no better shape than I was when I walked away from the very people I live and breathe for, ruining the best thing that ever happened to my miserable life. It's exactly what I deserve.

After snapping at everyone out in the gym and scaring the clients, I decided to lock myself in the office before I fuck up worse than I already have. Though, I'm not sure that's even possible.

The monster that has surfaced continues to rage, bringing a good dose of self-loathing with it when I think about what I did to Faith. It's bad enough I ruined the kid's birthday but then I had to take her like a fucking savage while the monster had me. Her eyes had pled for more. For the man she deserves, but the sad truth is, I'll never be the one she deserves. I'm incapable and Saturday only proved that.

The organ in my chest is dead and gone and it's how it will stay from now on because it's safer that way for everyone. Especially the people I love. Knowing that though doesn't make this any easier. I miss them, miss everything about them and the life we had begun to build.

A light tap sounds on the door, yanking me from my miserable thoughts.

"What?" I bark.

It opens to reveal Christopher. Shock courses through me before guilt quickly follows. By the hard look in his eyes, I'll say he's as pissed off at me as I am at myself.

"I didn't expect you to show up today." My voice is rough, sounding exactly how I feel.

"Why, because you ran off on your responsibilities you think I am going to as well?"

As much as I want to explain, to give him the apology he deserves, I can't. Not now, my head isn't on straight. My emotions are a mess waiting to explode with the beast I keep locked inside.

"Go home, kid. Go be with Faith and your sister today." Just saying their names has my black heart squeezing painfully in my chest.

The request only pisses him off more. He storms up to my desk, sweeping his hand over it and knocking everything to the floor. "You should be with them! You promised you wouldn't hurt her and now, for the last two nights, I have to hear both of them cry themselves to sleep because of you!"

Agony sears my chest, knowing the pain I've caused them all. Instead of finding a way to make things right, I remain quiet, knowing it's for the best.

He steps back, throwing his hands up. "You know what? Fuck you. We don't need you. We never needed you." Despite that statement, his voice cracks.

My teeth grind at the pain but I let the rage overpower it because it hurts so much less. Eventually, he storms out, slamming the door behind him.

The booming sound is the final nail in my coffin. Climbing to my feet, I start packing up my shit, needing to get the fuck out of here.

The door flies open and I expect it to be Christopher again, but it ends up being Sawyer.

The fury on his expression fuels the one dueling in my veins. "What the fuck do you think you're doing?"

"Stay out of it, Evans."

"I'm not staying out of this, not this time. My whole life I've watched you destroy yourself; I've even left you alone to do it, but no more. Not when you are fucking up other people's lives. You put yourself in those kids' lives and Faith's, you can't just walk away."

Fury boils beneath the surface, threatening to explode at any given moment. "I'm warning you, now is not the time to fuck with me." I move to walk past him but he shoves me back, shocking the hell out of me.

"It never is and it never will be. You need to get over it, man," he says, stepping into dangerous territory. "We all miss her, but she's gone and she isn't ever coming back."

My blood roars, washing out everything else but fury as I lunge at him. He braces himself, expecting it, but the hard right hook to his face still knocks him back a step.

We move at the same time, bodies colliding in a fit of rage. We land on the floor outside the door, fists flying.

Jaxson manages to pry us apart, his arms locking around my thrashing body as I fight to unleash this never-ending anger and despair.

"Enough," he bellows, locking me tighter in his grip. "You need to calm down, man, this is our workplace. Pull yourself together."

I nod, my breathing ragged.

When he releases me, I swipe at my mouth to find a lot more blood than I expected. I look at Sawyer and see him in the same condition. My best friend, the guy who has been through it all with me, and I did that to him. It's like a douse of cold water.

"Come into the office and get cleaned up," Jaxson says, grabbing my shoulder.

I shake my head. "No, I'm out of here, I'll be back tomorrow."

I walk out and don't look back, unable to witness the destruction I've caused, my soul drowning in a pool of darkness.

CHAPTER 37

Faith

Worry plagues me when I glance at the clock and realize Christopher should have been home by now. He was going to visit Alissa after his shift at the gym but said he would be home before dark and the sun has long fallen.

"Otay, all done." Ruthie walks into her room after brushing her teeth, wearing Cade's white muscle tank and her black beanie. It's become her night attire and makes my hurting heart warm.

"Come on, I'll lie with you for a bit." I turn down her bed, waiting for her to crawl in before climbing in next to her with my cellphone in hand. I put in another call to Christopher but it goes straight to voicemail. The first time it happened, I figured it died, but now I'm worried something more is going on.

That dreaded feeling only grows when I call Alissa and she says he never showed up to her house. She also says she has been trying to get ahold of him.

"Is Twistipwhor otay?" Ruthie asks, when I hang up.

I flash her a reassuring smile that I don't feel. "I'm sure he's fine. I'm going to call the gym." My pulse thrums rapidly as the phone rings, a part of me praying Cade will answer, my soul aching to hear his voice. These past few days without him have been absolute torture.

Unfortunately, it's not him who picks up, it's Jaxson. When he tells me Christopher isn't there and gives me the rundown of what happened, my heart breaks. I hate to hear he and Cade fought but I'm also not surprised. I think Christopher is as hurt as Ruthie and me. That must be why he never showed up to Alissa's. He probably wants to be alone.

Despite that thought, I still worry. After thanking Jaxson, I decide to call Cooper.

"McKay," he answers on the first ring.

"Cooper, hi, it's Faith. I hope I'm not disturbing you?"

"Not at all. Everything okay?"

"I hope so, but Christopher hasn't come home yet." I explain to him about all the phone calls I made and what Jaxson told me. "I'm worried since his phone is off. Would you mind driving by the skateboard park to see if he's there? If you're busy I understand, I can ask Katelyn to come stay with Ruthie and I'll go look."

"No, it's fine, I'm getting in my truck now. Keep your cell with you, and I'll call you when I find him."

"Thanks, Cooper, I appreciate it."

"No problem. Hang tight. I'll call you back soon."

After hanging up, Ruthie peers up at me, looking as sad and worried as I feel. "Tade and Twistphwor got into a fight?"

"More of an argument than a fight," I say, trying to lighten the blow.

"Dat mates me sad."

"Me too," I admit on a whisper.

"I shoure do miss de Big Guy."

I swallow thickly, unable to tell her how much I miss him, too. If I even think about it right now I will burst into tears and I have to be strong for her. For us all.

"We need to be patient right now and have faith that everything will work out. We have to remember he's hurting also and he needs time to work through it, but I know he's missing you too."

After that disaster of a dinner, I told Ruthie all about Cade's sister and the loss he suffered, at least a version she could understand. I felt bad betraying him but she deserved to know why he acted the way he did, why he feels the way he does, and why he lashed out at my father like that.

Before either of us can say more, a loud thump sounds from the back of my house.

"What was dat?"

Frowning, I sit up and peek out her bedroom window that overlooks the backyard. There, I find two men dressed in black from head to toe, trying to get in the back door.

Fear paralyzes me for all of a second before I spring into action. "Ruthie. Come now!" Without waiting for her to obey, I pick her up and run for her closet.

"What's going on?" she asks, voice trembling.

I place her in the far back corner and cup her scared, pale face. "I need you to listen to me right now and do exactly what I say."

At her nod, I hand her my phone.

"I want you to call Sheriff Cooper and ever so quietly tell him that he needs to come here right away."

A small sob slips past her lips.

"It's okay. Everything is going to be okay, I promise, but I need you to be strong right now."

"Otay."

"No matter what happens, no matter what you hear, you do not leave this spot until Sheriff Cooper comes and gets you. Do you understand?"

She nods, sucking in a harsh breath.

The sound of glass shattering has my already terrified heart thrashing in my chest. "Remember what I said, don't leave this spot until the sheriff comes. I love you. I promise everything will be okay."

I hit the redial button on my phone then put the clothes hamper in front of her before closing her in the closet. Without wasting another precious second, I dash from her room and into mine, going for the gun that Cade keeps there. Footsteps pound up my stairs, followed by male voices as I frantically search under the mattress for the gun, a frustrated cry escaping me when I don't feel it.

Come on, where the hell is it?

Two men charge in, stopping just inside the door. Despite being fully covered, I recognize Floyd Dennison and his friend, Spike.

"Your time has come, bitch."

At that precise moment, my hand comes into contact with the cold steel. I pull the gun out, gripping it firmly, but before I can even raise it, Floyd pushes forward, backhanding me across the face. The gun flies out of my hand, the painful blow sending me into the nightstand and making my world spin.

"Go find Ruth Jean," he orders Spike before grabbing me by my throat and throwing me to my bed.

I thrash beneath him, clawing at his hand as he robs me of air. My fingers collide with his face, nails gouging the skin on his cheek as I continue to fight. He sends another slap, hard enough that it renders me helpless.

Spike comes running back into the room. "I can't find her."

A small measure of relief washes over me, and I pray for Cooper to hurry.

Floyd leans over me, his eyes wild and crazed. "Where's my daughter, bitch?"

"She isn't here," I choke past the blood filling my mouth.

"Liar!" He raises his hand for another blow.

"No, I'm not. I swear. She's with Cade."

His fist pauses, gaze snapping to Spike. "I thought you said that asshole was alone?"

"No, I said I thought he was, but I couldn't be sure."

"Fuck!" he rages before looking back at me. "Well, let's hope your rich granddaddy is still willing to pay a pretty penny for you and my worthless, piece of shit son."

"Oh god," I sob, realizing he has Christopher. "What have you done to him?"

The only answer I get is a malicious smile before he sends another blow to my face, turning my world black.

CHAPTER 38

Cade

Shrouded in darkness, I lie in bed, feeling nothing but cold and numb. I welcome it as it masks the pain that's been trying to fight its way to the surface. I haven't moved in hours, the dark ceiling transpiring images of everything I miss yet am unworthy of.

My cell phone buzzes next to me once again but I continue to ignore it, not wanting to leave this numb state I've found myself in. It isn't until a pounding starts on my door minutes later that I can no longer ignore it.

"Walker, man, open up. Something's happened." The urgency in Jaxson's voice snaps me out of my fog and sends me to my feet.

My steps are quick as I move for the door. The moment I open it, I know something has happened, something bad.

"What is it?" I ask.

"You have to get to Faith's. She and Christopher are missing."

I shake my head, thinking I misunderstood him. "What the fuck are you talking about? What do you mean, missing?"

"Look, man, I don't have all the details yet. All I know is Faith was taken from the house and they think it was Dennison."

Dread grips my chest, its icy fingers unforgiving. I'm out the door before he can even finish, urgency propelling me forward. Jaxson catches up quickly, both of us hopping into his truck since it's parked right out front.

"Tell me everything," I demand, as he speeds through the night.

"Christopher never came home after the gym," he informs me. "Then Ruthie called in about Faith. She's unharmed but…"

"But what?" I ask, my breath stalling in fear.

"Faith hid her in the closet and she hasn't left there. She's terrified, man. No one can get her to talk, not even Faith's parents or Katelyn."

My hands clench on my knees, fear and rage colliding within. If I had been there none of this would have happened.

"Fuck!" I bellow, sending my fist into the dash. "If he's hurt either of them, I will fucking kill him."

Jaxson nods, his own expression tight with anger.

Flashing lights meet us as we turn down the street, a dozen cop cars lined up on either side. Jaxson barely slows to a stop before I jump from the truck, my feet pounding the cement as I race toward the house. Ruthie's sobs can be heard the moment I enter.

"Ruthie!" I yell, running for the stairs.

"Hey, wait, who are you?" A cop attempts to intercept me, but I send him to the ground, my quick feet never faltering until I reach Ruthie's room and find it crowded with people. I shove my way through without apology.

"Ruthie, where are you?" The moment I turn the corner, I find the most heartbreaking sight—my girl huddled in the closet, her face pale with fear and body trembling with sobs.

Her sad eyes widen in disbelief. "Tade?" she asks on a whisper.

"Yeah, kid, it's me, come here." I bend down, opening my arms for her.

She crawls toward me on a sob and I don't miss the fact that one of my shirts is engulfing her tiny form. I scoop her up then cup her face, forcing her to look at me. "Are you okay? Are you hurt?"

She shakes her head before burying it in my neck, crying hysterically.

I hold her close, trying to soothe her. "It's okay, baby. I got you. Everything is going to be okay."

Cooper touches my shoulder, his expression grim. "We need her to talk, man. We don't know anything. I've been going off assumption and what I heard in the background on the phone."

I nod then force her to look at me again. "Tell me what happened."

Her breath hitches as I wipe her tears. "Me and Faif was wayin' in bed when we hweard someone twyin' to get in de house. She hid me in de cwoset and told me to tawl Mr. Shewiff. She made me pwomise dat no matter what I wouldn't tome out, so I didn't, but I tould hewe her scweaming." Another heartbreaking sob leaves her. "It was my daddy and Spite. I heawd dem and dey was huwting her."

That familiar darkness that I have tried so hard to keep hidden emerges with a vengeance.

"Please, Cooper, you have to help her." Katelyn's plea pulls my attention to the left where I find her and Faith's mom huddled against Joshua William's chest. I wait for that hatred to hit me but it never comes. Maybe it's because of the pain and fear in his eyes, the same one I'm feeling this very moment.

The grandfather stands next to them, his body practically vibrating in fury. By his icy glare, there is no doubt where he lays blame and I can't deny he's right. Without a word, he storms past me, heading into Faith's room across the hall.

"Did they say where they were taking her, Ruthie?" Cooper asks calmly.

She shakes her head. "I touldn't tell what dey was sayin', I tould just heaw deir voices."

Cooper brings his attention to me. "I heard a little in the background while I was on the phone with her. I could tell it was Dennison but not much else. I already had cops search his place and Spike's, there's no one there."

"Have you looked into other properties he owns?" Sawyer asks. It isn't until that one question that I realize he's here with Grace. I shouldn't be surprised. He's always been a way better friend than me.

"Not yet," Cooper answers. "I have deputies looking into it though. It's highly unlikely, Dennison is poor as dirt and Spike isn't much better off."

Their conversation fades out when my gaze lands on the old man in the room across the hall as he answers his cell phone. Something in his tense shoulders has me pushing forward.

Cooper and the others follow behind.

George holds his hand up, motioning for us to be quiet as we enter the room. "I can do that. I can get you that amount no problem, just let me talk to my granddaughter so I know she's okay."

My heart stalls as I wait to see if Faith comes on the line. Fists clenched at my sides, I get the overwhelming urge to rip the fucking phone from him.

"If you don't let me talk to her, how do I know she's alive?"

An agonized scream comes from the receiver, loud enough for us all to hear, and the painful sound of it has rage thrashing through my veins.

"No, stop, that's enough. I get the point, and I'll get you the money, just don't hurt them."

There's a brief pause.

"Yes, I understand." He hangs up, his expression solemn. "He's giving me twenty-four hours to get him three million dollars. He has Christopher, too."

My eyes close, teeth grinding as I try to breathe through the guilt constricting my chest, especially when I think about my last encounter with him.

"Do you have that much?" Sawyer asks.

"Yes, but we all know I'm not giving him a goddamn penny. He will only kill them."

Cooper nods his agreement. "Did he say where he wants the drop?"

He shakes his head. "He said he would call me back to tell me where. Obviously, he said no cops, too. The bastard is an amateur, it's as if he was quoting shit from a movie. It's the dumbest move he could have made because he has no idea who he's fucking with." The older man steps closer, his finger jabbing Cooper in the chest. "I'm telling you right now, Sheriff, you better find him soon or I will, and when I get ahold of him I'm going to blow the motherfucker away."

He can get in line, because if anyone is killing him, it's me.

"Dad, just take it easy. We have to let the sheriff do his job and have faith that it will work out." Joshua's voice wavers, his fear for his daughter apparent. "What's your plan?" he asks Cooper. "We wait for the phone call?"

"We aren't waiting twenty-four hours to find them," I reply, sending a look Sawyer and Jaxson's way.

Both of them nod at our silent exchange.

I press a kiss to Ruthie's head. "I need to go, baby."

Her arms tighten around my neck. "Pwease, don't weave me."

The plea shreds my heart in half, a part of me never wanting to let go. "It's going to be okay, kid, but I have to go. I'm going to get them back but I need you to be strong and stay here with Katelyn and the others, okay?"

She finally nods but a small sob falls from her. "Be tarefwul, Big Guy."

"Always." After one last kiss, I pass her off to Katelyn's waiting arms then leave the room, feeling Jaxson and Sawyer follow.

Before we make it far, I'm yanked back by an enraged Cooper. "You're not going anywhere without me. Got it?"

My chest heaves as I fight to not drop another friend to the ground. "Then I guess you better keep up and prepare yourself, Sheriff. Because I have only one goal, and that's getting them back alive at any cost."

"Don't you pull that sheriff bullshit with me!" he seethes, getting into my face. "I'm your goddamn friend and their lives mean just as much to me as they do you. But this isn't a fucking war zone; this is *my town* and *my rules*. So, you toe the fucking line or else—"

I grab him by the shirt and pin him up against the wall. "Fuck you! I don't follow anyone's rules when it comes to my woman and kids. You hear me?"

"Lay off, Walker." Jaxson inserts himself between us, pushing me back.

"Both of you need to rein it in," Sawyer says. "We're wasting time. You"—he points at Cooper—"need to lay off him. We all know what kind of rules you would follow if this was Kayla."

A thick moment of silence fills the air as Cooper and me continue to face off.

"I know a place where they both go to drink," he says. "It's a biker bar just off the interstate. I know one guy in particular who's close with Spike that might even know where they are."

I nod, our truce unspoken. "Then let's go."

CHAPTER 39

Faith

My body aches, head throbbing violently from the blow Floyd delivered minutes ago as he spoke with my papa. I have no idea how long we drove for before we showed up here. A remote location out in the middle of nowhere, the small cabin nestled deep in the woods.

I brace myself as they pull me from the truck, their rough hands yanking me out by my hair. A cry of pain lodges in my throat as I fight to keep my balance, stumbling toward the run-down, abandoned cabin with my hands cuffed in front of me. I scan my surroundings, trying to get a sense of direction, any means at escape.

"Whatever you're thinking you can forget it," Floyd says, sensing my thoughts. "There's nothing around here for miles. I can make you scream like a fucking pig and no one will hear you."

Icy fear flows through my veins at the thought of what they will do to me if someone doesn't find me soon.

"Lock her up with him," Floyd orders Spike, shoving me into his chest.

I don't miss the glare Spike sends his way. It's obvious who is calling the shots here. He leads me around back, the night falling even darker as the dim light from the cabin fades.

"Please, if you help me, I'll have my papa pay you double what Floyd is," I whisper, grasping at straws.

He grunts, not believing me. "I don't think so. I'm going to get my money and enjoy making you and your family suffer."

Anger begins overriding my fear. It's then a small wooden shack appears, a large chain banded across the doors with a heavy padlock.

He uses a key to unlock it then swings open the door, the disgusting smell overwhelming my senses. A small lantern in the top right corner gives off a faint glow in the dark, dank space, but it's enough for me to see the shadow of a boy huddled in the corner with his head down and arms wrapped around his knees.

"Christopher?" I sob in relief, my feet propelling me forward.

"That was easy," Spike chuckles before slamming the door and bolting the lock back in place.

The final click falls on deaf ears, my attention only on Christopher as I kneel down next to him. "Are you okay?" I ask but get nothing in return, only the sound of him sniffling. It doesn't take long before I realize he's crying. "Christopher, please look at me, are you hurt?"

He shakes his head, mumbling words I can't quite catch.

"I can't understand you."

His face lifts, my heart swelling at the battered mess of tears. It's the first time I've ever seen him cry, and he looks absolutely devastated.

"He killed her," he chokes out roughly.

My heart stops at the revelation. "Who?"

"My mom!" he says, an agonized sound falling with it.

I shake my head, not understanding. "What do you mean? I thought she left."

"I thought so too but she didn't. She's," he pauses, swallowing thickly, his expression twisted with grief, "she's here."

Before I can even ask what on earth he's talking about, he points to the corner. I turn around, moving closer to get a better look but find nothing except some sticks piled together.

"It's human bones, Faith."

A scream of horror lodges in my throat as I scatter back. At the sound of Christopher's pain, I pull myself together and wrap my arms around him. "It's okay, it's going to be okay."

"This entire time I thought she left us. I couldn't understand how she could just leave us with him but she never did."

"Are you sure it's her?"

"Her ring is beside it, and I heard him tell Spike he caught her trying to take Ruthie and me. She was going to take us with her." His harsh sobs completely break my heart.

"I'm so sorry, Christopher. So, sorry," I choke past my own grief. "I promise we'll get through this. I'll help you."

For the next few minutes I just hold him, trying to bring any comfort I can. When he's a little calmer, he sits up and looks at me. "Are you okay? Where's Ruthie? They said they were going to grab both of you."

His questions trigger many of my own but I decide to answer his first. "She's okay. I hid her just before your father broke in. How did they get to you?"

"They followed me from the gym. I turned down a back alley a couple blocks away and that's how they got me." His jaw locks, anger and shame gripping his face.

My hand moves to his shoulder. "We're going to get out of here. Do you have any idea where we are?"

He nods. "This cabin belonged to my mother, it was her parents'. I've only been here a few times. I didn't think we still owned it. Now I know why it was kept a secret." He shakes his head in disgust.

Knowing that Floyd Dennison is capable of murder, I realize we are in even more danger than I originally thought. "Okay, listen, they have asked Papa for ransom money, and I have no doubt we have a lot of people looking for us. But we have to try getting ourselves out of here, in case it takes them a while to find us."

He nods. "I've already started working in this corner." He slides over and shoves his hand underneath a board. "The bottom wood is wet and rotted. We just need a big enough space to slide underneath."

A surge of hope sparks within me. "Yes. If we can make something big enough to get under, do you know anywhere that is close enough to run to?"

He shakes his head.

"That's fine. All we need to do is get out of here and stay hidden until someone can find us, and I know someone will. I have no doubt Cooper has every man on it."

"Well, let's just hope Cade is one of them, because we know that guy gets good results in the end."

My heart falters at the mention of him, rendering me speechless for a solid moment. "I know he'll be the first in line looking for us." The words are out of my mouth without a second thought. Deep down, embedded in my heart, I'm sure of it.

"I wish my last words to him weren't telling him to go fuck himself."

I give him a sad smile and think about our last encounter, too. "He knows you care about him, Christopher. He knows we all do. Nothing will ever change that."

Even after everything that's happened, there is no way he isn't leading the manhunt. He saved me once and I know he will risk everything to do it again. Let's just hope this comes with a lot less sacrifice because I did not escape hell just to be thrown back into it.

CHAPTER 40

Cade

The bar resides just off I-90, the parking lot filled with motorcycles. We all drove with Cooper, wanting to stick together since he has deputies searching for any other clues as to where they could have possibly taken them. In the thirty minutes it took to get here, the anger I've been trying to keep concealed has only grown, spinning into a black spool of rage.

"Tell us who we're dealing with here, Coop," Sawyer speaks. "Are we dealing with types like *Wild Hogs*? Or are we dealing with serious badass dudes like *Sons of Anarchy*?"

All of our attentions shift to him.

"What? It's actually a pretty good show and those assholes are seriously badass, they'll kill you just for sneezing too loud. I want to make sure if that's what I'm dealing with then I'm prepared to be the one doing the killing."

"No one is killing anyone," Cooper states. "These guys are mostly into the drug scene, they are low on the totem pole. There's one guy in particular who is close with Spike and Dennison that might know something, but he won't talk easily."

"He'll talk," I reply, before climbing out of the squad truck. Across the parking lot, sitting on one of the parked bikes, a girl gets fucked hard, her annoying screams filling the night.

Cooper catches up quickly, pulling me back. "Look, let me do this my way first. If he doesn't talk then you can have at him. Deal?"

I nod and hope I can be patient long enough to keep that promise.

The four of us enter the dimly lit bar, walking into a cloud of smoke. Every single person stops what they're doing, their gazes locking on us like the outsiders we are.

"Pig," someone calls out, while others make snorting noises.

Coop looks over at me, his expression bored. "So original." His gaze scans the bar until it lands on one person. He nods to a guy who sits at the end of the counter alone, a mug of beer in front of him.

The three of us follow, keeping our eyes on our surroundings, especially the assholes who are eyeing us like they want to try something stupid. Little do they know, tonight is not the night to fuck with me. The darkness I keep locked in is ready to emerge at any second, when I unleash it, I know it will result in nothing short of another bloodbath.

"Silas," Cooper greets a short, pudgy guy with long, greasy hair, and the most pathetic skull tattoo I've ever seen on his meaty bicep.

"Sheriff," he mimics back with a smirk.

"Do you have any idea where Spike and Dennison are tonight."

"Nope," he answers quickly, too quickly.

"So you don't know anything about the kidnapping of a woman and kid they did tonight, or where they might be holding them?"

"Nope, and I wouldn't fucking tell a pig like you even if I did."

My temper spikes, patience wearing thin. I push forward but Cooper holds me back, signaling one more chance.

"Here's the thing, Silas. I'm not here as a cop tonight. I'm here with some friends of mine, friends who will eat you up and spit you out if you don't tell them what we want to know. We both know you have the information we need. I suggest you start talking and quickly."

The guy flicks an annoyed glance his way before taking a long pull of his beer.

That's when I intervene and this time, no one stops me. "Time's up." I knock the bottle from his mouth, catching it before slamming his head into the counter.

Blood sprays from his nose, the warmth of it hitting my face. Gripping his throat, I lift him out of his seat and slam his back to one of the tables. Chaos erupts behind me that has Jaxson, Sawyer, and Cooper pulling their guns.

I shatter the bottle I still hold in my hand, holding the severed glass to his neck. "You tell me where my woman and kid are or I will gut you like a fucking pig."

"I don't know anything," he spits, his face turning purple.

I make a small incision against his neck, making him cry out. "That is inches from the spot that will take your life. I am giving you one more chance to tell me what I want to know or you will bleed out your death right here and now."

When he remains silent, I drag the edged glass closer, the first sign of fear sparking in his eyes.

"No, wait! Please, I'll tell you what you want to know."

I still, keeping the glass against his sensitive skin.

"Look, I had nothing to do with it, I swear. They asked me if I wanted in. Dennison said we'd split the three mil equally but I turned them down, I'm not into hurtin' kids, man."

"Tell me where he's keeping them."

His body trembles as I press the glass deeper. "Dennison has a cabin about thirty minutes from here. It used to belong to his wife; Spike said that's where they were keeping them. I swear I know nothing else."

I lift him by his bloody throat, dragging him back to the bar, and shoving a napkin in front of him. "Directions."

"I don't have a pen."

The bartender throws him one. "Hurry up and give them what they want before my bar is destroyed."

He writes down the directions quickly, his hand trembling.

Afterward, I take it from him, handing it off to Cooper. "You better not be lying to me, because if they aren't there, I will come back and gut you of every fucking organ you possess. Do you understand?"

He nods, but refuses eye contact.

"Let's go."

The four of us climb back in Coop's truck. He radios in backup as he guns it out of the parking lot. "If we're lucky I can make it there in under twenty minutes."

"Make it ten," I tell him, fearing we're running out of time.

CHAPTER 41

Faith

Pain slices through my bloody fingertips as I fight to break through board by board. "We're almost there, Christopher, a little more and I think we can make it out."

The problem is the higher we get, the dryer the wood is, and that is not as easy.

Christopher lets out a heated curse when the next board won't pull. He shakes his head in frustration, his body as exhausted as mine. "Back up," he says.

I move out of the way as he starts kicking it with his foot. It does more than what our hands were doing. Moments later, it finally gives.

We both scramble forward, pulling the rest of it off with our hands.

He looks over at me, his expression doubtful. "Think we can make it under this?"

"We have no choice."

He nods. "I'll go first then I can help you from the other side."

"Be careful and go slow."

His head turns as he looks over his shoulder at the scattered human bones in the corner. He crawls over there first, picking up the ring that lies in the midst and shoving it into his pocket, before making his was back to the hole we made. After a brief hug from me, he lowers onto his belly and maneuvers himself every which way until he gets his head and shoulders on the other side.

I push the bottom of his sneakers with my cuffed hands, hoping the extra shove will help and it does. A moment later he's out. I send a silent prayer above then try to follow but have a much more difficult time since my hands are still cuffed.

Mud coats my face, the rough wood scraping against my cheek. Once my top half is out, I lift to my elbows then gasp in pain from the pressure on my lower back.

"Lie completely flat," Christopher whispers.

I comply and feel him grasp my wrists, slowly pulling me the rest of the way out.

"Oh my god, we did it," I breathe, slinging my bound wrists around his neck.

He hugs me back. "Come on, let's get the hell out of here."

We crouch low, heading for the side of the house. "Let's try to get to a main road," I whisper. "Flag someone down for help."

He nods in agreement then grabs my arm, pulling me with him to keep me close. He's able to move quicker than I am since his wrists aren't cuffed. We don't make it far when the back door to the cabin flies open.

Christopher pins me to the side of the cabin, hidden in the shadows.

"How long did he say we have?" Floyd asks. Anger edges his voice but beyond that is panic.

"I don't know. He just said the cop and three guys came to the bar, the one sounded like that boyfriend of hers, and, supposedly, the bastard almost fucking sliced open Silas's throat until he gave up our location."

Cade!

Christopher and I share a look, our hope reflecting the other's.

"I knew we shouldn't have said anything to that asshole," Floyd seethes, his voice sounding further away.

Christopher takes my arm again, signaling to move. We run faster this time, knowing we are only seconds away from being found out.

A furious roar tears through the air, followed by a loud bang. "Fuck! How the hell did they escape?"

"Come on, Faith, we have to move faster," Christopher breathes, ushering me forward.

"There they are!" Spike bellows.

A quick glance over my shoulder reveals they are headed our way, Floyd raising a gun in our direction.

"Christopher!" His name rips from my throat, piercing the air just as the shot is fired off.

"Don't look behind you, just keep moving!"

It's faster than what I'm capable of. I trip over my own feet, landing painfully on my stomach.

Christopher lifts me, helping me right myself before changing directions and leading us into the woods.

"If that happens again you keep going," I tell him, angry with myself.

"Never. I won't leave you."

Just as we make it into the dense woods, another shot fires off, the bullet striking a tree close to me. A whimper of fear rips from my throat, but I continue to push myself, ignoring the sharp pieces of earth biting into the bottoms of my feet.

Christopher pulls us to the side, hiding behind one of the trees. I'm thankful for the reprieve, my lungs restricting painfully as I try to take in air.

"Forget them, man!" Spike says, sounding closer than he was a moment ago. "Let's just get the fuck out of here before the cops show up."

"No. We're not leaving without them. I want my fucking money."

Their approaching footsteps are too close for comfort. I squeeze my eyes shut, fighting to keep myself still and quiet.

"There is nowhere to hide, you little shit," Floyd says, speaking only to Christopher. "I know these woods like the back of my hand. If you don't surrender now, when I do catch you, I will make you fucking suffer just like I did your bitch of a mother."

Christopher tenses next to me, his jaw ticking in anger. He leans in close, his lips right at my ear. "I'm going to lead them away."

I shake my head, rejecting the idea immediately.

"Yes. This is our only choice, and I can run faster than you right now. Cade and the others will be here soon, we just need to hold out until then. It will be okay, I promise."

Before I can protest again, he's gone.

"There!" Several branches snap from fast and heavy boot falls as they both run after Christopher, a gunshot firing in his direction.

I cover my mouth with my hand, stifling a cry of fear.

Within seconds, everything falls silent.

I keep my hand over my mouth, listening for any signs of life. Just then a loud crack sounds, followed by Christopher crying out in pain.

Terror grips me when I realize they have found him.

"Come out, bitch, or I kill him right here, right now."

"Don't do it, Faith, stay where you are!"

He strikes Christopher again. "You have three seconds to come out or I will put a fucking bullet in his head. One!"

"Don't do it, Faith!"

I cry in defeat, knowing I can't take the chance.

"Two!"

"Stop, I'm here," I yell, stepping out from behind the tree. "I'm right here. Please don't hurt him."

"Grab her!" he orders Spike, who's already headed straight for me.

I have no time to prepare myself for the fist he throws at my face. The hit is so powerful it knocks me to the ground, making my ears ring for seconds later. "Your damn boyfriend is a real pain in the ass, lady."

He grabs a fistful of my hair, dragging me out of the woods, the tiny strands severing from my scalp. My frustrated cries shatter the night as I thrash against the painful hold he has on me.

"Let her go, asshole!" Christopher struggles against his father's grip, Floyd's arm wrapped around his neck.

Spike eventually yanks me to my feet, realizing it's easier on the both of us. Halfway to the truck, a bright light falls from the sky, the noise of a chopper sounding above us.

"Shit!" Spike bellows, his panic unmistakable. "They're here."

Just at that moment, a truck speeds up the driveway, its bright headlights and loud siren adding to the agony of my head.

A bunch of bodies tumble out into the dark night, disappearing out of sight as Cooper steps into the light, his gun trained directly at us. "Drop your weapons, now!"

I sob in relief, but it's short-lived when I'm shoved to my knees and feel the sharp blade of Spike's knife pressing against my throat.

Floyd does the same thing to Christopher, holding a gun to the top of his head. "Back up or I shoot." The threat sends my terrified heart plummeting straight to my stomach.

"It doesn't have to be like this, Dennison," Cooper says, his voice calm. "There's still time for you to do the right thing. You're already surrounded, don't add to your list of charges."

"Fuck you! You think I care? If I'm going down for this I'm making sure to take him with me."

"Please just stop," I plead, unable to bear the thought of watching another boy die in front of me.

"I mean it, you let us out of here and we will let them go. If you don't, I take them down with me. Your choice, Sheriff."

Cooper shakes his head. "I can't do that, Dennison, but if you let them go now, unharmed, we can work something out."

"No, that's the only fucking deal I will make. You have seconds before I pull the goddamn trigger."

"Shit!" Spike curses. "What the fuck are you doing, man?"

"Please," I sob again, fearing for the next several seconds.

Christopher reaches over, grabbing one of my cuffed hands. I grip his tightly, crying even harder as despair grips my heart.

"Hey, asshole."

My head snaps to the left, watching Sawyer step out of the shadows. Floyd swings his gun over at him, a gunshot firing off.

A scream bubbles up my throat, my heart coming to a fearful stop. Only Sawyer isn't the one to fall to the ground, Floyd does.

"What the fuck?" Spike rushes out in a panic.

I barely have time to comprehend what happened before I'm yanked to my feet, an arm locking around my throat as I'm dragged backward.

I gasp for every precious breath, darkness dancing at the edge of my vision. Everything suddenly moves into slow motion. Christopher lunges for me, tears streaming down his face as Sawyer holds him back. Cooper barks orders but I hear none of it, only his mouth moving. It's like a dream, a nightmare I can't wake up from.

My eyes flutter closed, as I begin to lose consciousness. Just as I'm about to succumb to the darkness, an unbelievable force slams into me, ripping me from Spike's hold and sending me flying. I land on the ground with jarring impact, pain radiating through my head.

I roll to my side, vision blurring from the agony. I watch Cade, unfocused, his face savage as he rains blow after blow down on Spike. He looks more like a machine than human in this moment, very much like the warrior I saw all those years ago.

Christopher suddenly comes into view, despair twisting his expression. I blink for what only feels like a second but when I reopen Cade is there, kneeling next to me. His hard expression soft with worry.

There's so much I want to say, so much I want to tell him, but I'm unable to speak, reality feeling so far away.

"Can you hear me, Red? What hurts, baby?" His voice is distant and muffled.

I open my mouth to speak but nothing comes out.

He puts my cuffed wrists around his neck then picks me up, cradling me in his strong arms. My favorite place to be. Just as that thought emerges, I let myself succumb to the darkness, letting it swallow me whole.

CHAPTER 42

Cade

Silence consumes the hospital room but the guilt plaguing me is deafening. I sit next to her bed, holding her battered hand. It's been twelve hours since she was brought here and I haven't left her side. She has woken only a few times, disoriented and mumbling incoherently before going back to sleep.

The doctor says sleep is the best thing for her right now and that she's lucky the concussion is the only thing she suffered. The truth is she shouldn't have suffered at all. I promised her she never would again, and I broke that promise.

"Cade?"

My head snaps up at the soft sound of my name, my gaze landing on her swollen face. She looks a little more alert this time. "Hey, Red," I murmur, shocked to hear how gruff my voice sounds. "How are you feeling?"

"All right. The pain in my head isn't as bad as it was the last time I woke up."

I nod, feeling lost for words when there's so much I need to say, so many things I need to make right but they all evade me, nothing feeling adequate enough. Instead, I lift her hand to my lips, pressing a gentle kiss.

"You look so tired," she says sadly. "Have you slept at all?"

I shake my head. "I'm fine. I've been going back and forth, also checking on Christopher."

"Is he okay?" she asks, tears immediately forming in her eyes.

"Yeah, Red, he's good. He's a tough kid. The doctors have him on some pain meds so he's sleeping a lot like you, but Katelyn's been staying in the room with him."

"Good. What about Ruthie? I briefly remember seeing her one of the times I woke up but I don't remember much."

"She's worried about you and Christopher, but she's good. Sawyer and Grace have her. He texted me a few minutes ago and told me they'll be coming by in a bit, they're grabbing breakfast first."

She watches me, her expression becoming even more somber. "And how about you, Cade? How are you doing?"

I drop my head, not knowing how she can care about me after everything I've done, but this is Faith. I guess I shouldn't be surprised.

Her hand cups the side of my face, soothing the beast that lives within. "Look at me."

I lift my face and stare into her soft, understanding eyes.

"It's not your fault," she says.

A disbelieving breath escapes the confines of my chest. "Yeah, it is. We both know none of this would have happened if I had been there."

"They would have found another way. You weren't with us twenty-four seven. They could have tried to take Christopher after school; they could have taken me during the day from the house. They would have found a way."

I don't respond because I disagree. They came for her because they knew I wasn't there. Instead, I was holed up in my apartment, trying to escape life and not deal with something I should have dealt with a long time ago.

She swallows thickly before asking the next question. "Is…Is Floyd dead?"

"Yes."

She nods, relief filling her expression. "And Spike?"

I remain silent for a moment, wondering how much I should tell her. "He's not dead but he's not doing great either. He'll be in the hospital for a while recovering before trial."

"Has Christopher told anyone about his mom?"

"Yeah, Cooper knows about the shed, we're waiting for verification that it's her, but considering what Christopher has said, it sounds like it will be."

"He was devastated when I found him," she chokes out softly. "My heart is absolutely breaking for him, but I'll help him get through it, and when it's confirmed that it's her I'll make sure we have a nice funeral for her."

There is no one better who walks this earth than this woman right here. "I know you will, Red. He's lucky to have you and so is Ruthie."

The tears that have been welling in her eyes begin to escape the corners, tumbling down her cheeks. "You have me too, if you want me."

Fire erupts in my throat. "I don't deserve you."

A quiet cry escapes her, cracking my tortured heart in half. I push to my feet, moving to sit beside her on the bed before pressing my lips to hers gently, careful to avoid any wounds.

All my caution is thrown out the window when she pulls me harder against her mouth. I kiss her like I've been aching to since the night she left me at the gym. I inhale her sobs, taste her tears, and take them as my own, letting it settle deep into my bones like the rest of her, even though I deserve none of it. Not yet but I will.

With that thought surfacing, I pull back and rest my forehead on hers. Her eyes flutter open, breath racing past her lips, tempting me with everything I want forever.

"Listen, Red. Once I get you home and settled Sawyer and Grace are going to stay with you and the kids for a while."

Surprise sparks in her pretty eyes. "Why? Where are you going?"

"Colorado. There's something I need to take care of."

I don't need to explain further. I'm sure she has a pretty good idea why I'm headed there.

"For how long?" she asks.

"I'm not sure."

Her breath hitches. "Are you coming back?" The fear in her voice only adds to the remorse flowing through my veins.

"Yeah, baby, I'll be back."

She nods, relief blanketing her expression. "Sawyer and Grace don't have to stay with us. We will be okay on our own, or I'm sure we could stay with my parents."

I shake my head. "Everything is already set. I need him there with you, Red. I need to know you guys are safe."

She gazes back at me, her sad expression softening. "I love you, Cade Walker. I'll be waiting for you. Please don't make me wait long."

I seal my promise with another kiss, the taste of my redemption so close.

I'm going to fix this if it's the last thing I do.

CHAPTER 43

Cade

Everything in this moment hurts. A pain in my chest like I've never known, or maybe just forgot. It passes back and forth like a ball of fire as I stand at the long cement pathway that leads to a place I've never been to, but one I should have visited a long time ago.

I never went to my sister's funeral for two reasons. One—because my bitch of a mother had it in a church despite the circumstances surrounding her death, and two—because the thought of watching her small, innocent body get lowered in the ground would have been the final nail in my coffin, too. From the way I'm feeling right now, it still might.

Knowing I can't prolong this moment any longer, I put one foot in front of the other, ignoring all the headstones I pass, interested in only one. Images of a sweet face I have pushed away for so long emerge, bringing some beautiful yet painful memories with it.

The way her big, innocent, brown eyes watched me with trust and loved me for reasons I will never understand. The way her tiny body fit in my arms when she was scared or sad and needed someone to hold her. She was a little girl who had the kindest heart and didn't deserve to be ripped away from the world in the most vile way.

By the time I reach her headstone, I can barely read the script through my blurred vision.

In Loving Memory

Of

Mia Elle Walker

May you rest peacefully in

God's loving arms.

Do you think I'm a good enough girl to go to heaven when I die? Her words fill my head like a beautiful disease.

I grind my teeth and try to breathe through the ache in my chest. Images of her small body, bloody and violated, make its way to the surface next, taking me back to that fateful day.

Why didn't you tell me?

I'm sorry, Cade, he said he'd kill you if I ever told.

The guilt is what finishes me, shredding the little composure I had up until this point. My legs give out as I fall to my knees in agony, my forehead dropping on the headstone. "I'm so sorry, so fucking sorry I wasn't there." The words barely making it past the excruciating burn in my throat. "I'm sorry that I didn't know sooner. I should have protected you." All the words I've always wanted to say to her pour out of me, until there is nothing left to say. Until the foreign tears and sobs subside to nothing but numbness.

Time becomes nothing more than an afterthought, the night filled with nothing but my despair and regret. Everything is calm and quiet as I rest against the headstone behind me, my gaze up on the Colorado sky that's painted with the sunset.

I love you, Cade.

Her words come out of nowhere, filling my mind and heart. Just then, a sudden gust of wind picks up, something soft grazing my hand. When I look down, my heart stops beating altogether.

A white ribbon lays across my hand, the same one I'd swear I've seen before. I jump to my feet quickly, my gaze scanning the deserted graveyard.

It can't be. Someone has to be here.

I clutch the ribbon in my hand, doing a quick walk around the cemetery but find no sign of anyone. I begin to worry I'm crazy, that coming here was too much and I've lost my fucking mind but there is no denying what I hold in my hand nor the scent it holds. A shampoo I could never forget.

Was it here the whole time and I missed it?

I shove the thought away, knowing this is something I wouldn't have missed. Disbelief courses through me as I walk back to her headstone, staring down at it long and hard before kneeling once again. I rest my forehead on it, saying one final goodbye. "I'll never stop thinking of you again. I love you, Mia. Forever."

I push to stand and walk away with an ache in my chest that I know will never fade but somehow feels more manageable. After climbing into my rental vehicle, I head to my next destination, dread sinking into my gut with every minute that passes. It isn't long before I pull up to the small run-down house I haven't seen in twelve years. If it weren't for Catherine Evans, I wouldn't have known the woman inside still lived here.

I walk up the familiar, cracked cement steps and knock on the broken screen door. When it swings open, I'm met by the one woman I resent most in this world. Maria Walker looks mostly the same, but older, and more worn. Her bloodshot eyes tell me she's just as much of a junkie now as she was back then.

Shock registers in her eyes seconds before they narrow in hatred. It's a look I remember well, the only way she's ever looked at me.

"What the hell are you doing here?" she bites out.

You would think her greeting would hurt me, that the woman who is supposed to love me unconditionally can barely stand the sight of me, but it doesn't. If anything, it makes it easier to forget about her.

Without waiting for an invite, I push my way past her and enter inside. "I'm here to pick up something of Mia's that I want."

"You are not taking a single thing. You don't deserve anything of hers."

I ignore her and head straight for my sister's room.

She follows me, her steps quick as she grabs my arm. "I mean it, you're not—"

"Don't put your fucking hands on me." I turn on her quickly, forcing her back a step. "I'm taking the rabbit I gave her for her birthday, and if you try to stop me again you will live to regret it."

Fear enters her cold eyes and she doesn't stop me again.

My sister's room is exactly how I remember it, nothing out of place. The rabbit sits in the middle with all her other stuffed animals. As I grab it, I come across the picture that sits next to her bed on the nightstand, the sight of it stopping me cold.

It's the one of us when I took her to the fair. She's on my back, her small face next to mine with the biggest smile; it's one I rarely saw because the house we lived in was never happy. But for that one night she was happy, and it makes me feel good to know I was the one who put it there. Feeling a burn in my throat, I grab the picture too, knowing Maria couldn't give a shit about it and walk out.

I pass by her in the living room, ignoring her death glare. Before I leave, I ask one question I have to know. "Did you put the ribbon at her grave?"

"What ribbon?" she sneers. "What the hell are you talking about?"

I figured it wasn't her but I had to be sure. I don't bother to explain and reach for the door but stop short with what she says next.

"It should have been you not her."

I turn back around and find her eyes filled with so much hatred. It makes me wonder how a mother can hate her own child so much, a child who never did anything but live and breathe. I think of Red, of how she is with Christopher and Ruthie and the way she loves them unconditionally. She's everything a mother should be and everything this mother isn't. For the first time I'm struck with the realization that I may be all sorts of fucked-up but I know I'm nothing like this bitch or my father.

"If I could have traded places with her I would have," I tell her honestly. "I would have died for her, but as it happened you killed her instead. All because you're nothing but a no-good fucking junkie who wanted attention and let some asshole who was screwing you, screw with your daughter."

Pain flashes in her angry eyes but I couldn't give a shit because all of it is the truth. She picks up an empty drinking glass and throws it my way. I duck just in time, feeling the glass shatter around me.

"Get out!" she wails, "and never come back."

"Don't worry, you will never see me again." With that last remark, I get the hell out of there and drive to the airport, hoping there will be a flight out sooner rather than later. There are things I need to finish putting in place, things I need to do before I can move on with my life and right the wrongs I've done.

CHAPTER 44

Cade

The past week has been one hell of an emotional roller coaster, which takes a lot out of a guy who never used to feel anything. Until one woman changed that.

I've missed Faith like fucking crazy this past week. Evans has been giving me daily updates but it hasn't helped. As much as I appreciate what he has done, I want to be the one eating dinner with them and going to bed every night there only to wake up and have breakfast with my family. My family, something I haven't had since my sister's death.

Everything I want is within reach. I've spent every day getting what I need in order except for a couple more things. This next wrong I need to right won't be easy.

I pull up to the two-story home and am thankful to see Faith's father's car on the driveway. I didn't call, worrying he would refuse to see me. Unfortunately, I can't give him that option. For Faith's sake, I have to mend this.

With that thought in mind, I climb out of my truck and walk up the front steps. My fist is heavy and hard as I rap on the door.

It opens moments later, revealing the man I came to speak with. "Cade," Joshua Williams greets me, his shock evident.

"Joshua." I nod. "Sorry to stop by unannounced. Do you have a minute?"

He stares at me for a long hard second before finally stepping back. "Of course, please come in."

Relief fills my chest, knowing getting through this door would be my hardest obstacle.

Just as I step inside, George Williams comes walking out of the kitchen. His eyes widen in shock before they narrow. "What the hell are you doing here?"

I'm not surprised by the hostile greeting and know I deserve it.

Before I can say anything though, Joshua does. "Don't be rude, Dad, he's here to speak with me."

"Rude?" the old man bellows. "I'll show you rude when I pull out my shotgun on this asshole for making my Shortcake cry."

Joshua scolds him again before turning to me. "Why don't we go to my office to speak?"

After a nod in his direction, I begin to follow him up the stairs, briefly glancing over my shoulder to find George still glaring at me, his disapproval noted. He tosses me the I'm-watching-you signal before I turn around.

I grunt, getting the message loud and clear.

The moment we enter Joshua William's office, I'm surrounded by all things religion. Pictures, plaques, crosses, bible scriptures. That familiar resentment builds inside of me but more than anything is questions. So many questions I have that I will never ask since walking away from my sister's grave.

On the wall, a massive picture hangs, a blue sky with rays of sunshine along with a long white staircase. What captures my attention isn't the picture, it's the quote.

A little faith will bring your soul to heaven, but a lot of faith will bring heaven to your soul.[2]

"What can I do for you, Cade?" Joshua asks, yanking my attention away as he sits behind his desk.

I open my mouth to say the apology I came for but instead, I end up doing something completely different. Something I never thought I'd do. Reaching inside my pocket, I pull out the white ribbon that I haven't parted with since it landed on me and slam it down on his desk. "I want you to tell me how the hell this ended up in my hands when I haven't seen it in twelve years."

He frowns, confused as he stares down at the ribbon before looking back up at me. "I don't understand. What is it?"

"It was my sister's. She used to wear this in her hair every night. I went to her grave for the first time a few days ago and somehow, this landed on me right out of thin fucking air."

If my language offends him, he doesn't show it. I expect him to look at me like I'm completely crazy for asking him this question but he doesn't. Instead, he leans back in his chair and watches me patiently. "What is it you want me to tell you, Cade?"

I can't answer that because I don't know. I feel like I don't know anything anymore.

"I can tell you what I think, but it probably isn't something you want to hear."

"And what's that?" I ask, surprised how level my voice is despite the turbulent emotions I'm feeling.

"I'd say that is your sister telling you she sees you and that she's okay."

"That's impossible," I snap, though I can't deny the hope it instills. It's all I've ever wanted, for my sister to be okay. To not be hurting like her final moments on this earth.

"Nothing is impossible when it comes to God, but I also know how you feel on the subject, which is why I didn't want to tell you my opinion."

I stare back at him, waiting for judgment to come but it never does. Life father like daughter.

"How the hell can you still believe in him after what happened to your daughter?"

I regret the question when pain darkens his expression. I'm about to apologize but don't get the chance before he answers.

"Because I have faith."

I don't miss the double meaning that answer holds.

"Look, I'd be lying if I told you it was easy for me to always remember that, because it's not. It still kills me to know what happened to my daughter, but I know where there's good there is also evil. And I believe the bastards who hurt her are in hell right alongside the man who hurt your sister."

I drop into the chair across from him, my head falling into my hands as I become more conflicted than ever before.

There's a moment of silence before he speaks again. "I don't know much about what happened to your sister, just the little that Faith has told me, and I want you to know how sorry I am. I know it doesn't mean much and it doesn't make it feel better, but you need to know, Cade, that I am nothing like that man."

My head snaps up to find him watching, regret etched on his face.

"I don't know who he was but I can assure you he was not a man of God."

I nod. "I understand that now and that's why I came here, to apologize about the way I treated you. It's difficult for me to accept that there's this great power out there, after all the awful shit that goes on in this world. Regardless, I shouldn't have taken out my issues on you and for that, I am sorry."

"I can understand where your doubt comes from, but again that's where faith comes in," he says, adding a wink. "You see, God works in mysterious ways. I believe he still fights the battle of evil and his weapons are people like you and your friends, or even my father for that matter, and people like me."

I quirk a brow, wondering where he's going with this.

"While you rid the world of evil and keep it safe, I'm here to keep God alive by faith. Are you getting why I named my girl that?" he asks, a hint of a smirk lifting his mouth. "I always knew she was going to be something great, that one day she was going to change the lives of many just like she did mine, and I was right. You, Christopher, and Ruthie are products of that, and I know there is more and will always be more, because she is special."

"Turns out we actually do agree on something," I say, relaxing back into my chair.

He smiles but it fades quickly. "Have you been to see her yet?"

"No, but I plan to soon. I had to take care of some stuff first but I'd appreciate it if you don't tell her that I came here, I'd like to do that."

"All right, just don't wait too much longer, she misses you and she needs you."

"Trust me, I need her more." I stand just then and decide before I leave, I should let him know of my plans. "I'm going to ask her to marry me."

He doesn't look the least bit surprised. "Are you telling me or asking me?"

"I thought about asking you," I admit, "but figured I should just tell you since it wouldn't matter what you said because I'd ask her anyway."

He smiles, seeming content with that answer. "Fair enough."

I offer him my hand and he clasps it firmly, a truce of silence. "I know I'm not good enough for your daughter, but I promise to take care of her and keep her safe, always."

"Obviously, as her father, I think no one is good enough for her, but as a man, I will tell you I think you are worthy of her." His response surprises me. "However, I should warn you, if you mess up again there will be no stopping my dad and I won't try."

I grunt, having no fucking doubt about that. "If I ever hurt her again, I'll beat the shit out of myself. That's a promise."

He chuckles then claps me on the back before walking me out. I drive away with only one more thing to do, and then, hopefully, Red will be mine and I will have my family back.

CHAPTER 45

Faith

Butterflies dance in my belly as Christopher and I wait in the back of the church to be called upon by my father for our first performance. A performance that will hopefully draw in crowds for my music school, a dream I've had for longer than I can remember.

"I'm not sure I can do this, Faith," Christopher worries, his feet eating a hole in the floor as he paces back and forth nervously.

I grab his shoulders and look back at him with more confidence than I feel. "Yes, you can. We're going to do this, Christopher, and we're going to be amazing, because together we make one heck of a team and you know it."

"Yeah, we make one heck of a team all right, especially sporting our matching, fading bruises."

A sad smile graces my face as he tries to lighten the moment. "It means we're survivors, sport them proudly."

"I'm proud to go out there with you," he says, making my nervous heart jump in my chest.

Ever since we made it out of that catastrophe alive, he has opened up so much more to me, trusted me more than ever before. We're close, more than friends—we are family.

"Have you heard anything from him yet?" he asks, causing my warm smile to fade.

Sadness consumes my soul as I ache for the man I haven't seen or heard from in weeks. "Not yet but I know I will."

Cade Walker is a man of his word. He promised to come back to me and I know he will. It's the only thing that has kept my hope alive. I just pray it happens soon. I miss him so much it hurts. I've used this time though for the kids and I to heal and become whole again after everything that's happened. Something we desperately needed. Just as much as we need our missing piece—Cade.

Alissa pops her head in the back room, her eyes and smile for Christopher only. "We're ready when you guys are."

"Thanks." At Christopher's nod, she backs out.

I turn to face him, inhaling a deep breath. "You ready?"

"Nope, but I'm going to do it anyway. I just pray Alissa still thinks I'm hot after this."

The remark has me breaking into laughter. "She will find you even sexier, I know it."

He grunts, refusing to believe me.

My laughter fades as I step forward, cupping his healing face. "I love you, Christopher."

He clears his throat, his expression solemn. "I love you, too. Now let's get this over with before I back out on you."

Hand in hand we walk out, joined as forces who will hopefully make some history with our talent.

Cade

My heart pounds in my chest like a fucking jackhammer as I stand outside the church, the white building making me feel like I might get sick. I'm not really sure what's scaring me most. If it's the fact I am about to walk into the one place I swore I would never step foot in since my sister's death or if it's fear of being rejected by the woman I love and family I now live for.

Knowing there's only one way to find out, I pull myself together and walk in, finding the place packed. Every pew is filled with people as Faith's father preaches before them. The heavy wooden door closes behind me, drawing attention. Everyone turns to check out the newcomer, looking at me like the outcast I am. All but one.

"Tade!" The excited whisper comes from the center of the room as Ruthie crawls over the people she's with. All my friends help her as she jumps from lap to lap before she makes it to the other side.

She wastes no time running straight for me and I can't help but smirk at the white dress she wears with the black beanie.

That's my girl.

I bend down, arms open. I've been waiting for this moment as much as I have been waiting for my moment with Faith.

She slams into my chest, arms locking tightly around my neck. "I've missed you so much, Big Guy," she whispers into my shoulder.

My arms hug her tighter as I climb to my feet. "I've missed you too, kid," I tell her, voice gruff. "I'm sorry it took me so long but there was something I had to do."

She leans back, looking at me with big, blue, watery eyes. "It's otay, Faif said you wuved me and dat you'd be back."

"I love all of you, and I promise I'm back for good."

Her smile lights up the entire room. It's not long after that I notice the place has fallen silent, everyone's attention being on us.

Joshua smiles, giving me a nod of approval before he continues his sermon. With Ruthie in my arms, I walk to the pew my friends sit at, taking the spot next to Sawyer.

Faith's mom and Katelyn wave at me from the other end of the bench while her Papa gives me the whole I'm-watching-you signal again. It makes me wish he were as forgiving as his son and granddaughter.

Everyone else acknowledges me with a wave, except for Grace. She leans over Sawyer, placing her hand on my leg. "I'm so proud of you, Cade." Her praise makes the whole situation even more awkward, but I nod, not wanting to be an asshole.

"I'm proud of you, too," Sawyer mocks. "Look at you all grown up, such a big boy now."

"Shut up," I return quietly, my eyes narrowing at his stupid smirk.

We fall silent just as Joshua finishes his sermon. "To end today's service we have a special performance. As many of you know, my daughter will be opening a music school here in the fall. I was told very sternly by her not to call it a choir or she said no one would join."

Laughter fills the room, including my own, knowing that's something she would say.

"Her performance will be a good representation of what you can expect if you wish to sign up and be a part of it. Without further ado, please welcome my daughter, Faith, and her boy, Christopher."

My heart thumps wildly, anticipation heating my blood as I wait to finally see the one woman I've missed more than anyone. She and Christopher walk out hand in hand, the entire church breaking out into a welcoming applause.

Though I braced myself for it, the impact I have at the first sight of her completely takes my breath away, everyone around us falling away.

She's as beautiful as always, wearing a simple white sundress with dark brown cowgirl boots and her long, red hair falling in loose waves around her shoulders. It takes every bit of willpower I possess not to walk up there and carry her out of here with me.

My gaze moves to Christopher next, a surge of pride filling my chest at his bravery for being up there, knowing this isn't easy for him.

Faith whispers something to the elderly lady at the piano before taking her spot next to Christopher again. They look out over the crowd but never focus on one person, which is probably a good thing because I don't want her to see me in the middle of singing and have it throw her off. It's something I probably should have thought about. Hopefully, she won't know any different until after the performance.

The piano comes to life and I quickly recognize the tune to "Lean on Me". Christopher starts the first chorus and the moment the first word falls from him, I'm stunned, completely dumbstruck. I hadn't heard him up until this point. Faith said he was good but never did I think he was this good. He's as talented as Faith, something I didn't think was possible.

"Holy shiii… crap," Sawyer whispers, catching himself. "He's incredible."

"Dats my Twistphwor," Ruthie claims proudly, and I can't help but feel the same way. I'm proud to know him too, proud to call him family.

Christopher eventually fades out, leaving the next chorus all to Red, and like always, her voice rivets me, changing the world as I know it.

As the song goes on they take turns, singing separately and together, their voices mingling in harmony. The two of them are a powerhouse, blowing every single person away.

Once the song finishes, everyone jumps to their feet, giving a standing ovation. Red launches herself excitedly at Christopher and he catches her with a laugh, looking damn proud of himself, as he should be.

"Dey was amazing, wewn't dey, Big Guy."

I don't take my eyes off them as I reply, "Yeah, kid, they were incredible."

Christopher is still hugging Faith when he looks over at our pew and spots me, his expression transforming to one of shock.

I try to gauge his reaction and he must stiffen because Red notices. She steps back, looking up at him. He lifts his arm and points me out. That's when she turns around, her beautiful emerald eyes colliding with mine.

The first reaction to cross her face is utter disbelief, not that I can blame her, but eventually, a myriad of other emotions are soon to follow.

Christopher snaps back into himself when Alissa wraps her arms around him. He lifts her off her feet, hugging her back. Faith hasn't moved or taken her eyes off me; I don't think she has even blinked.

Christopher tugs her hand, dragging her behind him as they make their way through the crowd. Everyone congratulates them as they pass by, telling them how amazing they were.

Once they reach our pew, Katelyn and her mom are the first to hug them, then are followed by all the others. Through it all, Faith's shocked gaze never leaves mine.

When everyone has had their turn, I make my way down, extending my hand to Christopher first. "I'm impressed, kid. You were incredible and you should be really proud."

"Thanks. It's good to see you, I'm glad you came."

It's not until this moment I realize how worried I was about his reception. "Me, too." My eyes shift to Red now, finding her a few feet away, tears welling in her pretty eyes.

"Go get 'er, Big Guy," Ruthie whispers, punching me in the arm. I look down at her as she stands on the pew, offering a smirk before I get my feet moving, everything I have worked for the past few weeks all leading up to this one moment.

"Hey, Red," I greet softly, stopping just in front of her.

She doesn't say hi back, only gapes at me. "You're in a church."

I nod, clearing my throat. "And the building didn't even catch fire. Go figure."

She bursts into a fit of laughter. It's a laugh that warms every cold place inside of me and one I've missed like crazy. But it quickly trails into sobs, the entire realization catching up with her.

I don't waste another second taking her into my arms, lifting her off her feet. She hugs me back, burying her face in my neck. "I've missed you so much," she cries.

"I missed you too, baby." Placing her down on her feet, I cup her face, lifting it to mine. "Leave here with me. I have something to show you."

"Now?"

"Yeah, now."

She hesitates, looking over at the kids.

"Go on, Faith," Katelyn says, giving her the push she needs. "I got them. We'll go grab lunch and meet up with you later."

Her gaze comes back to mine. "Okay, let's go."

Grabbing her hand, I lead her out of the church, my feet quick. The moment we make it outside, I reel her in again, kissing her like I've been aching to. Her arms lock around my neck, lips as desperate as mine. The sweet taste of her, the one I have come to crave, settles deep into my chest.

Eventually I pull back, forehead resting on hers. "I'm sorry it took me so long."

"It doesn't matter. All that matters is you're here now."

I have no idea what I did to deserve this woman but now that I have her, I'm never letting go. Not ever again and it's time to prove it.

CHAPTER 46

Faith

The truck is filled with silence as we drive into the country, my body fully aware of the man next to me. Every part of my skin tingles to touch his, my heart yearning for so much more than the kiss he gave me outside the church.

I can't even begin to describe how I felt when Christopher pointed him out to me in the crowd, not only was I surprised by his return, but I was stunned he was in that church. The fact the he made that big of a leap for me means more than he will ever know.

My curiosity piques when he turns down the same gravel road that Jaxson and Julia live on. "Where are you taking me?"

"You'll see."

The cryptic answer leaves me even more intrigued but I don't have to wait long before he turns down a long driveway, leading to the most beautiful Victorian-styled house. It's white with burgundy trim and has a massive wrap-around porch that takes my breath away. What has my heart skipping a beat though is the SOLD sign that's staked in the front lawn.

My eyes shift to Cade as he parks, waiting for an explanation, but I still don't get one. Instead, he climbs out and walks around to my side, opening my door and offering me his hand. "Walk with me."

Without hesitation, I place my hand in his and wonder what's going on as he starts walking us across the large property toward the barn in the distance.

"I visited my sister's grave for the first time," he tells me, pain lacing his voice.

"I would have come with you. You know that, right?"

"I know but it's something I had to do myself."

I nod, completely understanding that. Even though I would have liked to have been there to comfort him, I believe he had to do this on his own, to grieve with no one watching.

"How did it go?" I ask softly.

"It hurt like a motherfucker; it still does." His gruff voice has tears stinging my eyes. I wish more than anything I could take his pain away.

"I'm sorry," I choke out, knowing it means nothing.

Once we reach the barn, he releases my hand and leans back against it. He shoves his hands in his pockets and stares at the ground as he kicks the dirt. He looks like a vulnerable boy rather than the strong man I know.

"I'm not sure what's worse, finally dealing with the fact that she's dead and never coming back or that I never went to see her before because it hurt too much."

I step into him, wrapping my arms around his waist as I peer up into his heart-broken face. "She knows you love her, Cade. She's always known that."

"How, Red?" he asks, the question choking past him. "How would she know that? I never even let myself fucking think about her. I pretended she didn't exist because it hurt too bad, it still does, and I'm not sure it will ever stop hurting." He looks away but not before I witness tears brimming in his eyes, something I never thought he was capable of.

"It's going to hurt a lot right now, because even though she's been gone a long time, you're just starting to accept it."

His jaw clenches as he struggles to hold in his pain, but no matter how hard he tries, a single tear slips past the corner of his eye. It has me close to breaking into a blubbering mess.

I frame his face between my hands, forcing him to look at me. "I'm so sorry you're hurting right now, but I promise, as time goes on it will get a little better. You're always going to miss her, and I'm sure it will always hurt but not this much. It still pains me to think about Aadil, but ever since you and the kids it's been getting better. You all have healed my heart in so many ways; let us do the same for you."

He drops his forehead on mine. "That's why I went. I knew I had to deal with her death, and I'm trying, but…"

"What?" I ask when he trails off.

"It's the fucking guilt, Red. It's been eating at me for twelve years and that's the hardest part, trying to forgive myself."

"Forgive yourself for what?" I ask, feeling confused.

"For not stopping it, for not making it in time."

"No," I interrupt before he can go further. "None of what happened was your fault, you were just a child."

"I was fifteen!"

"Exactly! Look at Christopher, would you blame him if this were Ruthie?"

"This is different."

"How?" I ask. "How is this any different?"

"Because I knew what kind of person my mother was, knew the guy was a fucking nut job, but I didn't know he was ever alone with her, that he had been messing with her."

"How could you? What happened to her was his fault, not yours."

He shakes his head.

"Yes," I counter, refusing to let him take on this blame. "Listen to me. Your sister knew you loved her and she wouldn't want you to blame yourself for this. I know we don't view things in life the same way but I really do believe she's okay, and that she's at peace."

Something passes over his expression, something I can't decipher. "Funny you should mention that…" He reaches into his pocket, pulling out a long, white ribbon before passing it to me.

I take the delicate piece, holding it in my hand. "What is it?"

"It was my sister's. At least I think it was…" He pauses, seeming agitated now. "Jesus. I don't fucking know what to think, Faith."

"Tell me," I plead, trying to follow what he's saying.

"I was sitting at her grave for hours, just sitting there while memories of her ran through my head, they were so clear I swear I could hear her voice, as if she were right beside me. And then, all of a sudden, this thing came out of nowhere and landed right in my fucking hand."

My heart stops beating altogether, a beautiful emotion taking its place. "Oh my gosh, Cade. That's amazing."

"Amazing?" he repeats. "I just told you my sister's ribbon that she used to wear in her hair flew out of thin air and landed in my hand, and you tell me this is amazing?"

His brash tone doesn't deter me in the least. "Don't you see? It was her telling you she sees you and that she's at peace. Do you have any idea how many people would love to have someone, who they miss dearly, send them something as precious as this from beyond?"

"You sound like your father."

I tense. "My father?"

"Yeah, he said the same thing to me."

"You spoke with him?" I ask, shocked.

He nods. "I gave him the apology he deserved. I fucked up at Christopher's birthday, Red, and I know it. I'm so sorry I said the things I did. I just…I couldn't seem to help it. All I could picture was that bastard hurting my sister."

"He's a good man, Cade," I tell him sadly. "He'd never hurt anyone."

He reaches up, cupping my cheek. "I know, baby. I see that now and I know how wrong I've been. It's why I went to her grave. I knew I had to deal with it if I wanted to keep you and the kids."

"Is that what you want? Me and the kids?" I ask, my breath stalling in hope.

"I don't just want you. I need you. I can't live without you."

His words do so much to mend my broken heart and have me breaking out into a blubbering mess. He kisses my flowing tears, trailing his lips across my cheek until his mouth reaches my ear. "Live here with me, Red. Marry me."

Every muscle in my body stiffens, my eyes snapping up to his. "Wha—what?" I ask, fearing I misheard him.

His hand disappears into his other pocket, pulling out a small velvet box. He opens it, revealing the most breathtaking engagement ring, the large diamond colored red. "Marry me, Faith. Be mine forever."

"I thought you didn't believe in love?" I blurt out stupidly, my mind scrambling to catch up with what's happening.

"Yeah, well some redheaded country girl may have changed my mind about that"

"May have?" I ask, feeling a smile touch my lips.

The joke falls flat though, his gaze never wavering from mine. "You did. You made me realize I'm not so broken after all."

The softest breath impales my lungs, my breath catching with emotion. "You're not broken, you're perfect."

"I'm nothing without you. Say yes, Red."

"Yes, Red," I tease, a giggle sliding from my throat at the glare he shoots me. I take pity on him, giving him the answer we both want, my entire world falling into place with it. "Yes, Cade. I already told you, I'd follow you anywhere."

"Good because I wasn't going to give you a choice."

After he slides the ring on my finger, I launch myself into his arms, kissing him with a love I feel all the way down to my soul. Growling, he lifts me off my feet, pinning me against the barn, his erection pressing against the one spot I crave to feel him most, but before things can get too heated, a noise sounds from inside the barn, yanking us from the moment.

We both pause, my head pulling back. "What the heck was that?"

"Nothing," he says quickly, but there's an unmistakable knowledge in his eyes.

The noise happens again. A sound that's impossible to distinguish.

"That is definitely something."

He clears his throat, seeming nervous for some reason. "I bought you something but I don't want to give it to you anymore."

"Why?"

"Because it's stupid."

"Impossible," I tell him, meaning it.

"Believe me, Red, this is dumb."

"I have loved everything you've given me so far."

When he makes no move to give me what I want, I push away from him and walk to the large wooden doors before opening them. The sight I'm met with has a gasp leaving my throat. "Cade, you didn't!"

I run inside, kneeling before the adorable brown calf that's gated in a stable. He's the cutest thing I've ever seen; with big brown eyes and even bigger ears. His head tilts to one side as he gazes back at me.

I run my hand through his soft, fine coat, pressing a kiss to his nose. "Well, aren't you just the most precious thing ever."

He releases another noise, rubbing against my touch. My hand strokes down his neck and hits the big brass bell around his neck. With a closer look, I find the word *Hank* engraved on it.

I burst out laughing and turn back to see Cade standing at the door watching me.

"You bought me a cow named Hank?" I ask, unbelieving he would remember something so minor I told him years ago.

"I told you it was stupid," he grumbles, looking unsure of himself.

Giving Hank one more kiss on the head, I stand, my feet eating up the distance between us.

Cade's eyes sweep down my body like a dark hurricane, making my skin burn for his touch. Rising to the tips of my toes, I wrap my arms around his neck. "It's not stupid. I love him and I love you with my whole heart."

"I love you too."

I smile, knowing I will never tire of hearing him say that to me. My lips brush his, just a feather of a touch, but they ache for so much more. "Make love to me, Walker. Right here. Right now."

His response is a growl as he takes me to the ground within seconds. My back meets the loose straw, hay bales surrounding us as he comes over top of me, his body blanketing mine, igniting a warmth all the way to my soul.

His mouth claims mine before his lips descend down my neck, building an inferno in my body and heart. Our clothes are gone next, our skin colliding seconds before he slides into me, completing me body and soul.

"I missed you so much," I cry, wanting him to know I need him as much as he does me.

"Me too, Red. I thought about you every fucking second I was away from you." His hips surge forward, cock thrusting hard and deep. Sweat begins to coat my skin, our bodies moving in harmony, communicating in a way that only we can.

"Don't ever stop," I plead, clinging to his shoulders.

"Never, baby. I'll never stop."

It's a vow I hold close to my heart, letting it heal the remainder of any cracks it had.

All too soon, that familiar feeling builds low in my tummy, catapulting me into the universe where only Cade and I exist.

"That's it, Red. Give it to me, baby. I want all of you."

He has me. My body and heart, now until the end of time.

It isn't long before he follows suit, groaning out his own pleasure. I hold him through it, loving him through the emotions he allows himself to feel for these few short moments in time.

Our heartbeats slow, drumming to the same rhythm as my hands run along his mangled back, feeling the puckered skin of his scars. It's a heavy reminder of just how far we've come, of the hell we escaped only to find this kind of heaven with one another.

"You've made me the happiest woman in the world, Cade Walker," I whisper, holding him close.

He lifts his head from my shoulder, eyes penetrating the deepest parts of my soul. His hand cups my cheek, thumb stroking my skin. "I promise to make you happy like this always. I'll take care of you, Faith, and our family. You'll never want for anything and I swear you will never hurt."

I peer back into his hazel eyes and realize this is my life. My happily ever after that I've dreamt about since I was a little girl. Having no words to adequately describe just how he makes me feel, I bring his lips upon mine, knowing our love will conquer anything this world throws at us because it already has.

EPILOGUE

Cade

Two years later

Our yard is filled with our closest family and friends as we celebrate Christopher's high school graduation, a monumental moment in his life that I am lucky enough to be apart of. I couldn't be more proud of the man he has become and I'm fortunate to call him family. Fortunate for the second chance I've been given, something I will never take for granted again.

"Come on, Faith. How many more pictures are you going to take?" he complains, walking hand in hand with Alissa.

"Just one more, I promise."

"That's what you said the last twenty times," he reminds her.

"I know but I'm telling the truth this time."

Chuckles float through the air and I can't help but smirk. She's been making the poor kid pose and smile for hours.

"Stop your grumbling," Katelyn intervenes. "This is one of the biggest days of your life."

Faith lifts her chin. "Exactly, and I have not been that bad."

"Not that bad?" he replies, exasperated. "Are you kidding me? All of you girls stood up and screamed so loud when my name was called that the whole town probably heard you."

"That's true, you girls were pretty over the top," Sawyer pipes in, holding his one-year-old daughter, Hope, while Grace stands next to him, holding the other twin, their son, Parker.

"We were excited for him," Julia argues back, standing next to Jaxson who has their two-year-old daughter, Annabelle, on his shoulders.

"Yeah, and it could have been worse, we could have stolen the sheriff department's megaphone like we were going to and really announce you," Kayla adds, sitting on Cooper's lap while holding their one-year-old son, Beckett.

Cooper leans back to look at her. "Why would you have stolen it? Why wouldn't you just ask me?"

"Because it's much more fun to steal it then see your face when we use it," she replies, not bothering to hold back her amusement.

His eyes narrow as he grumbles something intangible.

"You have to admit that it's better to have someone cheering for you than no one at all," Joshua adds, being the logical one as always. His wife smiles up at him while

Papa George grunts in disagreement.

"That's very true, now enough stalling," Faith says, getting back on topic. "Put your arm around Alissa and smile this time."

The kid huffs out a breath but does as she asks, though the smile is half-ass if you ask me but it's okay because Alissa's has been big enough for the both of them.

After Red snaps the picture, she gives him a watery smile and starts wiping her cheeks again.

The kid rolls his eyes but his expression softens. "Come on, Faith, please don't cry again," he pleads but pulls her in for a hug. No matter how much she embarrasses him, there is no denying he has a soft spot for her. It's something he and I have in common.

"I'm sorry," she apologizes tearfully. "I'm just so proud of you. You have come so far."

My attention is drawn away when I feel small fingers grip my hand. "Hey, Big Guy."

I look down at the little girl who has healed my heart just as much as Red has. Bending down, I swing her up in my arms. "How's my girl?"

She gives me a bright smile that still causes a shift in my chest. "Good. She sure does cwy a lot nowadays, doesn't she?" she says, nodding over at Red.

I still find myself impressed at how far she has come with her speech, something she's been working hard at with a therapist for the past two years. It's those R's she still struggles with.

"It's pregnancy tears, kid," Sawyer says. "Believe me there's much more to come."

All the guys grunt in agreement while Grace elbows him. "Don't even go there, Sawyer."

"Don't worry, Cupcake, I wasn't meaning you. I was talking about every other pregnant woman."

She shakes her head but can't hide her smile.

For once I agree with him. Red has definitely become more sensitive since being pregnant, but I wouldn't change it for the world. She's carrying my second daughter, our third child, one we have decided to name after my sister.

"Okay, one more picture," Faith says, which has Christopher throwing up his hands in exasperation. "I know, I'm sorry, but I want one of our family."

"Come on, Red, that's enough, baby," I cut in, trying to help the kid. "We took some at the school."

"I know, but I want one of us in front of the tree. Please?" she pleads softly when we don't budge.

I clap Christopher on the shoulder. "Come on, one more," I tell him, willing to suffer through anything if it means putting a smile back on her face.

"I'll take it," Katelyn says, taking the camera from Faith.

We all walk toward the huge oak tree that was planted in memory of my sister, Aadil, and the children's mom. All of their names are engraved on it. Faith insisted, saying it was a way to keep them all a part of our family.

I hold Ruthie, shifting her to my one side so I can put my other arm around Faith while Christopher stands on the other side of her.

"Your mom would be so proud of you, Christopher," she tells him softly. "I know she's smiling down on you today from heaven like she does every day."

"Thanks, Faith," he says, clearing his throat.

It's been harder on him than it was on Ruthie since she doesn't remember her mother, but he's come a long way in his grieving process like I have. However, that pain will always be there for the both of us, one no one can understand unless they have gone through it.

"Well, Big Guy, I guess this will pwobably be the last family picture we will have where you will be holding me," Ruthie says, a sudden sadness edging her voice.

Red and I share a look before turning our attentions on her.

"Why would you think that?" I ask.

"Because, once the baby is bown you will pwobably always want to hold her, since she's your weal daughter."

The words are like a knife to the chest, slicing me open.

"Oh, Ruthie," Faith sighs, "that's not true. Sure Cade will want to hold Mia too, but that doesn't mean he will hold you any less. And who knows, maybe Mia will always want you to hold her?"

A smile brightens her face. Clearly she never thought of that.

"She may be the baby but you are my first," I add, "Nothing will ever change that, kid. I will gladly haul you around for as long as you will let me. Even if that means carrying you into high school."

It's the truth. I will never give this up. The thought of her growing up and not thinking I'm as cool as she does right now…it brings a panic I don't like to think about.

She gives me a big, sloppy kiss on the cheek. "I'll never want you to stop carrying me for the west of my life, and I don't even care if kids make fun of me for it."

Christopher grunts. "No one will make fun of you when they get a look at him."

Faith chuckles. "That's very true."

"All right, everyone, look over here and say cheese," Katelyn orders, bringing us all forward. "Cade, can you at least look like you're happy?"

"I am happy," I shoot back.

"Well, you don't look it, people who are happy smile."

"This is my smile."

She rolls her eyes and that's when Faith intervenes.

"Ruthie, tell Cade you love him."

"I love you, Big Guy," she whispers, before dramatically squishing her nose into the side of my cheek.

"Perfect!" Katelyn snaps the picture then hands it back to Faith. "You can't see Ruthie's face but at least he's smiling."

I glare at her sassy smile as she takes the kid from me. "Come on, sweetness, let's go eat cake."

Before she makes it too far, I catch up and plant a quick kiss on Ruthie's cheek. "I love you too, kid. Forever."

She smiles at me over Katelyn's shoulder as they head back to the picnic table where Faith's mom is dishing out the cake.

Faith comes up behind me, wrapping her arms around my waist. My cock jerks when she slides her warm hands beneath my shirt.

"Red," I growl before turning around, pulling her into my arms.

"Walker," she mocks back, trying to keep the smile off her face.

"Don't pull that shit in front of people, because you know I will haul your ass behind closed doors and give it to you."

She steps in even closer, peering up at me with need in her pretty green eyes. "I just can't help myself, you're so darn sexy today."

I pick her up gently, her feet dangling and slightly rounded tummy against my hard one. It has another surge of heat shooting straight to my groin. Knowing she's carrying my child drives me fucking insane with the need to claim.

"You're the sexy one, Red, and I'm going to show you just how sexy I think you are as soon as everyone leaves."

Her brow lifts. "I guess it's a good thing Ruthie is staying the night at my parents' house tonight, isn't it?"

"Damn right. I'm going to make you scream so goddamn loud you will wake the fucking neighbors."

"Our nearest neighbor is a mile away," she reminds me.

"Exactly."

She throws her head back and laughs, which has my own lips twitching with a smile, something that isn't so unusual anymore. Not when I'm around her.

She brings her sparkling emerald eyes back to mine, her smile as beautiful as the rest of her. I lean in to give her a quick kiss, but like always, I can't help myself and end up taking more. Always more.

"Hey, there are children at this party, the least you can do is go into the barn," Sawyer belts out from across the lawn, drawing attention to us.

It leaves me no choice but to place Faith back on her feet. "I really hate that guy."

"No, you don't, you love him. He is your best friend."

"No, I don't, I hate him," I argue back.

She shakes her head, knowing I'm full of shit, and she's right. No matter how much Sawyer pushes every one of my buttons, he and Jaxson will always be the brothers I never had. They are the two guys who lived through hell with me to help save the only woman who ever mattered to me, and I know they would do it again in a heartbeat, just like I would for them. We will always have each other's backs and protect one another's family. It's an unspoken bond, one that will never die.

"Come on, Walker, we'll finish this later." She tugs on my hand, leading me back to the picnic table.

"I think Norman wants to join us," Sawyer says, pointing over at the cow as he watches us through the white fence.

"His name is Hank," Faith says, barely holding back a laugh. "I tell you this all the time."

He shrugs. "Hank, Norman, either way it's a cow, and I'm still trying to understand your logic on this so-called present, Walker," he says, continuing to bust my balls. "He buys his woman a tree from her childhood"—he points at Jaxson—"I buy my woman the bakery she always wanted, and you buy your woman a cow?"

A couple of the guys chuckle, which only makes me want to punch the smug smile off his face that much more.

"You're lucky you're holding your daughter right now, *Sexy Sawyer*, or I would lay your ass out right here."

"Oh, Cade, stop," Faith says. "He's just teasing."

"Yeah, I was only kidding, don't have a cow, man," he laughs hysterically, thinking he's the funniest asshole alive.

I'm just about to knock him upside the head when Red gets between us. "All right, now that's enough," she scolds, but can't stop herself from laughing either.

Clearly, I'm the only one who doesn't find him very funny.

"And for the record, I love Hank as much as Grace loves her bakery and Julia loves her swing." She leans down, dropping a kiss on my lips. "I'm going to bring him over so he can hang out with us."

The other women get up to follow, leaving the few of us guys alone. At least until Ruthie joins us, hopping up on my lap. "Did Papa Joshua talk to you yet?"

"About what?" I ask, looking over at Joshua for the answer.

He clears his throat, shifting in his seat. "There's an overnight convention in Greenville I'm going to, and there's a fun camp going on for any of us who have grandkids. I thought Ruthie might like to join me. Of course, only if it's okay with you and Faith."

My immediate instinct is to say no, and Joshua knows it too.

"I would be with her the entire time," he adds reassuringly.

I look back at Ruthie who watches me hopefully. "Do you want to go?"

"Oh yes, I think me and Papa Joshua would have a lot of fun, and my friend Morgan from Sunday school is going to be there, too."

The entire thought leaves me nauseous but I've come to trust Joshua and I need to give Ruthie this chance. "If it's all right with Faith then it's okay with me."

"Yay!" She wraps her arms around my neck. "Thank you, thank you, thank you."

"You're welcome, but remember, Faith has to say yes first."

"I Understand." She jumps off my lap, running toward the pasture.

Joshua nods at me. "I'll take good care of her, I promise."

"I know."

Conversation picks up but I'm distracted by the sound of Red's laughter. I look over to see her laughing as Hank rubs his big, goofy face against her slightly rounded stomach. The sun shines down on her, showcasing a beauty that I never knew existed until her. It's this image that makes me see just how wrong I've been.

The thing is, I will probably always have some concerns when it comes to religion, because of what happened to my sister, but one thing I have been doubting less of is God. Because I know, without a doubt, that something pretty powerful had to create someone as extraordinary as her. I have no idea how I got to be lucky enough to have her, but I do know I will spend every day making sure to appreciate one of life's best creations.

The Final Temptation

Men of Honor Series

K.C. LYNN

The Final Temptation

Published by K.C. Lynn

Cover Art by: Vanilla Lily Designs
Formatting: BB eBooks

Dedication

Dedicated to the star herself, my girl Kayla. You have been my biggest cheerleader from the very beginning. Who knew that when I wrote you into *Fighting Temptation*, that my readers would beg for you to have your own story? Though I'm not surprised; you are easy to love. Thank you for always being there. Kayla and Cooper are for you.

CHAPTER 1

Kayla

There are certain moments in life that we will remember forever. Some may be a memorable birthday from our childhood, one that stood out a little more than the rest of them; that awkward moment with the first boy you ever kissed; or times with your best friend where you laughed so hard that you cried. Or, in Julia's and my case, times where I got us into deep shit thanks to my dumb ideas and hot temper. And then there were moments that altered the course of your life. They touched you so deeply that every time you think about them, you can still feel what you felt in that moment just as strongly as you did all those years ago.

I'm lucky enough to have a few of those moments, and one of them was the night of my senior prom. Though not because of my success of getting through twelve years of school—nope. It's because it was that night when I found out the one guy, who I had been in love with since I was fourteen years old, returned my feelings. The same one who lived next door to me and tempted my teenage hormones on a regular basis. He's a guy that was born with natural good looks, like insane good looks, like so damn sexy that it should be illegal to look that good. He could charm the panties off any girl who came within reach of him… *Don't think about that part, Kayla.*

He was a natural at sports, good in school, and was loved by everyone—still is. You know that term, *the All-American boy next door*? Well, that was Cooper McKay. But the attributes I just listed are only a very small part of why I fell in love with him. The one thing I love most about Cooper—other than his delectable body of course—is his heart. He is the most honorable and courageous man I've ever known. A man who puts his life on the line every day, and damn does he look good doing it too, uniform and all… *Head out of the gutter, Kayla.*

Okay, in all seriousness, it's his integrity that made me fall madly in love with him. The way he takes care of me and protects me, my friends, and all the other citizens of Sunset Bay. The guy will go to Grams's senior home every time Gladys thinks someone is stealing her panties for crying out loud. Now how many guys do you know that would do that? None, zero, zip, nada—but my Coop will. We all know the real reason why Gladys calls the good sheriff time and time again, and it ain't because she thinks anyone is stealing her panties. She just wants to get a look at the goods, and can you really blame her? I most certainly don't. Though, if she were about forty years younger and looked like Megan Fox, the bitch and I would be having words.

"You look so darn beautiful, Kayla," Grace says softly, breaking into my thoughts.

I smile at her reflection in the mirror as she stands behind me. "Thanks, Grace."

Today I will be adding to those memorable moments in my life, because I am finally going to marry the man I'm madly in love with. Ever since I was a little girl, I dreamed about this day, and I have to admit as I look at my reflection, what I see staring back at me is exactly how I pictured myself. With my white, strapless, poufy dress, high veil, and classy shoes I feel like a modern-day Cinderella. Add along the plantation we chose, which has a beautiful outdoor garden, and of course my very own Prince Charming, it's my dream wedding come true. Although, Cooper is a little more on the rugged side for a prince, but I'll bet good ol' Prince Charming can't do half of the things Coop can with his mouth…

"Miss Gwace is wight. You wook boutiful," Ruthie chimes in, cutting off my perverted thoughts.

With a smile, I turn around and hunch down to her level. "And you look so beautiful too, Ruthie. Thank you for agreeing to be my flower girl, and thank you for parting with your beanie. I know that must have been difficult. But I promise as soon as the ceremony and pictures are finished you can put it right back on."

She gives me a big, gap-toothed grin. "No pwobwem. Da Big Guy and me talked about it and decided it was a small sacwifice to make fwor just one day." All of us bite back a chuckle, knowing how serious her and Cade's beanie obsession is. It's adorable how much she tries to be just like him.

I look around at the beautiful ladies who surround me in this room and feel so blessed. Grace, Katelyn, and Faith all agreed to be my bridesmaids, while Ruthie and Annabelle are my flower girls. And, of course, Julia is my matron of honor. They all look stunning in their pink, silk, strapless dresses, and I know the guys with their pink ties are going to compliment them nicely. I feel my lips tilt with a smirk at the thought. I bet the guys have been grumbling all morning about that, but Coop put up and shut up because it made me happy. One of the other things I love about him so much.

I'm brought out of my thoughts when the bathroom door swings open to reveal a smiling Julia. My heart immediately thrums in anticipation for what she's about to tell me. "So? What does it say?" I ask, but by her expression I already know the answer.

"It's positive," she responds softly.

Silence fills the room as I stare at her. Everyone awaits my reaction, not knowing what to expect. "Positive?" I repeat, making sure I heard her right.

She nods.

I blow out a heavy breath and feel tears blur my eyes but I hold them back, not wanting to ruin my makeup. Walking over, I snatch the pregnancy test from her and stare at the blue plus sign. "Oh my god. Coop and I are going to have a baby," I whisper.

The girls remain quiet, trying to gauge my reaction. Katelyn is finally the one to break the silence. "So, how do you feel about it?"

I think about it for a moment. "I'm really surprised. I didn't think it would happen so soon. I just went off the pill last month, and I heard it usually takes a while for it to leave your system." I pause then look up at them all with a smile. "But I'm really happy."

Everyone rushes over and wraps me in their arms. "Congratulations, Kayla, I'm so happy for both you and Cooper," Faith says, her voice soft and sincere, as always.

A chorus of agreements follow before Grace breaks in. "I can't believe we're gonna have babies together. This is so darn excitin', Kayla." Grace and Sawyer just found out last month that not only are they expecting, but they are also having twins.

"I'm so excited that Annabelle is going to have more play buddies," Julia adds.

"Me, too." I walk over and sit at the end of the bed then stare down at the test, still feeling in utter shock. Although, I guess I shouldn't. I have suspected this the last few days.

"What do you think Cooper will say?" Katelyn asks as she takes the seat next to me.

I feel bad everyone here knows before him, but when I voiced my suspicion to Grace and Julia early this morning they suggested I take a pregnancy test. The need to know one way or another became so overwhelming that I couldn't wait. I didn't want the question on my mind all day.

"I think he will be happy. We talked about not waiting too long, which is why I went off the pill last month, but we also didn't think it would happen this fast." I shrug. "I guess it's meant to be."

"Coop is going to be ecstatic, I know it," Julia says with confidence. "Let's just hope that when you go into labor, he and Jaxson aren't together. Lord knows what would happen after last time."

We both burst out laughing from the memory of the guys being complete lunatics when Julia went into labor with Annabelle. Everyone looks at us in confusion so we fill them in on what happened. I tell them how they both almost drove off without us because they were in such a mad rush, thinking the baby was just going to fall out of Julia at any given second. It isn't long before everyone is laughing just as hard as Julia and me.

"How did you and Mistwer Shewiff meet?" Ruthie asks.

I smile at the memory. "He moved in next door to me when I was fourteen years old. Then it was hook, line, and sinker for that guy."

"Yeah, about three years later and with a little push, or should I say shove, from this girl," Julia says, pointing at me with a giggle.

I shrug but can't suppress my own chuckle. "What can I say, I'm a persistent one when I want something, and that guy didn't stand a chance. Little did I know though, he felt the same way."

"Oh, this sounds like a good story that you must share," Faith says, taking a seat on the other side of the bed, then lifts Ruthie up to sit on her lap.

"Sure, I'd love to share it with you guys."

"It's definitely an entertaining one," Julia adds as she takes her own seat. Grace follows suit and gets comfortable, then everyone waits for me to begin.

"Okay, as I said, Coop moved in next door to me when I was only fourteen. He was seventeen, and let me tell you, he was as sexy then as he is now. The first day I laid eyes on him—it was a sweltering, hot summer day. He was carrying boxes in from the moving truck, with no shirt on, his bronzed skin and toned muscles were flexing with every..." I trail off and look at Ruthie who watches me with a big smile.

Yeah, I'm going to have to be careful how I word this story.

"Anyway..." I cut my hand through the air and move on. "As I watched him that day, I told myself I was going to marry him. I didn't care what it took, I was going to make it happen." I think about that for a second. "Okay, it sounds kinda creepy right now but remember, I was fourteen at the time."

"You were the same way at seventeen, too," Julia reminds me, her voice laced with amusement.

"This is true," I admit, completely unashamed. "But with Coop, I can't explain it. My crush for him at fourteen was different than it was for any other crush I'd had. Then as the years went on, and I got to know him, my crush turned into love. Unfortunately, he didn't live next door for very long since he moved out with Jaxson after they graduated, but that didn't stop me from trying to see him every chance I could."

Julia giggles and I look at her with a smile as I go back to a time that was frustrating, emotional, and downright beautiful…

I glance at my clock with bleary eyes and realize I'm late. "Shit!" Shooting out of bed with a speed that shocks even myself, I get presentable for school in record time.

I rush into the kitchen and kiss my mom's cheek just before I dash out of the house with an apple in my hand.

"No speeding, Kayla," she yells at me through the window. I wave her off, unconcerned, then send a quick text to Julia, letting her know I'm on my way.

As I get into my vehicle, I notice Cooper's squad car isn't parked outside his parents' house anymore, and I don't know if I'm relieved or disappointed. It's his fault I slept like shit last night. He had my hormones on high alert all damn night.

When I found out he was house-sitting for his parents, while they were on vacation for the next week, I knew it was time to make my move. But no matter how many seductive attempts I've made, the guy hasn't come near me. So last night I pulled out the big guns by prancing around my backyard in the skimpiest bikini I owned. I soaked in the hot tub until my skin was wrinkled to a prune, but the bastard still didn't come over. I know he saw me though; I caught him watching me from his upstairs window, his expression as hard as granite. I'm sure it's because he was just as worked up as me. I see the way he looks at me; I know he wants me just as bad as I want him.

So, why the hell is he holding back and fighting this?

I shake myself from my frustrated thoughts when I pull up to Julia's. She's waiting patiently on the driveway and hops in just as I come to a stop.

"I'm so sorry, I slept in," I apologize, knowing it's a shitty explanation. I hate being late.

Of course, being Julia, she doesn't get mad. "No problem, it happens. I'm hoping you're going to tell me it's because you were up late, making out with Coop." She inquires with a hopeful smile.

I harrumph as I hit the gas and drive a little faster than I should. "No. I wish it were because of that."

"Seriously?" she asks in surprise. "Did you go into the hot tub like we talked about?"

"Yep. I even wore my skimpiest bikini, and the bastard still didn't bite."

She reaches over and touches my arm gently. "I'm sorry, Kayla. If it's any consolation, I know how you feel," she says, referring to Jaxson.

"Yeah, well at least Jaxson still hangs out with you. For the last year it seems all Cooper does is completely avoid me, and I don't understand why. We used to be friends until he dated that bitch Brittany." Just thinking about that whore has anger rushing through my system hot and fast. They dated over a year ago and it still infuriates me to think about. She's probably the biggest bitch I've ever met, and she always made sure to rub Cooper in my face. Thankfully, they only lasted a short month, like most of Coop's relationships over the last few years. It was the happiest day of my life when he broke up with her.

"Well, tonight you could always..." Julia trails off at the sound of police sirens and glances behind us. "Uh-oh."

I look down at my speedometer to see I'm only going seven miles over the legal limit. I growl in frustration and pull over, not happy that we're now going to be even later for school. The cop pulls up behind me, and I stare in complete shock as Cooper steps out of the car.

Are you freaking kidding me?

My stomach does its usual flip as I watch his gorgeous ass make his way over.

Hmmm, maybe this isn't such a bad thing after all.

Getting my wits about me, I roll down my window then stick my head out and give him my best smile. "Well, hey there, Officer Sexy."

With his aviators in place, Cooper stares down at me, his expression unimpressed. "Kayla," he greets in irritation before nodding over at Julia. "How's it going, Julia?"

"Hey, Cooper."

I'm annoyed that his greeting to her is friendlier than mine, but I shrug it off and decide to push his buttons like I always do. Reaching over, I finger his handcuffs at the side of his belt and give him a suggestive smile. "Nice cuffs, Coop. I've always wondered what it would be like to be cuffed to a bed. Maybe you can lock me up sometime."

I hear Julia muffle her laughter, but I don't take my eyes off of him. His expression never wavers, but I know I got to him because his jaw flexes. I love riling him up like this. I'm hoping one day it will finally make him crack and he will let all that frustration loose on me in the dirtiest ways possible.

"License and registration," he says, ignoring my comment.

I tense. "What? Why?"

"Because you were speeding, and I'm going to give you a ticket."

My mouth drops in shock. "You can't be serious."

Now it's his turn to smirk. "I'm very serious."

"Give me a break, Coop, I was going seven over. You have to at least be going ten over to get a ticket."

He stares at me like I'm an idiot. "I can give you a ticket for going one over the legal limit."

I try to gauge his expression, still thinking he can't be serious.

He wouldn't give me a ticket, would he?

No, he wouldn't, he's just screwing with me, I know it. "All right, Officer Romeeooo," I croon, dragging out the name. "Let's be honest here, you really pulled me over because you missed my pretty face this morning. I missed yours too, but this"—I gesture between us—"will have to wait because I'm late for school."

Julia snickers again, but unfortunately Cooper doesn't find it as funny. "You're going to be even later if you don't stop stalling. Give me your license and registration, Kayla. Now."

I gape at him as I realize he's completely serious. With a huff, I pull out my license and registration then hand it to him, knowing I need to get my ass to school. He takes it with a smirk then walks back to his squad car.

I look over at Julia. "I can't believe he's really going to give me a fucking ticket."

She shrugs. "Maybe he's just messing with you to prove a point and he won't actually give you one."

I shake my head, knowing he's going to. He wouldn't do all this then not follow through. Sure enough, he walks back a couple of minutes later and hands me back my license and registration. I don't bother to look at him as I rip them from him. When I go to snatch the ticket out of his hand, his grip tightens on it, not letting go.

My irritation quickly vanishes when he bends down and leans in my window. His delicious, masculine scent penetrates my senses and completely short-circuits my brain. My heart pounds wildly and my breath catches in my throat, as he trails his nose along the side of my cheek until his lips are at my ear. "You need to be careful of the games you keep playing with me and my dick," he whispers, his tone as smooth as whiskey. "Because next time, Kayla, I will not be responsible for my actions, and believe me when I tell you, you are not ready for me, baby. Not yet."

With that, he presses the softest kiss to my cheek and drops the ticket on my lap before strutting his sexy ass away, as if he didn't just completely tilt my world on its axis. I sit stunned for a long moment, wondering if I just imagined his words.

"Whoa." Julia fans herself. "What the heck was that all about?"

She couldn't have heard him, but I'm sure she felt the sexual tension. She had to; it still lingers heavily in the car. I pick up the ticket and see the amount for *one hundred thirty dollars.*

Instead of feeling pissed like I ought to, the biggest smile takes over my face. I think today is going to be a great day after all.

CHAPTER 2

After school lets out, Julia and I grab an ice cream then head over to the ball diamond. "Tell me again why we're coming here?" she asks as we get out of the car.

"Because it's the baseball game of the year—the sheriff's department against the fire department. Sweaty, shirtless hotties with bronzed skin and toned muscles." I shiver just thinking about it. "This is shit we do not want to miss." Although, my eyes will be for one guy only.

My heart rate kicks up in anticipation at getting to see Cooper again. His words have been replaying in my head all day since our run-in earlier.

Next time, Kayla, I will not be responsible for my actions, and believe me when I tell you, you are not ready for me, baby. Not yet.

Oh boy is he wrong. I'm more than ready for his sexy ass. I've had a throbbing between my legs since this morning, hell, for the last three years. He is close to cracking, I can feel it. I just have to figure out what is holding him back.

I used to think it was our age difference; it's almost three years, which is squat in my opinion. He never came right out and said it, but he would make the odd remark about it. I turn eighteen in a few weeks, the day after prom, so there is no way it can be that.

But what the hell is it then?

Julia and I grab a seat up high on the metal bleachers with our ice creams and soak in the incredible view before us. My eyes sift through the shirtless hotties and immediately find the man I came to see, instantly recognizing his body and the tattoo that marks his defined shoulder blade. The American Flag, with the overlying script—*To Serve With Honor*—suits him perfectly. Cooper is the most honorable guy I've ever met. His integrity is what made me fall madly in love with him, and I know he's going to make an incredible sheriff one day.

I watch him tense suddenly then, as if feeling the weight of my stare, he turns around. I can't see his eyes because of his aviators but I feel them as if it were his hands. We watch each other, a long moment stretching between us. He keeps his expression schooled, but it doesn't last long. Giving him a flirtatious smile, I lick my ice cream the same way I want to lick his delectable, hard body.

Even from here I can see his nostrils flare and his jaw flex. I give him a sassy little wave with my fingers, enjoying his torment. He shakes his head in frustration then turns back around, dismissing me.

I look over at Julia and we both laugh. "Lord, girl, one day you're going to push that man too far."

"That's the plan," I tell her truthfully, without feeling an ounce of shame.

"So I heard Matt Greenwood asked you to prom today," she says, quirking an eyebrow in question.

"Yep, but of course I said no. Which probably wasn't a smart idea, considering I haven't been making any headway with you know who." I nod to where Coop is throwing a ball back and forth with another guy from the police department. "I may just end up dateless if I don't think of something soon." The entire thought is depressing. I've thought about just straight out asking Cooper, but I want to be certain of his feelings for me before I do. However, I'm running out of time and I may need to just bite the bullet and do it regardless.

"Well, at least you have been asked. No one has even attempted to ask me," she says sadly. "I don't know why, I mean, I know I'm not a knockout or anything, but I'm a pretty nice girl and I can be a lot of fun to hang out with. Can't I?"

"Of course you are," I tell her truthfully; the girl is full of shit, she's a knockout but she doesn't know it, which only makes her more attractive. "I keep telling you, no one is asking because they're terrified of Jaxson."

"Why would Jaxson care?"

I roll my eyes. I love this girl to death but she is incredibly naïve. "Because he wants you to himself." She shakes her head, dismissing my theory right away. "Yes, he does. I tell you this all the time, Julia. The guy has it bad for you, but he's too fucked up to admit it. Why do you think any guy who has ever remotely tried to ask you out never looks at you again? I'm telling you, Jaxson has laid claim, you just don't know it."

"I wish," she mumbles.

"Trust me, I'm right. Either way, I thought you were going to ask him to go to prom with you?"

"I really want to but I know it's not his thing. He didn't even go to his own prom, so I doubt he would come with me."

I shrug. "You don't know unless you ask."

"Yeah, but I'm a coward. The entire thought of his rejection stings a little too much."

I nod in understanding because I feel the exact same way with Cooper. "Well, if all else fails we can go together?"

She smiles. "I love that idea."

Before we can say more, Mark Stevens climbs up the bleachers and takes a seat between us. *Great!*

"Well hello, ladies," he greets as he throws an arm around each of us, his clothes reeking of marijuana.

"Mark," I acknowledge, before glancing nervously over at Cooper. I see him watching us, his entire demeanor looking downright lethal. *Crap!* I was hoping he wouldn't notice, he hates Mark and I don't want him in a pissy mood after this. Looking away, I bring my attention back to Mark. "What are you doing here? Came to scope out the hotties like the rest of us?"

He grunts. "Fuck that! Like I want to be around a bunch of pigs."

I tense, taking offense to that term. The only reason he doesn't like cops is because he deals with them often over his alleged little side business. The asshole's only savior is his dad, who's a high profile lawyer. Most of the girls in our school play up to him because of his money and status, when in reality he's nothing but an arrogant jerk.

"I'm actually here to meet up with Scott, but since I saw you two beautiful ladies sitting here I decided to personally invite you to this." He hands each of us a printed postcard.

I read it and see it's an invitation to a party this coming weekend in the next town over. "A party in Callingwood?" I ask.

"Yep, and it's not just any party, it's going to be the party of the century. We are combining the graduates of Sunset Bay along with Callingwood and throwing one hell of a farewell party to the life of high school. My buddy's parents own some land buried in the bush, that's where it's being held. There will be kegs, music, a bonfire, and best of all—me." He gestures to himself in arrogance.

I roll my eyes, but have to admit it sounds fun. Well, except for the part that he's going to be there. Suddenly, I feel Mark tense next to me. I glance up to see his face pale as he stares at something ahead. I look over to where his attention is and see Jaxson striding toward us with a look of intent to kill.

"That's my cue, ladies. I'll see you this weekend," he says, then hightails his ass down the back of the bleachers, avoiding trouble altogether.

Jaxson makes his way over, looking pissed.

Yeah right, the asshole hasn't laid claim. Just look at the way Mark hightailed it out of here.

"Hey, Jax," Julia greets him quietly, and moves over for him to sit next to her.

His expression softens marginally. "Hey, Jules." He gives her the usual kiss on her forehead then takes the seat next to her. "Hey, Kayla." He acknowledges me with a nod.

"Hey."

He looks back to Julia. "What the fuck was Mark Stevens doing up here with you guys?"

She shrugs. "He just handed us an invitation for a big, senior class party."

He takes the invitation out of her hand and reads it. "This is in Callingwood," he says, stating something we already know.

"Yep," she replies easily.

"You're not going."

I tense, and Julia falters slightly at his tone. "Excuse me, and why not?"

"Because I don't fucking like that guy. He's bad news."

Julia stares back at him aghast, and I watch her aquamarine eyes flare with irritation. "Well, I'm not going for him. If Kayla and I decide to go it will be because we want to hang out with our graduating class. You do not have a say, Jaxson."

His eyes turn downright lethal. He turns and puts his hands on either side of her hips, caging her in, then leans in close and brings his face only an inch from hers. "Don't push me on this, Julia, I'm serious. I work late that night, and I can't be there to look out for you."

"I don't need a babysitter!" she snaps.

They stare each other down, and I swear you can feel the sexual tension roll off of them in waves.

They seriously just need to get it over with and fuck already.

"Stop being bossy." She pushes against his forehead and moves him out of her personal space.

He relents with a grunt, but we all know this argument is far from over.

Shaking my head, I turn my attention back to the ball diamond. We watch most of the game in silence, except for when I'm cheering my ass off for Cooper, using every kind of pet name I can think of, which ticks him right off. Jaxson chuckles a few times and warns me of the buttons I'm pushing. I just give him a wink, letting him know my intention, and don't let up.

After the game, we make our way down to the chain link fence. My gaze takes in all of Cooper's hot and sweaty, half naked glory as he strides toward us. His shaggy, light brown hair pokes out of the sides of his baseball cap while his long, lean muscles and eight pack are on full display. I get the sudden urge to lick every line and definition, wanting to know if he tastes as good as he looks.

The man is seriously one sexy son of a bitch.

By his expression I can tell he's not happy, probably about my catcalling him throughout the game. I ignore his brooding demeanor and give him a bright, innocent smile. Then I put one foot in the hole of the chain link and boost myself up. As soon as he reaches us, I lean over and give him a swat on the ass. "Good game, Officer Sexy."

He falters, obviously not expecting the love tap, but keeps his expression schooled. Jaxson and Julia both try to cover their amusement, but one of the guys from his department overhears me and doesn't bother to hide his.

"Officer Sexy." The guy points, proceeding to laugh his ass off.

I start to feel bad about others ribbing him; it's only okay for me to do it, not anyone else. But then I remember the ticket in my car and my guilt fades.

Cooper shoots him a death glare and the guy quickly shuts up, then he brings his attention back at me. My heart pounds wildly as he steps closer, stopping when his face is only a mere inch from mine. Reaching up he takes his aviators off, and I suck in a sharp breath at the intense hunger in his gaze. My smile spreads, knowing my plan is working, but before I can think of anything witty to say he speaks first. "What was Mark Stevens doing with you, and why the fuck were his hands all over you?"

I rear back, not only surprised by his question, but also shocked at how angry he sounds. I know he doesn't like the guy, but I didn't expect him to be this mad.

"He invited them to a bush party out in Callingwood," Jaxson responds before I can.

I glare over at him, not appreciating that he replied to *my* question.

I look back to Coop but once again, before I can get a word in edgewise, he speaks. "You're not going anywhere near there. Do you hear me?"

I tense at the order. "Excuse me?"

"You heard me, Kayla."

Oh, I don't think so.

The only time he can order me around is if he's telling me to shed my clothes. I give him my best glare, not bothering to hide my irritation. "Listen here, buddy, I'm going to tell you the same thing that Julia already told Bossy McBosserson over there," I snap, gesturing behind me to Jaxson. "If we decide to go to that party it's our decision. You have no say."

His eyes turn fierce and his teeth clench until I think his jaw is going to snap. "I know shit about him that you don't. He's not a good guy to be around."

"I wouldn't be hanging out with him. I'd be going to hang out with others from my graduating class."

He shakes his head. "It doesn't matter. Anywhere that guy goes he brings trouble, it's not safe for you."

I soften a little at his concern. "Don't worry, Officer Romeeoo, I can take care of myself." I can tell he's about to argue but I don't give him the chance. "I need to get going, but I'll be in the hot tub again tonight if you want to join me," I inform him with a sassy smile. Then, leaning closer, I whisper, "Except this time I'll give you a better show and take my top off."

A low growl erupts from his chest and the deep, sexy sound of it hits me between the legs.

Being bolder than usual, I turn my face and lay a loud smacking kiss right on his stubbly cheek. Before I end up mauling the poor bastard like I really want to, I force myself to jump down.

I look over at Julia to see her and Jaxson watching us with amusement. I nod at her, signaling it's time to go. She gives Jaxson a hug then follows me. Once we're a little distance away, I turn back around to see Cooper staring at me, his expression holding a promise for retribution, which completely excites me. I blow him a kiss then wink before turning around and heading to my car.

I'm wrapped up in my thoughts, thinking about what my next move will be tonight, when I feel Julia come to an abrupt halt. "Uh-oh," she mumbles nervously.

"What?" I look to where her attention is riveted and my good mood sours quickly when I see Brittany fucking Vail next to my car. She's bent over, looking in my side mirror as she puts on lipstick. The sight of her has fury rushing through me.

Sensing my presence, she looks over at us and gives me a snide smirk.

I'm so not in the mood for her shit today.

The bitch stands and leans against my car, cocking a hip and sticking her fake tits out for the world to notice. I stride toward her easily, trying to calm my angry heartbeat. I hate that she gets to me, and I hate even more to know that Coop has been with her, touched her…

Ugh, don't think about it, Kayla.

"You lost, Brittany? Your street corner is that way." I point off to the left.

She glares at me with the same hatred I feel. "For your information, I'm here to see Cooper, we have plans."

I try to keep my cool because I know she's full of shit. Cooper has nothing to do with her anymore… I don't think.

"But the question is, what are you doing here? Shouldn't you two be at home, getting ready for bed?"

I roll my eyes at her lame insult about our age. She acts like she's ten years older than us rather than two. "Give it a rest, Brittany, and fuck off. Don't you have something better to do than annoy me?"

"Actually, yes, I do. Cooper," she retorts with a smirk, making me want to yank one of her lame pigtails right out of her fucking head.

"You're full of shit. He broke up with you a year ago, and it's time you move on. Clinginess doesn't look good on you, though not much does," I add, taking in her too short top and her barely there skirt.

"Just because we broke up doesn't mean we've stopped fucking."

Her words hit me like a painful blow to the stomach, no matter how hard I try not to let them.

"She's lying. Don't listen to her," Julia whispers next to me.

Brittany releases a snotty laugh. "Oh she wishes, just like I'm sure you wish I never fucked Jaxson."

I feel Julia tense next to me, and my fury spikes to a whole new level now that she's brought her into this. "I'm giving you fair warning, bitch, if you don't get out of my face in the next five seconds, you won't need your circus makeup any longer, because the damage I'll do to you will permanently decorate your face."

She glares back at me, but there is no denying the trepidation in her eyes. She knows I'm serious, and for all of our sakes I hope she listens. With a scoff she pushes off my car and stalks past me, but not before one last blow. "Go home and leave the guys for the girls who know what to do with them."

I clench my fists and restrain myself from turning around to watch her retreating back, knowing if I do I will tackle the bitch. I stand frozen for a long second and stare at my car, hating the sick feeling that's plaguing me right now.

"What a lying slut," Julia seethes. When I don't respond, and remain still, she touches my arm gently. "She's lying, Kayla, I know it."

I nod and give her a small smile, though not a convincing one. I want to believe Cooper would have nothing to do with her, but why else would she have come here?

We both get into the car, and as soon as I close my door, something on my side mirror catches my attention. "Ugh, that bitch!" I growl, staring at the bright red lipstick on my mirror that spells out *SLUT*.

"Are you serious?" Julia asks, aghast. "She has some nerve!"

I rip some tissue out of my purse and try wiping it off, but it only smears and makes a mess. I give up and toss the garbage in my backseat, then make the mistake of looking toward the ball diamond to see the whore rubbing herself all over Cooper. I quickly look away, because the pain lancing me is heart-stopping.

"If you want to change your mind about taking the bitch out, I got your back," Julia offers, trying to lighten the mood.

I release a slight chuckle and look over at her. One of the best things that happened to me was her moving here two years ago. We always have each other's back, and even though she could never hurt a fly, I know she would swing her fists and try her best just for me. I'd love nothing more than to kick Brittany's ass, but the charges wouldn't be worth it. I have to tread carefully; my dad's trying to get her dad as a client. But the bitch needs to be taught a lesson… Suddenly, an idea forms, and it's a really good one. I give Julia a mischievous smile.

"Uh-oh, why are you smiling like that?" she asks nervously.

"Be ready late tonight and dress in dark clothes."

"Why, what are we doing?"

I feel my smile spread. "We're going to get even."

CHAPTER 3

I decided to have Julia meet me at the park late that night, knowing it wouldn't be smart for either of us to have our cars for this.

At five after eleven she comes jogging down the dark path that's marginally lit up by the houses on either side. She's out of breath by the time she reaches me. "Okay, I'm here. Sorry I'm late, I was with Jax."

"It's all right. It's better that we're later anyway. Come on."

We start walking toward Brittany's house and she eyes the bag in my hand with curiosity. "What's in there?"

"Our props." When I feel her continue to stare at me with questions, I give her a few more details. "We're going to fuck with her car like she did mine."

She stops abruptly. "Oh, Kayla, I don't think this is a good idea. I hate her as much as you, but what happens if we get caught?"

"We won't. Her place is massive so her neighbors aren't that close."

She eyes me hesitantly.

"Look, someone needs to teach this bitch a lesson and I'm going to do it. You don't have to come if you don't want to. I will completely understand. Or you can just stand and keep watch."

She blows out a breath. "No, of course I'm coming with you. I'm just scared of getting caught. Jax will kill me."

I roll my eyes. "Well, tell the guy he has no say in your life unless he's fucking you."

Her cheeks turn pink and she bites her lip. "Do you think he finally would if I said that?"

We stare at each other for a long moment then burst into a fit of laughter and start walking again. "He will come around one day. I know he cares about you, you can see it every time he looks at you."

She shrugs and I know it's because she doesn't believe me. "I talked to him about what happened with Brittany earlier," she starts quietly. "We were right, she lied. He never slept with her and he was pissed when I told him what she said to us. He also said, as far as he knows, Cooper hasn't had anything to do with her since they broke up."

As glad as I am to hear that I'd rather hear it from Cooper, to know it's the truth. "I hope that's the case, because if not, Julia, then I will have to make the decision to give up and move on. It was hard enough on me when he dated her, but if he's been screwing her for the last year, after knowing my feelings for him…" I shake my head, unable to say it. I can't even think it.

She links her arm with mine to offer comfort and we walk the rest of the way in silence. A few minutes later we turn down the street with big, fancy houses, and I'm thankful to see Brittany's lame, pink BMW is parked on her driveway and not in her garage.

"Come on." I start jogging, pulling Julia with me.

"Oh god, oh god, I'm so scared for this," she whispers, trying to keep up.

I roll my eyes at what a worrywart she is. "Would you stop worrying? We will do this quick—it will be done and over with before you know it."

I get down on my knees next to the driver's side door and Julia follows suit. "Okay, what are we doing?"

I hand her the jar of peanut butter and a knife. "Put this under the handle of her door."

With a giggle she takes the peanut butter and does what I say.

Next, I reach in and grab a baggie filled with small rocks I gathered earlier, and proceed to put them into the small holes of her hubcaps.

"What does that do?" she asks, moving closer to me.

"It makes a bunch of racket and sounds like her tires are about to fall off." I shrug. "I did some research in a quick amount of time."

"It won't cause an accident, will it?"

"No, of course not. I want to teach the bitch a lesson, not kill her, or more importantly, someone else."

She nods. "I didn't think so, but just wanted to double-check."

We both giggle then after we finish with the rocks, I reach in and pull out a pair of rubber gloves and a brown paper bag. "You might want to hold your breath for this," I warn her as I put the gloves on.

"Why, what's in it?"

"Dog shit," I reply, barely containing my laugh.

"What? How on earth did you get dog poop? You don't even own a dog."

"A neighbor a few houses down from me has one. It was a nasty task, but it will be worth it." Holding my breath, I open the bag then put my hand on the bottom of it and turn it inside out, using it as a tool to smear the shit all over the side of her car.

"Oh god, that smells so bad." Julia pinches her nose with a chuckle and backs up.

I finish quickly since I'm about to pass out from lack of oxygen, then throw the paper bag along with the nasty gloves back into the plastic bag and tie it in a knot. Glancing around, I quickly run and throw it in their garbage can, making sure to shuffle the trash around so it's buried. I don't breathe again until I have my sanitizer out and am dousing my hands in it.

"Okay, is that it? Can we go now?" Julia asks hopefully.

"No, one last thing." Reaching into my purse, I pull out two black markers and hand one to her. She looks at it curiously then follows me as I walk to the back of her car. Across the rear of the trunk I write, *penis swallower*, knowing everyone who drives behind her will see it.

"Oh my god." Julia covers her mouth in horror but can't contain her snicker.

"What? It's not permanent, it will wash off, just hopefully not before others see it." I nod at her hand. "Write something for what she said about Jax. Believe me, it will make you feel better."

With a grin plastered on her face she writes, *I'm as fake as my boobs.*

I burst out laughing. "Good one."

"Thanks, and you're right, I do feel better."

We begin to laugh uncontrollably, and are so caught up in our amusement that we don't hear anyone come up behind us until it's too late. "What the fuck do you guys think you're doing?"

A startled scream rips from us both as we flip around and land painfully on our butts. As soon as I get my wits about me, I quickly slap a hand over Julia's mouth, since she's still screaming, and look up at a very pissed off Cooper.

Oh shit!

I stare at him, wondering how I should start.

He shifts his focus to the writing behind us then leans to the side and looks at the dog shit smeared on her car. "You have got to be fucking kidding me." He expels a laugh that doesn't sound funny at all and shakes his head.

"Coop, I can explain."

"Not here!" he snaps and hauls us both up by our arms. "Get into my fucking car before anyone else sees you guys."

He starts to drag us toward his squad car, that's parked across the street, but I dig my heels in. "Wait." I rip out of his grasp then run back a couple of steps to pick up my pens. "Uh, don't want to leave any evidence behind." I hold up the markers briefly before putting them in my purse.

Julia tries to bite back her chuckle but fails miserably. Unfortunately, Cooper doesn't find anything funny about it. I swear, if steam could blow out of his ears right now it would. I get my ass in gear and link arms with Julia as we make our way to his car. I take notice that his lights are off, probably to make sure we wouldn't know he was coming.

The tricky bastard.

"You don't think he's going to arrest us, do you?" Julia whispers, seeming terrified at the thought. I shake my head. He wouldn't do that…I don't think.

He opens the back door for us and Julia crawls in first. I think about asking if I can sit up front with him, but with one look at his expression, I decide against it and follow in behind her. We both jump when he slams the door.

"Oh man, we are in so much trouble," Julia whispers shakily.

"I got this. Just play it cool."

Cooper slams his door as he gets in. As he pulls away, he wastes no time laying into us. "What the fuck do you girls think you're doing?"

"Okay, now just calm down, I can explain."

He falls silent, and I try to think of where to start but have a hard time finding words. "I'm waiting!" he snaps.

I clear my throat. "Well, for starters, the bitch deserved it."

A bitter laugh escapes him. "Well that just clears it right the fuck up, doesn't it?"

I glare at him, not appreciating his attitude.

"And you?" He gestures to Julia. "I thought you were with Jaxson tonight. Does he know about this? I'm going to assume not or else he would have stopped you."

Julia tenses, the comment clearly pissing her off, like it does me. "Jaxson has no say in what I do unless he's fucking me," she snaps.

I give her a proud punch in the arm for telling him like it is and she nods in return.

Cooper sees our exchange in the rearview mirror and shakes his head. "Jesus, do you girls even realize that you just committed a fucking crime?"

"Oh give me a break, Coop, it's not like we cut her brakes, for god's sake. All we did is smear some dog shit and peanut butter on her car."

"And the marker, don't forget the marker," Julia whispers, which has us both bursting into a fit of giggles at a really bad time.

"I'm glad you girls are finding this shit so funny." I roll my eyes, but before I can say anything, he whips out his phone and calls someone. "I'm bringing Julia by so you can drive her home," he says, to who I'm assuming is Jaxson.

"Uh-oh," Julia whispers nervously.

"I'll let her tell you the fucking story… Yeah, we're almost there."

After he hangs up I let him have it. "You didn't need to bring Jaxson into this. It's none of his business."

His angry eyes snap to mine in the rearview mirror. "Would you rather I drive her home myself so Margaret can ask why she's in the back of my cop car?"

Good point, but I don't bother to voice that.

We pull up to Jax and Coop's apartment building just a short two minutes later and see a concerned Jaxson waiting outside. I reach over and grab Julia's hand when Coop gets out of the car. "Stay strong, don't take no shit. The bitch deserved it."

She nods then we both step out of the car as Cooper opens the back door.

"Jules, what's going on?" Jaxson asks, rushing over to her. "I thought you said you were going home to bed?"

"Well—I—um—I," she stammers then blows out a breath. "I lied because I had plans with Kayla that I couldn't tell you about. I'm sorry." Her voice is soft and drips with guilt.

"What do you mean you fucking lied?" he asks, clearly pissed.

"Just like she said. She lied because she couldn't tell you. Now back off!"

He rears back at my outburst but I've had enough of both him and Cooper.

The bossy assholes.

"Stay out of it, Kayla, and get back in the car," Cooper orders.

My fists clench at my sides, and I'm just about to tell him where he can go but Julia ends up stopping me by pulling me into a hug. "Go. I'll be okay, I promise. I'll text you later."

My anger evaporates, and I hug her back tightly. "I'm sorry we got busted. I'll take the heat if it comes down to it," I whisper, feeling like shit since she didn't want to do it in the first place and it was my idea.

"No. No matter what happens we're in this together. But I'm sure it will work out."

I nod, but don't feel very confident with how mad Cooper is.

I get back in the car but this time in the passenger side. No way am I going in the back again. Angry silence weighs heavily in the car when Cooper pulls away. He doesn't look over at me once; he stares straight ahead and completely ignores me.

"Don't you think you're overreacting just a little bit, Cooper? It was fucking peanut butter and dog shit."

"It doesn't matter. It's still vandalism, Kayla, what part of that do you not understand?"

"The bitch needed to be taught a lesson!"

He shakes his head as if I'm being ridiculous.

"You know, it's really nice how fast you jump to her defense and blame everything on me." Hurt starts creeping in, mixing with my anger.

He throws his hands up. "What the hell are you talking about? I caught you red-handed committing a crime, how the fuck is it not your fault?"

"She fucked with my car first!"

"Then report it. Don't act like an immature adolescent!"

I grind my teeth, his comment taking my anger to a whole new level. "Of course you're taking her side. I guess I shouldn't be surprised since you're still fucking her."

He tenses, clearly caught off guard by my statement. "What did you just say?" he asks, his tone deadly calm.

"You heard me." Now that I think about it, it makes sense. Why else would he be there? "Did I ruin your booty call for you, Cooper? Is that what you're so pissed off about?" Just the thought has me feeling sick to my stomach.

"Watch it, Kayla, you don't know what the fuck you're talking about."

"No? I had a nice little visit from her today after your game. She waited by my car just to tell me how you guys are still screwing. Of course, that was after she wrote *slut* on my side mirror with her lipstick."

Out of the corner of my eye, I see his grip tighten on the steering wheel, but I don't look over at him—too afraid of what I will see. Is he mad because it's a lie, or is he mad because I found out? I think about the way she hung on him today at the ball diamond and how he didn't push her away.

His silence is all the confirmation I need, and the pain that slices through me is so intense it hurts. I try to hold on to my composure, not wanting him to know how much he has hurt me.

I'm thankful when we finally pull up into his parents' driveway a minute later. I bolt out of the car and quickly rush over to my house, not wanting to be around him for another second, but he intercepts me by grabbing my arm. "Whoa, hold up, baby, we are nowhere near fucking done here."

His 'baby' has me losing all control. I rip out of his grasp and spin around. "What?" I spread my arms out wide. "You gonna arrest me, Cooper? Over fucking peanut butter and dog shit!"

"Would you stop shouting and listen to me for a goddamn minute?" he snaps under his breath.

"No! I don't want to hear any more. You can go fuck yourself!" I turn back around and start off again but I don't make it far.

With a low growl he grabs me from behind, then picks me up and hauls me toward his house.

"What are you doing? Let go of me!" I kick and fight, needing to be away from him. I'm so close to losing it; I can feel tears flooding my eyes, and I don't know how much longer I can keep them from falling. He plows through his back door, almost knocking the thing off its hinges, then hauls me into his kitchen. "I mean it, Cooper, let go of me." I fight harder, even more desperate for escape when I feel hot tears slipping down my cheeks.

"No, you are not going anywhere until you fucking hear me out!" He spins me around, his expression fierce, but it immediately softens when he sees my tears. "Jesus, Kayla, I'm not fucking her."

"Don't lie!" I grind out through the burning ache in my throat. "I saw her hanging all over you after the game."

"Then you didn't look for very long or you would have seen me push her away! I've had nothing to do with her since I broke up with her and I don't want to. I haven't fucked anyone in the last year because some pain in the ass blonde has been consuming my every fucking thought!"

I gape at him, almost certain that he's talking about me. At least he better be, or the other blonde pain in the ass is going to be hearing from me.

We stare at each other for a long moment, the air thick with tension. His hands still grip my arms tightly when something passes between us, something powerful.

"You know what? Fuck it!" Then suddenly it happens, the one thing I have been wanting from him for three long years. He kisses me, his mouth crashing to mine—hard, hot, and demanding.

Oh god.

My knees go weak and a whimper escapes me at the first sweep of his tongue. His taste—his incredible, masculine taste—floods my senses and sets my body on fire. I waste no time giving just as good as I get. My fingers weave into his hair with a grip that draws a growl from him, and I match him stroke for every desperate stroke, taking what I have ached for, what I have dreamed about for so long.

Catching me off guard, he picks me up by my ass and walks us a few steps. I hear a bunch of shit crash to the floor before my back suddenly meets the cold, hard surface of his kitchen table. We never break the kiss, our mouths devouring one another, our tongues dueling a beautiful battle of frustration and pure, hot lust. My lungs crave oxygen but I can't stop, I don't want to, I need more. I rip open his uniform shirt and the tiny buttons fly all over the place. My hands slip beneath his undershirt and roam over the smooth, hard plains of his abs.

With a groan he rips his mouth from mine, and starts trailing his lips down my throat. "You drive me fucking crazy!" he growls. "The way you torment my dick, prancing around this tight, little body of yours. Testing every measure of my control."

And I finally snapped it. Thank the Lord!

Before I can put that thought into words, he rips the top of my tank top down and immediately frees my breasts from the pink lace confines of my bra.

"Look how pretty your tits are," he croons, his dirty words intensifying the throbbing between my legs. "Even fucking better than I imagined."

I'm so drunk with desire that I can't form a coherent word, let alone a witty reply. Cupping the swollen, achy mounds, he leans in and takes a tortured bud between his warm, firm lips.

"Oh god, yes." I arch into his mouth as the most amazing sensations flow through me. His teeth graze my sensitive tip while his fingers work my other, pinching with a force that has my pussy clenching with an intensity that hurts. Lifting my hips, I grind against his erection and whimper when I feel how hard he is. "Cooper, please," I beg with a whimper. "I ache so bad."

Growling, he reaches down and cups me through my yoga pants. "Oh yeah? Has this sweet little pussy been wet and aching for me, baby?"

His words send another wave of heat to soar through me. "Yes. So bad, and for so long," I confess on a moan.

"Good!" he snaps. "Because that's what you do to me. You've been torturing my dick for years with that smart mouth of yours."

I falter, his words bringing joy to explode through my chest. Okay, so it isn't *I love you* but at least I know he has been wanting me as bad as I've been wanting him.

"Well then, what are we waiting for?" I reach for his pants, ready to get this show on the road, but he stops my attempt with a growl and locks my arms above my head.

"No! The only one who will be doing the touching tonight is me." I scoff at that and go to reach for him again, but his grip tightens on my wrists and his jaw clenches in restraint. "I mean it, Kayla. Only me, or everything stops now."

I stare at him and quickly realize he's serious. I'm about to argue but he doesn't give me the chance. Leaning down, he takes a nipple into his mouth again while his hand slips into my pants and his fingers glide through my wet flesh. A fiery whimper escapes me as he skims over my swollen clit, just before he thrusts two fingers inside of me. I gasp and arch at the sweet invasion.

"Ah yeah," he groans. "As tight as I knew you would be. That's because no one else has been here. Right, baby?" I nod in response because I'm too lost in my desire to speak. "That's right. Because this is fucking mine!"

"Yes," I moan breathlessly. Little does he know, I'm all his—body and soul—but I decide to keep that to myself for now. The man already has enough power over me, and quite frankly it's a little scary.

"Do you have any idea what you've been doing to me these last few days? Hell, the last few years. Watching you in that fucking hot tub last night, having to jack off for any relief so I didn't come down there and bend you over the side of it, and fuck you from behind like the animal you're making me."

Oh god.

The image in my head, along with the pleasure of his fingers, has my body feeling like it's about to combust. I try to wiggle closer to him, wanting so desperately to touch him, but he won't release my wrists.

"Cooper, please," I plead. "I want to touch you, too."

He smirks down at me. "You wanted to know what it feels like to be cuffed, baby. Isn't that what you said?"

Oh, he does not want to play this game with me, because I will play right back. I try to clear the fog of arousal clouding my head. "Yes, but that's in your bed when you are fucking me with your cock, not your fingers."

His heavy-lidded eyes turn wild as he expels a mumbled chuckle. "You and that sassy fucking mouth of yours. Soon, Kayla. Soon you will find out what I'm going to do to it, and you will learn quickly just who's in charge here. During the day you can run your mouth all you want, but when your clothes are off and my cock is inside of you, that's my territory, baby."

Holy hell he can be sexy when he's arrogant, but as much as I love his demand right now, I want something more from him. I need it to be more. "If you won't let me touch you, will you at least kiss me?" I whisper, hoping I don't sound as vulnerable as I feel.

His expression softens just before he leans down and gives me his mouth. Our tongues intertwine again, but this time the pace is slower and more intimate, giving me the connection I crave. He finally releases my wrists and allows me to wrap my arms around his neck. I decide not to push my luck, not wanting him to stop me from holding him close.

I gasp when his fingers speed up their delicious assault, stroking a part inside of me I never knew existed. Moaning into the kiss, I hook my legs around his lower back to bring him closer. My hips start rocking to the rhythm of his hand with desperation as I feel myself teeter on the edge.

His growl vibrates against my lips. "That a girl, I can feel how close you are, Kayla, give it to me, let me feel it all over my hand, baby." As soon as he mumbles the words, his free hand cups the soft weight of my breast and his fingers pinch my sensitive nipple with a force that sends me crashing over the edge.

White lights explode behind my eyes and ecstasy rushes through every vein in my body, stealing the breath from my lungs. Cooper swallows my cries of release until every last ounce of pleasure spills from my body.

As I float down from my high and back to reality, I feel him remove his hand quickly. Before he can pull away, I tighten my hold on his neck and kiss him for all I'm worth, not wanting this connection with him to end, but unfortunately, it does, and all too soon.

With a groan, he reaches up and forcibly unlinks my hold from around his neck then walks to the other side of the kitchen. He braces his arms on the counter, keeping his back to me, and drops his head in defeat.

"Cooper, what is it?" I ask, confused at his sudden turmoil. His silence has a sick feeling forming in the pit of my stomach. I quickly put my bra back in place and right my shirt before hopping off the table. I walk toward him slowly, then lay my hand tentatively on his heaving back and feel him tense. "What? Did I do something wrong?" My question drips with insecurity, which bothers me because I am not an insecure person.

"Jesus, no," he breathes out before spinning around and pulling me against him. I feel his erection against my stomach and his body wound tight. I wrap my arms around his waist and soak in his warmth. "Kayla, as much as I want you to stay right now, baby, I need you to leave."

At the restraint in his tone, I look up at him and suck in a sharp breath at his tortured expression. Without hesitation, I reach up and cup the side of his face. "Coop, talk to me."

He watches me for a moment, his jaw flexed and his eyes ablaze. "I'm barely holding on to my control right now." Every word he breathes is through clenched teeth. "If I fuck up here I could lose my job. Do you understand?"

I do now. It finally dawns on me—it's because I'm underage, that's what's been holding him back. Even though I am only weeks away from my eighteenth birthday that doesn't matter to Cooper. His oath to uphold the law weighs heavily on him, and I've been tormenting him to break that oath without realizing it.

"I'm sorry," I whisper guiltily. "I wasn't thinking."

He shakes his head, seeming like he wants to say something but holds back. Instead, he leans down and presses a hard kiss to my forehead. He turns to walk away but I grab his shirt before he can escape and stare up at him.

My heart pounds in my chest for what I'm about to ask but I feel like it's now or never. "Come to prom with me." His eyes widen in surprise, but before he can answer I slap my hand over his mouth. "Don't answer yet, just think about it. Please." I pause and lick my lips nervously. "I've turned down a lot of offers, Cooper, because I want you to take me. I don't want to go with anyone else. I understand your reasoning for all of this now." I gesture between us. "And I don't expect anything from you but to be my date. Although, I will remind you that I turn eighteen at midnight that night, so…" I trail off with a smirk.

Removing my hand, I reach up on my tiptoes and kiss his jaw before slipping past him. Just as I make it to his door, he calls out to me. I stop and look back at him.

"Promise me you won't go to that party this weekend."

"Coop…" I breathe out and shake my head, not understanding why he's being so stubborn about this.

"Please, Kayla."

It's easy to see how concerned he is about it, and since it really isn't a huge deal to me if I go, I relent with a nod. "Okay. I promise."

Walking out the door, I make my way across the driveway to my house. Just as I'm about to walk in, I feel his eyes on me, and turn to see him watching me from his back door, making sure I get in safely. With a smile, I blow him a kiss and don't miss his small smirk in return.

After a hot shower I get settled into bed, my body feeling the most satisfied it ever has, but unfortunately, my heart does not, and I know it won't until I finally have all of Cooper, body and soul.

CHAPTER 4

Saturday morning I walk down the stairs to see my mom and dad sitting at the kitchen table eating breakfast.

"Hi, honey, have a seat. I made pancakes," my mom says, immediately dishing me a plate.

As I take the chair next to my dad, he leans over and kisses my cheek. "Morning. How's my girl?"

I smile and return his kiss. "Good. You aren't working this weekend? Should I have a heart attack?"

I love my father, but he's a workaholic. It's rare to see him on a Saturday morning but I know it comes with owning your own business. He runs the best construction company around, and I'm really proud of him for all of his success.

"Ha, ha," he replies with an amused smirk. I get my smart-ass attitude from him so he knows I'm just messin' with him. "Actually, I took the day off since I have a meeting tonight." He pauses, suddenly seeming uncomfortable. "I'm having a prospective client and his family over for supper. I'm hoping you will be around to join us?"

I shrug. "Sure. Who is it? Do I know them?" I'm assuming I do since everyone knows everyone in this town.

I can tell by my parents' expressions that I'm not going to like this. "Yes, actually, you do. It's the Vails."

"What?" I shout in outrage. "No, Dad! No way is that bitch sitting at my kitchen table."

"Kayla, language," my mom scolds, but I ignore her.

"How could you invite them here for supper? You know how much I hate Brittany."

My dad's expression turns remorseful. "It was her father who suggested it. He thought our families could get to know each other while we talked business."

"Hell no! I already know her, and like I said, she's a class A bitch."

My mom cuts in now. "Honey, why don't you give her a chance? Who knows, it might surprise you and y'all could end up becoming really good friends."

I roll my eyes at how delusional she can be. "Trust me, I will never, ever be friends with her."

"She can't be that horrible if Cooper dated her."

I stiffen and feel as if someone just kicked me in the stomach. My teeth grind, and I try to remember that my mom doesn't know about my feelings for Cooper. I haven't purposely kept it from them; I just haven't exactly found the right time to bring it up. Although, I am a little surprised they haven't caught on.

I shake my head vehemently, not wanting to see that bitch ever again, let alone in my own house.

My father reaches over and puts his hand gently on my arm. "Can you please put aside your differences for tonight? This will be a huge contract for my company if I get it, Kayla. It would be years of work for us. Please, honey, can you do this for me?"

I stare into my dad's pleading blue eyes, which are the same color as mine, and feel my resolve slipping. He's wanted the contracts on the Vail's malls for so long. He's given me so much and has worked hard to make sure my mom and I could have everything we've ever needed. No matter how much I want to, I can't say no to him.

"Fine," I relent on a sigh. "But I'm not staying long, Dad, I will only be able to put up with her for so long. Also, I have plans with Julia, so if it's all right I'm going to invite her, too."

He nods and gives me a relieved smile. "Yes, of course. She's always welcome here, and I promise just a couple of hours then you can go." Leaning over, he kisses my cheek again. "Thank you, sweetheart."

Yeah, well, he better not thank me yet. I just pray I can bite my tongue long enough to get through this. I suddenly think about what I did to her car the other night and realize this could get very ugly.

Yep, just like I expected, a giant clusterfuck. Right when I thought there was no way this night could get any worse, I was wrong. Because my mom ended up inviting Cooper over at the last minute to join us, thinking it would be nice for him to have a home-cooked meal since he will be going back to his apartment soon. He was completely caught off guard when he walked in to see the Vails. But Brittany? Oh, the bitch was overjoyed, and before I could take the seat next to him, she did, which left Julia and me to sit directly across from them. To say you can cut the tension with a knife is a huge understatement.

I watch her sidle up close to the man I have been in love with for three years, the same one who gave me the best orgasm of my life just the other night. My heart pounds in fury and my body vibrates with the urge to punch her out when she leans over and whispers suggestively in his ear with a giggle. Even though it's apparent that Cooper is uncomfortable with how she's acting, he doesn't push her away. I assume he doesn't want to cause a scene, but regardless, it pisses me right off. I glare at him, not bothering to hide my irritation, and feel Julia put her hand on my bouncing knee in comfort; I'm sure she can tell I'm about ready to commit murder.

Small talk happens amongst the parents, but I do nothing except shovel heap loads of food in my mouth, hoping it will keep me quiet long enough to get through this disaster and not ruin the night for my dad. But I'm finding it very difficult when all I keep hearing is that bitch giggling. I don't bother to glance up, not wanting to know what she's giggling about.

"Did James tell you Brittany's car was vandalized the other night?" Mrs. Vail asks my parents.

Julia and I both tense and my mother gasps in horror. "Oh my gosh. No, he didn't, that's horrible."

"What did they do to it?" my father asks.

Mrs. Vail clears her throat, and I take a sip of my drink, suddenly needing to wash down the thickness in my throat. "They wrote obscene messages on the trunk of her car and spread feces on it."

I should have never taken that drink, because, before I can stop myself, I choke on the smooth liquid. I slap a hand over my mouth, trying to cover the laugh bubbling up from my throat. Julia pats me on the back, and I can tell she's having a hard time containing herself, too.

"Honey, are you all right?" my mom asks in concern, completely oblivious.

I finally manage to pull myself together. "Yes, sorry, it just caught me off guard," I mumble then glance at Brittany to see her glaring at Julia and me. I bite back a smirk and just can't refrain myself from saying, "That really is awful. Why do you think someone would do that to you?"

"I have no idea," she grinds out. "But I know Coop will find out who did it and make them pay. Won't you, baby?" she croons, leaning closer to him.

My amusement vanishes and my fists clench under the table with the need to punch her smug face that's decorated with clown makeup, like usual. I quirk a brow at Cooper and wait for him to say or do something. He shifts in his seat but I'm not sure if it's to move away from her or because he's uncomfortable. Either way, the fact that he isn't outright pushing her away has my anger reaching a whole new level.

"Well, I'm glad nothing too serious was done and she wasn't injured," my father says, trying to break the awkward tension that has settled over the table once again.

Mr. Vail nods. "Yes, us too, and we feel very confident with Cooper's ability to catch the hooligans who did this."

Even though I'm incredibly pissed off right now at Cooper, I still can't help but feel guilty for the position he's in.

"So, Kayla, what are your plans after graduation?" Mrs. Vail asks, changing the subject. "What college are you attending?"

I take a deep breath and try to calm the storm of conflicting emotions swirling inside of me. "Actually, I'm not going to college. I plan to take the massage therapy program at the health and wellness center in Charleston in the fall."

"You want to be a massage therapist?" she asks, as if not understanding that concept.

I try to be as polite as I can and not show my irritation. "Yes, ma'am, I'm also planning to practice Chinese medicine and do acupuncture."

"Oh, well… That's nice, dear." I don't look up from my plate, suddenly feeling uncomfortable, like my choice to not go to some Ivy League college makes me inferior.

"Yes, very nice," Brittany adds snidely, which has my heart rate thumping madly again.

"I think it's something you will be really good at."

My head snaps up in surprise at Cooper's words and my heart warms. I also get a small level of satisfaction at the jealousy on Brittany's expression.

"I agree," my mother says, cutting in. "This is something Kayla has always been passionate about. Ever since she was a little girl, she has always wanted to help people. She will be graduating with honors and we are very proud of her."

I look over at my mother and smile, her words meaning a lot to me in this moment.

"Well, that's great." Mr. Vail joins in on the conversation now. "And you know, there isn't a massage therapy clinic here in Sunset Bay, so you could even open your own business if you wanted."

"That's my plan one day," I tell him truthfully. "And I know just the man to build it for me." I look over at my father with a smile and he winks at me.

"And what about you, dear?" Mrs. Vail asks Julia.

"Oh—well," Julia stammers nervously, never liking to be the center of attention. "I'm hoping I get accepted to the University of Charleston. I want to get my teaching degree."

"A teacher?"

Julia nods. "Yes, I would love to teach elementary school one day like my mother did."

"And you will be the best teacher any kid can have," I chime in, slinging an arm over her shoulder.

She smiles back at me. "Thanks."

"How about you, Brittany?" my mom asks. "Your mother said you are attending the University of Charleston. What is your major?"

"Business," she boasts proudly in her usual annoying voice. "I plan to start my own company as well, though not anything like Kayla. My plan is to open a high-end, successful fashion boutique."

I don't miss her not-so-subtle hint, and before I can stop myself, I snort. The only business that girl could run successfully is a whorehouse.

The room falls silent again, and I feel Brittany's glare on me.

Oops.

"I was actually just telling Cooper all about my plans last night over supper, and he liked my ideas."

I falter at her words and feel like I've just been slapped in the face. My eyes snap to Cooper, and I see his head fall back in defeat, looking rather upset that he's been busted. The bastard lied to me. Something I didn't think he would ever do.

"Wow, two nights in a row for supper together?" I ask, trying to keep the hurt and anger out of my tone, but know I don't succeed.

He is about to say something but Mrs. Vail cuts him off. "Oh yes, Cooper is at our house often for supper, and we always enjoy having him."

I try to rein in the pain and fury rushing through me right now, but my control finally snaps when Brittany leans over and kisses his cheek. "I hope you're still coming to the lake house with us next weekend."

Okay, that's fucking it.

I lean over, pretending to reach for the butter, and knock her full glass of red wine over, making sure it spills on both of them, which isn't hard since she's practically on top of him. Brittany gasps and flies backward.

"Oops. Sorry 'bout that," I deadpan, clearly not meaning it.

"Uh-oh," Julia mumbles.

"You bitch, you ruined my brand new Vera Wang top."

"Brittany!" her father scolds.

The room erupts in chaos as everyone rushes to Brittany's aid. I feel Cooper's eyes on me but I don't look at him, I can't, and I can't look at my father either.

"Come on." I grab Julia's hand, needing to get the hell out of here. "I'm sorry, Dad," I whisper as I rush past him.

"Kayla, where are you going?" my mom calls out, but I don't stop and answer her, my throat getting tighter by the second.

Julia swipes her purse from the couch as we make our way to the door. I decide to forgo mine, not wanting to run to my room to get it. Once we're outside, I tug Julia behind me, urging her to move faster to my car.

"Kayla, wait! Get back here!" Cooper shouts as he chases after us, but again, I don't stop. I get in and immediately start the car, then as soon as Julia's ass hits her seat, I'm peeling out of my driveway. "Fuck!" I faintly hear his curse through my open window as I speed down the street.

It isn't until I'm far enough away that I finally take a deep breath, though it's a struggle through the lump that's lodged in my throat.

"Well, that was intense," Julia whispers, trying to find words for the clusterfuck we just left behind. I don't say anything, I stare straight ahead, the road blurring in front of me from the tears clouding my eyes. She reaches over and places a hand on my leg. "Are you okay?"

I shake my head, because I'm not. I'm angry, hurt, confused, and most of all, I feel guilty for just ruining everything for my father.

"She was just doing it to hurt you, Kayla. Don't let her win. It was easy to tell she was making Cooper uncomfortable, too."

I choke out a bitter laugh. "Yeah, well, not uncomfortable enough, considering he didn't push her away."

"You're right. He should have."

"He fucking lied to me, Julia. He said he hasn't had anything to do with her since they broke up."

"Maybe he was over at her house for another reason?"

I shake my head, dismissing the suggestion immediately. No way, it didn't sound like that at all. I glance over at her. "Do you still have the invitation to that party in Callingwood?"

She hesitates. "Yes. It's in my purse, but I sort of told Jax I wouldn't go since you told Cooper you weren't going."

"Yeah, well, that promise to him is out the fucking window now, but you don't have to come. I can drop you off at home on my way. I would completely understand, but I need to get out of here, Jules. I need to get my mind off of what just happened back there."

She shakes her head. "Of course I'm coming. I'll drive home if you want to have a few drinks."

"Thanks," I whisper, glad that she always has my back. Because that is exactly what I want to do—I want to party my ass off and forget this night ever happened, and more importantly, I want to forget about Cooper McKay. Though I doubt any amount of alcohol will ever erase him from me, especially my heart.

An hour later, I realize this was a mistake, because no matter how much I drink or how much I try to mingle, nothing lifts the heaviness that's weighing down on my chest.

People bump into me from either side as I make my way through the heavy crowd to find Julia. Some stop to hug me and ask how I'm doing, some try to get me to join their drinking game, and suddenly it all becomes too much.

I dart to the left and push my way through the crowded bodies until I finally make it into the deserted woods. The loud music starts to fade as I walk a little ways in, finding the privacy I need. I take a seat against one of the big oak trees and try to get my head together, but the quiet has me thinking about the night's earlier events. Hugging my knees to my chest, I let my tears flow freely, and try to think of how I'm going to make it up to my parents. As for Cooper… I shake my head, the pain is too much to think about it right now, but I know what I have to do.

The sound of a branch snapping has my head shooting up, and I see none other than Mark fucking Stevens stumbling toward me.

Great, just what I need.

"Well, hey there, Goldilocks." The nickname I was given back in grade school by my peers slurs out of his drunk mouth.

"Keep walking, Mark, I'm not in the mood for your shit tonight," I mumble and swipe at my wet cheeks, hating for anyone to see me cry.

He clutches at his chest dramatically. "Your words cut me deep."

I roll my eyes at his theatrics.

He makes his way over to me, completely ignoring my brush-off, and takes the spot next to me. "Here, have some of this. It will make you feel better," he says, thrusting his drink toward me.

"No, thanks."

He dances the cup closer to my face. "Come on, take it, I know you want it."

I push his wrist away with a chuckle. "Get the hell out of here. God, you're annoying. Anyone ever tell you that?"

"Only the ladies that want me." I shake my head at his arrogance. "What's going on, Kellar? Not like you to cry."

"Yeah, because you know me so well."

"I do," he replies insulted. "I've known you almost my entire life."

"You have gone to school with me most of your life, that doesn't mean you know me."

"I know you never cry, and I know that Julia is your best friend." I quirk a brow at him. "I'm not just a pretty face," he says, tapping his cheek. I turn my face away, trying to hide my smile from him. "I can actually be a good listener, if you give me a chance."

Silence consumes us as I think about it. Am I seriously considering talking to him about this? I look back at him to see him watching me, and he smirks when he knows he's got me.

I grab his drink from him and take a hefty sip of some nasty shit then hand it back. Blowing out a heavy breath, I drop my head back on the tree, look up at the starlit sky, and think about tonight's events. "Have you ever done something you aren't proud of, no matter how good it felt at the time?" I think about my question then laugh. "Never mind, what am I saying—of course you have."

He grunts, clearly not finding my remark as funny as me. "Nope, I don't waste my time regretting shit, Goldilocks, and you shouldn't either. Life is too short. Besides, whatever you did, I'm sure it's not that bad."

I keep silent, because I disagree. What I did probably ruined any chance of my father getting that contract, something he deserves to have, and it was all done out of pain and anger.

"Is this about that pig you have a thing for?"

I tense at his remark about Cooper. "Don't talk about him like that. Not ever, and especially not to me."

He grunts again. "I figured. You need to get over him, Goldilocks, that prick is so full of himself, you will never be good enough for him."

I try not to let his words cut me but they do, deeply. I glare back at him. "You're a real asshole, you know that?"

I begin to get up but he grabs my arm and pulls me back down. "Whoa, hold up now. I didn't mean it because you aren't good enough. I just meant that, to him, you never will be. That asshole thinks his shit don't stink, and it's because he's been labeled the town golden boy ever since he moved here, all because of who his daddy is."

I think about his statement and realize it's partly true. Cooper's dad grew up here and was the town's legend when it came to football. He even went on to play pro for a few years. When the star quarterback returned to coach the high school football team, Cooper was immediately lumped into the same category as his father. Especially after proving his talents on the field by bringing home state championships two years in a row. I guess Cooper is partly labeled the town golden boy because of his father but he also deserves that title. Even though I am pissed at him, there is no denying that he is a good guy. One day he will become Sunset Bay's sheriff and I have no doubt he will be a good one. Besides my father, he's the best man I know… Ugh! Now I feel like crying all over again.

I'm suddenly pulled out of my thoughts when I feel Mark's hand grasp the inside of my thigh. I immediately slap it away and glare at him. "What the hell are you doing?"

An irritating smirk tilts his lips. "I'm trying to get your mind off your troubles. Come on, Goldilocks, fuck him out of your system, I'm a willing participant."

I gape at him when I realize he's completely serious. Shaking my head, I expel a bitter laugh. "God, and here I thought just maybe you actually had a decent bone in your body, but I guess not." I try to get up again but he grabs my arm, a little rougher than before, and pulls me back down. "Get your fucking hand off me before I break it."

"Come on, don't be like that." He leans in to kiss me, and I smack him across the face, hard enough that it stings my hand.

"I told you to back off!"

I attempt to stand again but this time he grabs me by my hair. "I don't think so, bitch." He yanks me back down, drawing a startled cry from me. All of a sudden I'm on my stomach with his weight over top of me and panic immediately floods my system.

"Get off of me!" I kick and fight with everything I have to get free but I'm not strong enough, and I quickly realize I'm in real trouble here. I start to scream but he shoves my face into the ground, the rough earth biting painfully into my cheek.

"Just stay still, and I promise I will make it better."

My teeth clench in rage. I quickly spot a big rock only an arm's length away. As he fumbles with my pants, I'm able to slip my arm out from under me and grab it. Somehow, I manage to wiggle and turn myself over just enough so that I can swing the rock and connect it with his face. A painful howl leaves him, and I take quick advantage of his shock to slide myself out from underneath him. He grabs my ankle to drag me back but I'm able to kick free. As soon as I get on my feet, I haul ass.

"You fucking bitch!"

I glance back and see him getting up to chase after me. Panic has me pushing myself faster. I begin screaming, as I get closer to the party, hoping someone will hear me. I turn back to find out how close Mark is but I don't see him, then suddenly, I slam into a brick wall. Arms quickly grab me to steady me, and my fear has me fighting to get free, thinking somehow he ended up in front of me.

"Kayla! Stop, it's me!"

I look up through my blurry vision and realize it's Cooper. "Oh thank god," I sob in relief.

He grasps my chin and his eyes widen in alarm when he sees my face. "What the fuck happened to you?"

Before I can explain, Jaxson and Julia come running up. "Oh my god, Kayla, are you okay?" Julia asks.

I nod through my tears, my chest still heaving for breath. Cooper's gaze trains on something behind me, his eyes turning wild with rage.

I spin around to see Mark come to an abrupt stop, not looking much better than me. "You have got to be shitting me," he says in disbelief.

Cooper quickly puts the pieces together and starts toward him. "You're fucking dead!" He grabs Mark by the shirt and throws him up against the closest tree.

Jaxson moves fast and pulls him back before he can do any real damage. "Easy, man, find your control, there is a lot at stake here."

Cooper pushes away from him but Jaxson makes sure to stay close.

"What are you going to do?" Mark asks with a cocky smirk, spreading his arms out at his sides. "You gonna hit me, pig? Do it. I fucking dare you."

Even from here I can see Cooper's body vibrating with fury. I start over as he takes another step toward Mark and put my hand on his chest. "Don't, he's only trying to bait you. Let's just get out of here. Please."

Mark chuckles. "Listen to the bitch and leave, because we both know you can't do shit."

In one heart-stopping second, I see Cooper wind back, and I know he's going to hit him. Panic has my protest lodging in my throat, but thankfully, Jaxson is quicker than Cooper. "He can't, but I can." A split second later you hear fist connecting with flesh and Mark falls to the ground from Jaxson's blow, blood pouring from his nose.

"Fuck! You broke my nose, you asshole! I'm pressing charges."

Cooper drops down to look him in the face. "You're not going to do anything because there are no witnesses to back up your story, but I wonder what your daddy will say when he has to try and dismiss an attempted rape charge from your record." He grabs Mark's jaw now, and by the whimper that escapes him, I can tell it's hard. "Listen up, you little fuck. If you ever come near her again, I will make sure you regret it for the rest of your life. There is only so far I will be pushed, and believe me when I say this is not over." Cooper shoves his head down in the ground as he stands then looks over at me, his eyes flat and void of any emotion. "Let's go."

"Cooper…" I start with a whisper, but he doesn't give me a chance to speak.

"No! We aren't talking about this right now. Go!"

I swallow past the urge to argue, but know now is not the time. Julia links arms with me as we start to walk off with Cooper and Jaxson following close behind. I hear them talking in hushed tones, and although I can't hear what they're saying, there is no denying the quiet fury in Cooper's voice.

As soon as we make it to the party, I ignore everyone and beeline for my car, making Julia jog to have to keep up.

"Jules! You come with me." I glance over at Jaxson to see him wave her over to Cooper's truck that is parked in front of mine.

"Do you want me to stay with you? I will and tell Jax no. He's pissed at me anyway."

I look over at Cooper to see him on his phone, and vaguely hear him reporting the party. He shakes his head at me, as if he knows what I'm thinking, then makes his way over to us. "Yeah, and find Stevens as soon as you get here and search him. I'll meet up with you in a bit."

I tune him out then look back at Julia. "No, it's okay, go ahead. I'm sorry I got you into shit for the second time this week," I whisper, feeling guilty.

She pulls me into a hug. "You didn't. We did nothing wrong coming here, Kayla. Call me when you get home and we will talk about what happened with Mark, okay?"

I nod and hug her tighter, not wanting to let her go because I'm not ready to deal with Cooper quite yet. She kisses my cheek before stepping back, but hesitates to walk away when she sees my face. "Kayla, are you sure? I'll drive you home and we can talk. The guys will get over it."

I attempt to give her a reassuring smile. "I'm sure. Really, it's fine. I need to talk to him anyway."

"Okay, make sure you call me as soon as you get home."

"I will."

She starts off toward Jaxson and I get in the passenger side of my car since Cooper is in the driver's seat. I hand him my keys and he takes them in silence, then pulls away and stares straight ahead. The confined space is thick with tension but it's a different tension than what it was a few days ago, after Brittany's car incident. I glance at him and my stomach twists at his stoic expression. I've seen him mad before, but nothing like this. I swipe at my subsiding tears, flinching as I pass over my sore cheek.

When we are over halfway home, and he still hasn't said anything, I decide to break the silence. "So what, Cooper, you came all this way and you're not even going to say anything to me?"

"It's best if we don't talk right now." His response has my irritation reaching a whole new level.

"For who? You?"

"No! For you!" I flinch at his angry bellow. There is a moment of silence before he slams his fist down on the steering wheel. "Fuck!" He runs his hand through his hair in frustration, his breathing fast and heavy. "You fucking promised me you wouldn't go!"

I grind my teeth and try to keep my temper in check. "Yeah, well you promised me things too, and you lied."

"I never lied to you!"

"Yes, you did! You said you had nothing to do with her since you broke up. Oh, but I guess going to her house for supper and her lake house with her doesn't count, huh?"

His jaw flexes. "She's full of shit! I was at her house for supper because of the fucking vandalism on her car and her parents asked me to stay. Any time before that was business, since her dad is on the town council. And I wasn't there alone, I was there with Sheriff Lancaster. It was her parents who invited me to their lake house at supper last night and I declined. This is all shit you would have known if you stuck around to hear me out."

"What do you expect, Cooper? Not even two nights ago you had your fingers inside of me, and then I was subjected to watching her put her hands all over you, without you even attempting to stop it."

"You think that shit wasn't uncomfortable for me, too?"

"Oh yeah, you looked really uncomfortable."

"What the fuck was I supposed to do? I didn't want to ruin supper for your parents. If I had known they were going to be there then I wouldn't have come!"

"You should have pushed her away regardless. Try being in my position. Do you really think I was going to stay a second longer to witness any more of that shit?"

"If you would have stuck around then you would have heard me lay into her, right in front of everyone for what she did. And you would have also seen your dad go to bat for you, too. But no, you had to be fucking impulsive again, like always, and let your emotions get the better of you."

My anger deflates fast, and I sit in stunned silence as we pull onto my driveway. I'm shocked to know that not only did Cooper stand up for me in front of everyone, but so did my dad. Guilt plagues me, and I'm just about to thank him but he doesn't give me the chance.

"Do you have any idea the positions you put me in because you can't ever think shit through? I lied about not knowing who did that shit to her car, which is the first time I have ever done that, and I fucking hate it. Now, I almost just beat the shit out of a kid because you took off on a tantrum and got yourself into trouble that I warned you from to begin with. I mean jesus, it's like fucking poison wherever you go!"

The last of his words strike me like a painful blow. It's so intense I swear my heart just stopped beating and I have a hard time pulling in a breath. Mark's remark earlier about not being good enough for him rings loudly in my ears, and I'm not sure what hurts more—that he was right or that Cooper really does think this.

I do everything in my power to hold my tears back and swallow past the excruciating burn in my throat. "You're right," I whisper, staring straight ahead. "I am impulsive, especially when I'm hurt. I have a temper that spikes from zero to ten in one second and sometimes that makes it really hard to think things through. But what you're most right about is I am not good for you. Or maybe I should say not good *enough* for you." I laugh bitterly. "Who the fuck knew that Mark would be right about something tonight after all."

I open the car door and hear him expel a heavy breath. "Kayla."

"I will fix the mess I made, and I promise to stay the hell away from you and not subject you to my *poison* ever again."

I slam the door and rush into my house, refraining from looking back, the heartache that's crawling up my throat threatening to choke me. I enter the kitchen on the way to my room and see my parents waiting for me at the table.

I stop to face them but have a hard time looking at them, especially my dad. My mom gasps when she sees my face, but I'm not sure if it's because of my bruised cheek or if the pain I'm feeling is apparent.

"Honey, what happened to you? Where did you go?" she asks.

I open my mouth to try and explain but then snap it shut as I feel my heartbreak erupting to the surface. I swallow and try again, but look at my dad this time. "I'm sorry, dad. I'm so sorry." He moves to stand, but I shake my head at him. "No, please. I—I can't talk right now. I will explain everything later, I promise, but I just can't right now."

I rush up to my room as a strangled noise leaves my throat, but manage to hold the dam off until I fall into bed. I hug my pillow close and try to muffle my sobs. I let everything pour out of me. My humiliation and guilt for what happened at supper, my anger at Mark, but mostly I cry my heart out over Cooper. For the fact that I wasted three years loving someone who never thought I was good enough anyway.

I mean jesus, it's like fucking poison wherever you go!

I meant what I said—I will fix the mess I made, then I will make sure to never taint him again.

CHAPTER 5

A couple nights later, I'm sitting out on the back patio in my sweats with a blanket draped around me, the warm night and clear starlit sky doing nothing for my heavy heart. I hear the back door open, then a second later my mom takes the chair next to me and hands me a cup of tea. I smile at her as I take the steaming mug then curl my feet under me and look ahead into the distance again. I feel her watch me and know we are about to have the talk that I've been stalling.

"Mr. Vail called your father." I falter, not expecting her to start with that. "He said you went there today and apologized, not only about what happened at supper but also about Brittany's car."

My blood heats when I think about apologizing to that bitch. Her parents were good about it, but she was smug as shit and enjoyed every minute of my humiliation. I hate that my parents found out from Mr. Vail and not me. I didn't think he would call them, especially not so soon.

"Yeah, it wasn't easy but I knew it was the right thing to do," I admit.

"Yes, it was the right thing to do, but I wouldn't have held it against you if you didn't."

I tear my gaze away from the darkness and look at my mom now, surprised by her comment. "You wouldn't?"

"No, because you're right, Brittany is a class A bitch."

I rear back, shocked by her language. A moment of stunned silence stretches between us before we both burst out laughing. It's the first time I've laughed or smiled in days and it feels really good, but I sober quickly. "Yeah, she is, but I shouldn't have let her bait me like that. I hate that I ruined things for Dad."

She shakes her head with a smile. "You didn't ruin anything, honey. Your dad got that contract."

"He did?"

"He did. That is partly why Mr. Vail called him. He also told your father that he had a very courageous daughter and that he should be really proud of her. Of course, we both already knew that."

I smile and feel some of the guilt lift from me, knowing that I didn't screw things up beyond repair. "Well, I'm glad one good thing came out of this."

My mom's expression softens and I already know what she's about to say before she says it. "How on earth did I not know about your feelings for Cooper?"

Just the sound of his name is like a blow to the stomach. "It's not like I was really forthcoming about it."

"No, but when I think about it now, it's clear as day. I hate how oblivious I was and that I didn't know my baby was in love."

I swallow thickly and feel tears sting my eyes but I hold them back, I've shed enough over the last few days.

"I really hate that I invited him here with the Vails. I hope you know I would have never done that had I known."

"Of course I do. Don't worry about it, Mom, none of it matters anymore anyway," I tell her softly.

"Oh, and why do you say that?"

It takes me a minute to find my words. "Because I'm not good enough for him, and in his eyes I never will be." I turn my face away and bite my lip, trying to stop it from quivering.

"Kayla Kellar, look at me right now!" I turn back to her with a blurry gaze and swipe at the single tear that manages to slip free. My mom's expression is sad as she cups my face. "You listen to me, you are wrong. You're more than good enough for Cooper."

"We are so different, too different. Cooper is so levelheaded and I'm…not."

"Of course you're different. It wouldn't be fun otherwise." I shake my head but she doesn't let me speak. "Yes, you have a hot temper, and sometimes that makes you react without thinking, but you come by it honestly, and you have your father to thank for it." I can't help but smile at that because I know it's the truth. "Never doubt your self-worth, Kayla. I think you and Cooper are perfect for each other, and I'm happy to know out of all the people you could have fallen for it was him."

My smile vanishes and pain lances through me again. "It doesn't matter. Not anymore. He doesn't feel the same way."

"You're wrong. I saw it that night. He was so panicked when you ran out like that. He really laid into Brittany and so did your father. He wouldn't have done that if he didn't care." I don't say anything because I know she doesn't understand and she isn't going to. "I don't know what happened with you guys the other night, but I hate seeing you so heartbroken. Whatever it is, I know y'all can fix it."

I shake my head again, my throat too tight to speak. Some things can't be undone.

She expels a heavy breath then leans in and kisses my cheek. "Just think about it, sweetheart. Finish your tea then come inside and see your father. He's worried about you."

I nod. "Okay, I will."

She gives me one more kiss then goes inside. I stare into the darkness again and think about everything she had to say. She doesn't understand because she doesn't know what he said. And when I really think about it, I'm starting to realize this is all for the best, no matter how much it hurts. I am irrational and let my emotions get the best of me. It's just how I'm wired, and the future sheriff of Sunset Bay doesn't need that kind of hassle. He is going to have responsibilities and an image to uphold, he doesn't need my *poison*.

I shake myself out of my thoughts and worry about a different set of problems, like the fact that prom is this coming weekend and I'm all alone with no date, and I have no one to blame but myself. I was so happy for Julia that she finally got the courage to ask Jaxson, and even more elated that he said yes. She told me to come with them, but no way in hell am I being their third wheel. There isn't enough time for me to find anyone else to go with, everyone already has dates. Well, maybe not Timmy

Dickerhoff, but there is no way I'm going to subject myself to his creepiness just so I'm not dateless. I'd rather not go at all.

The sound of a familiar truck pulls in next door, and I immediately get the urge to run into the house but I don't want to give him the satisfaction. I'm glad his parents get home tomorrow and I won't have to see him so often anymore. I tense in surprise at the sound of my gate opening and my heart races anxiously.

Why the hell is he coming over here?

I feel his gaze on me as he makes his way over, and I curse my body's reaction to it.

"Hey," he greets quietly.

"Hi."

I hear him take the seat next to me, but I keep my eyes forward and don't look over at him. "How have you been?"

"Fine."

In my peripheral vision I see him shift uncomfortably. "We didn't get a chance to talk about what happened with Mark the other night."

I tense, not wanting to have this conversation with him. "I don't want to talk about it, Cooper. Especially with you."

He releases a frustrated breath. "Then will you at least go to the station tomorrow and talk to someone else? Leave a statement? He was arrested that night for having drugs on him, but he needs to pay for what he did to you, Kayla. For whatever the fuck happened. And since I can't punish him with my fists, I will make him pay with the law."

I take a moment to think about this. I haven't told my parents yet about what happened with Mark, but Cooper is right, I do need to make a statement. The last thing I want to happen is for Mark to do this to some other girl because I never spoke up. Hell, who's to say he hasn't already done this to someone else. They just may not have been as lucky as I was.

"I'll go tomorrow."

I hear him expel another breath, this one sounding more like relief. "Good. Thanks." When I stay silent, he clears his throat. "So, I heard you went and saw the Vails today."

Of course he did.

"Yep, but don't worry, I didn't say you caught us. I left yours and Julia's name out of it."

I feel the intensity of his eyes as he watches me, and I desperately want to look over at him but I don't, knowing it will only make it harder. Even his delicious scent is getting to me right now, making it difficult to hold on to my resolve, and that just jacks my annoyance up another notch.

"I didn't think you would have."

"No?" I question, trying to keep the sarcasm out of my tone. "Then why are you bringing it up? Shocked that I have a decent bone in my body, Cooper?"

"Jesus, no, that's not it. I—"

"Save it. I don't care, it doesn't matter anymore."

"The hell it doesn't! Would you fucking look at me?"

I shake my head and stand, not wanting to be around him right now. I'm still too upset to talk to him. He grabs my wrist with a frustrated growl and electricity shoots through my arm like a bolt of lightning. I look at where he has me grasped, then for the first time I look up at him, and like I thought, just the sight of him hurts. "Better be careful, Cooper, there's only so much *poison* someone can take before it kills them." I know it's a bitter thing to say but I can't help it, I'm still so hurt by his words. Words I will never forget.

I ignore the guilt that washes over his expression. "I didn't mean it, Kayla."

"Yes, you did. Because, unlike me, you aren't irrational, and you only ever say what you mean."

I rip out of his grasp and rush into my house, ignoring him when he calls me back. It hurts like hell but I know in the end it's better this way. I can't let myself love him anymore; he already made it clear that I'm not good enough. Prolonging this will only end up breaking me in the end.

CHAPTER 6

My heart races and my stomach twists anxiously as I pull up in front of the banquet hall. My phone buzzes like crazy but I don't look at it, knowing it's probably Julia. I feel so guilty for telling her last minute that I would just meet her here and not go to her house first, but I just couldn't show up with her and Jaxson. I would have felt like a complete idiot. Though, maybe it wouldn't have mattered, because as I get out of my car and see all the couples laughing and walking up to the front doors, I still feel like an idiot.

I feel a panic attack coming on and second-guess the decision I made to come here. So instead of heading into the hall, I dart to the right and follow the stone path that leads to a beautiful garden lit up with white lights. I come to a sudden stop when I see a couple kissing, thinking they're in privacy. I'm about to turn back around but they end up breaking apart and start leaving first.

"Hey, Kayla," Suzy greets me with a blissful smile. "You look amazing, I love your dress."

I glance down at my dress, the one my mom and I shopped hours for. At the time I had hoped to find something that would knock Cooper on his ass. The soft, black silk hugs my body in all the right places and falls effortlessly in others. The trim of rhinestones lay delicately along the swells of my breasts then follows a path along the straps and outlines the seams of the open back. Yep, it's pretty fucking epic, and I have no one to impress with it.

Ugh, get over it, Kayla.

I paste a fake smile on my face. "Thanks, I love yours, too. You guys both look great."

"Thanks." They head to the back entrance, and I hear the music faintly as he opens the door for her and they enter the hall.

Blowing out a heavy breath, I go take a seat on the cement bench that's in front of a small fountain. The sound of the water and the warmth of the surrounding white lights begin to calm my erratic heartbeat.

God, what was I thinking coming here? Would it really have mattered to miss my own prom?

My entire week has already been shit; missing this wouldn't have made it much worse. Between having to tell my parents about what happened with Mark, going to the police station to file a report, and ensuring Cooper wouldn't be there at the same time has left me completely drained. I should have just stayed home, curled up in bed, and watched *Dirty Dancing* while vegging out and cursing a certain sexy cop. The idea sounds more appealing by the second and I decide that's exactly what I'm going to do. I'm in no mood to be here and my pity party is only going to wreck it for others.

Standing, I turn and start walking but come to an abrupt halt when I see someone come charging in frantically. "There you are!"

My eyes widen in shock, and I blink several times, thinking I'm hallucinating the person in front of me.

"Why aren't you answering your damn phone?" Cooper asks through labored breaths. He's bent down with his hands on his knees, looking like he just ran a marathon. He holds a corsage in his hand that looks a little worse for wear.

Silence surrounds us as I gape at him, still not believing what I'm seeing.

After catching his breath, he stands to his full height and his eyes sweep down my body. "Jesus, you look fucking incredible."

My stomach does a flip at his compliment and blatant appreciation, but I wish it didn't. *Bastard.* He's a sexy bastard, especially all dressed up, but still…

"What are you doing here?" I ask, finally finding my words.

He starts toward me, or maybe stalks is a better word. His eyes are narrowed and he looks insanely pissed. "You were supposed to go to Julia's first. You ruined my plan."

I rear back, aghast at his reply. "Well, I changed my mind. You and your plans weren't a part of it. Just like they aren't now, which is why I'm leaving."

I move to walk around him but before I can make it past him, he wraps an arm around my waist and pulls me back against him. Heat rushes through my veins, and I suck in a sharp breath when I feel his erection against my lower back.

"Cooper, let me go." The protest is weak at best. My heart has me never wanting to leave this spot in his arms, but my pride and hurt feelings tell me to run as fast and far as I can.

"No! I'm not letting you run away again."

"Please don't do this," I plead on a shaky whisper. "I can't take any more this week."

I feel his body soften behind me. "Please just hear me out, baby."

Oh the bastard just had to use 'baby', didn't he?

He takes my silence as a yes, which I guess it is, then takes a seat on the bench where I was just sitting and pulls me down on his lap, his obvious erection now nestled along my ass. The stubborn side of me wants to wiggle my way out of his arms but the other side, the wounded one that has missed him so much, wants to burrow closer. Instead, I sit stock-still, stare at the flowing water and try to steel myself against the conflicting emotions battling inside of me. But I don't have much luck when his arms hug me closer and I feel his lips on my bare back.

"I'm sorry, Kayla. I'm so sorry for what I said, I didn't mean it." I open my mouth to argue but he quickly claps a hand over it. "Please, just let me finish, if you still want to yell at me after I'm done then fine. But just hear me out first."

My protest deflates and I slump in his arms.

He removes his hand and continues. "I was really pissed off that night, and I wasn't even all that upset at you. I was mad at Brittany for being a bitch and hurting you. I was pissed off and worried when I found out from Jaxson that you were at that party. Then when I found you there, running scared, with your face messed up like that…" He trails off and drops his forehead on my back with a heavy breath. "I was furious, Kayla, and I snapped. I fucking hated that I couldn't beat the shit out of that prick, and hated even more that I almost lost control, which would have ended my career. The entire night was a giant clusterfuck, and I said things that I didn't mean."

I take a moment to absorb everything he just said. I get it. If anyone understands saying things in the heat of the moment it's me, but it doesn't lessen the sting of what he said. "I understand how you were feeling, because I felt the exact same way most of the night, but what you said, Cooper, was harsh and it really hurt me."

"I know. I swear if I could take it back—"

I turn and cut him off by putting my hand over his mouth. "It's my turn now."

I feel him grin. "Sorry, baby, continue."

I begin to remove my hand but before I can, he encloses his fingers around my wrist and kisses my palm, the entire gesture warming my heart. His light green eyes are soft and pleading, but I try to steel myself against it because this needs to be said.

"I'm not sure it matters anymore, because I'm never going to change. This is who I am. I'm irrational, and I get pissed off quickly. I jump to conclusions, and I really don't have much self-control, but that's not all of who I am. I'm a good person, Cooper, despite what you think, and I usually only get irrational like that when it comes to people I care about."

His eyes fall closed and he drops his forehead on my shoulder again, but not before I see pain flash through them. "You're the best person I know, Kayla, and I fucking hate that I made you think otherwise. If I could take it back I would, but I swear I'll make it up to you. I promise to make sure you never doubt my feelings again."

"And what are your feelings?" His head snaps up, and I force myself to hold his gaze, then taking a deep breath, I gather my courage and voice my feelings. "As much as I want you, I need to understand where you're coming from. This isn't some crush for me, I've loved you for a long time," I admit softly. "And if you don't intend for this to be more than you working me out of your system then I can't do it. I'm sorry but I can't."

His eyes bore into mine and my heart jackhammers in my chest as I wait to see if I will be rejected. I expected to see some alarm in his gaze from my admission of the 'L' word, but shockingly, I don't.

He reaches up and cups the side of my face, his thumb tracing delicately along my bottom lip. "You are the biggest pain in the ass." I frown at his unexpected response. "But you are my pain in the ass," he quickly adds with a smirk. "You always have been, and I don't want you to change for anything." His smile vanishes as he lets out a heavy breath. "There are reasons why we couldn't be together until now, ones that really matter to me. Yeah, I could have dated you, but I know that I wouldn't have had the self-control to keep my dick in my pants. But make no mistake of my feelings for you, Kayla. You've weaved your stubborn ass so deep inside of me there will be no working you out of my system, baby, and tonight everything changes for us."

Joy explodes through my chest, and I drop my forehead on his with relief. I stare into his intense gaze, my lips only a breath from his. "I'm good at weaving my stubborn ass inside of people, it's a gift."

He smirks then turns his face into the side of my neck and trails his lips up my throat. "Do you forgive me, baby?"

"Mmm, maybe," I whisper as I tilt my head to the side for him.

"Come on, even perfect assholes like me make mistakes sometimes."

"Pffft," I harrumph.

With a chuckle, he leans back then frames my face before drawing my mouth down to his. I gasp at the first touch of his lips, it's completely electrifying and soul touching. I weave my fingers through his hair to hold him close and let his kiss ease the wounds that were engraved on my heart this past week.

His tongue wastes no time thrusting past my lips, demanding more, and I happily give him the access he wants. I whimper as his delicious flavor floods my senses, one that I have craved and dreamed about since that night on his parents' kitchen table. "Goddamn, I love the way you taste." His big, warm hand slides up my high slit and grasps my upper thigh. "And this dress is going to drive me fucking crazy all damn night."

"It doesn't have to," I mumble breathlessly. "Let's go back to your place and you can rip it off me, or hell, just hike that shit up and do all the dirty things you want to me."

He chuckles but it trails off into a groan. "No, I'm not letting you miss your prom, but I promise, baby, you're going to feel me tonight. Everywhere. My mouth, my hands, my cock—all of it. I'm going to claim what's mine, what has always been mine."

My panties flood with arousal at his possessive words, and I desperately want to hike my dress up, crawl on top of him, and have him claim every part of me right here, right now. I consider doing just that but he ends up pulling away and stands us up.

"No, don't stop." I jump and cling to him like a dog in heat then crush my mouth to his again.

His hands cup my silk-covered ass as he lifts me off my feet with a growl. "We have to stop or I'm going to come in my fucking pants."

"That's okay, it will feel good, take the edge off until we go back to your place."

He expels a tortured groan. "Jesus, Kayla, I'm trying to do the right thing here, help a guy out."

"Sometimes it pays to be bad, Coop." I press on, hoping to convince him.

"Oh believe me, there is nothing good about anything I plan to do to you tonight, but"—he drops me back down to my feet—"not until midnight."

I huff in frustration and blow a stray curl out of my face. "Fine, then let's get this show on the road so we can get out of here." I grab his hand to drag him behind me but he doesn't budge and ends up yanking me back against him.

"Hold up," he whispers in my ear, sending shivers along my spine. "I have something for you." He picks up the mangled looking corsage off the bench and slides it on my wrist. "Sorry it's a fucking mess, it got wrecked when I was running from my truck that I had to park a mile away."

I smile down at it. "It's perfect."

"You're lying, it's shit."

"You're right, it is," I admit with a giggle. "But it is perfect to me because it's from you."

I feel his smile against my cheek before his lips brush it softly. "Come on, baby, let's go inside. Jaxson and Julia are saving seats for us." Linking our fingers together, I start leading the way, when suddenly I hear him groan behind me. I glance back to see him staring at the open back of my dress. "This is going to be the longest fucking night of my life."

He's got that right.

We make our way into the banquet hall and are immediately assaulted with loud music and a sea of bodies. We wind our way through the crowd to find Jaxson and Julia at one of the tables in the center of the room. Julia stands then meets me halfway and pulls me in for a hug. "Everything okay?" she asks in my ear.

I squeeze her back tightly. "Yeah, actually, everything is perfect."

She steps back and gives me a big smile. "Looks like we got our wish," she says, glancing over at the guys. "Well, you got yours, I only got half of mine, but at least he's here with me."

"It will happen one day, Jules, I know it." And I do, because I see the way he looks at her, everyone does. "Come on." I sling my arm around her shoulders as we walk over to the table.

The first half of the night surprisingly speeds along and I'm having a good time. We take pictures, Julia and I dance while the guys glare at anyone who comes near us. At one point I thought Bobby Wright was a dead man when he started dancing behind Julia, but with one look from Jaxson he backed his ass right to the other side of the dance floor. As the night wears on, I become more anxious for midnight to hit. Every time Cooper looks at me, his eyes are intense and hold promise. Every gentle touch, whether it is on my leg or back, has tremors racing along my skin and my body humming with arousal.

After the announcement of prom queen and king, we decided to pick up a pizza and go to the beach where Jaxson and Julia always hang out. Cooper and I went in my car while Jaxson drove his truck, and it took some major self-control on my part not to maul the sexy bastard on the way over. But I knew it would only make it harder on the both of us. I understand now how important it is for him to wait until that clock strikes midnight.

So here we are, the four of us sitting in front of the ocean, our feet in the warm sand and the ocean breeze misting across our faces while we chow down on pizza from Antonio's. Both Julia and I are wearing the guys' jackets since it's a little cooler this close to the water.

Once we finish eating, Cooper pulls me between his legs. I lean back against his hard chest and try not to moan when I feel his erection against my lower back.

Jesus, has that bad boy been like this all night?

When Julia walks back from throwing out our garbage, she goes to take the seat next to Jaxson but he surprises us both by pulling her in the same way Cooper has me. I watch her soft expression break out into the biggest smile.

"So, girls, how does it feel to almost be done with school for the rest of your lives?" Cooper asks.

"It feels a little weird," I reply first. "If you think about it we have been in the same routine for the last twelve years, thirteen if you want to count kindergarten. Wake up early and go to school, every Monday you pray for it to be Friday, you look forward to the weekends and summers but also love seeing your friends at school every day. As much as I'm going to enjoy not having schoolwork anymore, I don't think I'm really feeling this bill business that will start coming my way soon. I'm quite content to have my dad still buy me everything."

They all chuckle but what they don't realize is I'm partly serious.

Who the hell wants to grow up and have more responsibilities?

Well, okay, Cooper makes it a little more appealing. I'm assuming he wouldn't be cool with me living off my dad forever.

"Well, I'm not done with school yet," Julia says, cutting into my thoughts. "If I get into the University of Charleston I will have four more years of it. But I have decided to take a year off because, like you said, I need a break after twelve years.

"You didn't tell me that," Jaxson says in surprise.

"I just decided a few days ago after talking with Grams about it." She pauses then turns back to look up at him. "Why? You don't think it's a good idea?"

"I think it's a great idea. Take a break, have fun for a year then go to college. I have no doubt that you will get in and end up being the best teacher any kid can have."

She smiles up at him. "Thanks, Jax."

He leans down and gives her a kiss on the forehead.

I roll my eyes and shake my head. Seriously, how can she not see this shit?

"Have you given any more thought to those business courses? It sounds like Eddie really wants you to take over the shop for him," she says, talking about the mechanic shop he works at.

There's a slight pause, and out of the corner of my eye I see him briefly glance over at Cooper before he clears his throat. "No, not yet."

What is that all about?

"That's okay, you have time," she replies with a shrug, missing the exchange.

A comfortable silence settles over us as we listen to the sound of the waves crash against the shore, but I swear I can hear a clock ticking every second. I know Cooper does too, since he's checking his watch constantly. The last time he checks it, I lean over and see we still have a half hour. I hear him blow out a frustrated breath behind me. "You know what, fuck it." Before I can register his words, he hauls me up to my feet. "We're out of here, we'll catch up with you guys tomorrow."

He yanks on my hand to propel me forward but I plant my feet in the sand then reach down and swipe my shoes. I barely have them snagged when he pulls on me again. "Bye," I yell back to Jaxson and Julia with a wave.

"Yeah, I won't be going home tonight," Jaxson grumbles behind me.

I hear Julia giggle but can't make out what she says since Cooper is pulling me at a fast pace.

"Coop, slow down, this dress wasn't made for running."

Instead of listening, he turns back and catches me off guard by picking me up around the waist. With a squeal of surprise, I wrap my arms around his neck and laugh as he races to the car. I expect him to throw me in but instead he pins me against it then his mouth descends on mine. Moaning, I kiss him with the same desperation.

"I can't wait any longer," he mumbles against my lips. "I'll take you home and start fucking you with my mouth and hands until midnight, then you better be ready, baby, because it will be my cock next, and I have years of need to work out." He drives his statement home with a hard thrust against me, his erection hitting the little spot that has electricity shooting through every nerve ending in my body.

I'm about to beg him for it right here, right now, but I don't get the chance because he quickly deposits me in the car. When he peels away, I look over and see that he's going seven over the legal limit, the exact same speed he gave me a ticket for.

"Better be careful, Coop, or I will have to call you in. I know this cop who is a real stickler with that shit around these parts."

He grunts, not finding my sarcasm funny.

I think about the ticket that is sitting in my car. "I still can't believe you actually gave me a ticket."

There's a slight twitch to his lips. "If you would have gone to pay for the ticket already you would know it doesn't exist."

"Come again?" I ask, thinking I misunderstood him. "What do you mean it doesn't exist?"

"I mean exactly that. It's a fake."

My mouth drops open in shock. "Then why the hell did you even bother to give me one?"

"Because you needed to be put in your place for fucking with me like you did. And since I couldn't fuck the sass out of you, I decided to join in and play your little game." He looks over at me, his smirk spreading. "Except my way."

I gape at him, aghast. "What if I had gone to pay for it?"

He shrugs. "I made sure Cliff knew about it. I also told him that when you came in to make sure he called me. I didn't want to miss your reaction."

My eyes narrow at his smugness. *Why, the sneaky, clever bastard.*

Leaning over, my hand finds his erection through his dress pants. His grin vanishes, and I hear him inhale sharply.

"Mmm, too bad I didn't find out about this sooner, because I would have paid you back so good," I whisper in his ear. "If you thought the bikini in my hot tub was torture that's nothing to what you would have come home to find." I lick his earlobe. "Me, in your bed." *Nip.* "Waiting for you all naked and needy." *Nip.* "And since you wouldn't have touched me, I would have done it myself. I would have shown you exactly what I've done to myself for the last three years every time I thought about you."

Nothing less than a sound that you could describe as animalistic erupts deep from within his chest before he rips my hand away from him. "Oh, Kayla, you just played with some serious fire, baby, and you are going to get burned for it."

His threat has a fierce ache igniting between my thighs. Thankfully, we pull up to his place only a short minute later. Just as we enter his building, he picks me up then our hands and mouths are out of control once again. We bang against the hallway walls as we make our way to his door, refusing to have our lips apart from one another.

I release a startled yelp when he stumbles.

"Shit, fuck," he curses, but gains his footing quickly. "Sorry, baby, pretend that didn't happen."

I laugh into our kiss, loving that I make him feel this way—out of control, frantic, desperate—the same way he has always made me feel.

He pins me against the door as he fumbles to unlock it, then once we're in he slams it behind him. I feel us rush through his apartment just before the cool, soft mattress of his bed meets my back. I try to keep him close, but he doesn't allow it. He releases my mouth and quickly slips out of my arms, drawing a disappointed moan from me. I recover from it quickly though when his lips find the swells of my breasts. My nipples strain painfully under the silk of my dress, craving his attention. I push his head down when he takes too long, and feel him smile against my supple flesh just before his teeth graze my stiff peak through the thin material.

With a fiery moan I arch up for more, but he doesn't give it to me. Instead, the fucker tortures me, only giving me a tease over my dress, then lowers himself down my silk-covered body, bringing his mouth to the spot that I ache for him most. I feel his hands go to the slit just before he tears it higher, revealing my black panties. He brings his mouth against the wet lace and gives me a gentle kiss.

"Please, Cooper, I want more. I need more," I plead with a whimper.

"Soon, baby, but first you're going to back up that mouth of yours." I barely comprehend his words before he shreds my panties from my hips with one swift pull.

I gasp at the unexpected act but it quickly trails off on a moan.

Oh shit, that was so damn hot.

"Jesus, you're fucking perfect." My eyes fall closed when I feel his warm breath hit my bare center, and my hips rise—seeking his pleasure. When he doesn't give me the attention I want, I open my eyes to see him on his knees, staring up at me, right over my most intimate part. "Touch yourself, Kayla, show me how you have pleasured this sweet pussy while waiting for me."

Heat explodes through me at his erotic words. "I'll do it if you show me, too." I challenge.

He smiles at me, and it's a smile that has my heart skipping a beat. "You wanna see me stroke my cock, baby?"

I nod, my throat suddenly too dry to speak. He stands with confidence and rids himself of his shirt first, giving me a view that has my heart stalling in my chest.

God, he is beautiful.

His shoulders are broad and strong, his chest defined and his abs perfectly cut until they taper off into that sexy v—

"Get moving, Kayla."

My eyes snap to his, and I quirk a brow at the order. "My you're awfully bossy."

"I told you, baby, that's the only way it works with me in here."

"Hmmm, that you did. But just an FYI, the only time this is acceptable is when our clothes are off. Otherwise, don't press your luck."

"Like you are right now with that mouth of yours?"

I give him a wink, letting him know that's exactly what I'm doing.

"Stop stalling, Kayla."

I can tell I'm pushing it, so with a smile, I give him what he wants. I slowly trail my hand down between the center of my breasts and over the silk material. His heated gaze follows my path, warming me from the inside out. My hand freezes, hovering just above my destination, when Cooper moves to undo his belt, and I wait with bated breath for what I'm sure is going to be the sexiest thing I will ever see in my life. He unbuttons his dress slacks then drops his pants only enough to free himself.

All the air leaves my lungs at the first sight of his cock.

Oh sweet baby jesus and all that is holy, it's even bigger and hotter than I thought it would be.

"Now, Kayla, give me what I want." His gruff demand penetrates through my sexual fog. Continuing my descent, I reach down and slide two of my fingers through my wet flesh. A strangled noise escapes me as I find the bundle of nerves that's screaming for attention. "No. Don't stay there, keep moving, baby. Go inside. I wanna see your fingers fuck your tight little pussy."

I whimper, both at his dirty words and in need for wanting to give myself release, but I do as he says and enter both of my fingers deep inside of me. I gasp in pleasure at the snug feel and arch up into my hand.

A low growl penetrates through the heated silence. "That a girl, show me what you did while thinking about me." I pump my fingers in and out, all the while watching with rapt fascination as he strokes himself. "Do you like watching me stroke my cock, Kayla?"

"Yes," I answer truthfully, my voice barely above a whisper.

"This is what I have done almost every night while thinking about all the ways I was going to fuck you."

His words have fire erupting inside of me, my need for release so strong that it's painful. I bring the heel of my hand to grind against my throbbing clit. My stomach tightens and my breathing accelerates with my impending orgasm.

"No, stop." Cooper rips my hand away just before I detonate and it's enough to make me cry.

"Cooper, please. I—"

"Shhh. I got you." He drops to his knees in front of me then takes my two fingers into his mouth, sucking my arousal off of them and groans. "You taste as fucking good as I knew you would." Leaning down, he runs his warm, wet tongue through my aching center.

My entire body jolts off the bed and my fingers wind in his hair tightly, forcing him to stay exactly where he is.

He splays his hand along my lower tummy and holds me in place while he devours me like a starved man. I was already so close to exploding that I know I'm going to erupt at any moment. My feet find their place on his broad shoulders, and I thrust up against the perfection of his mouth.

"That's it, baby, fuck my mouth." His words vibrate against my clit and reverberate through my entire body.

"Oh god, I'm going to come. Right now." As soon as the words escape past my lips, he thrusts a single finger inside of me and it sends me crashing over the edge with an intensity that steals my breath. Ecstasy rushes through every nerve ending in my body and Cooper draws out my orgasm, making it last so long I think I could die from it. Once my final tremors subside, he eases his mouth away and kisses the inside of my thigh. I take a moment to try and steady my breathing as I float back down from the most intense orgasm I've ever had.

He stands, his pants still undone but his cock now back in his underwear. My eyes travel up his hard, bare body that is nothing short of perfection—a body that I have wanted to touch and taste for so long. I glance over at his bedside clock and see we have five minutes. Looking back at him, my gaze collides with his intense one as he stares down at me with undisguised hunger, and I feel a smile tug at my lips.

"Mmm, I always knew that mouth of yours was capable of the best things." Getting to my knees, I reach for the side zipper, underneath my arm, and unzip my dress. The straps slip down my shoulders and the silk falls away easily, leaving me completely bare. His eyes turn to liquid fire as he devours my naked body.

I crawl over top of the soft material until I'm directly in front of him and reach out tentatively to touch him. I'm a little worried that he won't let me, like last time, but he grabs my wrist and guides my hand to rest on his hard, defined abdomen. His gaze never wavers from mine as he leans down and claims my mouth. It isn't like any of the kisses we've had yet. It's not frantic and desperate; it's slow and deliberate. It sends warmth through my entire body and my heart into a tailspin.

When he pulls back, I take a minute before opening my eyes, wanting to bask in this moment as long as possible. When I eventually open them, I see him watching me with a small smile, and I can't help but return one of my own.

"You really can do wonders with that mouth of yours, McKay, and now I'm going to show you what mine is capable of."

Leaning down, I kiss his toned stomach before trailing my tongue along the contours of his abs. As much as I would like to take hours to explore every inch of his body, I know I don't have much time before he will have me on my back again, so I head right to the good stuff. I hook my thumbs on the inside of his waistband and pull his pants down just enough for his erection to spring free. I don't bother to finish ridding him of them before fisting his thick cock in my hand, loving the smooth, hard feel of it. He hisses out a breath and pumps himself into my firm grasp. When a pearl of clear fluid leaks from the tip, I lean in and lick it clean, loving the salty taste of him.

With a growl, he weaves his fingers in my hair and the firm grip stings my scalp in the best way. "Take me in, Kayla. All of me."

He doesn't need to tell me twice. Looking up at him with a smirk, I take him all the way in until he hits the back of my throat, then I suck back to the tip, making sure to run my tongue on the underside of it.

"Ah fuck, yeah. That's it, baby, suck my dick just like that."

I move to repeat the motion but he beats me to it and thrusts back in. A whimper escapes me and my clit flares to life again from his control. He sets the pace, which is hard and fast. I relax my throat and take him as far as I can and grip the base where my mouth can't reach.

He tugs my head back a bit so our gazes collide and keeps his pace, his eyes wild with lust. "You like it when I fuck this sassy mouth of yours, Kayla?"

I moan, letting him know that I love it, and I do. I usually don't like to be told what to do, but this guy can do anything he wants to me when our clothes are off. Hell, even with our clothes on I think I would do anything he says, which is a little scary.

"This is what I pictured doing to you every time you mouthed off to me. It drove me fucking crazy and you knew it."

Yes, I did. It's why I loved riling him up, because I knew one day he would make me pay for it in the dirtiest ways possible.

I feel him grow harder just before he pulls out of my mouth with lightning speed. "Why are you stopping?" I ask through labored breaths, my mouth watering for his taste.

"Because it's almost time and there is nothing in the world that will stop me from claiming what I have been waiting years to do." He leans down and pulls something from his pants pocket before putting a hand on my chest and coaxing me to lie down.

I scoot back a little closer to the headboard then watch him as he opens the condom and sheathes himself. His gaze is fierce as he crawls over top of me, his hard, bare body blanketing mine, sending a beautiful warmth flowing through me. I feel his erection on the inside of my thigh and my heart rate speeds up in anticipation. I'm not nervous though; I have wanted this for too damn long.

Cooper's expression softens as he reaches up and brushes a strand of hair out of my face. "There are so many ways I want to take you, so many things I want to do to you. But for now, I'm going to go slow and savor every minute of it, and I'll try to make it as painless as possible for you."

As much as I like his dominant side, I love this side of him too—his softer side. "It will be perfect because it's with you," I tell him truthfully.

He presses a kiss to my forehead then rises up on one arm and runs his erection through my wet flesh, coating it with my arousal. I moan when he grazes my sensitive clit. We both glance at the clock to see it's one minute after midnight.

"Kayla?" I look back at him to see a small smile on his face. "Happy birthday, baby." Then he enters me with one smooth thrust.

I gasp. The sting of pain is the most exquisite I've ever felt.

A deep groan erupts from his chest as he stills and gives me time to adjust. His back muscles are tight and strained under my fingertips. "Shit. Just relax, baby." I relax my knees that have a strong grip on his hips and breathe through the fullness of him. "Better?" he asks a moment later.

"Yes."

Rising up, he begins thrusting inside of me with slow, deliberate strokes. It's tight, a little painful, and absolutely beautiful. "Jesus, you feel fucking incredible."

I reach up and frame his face between both of my hands, and pull him closer until his lips are only a breath from mine. As I stare into his warm, green eyes, I let it sink in that I am finally having the only man I've ever wanted. And now that I have him, I know that everything I have gone through, up until this point, was meant to lead me here—to this one person.

"What are you thinking?" he asks softly, as if sensing my thoughts.

I debate on how much to tell him then decide on the truth. "I'm pretty sure I've waited my whole life for this moment with you."

He falters and my heart thrums at a fast pace, scared that I just ruined the moment, but my fear vanishes when he gives me a small, genuine smile. "I have no doubt, Kayla, that you were made just for me." I feel the biggest, silliest smile take over my own face. "You and your sassy mouth that drives me fucking crazy."

"Mmm, you love my mouth," I throw back.

He grunts. "Now that I can do something with it I do."

A giggle escapes me, and we both groan when I clench around him. I feel his body begin to shake with restraint from holding back. Linking my arms around his neck, I hitch a leg up on his lower back, bringing him deeper. "Kiss me, McKay, then fuck me like you mean it."

With a growl, he claims my mouth then unwraps my arms from around his neck and pins them above my head. He pulls out so only the tip of him is inside of me then he slams back in. I gasp and arch up into him as tingles explode through my body.

"That okay?"

"God yes, keep going."

"My fucking pleasure." He pulls back again until he's almost out then slams back into me. He does this over and over, rocking my body with the best sensations. Our fingers link above my head and our bodies begin to stick from sweat. I finally find rhythm with him and thrust up into his beautiful, relentless assault. "That a girl, take me, Kayla, all of me."

I feel my tummy pull tight with my impending orgasm, and I begin to flutter around him.

He feels it and groans. "Yes, give it to me. Let me feel it, baby."

"Cooper?" I barely get his name out—I'm so enraptured in the moment—I'm not even certain of what I'm asking for. My fingers dig into his back as I feel my body teeter on the edge. I'm so close but can't grasp it.

"I got you." He changes the angle of his thrusts, hitting that spot deep inside of me at a hard, fast pace.

I can do nothing else but take it, and it feels incredible. "Oh god, oh god."

Unlinking one of his hands from mine, he moves it down to cup my breast and pinches my sensitive nipple with a force that has me detonating.

"Fuck yes!" Cooper increases his pace, faster than I thought possible, and fucks me through the intensity of my pleasure. I'm barely coming back down from my high when he stills deep inside of me and groans out his own pleasure.

We lie together in a sweat-tangled mess as we try to catch our breaths, our hearts beating together as one. I hold him as close as humanly possible, never wanting him to leave this spot inside of me. I feel his lips press gently against the corner of my forehead.

"You okay?" he asks, sounding a little concerned.

"Mmmhmmm," I hum, having a hard time forming words.

With a chuckle he pulls out of me, and we both groan at the disconnection. "I'll be right back."

Once he stands, I pull the blanket up to keep warm, since I no longer have his body heat, then enjoy the view as he walks to the bathroom. He comes back in his underwear a few minutes later, and begins to clean me with a warm washcloth. I tense at the awkwardness of it, but he puts me at ease when he presses a kiss to the inside of my thigh.

After he finishes, he throws it in his laundry hamper then crawls back in beside me and pulls me against him so we're face to face. We stare at each other for a long, silent moment and I can't help but smile. "Happy birthday to me."

He chuckles and presses a kiss to my forehead. "Yeah, baby. Happy birthday to you, and it's about fucking time."

I giggle and wrap my arms around his neck to bring him closer. "Mmm, agreed, and this was, by far, my favorite birthday gift ever."

His lips tilt with a mischievous smile. "That wasn't your birthday gift."

I quirk a brow. "No? You got something more for me, McKay?"

"Maybe," he replies secretively.

"It's handcuffs, isn't it? Let's put that shit to use right now."

He belts out a laugh and cups my ass in his big hands. "I don't need to buy you handcuffs. I get that shit for free."

I wait for him to say more but he doesn't. He only stares at me with a sly smile.

"Well, come on, give it to me already."

"Oh, I'll give it to you." With lightning speed he flips me to my back and comes over top of me, then kisses the living daylights out of me.

I sigh and decide I will never tire of him. Not ever. I distantly feel him reach over and hear the sound of a drawer being opened. Then before we can get caught up in our passion, he rolls off of me and leaves a small wrapped present on my chest.

I stare at it, wondering what it could be. "You didn't have to get me anything."

"I know, I wanted to. I've had it for a while."

I look over at him in surprise, my heart warming at that small tidbit of information. With giddy excitement I sit up, making sure the sheet is wrapped around me, and start opening it. My curiosity peeks at the small, velvet jewelry box. "You asking me to marry you already? I love it, Coop, but maybe we should wait until after graduation."

"Ha ha," he replies, deadpanned. "Just open it, smart-ass."

I open the box with a smile and falter when I get a look at the authentic, platinum Pandora charm bracelet. "Whoa," I whisper, not really knowing what else to say. I don't think there are any words to describe the beauty of this bracelet.

Cooper pulls it out of the box then takes my hand and puts it on my wrist. I start fingering the charms. The first one is a light pink heart. Next to it is the number three. "For three years." I glance over at him for confirmation, which he confirms with a nod. I touch the simple, deep blue charm beside it, trying to think of what it could mean, and he ends up answering my silent thought.

"For the color of your eyes."

I smile, my heart melting into a serious gigantic puddle. When I finger the next charm I burst into a fit of laughter at the small set of handcuffs. I look over at him to see a sly smile on his face. "Hmm, and you said you didn't get me handcuffs, you liar."

He gives me a sexy wink that has my heart flipping over in my chest. The sexy bastard. I glance down at the last charm and my head tilts in confusion as I study the ice cream cone, wondering what it could mean. I look over at him for the answer.

"There's actually a story behind that one," he says quietly then clears his throat, suddenly seeming nervous. "It's from the first time I saw you."

I frown at the charm, and remember the first time we ever met was when he moved in next door to me. "I didn't have an ice cream that day."

He watches me for a moment, and I wait for him to explain but what he says next is something I could have never expected. "I was pissed when my parents said we were moving back to my dad's hometown. I had it good where I lived before—star quarterback of the football team, lots of friends. I didn't want to come here and start all over. A few days before we moved, we were driving through town; my dad was taking us to see the house. It was a really hot day and I had my window down. We came to a stop at a red light when I suddenly heard some girl, yelling up a storm. I looked over to see what the ruckus was about and saw this beautiful blonde firecracker, who didn't look much younger than me, giving some guy shit for picking on another kid. They were in the parking lot of the ice cream shop and she was waving her pink ice cream cone all over the place. I actually thought she was going to throw it at the guy. When the asshole left and she turned around to help the kid up, the full view I got of her was like a punch to the chest. She was the prettiest girl I had ever laid eyes on. I hated it when that light turned green. I was tempted to jump out of my parents' car and run to meet this fiercely pissed off girl who looked like an angel but had the mouth of a sailor."

He pauses for only a brief second.

"Three days later we moved into the house. As I was carrying boxes, I felt someone's eyes on me. I looked up at the house next door and low and behold, the one girl I couldn't stop thinking about was staring down at me from her bedroom window. That day I realized that moving to this town wasn't going to be so bad after all, and it actually turned out to be the best thing that ever happened to me."

I gape at him in complete and utter shock, my vision blurry with unshed tears. I don't move, I can't. I am completely frozen in place, and I swear my heart literally stopped beating the moment he started his story. I remember that day at the ice cream parlor, when Jacob Larson was picking on Timmy Dickerhoff. He was even more mean than usual and pushed him down to look cool in front of his friend. Little did I know, that the guy I would become infatuated with saw me that day, waving my ice cream around like a lunatic.

When I don't say anything and continue to stare at him, Cooper reaches up and wipes my wet cheek before cupping it in his large hand. "That's why it killed me to think I made you feel like a bad person after our fight. Like you weren't good enough for me. That day I saw a girl who could have minded her own business but instead stopped to help someone and didn't care what anyone thought." Without taking his hand from my cheek, he sits up and moves in close, then drops his forehead on mine, his warm gaze penetrating. "The truth is, you're the best person I've ever known, Kayla, better than me. And I promise to make sure you always know it."

My breath hitches with emotion, and since I can't form any words at the moment, I crush my lips to his and kiss him for all I'm worth. My arms wrap tightly around his neck and he lies down, bringing me on top of him. Our mouths create a beautiful passion, my tears mixing in with the sweet taste we make together. I pull back a long moment later when my lungs desperately crave air but only slightly, making sure to keep our lips only a breath away from one another. I stare back into his warm, green eyes and try to think of the right thing to say, but there are no words to describe what I'm feeling. So with a small smile I decide to let him in on my future plans. "I'm going to marry you one day, Cooper McKay, so you better be ready for me."

He gives me his trademark sexy smile. "I'm never prepared when it comes to you, baby, but I wouldn't have it any other way."

With a giggle I attack his mouth again, but this time he flips me over and takes control. Just the way I like.

What started off being a terrible day turned out to be one of the best nights of my life…

I come back to the present and look around at all the girls who are sitting around me, hoping my face isn't as red as it feels when I think about what Coop did to me later that night. Obviously, I kept this story PG for Ruthie's sake.

"That is the most beautiful, real-life love story I've ever heard," Grace says with a hand over her heart.

I look down and finger the bracelet that is now loaded with charms; including the baseball bat to signify when I beat his truck after thinking he was cheating on me. I still feel like crap over it, but like Grams says, desperate times call for desperate measures.

"Well, I don't know about that, but it's my and Cooper's story, so it's perfect to me."

Just thinking about it has me craving to see him. We didn't sleep together last night since all of us girls stayed together. It's the first night we've been away from each other in, well, ever. I missed him like crazy, missed the safety of his arms and the feel of his hard, warm body wrapped protectively around me. Oh hell, I just missed every damn thing about him.

"God I'm so jealous," Katelyn says, almost sounding wistful. "Don't get me wrong, I'm happy for you all, but jealous as hell. You are all lucky to have found such amazing men who worship the ground you walk on."

"You will find your guy one day, Katelyn. I know it." Julia assures her with a soft smile.

"Not unless his name is Nick Stone." All of our eyes snap to Faith at her mumbled comment.

"Nick Stone? Who's Nick Stone, and why have I never heard of this guy?" I ask, my curiosity piquing at full intensity.

Katelyn glares over at Faith. "No one important. Just someone I used to know. He was one of Kolan's friends back in Montana."

I can tell he's a lot more than that, but there's no denying the flash of pain in her eyes as she talks about him, so I don't press. I don't know much about her past before coming here but I do know it wasn't pretty. Her brother, Kolan, is extremely protective over her. I've only met him a few times and he's really not all that friendly. I've also witnessed what he can do in the ring, and there is no denying the guy is lethal. Faith once told me he's very complicated. She said, other than her and Katelyn, he likes to keep to himself and ensures his life stays private. It surprised me considering he's in the media often for all of his fights. He's one of the best in the industry right now and is rising to the top fast.

Suddenly, Ruthie crawls over onto Katelyn's lap and slings an arm around her neck. "Don't worwy, Auntie Katewyn, you always have me, and I woship you."

All of us look at each other with a smile. Ruthie has the most beautiful heart of anyone I've ever known.

Katelyn's expression turns soft as she hugs her. "Thanks, sweetheart. I worship you, too."

Julia's phone dings with a text, interrupting the moment. She looks at it and gets the biggest smile. "Oh my god, you guys, look at Anna in her prom dress."

We all lean over to look at the picture of her and Logan. "They both look stunning," I say quietly.

"I sent her a picture of you already and told her I would send more as the night went on. She says you look beautiful."

I nod, hating that her prom fell on the same day as my wedding. She is a big part of our group and is important to us all, especially Julia and Jaxson. I wish she could have been here to celebrate with us, but I'm glad to see she's having a great time, if the smile on her face is anything to go by.

I glance back down at the pregnancy test and feel butterflies swirling around in my tummy again.

"Did you want to talk to Cooper before the wedding?" Julia asks. "I can go get him or text Jaxson to tell him to meet you somewhere."

I seriously consider it but quickly decide against it. There isn't much time before the ceremony, and I don't want him to see me before the wedding. I'm pretty sure he's going to be happy about the baby, like me, but I want to tell him when we have time to enjoy the news together. Not, *hey, babe, I just wanted to let you know that I'm pregnant. See ya down the aisle in a few minutes.*

I shake my head at Julia. "Nah. I'll tell him tonight after the ceremony. But can you pass me that empty gift bag there?" I ask, pointing to the bag that my garter came in. She passes it to me, and I put the test in then close it up. "Would someone mind taking this to our room for me?"

"I will," Katelyn says, standing. I give her my room key, once again thankful that we decided to have the entire wedding at the plantation for the sheer convenience of having it in one place.

Faith and Ruthie decide to go with her, and as soon as they open the door to leave, I hear my mom's voice. "Oh my gosh. Look at how stunning you girls are," she gushes. "Is my girl ready in there? Is everyone decent?"

I speak up before Katelyn can answer. "Yes, Mom, we're decent, you can come in."

She plows into the room and gasps when she sees me. "Oh my god, you look so beautiful," she blubbers and pulls me against her in a gripping hug.

I roll my eyes but can't deny the thickness I feel in my throat as I pat her back. "Thanks, Mom. You look beautiful, too."

Both her and Cooper's mom are wearing pink dresses too, but where my bridesmaid's dresses are silk, theirs are chiffon and a lighter tone of pink.

Suddenly, I catch sight of my dad as he walks in. "Whoa." He comes to an abrupt halt and puts a hand to his chest.

"Hey, Dad," I whisper, feeling my cheeks heat at his heart-stopping reaction.

After a long moment of staring at me, he walks over and pulls me into his arms. I breathe in deeply, taking in the safety and familiarity of his embrace. No matter how old I get, there is nothing more heartwarming than feeling my dad's arms around me. He was the first man I ever loved, and I'm so glad I found someone as amazing and honorable as him. "You're the most beautiful bride I've ever seen, next to your mother of course."

"Thank you." I feel him reach over and bring my mom into our hug then I hear a picture being snapped. Probably Julia.

"Isn't she beautiful?" my mom says, her voice laced with emotion. "Cooper isn't going to know what hit him."

I smile. Well, if my dress doesn't make his jaw drop, the baby news definitely will.

CHAPTER 7

Cooper

"I still can't believe she talked you into making us wear pink fucking ties. I swear my balls are shrinking by the second," Sawyer complains as he adjusts his tie in the mirror.

Yeah, well I don't like it either, but Kayla really wanted it and anything my girl wants I give her. Hell, I probably would have worn a pink fucking suit if it made her happy.

"Good," Jaxson says, clapping him on the back. "Now they will match your small dick."

All of us chuckle but Sawyer. "My dick is far from small, asshole. Just ask—"

A knock on the side door interrupts whatever arrogant remark was about to be made and opens to reveal Christopher. "Hey, some lady named Gladys out here is confused on what side she should sit on. I told her if she's friends with both of you she can pick anywhere, but she's insisting I ask you where you want her seated. She said she doesn't want to make Kayla jealous."

I groan and shake my head but everyone else seems to find it fucking hilarious. "Seat her on Kayla's side, next to Grams."

"Okay, I will, but I'll let Alissa deal with her. That old lady is grabby."

Don't I know it.

"Thanks, Christopher."

He nods then backs away, but before the door can close my mom comes barging in. "Oh my, look at how handsome all of you boys are." Strolling over, she grabs the lapels of my jacket then pulls me down and kisses my cheek. "I can't believe my baby boy is getting married today," she says with a quivering lip.

Oh jesus.

I'm just about to ask why she isn't with the girls but Evans walks over and grabs my face. "I know. I can't believe our baby is all grown up, pink ties and all."

I slap his hand away and shove him. "Get the fuck off of me."

"Cooper!" my mom gasps. "Don't talk to your friends like that or you won't have any at all."

I roll my eyes, but before I can respond Evans does. "Yeah, that really hurt my feelings, I might just up and leave you one man down."

I grunt. "You do that and I'll make sure to find the perfect guy to walk your Cupcake down the aisle."

His amusement vanishes in an instant and he points his finger at me. "That shit's not funny."

The rest of us chuckle, thinking it is.

"Okay, that's enough, boys, be nice to each other," my mom says as she starts adjusting my tie, her expression becoming somber. "I still can't believe your sister is missing your wedding."

"Mom, we've talked about this. She has a year left on her teaching contract then she will move here and we will see her all the time. I spoke with her this morning. It's all good, I promise."

She shakes her head, still not liking it, but I am fine with it. I've never been that close with my sister. I mean, she's awesome and all, but she's five years older than me and was in college when we moved to Sunset Bay. After getting her degree she travelled the world, teaching English abroad. She couldn't leave Korea to come today or else it would have been a breach in her contract. Kayla and I thought about waiting but I didn't want to, I've waited long enough. My sister and I are fine with it; my mom, however, is not.

"Aren't you supposed to be with the girls?" I ask, trying to bring her out of her thoughts.

"Yes, I'm on my way, but I wanted to quickly stop in and see my boys." She walks up to Jaxson and pulls him down for a hug. "You look as handsome as always. Julia and Annabelle are so lucky to have you."

Jaxson hugs her back easily, used to her affection. After his useless dad split on him, my parents insisted he live with us and they made him a part of the family. He's not only my best friend but also the closest person I have to a brother.

"Thanks, but I'm the lucky one."

My mom smiles at his response then walks over to my cousin Shawn next. "My favorite nephew. I'm so glad you could come and stand with Cooper on his special day."

I roll my eyes again. *Jesus, does she have to talk like we're fucking ten?*

"I'm your only nephew," he replies with a smirk.

"True, but you're still my favorite." She chuckles then moves on to Cade for a hug, which makes him uncomfortable but he's polite about it. The guy has gotten better, but if it isn't Faith or Ruthie he's still not all that comfortable with affection. Sawyer, of course, eats that shit up.

"All right, and one more for my boy before I go." She walks back over to me and wraps her arms around my waist. "I love you, and I'm so proud of you."

"Thanks, Mom," I mumble uncomfortably and want to punch Evans in the face at his smirk. Thankfully, my dad walks in and breaks up the awkward moment.

"Hey, Coach." Everyone greets him.

"How goes it, boys?" He shakes their hands and gives them a clap on the back. "All right, Arlene, let the boy go and head on over to the girls' suite. I just spoke with Pastor Williams and we're ready in five minutes."

"Okay, okay." She squeezes me one more time then looks up at me with a smile. "I'm excited to see Kayla, I know she's going to be beautiful today."

"She's beautiful every day." I answer honestly because it's the damn truth. No one, and I mean *no one*, holds a candle to her. She's the most beautiful girl in the world, inside and out. Even when she's a pain in the ass she's still sexy as hell, and fuck did I miss her sassy ass last night. I didn't sleep worth a shit without her and I never want to do that again. Not under any circumstance. I can't wait until the wedding is over so I can haul her ass upstairs to our room and show her how much I missed her.

"That certainly is true," my mother replies, snapping me from my thoughts. "Okay, I'm going now. Want me to give Kayla a message from you?"

I shake my head. The message I have for her is completely inappropriate for my mom to know.

"All right." She gives my father a kiss then waves one last time before walking out of the room.

My dad walks up to me now and claps me firmly on the back, like he did the others. "How are you doing? You nervous?"

I shake my head. "Nah, I'm ready."

That is a major understatement. I swear I was born ready for this moment.

My father nods. "Good. I promise not to get all mushy like your mom. Just know I'm proud of you too, kid."

"Thanks, Dad."

He pulls me in for a quick hug. "All right, let's go. Pastor Williams is waiting."

All of us head to the side door that leads to the outdoor garden where the ceremony is being held. Just as everyone walks out Jaxson holds me back. "Wait up a sec."

I turn to him. He shifts nervously, and I quickly realize shit's about to get uncomfortable again. "Listen, I just want to say…uh…" He rubs the back of his neck. "Fuck, I suck at this shit!"

"You're not going to kiss me, are you?" I joke with a smirk, trying to lift the awkwardness of the moment.

He grunts then takes a moment as he finds his words. "I just want to say thanks…for everything. I owe a lot to you and your parents. If it hadn't been for you, I probably wouldn't have finished high school. You took care of Julia for me when I left, you beat the shit out of me when I needed it, and you've stuck with me through some of the worst moments of my life. You're the brother I never had, and I guess I just…I wanted to say thank you. For all of it. And I'm glad I'm standing beside you today like you did me."

I clap him on the shoulder. "You don't need to thank me, you've done the same for me over the years. Although, you could have tried a little harder when my woman beat the fuck out of my truck that night, but hey…" I trail off with a shrug.

He grunts. "She threatened to bash my head in with that bat and we both know she would have."

I chuckle. Yeah, I have no doubt she would have; she was pissed. It's something I can joke about now but at the time it wasn't funny. Not the damage to my truck, I didn't care about that, but the fact that she thought I would cheat on her… I shake myself from the memory—the thought still bothers me.

Jaxson gives me a punch on the arm. "Come on, let's get out there before you're late for your own wedding."

We head outside to see over two hundred friends and family seated on white, fancy chairs that have big fucking pink bows tied to them. I smile and nod at a few people as we walk down the aisle informally and take our spots next to Pastor Williams and the groomsmen. I turn to Faith's father and clasp his hand. "Pastor, thank you again for being here with Kayla and me. We really appreciate it."

"You're welcome. I'm honored you guys asked me to be a part of it."

"Oh, Sheriff!" The old lady voice interrupts our greeting, and I look over nervously to where Gladys is sitting with Grams, waving at me with a coy smile.

I clear my throat awkwardly and give her a brief flick of my hand, which clearly is a mistake since she takes that as a sign to blow me a kiss.

"Damn, that lady is relentless," I mumble.

Jaxson slings an arm around my shoulders. "I told you, man, you need to stop going over there every time she tells you her panties have been stolen. You're leading the poor lady on." He chuckles.

I'm just about to tell him I do no such thing but the music begins playing, signaling it's time to start. I stand up straighter and watch both Kayla's mom and my mom take their seats up front. Kayla's mom waves and blows me a kiss then pulls some tissue out of her purse, taking one for herself then handing one to my mom.

Oh jesus, they are both going to be a blubbering mess the entire wedding. I know it.

Katelyn makes her way down the aisle first. I catch her make eye contact with my cousin, whom she will be walking back down with, and I look over to see him wink at her. When he looks at me, I give a subtle shake of my head, letting him know to back off. I warned him earlier to stay away from her. He's the biggest whore I know, and that girl has gone through enough shit, she doesn't need to deal with his, too.

Faith walks down next and blows a subtle kiss to Cade before taking her place beside Katelyn. Then it's Grace. She smiles shyly at Sawyer. I don't look over at his response, but whatever it is has her blushing furiously.

Go figure.

Julia follows in next, and I hear Jaxson exhale a breath. "I swear I'm the luckiest motherfucker alive."

"Yeah, you are," Sawyer adds, slightly above a whisper. "I still have no idea what she sees in you."

All of us chuckle under our breath, including Jaxson. Before Julia walks past me, she stops and kisses my cheek. "I can't wait for you to see her. She's perfect."

"She always is." I have no doubt that she looks incredible, but I've already seen her at her best. Naked, with me on top of her, inside of her, connected to her… *Oh shit.* I shift uncomfortably and pull myself from my thoughts before I get a boner in front of hundreds of people.

Julia steps back then turns to wait for Ruthie and Annabelle to make their way down. Ruthie holds Annabelle's hand as she walks slowly and unsteadily down the aisle. Everyone gushes and snaps a million pictures. Once they reach the end, Julia bends down and sweeps Annabelle up in her arms and kisses her cheek.

"You did so good, baby girl." She walks Annabelle over to Jaxson so he can kiss her too, then she takes her over to Grams's waiting arms.

Ruthie walks up to Cade before taking her spot next to the girls. "Wookin' good, Big Guy." All of us bite back a smile as she holds her fist out for a knuckle-bump.

"You too, kid. Always," he replies, knocking fists with her.

With a bright smile, she skips over to her spot and gives me a light punch in the arm as she passes by. "Goodwuck, Mister Shewiff."

"Thanks. Do you think I'm going to need it?"

"Well, she is hopin' to knock you on yowr ass."

We all burst into a fit of laughter, including Pastor Williams.

Faith leans down and pulls Ruthie in next to her. "Butt, honey, remember it's *butt* for you."

"Oh yeah, wight, sowwy."

Faith kisses her cheek, letting her know it's okay.

When the music changes and everyone stands, I swing my attention back to the aisle and suck in a sharp breath at the sight before me.

Ho-ly shit.

All the oxygen leaves my lungs as I stare awestruck at the girl whose arm is linked with her father's, as she walks toward me. I knew she would look amazing, but jesus…she looks like an angel, an innocent one, except I know she is anything but. I have corrupted her way too many times for her to be innocent any more. But as I take in her white, strapless dress, long blonde hair flowing down past her slender shoulders in big, loose curls and the veil high on her head—she looks like the most innocent angel that God has ever created. That's until her sweet, soft smile turns into something else the closer she gets. It's a smile that tells me she's up to something.

Stopping a short distance in front of me, her dad leans down and kisses her cheek. Just as he's about to pass me her hand, she pulls free and launches herself at me. I catch her in surprise with a grunted chuckle that quickly vanishes when she gives me one hot fucking kiss. I snap out of my shock quickly then take control, like always. A low growl escapes my throat as soon as her sweet taste touches my tongue, the deep sound is covered from everyone hooting and hollering at her unexpected act.

Kayla is the one to break the kiss first, and thank god she does because I probably would have never stopped. I keep hold of her, her feet still dangling off the ground and stare into her smiling face.

"I think the kiss comes at the end," I tell her with a smirk.

"I've never been one to follow the rules, Sheriff. You know that." She leans in closer then whispers, "But you can punish me for it later."

My amusement vanishes and I groan inwardly. "You can count on it. I have lost time to make up for. I missed you last night."

"Me, too," she replies softly.

I press a kiss to her forehead then drop her back on her feet.

"You like my dress?" she asks, giving me a little twirl.

Chuckles fill the air around us, including mine. "Yeah, baby." I pull her back in to me. "You look beautiful, just like always, but you're going to look even better when I take it off of you tonight."

"Mmmm, agreed." She reaches up and gives me another kiss, but this one ends much quicker than the last, much to my disappointment. Kayla steps back then looks up at Pastor Williams with a smile. "Sorry, Pastor, I just couldn't help myself. He looks so darn good in this suit of his."

She gives me a sassy wink that makes me want to haul her ass up to our room and say *fuck all this* and just sign the papers tomorrow. Somehow, I manage to restrain myself. It's what this woman does to me, what she has always done to me. She pushes every button I have with just a look, a wink, or a sassy remark—all to get a rise out of me. And she loves when I take it out on her later, when we are alone and—

"No problem. Whenever you're ready we can start," the pastor replies, interrupting my perverted thoughts.

"I'm ready," she says, then looks at me. "You ready?"

"I was born ready, baby."

She smiles. "Good answer."

With a chuckle the pastor starts, and thankfully the ceremony is fairly quick, which is what we wanted because South Carolina in June is hotter than hell. After the signing of the papers, exchange of rings, and vows, Pastor Williams finishes it with, "Now, by the power vested in me by the state of South Carolina, and as a minister of the gospel, I now pronounce you husband and wife. You may kiss—"

That's the last thing I catch before Kayla launches herself at me again. This time though, I'm prepared for her. I lift her off her feet once again and claim her mouth first. Our kiss is slower and more intimate than the last, and I get completely lost in her, like always. It doesn't matter how many times I've kissed this girl, I can never get enough of her.

She pulls back and drops her forehead on mine with a smile. "I told you I was going to marry you one day, Cooper McKay."

I return her smile with a smirk. "You did, but little did you know that was my plan long before yours."

With a sweet giggle, she leans in and kisses me again. "I love you, Officer Sexy," she mumbles against my lips.

"I love you too, baby."

CHAPTER 8

From the moment that kiss ended everything turned into chaos—from pictures in the smoldering heat, to supper, speeches, and now the first dance. I'm not a big dancer. Actually, I don't like it at all, but right now, as I hold Kayla's soft, slender body close to mine, I decide it's not such a bad thing after all. Even though we have hundreds of people watching us, I feel like, for the first time today, it's just her and me, and I'm thankful for the small reprieve.

"So, has it been everything you hoped it would be?" I ask.

She nods softly. "Yes, actually even more than I had hoped it would be." For some reason I get the feeling that her words hold meaning, but before I can think more of it, she reaches up and wraps her arms around my neck. "What about you?"

Most guys don't give a shit about things like this. I know girls think about this moment from the time they are kids, but us guys don't. Well, maybe the wedding night, but not the actual wedding. I couldn't have cared less what we did or where we had our wedding just as long as she was here. "Yeah, baby, because all I need is you."

"Well, yeah, it wouldn't have been anyone else or I would have cut a bitch."

I bust out laughing, knowing it's true. "I wish you would be more possessive where Gladys is concerned. Jesus, that lady has been relentless all night. Where are your ass kickin' skills when I need them?"

"Now come on, Coop, you don't really want me to kick an old lady's ass, do you? You should be flattered, Sheriff. I mean, she could call anyone to come find her panties, but she trusts your investigatin' skills to get the job done."

I grunt at her sarcasm, not finding it very funny, which only makes her laugh.

Unfortunately, that is not where my torment ends when it comes to Gladys. An hour later, when I'm sitting at a table with all the guys, she comes up to me, looking excited as shit because my wife just told her that I would dance with her. My eyes snap to Kayla on the dance floor, where she's dancing with the girls, and she gives me a sassy little wave of her fingers.

Oh, she is going to fucking pay for this.

I look back up at Gladys's hopeful expression and try to figure out how the fuck I'm going to get out of this. "Well, that's real nice of you, Miss Gladys, but unfortunately, I'm not a very good dancer." Her face falls, making me feel like shit, so I add, "But Sawyer here loves to dance."

Her face lights back up, and I feel Sawyer's hard gaze on me, but I don't acknowledge him. That will teach the fucker for messing with me about the pink ties.

"Oh, he will work just fine, too." She turns to Sawyer. "What's your favorite dance, sugar?"

Jaxson chuckles next to me, and when I glance over at Sawyer, I swear if looks could kill I would be ten feet under right now. He snaps out of it quickly and pastes a smile on his face. "Sorry, but I'm only allowed to dance with my Cupcake. She gets really mad if I dance with other women, especially ones as beautiful as you, and I sure wouldn't want to hurt her feelings."

What a smooth motherfucker.

Gladys nods, as if fully understanding this. "Oh yes, I get that a lot. It seems the younger ladies do find me a little threatening, and I love Miss Grace. I wouldn't want her feelings hurt either."

You have got to be shittin' me.

I start feeling like an ass as she watches us eagerly, waiting for one of us to fill the role. Right when I think I'm fucked and have no other choice but to dance with her, old Gus, Kayla's grandpa, comes walking over and asks her. She's caught off guard but happily accepts then walks off arm in arm with him.

Thank fuck!

I glance back to Kayla to see her looking amused as shit. When she gives me a wink, I shake my head to let her know she's going to pay for this later. Suddenly, a napkin gets thrown at me from across the table and pulls me from our stare down.

"You fucker!" Sawyer berates me under his breath. "Why the hell did you throw me under the bus? Why not him?" He points to Jaxson.

I whip the napkin back at him. "Because he hasn't been annoying me by running his mouth all day about the pink fucking ties."

He grunts. "That's because he enjoys dressing like a chick, too." Jaxson throws his napkin at him now, which he catches with a laugh. "Oh calm your shit, ladies, I'm kidding. And what the hell are you thinking inviting that lady anyway? I mean, jesus, she is off her fucking rocker and you know it."

"Yeah, but she's harmless…most of the time, and Kayla said we had to since she's Grams's friend."

It's pretty much the only reason I agreed to it.

Before anyone can say more, Ruthie comes skipping over and jumps up on Cade's lap. Her beanie is now back on her head, even though she's still in her flower girl dress, but I have to admit, if anyone can pull it off it's her. "Hey, Big Guy, you havin' fun?" she asks Cade.

"Yeah. How about you?"

"Oh yes. I tan't wait until you and Faif get married, and I weally tan't wait to be your best man, or I guess I should say best girl," she adds with a giggle.

He smirks. "Me too, kid."

Cade and Faith's wedding is in a few months. Sawyer was always his best man while Jaxson, Christopher, and I are his groomsmen. Then Ruthie told him that the best man is supposed to be his best friend, and since she's his best friend she asked if she could stand next to him. Of course he said yes. Who could say no to her? However, we have all agreed that Sawyer is still in charge of the bachelor party.

The conversation gets broken up when the music suddenly switches from a slow song to a fast one, "I'm Sexy and I Know It", blaring loudly from the speakers.

"Oh my gosh, Sawyer." Grace squeals from across the dance floor, drawing all of our attention. "It's your song," she yells with a laugh then turns to him and starts dancing along. When she kisses each of her biceps we all burst into a fit of laughter.

Sawyer isn't fazed in the least—he's too arrogant. Instead, he watches her with an amused smirk then gets up and makes his way to the dance floor. We all groan because we know what's coming and so does Grace, if her attempt to dodge him is any indication. Of course she isn't able to make her escape. Bending down, he picks her up, sweeping her off her feet.

"Put me down, Sawyer!" she demands with a laugh.

"Sorry, Cupcake, but no can do. We have some business to take care of."

We all shake our heads as he walks out of the tent.

"Where's he takin' her?" Ruthie asks.

"Nowhere!" All of us shout at once.

I hope wherever he's taking her, he has the decency to go somewhere private, or better yet their room.

Ruthie lets out a big yawn and drops her head on Cade's chest, her eyes getting droopy. "You tired, kid? Want Christopher and Alissa to take you to bed?"

"No, I'm okay," she replies sleepily, then passes out not even two minutes later. Christopher and Alissa carry her to the suite Cade and Faith rented, and take Annabelle with them also.

Sawyer and Grace return thirty minutes later, Sawyer looking cocky and Grace looking…well, satisfied but clearly embarrassed, if her red cheeks and lack of eye contact with any of us guys is anything to go by.

At the very end of the night, after everyone has cleared out and the staff is cleaning up, all of us friends walk out to the garden for one last drink. Katelyn headed up to her room a little while ago, while my cousin left with some chick Kayla works with. Us guys are sitting on the stone steps to the fountain while the girls sit on our laps and talk about the day's events.

"It really was an amazing day. Thank you for letting us be a part of it," Faith says, and a chorus of agreement goes around.

"No, thank you, all of you," Kayla speaks for the both of us. "We couldn't have asked for a better wedding party. Coop and I are very thankful for you guys… Even you, Hulk," she adds, glancing over at Jaxson. "And to think, you didn't turn green once today, I'm so damn proud of you."

He grunts at her smart mouth. "I guess we both deserve a pat on the back then, because just think—you didn't take a bat to anyone's truck tonight."

She punches him in the arm. "Well, the night's not over yet. Where did you park again?"

All of us chuckle at their usual bantering.

"We definitely have been through a lot together," Julia says softly, steering the conversation back to the original topic. "I tell Jaxson all the time how blessed we are to have each other. We're more than friends, we're family, and I know our kids will grow up to be close, too."

Sawyer points at me with a smirk. "I guess it's time for you to get cracking on your baby-making skills, Sheriff."

I grunt. "Not yet."

Kayla tenses on me, but before I can think too much of it, the shrill ringing of a cell phone sounds. With a confused frown, Jaxson pulls his phone out of his pocket and glances at the number before answering. "Anna?" His expression immediately puts me on alert. "Whoa, calm down. I can't understand anything you're saying. Just take a deep breath." He puts a finger to his ear, trying to hear her better.

All of us look at each other, as we can hear a hysterical Anna on the other end of the line but can't make out what she's saying.

"What! What do you mean? How… Okay, okay, calm down. Just sit tight. I'm on my way." Jaxson hangs up and stands up quickly, lifting Julia to her feet.

"Jax, what's going on?" she asks in concern.

"That was Anna. She's at the police station." He pauses and looks at all of us, his expression unreadable. "Logan has been arrested for murder."

"What!" We all shout at the same time.

"I don't know what happened, she was so hysterical that I could barely understand her, but she wants me to come there." He looks at Julia. "I told her I would come. Can you go get Annabelle? Then we'll go home and pack a bag."

"Jax, that might take too long, and she's sleeping. Why don't you go tonight and Annabelle and I will come tomorrow?"

He shakes his head. "No. I don't want to leave you two, and I don't want you driving yourself there."

"Grace and I will stay with her," Sawyer offers. "I can drive them up tomorrow if you're still there."

"You sure?"

Instead of repeating himself, he replies with a nod. Jaxson is still reluctant but Julia convinces him it's for the best.

"All right." He leans down and kisses her. "I'll see you tomorrow, baby."

"Drive carefully," she says softly. "Text me when you get there and tell Anna I love her."

He nods then glances at me but I wave him away. "Go, just call me tomorrow and fill me in on what's going on. You know I'll help any way I can."

"Thanks." After a quick good-bye to everyone else he's gone.

We all get up to head to our rooms now, everyone silent while we ponder what could have happened. It's clear Logan has been through some shit, but I would never peg him for killing someone in cold blood. I shake my head. No, he wouldn't. I've gotten to know him well enough over the last two years, and I know he wouldn't do that. Something else is going on.

After one last good-bye to the others, Kayla and I walk to our room that's on the opposite side of the house. Closing the door behind me, I turn to see her standing in the middle of the room, looking tired and upset. I walk over and pull her in my arms. "You okay, baby?"

"Yeah, I'm just worried about Anna and Logan. I hope they're okay."

"They will be. Jaxson will make sure of it."

She looks up at me with a soft smile and nods. "Yeah, you're right."

I cup the side of her face and brush my thumb across her lush bottom lip. She turns her face to the side and kisses my palm. Just as I lean down to claim her mouth, she slaps a hand over my lips, stopping my attempt. "Hold it right there, Officer Sexy. Keep that delicious mouth away for just a moment. I have something that I need to tell you first."

I ignore her protest and pull her hand away. "We can talk later, baby."

She shakes her head. "No, we can't. It's important, Cooper."

I immediately back off at her underlying tone. "What's wrong?"

"Nothing is wrong, per se." She bites her thumbnail nervously, taking my concern to a whole new level.

"Kayla…"

"Can I ask you something?"

The vulnerability in her voice is starting to scare the shit out of me. "Always, baby, you know that."

She clears her throat and nods. "What did you mean down there when Sawyer said it was time for us to make a baby and you said 'not yet'?"

I rear back, caught off guard by the question and the fact that she seems upset by it. "I didn't mean anything. We talked about starting a family in a year or so and you just went off the pill—"

"Well, sometimes things change."

My brow furrows at her quiet reply. "Yeah, I guess it can." I shrug, still trying to figure out where this is all coming from. "Where are you going with this, Kayla?"

Her gaze focuses to something behind me, then she heads over to the antique dresser and grabs a small, silver gift bag off the top of it. She walks back up to me warily and hands it to me. "Here, open it. It's uh, it's kind of my wedding gift to you."

Oh shit!

"We're supposed to get each other gifts? I didn't know that."

She smiles at my sudden panic. "No, we aren't supposed to, but this was a surprise present for me this morning and now I'm gifting it to you."

Okay, now I'm completely intrigued. Taking a seat at the end of the bed, I open the bag and pull out a white stick that has a blue plus sign in the window. I tense and my eyes shoot to Kayla to see her watching me nervously. "What's this?" I ask, even though I know exactly what it is.

"A pregnancy test… *My* pregnancy test."

"You're pregnant?" I ask in shock.

She nods. "I found out this morning. I wanted to tell you earlier, but I thought it was best to wait until we were alone so we could talk about it."

I glance back down at the test and try to let it sink in that we're going to have a baby. I guess I shouldn't be surprised, considering she went off the pill, but the doctor said it could take up to a year to conceive.

"Say something," she whispers, her voice thick with worry.

I look back up at her and my chest constricts at her expression. "Jesus, Kayla." Reaching out, I grab her wrist and pull her to stand between my legs. "Why are you so nervous about my reaction? You have to know I'm not upset about this."

She expels a relieved breath then shrugs. "Well, I didn't think you would be, but then downstairs you said that to Sawyer, and I—I got worried." She shakes her head. "I don't know. I'm being stupid, I'm sorry."

"No, I'm sorry. I didn't mean anything by it. I'm happy, baby. Surprised as hell, but…really happy."

And a little fucking scared, but I decide to keep that part to myself.

I'm not scared for the responsibility, I'm more so worried about bringing a life into a world that can be very ugly at times. It's something I see on a regular basis. The thought of something happening to anyone I care about scares me, but the thought of it happening to Kayla or our future family is completely fucking terrifying.

Wrapping my arms around her waist, I drop my forehead to her stomach. "I promise I'll take really good care of our family, Kayla. I'll always protect you guys."

Her slender fingers thread through my hair as she holds me close. "I never doubted that for one second. I know you will take good care of us like you do everyone else in this town."

I glance back up at her. "Yeah, but you will always be my first priority. You know that, right?" I mean that with everything I am. My job means a lot to me and I will always uphold it, but my family will always come first—she will always come first.

"Yeah, Coop, I know that. I have no doubt you're going to be the best father our kids can ever have." Suddenly, a smile graces her lips. "Let's just hope they are like you and nothing like me, or you're in some serious trouble."

The thought of having a bunch of sassy little Kaylas running around does kind of scare the shit out of me.

She senses my thoughts and bursts out laughing. "I love your silence."

"Sorry," I apologize with a smirk. "But the thought is a little terrifying. My hands are full enough with just one of you."

"Mmm, don't be sorry." She backs out of my arms with a saucy smile. "I like it when your hands are full of me." My dick comes roaring to life as I watch her reach behind her back to undo her dress. I begin to stand up but she shakes her head. "Uh-uh, stay there. I have something to show you."

I already know exactly what she has under there; just the thought of it has fire pumping through my blood. But I sit back down then rid myself of my jacket, shirt, and tie, making sure my eyes never leave her body. My cock twitches at her blatant eye-fuck of my shirtless state. She takes her time ridding herself of the dress, trying to give me a show, but I'm way too impatient for that right now.

"Kayla, hurry the fuck up before I rip that thing off of you myself."

"Mmmm, a little impatient are we, Sheriff?" She mouths back, jacking my dick up another notch.

"Yeah, baby, I'm always impatient for your pussy." Undoing my pants, I free myself then take my cock into my hand with a firm grip. She freezes and her eyes glaze over with lust as she watches me stroke myself. A low groan rumbles deep in my throat. "Drop the dress, Kayla, now."

She quickly follows my order and I inhale a swift, sharp breath at what she reveals—her tight, fuckable body encased in a strapless, white lace bra and matching panties that are attached to a garter belt and stockings. My eyes sweep down the length of her, taking in her perfection. Her veil still drapes down her hair, and once again she looks angelic and innocent when I know she's really a vixen.

"I kept it simple so it wouldn't take you too long to get it off of me."

My gaze snaps back to her face to see a brazen smile tilting her lips. "Come here," I demand gruffly. She does as I tell her and comes to stand between my legs. I release my cock then cup her firm, round ass and groan when I realize she's wearing a thong. Leaning in, I press a kiss to her soft, toned stomach. "Do you have any idea how hard it makes me to know my baby is growing inside of this beautiful body of yours?"

I feel her shiver at my breath on her skin. "No, but I'm glad to hear it, because this body is going to be making some changes over the next nine months. And you better still find my ass sexy, because I have no plans to stop jumping your bones every chance I get."

I chuckle but it trails off on a groan when I think about all the times she surprises me at work because she doesn't want to wait until I get home. Those are always the best fucking days.

"Believe me, baby, you're going to be even more beautiful, if that's possible." I circle her naval with my tongue, loving the taste of her skin. "Know why?"

"No, why?" she whispers as her hands find my shoulders to keep balance.

"Because no matter where you are, what you're doing, or who you're with, there will always be a part of me inside of you, and there is nothing fucking hotter than that."

"Mmmm, well when you put it like that, that's downright beautiful."

"Yeah, baby, you're beautiful, always." I trail my lips lower, bringing them to the center of her panties, then skim my nose along the damp lace and breathe in deeply. Her sweet aroma penetrates my senses and my mouth instantly waters for a taste of her.

"Cooper." She moans while her fingernails bite into my shoulders.

"What do you want, Kayla, hmmm?" I hum against her. "You want my tongue buried deep in this sweet pussy of yours."

"God, yes." She whimpers and thrusts against my mouth.

My hand moves behind one of her knees and I lift it up to prop her foot on the bed, next to me, opening her up more to my view. She reaches up to take off her veil but I grab her wrist and stop her. "Leave it on."

She quirks a brow. "Whatever you say, Sheriff."

Leaning in, I nip the inside of her thigh just above where her stocking ends and watch goose bumps break out over her soft, delicate skin. She inhales sharply and her breathing turns ragged. I glance up at her just before I rip the garter belt and panties from her body with one swift pull. Her gasp trails off into a moan, and I grip her hips when she loses her balance.

A low growl erupts from me when I take in her slick, bare folds that glisten with her arousal. "Such a pretty pussy," I murmur. "And it's all mine, isn't that right?"

"Yes, yours, always." Her voice drops to a whisper.

"That's right, for fucking ever, until death do us part." I spread her open with my fingers and blow gently on her clit. Her knees buckle, but I quickly grab her ass to hold her up.

"Oh god, please, Cooper," she pleads on a moan, bringing my restraint to its breaking point.

"Please what?" I ask, glancing up at her again.

She stares down at me with her cheeks flushed and eyes glazed with naked lust, knowing exactly what I want to hear. She licks her lips, making my cock jerk at the sight of it. "Please lick my pussy."

I groan at her soft words. "My fucking pleasure." Leaning in, I take a long, leisurely lick of her warm, wet flesh and growl as her flavor explodes on my tongue.

"Ah yes!" she cries out. Her stance weakens again, but I cup her ass tighter to keep her from falling. I hear something drop to the floor and look up to see she rid herself of her bra, her perfect tits filling her hands. The sight of her is almost enough to make me come.

Her hips start rocking at a frantic pace as I devour her. "That a girl, fuck my mouth."

"Oh god. It feels so good," she confesses with a whimper. I feel her clit start to swell so I bring my hand up behind her and drag two fingers along the crevice of her ass before slamming them deep inside of her. "Ahhh!" As soon as her inner walls lock down on me, I catch her fluttering bud between my lips and send her over the edge. Her fingers grip my hair and her head falls back on a cry as ecstasy washes over her face. I don't let up until every ounce of pleasure has spilled from her.

She drops down and straddles me, her stocking-covered thighs on either side of my hips. Her arms wrap around my neck and our mouths meet frantically. I thread my hand through her thick, curly locks, and pull her head back to deepen the kiss.

Unable to withstand not being inside of her for another second, I shove my pants further down my legs and slip inside of her tight heat without breaking contact with her mouth.

"Ah, fuck you're perfect." I groan as heat explodes through my entire body, her pussy gripping me like a tight vise. I swear there is nothing in the world that is better than being inside of this girl. I have been fucking her for years and every time I enter her it feels like the first time.

"I love you so much," she whispers against my mouth.

"I love you, too, baby. Forever."

"Yes, forever."

Damn fucking straight. I will never tire of her—not her smile, her body, or her sassy mouth. Not even a lifetime with her will be enough.

Bringing my hand up, I cup the heavy weight of one of her firm, round tits and brush my thumb over the hard tip. Her head falls back in pleasure and she arches into my touch, giving me the perfect opportunity to lean in and take her other nipple into my mouth.

"Oh god, yes." Her fingers wind in my hair with a painful grip that shoots straight to my cock and her hips pick up rhythm.

"That's right, baby, fuck me." I lean back on my arms to bring her deeper, then slam up inside of her. All the breath leaves her lungs and she falls forward, bracing her hands on my stomach.

"Yes, again!"

I groan. "You want it hard and fast, Kayla?"

"Yes! I want it all."

With a growl, I grip her hips and start fucking her with an urgency that makes me feel like an animal, pounding up into her relentlessly. Pleasured cries spill past her lips as she claws at my chest to hang on, her nails marking me while her tits bounce enticingly in my face. Feeling close to exploding already, I change the angle of my thrusts and hit her sweet spot. Her pussy starts to flutter around me, warning me of her impending orgasm.

"That's it, give me another one, baby. Let me feel this pussy milk my cock."

I reach up and deliver a light slap to her tit, right over her beaded nipple, and it was all she needed. Her inner walls clamp down on me and send me over the edge with her. Ecstasy rushes through my veins as I continue my pace, fucking her hard and fast through our orgasms.

When we're both spent, she drops down on top of me, our sweat-slicked bodies molding together. I wrap my arms tightly around her and hold her close as we catch our breaths, our hearts pounding against one another. I drag my fingers along her back as we lie in comfortable silence—no words needed.

A few minutes later, I kiss the top of her head. "Come on, baby, let's shower before we fall asleep." Just as I sit us up, a big bang has me struggling to maintain balance to stop us from rolling off the bed.

Kayla gasps. "Oh shit! Did we break the bed?" She jumps off and looks underneath it then glances back up at me in horror. "Oh my god, we did! We broke the bed!"

"What? What kind of bed can't withstand a good fuck?"

A long bout of silence stretches between us before we both burst out laughing. "Damn it! They are going to charge us a fortune for this, I know it." Her voice has an edge of worry to it as she rips her veil off her head.

"At least it was money well spent."

She laughs again like I hoped for her to.

Bending down, I scoop her up in my arms then walk to the bathroom. "Don't worry, baby, we'll figure it out."

"Speak for yourself, buddy. I'm bailing early in the morning and totally blaming the whole thing on you."

I grunt, not putting it past her.

We shower and dry off quickly, both of us exhausted from the day's events. When we walk back out to the room, I use a phone book to prop up the broken side of the bed, making it close to level. Then I crawl in next to Kayla and pull her warm, naked body against mine. She looks up at me, her expression unreadable.

"We're married," she whispers, her tone serious.

"Yeah..." I reply slowly and stare down at her, unsure of where she's going with this.

"That means I'm your wife. Forever. Until you die." Her head tilts and her eyes turn crazy. "You are mine and there is no escape for you, Cooper. Do you understand? If you ever try to leave me, I will find you, and I will kill you!"

I roll my eyes at her dramatics and lay a hand over her face, covering up her crazy-ass expression. "Thanks for the warning, Black Widow, but I don't plan on going anywhere. I like my new truck too much," I add with a smirk.

She laughs and slaps my hand away from her face. I keep hold of her hand and twine our fingers together to see how our rings look next to each other. "Do you feel different?" she asks quietly.

"What do you mean?"

"I don't know. We're married now and just found out we're having a baby; shouldn't we feel different?"

I shrug. "I don't see why. We always knew our lives were headed in this direction, and I love you the same as I did yesterday."

"Shouldn't you love me more every day?" she teases, quirking a brow at me.

"That's impossible, because I've loved you with everything I have from the day I made you mine, and I will for the rest of my life. Nothing—or no one—will ever change that, Kayla," I tell her truthfully.

She smiles softly; it's one of those smiles that constricts my chest and makes it difficult to breathe. "You always know the right thing to say to me." She leans in and places a kiss over my heart. "I'll never stop loving you either."

"Damn straight, or I will find you, and I will kill you," I mock back the teasing threat to her.

She giggles and we fall back into a comfortable silence again.

A few minutes later my eyes begin to feel heavy but I force them to stay open, wanting to say one last thing to her. "Kayla?" I whisper, not wanting to wake her if she's already fallen asleep.

"Yeah?" she replies just as quietly.

I reach down and place my hand flat against her stomach. "What I said earlier about the baby… I lied." She stiffens, but before she can say anything, I continue, "I hope all of our kids turn out just like you—kind, brave, generous, and a pain in the ass."

I feel her smile against my chest before she reaches down and places her hand over mine. "We're going to have a good life, Coop."

"Yeah, we are." Leaning down, I kiss the top of her head. "Sleep, baby." Are the last words I speak before I fall into a deep slumber.

I hear Cooper's breathing even out and his hand gets heavier on my tummy. Looking up, I see his handsome face soft with sleep, and I watch him for a moment, taking in his unguarded expression like I do on so many nights. This is also one of my favorite moments in life that I cherish—to watch him when the world isn't weighing so heavily on him, as he shoulders so much responsibility. What he doesn't know, is that while he's watching over everyone and taking care of everything, I'm watching out for him and I always will. I know there will be times throughout our life that won't always be easy, but I will never give up on us—never give up on him. He was the first man I ever loved and he will be my last. I will make sure that we share as many unforgettable moments as possible, ones that will stay with us to eternity.

THE END

Want more Men of Honor? Then keep reading for an excerpt from Logan and Anna's story *An Act of Redemption*. Book one in the *Acts of Honor series,* spin-off series from the *Men of Honor*.

In this series, you get to keep up with all the Men of Honor characters and their families while also meeting new characters that will steal your heart and add to this amazing found family.

You can also find fun bonus scenes about these characters on my website at www.authorkclynn.com.

PROLOGUE

Anna

At only fourteen years old I was abducted, brutalized and violated. It was the worst week of my life. If it wasn't for Jaxson Reid, who I now consider my big brother, and two other brave Navy SEALs, I would have never survived.

I didn't think I could overcome what happened to me, but I did, and I came out stronger.

I also fell in love.

Logan Knight was misunderstood and perceived as dangerous, but I've always known better. I saw in him what no one else did and we formed a connection, one that, even with a break in time, could never be severed.

In the beginning he was my salvation, but in the end I was his redemption.

This is our story.

Keep reading for a complete list of K.C. Lynn's books. Available on Amazon and Kindle Unlimited...

MEN OF HONOR SERIES

A small-town romantic suspense series of interconnected standalones.

Possessive alpha males, sweet heroines, found family, touch her & die, military heroes.

FIGHTING TEMPTATION
Friends-to-Lovers

SWEET TEMPTATION
Opposites Attract

RESISTING TEMPTATION
Grumpy X Sunshine

THE FINAL TEMPTATION
Opposites Attract

MEN OF HONOR BOX SET
Read the complete series in one!

ACTS OF HONOR SERIES

A spin-off series from the Men of Honor with interconnected characters.

Small-town romantic suspense.

Possessive alpha males, sweet innocent heroines, found family, touch her & die vibes

AN ACT OF REDEMPTION
Second Chance

AN ACT OF SALVATION
Brother's Best Friend

AN ACT OF OBSESSION
Heroine in Hiding

AN ACT OF COURAGE
Second Chance

FIGHTING WITH HONOR
A Men of Honor tie-in novella
(Best to read after An Act of Courage)

AN ACT OF LOVE
Van & Ruthie
Release date TBA

SWEET SERIES

A spin-off series from Sweet Temptation with interconnected standalones.

Contemporary small-town romance.

Protective alpha males, sweet innocent heroines, family Saga, emotional, spicy, family drama.

SWEET LOVE
Spin-off novella of Sawyer & Grace
Must read after Sweet Temptation

SWEET HAVEN
Enemies-to-Lovers

SWEET DESTINY
Sam & Jase's Wedding Novella

JESSE & MATT'S STORY
Title & Release TBA

SWEET CATCH
Title & Release TBA

SWEET LUCY
Title & Release TBA

CREED BROTHERS SERIES

A small-town romantic suspense series of interconnected standalones.

Possessive alpha males, sweet innocent heroines, found family, touch her & die vibes, military romance, foster brothers.

JUSTICE
Secret Baby Romance

BRAXTEN
Amnesia Romance

KNOX
Title & Release TBA

STANDALONE BOOKS

Both books have interconnected characters.

BEAUTIFULLY INSIGHTFUL
Second Chance Romantic Suspense

COCKLOFT
Enemies-to-Lovers Romantic Comedy

MEN OF COURAGE SERIES

A spin-off from the Sweet Series with interconnected characters and an interconnected suspense subplot that weaves through the series.

Small-town romantic suspense.

Possessive alpha males, sweet innocent heroines, found family, firefighter romance, touch her & die vibes.

ULTIMATE SACRIFICE
Friends-to-Lovers

ULTIMATE REVENGE
Title & Release TBA

ULTIMATE SACRIFICE
Title & Release TBA

HEART MOUNTAIN SERIES

Steamy contemporary small-town romance.

Protective alpha males, sweet innocent heroines, found family, friend group, blue collar, a mountain with a legend.

CONNECT WITH KC LYNN

Find release day info, bonus content, and more on my website:
www.authorkclynn.com

Subscribe to my Newsletter:
authorkclynn.com/newsletter
Join my Facebook Reader Group:
facebook.com/groups/KCLynnCupcakes
Follow me on Facebook:
facebook.com/authorkclynn
Follow me on Instagram:
instagram.com/authorkclynn_
Follow me on Book Bub:
bookbub.com/authors/k-c-lynn
Follow me on Tik Tok:
tiktok.com/@authorkclynn

Acknowledgements

So many people make this journey possible—my family, editor, betas, friends, bloggers, and readers around the world. Thank you. I love and cherish every single one of you.

Author Bio

K.C. Lynn is a small-town girl living in Western Canada. She grew up in a family of four children—two sisters and a brother. Her mother was the lady who baked homemade goods for everyone on the street, and her father was a respected man who worked in the RCMP. This being one of the things that inspires K.C. to write romantic suspense about the trials and triumphs of our heroes.

K.C. married her high school sweetheart, and they started a big family of their own—two adorable girls and a set of handsome twin boys. It was her love for romance books that gave K.C. the courage to sit down and write her own novel. It was then a beautiful world opened up, and she found what she was meant to do.

When K.C.'s not in the writing cave, she can be found watching a good, true crime documentary and exploring the picturesque landscapes of her own backyard in the Canadian Rockies with her husband and their four children.

Bibliography

1. Author Unknown. https://www.pinterest.ca/pin/584342120372885042/?lp=true

2. Spurgeon, C. https://quotefancy.com/quote/759647/Charles-H-Spurgeon-A-little-faith-will-bring-your-soul-to-heaven-a-great-faith-will-bring